HAWK QUEEN

Long minutes passed. Then he appeared, walking with care upon the ice. He was not as tall as she remembered, but then she had only looked upon him with the eyes of a child. Shorter than Fell, he was a stocky man, his belly straining at the red leather coat he wore. His hair was black, close-cropped, silver at the temples, his face fleshy and round. His leggings and boots were red, as was the ankle-length cloak he wore.

Sigarni drew back the bow-string, took careful aim, and waited as he approached. The man saw her, and continued to move closer. Forty feet, thirty. He looked up and smiled. Sigarni let fly and the arrow flashed through the air. He raised his hand and the shaft burst into flame. She notched another.

D1344950

9112000326137

BY DAVID GEMMELL

Legend
The King Beyond the Gate
Waylander
Quest for Lost Heroes
Waylander II
The First Chronicles of Druss the Legend
Drenai Tales: Omnibus One
Drenai Tales: Omnibus Two

Wolf in Shadow
The Last Guardian
Bloodstone

Ghost King
Last Sword of Power

Lion of Macedon
Dark Prince

Ironhand's Daughter
The Hawk Eternal

Knights of Dark Renown

Morningstar

Hawk Queen: The Omnibus Edition
Stones of Power: The Omnibus Edition

DAVID GEMMELL

HAWK QUEEN

This omnibus edition includes

Ironhand's Daughter
The Hawk Eternal

orbit

www.orbitbooks.net

ORBIT

First published in Great Britain in 2014 by Orbit

5 7 9 11 12 10 8 6 4

Copyright © 2014 by David A. Gemmell

Ironhand's Daughter
First published in Great Britain in 1995 by Legend Books
Reprinted by Orbit in 1999, 2000 (twice), 2002, 2003,
2005, 2006, 2007, 2008, 2009 (twice), 2010
Copyright © 1995 by David A. Gemmell

The Hawk Eternal
First published in Great Britain in 1995 by Legend Books
Reprinted by Orbit in 1999, 2000, 2001, 2002, 2004,
2005, 2006, 2007, 2009 (twice)
Copyright © 1995 by David A. Gemmell

The moral right of the author has been asserted.

*All characters and events in this publication, other than those
clearly in the public domain, are fictitious and any resemblance
to real persons, living or dead, is purely coincidental.*

All rights reserved.
No part of this publication may be reproduced, stored in a
retrieval system, or transmitted, in any form or by any means, without
the prior permission in writing of the publisher, nor be otherwise circulated
in any form of binding or cover other than that in which it is published
and without a similar condition including this condition being
imposed on the subsequent purchaser.

A CIP catalogue record for this book is available from the British Library.

ISBN 978-0-356-50376-9

Typeset in Bembo MT by Hewer Text UK Ltd, Edinburgh
Printed in Great Britain by Clays Ltd, St Ives plc

Papers used by Orbit are from well-managed forests
and other responsible sources.

MIX
Paper from
responsible sources
FSC® C104740

Orbit
An imprint of
Little, Brown Book Group
Carmelite House
50 Victoria Embankment
London EC4Y 0DZ

An Hachette UK Company
www.hachette.co.uk

www.orbitbooks.net

Ironhand's Daughter

BRENT LIBRARIES	
WIL	
91120000326137	
Askews & Holts	05-May-2017
AF FAN	£10.99

PROLOGUE

Sunlight glinted on steel as the knife blade spun through the air to thud home in the chalk-circled centre of the board. The woman chuckled. 'You lose again, Ballistar,' she said.

'I let you win,' the dwarf told her. 'For I am a creature of legend, and my skills are second to none.' He smiled as he spoke, but there was sadness in his dark eyes and she reached out to cup her hand to his bearded cheek. He leaned in to her touch, twisting his head to kiss her palm.

'You are the finest of men,' she said softly, 'and the gods – if gods there be – have not been kind to you.'

Ballistar did not reply. Glancing up he drank in her beauty, the golden sheen of her skin, the haunting power of her pale blue-grey eyes. At nineteen Sigarni was the most beautiful woman Ballistar had ever seen, tall and slender, full-lipped and firm-breasted. Her only flaw was her close-cropped hair, which shone like silver in the sunlight. It had turned grey in her sixth year, after her parents were slain. The villagers called it the Night of the Slaughterers, and no one would speak of it. Pushing himself to his feet he walked to the fence post, climbing the rail to pull Sigarni's throwing knife from the board. She watched him stretching out his tiny arms, his stunted fingers unable to curl fully around the hilt of her blade. At last he wrenched it clear, then turned and jumped to the ground. He was no larger than a child of four, yet his head was huge and his face heavily bearded. Ballistar returned her blade and she slid it home into the sheath at her hip. Reaching to her right she lifted a pitcher of cool water and filled two clay goblets, passing one to the dwarf.

Ballistar gave a wide grin as he took it, then slowly passed his tiny hand across the surface of the water. She shook her head. 'You should not make those gestures, my friend,' she said seriously. 'If you were seen by the wrong man, you would be flogged.'

3

'I've been flogged before. Did I show you my scars?'

'Many times.'

'Then I shall not concern myself with fears of the lash,' he said, passing his hand once more over the drink. 'To the long-dead King over the water,' he said, lifting the goblet to his lips. A sleek black hound padded into sight. Heavy of shoulder, slim of flanks, she was a hare and rabbit hound, and her speed was legendary. Highland hunting hounds were bred for strength, stamina and obedience. But most of all they had to be fast. None was swifter than Sigarni's hound. Ballistar laid down his empty goblet and called to her. 'Here, Lady!' Her head came up and she loped to him, pushing her long muzzle into his beard, licking at his cheek. 'Women find me irresistible,' he said, as he stroked the hound's ears.

'I can see why,' Sigarni told him. 'You have a gentle touch.'

Ballistar stroked Lady's flanks and gazed down into her eyes. One eye was doe-brown, the other opal-grey. 'She has healed well,' he said, running his finger down the scar on the hound's cheek.

Sigarni nodded, and Ballistar saw the fresh flaring of anger in her eyes. 'Bernt is a fool. I should never have allowed him to come. Stupid man.'

'That *stupid* man loves you,' chided Ballistar. 'As do we all, princess.'

'Idiot!' she snapped, but the anger faded from her eyes. 'You know I have no right to such a title.'

'Not so, Sigarni. You have the blood of Gandarin in your veins.'

'Pah! Half the population have his blood. The man was a rutting ram. Gwalchmai told me about him; he said Gandarin could have raised an army of his bastard offspring. Even Bernt probably has a drop or two of Gandarin's blood.'

'You should forgive him,' advised Ballistar. 'He didn't mean it.' At that moment a red hawk swooped low over the clearing, coming to rest on a nearby bow perch. For a moment or two it pranced from foot to foot, then cocked its head and stared at the silver-haired woman. The hound gave a low growl, but slunk back close to Ballistar. Sigarni pulled on a long black gauntlet of polished leather and stood, arm outstretched. The hawk launched itself from the fence and flew to her.

'Ah, my beauty,' said Sigarni, reaching up and ruffling the russet-coloured feathers of the bird's breast. Taking a strip of rabbit meat from the pouch at her side, she fed it to the hawk. Swiftly and skilfully she attached two soft collars to the hawk's legs, then threaded short hunting jesses through brass-rimmed holes in the collars. Lastly she pulled a soft leather hood from the pouch at her side and smoothly stroked it into place over the bird's beak and eyes. The hawk sat motionless as the hood settled, and even turned her neck to allow Sigarni to lean forward and tighten the braces at the rear. The woman turned her gaze back to the dwarf and smiled. 'I know that Bernt acted from stupidity. And I am more angry with myself than with him. I told him to loose Lady only if there was a second hare. It was a simple instruction. But he was incapable even of that. And I will not have fools around me.'

Ballistar said nothing more. There were, he knew, only two creatures in all the world that Sigarni cared for – the hound, Lady, and the hawk, Abby. Sigarni had been training them both, determined that they would work together as a team. The training had gone well. Lady would seek out the hares and scatter them, while Abby swooped down from the trees in a kill that seemed swifter than an arrow. The danger area came when only a single quarry was sighted. Hawk and bird had raced each other to make the strike. Abby won both times. On the second occasion when Lady darted in to try to steal the kill, Abby had lashed out, her beak grazing the hound's flank. Sigarni had grabbed Lady's collar, dragging her back. In an effort to re-train Lady, Sigarni had allowed the cattle herder, Bernt, to accompany her on the training hunts. His duty was to keep Lady leashed, and only release her when more than one hare was sighted. He had failed. Excited by the hunt, Bernt had loosed the hound at first sight of a single hare. Abby had swooped upon it, and Lady had sped in to share the prize. The hawk had turned, lashing out with her cruel beak, piercing the hound's right eye.

'You are hunting today?' asked the dwarf.

'No. Abby is above her killing weight. I let her have the last hare we took yesterday. Today we'll just walk awhile, up to the High Druin. She likes to fly there.'

'Watch out for the sorcerer!' warned Ballistar.

'There is no need to fear him,' said Sigarni. 'I think he is a good man.'

'He's an Outlander, and his skin has been burned by sorcery. He makes me shudder.'

Sigarni's laughter pealed out. 'Oh, Ballistar, you fool! In his land all people have dark skins; they are not cursed.'

'He's a wizard! At nights he becomes a giant bird that flies across High Druin. Many have seen it: a great black raven, twice normal size. And his castle is full of grimoires and spells, and there are animals there – frozen. You know Marion – she was there! She told us all about a great black bear that just stands in the hallway, a spell upon it. You keep clear of him, Sigarni!'

She looked into his dark eyes and saw the reality of his fear. 'I shall be careful,' she said. 'You may rely on it. But I will not walk in fear, Ballistar. Have I not the blood of Gandarin in my veins?' Sigarni could not quite mask the smile as she spoke.

'You should not mock your friends!' he scolded. 'Magickers are to be avoided – anyone with sense knows that. And what is he doing here, in our high, lonely places? Eh? Why did he leave his land of black people and come here? What is he seeking? Or is he perhaps hiding from justice?'

'I shall ask him when next I see him,' she said. 'Come, Lady!' The hound rose warily and paced alongside the tall woman. Sigarni knelt and patted her flanks. 'You've learned to respect Abby now,' she whispered, 'though I fear she will never learn respect for you.'

'Why is that?' asked Ballistar. Sigarni looked up.

'It is the way of the hawk, my friend. It loves no one, needs no one, fears no one.'

'Does it not love you, Sigarni?'

'No. That is why she must never be called in vain. Each time she flies to the fist I feed her. The day I do not, she may decide never to return. Hawks know no loyalties. They stay because they choose to. No man – nor woman – can ever own one.'

Without a word of farewell the huntress strode off into the forest.

1

Tovi closed the double doors of his oven, removed his apron and wiped the flour from his face with a clean towel. The day's bread was laid out on wooden trays, stacked six high, and the smell of the baking filled his nostrils. Even after all these years he still loved that smell. Taking a sample loaf, he cut through the centre. It was rich and light, with no pockets of air. Behind him his apprentice, Stalf, breathed a silent sigh of relief. Tovi turned to the boy. 'Not bad,' he said. Cutting two thick slices, he smeared them with fresh butter and passed one to the boy.

Moving to the rear door, Tovi stepped outside. Above the stone and timber buildings of the village the dawn sun was clearing the peaks and a fresh breeze was blowing from the north. The bakery stood at the centre of the village, an old three-storey building that once had been the council house. In the days when we were allowed a council, thought Tovi sourly. The buildings surrounding the bakery were sturdily built, and old. Further down the hill were the simpler timber dwellings of the poorer folk. Tovi stepped out into the road and gazed down the hill to the river. The villagers were stirring and several women were already kneeling by the water-side, washing clothes and blankets, beating them against the white rocks at the water's edge. Tovi saw the black-clad Widow Maffrey making her way to the communal well. He waved and smiled and she nodded as she passed. The smith, Grame, was lighting his forge. Seeing Tovi, he strolled across. Soot had smeared the smith's thick white beard.

'Good day to you, Baker,' said Grame.

'And to you. It looks a fine one. Nary a cloud in sight. I see you have the Baron's greys in your stalls. Fine beasts.'

'Finer than the man who owns them. One of them has a split hoof, and both carry spur scars. No way to treat good horses. I'll take a loaf, if you please. One with a crust as black as sin and a centre as white as a nun's soul.'

Tovi shook his head. 'You'll take what I give you, man, and be glad of it, for you'll not taste a better piece of bread anywhere in the kingdom. Stalf! Fetch a loaf for the smith.'

The boy brought it out, wrapped in muslin. Dipping his huge hand into the pocket of his leather apron, Grame produced two small copper coins which he dropped into Stalf's outstretched palm. The boy bowed and backed away. 'It'll be a good summer,' said Grame, tearing off a chunk of bread and pushing it into his mouth.

'Let us hope so,' said Tovi.

The dwarf Ballistar approached them, labouring up the steep hill. He gave an elaborate bow. 'Good morning to you,' said Ballistar. 'Am I late for breakfast?'

'Not if you have coin, little man,' said Tovi, eyes narrowing. The dwarf made him feel uncomfortable, and he found himself growing irritable.

'No coin,' the dwarf told him affably, 'but I have three hares hanging.'

'Caught by Sigarni, no doubt!' snapped the baker. 'I don't know why she should be so generous with you.'

'Perhaps she likes me,' answered Ballistar, no trace of anger in his tone.

Tovi called for another loaf which he gave the dwarf. 'Bring me the best hare tonight,' he said.

'Why does he anger you so?' asked Grame, as the dwarf wandered away.

Tovi shrugged. 'He's cursed. He should have been laid aside at birth. What good is he to man or beast? He cannot hunt, cannot work. If not for Sigarni maybe he would leave the village. He could join a circus! Such as he could earn an honest living there, capering and the like.'

'You're turning into a sour old man, Tovi.'

'And you are getting fat!'

'Aye, that's the truth. But I still remember the wearing of the Red. That's something I'll take to the grave, with pride. As will you.'

The baker nodded, and his expression softened. 'Bonny days, Grame. They'll not come again.'

'We gave them a fight, though, eh?'

Tovi shook his head. 'We showed them how brave men die – that's not the same, my friend. Outnumbered and outclassed we were – their knights riding through our ranks, cutting and killing, our sword-blades clanging against their armour and causing no damage. Gods, man, it was slaughter that day! I wish to Heaven I had never seen it.'

'We were badly led,' whispered Grame. 'Gandarin did not pass his strength to his sons.'

The smith sighed. 'Ah, well, enough dismal talk. This is a new day, fresh and untainted.' Spinning on his heel, the burly blacksmith strode back to his forge.

The boy, Stalf, said nothing as Tovi re-entered the bakery. He could see his master was deep in thought, and he had heard a little of the conversation. It was hard to believe that Fat Tovi had once worn the Red, and had taken part in the Battle of Colden Moor. Stalf had visited the battle site last autumn. A huge plain, dotted with barrows, thirty-four in all. And each barrow held the dead of an entire clan's fighting men.

The wind had howled across Colden Moor and Stalf had been frightened by the power and the haunted wailing of it. His uncle, Mart One-arm, had stood with him, his bony hand on the boy's shoulder. 'This is the place where dreams end, boy. This is the resting place of hope.'

'How many died Uncle?'

'Scores of thousands.'

'But not the King.'

'No, not the King. He fled to a bright land beyond the water. But they found him there, and slew him. There are no Mountain Kings now.'

Uncle Mart walked him on to the moor, coming at last to a high barrow. 'This is where the Loda men stood, shoulder to shoulder, brothers in arms, brothers in death.' Lifting the stump of his left arm, he gave a crooked smile. 'Part of me is buried here too, boy.

And more than just my arm. My heart lies here, with my brothers, and cousins, and friends.'

Stalf dragged his mind back to the present. Tovi was standing by the window, his eyes showing the same faraway look he had seen that day on the face of Mart One-arm.

'Can I take some bread to me mam?' asked Stalf. Tovi nodded.

Stalf chose two loaves and wrapped them. He had reached the door when Tovi's voice stopped him. 'What do you want to be, lad, when you're grown?'

'A baker, sir. Skilled like you.' Tovi said no more, and the boy hurried from the bakery.

Sigarni loved the mountain lands, the lush valleys nestling between them, and the deep, dark forests that covered their flanks. But mostly she loved High Druin, the lonely peak which towered over the high lands, its summit lost in cloud, its shoulders cloaked in snow. There was, in High Druin, an elemental magnificence that radiated from its sharp, defiant crags, a magic that sang in the whispering of wind-breath before the winter storms. High Druin spoke to the heart. He said: 'I am Eternity in stone. I have always been here. I will always be here!'

The huntress let Abby soar into the air and watched her swoop over High Druin's lower flanks. Lady bounded out over the grass, her sleek black body alert, her one good eye scanning for sign of hare or rat. Sigarni sat by the Lake of Tears, watching the brightly coloured ducks on the banks of the small island at the centre of the lake. Abby circled high above them, also watching the birds. The hawk swooped down, coming to rest in a tree beside the lake. The ducks, suddenly aware of the hawk, took to the water.

Sigarni watched with interest. Roast duck would make a fine contrast to the hare meat she had eaten during the last fortnight. 'Here, Lady!' she called. The hound padded alongside and Sigarni pointed to the ducks. 'Go!' hissed Sigarni. Instantly the dog leapt into the water, paddling furiously towards the circling flock. Several of the birds took wing, putting flat distance between them and the hound, keeping low to the water. But one took off into the sky and instantly Abby launched herself in pursuit.

The duck was rising fast, and Abby hurtled down towards it with talons extended.

At the last possible moment the duck saw the bird of prey – and dived fast. For a heartbeat only Sigarni thought Abby had her prey, but then the duck hit the water, diving deep, confusing the hawk. Abby circled and returned to her branch.

The huntress gave a low whistle, summoning Lady back to the bank. The sound of a walking horse came to Sigarni then, and she rose and turned.

The horse was a tall chestnut, and upon it rode a black man, his cheeks, head and shoulders covered in a flowing white burnoose. A cloak of blue-dyed wool hung from his broad shoulders and a curved sword was scabbarded at his waist. He smiled as he saw the mountain woman.

'When hunting duck, it is better for the hawk to take it from below,' he said, swinging down from his saddle.

'We're still learning,' replied Sigarni affably. 'She is wedded to fur now, but it took time – as you said it would, Asmidir.'

The tall man sat down at the water's edge. Lady approached him gingerly, and he stroked her head. 'The eye is healing well. Has it affected her hunting?' Sigarni shook her head. 'And the bird? Hawks prefer to feed on feather. What is her killing weight?'

'Two pounds two ounces. But she has taken hare at two-four.'

'And what do you feed her?'

'No more than three ounces a day.'

The black man nodded. 'Once in a while you should catch her a rat. Nothing better for cleaning a bird's crop than a good rat.'

'Why is that, Asmidir?' asked Sigarni, sitting down beside the man.

'I don't know,' he admitted, with a broad smile. 'My father told me years ago. As you know the hawk swallows its prey – where it can – whole and the carcass is compressed, all the goodness squeezed out of it. It then vomits out the cast, the remnants. There is, I would imagine, something in the rat's pelt or skin that cleans the bird's crop as it exits.' Leaning back on his elbows, he narrowed his eyes and watched the distant hawk. 'How many kills so far?'

11

'Sixty-eight hares, twenty pigeons and a ferret.'

'You hunt ferret?' asked Asmidir, raising a quizzical eyebrow.

'It was a mistake. The ferret bolted a hare and Abby took the ferret.'

Asmidir chuckled. 'You have done well, Sigarni. I am glad I gave you the hawk.'

'Three times I thought I'd lost her. Always in the forest.'

'You may lose sight of her, child, but she will never lose sight of you. Come back to the castle, and I will prepare you a meal. And you too,' he said, scratching the hound's ears.

'I was told that you were a sorcerer, and that I must beware of you.'

'You should always heed the warnings of dwarves,' he said. 'Or any creature of legend.'

'How did you know it was Ballistar?'

'Because I am a sorcerer, my dear. We are expected to know things like that.'

'You always pause at my bear,' said Asmidir, gazing fondly at the silver-haired girl as Sigarni reached out and touched the fur of the beast's belly. It was a huge creature, its paws outstretched, talons bared, mouth open in a silent roar. 'It is wonderful,' she said. 'How is it done?'

'You do not believe it is a spell then?' he asked, smiling.

'No.'

'Well,' he said slowly, rubbing his chin, 'if it is not a spell, then it must be a stuffed bear. There are craftsmen in my land who work on carcasses, stripping away the inner meat, which can rot, and rebuilding the dead beasts with clay before wrapping them once more in their skins or fur. The results are remarkably lifelike.'

'And this then is a stuffed bear?'

'I did not say that,' he reminded her. 'Come, let us eat.'

Asmidir led her through the hallway and into the main hall. A log fire was burning merrily in the hearth and two servants were laying platters of meat and bread on the table. Both were tall dark-skinned men who worked silently, never once looking at their master or his guest. With the table laid, they silently withdrew.

'Your servants are not friendly,' commented Sigarni.

'They are efficient,' said Asmidir, seating himself at the table and filling a goblet with wine.

'Do they fear you?'

'A little fear is good for a servant.'

'Do they love you?'

'I am not a man easy to love. My servants are content. They are free to leave my service whenever it pleases them so to do; they are not slaves.' He offered Sigarni some wine, but she refused and he poured water into a glazed goblet which he passed to her. They ate in silence, then Asmidir moved to the fireside, beckoning Sigarni to join him.

'Do you have no fear?' the black man asked, as she sat cross-legged before him.

'Of what?' she countered.

'Of life. Of death. Of me.'

'Why would I fear you?'

'Why would you not? When we met last year I was a stranger in your land. Black and fearsome,' he said, widening his eyes and mimicking a snarl.

She laughed at him. 'You were never fearsome,' she said. 'Dangerous, yes. But never fearsome.'

'There is a difference?'

'Of course,' she told him, cocking her head to one side. 'I *like* dangerous men.'

He shook his head. 'You are incorrigible, Sigarni. The body of an angel and the mind of a whore. Usually that is considered a wonderful combination. That is, if you are contemplating the life of a courtesan, a prostitute or a slut. Is that your ambition?'

Sigarni yawned theatrically. 'I think it is time to go home,' she said, rising smoothly.

'Ah, I have offended you,' he said.

'Not at all,' she told him. 'But I expected better of you, Asmidir.'

'You should expect better of yourself, Sigarni. There are dark days looming. A leader is coming – a leader of noble blood. You will probably be called upon in those days to aid him. For you also

13

boast the blood of Gandarin. Men will follow an angel or a saint, they will follow a despot and a villain. But they will follow a whore only to the bedchamber.'

Her face flushed with anger. 'I'll take sermons from a priest – not from a man who was happy to cavort with me throughout the spring and summer, and now seeks to belittle me. I am not some milkmaid or tavern wench. I am Sigarni of the Mountains. What I do is my affair. I used you for pleasure, I admit it freely. You are a fine lover; you have strength and finesse. And you used me. That made it a balanced transaction, and neither of us was sullied by it. How dare you attempt to shame me?'

'Why would you see it as shame?' he countered. 'I am talking of perceptions – the perceptions of men. You think I look down upon you? I do not. I adore you. For your body *and* your mind. Further, I am probably – as much as I am capable of it – a little in love with you. But this is not why I spoke in the way I did.'

'I don't care,' she told him. 'Goodbye.'

Sigarni strode from the room and out past the great bear. A servant pushed open the double doors and she walked down the steps into the courtyard. Lady came bounding towards her. Another servant, a slim dark-eyed young man, was waiting at the foot of the steps with Abby hooded upon his wrist. Sigarni pulled on her hawking glove.

'You were waiting for me?' she asked the young man. He nodded. 'Why? I am usually here for hours.'

'The master said today would be a short visit,' he explained.

Sigarni untied the braces and slid the hood clear of Abby's eyes. The hawk looked around, them jumped to Sigarni's fist. When the huntress lifted her arm and called out 'Hai!', the hawk took off, heading south.

Sigarni flicked her fingers and Lady moved close to her side, awaiting instructions. 'What is your name?' she asked the servant, noting the sleekness of his skin and the taut muscles beneath his blue silk shirt. He shook his head and moved away from her.

Annoyed, the huntress walked from the old castle, crossing the rickety drawbridge and heading off into the woods. Her mood was dark and angry as she went. The mind of a whore, indeed. Her thoughts turned to Fell the Forester. Now there was a man who understood pleasure. She doubted if there was a single woman within a day's walk who hadn't succumbed to his advances. Did they call him a whore? No. It was 'Good old Fell, what a character, what a man!' Idiotic!

Asmidir's words rankled. She had thought him different, more . . . intelligent? Yes. Instead he proved to be like most men, caught between a need for fornication and a love of sermonizing.

Abby soared above her, and Lady ran to the side of the trail, seeking out hares. Sigarni pushed thoughts of the black man from her mind and walked on in the dusk, coming at last to the final hillside and gazing down on her cabin. A light was showing at the window and this annoyed her, for she wished to be alone this evening. If it was that fool, Bernt, she would give him the sharp side of her tongue.

Walking into the yard, she whistled for Abby. The hawk came in low, then spread her wings and settled on Sigarni's glove. Feeding her a strip of meat she removed the hunting jesses; then carrying her to the bow perch, she attached the mews ties, and turned towards the cabin.

Lady moved to the side of the building, lying down beside the door with her head on her paws.

Sigarni pushed open the door.

Fell was sitting by the fire, eyes closed, his long legs stretched out before the blaze. It angered her that she could feel a sense of rising excitement at his presence. He looked just the same as on that last day, his long black hair sleek and glowing with health, swept back from his brow and held in place by a leather headband, his beard close-trimmed and as soft as fur. Sigarni took a deep breath, trying to calm herself.

'What do you want here, Goat-brain?' she snapped.

Then she saw the blood.

There were wolves all around him, fangs bared, ready to rip and tear. A powerful beast leapt at him. Fell caught it by the throat, then spun on his heel hurling the creature into the pack. His limbs felt leaden, as if he were wading through water. The wolves blurred, shifting like smoke, becoming tall, fierce-eyed warriors holding knives of sharpened bronze. They moved in on him, smoothly, slowly. Fell's arms were paralyzed and he felt the first knife sink into his shoulder like a tongue of fire . . .

He opened his eyes. Sigarni was kneeling beside him with a needle in her hand, and he felt the flap of flesh on his shoulder drawn tight by the thread. Fell swore softly. 'Lie still,' she said and Fell obeyed her. His stomach felt uneasy. Snapping the thread with her teeth, she sat back. 'Looks like a sword cut.'

'Long knife,' he told her, taking a deep shuddering breath. He said no more for a while, resting his neck against the thick, cushioned hide of the chair's head-rest. Focusing his gaze on the far timbered wall he ran his eyes over the weapons hanging there – the long-handled broadsword with its leaf-shaped blade and hilt of leather, the bow of horn and the quiver of black-shafted arrows, the daggers and dirks and lastly the helm, with its crown and cheek-guards of black iron and the nasal guard and brows of polished brass. Not a speck of rust or tarnish showed on them.

'You keep your father's weapons in good condition,' he said.

'That's what Gwal taught me,' she told him. 'Who gave you the wound?'

'We didn't exchange names. There were two of them. Robbed a pilgrim on the Low Trail. I tracked them to Mas Gryff.'

'Where are they now?'

'Oh, they're still there. I returned the money to the pilgrim and made a report to the Watch.' His face darkened. 'Bastards! You could almost feel their disappointment.' He shook his head. 'It won't be much longer, you know. They'll look for any excuse.'

'You've lost a lot of blood,' she said. 'I'll make some broth.'

He watched her move away, his eyes lingered on the sway of her hips. 'You're a beautiful woman, Sigarni. Never saw the like!'

'Look on and weep for all you've lost,' she said, before disappearing into the back room.

'Amen to that,' he whispered. Resting his head once more, he remembered the last parting two years before, Sigarni standing straight and tall and proud . . . always so proud. Fell had walked across the glens to Cilfallen and paid bride-price for Gwendolyn. Sweet Gwen. In no way did she match the silver-haired woman he had left, save in one. Gwen could bear children, and a man needed sons. Ten months later Gwen was dead, the victim of a breech birth that killed both her and the infant.

Fell had buried them both in the Loda resting place on the western slope of High Druin.

Sigarni returned to his side. 'Flex the muscles of your arm,' she ordered.

He did so and winced. 'It's damned sore.'

'Good. I like to think of you in pain.'

'I buried my son, woman. I know what pain is. And I'd not wish it on a friend.'

'Neither would I,' she said. 'But you are no friend.'

'Your mood is foul,' he admonished her. 'Had a falling-out with your black man, have you?'

'Have you been spying on me, Fell?' It irritated him that she did not deny the association.

'It is my work, Sigarni. I patrol the forest and I have seen you enter the castle, and I have seen you leave. How could you rut with such as he?'

She laughed then, and his anger rose. 'Asmidir is a better man than you, Fell. In every way.' He wanted to strike her, to slap the smile from her face. But the growing nausea finally swamped him and with a groan he pushed himself from the chair, staggered to the door, and just made it to open ground before falling to earth and vomiting. Cold sweat shone upon his face in the moonlight, and he felt weak as a day-old calf as he struggled to rise. Sigarni appeared alongside him, taking his arm and looping it over her shoulder. 'Let's get you to bed,' she said, not unkindly.

Fell leaned in to her. The scent of her filled his nostrils. 'I loved you,' he said, as she half-carried him up the four steps to the doorway.

'You left me,' she said.

When he woke it was daylight, the rising sun shining through the open window. The sky was clear and Fell saw the hawk silhouetted briefly against the blue. With a groan he sat up. His shoulder was burning, and his ribs were badly bruised from the fight with the two Outland robbers.

Rising from the bed he moved to the window. Sigarni was standing in the sunlight, the hawk on her glove, the black hound lying at her feet. Fell's mouth was dry, and all his long-suppressed emotions surged to the surface. Of all the women he had known – and there had been many – he had loved only one. And in that moment he knew, with a sickening certainty, that it would always be thus. Oh, he would marry again, and he would have sons, but his heart would remain with this enigmatic mountain woman until the daggers of time stopped its beat.

Though still weak from loss of blood, Fell knew he could stay no longer in sight of Sigarni. Gathering his cloak of black leather he pulled on his boots, took up his longbow and quiver and walked from the rear of the cabin, heading back on the long trail to Cilfallen. There was a maid there, of marriageable age, whose father had set a bride price Fell could afford.

'I hate this place,' said the Baron Ranulph Gottasson, leaning on the wide parapet and staring out over the distant mountains. Asmidir said nothing. It was cold up here on the Citadel's high walls, the wind hissing down from the north, cutting through the warmest clothes. But the Baron seemed not to notice the inclemency of the weather. He was dressed in a simple shirt of black silk and a sleeveless jerkin of the finest black leather. He wore no adornments, no silver enhancements to his black leather leggings, no chains or ornate discs attached to his knee-length boots. As Asmidir stood shivering on the battlements, the Baron turned his pale hooded eyes on the black man. 'Not like Kushir, eh? Too cold, too bleak. Ever wish you were back home?'

'Sometimes,' Asmidir admitted.

'So do I. What is there here for a man like me? Where is the glory?'

'The kingdom is at peace, my lord,' said Asmidir softly. 'Thanks mainly to your good self and the Earl of Jastey.'

The Baron's lips thinned, the hooded eyes narrowing. 'Don't speak his name in my presence! I never met a man so gifted with luck. All his victories were hollow. Tell me what he has ever done to match my conquest of Ligia? Twenty-five thousand warriors against my two legions. Yet we crushed them, and took their capital. What can he offer against that? The Siege of Catium. Pah!'

'Indeed, sir,' said Asmidir smoothly, 'your deeds will echo through the pages of history. Now I am sure you have more important matters to attend to, so how may I be of service to you?'

The Baron turned and beckoned Asmidir to follow him into a small study. The black man stared longingly at the cold and empty fireplace. Does the man not feel the cold, he wondered? The Baron seated himself at a desk of oak. 'I want the red hawk,' he said. 'There is a tourney in two months and the red hawk could win it for me. Name a price.'

'Would that I could sir. But I sold the hawk last autumn.'

The Baron swore. 'Who to? I'll buy it back.'

'I wouldn't know where to find the man, sir,' Asmidir lied smoothly. 'He came to my castle last year. He was a traveller, I believe, perhaps a pilgrim. But if I see him again I shall direct him to you.'

The Baron swore again, then lashed his fist against the desk-top.

'All right, that will be all,' he said at last.

Asmidir bowed and left the study. Descending the spiral staircase he moved down into the belly of the fortress, emerging into the long hall where the feast was in progress. Red-liveried servants were carrying platters of food and drink and more than two score of knights and their ladies were seated at the three main tables. Fires were blazing merrily at both ends of the hall and minstrels sat in the high gallery, their soft music drowned by the chatter of the guests.

Asmidir was not hungry. Swiftly he walked from the hall, and down the long stairs to the lower chambers and the double-doored exit. His thoughts were sombre as he recalled the Baron's words. Asmidir remembered the conquest of Ligia, the battles and the massacres, the rapes and the mutilations, the torture and the

19

destruction. A rich, independent nation brought to its knees, humiliated and beggared, its libraries burned, its holy places desecrated. Oh yes, Ranulph, history will long remember your bloody name! Asmidir shivered.

Revenge, so the proverb claimed, is a dish best served cold. Is that true, he wondered? Will there be any satisfaction in bringing the man down?

Wrapping his cloak more tightly about his broad shoulders, Asmidir left the fortress building and moved across the courtyard. A young man hailed him and he turned and smiled at the newcomer – a tall young man, slender and brown-eyed, his long blond hair drawn back from his brow and tied in a tight ponytail. He was carrying an armful of rolled maps. 'Good afternoon, Leofric. You are missing the feast.'

'Yes, I know,' said the other dolefully. 'But the Baron wants to study these maps. It doesn't pay to keep him waiting.'

'They look old.'

'They are. They were commissioned some two hundred years ago by the Highland King, Gandarin the First. Fine work, most of them. Beautifully crafted. The map-makers also had some method of judging the height of mountains. Did you know that High Druin is nine thousand seven hundred and eighty-two feet high? Do you think it could be true, or did someone just invent the figure?'

Asmidir shrugged. 'It sounds too precise to be an invention. Still, I am glad you are enjoying your work.'

'I enjoy the detail,' said Leofric, chuckling. 'Not many do. It pleases me to know how many lances we have, and the state of our horses. I like working on projects like this. Did you know there are four hundred and twelve wagons employed around the Five Towns?' The young man laughed. 'Yes, I know, it is a little boring for most people. But you try to go on a campaign without wagons and the war is over before it begins.'

Asmidir chatted with the young man for several minutes, then bade him farewell and walked swiftly to the stable. The hostler bowed as he entered, then saddled the chestnut gelding. Asmidir gave the man a small silver coin.

'Thank you, sir,' he said, pocketing the coin with a swiftness that dazzled the eye.

Asmidir rode from the stable, through the portcullis gate and out into the wide streets of the town. He felt the eyes of the people upon him as he passed through the marketplace, and heard some children calling out names. A troop of soldiers marched past him and he pulled up his horse. The men were mercenaries; they looked weary, as if they had marched many miles. Leofric planning the logistics of war, more mercenaries arriving every day . . . The beast is not far off, thought Asmidir.

Passing through the north gate, Asmidir let the horse break into a run as it reached open ground. He rode thus for a mile, then slowed the beast. The chestnut was powerful, a horse bred for stamina, and he was not even breathing hard when Asmidir reined him in. The black man patted the gelding's neck.

'The dreams of men are born in blood,' he said softly.

Fell was sitting by the roadside, catching his breath, when the small two-wheeled cart moved into sight. Two huge grey wolfhounds were harnessed to it, and a silver-haired man sat at the front with a long stick in his hands. Seeing the forester, the old man tapped his stick lightly on the flanks of the hounds. 'Hold up there, Shamol. Hold up, Cabris. Good day to you, woodsman!'

Fell smiled. 'By Heaven, Gwalch, you look ridiculous sitting in that contraption.'

'Whisht, boy, at my age I don't give a care to how I look,' said the old man. 'What matters is that I can travel as far as I like, without troubling my old bones.' Leaning forward, he peered at the forester. 'You look greyer than a winter sky, boy. Are you ailing?'

'Wounded. And I've shed some blood. I'll be fine. Just need a rest, is all.'

'Heading for Cilfallen?'

'Aye.'

'Then climb aboard, young man. My hounds can pull two as well as one. Good exercise for them. We'll stop off at my cabin for

21

a dram. That's what you need, take my word for it: a little of the water of life. And I promise not to tell your fortune.'

'You *always* tell my fortune – and it never makes good listening. But, just this once, I'll take you up on your offer. I'll ride that idiotic wagon. But I'll pray to all the gods I know that no one sees me on it. I'd never live it down.'

The old man chuckled and moved to his right, making room for the forester. Fell laid his long bow and quiver in the back and stepped aboard. 'Home now, hounds!' said Gwalch. The dogs lurched into the traces and the little cart jerked forward. Fell laughed aloud. 'I thought nothing would amuse me today,' he said.

'You shouldn't have gone to her, boy,' said Gwalch.

'No fortunes, you said!' the forester snapped.

'Pah! That's not telling your fortune; that's a comment on moments past. And you can put the black man from your mind, as well. He'll not win her. She belongs to the land, Fell. In some ways she *is* the land. Sigarni the Hawk Queen, the hope of the Highlands.' The old man shook his head, and then laughed, as if at some private jest. Fell clung to the side of the cart as it rattled and jolted, the wheels dropping into ruts in the trail, half tipping the vehicle.

'By Heaven, Gwalch, it is a most uncomfortable ride,' complained the forester.

'You think this is uncomfortable?' retorted the old man. 'Wait till we get to the top of my hill. The hounds always break into a run for home. By Shemak's balls, boy, it'll turn your hair grey!'

The hounds toiled up the hill, pausing only briefly at the summit to catch their breaths. Then they moved on, rounding a last bend in the trail. Below them Gwalch's timber cabin came into sight and both dogs barked and began to run.

The cart bounced and lurched as the dogs gathered speed, faster and faster down the steep slope. Fell could feel his heart pounding and his knuckles were white as he gripped the side rail. Ahead of them was a towering oak, the trunk directly in their path. 'The tree!' shouted Fell.

'I know!' answered Gwalch. 'Best to jump!'

'Jump?' echoed Fell, swinging to see the old man following his own advice. At the last moment the dogs swerved towards the cabin. The cart tipped suddenly and Fell was hurled head-first from it, missing the oak by inches. He hit the ground hard, with the wind blasted from his lungs.

Fell forced himself to his knees just as Gwalch came ambling over. 'Great fun, isn't it?' said the old man, stooping to take Fell by the arm and pull him to his feet.

Fell looked into Gwalch's twinkling brown eyes. 'You are insane, Gwalch! You always were.'

'Life is to be lived, boy. Without danger there is no life. Come and have a dram. We'll talk, you and I, of life and love, of dreams and glory. I'll tell you tales to fire your blood.'

Fell found his longbow and quiver, gathered the fallen arrows and followed the old man inside. It was a simple one-roomed dwelling with a bed in one corner, a stone-built hearth in the north wall, and a rough-hewn table and two bench seats in the centre. Three rugs, two of ox-skin, one of bear, covered the dirt floor, and the walls were decorated with various weapons – two longbows, horn-tipped, several swords and a double-edged claymore. A mail shirt was hanging on a hook beside the fire, its rings still gleaming, not a speck of rust upon it. On a shelf sat a helm of black iron, embossed with brass and copper. A battle-axe was hanging over the fireplace, double-headed and gleaming.

'Ready for war, eh, old man?' asked Fell as he sat down at the table. Gwalch smiled, and filled a clay cup with amber liquid from a jug.

'Always ready – though no longer up to it,' said the old man sadly. 'And that is a crying shame, for there's a war coming.'

'There's no war!' said Fell irritably. 'There's no excuse for one. The Highlands are peaceful. We pay our taxes. We keep the roads safe.'

Gwalch filled a second cup and drained it in a single swallow. 'Those Outland bastards don't need an excuse, Fell. And I can smell blood in the air. But that's for another day, and it is a little way off, so I won't let it spoil our drinking. So tell me, how did she look?'

'I don't want to talk about her.'

'Ah, but you do. She's filling your mind. Women are like that, bless them! I knew a girl once – Maev, her name was. As bright and perfect a woman as ever walked the green hills. And hips! Oh, the sway of them! She moved in with a cattle-breeder from Gilcross. Eleven babies – and all survived to manhood. Now *that* was a woman!'

'You should have married her yourself,' said Fell.

'I did,' said Gwalch. 'Two years we were together. Great years. All but wore me out, she did. But then I had my skull caved in during the Battle at Iron Bridge, and after that the Talent was on me. Couldn't look at a man or woman without knowing what was going on in their minds. Oh, Fell, you've no idea how irksome it is.' Gwalch sat down and filled his cup for a third time. 'To be lying on top of a beautiful woman, feeling her warmth and the soft silkiness of her; to be aflame with passion and to know she's thinking of a sick cow with a dropping milk yield!' the old man laughed.

Fell shook his head, and smiled. 'Is that true?'

'As true as I'm sitting here. I said to her one day, "Do you love me, woman?" she looked me in the eye and she said, "Of course I do." And do you know, she was thinking of the cattle-breeder she'd met at the Summer Games. And into her mind came the memory of a roll in the hay with him.'

'You must have thought of killing her,' said Fell, embarrassed by the confession.

'Nah! Never was much of a lover. Roll on, roll off. She deserved a little happiness. I've seen her now and again. He's long dead, of course, but she goes on. Rich, now. A widow of property.'

'Are all the weapons yours?' asked Fell, changing the subject.

'Aye, and all been used. I fought for the old King, when we almost won, and I fought alongside the young fool who walked us on to Colden Moor and extermination. Still don't know how I battled clear of that one. I was already nigh on fifty. I won't be so lucky in the next one – though we'll have a better leader.'

'Who?'

The old man touched his nose. 'Now's not the time, Fell. And if I told you, you wouldn't believe me. Anyway I'd sooner talk about women. So tell me about Sigarni. You know you want to. Or shall I tell you what you're thinking?'

'No!' said Fell sharply. 'Fill another cup and I'll talk – though only the gods know why. It doesn't help.' Accepting the drink he swallowed deeply, feeling the fiery liquid burn his throat. 'Son of a whore, Gwalch! Is this made of rat's piss?'

'Only a touch,' said the old man. 'Just for colour. Now go on.'

'Why her? That's the question I ask myself. I've had more than my fair share of beautiful women. Why is it only she can fire my blood? *Why?*'

'Because she's special.' Gwalch rose from the table and moved to the hearth. A fire had been expertly laid and he ignited his tinder-box, holding it below the cast-iron fire-dog until flames began to lick at the dry twigs at the base. Kneeling, he blew on the tongues of flame until the thicker pieces caught. Then he stood. 'Women like her are rare, born for greatness. They're not made to be wives, old before their time, with dry breasts drooping like hanged men. She's starlight where other women are candle flames. You understand? You should feel privileged for having bedded her. She has the gift, Fell. The gift of eternity. You know what that means?'

'I don't know what *any* of this means,' admitted the forester.

'It means she'll live for ever. In a thousand years men will speak her name.'

Fell lifted his cup and stared into the amber liquid. 'Drinking this rots the brain, old man.'

'Aye, maybe it does. But I know what I know, Fell. I know you'll live for her. And I know you'll die for her. *Hold the right, Fell. Do it for me!* And they'll fall on you with their swords of fire, and their lances of pain, and their arrows of farewell. Will you hold, Fell, when she asks you?' Gwalch leaned forward and laid his head on his arms. 'Will you hold, Fell?'

'You're drunk, my friend. You're talking gibberish.'

Gwalch looked up, his eyes bleary. 'I wish I was young again, Fell. I'd stand alongside you. By God, I'd even take that arrow for you!'

25

Fell rose unsteadily, then helped Gwalch to his feet, carefully steered the old man to the bed and laid him down. Returning to the fire, he stretched himself out on the bearskin rug and slept.

It was the closest Sigarni could come to flight. She stood naked on the high rock beside the falls and edged forward, her toes curling over the weather-beaten edge. Sixty feet below the waters of the pool churned as the falls thundered into it. The sun was strong on her back, the sky as blue as gem-stone. Sigarni raised her arms and launched her body forward. Straight as an arrow she dived, arms flung back for balance, and watched the pool roar up to meet her. Bringing her arms forward at the last moment she struck the water cleanly, making barely a splash. Down, down she sank until her hands touched the stone at the base of the pool. Spinning, she used her feet to propel her body upwards. Once more on the surface she swam with lazy grace to the south of the pool, where Lady anxiously waited. Hauling herself clear of the water, she sat on a flat rock and shook the water from her hair. The sound of the falls was muted here, and the sunlight was streaming through the long leaves of a willow, dappling the water with flecks of gold. It would be easy to believe the legends on a day like today, she thought. It seems perfectly natural that a king should have chosen this place to leave the world of men, and journey into the lands of heaven. She could almost see him wading out, then turning, his great sword in his bloodstained hand, the baying of the hounds and the guttural cries of the killers ringing in his ears. Then, as the warriors moved in for the kill, the flash of light and the opening Gateway.

All nonsense. The greatest King of the Highlands had been slain here. Sorain Ironhand, known also as Fingersteel. Last spring, during one of her dives, Sigarni's hands had touched a bone at the bottom of the pool. Bringing it to the surface she found it to be a shoulder-blade. For an hour or more she scoured the bottom of the pool. Then she found him, or rather what was left of his skeleton, held to the pool floor by heavy rocks. The right hand was missing, but there were rust-discoloured screw holes in the bones of the wrist, and the last red remnants of his iron hand close by.

26

No Gateway to Heaven – well, not for his body anyway. Just a lonely death, slain by lesser men. Such is the fate of kings, she thought.

A light breeze touched her body and she shivered. 'Are you still here, Ironhand?' she asked aloud. 'Does your spirit haunt this place?'

'Only when the moon is full,' came a voice. Sigarni sprang to her feet and turned to see a tall man standing by the willow. He was leaning on a staff of oak, and smiling. Lady had ignored him and was still lying by the poolside, head on her paws. Sigarni reached down to where her clothes lay and drew her dagger from its sheath. 'Oh, you'll not need that, lady. I am no despoiler of women. I am merely a traveller who stopped for a drink of cool mountain water. My name is Loran.' Leaning his staff against the tree he moved past her and knelt at the water's edge, pausing to stroke Lady's flanks before he drank.

'She doesn't . . . usually . . . like strangers,' said Sigarni lamely.

'I have a way with animals.' He glanced up at her and gave a boyish grin. 'Perhaps you would feel more comfortable dressed.' He was a handsome man, slender and beardless, his hair corn-yellow, his eyes dark blue.

Sigarni decided that she liked his smile. 'Perhaps you would feel more comfortable undressed,' she said, her composure returning.

'Are you Loda people always so forward?' he asked her amiably.

Returning the knife to its sheath, she sat down. Lady stood and padded to her side. 'What clan are you?' she asked.

'Pallides,' he told her.

'Are all Pallides men so bashful?'

He laughed, the sound rich and merry. 'No. But we're a gentle folk who need to be treated with care and patience. How far is it to Cilfallen?' He stood and moved to a fallen tree, brushing away the loose dirt before seating himself.

Sigarni reached for her leggings and climbed into them. 'Half a day,' she told him, 'due south.' Her upper body was still damp and the white woollen shirt clung to her breasts. Belting on her dagger, she sat down once more. 'Why would a Pallides man be this far south?' she enquired.

'I am seeking Tovi Long-arm. I have a message from the Hunt Lord. Do you have a name, woman?'

'Yes.'

'Might I enquire what it is?'

'Sigarni.'

'Are you angry with me, Sigarni?' the words were softly spoken. She looked into his eyes and saw no hint of humour there. Yes, I am angry, she thought. Asmidir called me a whore, Fell left without a word of thanks or goodbye, and now this stranger had spurned her body. Of course I'm bloody angry!

'No,' she lied. He leaned back and stretched his arm along the tree trunk. Sigarni swept the dagger from the sheath, flipped the blade, then sent the weapon slashing through the air. It slammed into the trunk no more than two inches from his hand. Loran glanced down to see that the blade had cut cleanly through the head of a viper, the rest of its body was thrashing in its death throes. He drew back his hand.

'You are an impressive woman, Sigarni,' he said, reaching out and pulling clear the weapon. With one stroke he decapitated the snake, then cleaned the blade on the grass before returning it hilt first to the silver-haired huntress.

'I'll walk with you a-ways,' she said. 'I wouldn't want a Pallides man to get lost in the forest.'

'Impressive *and* blessed with kindness.'

Together they walked from the falls and up the main trail. The trees were thicker here, the leaves already beginning to turn to the burnished gold of autumn. 'Do you usually talk to ghosts?' asked Loran, as they walked.

'Ghosts?' she queried.

'Ironhand. You were talking to him when I arrived? Was that the magic pool where he crossed over?'

'Yes.'

'Do you believe the legend?'

'Why should I not?' she countered. 'No-one ever found a body, did they?'

He shrugged. 'He never came back either. But his life does make a wonderful story. The last great King before Gandarin. It is said he

28

killed seven of the men sent to murder him. No mean feat for a wounded man.' Loran laughed. 'Maybe they were all stronger and tougher two hundred years ago. That's what my grandfather told me, anyway. Days when men were men, he used to say. And he assured me that Ironhand was seven feet tall and his battle-axe weighed sixty pounds. I used to sit in my grandfather's kitchen and listen to the tallest stories, of dragons and witches, and heroes who stood a head and shoulders above other men. Anyone under six feet tall in those days was dubbed a dwarf, he told me. I believed it all. Never was a more gullible child.'

'Perhaps he was right,' said Sigarni. 'Maybe they were tougher.'

Loran nodded. 'It's possible, I suppose. But I was a Marshal at last year's games. The caber toss from Mereth Sharp-eye broke all records, and Mereth is only five inches above six feet tall. If they were all so strong and fast in those days, why do their records show them to be slower and less powerful than we are today?'

They crossed the last hill before Cilfallen and Sigarni paused. 'That is my home,' she said, pointing to the cabin by the stream. 'You need to follow this road south.'

He bowed and, taking her hand, kissed the palm. 'My thanks to you, Sigarni. You are a pleasant companion.'

She nodded. 'I fear you spurned the best of me,' she said, and was surprised to find herself able to smile at the memory.

Still holding to her hand he shook his head. 'I think no man has ever seen the best of you, woman. Fare thee well!' Loran moved away, but Sigarni called out to him and he turned.

'In the old days,' she said, 'the Highland peoples were free, independent and unbroken. Perhaps that is what makes them seem stronger, more golden and defiant. Their power did not derive from a hurled caber, but a vanquished enemy. They may not have all been seven feet tall. Maybe they just *felt* as if they were.'

He paused and considered her words. 'I would like to call upon you again,' he said, at last. 'Would I be welcome at your hearth?'

'Bring bread and salt, Pallides, and we shall see.'

2

If Loran was as disappointed in Fat Tovi the Baker, he took pains not to show it, for which Tovi himself was more than grateful. The Pallides clansman had bowed upon entering the old stone house, and had observed all the customs and rituals, referring to Tovi as Hunt Lord and bestowing upon him a deference he did not enjoy even among his own people.

Tovi led the clansman to the back room, laid a fire and asked his wife to bring them food and drink, and to keep the noise from the children to as low an ebb as was possible with seven youngsters ranging from the ages of twelve down to three.

'Your courtesy is most welcome,' said Tovi uncomfortably, as the tall young man stood in the centre of the room, declining a chair. 'But as you will already have noticed, the clan Loda no longer operates under the old rules. We are too close to the Lowlands, and our traditions have suffered the most from the conquest. The title of Hunt Lord is outlawed, and we are ruled by lawyers appointed by the Baron Ranulph. We have become a frightened people, Loran. There are fewer than three thousand of us now, spread all around the flanks of High Druin. Seventeen villages of which my own, Cilfallen, is the largest. There are no fighting men now, saving perhaps Fell and his foresters. And they report to the Baron's captain of the Watch. I fear, young man, that the old ways are as dead and buried as my comrades on Colden Moor.' Tovi sniffed loudly, and found himself unable to meet the clansman's steady stare. 'So, let us dispense with the formalities. Sit you down and tell me why you have come.'

Loran removed his leaf-green cloak and laid it over the back of a padded chair. Then he sat and stared into the fire for a few moments, gathering his thoughts. 'We of the Pallides,' he said at last, 'suffered great losses at Colden. But we are far back into the mountains and the old ways have survived better than here. Our young men are still trained to fight, and retain their pride. As you say, you are close to the Lowlands and the armies of the Outlands, and so I make this point without criticism. As to my visit, my Hunt Lord wishes me to tell you that the Gifted Ones of the Pallides have been experiencing dreams of blood. It is their belief that a new war is looming. They have seen blood-wolves upon the Highlands, and heard the cries of the dying. They have seen the Red Moon, and heard the wail of the Bai-sheen. My Hunt Lord wishes to know if your own Gifted Ones have dreamt these things.'

'We have only one man with the Gift, Loran. Once a warrior – and a mighty one – he now travels the mountains in a cart drawn by hounds. He is a drunkard and his dreams are not to be relied upon.'

The door opened and Tovi's wife entered, carrying a wooden tray on which sat two tankards of ale and a plate of bread and beef. Laying it down on the table she took one glance at her husband, smiled wearily and left without a word. From beyond the open doorway the sound of children playing could be heard, but the noise was cut off once more as the door closed behind her.

'Drunkard or no,' said Loran, 'has he dreamed?'

Tovi nodded. 'He says a great leader is coming, a warrior of the line of Ironhand. But it is nonsense, Loran. The Outlanders have five thousand men patrolling the Lowlands. Five thousand! If there was the merest hint of rebellion they could treble that number in a matter of weeks. All their wars are won. They have armies sitting idle.'

'That is precisely what troubles my Hunt Lord,' said Loran. 'A warrior race with no wars to fight? What can they do? Either they will turn on themselves like mad dogs, or they will find an enemy. What your drunkard says about a great leader is echoed by our own Gifted Ones; and also by the Seer of the Farlain. No one knows this leader's name, nor his clan. There is a mist shrouding him. Yet we must find him, Lord Tovi. All indications are that the Outlanders will lead an invasion force here in the spring. We have less than seven months to prepare.'

'To prepare?' stormed Tovi. 'For what, pray? Fell and his foresters number around sixty men. I could raise perhaps another two hundred, and some of those would either be greybeards or children. Prepare? If they come, we die. It is that simple. The Loda were never the largest of the clans. The Pallides and the Farlain always outnumbered us. Still do. And you have the high passes that can be defended, and the hidden valleys to hide your cattle and goats. What do we have? I was a warrior, boy. I was a captain. I know how to use land in war. If I had ten thousand men I couldn't protect my own villages. You want to talk of preparation? Talk of pleading with the Baron, of sending an entreaty to the Outland King, of dropping to our bended knees and begging for life. The first I'll accede to, the second I'll put my name to, and the third I'll never do! But they are our only options.'

Loran shook his head. 'I don't believe that to be true. If we can find the leader to unite us, we can formulate a strategy. The people of Loda could leave their homes and draw back into the deeper Highlands. We have the autumn before us and could move food and supplies further back into the mountains. If you agree, I can arrange for temporary homes to be erected in Pallides lands.'

Tovi shook his head. 'There must be another way, Loran. There must be! We cannot fight them with any hope of success. And what could they gain from invading the Highlands? There is no gold here, no plunder. Would you declare war to capture a few cattle herds?'

'No, I wouldn't,' agreed Loran. 'But armies are like swords. They must be kept sharp and in use. The Outlanders will, as I have said, need to find some enemy.'

Tovi sighed and rose from his chair, pausing before the fire and staring into the flames. 'I am not the Hunt Lord, man. I am the baker. I don't have power, and I don't have resources. I don't even have the will.'

'Damn you, man!' stormed Loran, rising from his chair. 'Have you lost so much? I met a whore on the road with more fire in her belly than you.' Tovi's face went white and he lunged forward, his

32

large hands grabbing the front of Loran's pale green tunic, dragging the younger man from his feet.

'How dare you?' hissed Tovi. 'I stood on Colden Moor, my sword dripping Outland blood. I watched my brothers cut down, my land swallowed by the enemy. Where were you when I fought my battles? I'll tell you – you were sucking on your mother's tit! I have lost much, boy, but don't presume to insult me.'

'My apologies, Hunt Lord,' said Loran softly, holding to Tovi's angry gaze. There was no hint of weakness in the mild manner in which Loran spoke, and Tovi's eyes narrowed.

'You did that on purpose, Pallides. You think to fire my blood through anger.' Tovi released the younger man, then nodded. 'And you were right.' Clumsily he tried to brush the creases from Loran's tunic. 'Damn it all, you are right. Live under the yoke long enough and you start to feel like an ox.' He laughed suddenly, the sound harsh. 'I do not know how gifted are your Gifted Ones, Loran, but we will lose nothing by at least sending supplies back into the high country. And tonight I will call a meeting of the Elders to discuss the rest of your proposal. You are welcome to stay here the night and meet them.'

'No,' the younger man told him. 'I want to see the drunkard you spoke of.'

'It is a long walk and it will soon be dusk.'

'Then I'd best finish this meal and be on my way.' Loran tore a chunk from the bread and bit off the crust as Tovi returned to his seat.

'You mentioned a whore? We have only one whore in Cilfallen, and she rarely leaves her house.'

'A young silver-haired woman. She offered herself to me without even asking a price.'

Tovi suddenly chuckled. 'You should consider yourself most fortunate that you did not call her a whore to her face.'

'How do you know I did not?'

'The last man who called her such a name had his jaw broken in three places. It took two men to pull Sigarni away from him; she was about to cut his tongue out.' The smile faded. 'She is the last of the true blood line of Gandarin. Any son of hers would be the undisputed heir to the crown. And it will never happen.'

'She is barren?'

'Aye. She was due to wed Fell, the Forest Captain. Old Gwalch, our Gifted One, proclaimed her infertile. She is no whore, Loran. True she has enjoyed many lovers, but she picks only men she likes, and there is no price to pay. She is a woman of fire and iron, that one, and well liked here.'

'You are saying I should feel flattered?'

'Did you not?' countered the baker, a twinkle in his eye.

'She is very beautiful. I watched her make a dive into Ironhand's pool and it took the breath away. I have always spurned those I thought to be whores. Now I am beginning to regret my decision.'

'You may never get another chance, boy.'

'We will see.'

The sandy-haired young man sat with his head in his hands, his eyes bleary with drink. Before him was a half-empty tankard. Ballistar climbed to the bench seat and then perched his small body at the edge of the table. 'Getting drunk won't solve anything, Bernt,' he said.

'She doesn't want to see me,' said Bernt. 'She says she will never see me again.' He looked across at the dwarf. 'I didn't mean to do it, Balli. I got excited. I wouldn't have hurt Lady, not for all the world. I just wasn't thinking. I was watching Sigarni. She looked so beautiful in the morning sunlight. So beautiful.' The young man drained the tankard and belched. Ballistar looked at him – the square face, the deep-set blue eyes, the powerful neck and broad shoulders – and knew envy. All that *height* wasted on a dullard like Bernt. Ballistar felt guilty at the thought, for he liked the young man. True, Bernt was not bright, yet he had a warmth and a compassion lacking in other, more intelligent men. In truth he was a sensitive soul.

'I think,' said the dwarf, 'that you should just lie low for a while. Lady is almost healed and she is hunting well. Wait for a little while, then go out and see Sigarni again. I expect she'll relent. You were always good for her.'

'*Was*. That's the word, isn't it? *Was*. I could never talk to her, you know. Didn't understand much of what she said. It all flew over my head. I didn't care, Balli. I was just happy to be with her. To . . . love her. I think all she needed from me was my body.' He laughed nervously and looked round to see if anyone was listening, but the two other drinkers in the tavern were sitting by the fire, talking in low tones. 'That's what she told me,' he continued.' "Bernt," she said, "this is your only skill." She said I took away all her tension. She was wrong, though, Balli. It's not my only skill. I was *there* for her. She couldn't see that. I don't know what I'm going to do!'

'There are other women,' said Ballistar softly. 'You are a good young man, strong, honest. You have a great deal to offer.'

'I don't want anyone else, Balli. I don't. All my waking moments are filled with thoughts of her. And when I sleep I dream of her. I never asked for anything, you know. I never . . . made demands. She didn't ever let me sleep in the bed, you know . . . afterwards. I always had to go home. It didn't matter what the weather was like. Once I even went home in a blizzard. Got lost, almost died. Almost died . . .' His voice faded away, and he bit his lip. 'She didn't care, not really. I always thought that I would, sort of grow on her. That she would realize I was . . . important. But I'm not important, am I? I'm just a cattle-herder.'

The dwarf shifted uneasily. 'As I said, Bernt, you should give her a little time. I know she likes you.'

'Has she spoken of me?' asked the young man, his eyes eager, his ears hungry for words of encouragement.

Ballistar looked away. 'I can tell, that's all. She's still angry, but underneath . . . just give it time.'

'She didn't say anything, did she, Balli? Except maybe that I was a fool.'

'She's still angry. Go home. Get something to eat.'

The young man smiled suddenly. 'Will you do something for me, Balli? Will you?'

'Of course,' answered the dwarf.

'Will you go to her and ask her to meet me at the old oak grove tonight, an hour after dark?'

'She won't come – you know that! And she doesn't keep clock candles, she has no use for them.'

'Well, soon after dusk then. But will you ask her? Tell her that it is so important to me. Even if she only comes to say goodbye. Will you tell her that? Will you? Tell her I have never asked for anything save this one time.'

'I'll go to her, Bernt. But you are only building up more pain for yourself.'

'Thank you, Balli. I'll take your advice now. I'll go home and eat.'

The young man levered himself up, staggered, grinned inanely and lurched from the tavern. Ballistar clambered down from the table and followed him.

It was a long walk on tiny legs to Sigarni's cabin, more than two hours. And it was such a waste, thought Ballistar.

The afternoon was warm, but a gentle breeze was blowing over High Druin as the dwarf ambled on. He walked for an hour, then sat for a while on a hillside resting his tired legs. In the distance he could see a walker heading off towards the higher hills. The man wore a leaf-green cloak and carried a long staff; Ballistar squinted, but could not reconize him. He was heading towards Gwalch's cabin. Ballistar chuckled. He wouldn't be walking that straight when he left!

Rising once more, he set off down the slope and along the deer trails to Sigarni's cabin. He found her sitting by the front door, cutting new flying jesses from strips of leather. Lady was nowhere to be seen, but Abby was sitting on her bow perch. She flapped her wings and pranced as she saw Ballistar. The dwarf gave a low bow to the bird. 'It is good to see you as well, Abby.'

'Just in time,' said Sigarni. 'You can make some herb tea. Somehow I never make it taste as good as yours.'

'My pleasure, princess.'

Ballistar climbed the steps and entered the cabin. An old iron kettle was hissing steam over the fire. Taking a cloth to protect his hands, he lifted it clear. In the back room he found the packs of dried herbs he and Sigarni had gathered in the spring. Mixing them by eye, he added hot water and cut a large portion of crystallized honey, which he dropped into the mixture. He stirred the tea with a long wooden spoon and sat quietly while it brewed. How to tackle Sigarni? How to convince the silver-haired huntress to meet the boy?

After several minutes he filled two large pottery cups with tea and carried them out into the afternoon sunlight. Sigarni took the first and sipped it. 'How do you make it taste like this?' she asked.

'Talent,' he assured her. 'Now, are you going to ask me why I have walked all this way?'

'I assume it was because you felt in need of my company.'

'Under normal circumstances that would be true, princess. But not today. I have a favour to ask.'

'Ask it – and I'll consider it,' she said.

'I was hoping for a little more than that,' he admitted.

'Just ask,' she said, a little coldly.

'I saw Bernt today . . .'

'The answer is no,' she said flatly.

'You don't know the question yet?'

'I can hazard a guess. He wants me to take him back.'

'No! Well . . . yes. But that is not the favour. He asks if you will meet him after dusk at the old oak grove. Even if it is only to say goodbye. He said it was vital to him.'

'I have already said goodbye.' Returning her attention to the leather jesses, she said nothing more.

Ballistar sighed. 'He also said that he had never asked you for anything – save this once.'

She looked up and he braced himself for her anger. But her words were spoken coldly, and without emotion. 'I owe him nothing. I owe you nothing. I owe no one. You understand? I did not ask him to love me, nor to follow me like a dog. He was an adequate lover, no more than that. And now he is part of my past. He has no place in the present. Is that clear?'

'Oh, it is clear, princess. Callous, unkind, unfeeling. But very *clear*. And of course it would be so time-consuming for you to walk to the oak grove. After all, it is more than a mile from here.'

She leaned back and looked into his face. 'Now we are both angry, little man. And for what? Bernt is a dolt. I have no need of fools around me. But, since it is a favour to you, I shall grant it. I shall go to Bernt, and I shall tell him goodbye. Does that satisfy you?'

He grinned and nodded. 'And as a reward I shall prepare you a meal. What provisions do you have?'

'Abby killed a duck this morning.'

'I shall cook it with a berry sauce,' he said.

They ate well, the duck being young and plump. Ballister cooked it to perfection; the skin was crisp and dark, the flesh moist, the red berry sauce complementing the flavour. Sigarni pushed aside her plate and licked her fingers. 'If I had an ounce of common sense I'd marry you,' she told the dwarf. 'I never knew a man who could make food taste so fine.'

Ballistar was sitting in the hide chair, his little legs jutting out. He nodded sagely. 'Well,' he said, at last, 'you could *ask* me. But I would only say no.'

Sigarni smiled. 'Not good enough for you, dwarf?'

'Too good, probably. Though that is not the reason. There is something about you, Sigarni. Like the Crown of Alwen – all men can see it, but none can touch it.'

'Nonsense. Men can touch me. I like men to touch me.'

'No, you don't,' he argued. 'I don't think you have ever allowed a man to touch your heart. No man has ever opened the window of your soul.'

She laughed at him then. 'The heart is a pump for moving blood around the body, and as to the soul . . . what is that exactly?' She held up her hand. 'No, don't try to explain it. Let it lie. The meal was too fine to finish on an argument. And you had better go, or you'll be walking back in the dark.'

The dwarf scrambled down from the chair, and gathered up the plates. 'Leave them,' said Sigarni. 'Be off with you, Ballistar. I have a need to be alone.'

'Don't be too hard on Bernt,' said Ballistar, from the doorway.

'I'll treat him like an injured puppy,' she promised.

After the dwarf had gone Sigarni cleaned the plates and built up the fire. She did not relish seeing the young cattle-herder, for she was determined never to renew their relationship. It was not that he was a poor lover, nor even that he was dull. In the early days, last autumn, she had enjoyed his quiet company. However, during the spring he had become like a weight around her neck, following her everywhere, declaring his love, sitting and staring at her, begging for love like a dog begs for scraps. She shuddered. Why could he not enjoy what they had? Why did he need more than she was prepared to give? Idiot!

Pouring herself a goblet of honey mead from a flagon that Gwalch had given her, she moved to the doorway and sat down beside Lady. The hound looked up, but did not move. Idly Sigarni stroked the soft fur behind the beast's ears. Lady lay still, enjoying the sensation for several minutes, then her head came up and she stared intently towards the tree line. 'What is it girl?' whispered Sigarni.

As horse and rider emerged from the trees, Sigarni swore softly. It was Asmidir. He was dressed now in clothes of black and riding a tall black gelding. His burnoose of black silk was held in place by a dark band of leather, with an opal set at the centre. The horse advanced into the yard. Abby spread her wings and let out a screech on her bow perch. Lady merely stood, alert and waiting.

'Come to see your whore?' asked Sigarni as the black man rode up. He smiled amiably, then dismounted. Draping the reins over the gelding's head, he climbed the three steps to the porch.

'You are too prickly, Sigarni. I need to speak with you. Shall we go inside? Your northern weather plays havoc with my equatorial bones.'

'I'm not sure you are welcome,' she told him, rising to stand before him in the doorway.

'Ah, but I am, for friends are rare in life, and not to be idly tossed aside. Also I can see from your eyes that you are pleased to see me, and I sense in you a tension only sex will resolve. Am I at fault in any of these observations?'

'Not so far,' she agreed, stepping aside and ushering him into the room. Once inside he stopped and sniffed.

'You have been having a feast,' he said, nostrils flaring. 'The aroma makes my mouth water. Duck, was it?'

'Yes. Ballistar cooked it for me. Now he is a true sorcerer when it comes to food. You should employ him.'

'I'll think on it,' he said, removing his cloak and laying it over the back of the chair. Sitting down by the fire he sat for a moment in silence staring into the flames. Sigarni sat on his lap, leaning to kiss his cheek.

'I'm glad you came,' she said. Reaching up, he ran his fingers through her silver hair and drew her close. Pushing one arm under her thighs, he stood and carried her through to the back bedroom.

For more than an hour they made love but, skilled as he was, Sigarni could feel a different tension within him. After her second orgasm she stopped him, pushing him gently to his back. 'What is wrong, my friend?' she asked him, rising up on her elbow and stroking the sleek dark skin of his chest. He closed his eyes.

'Everything,' he said. He reached for her, but she resisted him.

'Tell me,' she commanded.

'I would have thought,' he said, forcing a smile, 'that you would have the good grace to let me achieve my own climax before entering into a dialogue.'

She chuckled and bit his ear. 'Then be quick!' she told him, 'for I have other matters to attend to.'

'Your wish shall be obeyed, mistress!' he said, rolling over and pinning her shoulders.

Sigarni felt loose-limbed and wonderfully relaxed as she sat by the fire and sipped her mead. Relaxed in the chair, Asmidir sat naked, save for his cloak, which he had wrapped about his shoulders against the draught from the warped wood of the door.

'Now tell me,' she said.

'There is a war coming,' he told her.

'Where?'

'Here, Sigarni. I was at the Citadel a few days ago. I saw the mercenaries arriving, and I know the Baron is studying maps of all

40

the lands around High Druin. It is my belief that he intends to bring an army into the mountains.'

'That cannot be,' she said. 'There is no one to fight him.'

'That is largely immaterial. He hates his position here, and probably sees a Highland War as his best chance of being recalled south in triumph. It does not matter that he will face a rabble of poorly armed villagers. Who will know? He has his own historian. His army will be able to pillage and plunder the Highlands, and he will gather to himself a force to make him a power in the land. He may even be looking ahead and planning a civil war. It doesn't matter what his motives are.'

'And how does this concern you, Asmidir? You are not of this land, and you are a friend to the Outland king.'

'I served him, but he has no friends. The King is a hard, ruthless man, much like the Baron. No, for me it is . . . personal.' He smiled thinly. 'I came here because of a prophecy. It has not been fulfilled. Now I am lost.'

'What prophecy?'

He shrugged. 'It does not matter, does it? Even shamen can make mistakes, it seems. But I have grown to love this harsh, cold land with a fierceness that surprises me. It is as strong as my hatred for the Baron and all he represents.' He sighed and turned his head towards the fire. 'Why is it that wickedness always seems to triumph? Is it just that evil men freed from the constraints of basic morality are stronger than we?'

'It is probably just a question of timing,' she said and his head jerked round.

'Timing?'

'We have had two Kings of legend here, Gandarin and Ironhand. Both were good men, but they were also strong and fearless. Their enemies were scattered, and they ruled wisely and well. But this is the time of the Outland Kings, and not a good time for the peoples of the Highlands. Our time will come again. There will be a leader.'

'Now *is* the time,' he said. 'Where is the man? That was the prophecy that brought me here. A great leader will rise, wearing

41

the crown of Alwen. But I have travelled far, Sigarni, and heard no word of such a man.'

'What will you do when you find him?'

He chuckled. 'My skill is strategy. I am a student of war. I will teach him how to fight the Outlanders.'

'Highland men do not need to be taught how to fight.'

He shook his head. 'There you are wrong, Sigarni. Your whole history has been built on manly courage: assembling a host to sweep down on an enemy host, man against man, claymore crashing against claymore. But war is about more than battles. It is about logistics, supplies, communication, discipline. An army has to feed, commanders need to gather reports and intelligence and pass these on to generals. Apart from this there are other considerations – morale, motivation, belief. The Outlanders, as you call them, understand these things.'

'You are altogether too tense,' she told him, leaning forward and running her hand softly down the inside of his thigh. 'Come back to bed, and I will repay you for the pleasure you gave me.'

'What of these other matters you had to attend to?' he asked.

For a moment only she thought of Bernt, then brushed him from her mind. 'Nothing of importance,' she assured him.

At noon the following day Ballistar found Bernt hanging from the branch of a spreading oak. The young cattle-herder was dressed in his best tunic and leggings, though they were soiled now, for he had defecated in death. The boy's eyes were wide open and bulging, and his tongue was protruding from his mouth. When Ballistar arrived at the oak grove a crow was sitting on Bernt's shoulder, pecking at his right eye.

Below the corpse was a hawking glove, lovingly made and decorated with fine white beads. Urine from the corpse had dripped upon it, staining the hide.

3

The oxen found pulling the wide wagon too difficult over the narrow deer trails to Gwalch's cabin, so Tovi was forced to take the long route, down into the valley and up over the rocky roads once used by the Lowland miners when there was still a plentiful supply of coal to be found on the open hillsides. The baker had set off just after dawn. He always enjoyed these quarterly trips into Citadel town. Gwalch was an amusing, if irritating, companion, but the money they shared from their partnership helped Tovi to maintain a pleasant and comfortable lifestyle. Gwalch made honey mead of the finest quality, and much of it was shipped to the south at vastly inflated prices.

One of the oxen slipped on the rocky shale. 'Ho there, Flaxen! Concentrate now, girl!' shouted Tovi. The wagon lurched on, the empty barrels in the back clunking against one another. Tovi took a deep sniff of the mountain air, blowing cool over High Druin. At the top of the rise he halted the oxen, allowing them a breather before attempting the last climb into the forest. Tovi applied the brake, then swung to stare out over the landscape. Many years before he had marched with the Loda men down this long road. They were singing, he recalled; they had met the Pallides warriors down there by the fork in the stream. Seven thousand men – even before the Farlain warriors had joined them.

All dead now. Well . . . most of them anyway. Gwalch had been there. Fifty years old and straight as a long staff. The King had been mounted on a fine Southern horse, his bonnet adorned with a long eagle feather. Every inch a warrior he looked. But he had no real heart for it. Tovi hawked and spat, remembering the moment when the King fled the field leaving them to stand and die.

'Blood doesn't always run true,' he said softly. 'Heroes sire cowards, and cowards can sire kings.'

The air was crisp, the wind beginning to bite as Tovi wrapped his cloak across his chest. *Didn't feel the wind back then,* he thought. *I did a week later, though, as I fled from the hunters, crawling through the bracken, wading the streams, hiding in shallow caves, starving and cold. God's bones, I felt it then!*

High above him two eagles were flying the thermals, safe from the thoughts and arrows of men. Tovi released the brake and flicked the reins over the backs of the oxen. 'On now, my lads!' he called. 'It's an easier trip down for a while.'

Within the hour he arrived at Gwalch's cabin. The old man was sitting outside in the sunshine with a cup of mead in his hands. There were three horsemen close by, two grim-faced soldiers still sitting their saddles, and a cleric who was standing before the old man, arguing and gesticulating. The soldiers looked bored and cold, Tovi thought. The cleric was a man he recognized: Andolph the Census Taker, a small, fat individual with ginger hair and a face as white as Tovi's baking flour.

'It is not acceptable!' Tovi heard the cleric shout. 'And you could be in serious trouble. I don't know why I try to deal fairly with you Highlanders. You are a constant nuisance.'

Tovi halted the wagon and climbed down. 'Might I be of service, Census Taker?' he enquired. Andolph stepped back from the grinning Gwalch. 'I take it you know this man?'

'Indeed I do. He is an old friend. What is the problem?'

Andolph sighed theatrically. 'As you know, the new law states that all men must have surnames that give them individuality. It is no longer enough to be Dirk, son of Dirk. Gods, man, there are hundreds of those. It is not difficult, surely, therefore to find a name that would suffice. But not this old fool. Oh no! I am trying to be reasonable, Baker, and he will not have it. Look at this!' The little man stepped forward and thrust a long sheet of paper towards Tovi. The baker took it, read what was written there, and laughed aloud.

'Well, it *is* a name,' he offered.

'I can't put this forward to the Roll Makers. Can't you see that? They will accuse the old man of making a mockery of the law. And I will be summoned to answer for it. I came here in good faith; I like a jest as well as the next man, and it did make me laugh when first I saw it. But it cannot be allowed to stand. You see that, don't you?'

Tovi nodded. There was no malice in the little man and, as far as was possible with an Outlander, Tovi quite liked him. It was a thankless task trying to take a census in the Highlands, especially since the object was to find new tax-payers. 'I'll speak to him,' he said, handing back the paper and walking over to where Gwalch sat. The old man was staring at one of the soldiers, and the man was growing uncomfortable.

'Come on, Gwalch,' said Tovi soothingly, 'it is time for the fun to stop. What name will you choose?'

'What's wrong with Hare-turd?' countered Gwalch.

'I'll tell you what's wrong with it – it'll be carved on your tomb-stone. And you'll not be surprised when future generations fail to appreciate what a fine man you were. Now stop this nonsense.'

Gwalch sniffed loudly, then drained his mead. 'You choose!' he told Tovi, staring at the soldier.

The Baker turned to the Census Taker. 'When young he was known as *Fear-not*. Will that do?' Andolph nodded. From a leather bag he took a quill and a small bottle of ink. Resting the paper against his saddle, he made the change and called Gwalch to sign it. The old man gave a low curse, but he strolled to the horse and signed with his new name.

Andolph waved the paper in the air to dry the ink. 'My thanks to you, Tovi Baker, and goodbye to you . . . Gwalchmai Fear-not. I hope we will not meet again.'

'You and I won't,' said Gwalch, with a grin. 'And a word of advice, Andolph Census Taker: Trust not in dark-eyed women. Especially those who dance.'

Andolph blinked nervously, then climbed ponderously into his saddle. The three horsemen rode away, but the soldier Gwalch had been staring at swung round to look back. Gwalch waved at him. 'That is the man who will kill me,' said Gwalch, his smile fading. 'He and five others will come here. Do you think I could have changed the future if I had stabbed him today?'

45

Tovi shivered. 'Are we ready to load?' he asked.

'Aye. It's a good batch, but I'll not be needing the new barrels. This is our last trip, Tovi. Make the best of it.'

'What is the point of having the Gift if all it brings is gloom and doom?' stormed Tovi. 'And another thing, I do not believe that life is mapped out so simply. Men shape the future, and nothing is written in stone. You understand?'

'I don't argue with that, Tovi. Not at all. Sometimes I have dreamt of moments to come, and they have failed to arrive. Not often, mind, but sometimes. Like the young cattle-herder who loved Sigarni. Until yesterday I always saw him leaving the mountains to find employment in the Lowlands. Last night, though, I saw a different ending. And it has come to pass.'

'What are you talking about?'

'Bernt, the broad-shouldered young man who works for Grame the Smith . . .'

'I know him . . . what about him?'

'Hanged himself from a tree. Late last night. Dreamt it sitting in my chair.'

'Hell's teeth! And it has happened? You are sure?'

The old man nodded. 'What I am trying to say is that futures can be changed sometimes. Not often. He shouldn't be dead, but something happened, one small thing, and suddenly life was over for Bernt.'

'What happened?'

'A woman broke a promise,' said Gwalch. 'Now let's have a swift drink before loading. It'll help keep the cold at bay.'

'No!' said Tovi. 'I want to be at the market before mid-morning.' Gwalch swore and moved away to the barrel store, and together the two men loaded twelve casks of honey mead alongside the empty barrels Tovi had brought with him. 'Why don't you let me leave the empties here?' asked the baker. 'You might change your mind – or the dream may change.'

'This dream won't change, my friend. There'll be no market for our mead come springtime. You know that; you've spoken to the Pallides man.'

'What did you tell him?' asked Tovi as the two men clambered to the driving seat of the wagon.

'Nothing he didn't already know,' answered Gwalch. 'The Pallides Gifted Ones are quite correct.'

'And that was all?'

Gwalch shook his head. 'There is a leader coming. But I wouldn't tell him who, or when. It is not the right time. He impressed me, though. Sharp as a stone of flint, and hard too. He could have been a force one day. But he won't survive. You will, though, Tovi. You're going to be a man again.'

'I am already a man, Gwalchmai Hare-turd. And don't you forget it.'

In the pale moonlight the friendly willow took on a new identity, its long, wispy branches trailing the steel-coloured water like skeletal fingers. Even the sound of the falls was muted and strange, like the whispers of angry demons. The undergrowth rustled as the creatures of the night moved abroad on furtive paws, and Sigarni sat motionless by the waterside, watching the fragmented moon ripple on the surface.

She felt both numb and angry by turn; numbed by the death of the simple herder, and angry at the way the dwarf had treated her. Sigarni had spent three days in the mountains trapping fox and beaver, and had returned tired, wet and hungry to find Ballistar sitting by her door. Her spirits had lifted instantly; the little man was always good company, and his cooking was a treat to be enjoyed. Greeting him with a smile, Sigarni had dumped her furs on the wooden board and then returned Abby to her bow perch. Returning to the house, she saw that Ballistar had moved away from the door. He was standing stock-still, staring at her, his face set and serious, the expression in his eyes unfathomable. Sigarni saw that he was carrying a hawking glove of pale tan, beautifully decorated with white and blue beads.

'A present for me?' she asked. He nodded and tossed her the glove. It was well made of turned hide brushed to a sheen, the stiches small and tight, the beads forming a series of blue swirls over a white letter S. 'It's beautiful,' she said gaily. 'Why so glum? Did you think I wouldn't like it?' Slipping it on, she found it fitted perfectly.

'I never saw a crow peck out a man's eye before,' he said. 'It's curious how easily the orb comes away. Still, Bernt didn't mind. Even though he was in his best clothes. He didn't mind at all. Scarce noticed it.'

'What are you talking about?'

'Nothing of importance, Sigarni. So, how was Bernt when you saw him?'

'I didn't see him,' she snapped. 'I had other things to do. Now what is wrong with you? Are you drunk?'

The dwarf shook his head. 'No, I'm not drunk – but I will be in a while. I shall probably drink too much at the wake. I do that, you know. Funerals always upset me.' He pointed at the glove she wore. 'He made that for you. I suppose you could call it a love gift. He made it and he put on his best tunic. He wanted you to see him at his very best. But you didn't bother to go. So he waited until the dawn and then hanged himself from a tall tree in the oak grove. So, Sigarni, that's one fool you won't have to suffer again.'

She stood very still, then slowly peeled off the glove. 'It was on the ground below him,' said Ballistar, 'so you'll have to excuse the stains.'

Sigarni hurled the glove to the ground. 'Are you blaming me for his suicide?' she asked him.

'You, princess? No, not at all,' he told her, his voice rich with sarcasm. 'He just wanted to see you one last time. He asked me to tell you how important it was to him. And I did. But nothing is important to him any more.'

'Have you said all you want to say?' she asked, her voice soft but her eyes angry.

He did not reply, he merely turned and walked away.

Sigarni sat in the doorway for some time, trying to make some sense of the events. Ballistar obviously held her responsible for Bernt's death, but why? All she had done was rut with him for a while. Did that make her the guardian of his soul? I didn't ask him to fall in love with me, she thought. I didn't even work at it.

You could have gone to him as you promised, said the voice of her heart.

Sorrow touched her then and she stood and wandered away from the house, heading for the sanctuary of the waterfall pool. This was where she always came when events left her saddened or angry. It was here she had been found on that awful night when her parents were slain: she was just sitting by the willow, her eyes vacant, her blonde hair turned white as snow. Sigarni remembered nothing of that night, save that the pool was the one safe place in a world of uncertainty.

Only tonight there was no sanctuary. A man was dead, a good man, a kind man. That he was stupid counted for nothing now. She remembered his smile, the softness of his touch and his desperation to make her happy.

'It could never be you, Bernt,' she said aloud. 'You were not the man for me. I've yet to meet him, but I'll know him when I do.' Tears formed in her eyes, misting her vision. 'I'm sorry that you are dead,' she said. 'Truly I am. And I'm sorry that I didn't come to you. I thought you wanted to beg me back, and I didn't want that.'

Movement on the surface of the pool caught her eye. A mist was moving on the water, swirling and rising. It formed the figure of a man, blurred and indistinct. A slight breeze touched it, sending it moving towards her, and Sigarni scrambled to her feet and backed away.

'Do not run,' whispered a man's voice inside her mind.

But she did, turning and sprinting up over the rocks and away on to the old deer trail.

Sigarni did not stop until she had reached her cabin, and even then she barred the door and built a roaring fire. Focusing her gaze on the timbered wall, she scanned the weapons hanging there: the leaf-bladed broadsword, the bow of horn and the quiver of black-shafted arrows, the daggers and dirks and the helm, with its crown and cheek-guards of black iron and the nasal guard and brows of

49

polished brass. Moving to them she lifted down a long dagger, and sat honing its blade with a whetstone.

It was an hour before she stopped trembling.

Gwalchmai's mouth was dry, and his tongue felt as if he had spent the night chewing badger fur. The morning sunlight hurt his eyes, and the bouncing of the dog-cart caused his stomach to heave. He broke wind noisily, which eased the pressure on his belly. He always used to enjoy getting drunk in the morning, but during the last few years it had begun to seem like a chore. The great grey wolfhounds, Shamol and Cabris, paused in their pulling and the cart stopped. Shamol was looking to the left of the trail, his head still, dark eyes alert. Cabris squatted down, seemingly bored. 'No hares today, boys!' said Gwalch, flicking the reins. Reluctantly Shamol launched himself into the traces. Caught unawares, Cabris did not rise in time and almost went under the little cart. Angry, the hound took a nip at Shamol's flank. The two dogs began to snarl, their fur bristling.

'Quiet!' bellowed Gwalch. 'Hell's dungeons, I haven't had a headache like this since the axe broke my skull. So keep it down and behave yourselves.' Both hounds looked at him, then felt the light touch of the reins on their backs. Obediently they started to pull. Reaching behind him, Gwalch lifted a jug of honey mead and took a swallow.

Sigarni's cabin was in sight now, and he could see the black bitch, Lady, sitting in the dust before it. So could Shamol and Cabris and with a lunge they broke into a run. Gwalch was caught between the desire to save his bones and the need to protect his jug. He clung on grimly. The cart survived the race down the hill, and once on level ground Gwalch began to hope that the worst was over. But then Lady ran at the hounds, swerving at the last moment to race away into the meadow. Shamol and Cabris tried to follow her, the cart tipped and Gwalch flew through the air, still clutching his jug to his scrawny chest. Twisting, he struck the ground on his back, honey mead slurping from the jug to drench his green woollen tunic. Slowly he sat up, then took a long drink. The hounds were

50

now sitting quietly by the upturned cart, watching him gravely. Leaving the jug on the boardwalk, he stood and walked to where the cart lay. Righting it he moved to the dogs, untying the reins. Shamol nuzzled his hand, but Cabris took off immediately towards the woods in search of Lady. Shamol ambled after him.

Gwalch recovered his jug and went into the house. He found Sigarni sitting at the table, a dagger before her. Her hair was unwashed, her face drawn, her eyes tired. Gwalch gathered two clay cups and filled them both with mead, pushing one towards her. She shook her head. 'Drink it, girl,' he said sitting opposite her. 'It'll do you no harm.'

'Read my mind,' she commanded.

'No. You'll remember when you are ready.'

'Damn you, Gwalch! you're quick to tell everyone's fortune but mine. What happened that night when my parents were butchered? Tell me!'

'You know what happened. Your . . . father and his wife were killed. You survived. What else is there to know?'

'Why did my hair turn white? Why were the bodies buried so swiftly? I didn't even see them.'

'Tell me about last night.'

'Why should I? You already know. Bernt's ghost came to me at the pool.'

'No,' he said, 'that wasn't Bernt. Poor, sad Bernt is gone from the world. The spirit who spoke to you was from another time. Why did you run?'

'I was . . . frightened.' Her pale eyes locked to his, daring him to criticize her.

Gwalch smiled. 'Not easy to admit, is it? Not when you are Sigarni the Huntress, the woman who needs no one. Did you know this is my birthday? Seventy-eight years ago today I made my first cry. Killed my first man fourteen years later, a cattle raider. Tracked him for three days. He took my father's prize bull. It's been a long life, Sigarni. Long and irritatingly eventful.' Pouring the last of the mead, he drained it in a single swallow, then gazed longingly at the empty jug.

51

'Who was the ghost?' she asked

'Go and ask him, woman. Call for him.' She shivered and looked away.

'I can't.'

Gwalch chuckled. 'There is nothing you cannot do, Sigarni. Nothing.'

Reaching across the table she took his hand, stroking it tenderly. 'Oh, come on, Gwalch, are we not friends? Why won't you help me?'

'I *am* helping you. I am giving you good advice. You don't remember the night of the Slaughter. You will, when the time is right. I helped take the memory from you when I found you by the pool. Madness had come upon you, girl. You were sitting in a puddle of your own urine. Your eyes were blank, and you were slack-jawed. I had a friend with me; his name was Taliesen. It was he – and another – who slew the Slaughterers. Taliesen told me we were going to lock away the memory and bring you back to the world of the living. We did exactly that. The door will open one day, when you are strong enough to turn the key. That's what he told me.'

'So,' she said, snatching back her hand, 'your only advice is for me to return to the pool and face the ghost? Yes?'

'Yes,' he agreed.

'Well, I won't do it.'

'That is your choice, Sigarni. And perhaps it is the right one. Time will show. Are you angry with me?'

'Yes.'

'Too angry to fetch me the flagon of honey mead you have in the kitchen?'

Sigarni smiled then, and fetched the flagon. 'You are an old reprobate, and I don't know why you've lived so long. I think maybe you are just too stubborn to die.' Leaning forward she proffered the flagon, but as he reached for it she drew it back. 'One question you must answer. The Slaughterers were not human, were they?' He licked his lips, but his eyes remained fixed on the flagon. 'Were they?' she persisted.

'No,' he admitted. 'They were birthed in the Dark, Hollow-tooths sent to kill you.'

'Why me?'

'You said one question,' he reminded her, 'but I'll answer it. They came for you because of who you are. And that is all I will say now. But I promise you we will speak again soon.'

She handed him the flagon and sat down.

'I cannot go to the pool, Gwal. I cannot.'

Gwalchmai did not answer her. The mead was beginning to work its magic, and his mind swam.

The Baron Ranulph Gottasson ran a bony finger down the line on the map. 'And this represents what?' he asked the blond young man shivering before him. Leofric rubbed his cold hands together, thankful that he had had the common sense to wear a woollen undershirt below his tunic, and two pairs of thick socks. His fleece-lined gloves were in his pocket, and he wished he had the nerve to wear them. The Baron's study at the top of the Citadel was always cold, though a fire was permanently laid, as if to mock the Baron's servants. 'Are you listening, boy?' snarled the Baron.

Leofric leaned over the table and felt the cold breeze from the open window flicker against his back. 'That is the river Dranuin, sir. It starts on the northern flank of High Druin and meanders through the forest into the sea. That is in Pallides lands.'

The Baron glanced up and smiled. The boy's face was blue-tinged. 'Cold, Leofric?'

'Yes, sir.'

'A soldier learns to put aside thoughts of discomfort. Now tell me about the Pallides.'

I'm not a soldier, thought Leofric, I am a cleric. And there is a difference between the discomfort endured through necessity and the active enjoyment of it. But these thoughts he kept to himself. 'The largest of the clans, the Pallides number some six thousand people. It used to be more, but the Great War devastated them. In the main they are cattle-breeders, though there are some farms which grow oats and barley. In the far north there are two main fishing fleets. The Pallides are spread over some two hundred square miles and live in sixteen villages, the largest being Caswallir, named after a warrior of old who, legend claims, brought the Witch Queen to their aid in the Aenir Wars.'

'I don't care about legends. Just facts. How many people in Caswallir?'

'Around eleven hundred, sir, but it does depend on the time of the year. They have their Games in the autumn and there could be as many as five thousand people attending every day for ten days. Of course, these are not all Pallides. Loda, Farlain, and even some Wingoras will attend – though the Wingoras are all but finished now. Our census shows only around one hundred and forty remain in the remote Highlands.'

'How many fighting men?'

'Just the Pallides, sir?' asked Leofric, sitting down and opening a heavy leather-bound ledger. The Baron nodded. 'It is difficult to estimate, sir. After all, what constitutes a fighting man in a people with no army? If we are talking men and older boys capable of bearing arms, then the figure would be . . .' He flicked through three pages, making swift mental calculations, then went on: '. . . say . . . eighteen hundred. But of these around a thousand would be below the age of seventeen. Hardly veterans.'

'Who leads them?'

'Well, sir, as you know there is no longer an *official* Hunt Lord, but our spies tell us that the people still revere Fyon Sharp-axe, and treat him as if he still held the title.'

Lifting a quill pen, the Baron dipped the sharpened nib into a pot of ink and scrawled the name on a single sheet of paper. 'Go on.'

'What else can I tell you, sir?' asked Leofric, nonplussed.

'Who else do they revere?'

'Er . . . I don't have information on that sir. Merely statistics.'

The Baron's hooded eyes focused on the younger man's face. 'Find out, Leofric. All possible leaders. Names, directions to their homes or farms.'

'Might I ask, sir, why are we gathering this information? All our agents assure us there is no hint of rebellion in the Highlands. They do not have the men, the weapons, the training or the leaders.'

'Now tell me about the other clans,' said the Baron, his quill at the ready.

Ballistar sat perched on the saddle of the small grey pony and stared around at the village of Cilfallen. Despite his fears, he gazed with a sense of wonder at this unfamiliar view. The pony was only ten hands high, barrel-bellied with short stubby legs – a dwarf horse for a dwarf. And yet, Ballistar estimated, he was now viewing the world from around six feet high, seeing it as Fell or Sigarni would see it.

Fat Tovi emerged from his bakery, and smiled at the dwarf. 'What nonsense is this?' he asked, transferring his gaze to the man on the black gelding who was waiting patiently beyond Ballistar.

'The sorcerer Asmidir has asked me to cook for him,' said Ballistar boldly, though even the words sent a flicker of fear through him. 'And he has given me this pony. For my own.'

'It suits you,' said Tovi. 'It looks more like a large dog.'

Grame the Smith wandered over. 'She's a fine beast,' he said, stroking his thick white beard. 'In years gone by the Lowland chariots were drawn by such as she. Tough breed.'

'She's mine!' said Ballistar, grinning.

'We must leave,' said the man on the black gelding, his voice deep. 'The master is waiting.'

Ballistar tugged on the reins and tried to heel the pony forward, but his legs were so short that his feet did not extend past the saddle and the pony stood still. Grame chuckled and walked back to his forge, returning with a slender riding-crop.

'Give her just a touch with this,' he said. 'Not too hard, mind, and accompany it with a word – or sound – of command.'

Ballistar took the leather crop. 'Hiddy up!' he shouted, swiping the crop against the pony's rear. The little animal reared and sprinted and Ballistar tumbled backwards in a somersault. Grame stepped forward and caught the dwarf, then both fell to the ground. Ballistar, his bearded face crimson, struggled to his feet as Asmidir's servant rode after the pony and led her back. Tovi was beside himself with mirth, the booming sound of his laughter echoing through the village.

'Thank you, Grame,' said Ballistar, with as much dignity as he could muster. The smith pushed himself to his feet and dusted himself down.

'Think nothing of it,' he said. 'Come, try again!' Pushing his huge hands under Ballistar's armpits he hoisted the dwarf to the saddle. 'You'll get the hang of it soon enough. Now be off with you!'

'Hiddy up!' said Ballistar, more softly. The pony moved forward and Ballistar lurched to the left, but clung on to the pommel and righted himself.

With the village behind them Ballistar's fear returned. He had been sitting quietly behind the tavern when the dark-skinned servant found him. Had he been asked beforehand whether he would be interested in a journey to the wizard's castle, Ballistar would have answered with a curt shake of his head. But two gold pieces and a pony had changed his mind. Two gold pieces! More money than Ballistar had ever held. Enough to buy the little shack, instead of paying rent. More than enough to have the cobbler make him a new pair of boots.

If he doesn't sacrifice you to the demons!

Ballistar shivered. Glancing up at the man on the tall horse, he gave a nervous smile, but the man did not respond. 'Have you served your master long?' he enquired, trying to start a conversation.

'Yes.'

And that was it. The man touched heels to the gelding and moved ahead, Ballistar meekly following. They rode for more than an hour, moving through the trees and over the high hills. Towards mid-morning Ballistar saw Fell and two of his foresters, Gwyn Dark-eye and Bakris Tooth-gone; he waved and called out to them.

The three foresters converged on the dwarf, ignoring the dark-skinned rider. 'Good day to you, Fell,' said Ballistar. Fell grinned, and Ballistar experienced renewed pleasure in the fact that he could look the handsome forester straight in the eye.

'Good day to you, little friend. She is a fine pony.'

'She's mine. A gift from the sorcerer.'

'He is not a sorcerer!' snapped the servant. 'And I wish you would stop saying it.'

'The Black man wants me to cook for him. Duck! Sigarni told him about me; he's paid me with this pony.' Ballistar decided not to mention the gold pieces. Fell he liked above all men, and Gwyn Dark-eye had always been kind to him. But Bakris Tooth-gone was not a man Ballistar trusted.

'Are you sure he doesn't want to cook *you*?' asked Gwyn. A slightly smaller man than Fell, and round-shouldered, Gwyn was the finest archer among the Loda.

Ballistar looked down upon him and noticed the man had a bald spot beginning at his crown. 'On a day like today the thought does not concern me,' said Ballistar happily. 'Today I have seen the world as a tall man.'

'Enjoy it,' sneered Bakris. 'Because when you get off that midget horse you'll return, to the useless lump you've always been.' The words were harshly spoken, and they cut through Ballistar's good humour. Fell swung angrily on the forester but before he could speak Ballistar cut in.

'Don't worry about it, Fell. He's only angry because I've got a bigger prick than him. I don't know why it should concern him. Everyone else has too!'

Bakris lunged at the dwarf, but Fell caught him by the shoulder of his leather jerkin and dragged him back. 'That's enough!' roared Fell. The sudden commotion caused the pony to move forward. Asmidir's servant nudged his gelding alongside and the two riders continued on their way. Ballistar swung in the saddle and looked back at the foresters. When he saw Bakris staring after him he lifted his fist and waggled his little finger.

Asmidir's servant chuckled. 'You shouldn't be so swift to make enemies,' he observed.

'I don't care,' said Ballistar.

'And why is it that you Highlanders value so much the size of the male organ? Size is of no relevance, not to the act itself nor to the pleasure derived.'

Ballistar glanced up at the man. Ah, he thought, so you've got a small one too! Aloud he said, 'I wouldn't know. I have never had a woman.'

It was mid-afternoon when they topped the last rise before the castle. Ballistar had never travelled this far before and he halted his pony to stare down at the magnificent building. It was not a castle in the true sense, for it was indefensible, having wide-open gateways with no gates, and no moat surrounding it. It had once been the house of the Hunt Lord of the Grigors, but that clan had been annihilated in the Lowland wars, the few survivors becoming part of the Loda. A three-storied building, with a single tower by the north wall that rose to five storeys, it was built of grey granite, and the windows were of coloured glass joined by lead strips.

'We are late,' said the servant. 'Come!'

Ballistar's heart was pounding and his hands trembled as he flapped the reins against the pony's neck.

Two gold pieces seemed a tiny amount just then.

4

Autumn was not far off, but here in the Highlands even the last days of summer were touched by a bitter cold that warned of the terrible winters that lay ahead. Two fires blazed at either end of the long hall, and even the heavy velvet curtains shimmered against the cold fingers of the biting wind that sought out the cracks and gaps in the old window frames.

Asmidir pushed away his empty plate and leaned back in his chair. 'You are a fine cook,' he told the dwarf. Two servants entered, lighting lanterns that hung in iron brackets on the walls, and the hall was filled with a soft glow.

'Can I go now?' asked Ballistar. The little man was sitting at the table, on a chair set upon blocks of wood.

'My dear fellow, of course you can go. But it is already becoming dark and your pony is bedded down for the night in a comfortable stall. I have had a room prepared for you. There is a warm fire there, and a soft bed. Tomorrow one of my servants will cook you a breakfast and saddle your pony. How does that sound?'

'That is wondrous kind,' said Ballistar uneasily, 'but I would like to be on my way.'

'You fear me?' asked Asmidir mildly.

'A little,' admitted the dwarf.

'You think me a sorcerer. Yes I know. Sigarni told me. But I am not, Ballistar. I am merely a man. Oh, I know a few spells. In Kushir all the children of the rich are taught to make fire from air, and some can even shape dancing figures from the flames. I am not one of those. I was a nobleman – a warrior. Now I am a Highlander, albeit somewhat more dusky than most. And I would be your friend. I do not harm my friends, nor do I lie. Do you believe me?'

'What does it matter whether I believe you or not?' countered the dwarf. 'You will do as you wish.'

'It matters to me,' said Asmidir. 'In Kushir it was considered unacceptable for noblemen to lie. It was one of the reasons the Outlanders – as you call them – defeated the armies of the Kushir King. The Outlanders kept lying: they signed treaties they had no intention of honouring, made peace, then invaded. They used spies and agents, filling Kushir soldiers with fear and trembling. An appalling enemy with no sense of honour.'

'But you fought alongside them,' said Ballistar.

'Yes. It is a source of endless regret. Come, sit by the fire and we shall talk.' The black man rose and walked to the fireside, settling his long frame into a deep armchair of burnished leather. A servant appeared and drew back Ballistar's seat, allowing the little man to slide from his cushions to the floor. Asmidir watched as he climbed with difficulty into the opposite armchair, then, waving away the servant, he leaned forward. 'You treat your affliction with great courage, Ballistar. I respect that. Now what shall we speak of?'

'You could tell me why you served the Outlanders,' said the dwarf.

'Swift and to the point,' observed Asmidir, with an easy grin. 'It all came down to politics. My family were accused of treason by the Kushir King. He was hunting us down at the time the Outlanders invaded. My sister and my wife were executed by him, my father blinded and thrown into a dungeon. We have a saying in Kushir – *the enemy of my enemy must therefore be my friend*. So I joined with the Outlanders.'

'And now you regret it?'

'Of course. There is no genuine satisfaction in revenge, Ballistar. All a man unleashes is a beast which will destroy even those he loves. Cities were laid waste, the people slaughtered or sold into slavery. A rich, cultured nation was set back two hundred years. And even when they had won, the slaughter continued. The Outlanders are a barbaric people, with no understanding of the simplest economic realities. The Kushir was rich because of trade and commerce. The lines of trade were severed, and treaties with friendly nations broken. There was a Great Library at Coshantin,

60

the capital; the Outlanders burned it down.' Asmidir sighed and lifted an iron poker, idly stabbing at the burning logs.

'You grew to hate them?'

'Oh yes! Hatred as strong and tall as High Druin. But two men more than any other, the Baron Ranulph and the Earl of Jastey. The King himself is merely a merciless savage, holding power through ruthlessness and manipulation. The Baron and the Earl hold the balance of his power.'

'Why are you telling me this?' asked Ballistar. 'It is not wise.'

Asmidir smiled. 'It is a question of judgement, my friend. Do you trust Sigarni?'

'In what way?'

'Her instincts, her values, her courage . . . whatever?'

'She is intelligent and does not suffer fools. What has this to do with anything?'

'She *trusts* you, Ballistar. Therefore so do I. And as for the risk . . . well, all life is a risk. And time is running too short for me to remain conservative in my plans. Sigarni tells me you are a great storyteller, and somewhat of a historian. Tell me of the clans. Where are they from, how did they come here? Who are their heroes and why? What are their noble lines?'

'You are moving too fast for me,' said Ballistar. 'A moment ago we were talking of trust. Before that, revenge. Now you want a story. Tell me first your purpose.'

'A clear thinker . . . I like that. Very well. First I shall tell you a story.' Asmidir clapped his hands and a servant came forward bearing a tray on which were two golden goblets filled with fine red wine. Ballistar accepted the first, holding it carefully in both hands. As the servant departed Asmidir sipped his drink, then set the goblet aside. Leaning back, he rested his head on the high back of the chair. 'With Kushir in ruins I went home to my palace. An old man, dressed in a cloak of feathers, was waiting for me there. His face was seamed with wrinkles and lines, his hair and beard so thin they appeared to be fashioned from the memory of wood-smoke. He was sitting on the steps before my door. A servant told me he had arrived an hour before, and refused to be moved; they tried to

61

lay hands upon him, but could not approach him. Knowing him to be a wizard, they withdrew. I approached him and asked what he wanted. He stood and walked towards my home. The door opened for him, though there were no servants close, and he made his way to my study. Once there, he asked me what I felt about the destruction of my land and my part in it. I did not answer him, for my shame was too great. He said nothing for a moment, then he bade me sit and began to talk of history. It was fascinating, Ballistar. It was as if he had witnessed all the events himself. Perhaps he had. I don't know. He spoke of the growth of evil and how, like a plague, it spreads and destroys. It was vital, he said, that there should always be adequate counter-balances against the forces of wickedness.

'Yet he insisted, we had reached a period of history when there was no balance. The Outlanders and their allies were conquering all in their path. And those nations still resisting the advance of the Outlanders were doomed, for there were no great leaders among them. Then he told me of a conquered nation, and a commander yet to come. He said – and I believed him utterly – that here, in the north, I would find a prince of destiny, and from the ashes of Highland dreams would come a dynasty that would light our way forward into a better future. I came here with high hopes, Ballistar, and yet what do I find?

'There is no leader. There is no army. And in the spring the Outlanders will come here with fire and sword and exterminate hundreds, perhaps thousands, of peaceful farmers, cattle-men and villagers.' Asmidir threw a dry log to the dying blaze. 'I do not believe that the ancient one lied to me . . . and I cannot accept that he might have been mistaken. Somewhere in these lands there is a man born to be King. I must find him before midwinter.'

Ballistar drained his wine. It was rich and heavy and he felt his head swimming. 'And you think my stories might help you?' he asked.

'They might provide me with a clue.'

'I don't see how. Legend has it that our ancestors passed through a magic Gateway, but I suspect our history is no different from other migrating peoples. We probably came from a land across the water, originally as raiders. Some of our people then grew to love the mountains, and sent back ships for their families. For centuries the clans warred upon one another, but then another migrating group arrived. They were called the Aenir, ancestors of the Outlanders. There was a great war. After that the clans formed a loose-knit confederacy.'

'But you had kings? From where did they come?'

'The first true king was Sorain, known as Ironhand. He was from the Wingoras, a mighty warrior. Hundreds of years ago he led the clans against the Three Armies and destroyed them. Even the Lowland clans respected him, for he risked everything to free their towns. He vanished one day, but legend has it he will return when needed.'

Asmidir shook his head. 'I doubt that. Every nation I know of has a hero of myth, pledged to return. None of them do. Did he have heirs?'

'No. He had a child, but the babe disappeared – probably murdered and buried in the woods.'

'So what of the other kings?' enquired Asmidir.

'There was Gandarin, also known as the Crimson – another great warrior and statesman. He died too soon and his sons fought among themselves for the crown. Then the Outlanders invaded and the clans put on their red cloaks of war and were cut down on Colden Moor. That was years ago. The young King fled over the water, but he was murdered there. Anyone known to share the blood of Gandarin was also put to the sword. And the Wearing of the Crimson was banned. No Highlander can have even a scarf of that colour.'

'And there is no one left of his line?'

'As far as I know there is only Sigarni, and she is barren.'

Asmidir rubbed his tired eyes and tried to disguise the dejection he felt. 'He must be somewhere,' he whispered, 'and he will need me. The ancient one made that clear to me.'

'He could have been wrong,' volunteered Ballistar. 'Even Gwalch is wrong sometimes.'

'Gwalch?'

'The Clan Gifted One. He used to be a warrior, but he was wounded in the head and after that he became a prophet of sorts. People tend to avoid him. His visions are all doom-filled and gloomy. Maybe that's why he drinks so much!'

Asmidir's spirits lifted. 'Tell me where to find him,' he said.

Sigarni was angry with herself. Four times that morning she had flown Abby, and four times the red hawk had missed the kill. Abby was a little overweight, for there had been three days of solid rain and she had not flown, but even so she was acting sluggishly and the tourney was only two weeks away. Sigarni was angry because she didn't know what to do, and was loth to ask Asmidir. Could Abby be ill? She didn't think so, for the bird was flying beautifully, folding her wings and diving, swooping, turning. Only at the point of the kill did she fail. The pattern with the red hawk was always the same — swoop over the hare, flick her talons, tumbling the prey, then fastening to it. Sigarni would run forward, covering the hare with her glove, then casting a piece of meat some distance from the hawk. The bird would glance at the titbit, then leave the gloved hare to be killed and bagged by Sigarni. But not today.

Sigarni lifted her arm and whistled for Abby. The hawk dived obediently from the high branch and landed on the outstretched fist, her cruel beak fastening to the tiny amount of meat Sigarni held between her fingers.

'What's wrong with you, Abby?' whispered Sigarni, stroking the bird's breast with a long pigeon feather. 'Are you sick?' The golden eyes, bright and impenetrable, looked into her own.

Returning to the cabin, Sigarni did not take Abby to her bow perch but carried her inside and sat her on the high back of a wooden chair. The cabin was cold and Sigarni lit a fire, banking up the logs and adding two large lumps of coal from the sack given to her by Asmidir. From the cupboard she took her scales, hooking them to a broad beam across the centre of the cabin. Fetching Abby, she weighed her. Two pounds seven ounces: five ounces above her perfect killing weight.

'What am I to do with you, beauty?' she asked softly, stroking the bird's head and neck. 'To keep you obedient I must feed you, yet if you do not fly you get fat and lazy and are useless to me. If I starve you, all your training will disappear and I will be forced to start again as if it never was. Yet you are intelligent. I know this. Is your memory so short? Mmmm? Is that it, Abby?' Sigarni sighed. Taking the hawk's hood from the pouch at her belt, she stroked it into place. Abby sat quietly, blind now, but trusting. Sigarni sat by the fire, tired and listless.

Lady scratched at the door and Sigarni opened it, allowing the hound to pad inside and stretch her lean black frame in front of the fire. 'I hope you've already eaten,' she told the hound, 'since we've caught nothing today.' Lady's tail beat against the floor and she tilted back her head, looking at Sigarni through one huge, brown eye. 'Yes,' said the woman, 'I don't doubt you have. You're the best hare hound in the Highlands. You know that, don't you? Faster than the wind – though not as fast as Abby.'

The darkness was growing outside and Sigarni lit a small lamp which she hung over the fireplace. Stretching out her legs, she removed her wet doeskin boots and her oiled leather troos. The warm air from the fire touched the bare skin of her legs and she shivered with pleasure. 'If only I wasn't hungry,' she said aloud, stripping off her buckskin shirt and tossing it to the floor. The fire crackled and grew, casting dancing shadows on the walls of the cabin.

'I have the bells of Hell clanging in my head,' said Gwalch, walking from the bedroom, clutching his temples.

'Then you shouldn't drink so much, Gwal,' she said, with a smile.

'All right for you but I . . .' He stopped as he saw her nakedness. 'Jarka's balls, woman! That's not decent!'

'You said you'd be gone, old fool. It would be decent enough were I alone!'

'Ah, well,' he said, with a broad grin, 'I think I might as well make the best of it.' Pulling up a chair, he gazed with honest admiration at her fire-lit form. 'Wonderful creatures, women,' he said. 'If God ever made anything more beautiful He has never shown it to me.'

'Since your eyes are standing now on reed stalks, I take it that you are a breast man,' she said, with a laugh. 'Now Fell is a legs and hips man. His eyes are naturally drawn to a woman's buttocks. Strange beasts, men. If God ever made anything more ludicrous She's never shown it to me.'

Gwalch leaned back and roared with laughter. 'Blasphemy and indecency in the same breath. By Heavens, Sigarni, there is no one like you. Now, for the sake of an old man's feelings, will you cover yourself?'

'Feel the blood rising, old man?'

'No, and that is depressing. Dress for me, child. There's a good girl.'

Sigarni did not argue, but slipped a buckskin shirt over her head. It was almost as long as a tunic and covered her to her thighs. 'Is that better, Gwal? You weren't so worried when I lived with you, and you bathed me and washed my hair.'

'You were a child and titless. And you were hurt, lass.'

'How do you kill a demon, Gwal?' she asked softly.

He scratched at the white stubble on his chin. 'Is there no food in this house? By God, a man could die of starvation visiting you.'

'There's a little cold stew, and a spare flagon of your honey spirit. It's too fiery for my taste. You want that, or shall I heat up the stew?'

He gave a wicked grin and winked. 'No lass. Just fetch me a drop of the honeydew.'

'First a bargain.'

'No.' he said, his voice firm. 'I will tell you no more. Not yet. And if that means a dry night, then so be it.'

'When will you tell me?'

'Soon. Trust me.'

'Of all men I trust you most,' she said moving forward to kiss his brow. She fetched him the flagon and watched as he filled a clay cup. The liquid was thin and golden, and touched the throat like a flame. Gwalch drained the cup and leaned back with a sigh.

'Enough of this and a man would live for ever,' he said.

She shook her head. 'You are incorrigible. Do you know the legend of Ironhand?'

66

'Of course. Went through a Gateway, to return when we need him.'

'And will he return?'

'Yes. When the time is right.' He drank a second cup.

'That's not true, Gwalch. I found his bones.'

'Yes I know. Under several boulders in the pool of the falls. Why did you tell no one?'

Sigarni was surprised, though instantly she knew she should not have been. 'Why do you ask, when you already know the answer?' she countered.

'It is not polite to answer a question with a question, girl. You know that.'

'People need legends,' she told him. 'Who am I to rob them of their power? He was a great man, and it is nice for people to think that he actually managed to kill all the assassins, instead of being done to death by the murdering scum.'

'Oh, but he did kill them all! Seven of them, and him wounded unto death. Killed them, and their war-hounds. Then he sat by the pool, his strength fading. He was found by one of his retainers, a trusted man, loyal and steadfast. Ironhand told him to hide his body where none could find it until the chosen time. You see, he had the Gift. It came on him as he was dying. So the word went out that Ironhand had crossed the Gateway and would one day return. And so it will be.'

Gwalch filled a third cup and half drank it. Leaning forward, he placed the cup on the hearth-stone, then sank back, his breathing deepening.

'When will he come back, Gwalch?' whispered Sigarni.

'He already has once,' answered the old man, his voice slurring. 'On the night of the slaughter. It was he who killed the last demon.' The old man began to snore gently.

Fell loved the mountains, the high, lonely passes, the stands of pine and the sloping valleys, the snow-crowned peaks and the vast sweep of this harsh country. He stood now above the snow line on High Druin staring out to the north, the lands of the Pallides and further to the distant shimmering river that separated the Pallides clan from the quiet, grim men of the Farlain. This was a land that demanded much from a man. Farming was not easy here, for the winters were harsh beyond compare, the summers often wet and miserable, drowning the roots of most crops, bar oats which seemed to thrive in the Highlands. Cattle were bred in the valleys, hard, tough long-haired beasts with horns sweeping out, sharp as needles. Those horns needed to be sharp when the wolves came, or the black bears. And despite the long hair and the sturdiness of their powerful bodies, the vicious winters claimed a large percentage of the beasts – trapped in snow-drifts, or killed in falls from the icy ridges and steep rises.

It was no land for the weak of spirit, or the soft of body.

The cool dusk breeze brushed the skin of his face and he rubbed his chin. Soon he would let his close-cropped beard grow long, protecting his face and neck from the bitter bite of the winter winds.

Fell climbed on, traversing a treacherous ridge and climbing down towards the supply cave. He reached it just before nightfall. The flap which covered the narrow opening was rotting and he made a mental note to bring a new spread of canvas on his next visit. It wasn't much of a barrier, but it kept stray animals from using the cave as shelter, and on a cold night it helped to hold in the heat from the fire. The cave was deep, but narrow, and a rough-built hearth had been built some ten feet from the back wall below a natural chimney that filtered smoke up through the mountain. As was usual the fire was laid, ready for a traveller, with two flint rocks laid beside it. By the far wall was enough wood to keep a blaze burning for several nights. There was also a store cupboard containing oats and honey, and a small pot of salted beef. Alongside this were a dozen wax candles.

It was one of Fell's favourite places. Here, sitting quietly without interruption, he could think, or dream. Mostly he thought about his role as captain of the foresters; how best to patrol the forests and valleys, to cull the deer herds, and hunt the wolves. Tonight he wanted to dream, to sit idly in the cave and settle his spirit. Swiftly he lit a fire, then removed his cloak and pack and stood his longbow and quiver against the wall. From the pack he pulled a small pot and a sack of oats. When the fire had taken he placed the pot over it and made several trips outside, returning with handfuls of snow which he dropped into the pot. At last when there was enough water he added oats and a pinch of salt, stirring the contents with a wooden spoon. Fell preferred his porridge with honey, but he had brought none with him and was loth to raid the store. A man could never tell when he would need the provisions in the small store cupboard, and Fell did not want to be stuck on High Druin in the depths of winter, only to remember that on a calm night in late summer he had eaten the honey on a whim.

Instead he cooked his porridge unsweetened, then put it aside to cool.

Sigarni's face came unbidden to his mind and Fell swore softly. 'I must have sons,' he said aloud, surprised how defensive the words sounded.

'A man needs love also,' said a voice.

Fell's heart almost stopped beating. Leaping to his feet, he spun around. There was no one there. The forester drew his double-edged hunting knife.

'You'll have no need of that, boy,' said the voice, this time coming from his left. Fell turned to see, sitting quietly by the fire, the oldest man he had ever seen, his face a maze of fire-lit wrinkles, his skin sagging grotesquely around the chin. He was wearing a tunic and leggings of green plaid, and a cloak that seemed to be fashioned from feathers of every kind, pigeon, hawk, sparrow, raven . . . Fell flicked a glance at the canvas flap over the doorway. It was still pegged in place.

'How did you get in here?' he asked.

'By another doorway, Fell. Come, sit with me.' The old man stretched out a fleshless arm and gestured to the forester to join him.

'Are you a ghost?'

The old man thought about it. 'An interesting question. I am due to die long before you were born. So, in one sense, I suppose

I am already dead. But no, I am not a spirit. I am flesh and blood, though there is precious little flesh left. I am Taliesen the druid.'

Fell moved to the fire and squatted down opposite the old man. He seemed harmless enough, and was carrying no weapon but, even so, Fell kept his dagger in his hand. 'How is it that you know me?' he asked.

'Your father gave me bread and salt the last time I came here, nineteen years ago, by your reckoning. You were six. You looked at my face and asked me why it no longer fit me.' The old man gave a dry chuckle. 'I do so love the young. Their questions are so deliciously impertinent.'

'I don't remember it.'

'It was the night of the twin moons. I had another man with me; he was tall and recklessly handsome, and he wore a shirt of buckskin emblazoned with a red hawk motif.'

'I do remember,' said Fell, surprised. 'His name was Caswallon and he sat with me and taught me how to whistle through my teeth.'

The old man's face showed a look of exasperation. He shook his head and whispered something that sounded to Fell like a curse. Then he looked up. 'It was a night when two moons appeared in the sky, and the Gateways of time shimmered open causing a minor earthquake and several avalanches. But you remember it because you learned to whistle. Ah well, such, I fear, is the way of things. Do you intend to share that porridge?'

'Such was not my intention,' said Fell testily, 'but since you remind me of my manners I am obliged to offer you some.'

'It never does a man harm to be reminded of his manners,' said Taliesen. Fell rose and fetched two wooden bowls from the cupboard. There was only one spoon, which he offered to the old man. Taliesen ate slowly, then put aside his bowl half finished. 'I see you've lost the art of porridge in this time,' he said. 'Still, it will suffice to put a little energy into this old frame. Now . . . to the matter at hand. How is Sigarni?'

'She is well, old man. How do you know her?'

Talisen smiled. 'I don't. Well, not exactly. My friend with the hawk shirt brought her to the people who raised her. He risked much to do so, but then he was an incautious man, and one ruled by an iron morality. Such men are dangerous friends, but they make even more deadly enemies. Thankfully he was always more of a friend.'

'What do you mean *brought* her? She lived with her father and mother until . . .'

'The night of the slaughter . . . yes, yes, I know. But they were not her parents. Their child died in her cot. Sigarni was a . . . changeling. But that is all beside the point. I take it the invasion is not under way yet? No, of course it isn't. I may be getting old, but I still have a certain Talent when it comes to Gateways. It is now six days from the end of summer, yes?'

'Four days, but you make no sense, old man,' said Fell, adding more wood to the fire. 'What invasion?'

'Four days? Mmmmm. Ah well, close enough,' said The old man, looking down at his gnarled hand and tapping his thumb to each of the fingers, as if working on some simple calculation. He stood and wandered to the doorway, pulling back the flap and looking up at the sky, scanning the bright stars. 'Ah yes,' he said, returning to the fire. 'Four days. Quite right. Now, what was your question? The invasion. Mmmm. Where to begin? The descendants of the Aenir, the conquerers of the Lowlands. What do you call them . . . Outlanders? Yes, Outlanders. They will come in the spring with fire and sword. I know you suspect this already, young Fell. Still, that is not important at this moment, for we were speaking of Sigarni. Is she strong? Is she wilful and obstinate? Does she have a piercing stare that strikes fear into the hearts of strong men?'

Fell laughed suddenly. 'Yes, all of those.' His smile faded. 'But speak plainly, old man, for I wish to hear more of this invasion you speak of. Why would they invade?'

'Why indeed? What motivates the minds of evil men? Who can truly know, save another evil man. And, testy though I have been throughout my long life, I have never been evil, and therefore cannot answer your questions with any guarantee of accuracy. I can hazard a guess, however.'

71

'I never knew a man who could talk so long and say so little,' snapped Fell.

'Youth was always impatient,' Taliesen rebuked him mildly. 'There are two main reasons I can think of. One concerns a prophecy being talked of in the south, about a great leader who will rise among the peoples of the highlands. Prophecies of this nature are not usually welcomed by tyrants. Secondly, and probably more important, is the fact that the Baron Ranulph Gottasson is ambitious. He has two enemies, one is the King, and the other is the Earl Jastey. By raising an army in the Highlands he can make himself a power again in the capital – especially with a few victories to brag of.'

'How can he achieve victories when there is no army to fight him?'

Taliesen smiled and shook his head. 'For that very reason, how can he not?'

'But there is no leader. God's teeth, this is insane!'

'Wrong again, boy. There is a leader. That is why I am here, sitting in this cold, inhospitable cave, with its dull company and worse porridge. *There is a leader!*'

Fell stared at him. 'Me? You think it is *me?*'

'Do I look like an idiot, boy? No, Fell, you are not the leader. You are brave and intelligent, and you will be loyal.' He chuckled. 'But you are not gifted to command armies. You have not the talent, nor the will, nor the blood.'

'Thank you for your honesty,' said Fell, feeling both aggrieved and relieved. 'Then who is it?'

'You will see. In three days, outside the walls of Citadel town a sword will be raised, and the Red will be worn again. Be there, Fell. In three days, at dawn. By the light of the new sun you will see the birth of a legend.'

The old man stood and his joints cracked like dry twigs.

Fell rose also. 'If you are some sort of prophet, then you must know the outcome of the invasion. Will my people survive?'

'Some will, some won't. But it is not quite so simple, young man. There is only ever one past, but myriad futures, though sometimes the past can be another man's future. Now there is a riddle to spin your head like a top, eh?' The old man's features softened. 'I'm not trying to baffle you, Fell. But I have knowledge gained over twenty times your lifetime. I cannot impart it to you in the brief moment we have. Let us merely say that I know what *should* happen, and I know what *could* happen. I can therefore say with certainty what *might* happen. But never can I tell you what *will* happen!'

'Even Gwalch is more sure than that,' put in Fell, 'and he's drunk half the time.'

'Some events are set in stone, and a part of destiny,' agreed Taliesen, 'as you will see in three days at Citadel town. Others are more fluid.' He smiled. 'Don't even try to make sense of what I tell you. Just be close to Citadel town. And now I will show you something more memorable than teeth whistling. Watch carefully, Fell, for you will not see its like again.'

So saying, the old man walked towards the wall – and through it. Fell gasped, blinked, then pushed himself upright and ran to the wall.

It was solid rock.

But of the old man there was no sign. For a moment Fell stood there, his broad right hand resting on the rock. Then he turned and glanced back at the fire. It had died down. Adding more wood, he waited until the flames rose and flickered high, then settled down beside the fire. It was pitch-dark and icy cold outside the cave now, but he felt the heat from the blaze and was comfortable. And as he dropped into a deep and dreamless sleep he heard again the words of the old man.

'*Be there, Fell. In three days, at dawn. By the light of the new sun you will see the birth of a legend.*'

Will Stamper moved through the market crowds, scanning for signs of cut-purses or beggars. He had been Corporal of the Watch for two years now, and the burly soldier took his job very seriously. Beside him the shorter Relph Wittersson munched on an apple.

'More people this year,' said Relph, tossing away the core. A mangy mongrel sniffed at it then moved away.

'Population's growing,' Will told him, stroking a broad finger under the chin strap of his iron helmet 'All them new houses on East Street are sold now, and they're talking of building to the north. God knows why people want to come to this place.'

'You did,' Relph pointed out. Will nodded and was about to speak when he saw a small grey haired man in a dirty brown tunic moving at the edge of the crowd. The man saw him at the same instant and swiftly darted down an alleyway.

'Alyn Shortblade,' said Will. 'I'll have the old bastard one of these days. What was I saying?'

'Can't remember, something about buildings going up and immigrants coming in,' answered Relph, pausing at a meat stall and helping himself to a salt beef sausage. The stall holder said nothing and looked away. Relph bit into the sausage. 'Not bad,' he said, 'but too much cereal. Shouldn't be allowed. Can't rightly call it a sausage if there's more bread than meat in it.'

The two moved slowly through Market Street, then down Baker's Alley and into the main square, where the tents and marquees were being erected ready for Tournament Day. The sound of hammers on nails filled the square as workmen continued to build the high banked seats for the nobles and their ladies and Will saw the slight, blond Lord Leofric directing operations. Beside him stood the Captain of the Watch. Will cursed softly. Relph tapped Will's arm.

'Let's go back through Market Street,' he advised. Will was about to agree when the Captain saw them. With an imperious flick of his finger he summoned them over. Will took a deep breath. He had no liking for the Captain, and worse, no respect. The man was a career soldier, but he cared nothing for the well being of his men.

Redgaer Kushir-bane, Knight of the Court, son of the Earl of Cordenia, did not wait for the soldiers to reach him. Arms clasped behind his back he strode towards them, his red beard jutting. 'Well?' he asked. 'Caught any cutpurses?'

'Not yet, sir,' said Will, giving the clenched fist salute.

'Hmmm. Nor will you if that stomach keeps spreading, man. I'll have no lard bellies under my command.'

'Yes, sir.' It was futile to offer any form of argument, as Will Stamper had long ago discovered to his cost. Happily for Will the Captain turned his attention to Relph.

'There is no shine to your buckle, man, and your helmet plume looks like it's been used to wipe a horse's arse. That's a five copper fine, and you will report to my adjutant for extra duty.'

'Yes, sir,' said Relph meekly.

'Well, get on with your rounds,' commanded Redgaer spinning on his heel, his red cloak swirling out.

'What a goat-brain,' whispered Relph. *'Your plume looks like it's been used to wipe a horse's arse,'* he mimicked. 'More likely it was used to brush his tongue after he'd dropped on his knees to kiss the Baron's rear.' Will chuckled, and the two soldiers continued on their way through Tanner Street and back into the market.

'Whoa, look at that!' said Relph, pointing. Will saw the object of his attention and let out a low whistle. A tall woman was moving through the market, her hair shining silver despite her youth, and on her left fist sat a red hawk. 'Look at the legs on that girl, Will. All the way up to the neck. And what an arse, tight, firm. I tell you, I wouldn't crawl across her to get to you!'

'Bit thin for my taste,' said the older man, 'but she walks well, I'll say that. She's a Highlander.'

'How do you know? Just because she's wearing buckskins? Lot of Lowlanders wear buckskins.'

'Look at the way she moves,' said Will. 'Proud, arrogant. Nah . . . Highlander. They're all like that. I see she's not wearing a marriage bangle.' As they watched they saw the hawk suddenly bait, wings flapping in panic. The woman calmed it, gently stroking its red head.

'She could stroke me like that,' said Relph. 'A bit lower down, though. Come on, let's talk to her.'

'What for?'

'I go off duty at dusk. You never know your luck.'

'I'll bet that five-copper fine that she's not interested.'

'And I'll bet you I'll spear her by midnight!'

'You arrogant son of a bitch,' said Will, with a smile. 'I'm going to enjoy watching you cut down to size.' The two soldiers angled through the crowd, coming alongside the woman as she stood by the dried fruit stall.

'Good morning miss,' said Will. 'That's a fine bird.'

The woman offered a fleeting smile. 'She hunts well,' was all she said, then she turned away.

'Are you from the Highlands?' asked Relph.

The woman swung back. 'I am. Why do you ask?'

'My friend here had a little bet with me. I said you were mountain bred, he insisted you were a Lowlander. I told him you could always tell a Highland woman.'

'Tell her what?' countered the woman, turning her pale gaze on the soldier.

'No . . . I mean, recognize one. It's in the . . . er walk. Tell me, are you . . . er . . . staying on in Citadel tonight? There are some fine places to dine, and I'd be honoured to escort you.'

'No, I am not staying on. Good day to you.' She walked on, but Relph hurried alongside, taking hold of her arm. This made the hawk bait once more.

'You don't know what you're missing, sweet-thing. It's never wise to turn down a good opportunity.'

'Oh, I never do that,' said the woman. 'Goodbye.'

She strode off leaving Relph red-faced. 'Ah,' said Will, 'the sound of five fresh copper coins jingling in my palm. I can almost hear it.'

Relph swore. 'Who does the bitch think she is?'

'I told you, she's a Highlander. As far as she is concerned you are an occupying enemy soldier. And if she doesn't hate you – which she probably does – she despises you. Now let's move on, and you can figure out how to pay me.'

'How'd she get a hawk?' said Relph. 'I mean, a woman with a hawk. It's not proper. Maybe she stole it!'

'You can put that thought from your mind now, son,' said Will sternly. 'Just because a woman doesn't want to sleep with you, it doesn't mean you can just lock her up. I'll not have that kind of wrong-doing in my cells. Put it from your mind, and concentrate on the crowd. It'll be more than a five-copper fine if there's a purse cut while we're on duty. More like five lashes!'

'Yes,' said Relph. 'Plenty more sheep in the field anyway.' He laughed suddenly. 'Did you hear that Gryen picked up a dose of the clap from the whorehouse in North Street? His dick is covered in weeping sores. He's in a hell of a state. They put bloody leeches on it! Can you imagine that? Must be pretty small leeches, eh?'

'Serves him right,' said Will. He stopped outside the apothecary shop and stepped inside.

'What we looking for?' asked Relph.

'My youngest has the whooping-cough. Betsi asked me to pick up some herb syrup.'

'Always ailing, that boy, ever since the fever,' said Relph. 'You figure him to die?'

Will sighed. 'We lost two already, Relph. One in the plague back in Angosta, and the second when I was campaigning in Kushir. Yellow fever struck him down. I don't know whether the boy will survive or not. But he's a fighter, like his dad, so he's got an even chance.'

'You were lucky with Betsi,' said Relph, as Will waited for the apothecary to fill a small blue bottle with syrup. 'She's a good woman. Cooks up a fine stew, and your place is always so clean. I'd bet you could eat off the floor and not pick up a scrap of dust. Good woman.'

'The best,' agreed Will. 'I think when summer comes I'll try to relocate down south. Her folks is back there and she misses them. Might do that.'

'There's a rumour we'll be campaigning in spring. You heard it?'

'There's always rumours, son. I don't worry about them. One of the reasons I came here was for the quiet. Betsi was always worried that I'd be killed in a battle. 'Ain't no battles here, so who are we going to campaign against?'

'The Captain was saying that the Highland clans were getting ready for war, attacking merchants and travellers.'

Will shook his head. 'It's not true. There was one attack, but the Foresters caught the men and killed them. They weren't Highlanders. No, I'm looking forward to summer, son. I'll take the family south.'

The apothecary handed over the bottle and Will gave him two copper coins.

Outside Relph tapped him on the arm. 'How come you pay? I don't. Bastard townies can afford to look after us. After all, we look after them.'

'I always pay my way,' said Will. 'It's an old habit.'

Grame the Smith delivered the Baron's grey stallions and left the Citadel. It had been no surprise when the Baron failed to pay for the work, and Grame had been expecting nothing more. He wandered through the town, and considered buying a meal at the Blue Duck tavern. Roast pork with crackling was a speciality there. Grame tapped his ample stomach. 'You're getting old and fat,' he told himself. There was a time when he'd been considered one of the handsomest men in Cilfallen, and he had grown used to the eyes of women lingering on him as he passed. They didn't linger much now. His hair had long since departed his skull, and sprouted unattractively from his shoulders and back. He'd lost three front teeth and had his lips crushed at Colden Moor, the teeth smashed from his head by an iron club wielded by an Outland soldier. God, that hurt, he remembered. It was a kind of double pain. As he fell he knew his good looks were gone for ever.

Now he sported the bushiest white beard, with a long, drooping moustache to cover the mouth.

He reluctantly passed the Blue Duck and continued along Market Street, catching sight of Sigarni talking to two soldiers. The first was a tall man, middle-aged, with the look of the warrior about him. The second was smaller; this one took hold of Sigarni's arm, but she spoke to him and moved away. Grame saw the man's face turn crimson. The smith chuckled, and made his way to where Sigarni was standing before a knick-knack stall. She was examining a brass tail-bell.

'Good day to you,' said Grame. Sigarni gave him a friendly smile, but he saw her cast her eyes back towards where the two soldiers were standing.

'I'm thinking of buying Abby a bell,' she said. 'All the other hawks here have them.'

'For what purpose?' asked the smith, 'apart from the fact that all the others have them?'

Sigarni thought about it for a moment, then grinned. 'I don't know, Grame,' she admitted. 'But they are pretty, don't you think?'

Grame took the bell from her fingers and looked at it closely. 'They're well made,' he said, 'and they'd be silent in flight. Falconers use them to locate their birds. You can hear them when they land in a tree. Do you have trouble with Abby? Do you lose her?'

'Never.'

'Then you don't need a bell. What brings you to Citadel?'

'There is a hawking tourney, with a money prize of two gold guineas. I think Abby could win it.'

Grame scratched at his thick white beard. 'Maybe. It will depend on how they structure the contest. If obedience is marked highly you would have a good chance. But speed? The goshawk is lighter and faster than Abby.'

'You surprise me, Grame. I didn't know you understood falconry.'

'Had a gos myself once. Beautiful creature . . . but wilful. Lost her in the year before Colden. I take it you're trying to get Abby used to crowds before the tourney?'

'Yes,' answered Sigarni, stroking Abby's sleek head. 'They don't seem to bother her. She's baited a few times, but I think she'll perform well. I'll bring her again tomorrow.'

'Is there an entrance fee to this tournament?'

'Yes. One silver penny. I paid it this morning.' Sigarni's expression changed. 'The cleric had to get permission from the Captain of the Tourney to allow me to enter. He wasn't sure if women were permitted to take part.'

Grame chuckled. 'Well, it is unusual, girl. They don't understand that Highland women are . . . shall we say different.'

'From what?' she countered.

'From their own timid females,' said Grame. 'Their women have no rights. When they marry, all their fortunes become the property of their husbands. They can be beaten, humiliated and cast aside, with no recourse to the law.'

'That is awful. Why do the women stand for it?'

Grame shrugged. 'Habit? God only knows. Their fathers choose their husbands, their husbands dominate their lives. It's a world ruled by men. So, the Captain of the Tourney allowed your entry? He must be an enlightened man.'

'He was fascinated by Abby. I could tell. He asked me where I got her, and how many kills she had. That sort of thing. He said the Baron would be interested in her.'

Grame said nothing for a moment. Then, 'I'm not sure I like the sound of that, Sigarni.'

'Why?'

'You don't come to the Citadel much, do you? No, of course you don't. You sell your skins to the tanner and the furrier, and you buy your supplies – what . . . three times a year?'

'Four times. What does that matter?'

'The Baron is a keen falconer. He will certainly be *interested* in Abby. He may want her for his own.'

Well, he can't have her,' she said.

Grame smiled, but there was no humour in the expression. 'The Baron will have anything he desires. He is the Lord here. My advice is to forget the tourney and take Abby back into the mountains.'

'I paid my silver penny!'

Grame reached into his pouch and produced a coin. 'I'll pay that – aye and gladly.'

'I don't want your money, Grame – though I thank you for the offer. You think he would steal her from me?' Grame nodded. 'But how could he do this. By what right?'

'Conquest. You are a clan-woman. You have no rights, save those he allows.'

Sigarni's face darkened. 'By God, that is wrong!'

'I don't doubt that by *God* it is wrong. But it is not God who makes the laws here; it is the Baron. I have some business here, but

80

I will be ready to leave by dusk. My wagon is by the north wall, behind the armourer's shop. I'd be pleased to have the company, if you'd like a ride back to Cilfallen.'

'Yes, I would,' said Sigarni. 'I'll meet you there at dusk.'

Grame's words both irritated and upset Sigarni. She had wanted to compete, to show Abby's skills to a wider audience, to revel in their approbation. And she wanted to show that a woman could train a hawk as well as any man. Yet Grame was no fool. If he said she was in danger of losing Abby then she had to listen, and act accordingly. It was unfair, but then life was unfair. If not, then she would have loved Bernt, and he would still be alive.

Sigarni strolled through the crowds and on to Falcon Field, passing the rows of hutches containing the hares to be used in the falcon displays, snared over the past few days, the little beasts would be freed individually to dart and run across the field, seeking escape from the silent killers sent to despatch them. Abby's golden eyes focused on the cowering creatures. 'Not for you, pretty one,' said Sigarni. 'Not this time. No applause for my beautiful Abby.'

The cleric was still sitting at his desk on the outer edge of the field, and several falconers were waiting to sign their names, or make their marks on the broad ledger. A cadger had been set close by, hooded falcons sitting on the many perches. All were goshawks. Abby bridled and baited as she saw them, her wings flaring out. 'Hush, now,' whispered Sigarni. 'Best behaviour from you, sweet one.' Behind the cleric she saw the two soldiers who had spoken to her earlier. The big one was no problem, but the shorter man had mean eyes. Beyond them stood the Captain of the Tourney. She could not remember his name, save that it began with Red, which matched his beard and his complexion.

Taking her place behind the men, she waited her turn. One of the falconers looked closely at Abby. 'Fine creature,' he said. 'Never thought to see another. Kushir bird, ain't she?'

'Yes.'

'Good killers. Not as fast as my own bird, but she'll come to call a damn sight faster.' Reaching out, he stroked Abby's chest with a broad forefinger. To Sigarni's annoyance Abby allowed this treatment, even seemed to enjoy it.

'Next!' called the cleric. He was ginger-haired and Sigarni remembered him riding with an escort through Cilfallen, taking the census. What was his name? Andred? No . . . Andolph.

The falconer signed his name, paid his silver, and moved away to the cadger to collect his bird. Sigarni stepped forward and Andolph glanced up. 'Oh, 'tis you. You've already signed.'

'And now I wish to unsign. I cannot take part after all.'

'I see,' said Andolph, laying down his quill. 'I am afraid there are no allowances made for withdrawals. I take it you are seeking your money back?'

'Yes. Why pay for something I cannot do?'

'Why indeed? However, the rules are quite specific. If a falcon becomes ill, or the falconer fails to appear, then his entry fee is forfeit. You see it is the entry fee that creates the ultimate prize.'

'I only signed an hour ago,' she said, smiling sweetly. 'Can you not make an exception for a poor mountain girl?'

Andolph blushed. 'Well . . . as you say, it was only an hour since.' Reaching into the box at his left hand, he removed a silver penny and handed it to her. Abby baited once more and the little man dropped the coin in Sigarni's palm and snatched his hand away. 'I really don't like them,' he confided. 'I prefer the hares.'

'Hares were created for sport,' said Sigarni.

Four riders came galloping across the field, their horses' hooves drumming on the hard-packed clay. Abby fluffed up her feathers, but Sigarni held tightly to the flying jesses. The lead horseman, a man dressed all in black, dismounted from the grey stallion, tossing the reins to a second horseman. Sigarni stood silently, for all the men were now waiting, stiff-backed. Even the little cleric had risen from his seat. This then, she knew, must be the Baron. Inwardly Sigarni cursed herself for bothering about the entry fee, for the man was staring intently at Abby. He was a tall man, with sleek black hair drawn back tightly over his brow and tied in a short ponytail at the nape of his neck. He sported a thin, trident beard that gleamed as if oiled, and his eyes were large and wood-ash grey, hooded, and bulging from their sockets. His lips were thin, the mouth cruel, thought Sigarni.

'Where did you get the bird?' he asked, the voice so low that it was a moment before Sigarni realized he had spoken.

'A gift from a friend,' she answered him. The other riders dismounted and gathered in close. Sigarni felt hemmed in, but she stood her ground.

'In return for some sexual favour, I don't doubt,' said the Baron, his tone bored. 'Ah well, I expect you are here to sell the creature. I'll give you ten guineas for it – assuming you haven't ruined it.'

'She is not ruined, my lord, and she is not for sale,' said Sigarni. 'I trained her myself, and was planning to enter the tourney with her.'

The Baron appeared not to notice she had spoken. Turning to the man behind him, he called out, 'Ten guineas, if you please, Leofric. I'll reimburse you later. And remind me to speak to the black man next time he visits the town.'

'Yes, my lord,' said the blond rider, fishing in his purse for coins.

Sigarni stepped back. 'She is not for sale,' she said, her voice louder than she intended. This time the Baron turned and for the first time looked into her eyes.

'You are a Highlander, aren't you?' he announced.

'I am.'

'There are no noble houses in the Highlands, merely a motley group of inbred savages scraping a living from the mountainsides. The law is simple, woman. A yeoman may raise a goshawk. That is the only bird of prey allowed to those not of noble blood. The bird you hold is not a goshawk; therefore you cannot own the bird. Am I speaking too fast for you? Now take the money and hand the bird to my falconer.'

Sigarni knew that she should obey. It mattered not that it was unfair. Grame was right, the Baron was the law and to deny him would be futile. Yet something flickered deep within her, like the birth of a fire.

'I am of the blood of Gandarin the King,' she said, 'and the hawk is mine. Mine to keep, mine to free!' So saying, her arm swept up and she released the jesses. Surprised by the sudden movement Abby spread her wings and sailed into the air. Not even a glimmer of anger showed on the Baron's face. For several heartbeats no one moved, and all watched the hawk gliding up on the thermals. Then, without speed, almost casually, the Baron's black-gloved fist cracked against the side of Sigarni's face. Half stunned, she staggered back. The Baron moved in. Sigarni lashed out with her foot, aiming for his groin, but her aim was out and she kicked him in the thigh. 'Hold her!' said the Baron. She found her arms pinned and recognized the soldiers who had first spoken to her in the market square. The Baron hit her in the stomach, and she doubled forward. His voice echoed through her pain; it was not a raised voice, nor did it contain a hint of emotion. 'Stupid woman,' he said. 'Now you have forfeited your right to the ten guineas. Any more stupidity and you will face the lash. You understand me? Call the bird!'

Sigarni looked up into the hooded eyes. Her mouth tasted of blood. 'Call him yourself,' she said, then spat full in his face. Blood and saliva dripped to his cheek. Taking a black handkerchief from the pocket of his tunic, he slowly wiped the offending drops from his face. 'You see,' he said to the gathered men, 'with what we are dealing? A people who have no understanding of law, or good manners. They are barbarians, without culture, without breeding.' His hand lashed out in a backward strike that cannoned his knuckles against Sigarni's right cheek. 'Call the bird!' he ordered. 'And if you spit at me again I will have your tongue cut out!'

Sigarni remained silent. The Baron turned to his falconer, a short, wide-shouldered Lowlander. 'Can you call it in?' he asked.

'I'll do my best, my lord,' he answered, moving out on to the open ground with hawking glove aloft. He gave a long, thin whistle. High above, Abby banked and folded her wings into a stoop to dive like an arrow. Some sixty feet from the ground her wings spread again and she levelled out. 'She's coming in, sir!' shouted the falconer.

The Baron turned back to Sigarni. 'Ten lashes for you, I think, and a night in the cells. Perhaps you will learn from the experience, though I doubt it. You Highlanders never were given to learning from your mistakes. It is what makes you what you are.' Casually he struck her again, left and right, his arm rising and falling with a sickening lack of speed. Sigarni tried to roll her head with the blows, but the soldiers were holding hard to her arms.

And then it happened. No one watching quite understood why. Some blamed confusion in the mind of the hawk, others maintained the woman was a witch, the hawk her familiar. But Abby swept down, past the falconer's outstretched glove and straight towards Sigarni, talons extended for the landing. At that moment the Baron's fist came up to strike the woman again.

'The hawk, my lord!' shouted the falconer.

The Baron turned, arm still raised. Abby's razor-sharp talons tore into his face, hooking into the left eyebrow, raking down through the socket and tearing out his eye. He screamed as he fell back, the hawk still clinging to his face, her talons embedded in his left cheek. Abby's wings thrashed madly as she tried to free herself. The Baron's hands came up, grabbing the wings and ripping the bird clear. Blood gushed from the face wound. Staggering now he threw the bird to the ground, and Sigarni watched in horror as one of the riders drew a sword and hacked it through Abby's neck. The wings fluttered against the clay. Men gathered round the Baron, who had fallen to his knees, pressing the palm of his black glove against the now empty eye-socket.

The three riders who had arrived with him half carried him from the field.

The Captain of the Tourney moved in front of Sigarni. 'You'll suffer for that, bitch!' he told her. 'The Baron will have your eyes put out with hot coals, your hands and feet hacked off, and then you'll be hung outside the walls in an open cage for the crows to feast on you! But first you'll answer to me!'

Sigarni said nothing as she was dragged away by the soldiers. A crowd had gathered on the edge of the field, but she did not look at them. Holding her head high she stared impassively at the keep ahead, and the double doors of the outer wall. Abby was dead. Had she given her to the Baron, she would still be alive. She saw again the fluttering wings, and the iron sword cleaving down. Tears fell to her cheeks, the salt burning the cut under her eye.

The men marched her through the Citadel entrance and then turned left, cutting across the courtyard to a narrow door and a staircase leading down into the dark. Sigarni pulled back as the men tried to force her through. The soldier whose advances she had spurned struck her over the ear with his elbow. 'Git down there!' he hissed. She was propelled forward. The stairwell was dark, the stairs slippery. The soldier twisted her arm behind her back, the other man releasing his hold on her and moving ahead. For a short while they descended in total darkness, then the faint glow of a burning torch lit the bottom of the stairs and they emerged into a dungeon corridor. Two men were sitting at a table, playing dice. Both stood as the Captain strode into sight.

'Open a cell!' he ordered. The men hurried to obey.

Sigarni was still in a daze as they dragged her into the cell. It was large and grey, one wall wet with damp, and it stank of rats' droppings. There was a small cot in one corner, and there were rusted chains hanging from the walls.

'How do you like this, bitch?' sneered the red-bearded captain, moving in front of her. Sigarni did not reply. His hand reached out, cupping her breast and squeezing hard. She winced, then brought up her knee, hammering it into his groin. He groaned and fell back. The soldier to her right, the short man, punched her in the side of the head, and she was hurled across the cot.

'Strip her,' ordered the captain, 'and we'll see how much pleasure the whore can supply.'

Through her pain Sigarni heard the words, and the strength of panic surged through her. Launching herself from the cot she dived at the first soldier, but she was still groggy and he caught her by the hair. Hands grabbed at her body and she felt her leather leggings being dragged clear. Torchlight glittered from the captain's dagger.

'I'm going to put my mark on you, woman. And I'll hear you beg and scream before this night is over.'

5

Gwalchmai was sitting on the porch weeping when Asmidir rode up. As the black man climbed from the saddle and approached the old man, he could smell the fiery spirit on Gwalchmai's breath, and he saw the empty jug lying on its side. 'Where is Sigarni?' he asked.

The old man looked up, blinking. 'Suffering,' he said. 'She is the sword blade going through fire.'

'What are you talking about?'

'Why do we do it?' asked Gwal. 'What is it in our natures? When I was young we raided a Lowland village, stealing cattle. There was a young woman in a field. She had hidden in some bushes. But we found her. We raped her. It seemed good sport, and no harm done.' He shook his head. 'No *harm* done? Now that the Gift is upon me and I know the truth, I wonder if there will ever be forgiveness. Do you ever wonder that, Asmidir? Do you ever think of the Loabite woman you captured in the high mountains of Kushir? Do you lie awake at night and ask yourself why she slashed her wrists?'

Asmidir straightened as if struck, his dark eyes narrowing. 'You are the Gifted One?'

'Aye. That is my curse, black man. It is only marginally worse than yours.'

The sunlight was fading and Asmidir helped the old man to his feet, guiding him into the cabin where Lady was stretched out by the dying fire. Asmidir eased Gwalchmai into a chair, then sat opposite the man. Lady rose and put her head in Asmidir's lap, seeking a stroke. The black man idly patted her, rubbing his fingers behind her ears, and Lady's tail began to wag. 'I need your help,' Asmidir told Gwalchmai. 'I need to find a man.'

The old man leaned forward and gazed into the dying flames. 'No, you don't,' he said. 'On both counts. But I will help you,

Asmidir. Oh yes, I will. First, however, tell me why are we such savages. Tell me that!'

'What do you want from me, Gifted One? The answers to questions we all know? We do what we do because we *can*. We hunt and kill because we *can*. That which is in our power belongs to us, to be used as we desire. Whether it be a round of meat, a wild-born stag, an ancient tree, or a beautiful woman. Now what is it you want to hear?'

Gwalchmai gave a long sigh, and rubbed at weary, bloodshot eyes with a gnarled hand. 'As we sit and speak,' he said, 'in the warmth of this cabin, there is a woman in a cell, being beaten, brutalized and raped by five men. She is bleeding, she is hurt. One of the five is a nobleman, but he is filled with a lust for inflicting pain. But the others are all *ordinary* men. Men like you and me, Asmidir. I can feel their thoughts, taste their emotions. By God, I can also sense their arousal! and I would like to kill them. But am I different? Was I different in that field? Were you different with the Loabite woman?'

'She was part of the spoils of war,' said Asmidir, 'and no, I do not lie awake at night and think of her. She was used. We are all used. She chose to kill herself. Her choice, Gifted One. But I have no time for these games, nor am I concerned about some whore in a prison cell. Do you know the name of the leader who is coming, or not?'

Gwalchmai swung round, his eyes bright and glittering. 'Yes, I know. I have always known. From the night when the Gate was opened, when Taliesen came to me, and brought me the child to raise.'

'And will you tell me?' asked Asmidir, masking his impatience.

'It is not a man.'

'You make no sense, you drunken old fool. What is it then . . . a tree? A horse?'

'Are you so stupid that you cannot understand what has been said here?' asked Gwalchmai. 'Where are we, for God's sake? Can you not concentrate that fine mind for a moment?'

Asmidir sat back and took a deep breath. 'Humour me,' he said at last. 'Perhaps my mind is not as fine as you imagine.' But the old man said nothing and Asmidir took a deep breath. 'Very well, I will play this game. Where are we, you asked? We are in the Highlands, in the cabin of Sigarni the Huntress. And we have been talking about a woman in a cell . . .' He sat bolt upright. 'Sweet Heaven, Sigarni is in the cell?'

'Sigarni is in the cell,' echoed Gwalchmai, tossing a fresh log to the flames.

'Why?'

'The Baron desired her hawk. She refused to sell it. In the argument that followed the hawk tore out the Baron's left eye. Sigarni was dragged away.'

'But she lives. They have not killed her?'

'No, they have not killed her. But they are giving her scars she will carry all her life, and her pain will be visited a thousand times upon their countrymen.'

'What can I do? Tell me!'

'You can wait here, with me. All your questions will be answered, Asmidir. Every one.'

Will Stamper sat in the Blue Duck tavern staring into the tankard. It was the fifth jug of ale he had consumed, and it could not deaden the shame he felt. Relph pushed through the crowd and sat opposite him, a bright smile on his face.

'Looks like I don't owe you that five coppers any more, eh? Told you I'd spear her by midnight.'

'Shut up, for God's sake!'

'What's wrong with you, Will? It were great, weren't it? Nothing like it! And you had your share.' He chuckled. 'And the captain. Humping like a little bunny. Nice to know the nobles get boils on their arses, isn't it?'

Will lifted the tankard and half drained it. The ale was strong, and he felt his head swimming. 'I've never done that before,' he said. 'Never will again. I'm not going to wait for the summer. I'm going south tomorrow. I'm finished here. Wish I'd never come.'

'You've got blood on your hand,' said Relph. 'Did she bite you?'

Will jerked and rubbed the dried blood on to his leather leggings. 'No. It's not my blood.' He bit his lip and looked away, but Relph saw the tears spilling to his cheeks.

'What's got into you? Is it the boy? He'll get over the whoop, Will. I'm sure he will. Come on, mate, this isn't like you at all. Here, let me get you another drink.' Relph stood, but Will reached out and took hold of his arm.

'It doesn't bother you, does it? She was screaming. She was cut, bitten, thrashed. It doesn't bother you?'

'It didn't bother you at the time, either. And no, why should it worry me? Worse'll happen to her tomorrow. At least she went out with a good rut, eh? Anyway, the captain told us to. So why not? God's teeth, Will, she's only a whore. Whores were made for sport.'

Will released his hold and Relph moved back into the crowd. He gazed around him through bleary eyes, listening to the laughter of the revellers, and thought of Betsi; picturing her in that cell. Relph returned with two tankards. 'Here, get that down you, mate. You'll feel better. There's a dice game back at the barracks at midnight. You fancy a bet?'

'No. I'll get home. Got to get Betsi to pack ready for tomorrow.'

'You're not thinking this through, Will. No one will be taking on mercenaries down south. What will you do?'

'I don't care.'

Relph leaned forward. 'You have to care, Will. You have a family to support, and a sick son. You can't go dragging them out into the countryside. It's not fair on them. Look, I don't know why this has got to you so bad. You stuck a few inches of gristle into a few soft warm places. Now you want to ruin your life and your family's lives. It don't make no sense. You get home and get a good night's sleep. It'll all look different in the morning.'

Will shook his head. 'What will be different? I'm forty-two years old. I've lived my whole life by an iron set of rules which my dad beat into me. You ever heard me lie, Relph. You ever seen me steal?'

'No, you're a regular saint, mate. They ought to put up statues to you. But what's the point you're making?'

'I just betrayed everything I've lived for. *Everything*. What we did there was wrong. Worse than that, it was evil.'

'Now you're talking daft. What do you mean evil? She was a slag, and I'll bet she's been jumped before. What pigging difference does it make? She's dead anyway, come morning. You heard the captain, they're going to put out her eyes and hang her in the old cage. Bloody Hell, Will, you think what we done is any worse than that? Come on I'll walk you home. You look all in.'

Relph stood and helped Will to his feet. The big man staggered, then headed for the door.

'I should have stopped it,' mumbled Will. 'Not joined in. Oh God, what will I say to Betsi?'

'Nothing, mate. Nothing at all. You just go home, and you sleep.'

The relief guard was called Owen Hunter; the man he replaced told him of the sport he had missed. Owen was a Lowlander, married to a harridan named Clorrie who made his life a misery. As he sat at the dungeon table in the flickering torchlight, he tried to remember the last time he had enjoyed a woman. It was more than three years – if you didn't count the alley whore.

He had smiled when the guard told him of the afternoon's entertainment, and even managed to say, 'That's life,' when the man pointed out that it should have been Owen's shift, except that the Lowlander had swapped it earlier that day.

But now, as he sat alone, he allowed his bitterness to rise. Of all the women to choose he had married Clorrie: sharp-tongued, mean-spirited Clorrie. Life's a bastard and no mistake, thought Owen. Like the other soldiers, he had heard of the incident when the Baron lost his eye. Even now the surgeons were at work in the upper room of the keep, plugging the wound and feeding the Baron expensive opiates.

There was no sound in the dungeon corridor, save for the occasional hiss from the torches. Owen stood and stretched his legs, remembering the last words of the man he replaced: 'What an arse on her! I tell you, Owen, she was a jump to remember.'

Owen lifted a torch from its bracket and walked past the four empty cells to the locked door. Pulling open the grille he peered inside. There was no window to the cell and the torchlight did not pierce the gloom. Slipping the bolt, he opened the door. The woman was lying on the floor, her legs spread open. There was blood on her face and thighs, and one of her breasts was bleeding. Owen moved closer. She was still unconscious. Despite the blood he could see that she was beautiful, her hair gleaming silver and red in the torchlight. His eyes scanned her body. Even the hair of her pubic mound was silver, he noticed. She was slim and tall, her breasts firm. Owen saw that one of her nipples was bleeding, a thin trickle of red still running down to her side. Kneeling alongside her Owen ran his hand up her thigh, his fingers stroking the silver mound, his index finger slipping inside her.

He made his decision and rose, planting the torch in a wall bracket. Swiftly he stripped off his leather leggings and knelt between the open legs, pushing his hands under her thighs to draw her on to him. Why not, he thought? Everyone else has had their pleasure. Why not me? Why shouldn't Owen Hunter have a little fun?

His last sight was of the woman suddenly rearing up. His own hands were locked beneath her thighs, but he saw her right hand stab forward, felt the terrible pain as her first two fingers struck his eyes. Then all was pain and an explosion of light that was unbearable.

Sigarni dragged her fingers from the oozing sockets and groaned. Her ribs hurt, but that was as nothing compared with the pain within. She pushed the body of the guard from her, then rolled to her knees. Nausea rose in her throat and she vomited. Her head was pounding, her body begging her to lie down, to rest, to heal. Instead she forced herself to her feet. The guard began to moan. Dropping to her knees she pulled his dagger from his belt and plunged it through the nape of his neck. His legs spasmed, one foot striking the narrow cot. Blood filled the man's throat and he began to choke. Dragging the dagger clear she held the point over the centre of his back and threw her weight down upon it. The blade slid between his ribs, skewering the lungs. Now he was still. A pool of urine spread out from beneath him. Sigarni stood again, then sat on the cot looking round the cell, taking in every block and stone, every rat-hole. Her leggings had been thrown into a corner. Retrieving them, she dressed. The cord of the waist had been cut.

Dragging the guard's belt clear, she pierced a new buckle hole in the leather and strapped it to her waist.

Everything hurt. Her lips were swollen, her cheek cut and bruised. There was a knife-cut in her right buttock and another on her left thigh. The guard moaned again. Sigarni could not believe the man could still be alive. Taking hold of the jutting knife with both hands she wrenched it clear of his back, then knelt forward to slice the razor-sharp blade across his throat. Blood gushed to the stone floor. Grabbing him by the shoulders she rolled him to his back, slashing the sharp blade again and again across his lower body. At last, exhausted, she stopped, her hands drenched in blood.

'You've got to get out of here,' she told herself. 'You've got to find them.' She had feigned unconsciousness at the end, even when two of them had stood and urinated over her. She had heard the small man, Relph, talking about the Blue Duck tavern. She knew it – it was close to Market Street.

Knife in hand, Sigarni walked from the cell and out into the dungeon corridor. Her legs had no strength, and she fell to her knees and vomited once more. 'Don't be weak,' she scolded herself. 'You are Sigarni the Huntress. You are strong.'

Rising unsteadily, she managed to reach the stairs and started to climb up into the darkness. Halfway up she heard footfalls. Pushing herself back against the wall she waited. Then a man called out from some distance above, 'Hey Owen, I was on my way home when I thought it would be worth a second tilt at the bitch. You fancy a double, eh?'

From out of the darkness he appeared, a looming shape with a protruding belly. Sigarni rammed the blade into that belly, ripping it up towards the heart. He grunted and fell back to the stairs. 'Oh God! Oh God!' he screamed. Sigarni pulled the blade clear and stepped in close.

'You want to ride double with me, Outlander? You want to enjoy Sigarni?'

'Oh, please! Don't kill me!'

'You left teeth marks in my breast, you fat bastard. Now bite on this!' The knife slid between his teeth and Sigarni slammed it home to the hilt. His fat arms began to flail, but she knelt on his chest and cut his throat. Only when he was still did she mutilate him in the same way she had the first guard. Slowly she climbed the stairs, pushing open the door at the top. The courtyard was moonlit and deserted, save for a sentry sitting under the arch. He was facing out into the town. Sigarni stepped into the open air and walked across to the arch.

The sentry was not even aware of dying . . .

Blood-drenched and weak, Sigarni moved on into the silent town.

Abby was dead – killed trying to save her. And I am dead, she thought. They will kill me, for I have not the strength to find them all. Somehow the thought of dying held no fear for her. All that kept her moving on tottering feet was the need for vengence, a need as old as the Highlands themselves. Clan laws were not subtle, precedents were rarely cited, and there were no glib-tongued lawyers to represent the factions. Wrongdoers were punished by those they had wronged, or in the case of murder were hunted down by clan warriors selected by the Hunt Lord. Justice was sudden, harsh and final.

But Sigarni had no family, save old Gwal who had raised her after the Slaughter. There were no men to seek blood revenge.

Only me, she thought. Only Sigarni. The knife slipped from her fingers and clattered to the street. Stopping, she picked it up, then fell heavily. 'Damn!' she whispered. Twisting round, she sat for a while with her back against a cool stone wall. The stars were bright, the night cool with the promise of autumn. Some distance away she could hear the sound of revellers, and knew she was close to the Blue Duck tavern. What will you do, she wondered? Walk in, covered in blood, and move from table to table until you see them? What kind of a plan is that? And if you wait past the dawn they will find you anyway, and drag you back to that cell, and who knows what torture. Are you mad, girl? Leave this place. Get back into the Highlands were you can gather your strength.

Two of them are dead, she told herself. One more, at least, is in the tavern.

One more . . .

Forcing herself to her feet Sigarni groaned. Blood was trickling down her leg. She licked her lips with a dry tongue and tried to blank out the pain.

Women are made for sport.

The words flashed back into her memory. The short soldier had said them at some point during her ordeal. Laughter had followed his words, then more pain. Suddenly she remembered the little Census Taker and his revulsion and fear as Abby pecked at him. What was it he had said: 'I prefer the hares'? Hares are made for sport, Sigarni had told him.

Everything is made for sport, she realized, in a world ruled by Outlanders.

The rest had given her fresh strength and she walked on.

The Blue Duck tavern was an old building with frayed timbers and white walls. There were four windows on the ground floor, two either side of the old oak door. One of the windows was open and through it she could hear the sounds of the drinkers. Moving to the wall beside it, she glanced in. The place was packed and her keen eyes scanned the faces within. There were none she recognized, but then she could see only a section of the crowd. Dropping to her knees she crawled under the window, then rose and glanced in from the new angle. Two men were walking towards the door. Her heart, and her anger, lifted. Transferring the knife to her left hand, she wiped the sweat from her right, rubbing the palm down her leggings.

The door opened. 'That's it, Will, one foot in front of the other. That's the way to go, son.'

'Shut the bloody door!' said someone inside. Relph pulled shut the door as Will Stamper leaned against the wall.

'Be right with you, mate, but I've got to piss,' said Relph, opening the front of his leggings and urinating against the wall. Sigarni moved silently alongside the drunken Will and sliced the knife back across his throat. The skin flapped open, blood bubbling clear. Then she ran forward and plunged the blade into Relph's back. He reared up and grabbing his hair, she rammed his head against the wall. Falling to his knees Relph struggled to turn. Wrenching the knife clear Sigarni, still holding to his hair, dragged his head back to expose his throat. 'Women are made for sport,' said Sigarni, slashing open his jugular. Relph fell back, his arms and legs thrashing. Sigarni stepped clear and moved to where Will stood leaning against the wall, his blood gushing over the front of his tunic. Slowly he toppled to his knees and looked up at her. There was no hatred in his gaze, and no fear. He tried to speak, but could only mouth two words. Sigarni almost laughed. Then she leaned back and kicked him in the head and his body fell to the stones.

Only one more now, she thought. The captain.

But where would he be?

Are you insane, woman! came a voice inside her mind. *Leave now!*

'No!' she said aloud. 'I'll find him.'

'*Leave and he'll find you. I promise you! Stay and you will die and he will live. I promise you that too!*'

'Who are you? Where are you?' she asked, spinning round and scanning the shadows.

'*I am with you, girl, and I want your trust. Leave now. Believe me, you won't like being dead. I know, I've tried it. Now go!*'

Confused, Sigarni obeyed, cutting down through an alley towards the North Gate.

The bastards have unhinged my mind, she thought. Now I am hearing ghost voices.

From the citadel keep came the sound of clanging alarm bells.

I'll never get out now, she thought.

'*Yes, you will,*' said the voice. '*Your people need you.*'

Baron Ranulph Gottasson groaned. The pain had moved beyond pleasure to a burning point of agony that bordered on the exquisite. Narcotics flowed in his blood, and his waking dreams were vivid. He saw again the fall of the Kushite cities, refugees running panic-stricken from their burning homes, heard again the wailing of the soon-to-die, the piercing screams of city dwellers staring into the brutal faces of the conquering soldiers, feeling the cold bite of their blades into soft, yielding flesh.

Days of blood and glory, marching his men across inhospitable deserts, iron mountains and lush foreign plains.

And then it was over. No one left to conquer.

At first it had not seemed so onerous: the triumphant return to the capital, the cheering crowds choking the streets, the nights of celebration at the palace, the orgies . . . The Baron groaned again. He felt someone lift his head, and a cold metal goblet was placed against his lips. He swallowed and sank back.

Then had come the day when the organization of the empire was re-shaped. Plessius was made Governor General of Kushir and the east – a bumbling fool of a man with not an ounce of ambition in his fat head. A hardly surprising choice to rule a land three thousand leagues from the capital. The King had chosen wisely; there would be no rebellion from that quarter. Ranulph had let it be known he desired the north. There was nothing here of any worth, save cattle and timber. The climate was harsh in winter, perversely changeable in what passed for summer. A little coal was being mined, but there were no deposits of gold or silver, nor even iron. The people were poor and defeated.

Ranulph had waited for his appointment, sure in the knowledge that he would be offered anything *but* the north. The King possessed a mind of astonishing cunning, and would never offer any general the true object of his desires.

Ranulph's mind swam on a sea of delicious pain . . .

He had a spy in Jastey's household, and knew well that the Earl desired the west. Seventeen rich cities, scores of mines, seven ports, and a thriving commercial network. Together they created the perfect foundation for an assault on the King. Wealth to buy mercenaries, ships to ferry armies and keep them supplied.

Oh, how Ranulph had laughed when Jastey had been made High Sheriff of the Capital. Despite being a position of great influence, bringing immense wealth, it meant that Jastey was always at court and close to the King.

But Jastey's handsome face had worn a smile the following day, when Ranulph had been summoned to the palace. The memory brought a fresh spasm of agony. Ranulph had walked down the long aisle in the Chapel of the Blessed Blade, to where the King waited with his courtiers around him, Jastey at his right hand. Ranulph knelt before his sovereign, then gazed up into the dark, reptilian eyes.

'It is reported to me that you desire to govern the north, my good and dear friend,' said the King. 'Your services to the kingdom merit great rewards, and I can think of no greater reward than to bestow upon you that which you most desire. Rise, Baron Ranulph Gottasson, Earl of the North, Governor General of the Highlands.'

To his amazement Ranulph had managed a smile. It did not match the grin on Jastey's face. The west had gone to the King's new favourite, Estelm.

The feast which followed had been bitter hard for the new Baron. The King seated him next to Jastey, and that alone made the food taste of bile and ash.

'My congratulations, Ranulph,' said the Earl. 'I know we do not see eye to eye on many issues, but I would like you to know that I argued most strongly for you to be given the north. I thought it would perhaps ease the animosity between us.'

Ranulph looked into the man's dark eyes and saw the humour glinting there. 'Animosity, cousin? Surely not. Friendly rivalry would be more apt, I believe?'

'Perhaps,' agreed Jastey. 'However, that should now be behind us. You have your own kingdom, as it were, while I must remain in the capital making laws, sitting in judgement, surrounded by clerics. Ah, how I envy you!'

Ranulph smiled, and pictured sliding a red-hot dagger into Jastey's belly.

Returning to his town house he had walked into his library and stood gazing at the map stretched out on the far wall. The empire filled it, from ocean to ocean. Ranulph's mouth was dry, his hands trembling with suppressed tension. The skin of his back and buttocks was still tender, but he knew that he needed the release of the whip. Summoning a servant, he ordered him to fetch Koris.

The man's face paled. 'I am sorry, my lord, but Koris packed his belongings and left this morning.'

'Left? What do you mean *left?*'

The servant swallowed hard. 'He has taken up a new . . . appointment . . . lord.'

The shock hit him like ice upon hot skin. Koris, whom he had trusted above all men, and loved better than any woman. And he knew, without a shred of doubt, where the boy's appointment had taken him.

Jastey!

Dismissing the servant, the Baron moved to the window, opening it wide and breathing in the cold night air.

'*I don't want to go north, Ranulph. It's cold there – and there are no amusements.*'

'*We will not be going north, sweet boy.*'

'*But isn't that what you want?*'

'*Be patient and all will be revealed.*'

'*You don't trust me!*'

'*Of course I trust you. Now don't sulk! I hate that.*'

And he had explained his plans, talked of his dreams, secure in the knowledge that he was with the one person in all the empire who loved him.

Two nights later, bound, gagged and hooded, Koris had been carried down to the secret room below the town house. Ranulph had his arms tied to posts, his legs chained to the wall. Dismissing the soldiers who had brought him, he pulled the hood clear of the boy's beautiful face.

'Oh, Ranulph, please God, don't hurt me!'

The Baron drew his dagger and pushed the blade into a brazier of hot coals. 'While the blade heats,' he said softly, 'we will talk of love and trust.'

Semi-conscious now, the Baron felt the terrible stabs of fire in his eye socket, lancing their way through the opiates in his blood. Koris had been allowed no opiates throughout that long, long night.

Kollarin the Finder was comfortably asleep between the two whores when he heard the frenzied hammering at the tavern door below his room. He yawned and stretched, his right arm touching the fleshy shoulder of the plump young woman on his right. She moaned softly and turned over. The slender girl to his left awoke.

'What is happening?' she asked, sleepily.

Kollarin sat up. The room was cold, the fire long dead. 'I don't know, but someone is anxious to get in,' he said. He heard the innkeeper tramping down the stairs, cursing as he moved.

'All right! All right, I'm coming, damn you!'

The sound of bolts being drawn back drifted up to the room and Kollarin heard his name mentioned. Now it was his turn to curse. Clambering over the slender whore he grabbed his leggings and began to climb into them. Just then the door opened and a soldier entered.

'We need you, Finder,' said Captain Redgaer Kushir-bane. 'There has been an attack on the Citadel cells.'

The fat whore woke with a start and screamed. Kollarin's head was pounding. 'Be quiet, please!' he said, squeezing shut his eyes. 'My head is splitting.'

'Why is he here?' she asked, drawing the blanket over her large breasts. Kollarin smiled at this show of shyness. 'Employment, my pretty,' he said. 'This gentleman has come to offer me coin, with which to pay for your expert services. Now go back to sleep.' Kollarin continued to dress, pulling on a pair of brown leather boots over his green leggings. His shirt was of wool, dyed dark green, and over this he donned a sleeveless leather jerkin lined with fleece.

Moving past the captain, he descended the stairs. Two soldiers were idling there and the innkeeper was standing by, his expression cold.

'I must apologize,' said Kollarin, 'for the ruination of your rest, my friend. It appears there has been an emergency of some kind. I am sure the captain will reimburse you.'

'Fat chance of that,' snapped the innkeeper, walking to the door and holding it open.

Out in the street Redgaer started to explain, but Kollarin cut him short. 'No need for words, captain. Merely take me to the scene.'

They moved swiftly through the town up the short hill to the arched gateway where a corpse lay on the cold stone. Kollarin knelt beside the body, laying his right hand just above the gaping wound in the man's neck. 'This is not where it began,' he said, and rose to walk across the moonlit courtyard to the dungeon stairs. Here was a second corpse. Kollarin paused, laid his hand on the man's head, then walked on.

The soldiers and the captain trooped after him and Kollarin entered the small dungeon. On the floor was the last corpse. Kollarin stood for a moment staring down at the man. He had been castrated, and then the genitalia had been pushed into his open mouth. Kneeling beside him, Kollarin touched his hand to the cold stone floor and closed his eyes. Images poured into his mind. He let them flow for a few seconds, then closed them off. Remaining where he was for a moment more, he gathered his thoughts and rose, turning to face the captain. 'What do you wish to know?' he asked, keeping his tone neutral.

'How many were involved in the attack? Where are they now?'

'There was no attack, captain,' said Kollarin softly. 'The raped woman lay where this man is now, pretending to be unconscious. When he too desired a piece of the vile action she stabbed out his eyes – as you can see.' The captain did not look down. 'She used her fingers. Then she took his dagger and killed him with it. She was in great pain herself at the time – but then you know that.' Kollarin turned. 'She fell to her knees and vomited there, then sat for a moment or two upon the cot.' Moving past the captain he stepped out into the dungeon corridor. 'Still holding the dagger she made for the stairs. The other guard was returning. He said something, but it is unclear to me. She killed him, then made her way up the stairs.' Kollarin followed in her footsteps and found a smear of blood upon the stairwell wall. Touching his fingers to it he closed his eyes once more. The captain and the soldiers were pressing in close. 'Ah yes,' said Kollarin. 'Here she paused for a moment. She is thinking of three men, two soldiers . . . and you, captain. She has decided to seek them out and kill them. But she is weak, and bleeding. She castrates this guard too, but has little energy to spare. She is thinking of a tavern, trying to remember where it is. She has heard the men speak of spending the evening there.'

'The Blue Duck!' said one of the soldiers.

'And that's where she is heading?' asked Redgaer. Kollarin nodded.

'*Was* heading, captain. This was some while ago.'

Redgaer Kushir-bane pushed past the Finder and ran up the stairs, the soldiers pounding after him. Kollarin followed. The four men ran through the streets, arriving at the Blue Duck tavern in time to see the crowd gathered around the bodies of the two soldiers. Kollarin pushed through and squatted down by the bodies.

'When did this happen?' he heard Redgaer demand.

'Moments ago,' said a voice. 'It was a woman. We saw her making off.'

Kollarin touched his hand to the blood on the dead Will Stamper's throat. Then he jerked and almost fell. A voice boomed into his mind. *'Delay them!'* It was not a command, nor yet a plea. Kollarin was surprised, but not shocked. Spirits of the dead had spoken to him before. Yet none had been as powerful as this one. For one fleeting moment he saw a face, hawk-nosed, with deep-set grey eyes and a beard of bright silver. Then the face faded. Kollarin remained where he was for a few seconds more, gathering his thoughts. He was a Hunter, a Finder. His reputation was second to none, and he valued this above all else. Kollarin never failed. He had trailed killers and thieves, robbers and rapists, cattle thieves and assassins. Never before had he been asked to hunt down an innocent woman, brutalized by her captors. Never before had a long-dead spirit interceded on behalf of a victim.

Kollarin rose and stretched his back.

'Where is she heading, man?' demanded Redgaer.

'I can't say,' said the Finder. 'Her mind was very confused at this point.'

'Can't say?' sneered Redgaer. 'It's what you are paid for, man.' Kollarin knew just where she was, heading out through the open North Gate, with half a mile to go before the safety of the tree line. He looked at Redgaer and smiled.

'As she killed these men, captain, she was thinking of you. She was wondering how she could reach you, and draw a sharp knife across your testicles.' Redgaer winced. 'After that she wandered away into that alley there. Perhaps she is still there – waiting.'

'That leads to the North Gate, sir,' said one of the soldiers. 'There is a stable there. We could get horses.'

Redgaer nodded. 'Follow me,' he ordered, and ran off.

Kollarin remained where he was, staring down at the dead Will Stamper. The thoughts of dying men were often strange, almost mundane sometimes. But this man had tried to speak on the point of death. Two words. Kollarin shook his head.

What a time to say, '*I'm sorry.*'

The more Fell considered his encounter with the old man, the more he believed it was a dream. That being so, he asked himself, why are you sitting here in the cold waiting for dawn to rise over Citadel town? He smiled ruefully and poked the dying camp-fire with a long stick, trying to urge some life into the little blaze. Fell's sheepskin cloak was damp from the recent rain and the fire had not the strength to warm him. It spluttered and spat, fizzled and sank low. He glanced at the sky. Dawn was still an hour away. He was sitting with his back against the shallow depression of a deep boulder, the fire set against a second tall stone. The forester looked down at the last of the wood he had gathered. It was also damp. To his left Fell could see the twinkling lights of the *Cinder-wings*. He hoped they would come no closer. Fell had no wish to be visited by the ghosts of painful memories. The *Cinders* were clustered under an oak branch twisting and moving, their golden wings of light fluttering in the dark. When he was a child Fell had caught one of them, and rushed it home to his parents. In the light of the cabin it had proved to be nothing more than a moth, with wide, beautiful wings and a dark, hairy body. Lying dead in his hand it had seemed so ordinary, yet out in the woods, its wings glowing with bright light, it had been magical beyond imagining.

'You are lucky, boy,' his father told him. 'You are too young to have bad memories. Trust me, as you grow older you will avoid the *Cinders*.'

How true it was. When Fell was sixteen he had been walking through the night, following the trail of a lame wolf. He saw the flickering of *Cinder-wing* lights and walked in close to see them fly. Instantly the vision of Mattick's soon-to-be-drowned face filled his mind, the child reaching out to Fell as the undertow dragged him towards the rapids. Fell couldn't swim, and could only watch helplessly as the child was swept over the rocks, the white water thrashing around him. The face hovered in Fell's mind and he dropped to his knees, tears coursing his cheeks. 'It was not my fault!' he cried aloud, then scrambled back from the glowing insects. After that he gave the *Cinder-wings* a distant respect.

The rain began again, and the *Cinders* vanished from sight. Fell shook his head. 'A great fool you are,' he said, aloud, watching the drops of rain settling on the longbow. The bowstring was safe and dry in his belt pouch, his quiver of twelve shafts behind him and under his cloak, but Fell did not like to see his favourite hunting bow at the mercy of the weather. It was a fine bow, made by Kereth the Wingoran. Horn-tipped, it had a pull of more than ninety pounds. Fell, though not the finest of the Loda bowmen, had not missed a killing shot since purchasing the weapon. An arrow would sing from the string, streaking to its target and sinking deep through skin, flesh and muscle. It was important for a deer to die fast. Ideally the beast would be dead before it knew it, therefore the meat remained tender and succulent; whereas if the creature was frightened, its muscles would tense and harden and the meat would stay that way. Fell's bow supplied choice meat.

'What are you doing here, Fell? Following a dream you don't believe in?' he said aloud. The words of the dream man came back to him. '*In three days outside the walls of Citadel town a sword will be raised, and the Red will be worn again. Be there, Fell. In three days, at dawn. By the light of the new sun you will see the birth of a legend.*'

The rain eased once more and, as the moon showed through the break in the clouds, the *Cinders* glinted back into life. Fell hefted his bow and wiped the drops of water from its six-foot length. Amazingly the fire flared up, tongues of flame licking at the wood. Fell stretched out his hands and felt the welcome warmth.

'That is better,' said Taliesen. Fell's heart hammered and he jumped like a startled squirrel. The old man had appeared from nowhere, seeming to blink into existence. 'It used to be,' continued the druid, his cloak of feathers shining in the moonlight, 'that I enjoyed forest nights. But some time during the last hundred years or so my blood started to run thin.'

'Why can't you walk up to a fire like anyone else?' stormed Fell.

'Because I am not like everyone else. What point is there in possessing enormous talent if no one is given the opportunity to appreciate it? By Heaven, boy, but you scare easily.' Taliesen rubbed a gnarled hand over his wood-smoke whiskers. 'No food this time, eh? Well, I suppose that is a blessing.'

'You didn't touch it last time, so you have no way of knowing!' said Fell. 'You are not real, old man. You are not flesh and blood.' As he spoke Fell suddenly reached out and swept his hand across Taliesen's face. His fingers passed through the wrinkled skin, and he felt nothing but air against his palm.

'Good,' said Taliesen. 'You have intelligence. Yet you are still wrong. I *am* flesh and blood. But I am not flesh and blood *here*. I am sitting in my own cave in another place, and another time. The energy needed to open the Gateways for the flesh is immense; there is no need to waste it when an astral projection will serve the same purpose. And since my role is merely to speak with you, my spirit image must suffice.'

'You breed words like lice,' snapped Fell, still rattled. 'And I don't relish having wizards at my fire. So speak you piece and be gone.'

'Tish, boy, where are your manners? Elders are to be treated with respect, surely, even in this new and enlightened age? Did your parents teach you nothing? Your father, I recall, was a man of good breeding.'

'For pity's sake, just say what you came to say,' said Fell. 'I am already sick of your lectures.'

Taliesen was silent for a moment. 'Very well,' he said at last, 'but mark the words well. Firstly, when I leave, I want you to string your bow. The time is drawing near when you will have to use it. Secondly, you know the location of the Alwen Falls?'

'Of course, where Ironhand passed over. Every Loda child knows where it is.'

'When the arrows are loosed, and blood is upon the ground, you must take the Cloak Wearer there. You understand?'

'Understand? No, I understand nothing. Firstly I have no intention of loosing a shaft at anyone or anything, and secondly, who is the Cloak Wearer?'

'Have a little patience, Fell. And if you do not loose a shaft a loved one of yours will die. Take me at my word, boy. And remember the pool. That is vital!'

The old man vanished. The fire died instantly.

Fell sent a whispered curse after the man. Yet even as he spoke he drew the bowstring from his pouch and strung the bow.

The first light of pre-dawn was heralded by birdsong and Fell swung his quiver over his shoulder and walked to the top of the hill overlooking Citadel town.

There was nothing to see, save the grey walls and the rising stone of the Keep beyond the town's rooftops. Gradually the sky lightened and he saw a tiny figure emerge from the north gate and begin to run towards the hills. Fell squinted, but could not – at first – identify the runner.

Then, with a shock, he saw the dawn light glint on her silver hair. She was some three hundred yards on to open ground when the three horsemen rode from the town. The lead rider was a soldier in helm and breastplate, as was the third. But it was the second man, riding a grey stallion, who caught Fell's attention. He was brandishing a sword, and he wore a red cloak! His excitement soared.

Sigarni was running hard, but the horsemen were closing. Why do they have their swords drawn? thought Fell. And then it came to him in a sickening realization. They are chasing her. They mean to kill her!

The lead horseman was a mere fifty yards behind her when Fell drew a shaft and notched it to the bowstring. It was not an easy shot – a fast-moving horseman, downhill from him, and with the light still poor.

The enormity of what he was about to do filled Fell's mind, yet there was no hesitation. Smoothly he drew back the string until it nestled against his chin, then he took a deep breath and slowly let it out. Between breaths and utterly motionless, he sighted carefully and loosed the shaft. The arrow sang through the air. For a fraction of a heartbeat Fell thought he had missed, but the shaft slammed home in the lead rider's left eye, catapulting him from the saddle. Running forward, Fell notched a second arrow to the string; but he shot too swiftly, and the shaft flew past the red-cloaked officer and skimmed across the flank of the third man's horse. The beast reared, sending the soldier tumbling over its haunches in an ungainly somersault.

The red-cloaked officer was almost upon the fleeing woman. Fell saw her glance back once, then turn and leap at the grey horse, waving her arms and shouting loudly. The grey swerved to avoid her, pitching its rider to the left. Sigarni leapt at the man, a silver blade glinting in her right fist. Her left hand caught hold of his cloak, dragging him from the saddle. The knife rose and fell. Blood gouted from a wound in the man's neck and again and again the knife flashed.

Sigarni rose with the dead man's cloak in her hand. Fell watched as she gazed back at the Citadel town. Scores of people were lining the parapets now. Sigarni swirled the crimson cloak around her shoulders, retying the snapped neck cord. Then she raised the dead man's sword and pointed it at the spectators.

The sun finally rose and Sigarni was bathed in its golden light, the iron sword shining like a torch of silver to match her hair. For Fell it was as if time ceased to have meaning, and he knew that this scene would shine for ever in his memory. The cloak wearer was Sigarni. *She* was the legend. Fell let out a long, slow breath.

Sigarni plunged the sword into the ground, then turned and slowly mounted the grey stallion. The third soldier was sitting on the ground nearby. Sigarni ignored him and urged the horse on towards the trees and the waiting Fell.

He saw the blood upon her shirt and leggings, the bruises and cuts on her face.

But more than this, he saw the crimson cloak around her slender shoulders.

'What now for us all, Sigarni?' he asked, as she came closer. 'What now?'

Her eyes seemed unfocused, and she did not appear to hear him. Her face was losing its colour, the surface of the skin waxy and grey. The horse moved on, plodding into the trees. Fell ran after it, just in time to throw aside his bow and catch hold of Sigarni as she started to fall from the saddle. Pushing her foot clear of the stirrup, Fell levered himself to the stallion's back. With one arm holding the unconscious Sigarni to him, he took up the reins in his left hand and heeled the stallion forward.

The old wizard had urged him to take her to the falls, but if he did so now he would leave a clear trail behind him, the horse's hooves biting deeply into the damp earth.

The pursuit was probably already under way, and with little time to plan Fell urged the horse to greater speed and headed for the deeper forest. He rode for several miles, keeping to the deer trails, always climbing higher into the mountains. Glancing at the sky he saw thick clouds to the north, dark and angry, their tops flattened like an anvil. Fell breathed a prayer of thanks, for such clouds promised hail and thunder and powerful storms. Hauling on the reins he stepped down from the saddle, allowing Sigarni to fall into his arms and across his shoulder. The ground beneath his feet was rocky and firm, leaving no trace of his booted feet. He slapped the stallion firmly on the rump and the horse leapt forward in a run, heading on down the slope towards the valley below. Fell left the trail, forcing his way through deep undergrowth. The ground broke sharply to his right into a muddy slope; it was hard to keep his footing here, especially with the added burden of Sigarni. He moved on carefully, occasionally slithering and sliding, keeping close to the trees that grew on the hillside, using them as barriers to halt any out-of-control slide. He was halfway down the slope when he heard the sound of horsemen on the road above. Dropping to his knees behind a screen of bushes, he looked back and saw the soldiers galloping by. There were more than thirty in the group.

With a grunt Fell pushed himself to his feet and struggled on. By his own reckoning he was around four miles due east from the Alwen Falls. But that four miles would become at least six by the route he would be forced to travel, along winding trails, skirting the steeper slopes and the many acres of open grassland.

He was sweating heavily by the end of the first mile, and by the second he felt his legs trembling with the effort of carrying the unconscious woman. Sigarni had made no sound throughout and Fell paused by a stream, lowering her to the ground. Her colour was not good, and her pulse was faint and erratic. Carefully he examined her, opening her torn shirt. There were bloody teeth-marks on her breast, and a range of purple bruises on her ribcage and shoulders. But no deep wounds. She is in shock, he thought. It is vital to keep her warm; to find somewhere he could nurse her. Gently he stroked her bruised face. 'You are safe, my love,' he said, softly. 'Hold on for me.' She did not stir as Fell wrapped the crimson cloak around her, then lifted her to his shoulders. Almost two hours had passed already since the fight above the town, and there were still four miles to go. Fell took a deep breath and struggled on, trying not to think of his aching muscles, the burning in his calves and thighs.

For three more painful hours Fell carried Sigarni through the forest. In all that time she made no sound.

At last they arrived at the Alwen Falls.

There was no sign of the wizard.

In a shallow cave, a little way back from the pool, Fell built a fire. Removing his own sheepskin cloak he covered Sigarni with it and, holding her hand, talked to her as she slept. 'Well,' he said, squeezing her limp fingers, 'this is a sorry mess and no mistake. We're wolves' heads now, my love. I wish I knew why. Why were they chasing you? Who wounded you? Ah well, I expect you'll tell me in your own good time. Shame about the bow, though. Best I ever had. But I couldn't carry it, hold you and guide the horse at the same time.' Leaning forward, he stroked her brow. 'You are the most beautiful woman, Sigarni. I never saw the like. Was that what caused your pain? Did some Outland noble desire you so badly he

109

felt compelled to take you by force? Was it the red-bearded man whose throat you slashed to red ribbons?' Releasing her hand, he fed wood to the fire and rose, walking to the cave-mouth.

What now, he wondered? Where will we go?

He had relatives among the Wingoras and the Farlain, but with a price on his head he would only endanger them by seeking their aid. No, Fell, he told himself, you are a man alone now, friendless and hunted. You have killed an Outlander and they will hunt you to your dying day. A roll of thunder boomed across the sky and lightning forked across the heavens. Fell shivered and watched as the rain hammered down on the surface of the pool, falling in sheets, thick and impenetrable. Stepping back from the cave-mouth, he returned to the fire and the sleeping Sigarni.

'We will cross the sea, my love,' he said, 'and I'll do what I should have done. We'll marry and build a home in distant mountains.'

'No, you won't,' said Taliesen from the cave-mouth. Fell smiled and swung to see the old man, his feather cloak dripping water, his wispy hair plastered to his skull. In his hands he carried a long staff, wrapped in sacking cloth.

'That's a more pleasing entrance,' said the forester. '*Now* I believe you are flesh and blood.' Taliesen removed his cloak and draped it over a rock. Squatting by the fire, he held out his ancient hands to the flames.

'You did well, boy,' he said. 'You have evaded the first hunters. But they will send more, canny men, skilled in tracking. And with them will be a Finder, a seeker of souls, a reader of thoughts. If you survive this, which is doubtful at best, they will send the night-stalkers, creatures from the pit.'

'No, no,' said Fell, 'seek not to cheer me, old man, with your boundless optimism. I am a grown man, tell it to me straight.'

Taliesen hawked and spat. 'I have no time for your humour. We must protect her, Fell. Her importance cannot be overstated. You must go from here to her cabin. Gather her weapons and some spare clothes; give them to the dwarf. Tell him, and the others there, what has occurred. Then you must find the hunters and lead them deep into the mountains.'

Fell took a deep breath, fighting for calm. It didn't work. 'Find the hunters? Lead them? What say you I just attack the Citadel town single-handed and raze it to the ground? Or perhaps I could borrow your feather cloak and fly south, invading the Outland cities and slaying the King? Are you insane, old man? What do you expect me to do against thirty soldiers?'

'Whatever you can.' The old man looked into Fell's eyes, his expression as cold as ice on flint. 'You are dispensable, Fell,' said Taliesen. 'Your death will matter only to you. You can be replaced. Everything can be replaced, save Sigarni. You understand? You must earn her time, time to recover, time to learn. She is the leader your people have yearned for. Only she has the power to win freedom for the clans.'

'They'll never follow a woman! That much I know.'

Taliesen shook his head. 'They followed the Witch Queen four hundred years ago. They crossed the Gateways and died for her. They stood firm against the enemy, though they were outnumbered and faced slaughter. They will follow her, Fell.'

'The Witch Queen was a sorceress. Sigarni is merely a woman.'

'How blind you are,' said the old man, 'and rich indeed is your male conceit. This woman was dragged to a cell and raped, sodomized and beaten senseless by four men. Like animals they fell upon her . . .'

'I don't want to hear this!' roared Fell, half rising.

'But you shall!' stormed the wizard. 'They struck her with their fists, and they bit her. They cut her buttocks with their sharp knives, and forced her to unspeakable acts. Then they left her upon the floor of the cell, to lie on the cold stone floor in a pool of her own vomit and blood. Aye, well might you look shocked, for this was men at play, Fell. She lay there and after an hour or so a new guard came into the cell. He too wanted his piece of her flesh. She killed him, Fell. Then she hunted down the others. One she slew upon the dungeon stair. Two she killed outside a tavern. And the last? You saw him, in his fine red cloak of wool. Him she tore the throat from. Just a woman? By all the Gods of the Nine Worlds, boy, in her tortured condition she killed six strong men!'

111

Fell said nothing, and transferred his gaze to the sleeping woman. 'Aye, she's a Highlander,' he said, with pride. 'But even that will not make men follow her.'

'We will see,' said Taliesen. 'Now go to her cabin before the hunters reach it. Send the dwarf with weapons and clothes.'

'You will stay with her?'

'Indeed I will.'

Fell rose and swung his quiver over his shoulder, then gazed down at the unconscious Sigarni. 'I will keep her warm,' said Taliesen. 'Oh, and I retrieved your bow.' Lifting what Fell had believed to be a staff covered in sacking, Taliesen passed the weapon to the surprised forester.

'You even kept it dry. My thanks to you, wizard. I feel a whole man again.'

Taliesen ignored him and turned to the sleeping Sigarni, taking her long, slim hand into his own.

Swirling his cloak around his shoulders, Fell stepped out into the rain-drenched night.

Sigarni stood silently by the grey cave wall and listened as Fell and the old man spoke. She could hear their words, see their faces, and even – though she knew not how – feel their emotions. Fell was frightened and yet trying to maintain an air of male confidence. The old man – Taliesen? – was tired, yet filled with a barely suppressed excitement. And lying by the fire, looking so sad and used, she could see herself, wrapped in the rapist's red cloak, her face bruised and swollen. *I am dying,* she thought. *My spirit has left my body and now only the Void awaits.* There was no panic in her, no fear, only a sadness built of dreams never to be realized.

Fell took his bow from the old man and walked from the cave. Sigarni tried to call out to him but he did not hear her. No one could hear her, save maybe the dead.

But she was wrong. As soon as Fell walked out into the rain the old man looked up at her, his button-bright eyes focusing on her face. 'Well, now we can talk,' he said. 'How are you feeling?'

112

Sigarni was both surprised and confused. The old man was holding the hand of her body, yet looking directly into the eyes of her
spirit. It was disconcerting.

'I feel . . . nothing,' she said. 'Is this what death is like?'

He gave a dry chuckle, like the whispering of the wind across
dead leaves. 'You are talking to a man who has fought back death
for many centuries. I do not even wish to speculate on what death
is like. Do you remember the waking of your spirit?'

'Yes, someone called me, but when I opened my eyes he was not
here. How is this happening, old one?'

'I fear the answer may be too complicated for an untutored
Highlander to understand. Essentially your body has been so brutalized that your mind has reeled from thoughts of it. You have entered
a dream state which has freed your . . . soul, if you will. Now you
feel no pain, no shame, no guilt. And while we talk your body is
healing. I have, through my skill, increased the speed of the process.
Even so, when you do return to the prison of flesh you will feel –
shall we say – considerable discomfort.'

'Do I know you?' asked Sigarni.

'Do you think that you do?' he countered.

'I can remember being held close to your chest. You have a small
mole under the chin; I know this. And in looking at you I can see
another man, enormously tall, broad-shouldered, wearing a buckskin shirt with a red wing-spread hawk silhouette upon the breast.'

Taliesen nodded. 'Childhood memories. Yes, you know me,
child. The other man was Caswallon. One day, if God is kind, you
will meet him again.'

'You both saved me from the demons – out there by the pool.
Gwalchmai told me. Who are you, Taliesen? Why have you helped me?'

'I am merely a man – a great man, mind! And my reasons for
helping you are utterly selfish. But now is not the time to speak of
things past. The days of magick and power are upon us, Sigarni, the
days of blood and death are coming.'

'I want no part in them,' she said.

'You have little choice in the matter. And you will feel differently when you wake. In spirit form you are free of much more

113

than merely the flesh. The human body has many weapons. Rage, which increases muscle power; fear, which can hone the mind wonderfully; love, which binds with ties of iron; and hate, which can move mountains. There are many more. But in astral form you are connected only tenuously to these emotions. It was rage and the need for revenge which saved your life, which drove you on to wear the Red. That rage is still there, Sigarni, a fire that needs no kindling, an eternal blaze that will light the road to greatness. But it rests in the flesh, awaiting your return.'

'You were correct, old one. I do not understand all you say. How do I return to my flesh?'

'Not yet. First go from the cave. Walk to the pool.'

She shook her head. 'There is a ghost there.'

'Yes,' he said. 'Call him.'

Sigarni was on the point of refusing when Taliesen lifted his hand and pointed to the fire. The flames leapt up to form a sheer bright wall some four feet high. Then, at the centre, a small spot of colourless light appeared, opening to become a pale glistening circle. It glowed snow-white, then gently became the blue of a summer sky. Sigarni watched spellbound as the blue faded and she found herself staring through the now transparent circle into her own cabin. She was there, talking with Gwalchmai. The conversation whispered into her mind.

'Who was the ghost?' asked the image of Sigarni.

'Go and ask him, woman. Call for him.' She shivered and looked away. 'I can't.'

Gwalch chuckled. 'There is nothing you cannot do, Sigarni. Nothing.'

'Oh, come on, Gwalch, are we not friends? Why won't you help me?'

'I am helping you. I am giving you good advice. You don't remember the night of the Slaughter. You will, when the time is right. I helped take the memory from you when I found you by the pool. Madness had come upon you, girl. You were sitting in a puddle of your own urine. Your eyes were blank, and you were slack-jawed. I had a friend with me; his name was Taliesen. It was he – and another – who slew the Slaughterers. Taliesen told me we were going to lock away the memory and bring you back to the world of the living. We did exactly that. The

114

door will open one day, when you are strong enough to turn the key. That's what he told me.'

Now the circle shrank to a dot and the flames of the fire returned to normal. 'Am I strong enough to turn the key?' she asked Taliesen.

'Go to the pool and find out,' he advised. 'Call for him!'

Sigarni stood silently for a moment, then moved past the old man and out into the night. The rain was still hammering down, but she could not feel it nor, strangely, could she hear it. Water tumbled over the falls in spectacular silence, ferocious winds tore silently at the trees and their leaf-laden branches, lightning flared in the sky, but the voice of the accompanying thunder could not be heard.

The huntress moved to the poolside. 'I am here!' she called. There was no answer, no stirring upon the water. Merely silence.

'Call to him by name,' came the voice of Taliesen in her mind.

And she knew, and in knowing wondered how such an obvious realization should have escaped her so long. 'Ironhand!' she called. 'It is I, Sigarni. Ironhand!'

The waters bubbled and rose like a fountain, the spray forming an arched Gateway lit by an eldritch light. A giant of a man appeared in the Gateway, his silver beard in twin braids, his hair tied back at the nape of his neck. He wore silver-bright armour and carried a long, leaf-bladed broadsword that glistened as if it had been carved from moonlight. He raised the sword in greeting, and then sheathed it at his side and spoke, his voice rich and resonant. 'Come to me, Sigarni,' he said. 'Walk with me awhile.'

'You spoke to me in Citadel town,' she said. 'You urged me to flee.'

'Yes.'

'And you fought for me when I was a child. You slew the last Hollow-tooth.'

'That also.'

'Why?'

'For love, Sigarni. For a love that will not accept death. Will you walk with me awhile?'

'I will,' she said, tears brimming.

And she stepped forward to walk upon the water.

6

Despite the excruciating pain flaring from the empty eye-socket, the Baron Ranulph Gottasson enjoyed the awestruck and fearful expressions of the men before him. Idly the fingers of his left hand stroked the carved dragon claws on the arm of the ornate chair. Sharp they were, as they gripped the globe of ebony. The men waited silently below the dais. He knew their thoughts and, more importantly, their growing anxiety. They had failed – the woman who had robbed him of his eye was still at large. The Baron leaned back on the high carved chair and stared balefully down at the twenty men before him, his single eye blood-shot but its gaze piercing.

'So,' he said softly, his voice sibilant and chilling, 'tell me that you have captured the woman and the renegade.'

The officer before him, a tall man sporting a square-cut beard but no moustache, cleared his throat. His chainmail leggings were mud-smeared, and his right arm was clumsily bandaged. 'We have not caught them yet, my lord. I brought the men back for fresh supplies.'

'You did not catch them,' repeated the Baron, rising from his chair. 'One woman and a forester, riding double on a stolen stallion. But you did not catch them.' Slowly he descended the three steps from the dais and halted before the officer. The man dropped his head and mumbled something. 'Speak up, Chard. Let us all hear you!'

The officer reddened, but he raised his head and his voice boomed out. 'They fooled us. They turned the stallion loose and cut out across the valleys. Then the storm came and it was impossible to read sign. But we followed as best we could, thinking the woman would return to her people. The renegade forester, Fell, shot at us from ambush, wounding two of my men. We gave chase, my lord, but heavily armed riders are useless in the thickets. We left our horses and tried to follow on foot. It was like trying to catch a ghost. I had no archers with me. Three more men were struck by his arrows. Happily their armour saved them from serious injury, though the mercenary, Lava, still has an arrowhead lodged in his shoulder.' Chard fell silent.

The Baron nodded solemnly. 'So, what you are saying is that thirty Outland warriors are no match for a woman and a clansman.'

'No, my lord. I am saying . . .'

'Be silent, fool! Did you think, at any time during the four days you have been gone, to send back to Citadel for trackers? Did you not consider hiring the services of the Finder, Kollarin? Did you set the renegade's own people to hunt him?'

'His own people . . .'

The Baron half turned away, then swung back his fist, smashing the officer's lips against his teeth. The skin split and blood sprayed out as Chard was hurled backwards. He fell heavily, cracking his skull against the base of a statue. Chard gave out one grunting moan, then slid into unconsciousness. 'You have all failed me,' said the Baron, 'but his was the greatest sin. He will suffer for it. Now you!' he said, pointing to a burly soldier with close-cropped fair hair. 'You are Obrin the Southlander, yes?'

'Yes, my lord.' The man bowed.

'You have fought barbarians before, I understand. In Kushir, Palol, Umbria and Cleatia?'

'Yes, my lord. And served also in Pesht under your command. I was there when you stormed the wall, sir, though I was but a common soldier then.'

'And now you are a sergeant-at-arms. Answer me well and you shall assume command of the hunt, and become a captain. Tell us all now what errors were made by the idiot lying at your feet.'

Obrin drew a deep breath and was silent for a moment. The Baron smiled. He knew what was going through the man's mind. No enlisted soldier wished to be made an officer: the pay would not cover the mess bills, and from its meagre supply he would have to purchase his own horse and armour and hire a manservant. Obrin's round face paled; then he spoke. 'The trail was cold from the moment the storm broke, my lord. We should have headed for Cilfallen and taken hostages. Then the foresters themselves could have hunted down their comrade. I would also have posted a reward for their capture, just in case. There's not much coin in the Highlands. And there's always some bastard who'd sell his mother for a copper or two, if you take my meaning, my lord.' Obrin paused and rubbed his broad chin. 'You have already mentioned the Finder, Kollarin, but – I'll be honest with you, my lord – I would not have thought of him, sir. And, if it please you, I don't want captain Chard's command. I'm no nobleman. And I wouldn't fit in. I don't have the brains for it. But I am a good sergeant, sir.'

The Baron ignored the soldier and climbed to the dais to return to his seat. His eye-socket was throbbing and tongues of fire were lancing up into his skull. Yet he kept his expression even and showed no trace of the pain he was feeling. 'Find Kollarin and take him with you when you have your supplies. Take fifty men. Split them into two sections. One will ride to Cilfallen and post a reward of one hundred guineas; this group will also take four hostages and return them to Citadel. The second group, led by you, Obrin, will include Kollarin. You will start your search at the woman's cabin. And before you leave you will take the former Captain Chard to the whipping post, where you will apply fifty lashes to his naked back. With every lash I want you to consider this: Fail, and one of your men will be lashing you.'

'Yes, sir,' said Obrin miserably.

The Baron waved his hand, dismissing the men. 'Not you, Leofric,' he said, as the slender blond-haired cleric was about to leave. 'Shut the door and come to me in my study.' Leaving the dais the Baron strode across the hall and through a small side door, leading to a flight of steps that took him up to the parapet study. A goblet had been placed on the desk, filled with dark, noxious liquid. The Baron hated medicines of any kind, and pain-masking opiates in particular. But the injury was now interfering with his thought processes and he drained the foul brew and sat with his back to the open window.

Leofric knocked twice, then entered the study. 'I am sorry, cousin, for your pain and your disappointment,' he said uneasily.

'The pain is nothing, but I am not disappointed, boy,' the Baron told him, motioning the younger man to a seat opposite him. 'Far from it. The Highlands need to be purged, and the excuse has now fluttered in on the wings of a dead hawk. A woman rebel was arrested after attacking the King's Emissary. Highlanders raided the dungeons to release her. Then they attacked the King's soldiers. When word reaches the south the King will send another five thousand men to serve under me, and we will march from Citadel to the sea and wipe out the clans once and for all.'

'I don't understand,' said Leofric. 'How are the clans a danger to the empire? They have no military organization, indeed no army, and there is no insurrection.'

The Baron smiled. 'Then we cannot lose, can we, Leofric? And at the end I will have an army as large as Jastey's. The King grows old and soft. You think Jastey has no plans to seize the crown for himself? Of course he has. And I can do nothing to stop him while I am stuck away here in this God-forsaken wilderness. However, a war against the clans, well that has great merit. In the south they still fear these northerners, and old men recall with dread how the shrieking savages erupted from the mountains bringing fire and death to the Lowlands. You will see, Leofric. As soon as news reaches the south of this latest outrage, the price of land south of the border will plummet. The weak-hearted will sell up and move and panic will sweep through the immediate Lowland towns.'

'That I do understand,' said Leofric, 'but what if the Highlanders do hunt down this ... Fell ... and the woman? What if they surrender them to us to save the hostages?'

The Baron shook his head. 'It won't happen. I know these barbarians; they're all too proud. I'll hang the hostages as soon as they reach Citadel, and leave their bodies on the north wall for all to see. And if that doesn't force at least a show of resistance, I'll burn Cilfallen and a few of their towns.'

119

'And what task would you have me perform, my lord?' asked Leofric.

'There will be no major invasion of the Highlands until spring. We want time for the fear to grow back home. I intend to attack with six thousand fighting men and five hundred engineers. You must put your mind to the question of how we feed and supply this army all the way to the sea. Also, I want you to study the maps and locate three sites for our fixed camps and fortifications. You know what is required: the forts should be situated close to the lands of the Pallides and the Farlain. Choose open ground, yet close enough to the woods for the men to be able to gather timber for the walls. Questions?'

'Yes, my lord, the fortifications. I am well aware of the standard design used for the construction of temporary fortifications during punitive raids into hostile territory. But these are rough constructions, not intended for more than a few nights. Will they suffice?'

The Baron considered the question. The Highland winters were notoriously savage, and the forts would need to be manned throughout the long, bitter months until the invasion. More important than this, however, was the likelihood of Highlanders attacking the outposts. There would be no way to reinforce them once the snow blocked the passes.

'You misunderstood my use of the word *standard,*' said the Baron smoothly. 'This is not a punitive raid, but should be considered as a full invasion. The forts therefore will have regulation defences, earth barriers at least ten feet high, topped with timber walls to another fifteen feet. Weighted portcullis gates will also be constructed. You are familiar with the design?'

'Of course, my lord. It was devised by Driada during the Cleatian Wars in the last century, but was possibly based on an earlier . . .'

'I did not ask for a history lesson, Leofric. You will take two hundred engineers and three hundred infantrymen into the Highlands. Then you will oversee the building of these forts and within them storehouses for supplies. Make sure the storehouses are watertight. I want no rotting meat, nor mildewed cereal when I arrive with the army.'

120

Leofric stood and bowed. 'I thank you for your trust in me, cousin. I will not fail you.'

Sigarni opened her eyes and saw the flickering flame shadows on the cave ceiling. She watched them for a moment, then felt the onrush of pain from her wounded body. A voice spoke from her left. 'She is awake. Pour some broth for her.' Sigarni rolled her head towards the sound, focusing her eyes upon a wizened old man with deep-set pale eyes.

'Taliesen?' she whispered

'Aye, lass, Taliesen. How are you feeling?'

'Hurt. What happened to me?'

'You don't remember the attack in Citadel dungeons?'

She closed her eyes. 'Of course I do – but that was years ago. I meant why am I injured *now?*' Taliesen leaned forward and helped her to sit up. Pain lanced through Sigarni's right side and she groaned.

'One of your ribs is cracked. It will heal soon,' said Taliesen. Another figure moved into sight, child-small, yet bearded. Sitting at her right, Ballistar handed her a wooden bowl and spoon. The broth was thick and salty and Sigarni became acutely aware of her hunger. She ate in silence. When she had finished Ballistar took back the bowl. Sigarni felt her strength returning, but still she was confused.

'Why did you mention the . . . attack on me?' she asked Taliesen.

'Because it happened three days ago,' he said slowly. 'You have been spirit-wandering in a place where there is no time.'

'I remember,' she said. 'He took me by the hand.'

'Who took her?' asked Ballistar. Taliesen waved him to silence.

'Yes, you walked with him,' said the wizard, taking Sigarni's hand. She wrenched it back, her eyes blazing.

'Do not touch me! No man will ever touch me again!' The violence in her voice was startling, surprising Ballistar who dropped the empty bowl. It rolled across the cave floor, coming to rest against the far wall.

Taliesen seemed unmoved by the rebuff. 'I am sorry, my dear, that was remiss of me. Did you learn much in your time with him?'

'It is hazy now,' she said sleepily. 'But he said he would teach me . . . would always . . . be with me.' Sigarni stretched out again and closed her eyes. Taliesen covered her with a blanket of wool.

'What was she talking about?' asked Ballistar. 'When did she go walking? And who with?'

Taliesen rose and walked to the fire. 'Time to gather more wood,' he said.

'Who did she walk with?' repeated Ballistar.

'It's not for you to know, dwarf. Now go and fetch some wood. The black man will be here soon, and then you'll understand a little more of what is happening here.'

'I'm not your servant!' snapped Ballistar. 'I don't have to jump through hoops because you say so!'

'No,' agreed Taliesen, 'you don't. But I am trying to keep her warm, and I am a little too old to relish walking around a forest and stooping to collect dead wood. You, on the other hand, do not have far to stoop.'

'I'll do it for her,' said the dwarf. 'But know this, Taliesen, I do not like you. Not one bit.'

'How wise of you,' Taliesen told him.

Ballistar stomped from the cave and out into the afternoon sunlight. Fallen wood was plentiful, following the storm, and he spent an idle hour gathering armfuls of fuel and carrying them back to the cave. Taliesen spent the hour sitting silently beside the sleeping Sigarni. Bored now, Ballistar returned to the poolside and stared out over the water. It was smooth and motionless here, and the reflections of the trees on the opposite shore could be seen growing upside-down in the pool. Ballistar moved to the edge and knelt, leaning out over the water. His own face looked back at him, the deep-set brown eyes gazing into his.

'What's it like in an upside-down world?' he asked his reflection. 'Are you happy or sad?' The face in the pool mouthed the same words back to him. Ballistar moved back and sat with his back to the trunk of a weeping willow.

Asmidir came riding down the slope and Ballistar stood. The black man was wearing clothes of brown and russet, with a deep green cloak. He sported no burnoose and upon his head he wore a helm of burnished iron that rose to a glistening silver point at the crown. Seeing Ballistar, he drew rein and stepped from the saddle. 'Where is she?' he asked.

Ballistar pointed to the cave. 'There is a wizard with her. Unpleasant little man.'

'How is she?'

'Beaten and abused. She will get better though. I know it.'

The black man nodded. 'I know it also. What news of Fell?'

'I've heard nothing,' the dwarf told him. 'I've been here for three nights. But I don't think they'll catch him. A canny man is Fell, and stronger than he believes.'

'You see much, Ballistar. You are no man's fool. I shall be taking Sigarni to my house. You are welcome to join us. I think she will feel better with you there.'

'She may not want either of us,' said the dwarf. 'She just told Taliesen that no man will ever touch her again – she may hate us all for the sins of a few.'

Asmidir shook his head. 'She is too intelligent for that, my friend. Will you come?'

'Of course I will come. She is my friend.'

'Mine also,' said Asmidir softly. 'And I will defend her with my life. You believe me?'

Ballistar looked deeply into the man's dark eyes. 'Aye, I believe you, black man. I don't like you, but I believe you.'

'There is much in me to dislike, Ballistar. I have been a harsh man, and at times a cruel one. Despite this I have never betrayed a friend, and treachery is utterly alien to me. I intend to help Sigarni, to teach her all that I know.'

'About what?' asked Ballistar.

'About war,' Asmidir answered.

There was little conversation as the five men moved through the forest, each locked in his own thoughts. Fat Tovi the Baker kept thinking of his eldest son, and how proud he was of the boy. When the soldiers had selected him as one of the four hostages he had stood tall, straight of back, and he had shown no fear. Like me, when I was younger, thought Tovi. Then he shook his head. No, he's better than me. There's a lot of his mother in him, and she comes from good stock.

Beside him walked Grame the Smith, his thoughts dark and brooding. Grame stood by while the soldiers selected the hostages, but he was holding the forge hammer in his hand, and using all his iron will to stop himself from running forward and braining the grinning officer. That I should live to see this, he thought, foreigners riding into our villages unopposed and stealing away our people. The smith felt the shame as if it were his alone.

Ahead of the two old men walked the three foresters, Fell at the centre. Bakris Tooth-gone was to his left, Gwyn Dark-eye to the right. Gwyn's thoughts were all of Fell. He loved him better than he loved his own brothers, and was racking his brains for a fresh argument to use to stop Fell from surrendering to the Outlanders. But nothing would come. Four lives were at stake, Tovi's son, the Widow Maffrey, the cattle-herder Clemet, and Nami, the fat daughter of the shepherd Maccus. Fell was a man of honour, and once he had heard about the hostages there was only one course of action left to him. It broke Gwyn's heart to make this journey.

Bakris was thinking about what would happen once the arrogant Fell had been hanged. Surely his own skills would be recognized and he would be elected Captain of Foresters?

Fell himself could think only of Sigarni, and all that might have been. Taliesen had ordered him to lead the hunters deep into the forest, and this he had done, wounding several of them. They had almost caught him twice, but his woodcraft saved him – that and his fleetness of foot. What will happen now, Sigarni, he wondered? Will you remember me kindly?

In his mind's eye he could see himself standing on the scaffold, the hemp rope at his throat. Will you die like a man, Fell, he asked himself, standing tall and proud? In that moment he knew that he would. No Outland audience would see a Highland man scream and beg for his life.

124

Fell glanced up at the branches above him, the sun dappling them with gold and sending shafts of brilliance to the undergrowth below. Through a break in the trees he saw High Druin, rising majestically above the other peaks. 'Be with me, Father!' he whispered to the mountain.

'What's that, Fell?' asked Gwyn.

'Talking to myself, man. Ah, but it's a fine day for a walk, to be sure.'

'That it is, my friend, but I'd be happier if we were heading north.'

'I cannot do that. I'll let no Highlander die for my crimes.'

'Crimes? What crimes?' snorted Grame, moving alongside them. 'They raped her, for God's sake, and they hunted her down like an animal. Who do they think they are, these Outlanders? First the Baron tries to steal her hawk, then they rob her of her virtue . . .'

'What virtue?' sneered Bakris. 'Hell's teeth, man, that was gone long ago. She's had more pricks than an archery target.'

'That's enough,' hissed Fell as he swung on Grame. 'Who do they think they are? They are the conquerors, and they make the laws. You, me, the whole of the Highlands, are ruled at their whim.'

'There's supposed to be a leader coming,' said Tovi. 'I wish to God he would appear soon.'

'*She* already has,' said Fell. The other men looked at one another, then back at Fell. 'Aye, you'll think it nonsense,' he said. 'But an old sorcerer came to me, and told me to be at the Citadel town at dawn on a certain day. There I would see the Red worn again, and a sword held over the town. Well, my lads, I was there. And I saw Sigarni don the Red, and watched her kill an Outlander. She's the leader prophesied. I won't live to see it, but you will.'

'Have you gone mad, lad?' asked Grame. 'What does she know of war and battles? She's a child. Who'd follow her?'

'I would,' said Fell.

'If he would, so would I,' put in Gwyn.

Bakris gave a sneering laugh. 'I'd follow her into the bedroom. Any time.'

'You will all see it come true,' said Fell. 'Now let's be moving on. I have a wish to be in Citadel town before dusk.'

Tovi put his broad hand on Fell's shoulder. 'I'm not stopping you boy,' he said, his voice thick with emotion. 'I'd do anything to bring my son home. Yet, even now, if you choose to take a different path I'll think none the worse of you. You understand?'

Fell nodded. 'I understand, Hunt Lord. But I killed an Outlander, and they want blood. If they don't get mine they will seek it elsewhere. It is their way. I would ask you this, though – look to Sigarni, and help her all you can. Both you and Grame are battle-hardened warriors. You have lived what the rest of us only hear stories of. You know how the heart feels before a battle, and how a man's courage can turn to water. You know what it takes to stand against a foe. That knowledge will be vital in the days ahead. My death may give you breathing space to plan. But it will be no more than that.'

It may not even give us that,' said Gwyn. 'They want Sigarni too. They may just take you, and keep the hostages.'

'I've thought of that,' said Fell. 'Let us hope there is a spark of honour in the Baron.'

'You're doing the right thing, Fell,' said Bakris. 'I'd do the same in your place.'

'Then let's move on,' said Fell. 'One more hill, lads, and we'll be home.'

The five men trudged up the hill, cresting it just as the sun was turning to blood over the western mountain peaks. In the distance they could see the line of the wall around Citadel town, and the tall ramparts of the keep beyond.

By the north gate, in cages outside the wall, hung four bodies, and crows were thick around them. At this distance it was impossible to recognize faces, but all knew the worn-out black dress worn by the Widow Maffrey. 'God's heart!' whispered Grame. 'They've killed them already! But it has only been two days! They promised a week.'

'A spark of honour, you said, Fell,' muttered Gwyn. 'Now we all see what Outland honour is worth.'

'They'll pay for this a thousandfold,' said Fell. 'I swear it!'

*　　*　　*

126

Sigarni, her red cloak wrapped around her shoulders, sat on the mock ramparts of Asmidir's castle home and stared out over the rolling hills and woodlands to the south. Asmidir stood alongside her, leaning on the crenellated grey stone parapet. 'You understand your purpose?' he asked her.

'Yes,' she said, her voice cold. 'I am to kill Outlanders.'

Angrily he swung on her. 'No! That is the first lesson you must learn. War is not just a game of killing. Any commander who thinks in this way will be destroyed, if not by the enemy then by his – or her – own troops.'

'Troops? Are you insane?' she stormed. 'There are no soldiers, there is no army. There is only Sigarni. And all I live for now is to kill as many as I can.' Pushing herself to her feet she faced him, her own pale eyes locked to his dark orbs. 'You can have no understanding of what they did to me, or what they took from me. You are a man. This whole world has been created for your pleasures, while women are here merely for sport – either that or to carry your brats for nine months, ready to feed more souls to your games of slaughter in years to come. Well, Asmidir, Sigarni will carry no brats, but she *will* play your game.'

He smiled ruefully. 'You cannot play until you know what you are playing for. You must have an objective, Sigarni. How else can you plan?'

'An objective?' she mocked. 'I am alone, Asmidir. What would you have me do? Where is my army? You want an objective? To free the Highlands of Outland rule, to drive the enemy back into their own lands and beyond. To lead a hundred thousand men deep into their territory and sack their capital. Is that enough of an objective?'

'It is,' he said. 'Now examine how you will plan for this objective.'

Sigarni rose and faced him. 'I have no time for worthless games. There is no army.'

'Then build one,' he said, sternly.

Spinning on her heel Sigarni strode along the rampart, climbing down the stone stairway to the courtyard. A servant bowed as she passed him. Moving on, she entered the house where Ballistar was standing before the stuffed bear, staring up at it. 'It's so lifelike,' said the dwarf. 'Don't you think?'

Ignoring him, she walked into the hall and seated herself in a wide leather armchair set before the log fire. Asmidir followed her, with Ballistar just behind.

'Why are they bowing to me?' demanded Sigarni. 'All of them. They don't speak . . . but they bow.'

'I ordered them to,' said Asmidir. 'You must become familiar with such treatment. From now to the end of your life you will be separated from the common man. You will become a queen, Sigarni.'

'The Whore Queen, is that it? Is that how you see me, Asmidir? Or was it some other black bastard who named me a harlot?'

Asmidir pulled up a chair and sat down opposite her. 'Your anger is justified,' he said. 'I did not know then *that you* were the leader the prophecy spoke of. I ask your forgiveness for that. But I also ask that you focus your rage, and do not allow it to swamp your reason. If the prophecy was true – and I believe it to be so – then you must be ready to act. A wise general knows that men can be replaced, weapons can be replenished. But lost time cannot be regained.'

'And who will follow me, Asmidir?' she asked. 'Who will follow the whore, Sigarni?'

Ballistar moved between them and gave a low bow. 'I will follow you, Sigarni,' he said. 'Will you let me be the first?' Dropping to one knee he gazed up at her.

Sigarni felt her anger drain away. 'You are my friend,' she said wearily. 'Is that not enough?'

'No. I believe what he says. The wizard said the same. I know I am not built to be a warrior, or to lead men into battle. I can serve you, though. I can cook, and I can think. I am not a fool, Sigarni, though nature has gifted me the appearance of one. Other men will kneel before you, and you will gather an army from among the clans. And if we are all to die, let it be while fighting a vile enemy. For from now until then, at least we will live with pride.'

Sigarni stood and took his arms, helping him to his feet. 'You shall be the first, Ballistar,' she said. Seizing her hand he kissed it, then stepped back, blushing.

'I'll leave you now,' he said. 'I'll prepare breakfast. Planning should never be attempted on an empty stomach.'

As the dwarf departed Asmidir leaned forward. 'His words had great wisdom, Sigarni.'

She said nothing, but sat silently for a while staring into the flames, seeing again the sword that crushed the life from Abby, and then the terrible ordeal in the dungeon.

'What kind of army can we raise?' she asked.

Asmidir smiled. 'That is more like it! The Loda number less than two thousand people, of which no more than six hundred could fight, and only then for a short space of time, for the fields would have to be tilled and planted, crops gathered and so on. Realistically we could raise three hundred fighting men. The Pallides number more than six thousand, with approximately two thousand men between the ages of fifteen and sixty. I have no detailed information as yet about the Farlain, but judging by the areas they inhabit, there should be at least four thousand of them. The Wingoras are the smallest clan, but even they could put two hundred fighting men on the field of battle. All in all, perhaps four thousand in total.'

'Such a total could not be reached,' she said. 'You could not assemble all the clan's fighting men in one place. If the enemy were to avoid a confrontation, or slip by, all the villages and towns would be undefended.'

Asmidir clapped his hands together. 'Good!' he said. 'Now you are thinking! Tell me then, what is the most important matter to be studied first?'

'The enemy leader,' she said, without hesitation. Then she faltered, her brow furrowing.

'What is it?' he asked. 'Are you in pain again?'

'No. I am . . . remembering. How strange. It is like looking through a window and seeing myself from afar. And he is with me. Talking. Teaching. He is saying, *Know the enemy general for he is the heart and mind of the foe. The body may be of great power, and almost invincible, but if the heart and mind are not sound he will face defeat.'*

She saw that Asmidir was surprised. 'Who is saying this? And when?'

'The King who was,' she told him, 'and he spoke to me while I slept in the cave.'

'Now you are speaking in riddles.'

'Not at all, Asmidir, but let us leave it there, as a mystery for you. He also said there were five fundamentals to analyse before war was undertaken: moral influence, weather, terrain, command, and doctrine.'

Asmidir's surprise turned to astonishment. His eyes narrowed and he smiled. 'Did he also mention the seven elements?'

'No. He said he would leave that to you.'

'Are you making mock of me, woman?' he asked, his expression softening.

She shook her head. 'I am speaking the truth.' Rising smoothly she stood before him. 'And *woman* is no way to address a leader,' she said, smiling.

Asmidir did not return the smile. Instead he moved to his knees before her and bowed his head. 'I ask your forgiveness, my lady,' he said, 'and I further request that you allow me to be the second man to pledge his loyalty to you.'

'Now you are mocking *me*, Asmidir,' she admonished him.

He glanced up, his face set. 'I have never been more serious, Sigarni. I offer you my sword, my experience, and – if necessary – my life. All that I have is yours . . . now and for ever.'

'It shall be so,' she heard herself say.

At that moment a servant entered. He bowed low. 'Soldiers approaching, lord. Some thirty in number. With them rides the man you spoke of, dressed all in green.'

Asmidir swore softly. 'Remain in your room, Sigarni. This situation may become delicate.'

'Who is the man in green?' she asked.

'A Seeker, a Finder. His powers are strong, and he will sense your spirit. One of my servants will come to you. Follow where he leads, my lady, and I will come to you when I can.'

Obrin removed his iron helm and pushed back his chainmail head-and-shoulder-guard, allowing the mountain breeze to cool his face and blow through his short-cropped hair. Resting the helm on a flat stone beside the stream, he pulled off his riding gauntlets and laid them atop the helm. 'A beautiful land,' observed the Finder Kollarin, moving alongside him and splashing water to his face.

'Like my homeland,' replied the sergeant, scanning the mountains. Obrin said nothing more and moved away to check the horses. They had been picketed a little way upstream and a sentry was standing by them. 'Give them a while to cool down, then take them to water,' he told the young man.

'Yes, sir.'

'Yes, sergeant!' snapped Obrin. 'I'm not a bloody officer.'

'Yes, sergeant.'

Obrin's foul mood darkened further. It had started already. Word of his temporary promotion had spread fast and the men thought it humorous, but nothing could be further from the truth. As they were leaving the Citadel barracks Obrin had seen several officers watching him. They were laughing. One of them, Lieutenant Masrick – a potbellied second cousin of the Baron – cracked a joke, his thin voice carrying to the mounted soldiers waiting for Obrin: 'Put a pig in silk and it is still a pig, eh, my friends?'

Obrin pretended not to hear. It was the best policy. His short-lived appointment would soon be forgotten, but the emnity of a man like Masrick could see him humbled – or worse. Obrin pushed thoughts of Masrick from his mind.

He had camped his men in a hollow beside a stream. From here the camp-fires could be seen over no great distance and, with a sentry posted on the closest hill, they could have ample warning of any hostile approach. Not that Obrin expected an attempt to rescue the prisoner. However regulations demanded that, in the absence of a fortified camp, the officer in charge observed the proper precautions. The ground was rocky, but sheltered, and two campfires had already been lit. Cooking pots were in place above them and the smell of stew was beginning to fill the air. Obrin walked to the brow of a hill overlooking the campsite and sat down on a rock. From here he could see Kollarin sitting beside the stream, and the other men moving about their chores. The prisoner was seated by a slender elm at the edge of the camp, his hands and feet tied. There was blood on his face, and his left eye was blackened and swollen.

Obrin felt uncomfortable. He had known Fell for almost four years and he liked the man. A good judge of character, Obrin knew the clansman to be strong, proud and honest. He was no murderer, of that Obrin was sure. What difference does it make what you think, he asked himself? Who cares? You had a job to do and you did it. That's all that matters. Fell had said nothing since the capture. Kollarin had led them to a cave, in which Fell was sleeping. They had rushed him and overpowered him. But not before Fell had smashed Bakker's nose and broken the jaw of the new recruit, Klebb. Obrin grinned at the memory. There was little to like about Bakker, a loud, greasy whoreson with shifty eyes. The flattened nose had improved his looks tenfold!

Obrin saw Kollarin rise and begin to walk up the hill. He cursed inwardly for the man unnerved him. The sergeant did not care for magickers. Obrin made the Sign of the Protective Horn as the man approached. He did not do it covertly, but allowed Kollarin to see the gesture.

The man in green smiled and nodded. 'I only read minds when I am paid,' he said. 'Your secrets are quite safe.'

'I have no secrets, Finder. I tell no lies. I deceive no one – least of all myself.'

'Then why make the sign?' asked Kollarin, sitting alongside the soldier.

'A casual insult,' admitted Obrin, unconcerned over any possible reaction.

'You do not like me, sergeant. You believe Fell should have been given the chance to fight like a man, and not be taken in his sleep. You are probably right. I would go further, though. We are all reared on stories of heroes, great warriors, or poets, or philosophers. We are told that we must aspire to be just like these heroes, for only by so doing can we ensure the survival of civilization. It is very noble. Indeed it is laudable.' Kollarin chuckled. 'And then we become men, and we realize that it is all a nonsense.'

'It is not nonsense!' said Obrin. 'We need heroes.'

'Of course we do,' Kollarin agreed. 'The nonsense is that sometimes they are the enemy. What then do we do, Obrin?'

'I'm not a philosopher. I live by my own rules. I steal from no man, and I commit no evil. God will judge me on that when my time comes.'

'I am sure that He will judge all of us, my friend. Tell me, what do you think He will think of *us* when young Fell is brought before him? When his body lies broken and blinded on the Citadel rack and his spirit floats up to paradise?'

Obrin was growing more uneasy, yet he did not walk away, though he wanted to. 'How should I know?'

'I think you know,' said Kollarin sadly.

'What do you want me to say?' stormed Obrin. 'That he has been treated unjustly? Yes, he has. That he doesn't deserve to die? No, he doesn't. None of it matters. The Baron is the law, he gave me my orders and it is my duty to obey them. What of you? You took his money, and agreed to hunt down the clansman. Why did you do it?'

Kollarin smiled. 'I had my reasons, Obrin. Did you hear about what happened to the woman?'

'It is said they raped her but I find it hard to believe. Will Stamper was not that kind of man. We were friends, I knew him.'

'He did it,' said Kollarin. 'I was in that cell. I read it in the blood. They all did it. And they cut her, and they bit her, and they beat her with fists. And all because she tried to stop the Baron stealing her hawk. Heroic, eh?'

Obrin said nothing for a moment. The light was failing and the campfires cast a gentle glow over the hollow. 'I can't change the world,' he said sadly. 'Fell rescued the woman and I'm glad that he did. Now he has to pay for it, which saddens me. But in my life I've seen a lot of good men die, Kollarin. And a lot of evil men prosper. It is the way of things.'

'You'll see worse yet,' said Kollarin coldly.

'Like what?'

'The invasion in the spring, when the Baron leads an army to annihilate the Highlanders. You'll see the burning buildings, hear the screams of women and children, watch the crows feast on the bodies of farmers and shepherds.'

'That's just a rumour!' snapped Obrin. 'And a stupid one at that! There's no one for the army to fight here.'

'I am Kollarin the Finder,' said the man in green, rising. 'And I do not lie either.'

Obrin stood and walked down the hill. A soldier offered him a bowl of stew, which he accepted, and for a while he sat with his men, listening to them talk of whores they had known, or lands they had campaigned in. Then he ladled more stew into his bowl and walked to where Fell was tied. The clansman looked up at him, but said nothing.

Obrin squatted down. 'I have some food for you,' he said, lifting the bowl to Fell's lips. The clansman turned his head away and Obrin laid down the bowl. 'I'm sorry, Fell,' he said softly. 'I like you, man, and I think you did right. I hope to God the woman gets far away from here.' The clansman's eyes met his, but no words were spoken by him.

Returning to the fire, Obrin ordered the cooking pots cleaned and stowed, then set sentries for the night. Kollarin was once more sitting by the stream, his green cloak wrapped about his shoulders.

Using his saddle for a pillow, Obrin removed his chainmail shoulder-guard and his breastplate, unbuckled his sword and dagger belt and settled down to sleep. In all his seventeen years of soldiering sleep had always come easily. In the blazing heat of the Kushir plains, in the harsh, bone-biting cold of the Cleatian mountains, at sea in a gale-tossed ship, Obrin could just close his eyes and will his body to rest. It was, he knew, a vital skill for a veteran. In sleep a man regained his strength and rested his soul. In war a soldier's life depended on his power, speed and reflexes. There were few second chances for a tired warrior on a battlefield.

But sleep was slow to come tonight.

Obrin lay on his back, staring up at the bright stars and the lantern moon.

He was walking along a narrow trail, beneath an arched tunnel made up of the interlinked branches of colossal trees on both sides of the way. Obrin stopped and glanced back. The tunnel seemed to stretch on for ever, dark and gloomy, pierced occasionally by a shaft of moonlight through a gap in the branches.

Obrin walked on. There were no night sounds, no owl calls, no rustling of wind in the leaves. All was silence, save for his soft footfalls on the soft earth. Ahead was a brilliant shaft of moonlight, a beautiful column of light that shone upon a crossroads. Obrin approached it, and saw a warrior sitting on a rock by the wayside. The man was huge, his long white hair gleaming in the moonlight. He wore his beard in two white braids which hung to his silver breastplate. A double-handed claymore was plunged into the earth before him, its hilt a glistening silver, while a huge crimson stone was set into the pommel.

'It is a fine weapon,' said Obrin.

The man stood. He towered over Obrin by a good Southland foot. 'It has served me well,' he said, his voice rich and deep. Obrin looked up into his pale, deep-set eyes. They were the colour of a winter storm-cloud, grey and cold. Yet Obrin felt no fear.

'Where are we?' he asked.

The tall warrior extended his arm, sweeping it across the three paths that began in the pillar of light. 'We are at the crossroads,' said the warrior. Obrin's attention was caught by the man's single gauntlet of red iron. It was splendidly crafted, seemingly as supple as leather.

'Who are you?' he asked

'A man who once travelled,' answered the warrior. 'Many paths, many roads, many trails. I walked the mountains, Obrin, and I rode the lowlands. Many paths, some crooked, some straight. All were hard.'

'The warrior's paths,' said Obrin. 'Aye, I know them. No hearth, no home, no kin. Only the Way of Iron.' Weariness settled upon him and he sat down.

The warrior seated himself beside the Southlander. 'And which path do you walk now?' asked the stranger.

'I go where I am sent. What else can a soldier do? Seventeen years I have served the Baron. I have watched friends die, and my boots have collected the dust of many nations. Now I have an aching shoulder and a knee that does not like to march. In three years I can claim my hectare of land. Maybe I will – if I can still remember how to farm. What of you? Where are you going?'

Nowhere I haven't been,' answered the man. 'I too wanted to farm, and to breed cattle. But I was called upon to right a wrong. It was a small matter. A nobleman and his friends were hunting, and they rode through a field and trampled a child playing there. Her legs were broken badly and the family had no coin to pay for a Wycca man to heal her. I went to the nobleman and asked for justice.'

Obrin sighed. 'I could finish that story for you, man. There's no justice for the poor. Never was, never will be. Did he laugh in your face?'

The giant shook his head. 'He had me flogged for my impudence.'

'What happened to the girl?'

'She lived. I went back to the nobleman and this time he paid.'

'What brought about his change of heart?'

'There was no change of heart. I left his head on a spike, and I burned his home to the ground. It was a grand fire, which burned bright and lit the sky for many a mile. It also lit men's hearts, and that fire burned for thirty years.'

'By God, did they not hunt you?'

'Aye. And then I hunted them.'

'And you were victorious?'

'Always.' The warrior chuckled. 'Until the last day.'

'What happened then?'

Idly the warrior drew his sword from the earth and examined the glistening blade. The ruby shone like fresh blood, the blade gleaming like captured moonlight. 'The war was over. Victory was won. The land was at peace, and free. I thought my enemies were all dead. A dreadful mistake for a warrior. I was riding across my lands, gazing upon High Druin, watching the storm-clouds gather there. They surprised me. My horse was killed, but not before the gallant beast got me to the edge of the forest. They came at me in a pack: men I had fought alongside, even promoted. Not friends, you understand, but comrades-in-arms. My heart was wounded each time I killed one of them. The wounds to my body were as nothing to my grief.'

136

'Why did they turn on you?'

The warrior shrugged, then thrust the sword once more into the earth. 'I was a king, Obrin. And I was arrogant and sure. I treated some of them with disdain. Others I ignored. There were always ten men queuing for every favour I could grant. And I made mistakes. Once I had freed them from the tyranny of the oppressor I became a tyrant in their eyes. Who knows, maybe they were right. I do not judge them.'

'How did you survive alone against so many?'

'I did not.'

Obrin was shocked 'You . . . you are a spirit then?'

'We both are, Obrin. But you have a body of flesh to which you will return.'

'I don't understand. Why am I here?'

'I called you.'

'For what purpose?' asked Obrin. 'I am not a king, nor of any worth.'

'Do not be so harsh on yourself, man,' said the warrior, laying his iron gauntlet on Obrin's shoulder. 'You have merely lost your way. And now you are at the crossroads. You may choose a new path.'

Obrin gazed around him. All the pathways looked the same, interminable tunnels beneath arched trees. 'What difference does it make?' he asked. 'They are identical.'

The warrior nodded. 'Aye, that is true. All roads lead to death, Obrin. It is inescapable. Even so, there is a right path.'

Obrin laughed, but the sound was bitter and harsh. 'How would I know it?'

'If you cannot recognize it, then you must find a man already upon it and follow him. You will know, Obrin. Let the heart-light shine. It will light the way.'

Obrin awoke with a start. The dawn light was streaking the sky, though the stars had not yet faded. His thoughts were muddled and his mouth felt as if he'd swallowed a badger. With a groan he sat up. His right shoulder ached abominably. Rising from his blankets, he walked to a nearby tree and emptied his bladder. Everyone else was still asleep, including the prisoner. Obrin hawked and spat, then stretched his right arm over his head, seeking to ease the ache.

The hill sentry walked down and saluted. 'Nothing to report from the watch, sergeant,' he said, 'but there are riders to the south.'

'Clansmen?' This was unlikely, for there were few horses in the mountains.

'No, sir. Soldiers from Citadel, I think. Too far away to be sure.'

'Get a breakfast fire going,' ordered Obrin. Moving to the stream, he stripped to the waist and washed in the cold water, splashing it over his face and hair. Kollarin joined him.

'Sleep well, sergeant?'

'I always sleep well.'

'No dreams?'

Obrin cupped some water into his hands and drank noisily. There was an edge to the man's voice, like a plea of some kind. Obrin looked at him. 'Yes, I dreamt,' he said. 'You?'

Kollarin nodded. 'Did it make sense to you?'

'Are dreams supposed to make sense?'

Kollarin moved in close, his voice dropping to a whisper. 'He has come to me before – back in Citadel when I was hunting the woman. He told me to leave her be. That is why I only agreed to hunt down the man. Do you know who he is?'

'I thought you only read minds for coin,' Obrin reminded him. The sergeant stood and shivered as the cold morning breeze touched his wet skin. Hastily he donned his shirt, then returned to his blankets and put on his armour. Kollarin remained by the stream.

A soldier with a swollen nose approached Obrin. 'All quiet in the night,' he said, his voice thick and nasal.

'How's the nose, Bakker?'

'Hurts like hell. I was tempted to cut the bastard's throat last night, but I reckon I'll just get myself dungeon duty and watch the torturer at work on him.'

'We ride in one hour,' said Obrin.

They breakfasted on porridge and black bread, but the prisoner steadfastly refused the food Obrin brought to him. With the meal finished, the cooking pots cleaned and stowed, Obrin's men prepared for the journey back to Citadel.

'Riders coming!' shouted one of the men. Obrin wandered to the edge of the hollow and waited as the ten-man section rode in. They were led by Lieutenant Masrick. Obrin saluted as the man dismounted.

'I see you caught him,' said the officer, ignoring the salute. 'About time, sergeant. Has he told you where the girl is?'

'No sir. I was ordered to bring him back, not interrogate him.'

Masrick swung to Bakker, who was just about to douse the breakfast fire. 'You there! Keep that fire going.' Slipping his dagger from its sheath, he tossed it to Bakker. 'Heat the point. I want it glowing red.'

Masrick strode to where Fell was tied, then aimed a savage kick into the prisoner's belly, doubling him over. 'That,' said the officer, 'is for nothing at all. What follows will, however, have value. Are you listening, clansman?'

Fell raised his head and met the officer's stare. He said nothing. Masrick knelt before him and punched him full in the face. Fell's head snappped back, cannoning against the tree-trunk. 'You killed a cousin of mine. He was a wretch, but he owed me money. That was bad. But it will be worth much more to me to find the woman and bring her back to the Baron. I think you'll help me. All you clansmen think you are tough. But trust me, when I have burned out your left eye you'll do anything to save the sight in the other.'

The soldiers had gathered round the scene in a sweeping half-circle. Obrin gazed at their faces. They were eager for the entertainment. Kollarin was standing back from them, his expression impossible to read. Bakker brought the heated knife to the officer; the hilt was wrapped in a rag, the point hissing as Masrick took it.

'Lieutenant!' Obrin's voice barked out. Masrick was startled and he almost dropped the knife.

'What? Make it quick, man, the knife is cooling!'

'Leave him be!'

Masrick ignored him and knelt before Fell, the knife moving towards the forester's eyes. Obrin's foot rose and slammed into the officer's face, spinning him to the ground. There was a gasp from the soldiers. Masrick rolled to his knees, then screamed as his hand pressed down on the red-hot blade which was smouldering in the grass. He surged to his feet, his face crimson. 'By God you'll pay for that!'

'I am an acting captain,' said Obrin, 'promoted by the Baron himself. You are a lieutenant who just disobeyed an order from a *superior* officer. Where does that leave you, you jumped-up toad?'

'You have lost your mind,' sneered Masrick, 'and I will see you hang for your impertinence. No common man may strike a noble-man, be the common man a captain or a general. That kick is going to cost you dear!'

'Ah well,' said Obrin, with a broad smile, 'may as well be hung for a sheep as a lamb!' So saying, he took a step forward and slammed his fist into the officer's mouth, catapulting the man from his feet. Drawing his dagger, he moved in for the kill.

Something struck him a wicked blow on the skull and he staggered, half turning. He saw Bakker raise his arm, then the cudgel struck his temple and he fell into darkness.

When he awoke he found himself tied to his saddle. Masrick was leading the column and they were approaching a small castle. Fell was walking beside Obrin's mount, his hands tied behind him and a rope around his neck. The other end of the rope was being held by the rider in front.

'You really did it this time, sergeant,' said a voice from his left. Obrin turned in the saddle to see, riding alongside him, Bakker. 'Now they're going to hang you! Not before time, if you ask me. You always was a right pain in the groin. Never liked you.'

Obrin ignored him.

The castle gates loomed ahead.

7

Asmidir had never enjoyed great talent as a magicker. Though his powers of concentration were great, and his imagination powerful, he had always lacked what his tutors termed *ability of release*. Magic, he was told, involved the user surrendering control and merging his mind with the powers hovering beyond what the five senses could experience. For all his talent Asmidir had never been able to fully *release*. Now he sat in the main hall, a huge leather-bound book open on his lap. The script was in gold, carefully set upon bleached leather; it was an ancient Kushir script and he read it with difficulty.

Closing the book, he stood and moved to the long, oval table. Upon it was a golden dish, set on a stand above three small candles. Asmidir drew his dagger and began to speak. His eyes were closed, his spirit loose within the cage of his powerful body as his breathing deepened. The dagger blade cut into his forearm and blood welled, dripping into the heated dish where it sizzled and steamed. Asmidir's voice faded away. Opening his eyes, he took a deep, shuddering breath. It was done. Not brilliantly, not even expertly. Let it at least be adequate, he thought. Returning the dagger to its sheath he pressed his thumb against the shallow wound on his arm, applying pressure for some minutes. A dark-skinned servant stepped forward with a long linen bandage. Asmidir extended his arm, and the man skilfully applied it.

'Bring the officer here to me, Ari,' he told the servant. 'Also the man in green. You have prepared the refreshment I ordered for the soldiers?'

'Yes, lord. As you commanded.'

The servant took the bowl and departed the room. Asmidir returned to the log fire and settled himself into an armchair. He heard the sounds of hoofbeats on stone, and felt the cold blast of air as the main doors of the castle were pulled open to admit the soldiers.

Rising from his chair, he turned towards the door just as the potbellied Lieutenant Masrick strode into sight with Kollarin the Finder behind him. Masrick's face was discoloured, his lips thickened and split.

'Good day to you,' said Asmidir, stepping forward with an outstretched hand. 'It is good to see you again, Masrick.' The officer responded with a perfunctory handshake. A servant appeared. 'Fetch wine for our guests, Ari.' Masrick removed his iron helm and carelessly dropped it upon the highly polished table.

'The Baron wants to see you,' said Masrick. 'You are to return with us to Citadel.'

'I think you mean that the Baron has *requested* my presence,' said Asmidir coolly.

'No, I said what I meant. He told me to bring you, and that's what I'll do.' Masrick lifted a hand to his smashed lips, probing them. 'I have two prisoners with me. Does this place still boast a dungeon?'

'No,' Asmidir told him. He swung to Kollarin. 'And you must be the Finder,' he said, forcing a smile. 'I take it from the fact that you have prisoners that you have been successful.'

'Yes,' said Kollarin. He moved to the hearth and reached out to touch the leather-bound book on the small table. Idly the man in green flipped open the cover. 'Ah, a Kushir grimoire. A long time since I have seen such a work. The scripting is very fine – resin dusted with gold and then varnished. Exquisite!'

'You read Kushir?' asked Asmidir, holding his expression to one of mild interest, while his heart beat against his ribs like a drum of war.

'I read all known languages,' said Kollarin. 'I do not wish it to sound like a boast, since it is a Talent I have possessed all my life, and not the result of dedicated study.'

The servant, Ari, returned with a flagon of wine and two goblets. Masrick accepted his without a word of thanks. Kollarin smiled at Ari and gave a short bow of the head. 'Not drinking with us, Asmidir?' Masrick asked.

'No.' Turning back to Kollarin, he asked, 'What will you do now that your hunt has been successful?'

'Successful?' queried Kollarin.

'Two prisoners. I understood you were hunting for a man and a woman.'

'We haven't caught the woman yet,' said Masrick, cutting in, 'but we will. We have the forester, Fell. The other prisoner is a rene-gade. He struck me! Loosened several teeth. By God, he'll pay for it when I get him back to Citadel.'

'It does look sore,' agreed Asmidir. 'Ari, fetch some of the *special* camomile ointment for this gentleman.' As the servant departed Asmidir seated himself before the fire, trying not to look at Kollarin as the man slowly turned the pages of the grimoire. 'So,' he said to Masrick, 'why does the Baron request my presence so urgently?'

'That's for him to tell you,' muttered Masrick. 'Now where can I lodge these prisoners? Do you have no rooms with locks?'

'Sadly, no. I suggest you bring them in here. Then at least you can watch them until you leave.'

'Until *we* leave,' corrected Masrick.

Asmidir rose and approached the officer. The black man was at least a foot taller. 'At the moment, my dear Masrick, I am putting aside your bad manners on the grounds that the blow to your face, and the subsequent pain, has made you forget your breeding. Understand, however, that my patience is not limitless. Try to remember that you are an insignificant second cousin to the Baron, whereas I am a friend to the King. Now get out and fetch your prisoners. I wish to speak with the Finder.'

Masrick's mouth dropped open, and his eyes narrowed. Asmidir read the fury there. The black man leaned in close. 'Think carefully before you react, moron. It is considered deeply unlucky to be struck twice in the face on the same day.' Masrick swallowed hard and backed away. Asmidir swung away from him and crossed the room to where Kollarin waited. For a moment only Masrick hesi-tated, then he marched from the hall.

'You did not need the cloak spell,' said Kollarin softly. 'I refused to hunt the woman.'

'Very wise,' Asmidir told him, keeping his voice low. 'When you return to Citadel town I will see that one hundred silver pieces are delivered to you.'

'Very kind.' Kollarin's green eyes held Asmidir's gaze. 'But I shall not be returning to Citadel.'

'Neither shall I,' said Asmidir, with a wry smile.

Masrick returned to the hall and two soldiers led in the prisoners, ordering them to sit by the far wall. The officer marched up to Asmidir. 'I fear you were right, Lord Asmidir,' said Masrick. 'The events of the day shortened my temper. I ask your forgiveness for my . . . abrupt manner.' The anger was still present in his eyes, but Asmidir merely smiled.

'We will say no more about it, my dear Masrick. Are your men being fed?'

'Yes. Thank you. How soon will you be ready to leave?'

Asmidir did not answer, but strolled across the hall and stood before the prisoners. 'I know you,' he said, addressing Obrin. 'You were in the fist-fighting tourney last winter. You lost in the final – stumbled and went down with an overhand right.'

'You have a good memory for faces,' Obrin told him. 'Now if I'd managed to hit the Cleatian with the same power that I used on goat-face there, I would have won.'

Masrick ran forward and aimed a savage kick which thundered against Obrin's shoulder. 'Be silent, wretch!' he shouted.

'Even kicks like a goat,' sneered Obrin.

Masrick drew his dagger. 'I'll cut your bastard tongue out!' he threatened.

Asmidir laid his hand on the officer's arm. 'Not here my friend,' he said. 'The rugs were expensive, shipped all the way from Kushir.'

As Obrin's laughter sounded, Masrick paled, and his hand trembled. But he slammed the dagger back in its scabbard.

The servant returned, carrying a small enamelled pot. As he paused beside Masrick and bowed, the officer looked at the tall servant. 'Well, what do you want?'

Ari held out the pot. 'What is this?' Masrick asked Asmidir.

'A healing ointment. Apply it to the lips and you will see.'

Masrick took the pot and removed the lid. The ointment was cream-coloured. Dabbing a finger to it, he spread some on his injury. 'That is good,' he said. 'Soothing! Where did you obtain it?'

144

'My servants are all *Al-jiin*,' said Asmidir. 'They are very skilled with potions.'

Kollarin was only half listening to the exchange, but the *words Al-jiin* cut through him like a sword of ice. Standing beside the hearth he stiffened, his green eyes flicking to Ari. The man was tall and slender, his skin the colour of age-polished oak; he had a prominent nose, not like Asmidir, but curved and aquiline. In that moment Kollarin wondered how he could ever have been convinced the man was a servant. He glanced at his wine goblet. It was still almost full. How much had he drunk? One mouthful? Two?

Ari turned slowly, his deep dark stare pinning Kollarin. The servant seemed to glide across the room. 'Are you well, lord?' asked Ari. 'You are looking pale.'

'I am well at this moment,' said Kollarin. Reaching out with his Talent, he touched the other man's mind . . . and recoiled as if he had thrust his hand into a fire.

'Perhaps you should sit down, lord,' offered Ari.

'*Am I to die here?*' pulsed Kollarin.

'*If my Lord wills it so,*' came the response. 'If you will excuse me,' he said aloud, 'I have duties to attend to.'

'By all means,' said Kollarin. Ari turned and left the hall and once more Kollarin reached out, seeking not the mind of the servant but choosing instead the soldiers who were waiting outside. He pictured the solid cavalryman, Klebb.

Nothing. One by one he sought out the others.

Still nothing. Were their thoughts being shielded, he wondered?

Sitting by the fire he closed his eyes and dropped his spirit to the second level, opening his mind to more general astral emanations. He felt the castle and its great age, and beyond it the forest and the heartbeat of eternity.

From here it was a simple matter to find the third level. Kollarin gasped. Moving through the castle he could see the restless, disembodied shapes of lost spirits, murdered men who did not yet know they had died.

145

His eyes snapped open.

All dead. Twenty-eight soldiers, drugged and then strangled. All that remained were the two guards in the room, and Masrick himself. Kollarin's mouth was dry and he reached out for his wine. *What are you doing, fool?* Leaving the goblet where it stood, he rose and rubbed his hand across his mouth. Am I under sentence? he wondered.

Asmidir crossed the hall. 'You seem preoccupied, my boy,' he said.

Kollarin looked up into the black man's face, seeing the power there, and the cruelty. '*Your Al-jiin* have completed their work,' he said softly. 'Where does that leave me?'

'Where would you like to be left?' Asmidir asked.

'Alive would be pleasant.'

'What are you two whispering about?' asked Masrick, picking up Kollarin's goblet and draining it. He belched and then sat down.

'We were talking about life and death, Masrick,' said Asmidir, 'and the slender thread that separates both.'

'Nothing slender about it,' said the officer. 'It is all a question of skill and courage.'

'What about luck?' asked Asmidir. 'Being in the wrong place at the wrong time?'

'A man makes his own luck,' replied Masrick.

'I'm not sure that's true,' said Asmidir. 'But let us put it to the test. Would it be lucky or unlucky were you to find the woman, Sigarni?'

'Lucky, of course,' answered Masrick. 'You know where she is?'

'Indeed I do.' Asmidir clapped his hands twice. A line of warriors filed silently into the room; tall men in black cloaks and helms, all carrying sabres of shining steel. They wore black mail-shirts which extended to their thighs, and black boots reinforced with strips of black steel. Across their chests each wore a thick leather baldric, complete with three throwing knives in jet-black sheaths. Kollarin moved back against the wall as the warriors fanned out. He recognized the servant Ari, though the man now looked like a prince of legend.

Masrick was also watching them. 'What is the meaning of this?' he asked.

Asmidir chuckled and without turning his head he gave an order. 'Kill the guards,' he said, his voice even, almost regretful.

Kollarin watched as if in a dream. Two of the black-garbed warriors drew throwing knives from their sheaths and slowly turned. One of the guards, a man with a bruised and swollen nose, frantically tried to draw his sword; a knife-hilt appeared in his throat and he sank back against the wall. The second guard turned to run; a black knife slashed through the air taking him in the back of the neck and he fell forward, his face striking the edge of the table; the blow dislodged his helm which rolled across the tabletop. The two dark-skinned warriors retrieved their blades and returned to stand in line with their comrades.

Masrick's face was ashen. Kollarin almost felt pity for the man. 'Ari,' said Asmidir softly, 'is our guest ready to join us?'

'Yes, Lord.' Ari departed the hall and a terrible silence followed. Masrick was sweating now and Kollarin saw that the little man's hands were trembling. Despite his armour he looked nothing like a soldier.

'I . . . I . . . don't want to die, Asmidir,' he whimpered, tears spilling to his cheeks. The black man ignored him. 'Please don't kill me!' The hall door opened and Ari returned. Behind him came another warrior and Kollarin's breath caught in his throat. She was tall and slender, her hair silver-white like the chainmail tunic she wore. Thigh-length and split at the sides, the links gleamed like jewels. Her long legs were encased in glistening black leggings, delicately reinforced by more silver chain-links around the upper legs, and a crimson cloak hung from her shoulders. Kollarin had never seen a more beautiful woman. As she entered all the warriors, including Asmidir, bowed deeply. Kollarin followed their lead.

Masrick tried to stand, pushing his arms against the sides of the chair, but his legs would not move. He slumped back, then a convulsion jerked his body in several spasms. Asmidir leaned over him. 'Your hunt was successful, Masrick. You are in the presence of Sigarni. Die happy!'

Spittle frothed at Masrick's lips and his eyes bulged. Then he was still, the open eyes staring unfocused at the man before him. The silver-armoured woman approached the chair and stared down at the dead man. 'Did he die of fright?' she asked Asmidir.

'No. He smeared poison upon his lips.'

The woman looked at Kollarin, who bowed once more. 'Why does this one live?'

'In truth I am not sure,' said Asmidir. 'He refused to hunt you, and I do not know why. He is the Finder, Kollarin. Do you wish him slain?'

Kollarin waited, his green eyes watching the woman's face. 'Why did you refuse?' she asked him.

'That is not easy to answer, lady,' he told her, surprised that his voice remained steady. 'A man appeared to me and asked me to spare you.'

'Describe him.'

'The face was powerful, deep-set blue eyes. His hair was silver-white, like yours, and he wore his beard in two braids.'

She nodded, then swung to Asmidir. 'Let him live,' she said.

The black man was about to speak, yet held his silence. Stepping back, he allowed Sigarni to dominate the centre of the room. Her armour he had brought with him from Kushir, intended as a gift for the warrior king the seer had spoken of. Asmidir had always pictured it upon the muscular form of a young man. Yet now, as he gazed upon her martial beauty, he could scarce believe he had not purchased it with Sigarni in mind. Everything about her was regal, and he wondered how he had failed to notice it before.

His *Al-jiin* had cut the two prisoners free and both men were now standing and staring at the warrior woman. Fell bowed his head. Sigarni's eyes were fixed on the Outlander in the uniform of a soldier. Her hand closed around the hilt of her dagger, the blade whispering from its scabbard as she moved towards the man with deceptive grace. Only Fell recognized her intent. 'No, Sigarni,' he said, stepping in front of the soldier. 'This man saved me from torture at the risk of his own life.'

'No Outlander will live,' she said softly, almost without anger. 'Stand aside, Fell.'

'I claim the *Cormaach* on this man,' he said. Asmidir was puzzled, and he watched Sigarni's reaction carefully. She stood silently for a moment, then gave a cold smile.

'You would do this for an enemy?' she asked.

'I do. I sat with my arms bound and a glowing red–hot knife was before my eyes. Obrin stopped the officer, and struck him into the bargain. They were taking him back for torture and death. It would seem poor gratitude indeed if I stood by while he was casually slain. I ask for his life, Sigarni.'

'Stand aside, Fell, I would speak with this man.' Fell hesitated, for the dagger was still in her hand. For a moment only he failed to move, then he stepped back. Asmidir watched the soldier, Obrin. There was no sign of fear in the man.

'Are you aware,' asked Sigarni, 'of what has been said here? Do you understand the meaning of *Cormaach*?'

'I know nothing of your barbarian ways, madam,' said Obrin. 'I'm just a soldier, see. Untutored, you might say. So why don't you tell me?'

Asmidir could see Sigarni fighting for calm as she gazed upon this man in the hated uniform of those who had so brutally assaulted her. She'll kill him, he thought. She'll step in close and at his first wrong word ram the knife into his throat.

'He has offered to adopt you – to make you his son. How old are you?'

'Thirty-seven, by my own reckoning. I might be out by a year or two.'

'So, your new father is some fifteen years younger than you. You wish to be adopted, Outlander?'

'Is there a choice?' he asked.

'There are always choices,' she said, moving in close. 'You saved Fell, therefore I am in your debt. You may leave here and make your way wherever you choose. I would like to kill you, Outlander. I would like to see the blood gush from your neck. But my word is iron. Leave now and no one will harm you.'

'What's the other alternative?'

'You are not man enough for it!' she snapped. 'Leave before my patience is exhausted.'

'Become a clansman, is that it? A rebel against the Baron, and the King?' Obrin laughed, the sound rich and merry. 'So that's what he meant, is it? This is the crossroads.' He swung to Fell. 'Adopted me, did you, boy? Well, by God, you could have done worse. I'll walk your road — even though we all know where it will lead. So what do I do, lady? To whom do I pledge my sword?'

Sigarni was too surprised to answer, and Asmidir stepped forward swiftly. He spoke in Kushir and the twelve *Al-jiin* all dropped to their knees around the silver-armoured woman. 'You are in the presence,' he told Obrin, 'of the Lady Sigarni, War Chief of the clans. It is to her you pledge your loyalty.'

Obrin dropped to one knee before her, then lifted his hand to guide her dagger to his throat. With the point resting against his skin he spoke. 'This day I am become your carle, lady. I will live for you, and when the day comes I will die for you. This is the promise of Obrin, son of Engist, and sworn before God.'

Sigarni was silent, then looked to Fell, who still stood. As their eyes met, the tall forester dropped to his knees, 'My life is yours, Sigarni,' he said, 'now and for ever.'

Sigarni nodded, then approached Asmidir. 'We need to speak,' she said, and walked from the room. Asmidir followed her.

Obrin and Fell rose together. 'Thank you lad,' said the soldier. 'You'll not regret it.'

'I believe that,' Fell told him. 'But will you? How will you feel when your countrymen face you sword to sword? It is no small matter.'

Obrin shook his head. 'Put your mind at rest, Fell. To you we are all Outlanders, yet we come from many parts of the realm. My people were mountain folk, conquered a hundred years ago. And I am the only one from my tribe at Citadel. Even that, though, misses the point. There are some things a man *must* fight for. That, I believe, is what Kollarin was trying to tell me. Is that not so?' he asked the man in green.

'Indeed it was,' said Kollarin, crossing the room and stepping over the corpses of the soldiers. 'I always wondered what it would be like to be a hero.'

Behind them the twelve silent *Al-jiin* gathered up the bodies and left the hall.

Sigarni felt gripped by a sense of unreality as she climbed the carpeted steps to the upper balcony, and the room where Ari had shown her the armour. Beside her Asmidir said nothing as they walked. The room was small, fifteen feet by twenty, with one large window looking out over High Druin. Sigarni had donned the silver chainmail top coat, the armoured leggings and the boots, but the sword, breastplate and helm remained. The breastplate had been sculpted to resemble the athletic chest and belly of a young warrior, while the helm was too large for the silver-haired woman.

Sigarni walked to the window, pushing it open to allow the cool, yet gentle autumn breeze to whisper into the room. Abby was dead, and this she found almost as hurtful as the abuse she had endured. But more than this Sigarni felt a weight of sorrow for the life she would never know again, the quiet solitude of her mountain cabin, the morning hunt, and the silent nights. Grame had warned her of the Baron, and she wished now that she had heeded him. A few pennies lost and her life would have remained free. Now she was embarked on a course that could lead only to death and ruin for the people of the mountains. What are we, she thought? And the picture came to her mind of a mighty stag at bay in the Highlands, with the wolves closing in. We can run and live for a little longer, or we can fight and be dragged down.

Clouds were gathering above High Druin like a crown of grey above the white snow-capped peaks.

'Speak your thoughts, my lady,' said Asmidir.

'You don't need to give me pretty titles here,' she told him, still staring from the window. 'There is no one to hear them.'

'It has begun, Sigarni,' he said softly. 'It is time to make plans.'

'I know. What do you suggest?'

He shook his head. 'I will offer my advice in a moment,' he told her. 'First I would like to hear your views.'

Anger almost swamped her, but she fought it back. 'You are the warrior and the strategist – or so you tell me. What would you have me say, Asmidir?'

'Do not misunderstand me, Sigarni. This is not a game we are playing. You are the one the seer spoke of. Unless the gods are capricious – and perhaps they are – then you must have some special skill. If we are to form an army, if we are to defy the most brilliant military nation of the world, it will be because of *you* – you understand? At the moment you are full of bitterness and righteous rage. You must conquer that, you must reach inside yourself and find the Battle Queen. Without her we are lost even before we begin.'

Sigarni turned from the window and moved to a high-backed chair. 'I don't know what to say or where to begin,' she said. 'If there is a skill it is lost to me. I do not believe I am given to panic, Asmidir, but when I try to think of the way ahead my heart beats faster and I find myself short of breath. I look inside, but there is nothing there save regret and remembered pain.'

Asmidir seated himself before her. He reached out, but she instinctively drew back her hand; his face showed his hurt. 'Let us examine then the immediate priorities,' he said. 'My men have been scouting the valleys and passes south of here. The Baron has ordered campaign fortifications built. These are vital for an invading army. Stores and supplies will be left at these forts so that when the invasion force moves in they will have bases from which to sally forth into the mountains. The first is being constructed no more than ten miles from here, in the Dunach Valley. It could be argued that our first task should be to halt their work, to harry them. For that we will need men. We have already discussed where to find warriors. You must seek the aid of the Pallides Hunt Lord, Fyon Sharp-axe.'

Sigarni rose and returned to the window. Sunlight shone brilliantly through gaps in the distant storm-clouds, and the muted sound of far-off thunder rippled across the land. She shivered. 'No,' she said, at last. 'The fortifications must wait. If I were Fyon

Sharp-axe I would not turn over my men to an untried woman from another clan. Send Fell to me.'

'What are you planning?' he asked.

'We will discuss it later,' she told him. Asmidir smiled and rose, bowing deeply. After he had gone Sigarni drew the sword from its silver scabbard. It was a sabre, thirty inches long, the blade highly polished and razor-sharp, the hilt bound with strips of dark grey speckled skin, reinforced by silver wire. It was surprisingly light in her hand, and perfectly balanced. She swung the sword to the left. It sliced through the air, creating a low hissing sound. Hearing Fell approach she moved to the chair, laying the naked blade upon the table before her. The forester entered and bowed clumsily.

'A surprising turn of events,' she said. He grinned and nodded. His face was bruised and swollen, but as he smiled she saw again the handsome clansman she had loved. Motioning him to a seat she looked away, gathering her thoughts. 'How many of the foresters could you gather to us?' she asked.

'Not many,' he said. 'Perhaps six of the fifty. You have to understand, Sigarni, that they are men of family. They know a war against the Outlanders can end only one way. Most would therefore do anything to avoid such a war. Even after the murders.'

'What murders?'

Fell told her of the taking of hostages, and his decision to give himself up to the authorities. 'But they did not wait the promised four days. By the following morning all four were hanging from the walls of Citadel. I believe Tovi and Grame would join us, and perhaps half of the men of Cilfallen. What are you planning?'

'I want you to go from here. Now. Find the six men, and any others you trust. We will meet at my cabin in four days. Is that enough time for you?'

'Barely. But I will be there.'

'Go now,' she ordered him. 'And send the Outlander to me.'

Gwalchmai lifted his jug from the dog-cart and stared out over the hills towards Citadel town. The two hounds, Shamol and Cabris, were asleep in the sunshine. Gwalch pulled the cork from the jug and sat beside Tovi. The baker was silent, lost in thought. The sun was bright in a clear sky, the mountains shining in splendour, but Tovi was oblivious to the beauty and Gwalchmai felt for him. 'Your son was a fine boy,' said Gwalch, lifting the jug to his lips and taking three long swallows.

'You didn't know him,' said Tovi, tonelessly.

'I know you. And I can see him in your mind. You were proud of him – and rightly so.'

'None of that matters now, does it? His mother weeps all the time, and his brothers and sisters walk silently around the house. What manner of men are these, Gwalch, who could hang an innocent boy? Are they monsters? Demon-driven?'

The old man shook his head. 'All it takes is a monster in charge, Tovi. Like a pinch of poison in a jug of wine. Suddenly the wine is deadly. You want a drink?'

'No, I need to keep my eyes sharp for when the devils come. You know, I can't even hate them, Gwal. I feel nothing. Is that my age, do you think? Have I lost something during these years in the bakery?'

'We've all lost something, my friend. Maybe we'll find it again.' Gwalch lifted the jug to his lips – then paused. He pointed to the south. 'There! What do you see? My old eyes have dimmed.'

Tovi squinted. 'Flashes of sunlight upon metal. The enemy are coming. It will take them at least an hour to cross the valley floor.'

'How many?'

'They are too far away to count accurately. Go back to Cilfallen and tell them the Outlanders are coming.'

'What about you?' asked Gwalch, pushing himself to his feet. Behind him the grey hounds rose also.

'I'll wait awhile and count them. Then I'll join you.' Gwalch climbed into the cart, still nursing his jug. He flicked the reins and the two war-hounds lurched into the traces. Tovi watched as the little cart trundled out of view, then he stood and stretched. His thoughts flicked to the Pallides man, Loran, and his warnings concerning the Outlanders. He had hoped the clansman was wrong, but now he knew otherwise. A few weeks ago the world had been a calm and pleasant place, filled with the smell of fresh-baked bread and the laughter and noise of his children. Now the days of blood had dawned again.

Stooping, he picked up the old claymore and stood facing the south, his hands upon the hilt, the blade resting on the earth. It was a fine weapon, and had served him well all those years ago. Yet holding it now gave him no pleasure, no surging sense of pride. All he could feel was sorrow.

The line of riders came down the long hill into the valley. Now he could count them. One hundred and fifty men and five officers. Too large a group to have come for hostages. No, he told himself, this is a killing raid. One hundred and fifty-five soldiers for a village of forty-seven men, thirty-eight women and fifty-one children! As he thought of the little ones a spark of anger burned through his grief, flaming to life in his breast. His huge hands curled around the claymore, the blade flashing up. Once he could have taken three, maybe four enemy soldiers. Today he would find out how much he had lost.

Turning his back upon the distant enemy, Tovi laid the claymore blade on his shoulder and strode down the long road to home. He was high above Cilfallen and from here the buildings seemed tiny set against the green hills and the mighty mountains. Newer dwellings of stone alongside the older timbered houses, and ancient log cabins with roofs of turf, all clustered together in a friendly harmony of wood and stone. Aye, thought Tovi, that is the mark of Cilfallen. The village is friendly and welcoming. There were no walls, for up to now the people had lived without fear.

Cilfallen was indefensible. Tovi sighed, and paused for one last look at the village he had known all his life.

Never will you look the same to me again, he knew. For now I can see the lack of walls and parapets. I see hills from which cavalry can charge into our square. I see buildings with no strong doors, or bowmen's windows. There is no moat. Only the stream, and the white rocks upon which the women and children beat the clothes to wash them.

Tovi walked on, aware also of his own weakness, the large belly fed with too much fresh bread and country butter, and a right arm already tired from holding the claymore.

'I'll find the strength,' he said, aloud.

Captain Chard led his men down into the valley, riding slowly, stiff-backed in the saddle. Despite the honey salve on his back the whip wounds flared as if being constantly stung by angry wasps. The weight of his chainmail added tongues of flame to his shoulders, and his mood was foul. He knew that if Obrin had followed the Baron's orders with more relish he would not now be alive, for the three-pronged whip could kill a man within thirty lashes if delivered with venom. Obrin had been sparing with his strokes, but each of the whip-heads had a tiny piece of lead attached, adding weight to each lash, scoring the skin, opening the flesh. Chard felt sick as he remembered standing at the stake, biting into the leather belt, determined not to scream. But scream he did, until he passed out on the thirty-fourth stroke.

A mixture of honey and wine had been applied to his blood-drenched back. Three of the deeper cuts had needed stiches, twenty-two in all. Yet here he was, within a fortnight, sitting his saddle and leading his men.

He did not question the Baron's change of heart, and had accepted the commission with a burbled speech of gratitude that the Baron had cut short. 'Do not fail me again, Chard,' he had warned. 'How many men will you need?'

'Three hundred, sir.'

The Baron had laughed at him. 'For a village? why not take a thousand?'

'There are nearly two hundred of them, sir!'

The Baron had lifted a sheet of paper. 'One hundred and fifty, approximately. Fifty of them are children under the age of twelve. Around forty are women. The remainder are men. Farmers, cattle-herders – not a good sword among them. Take one hundred and fifty men. No prisoners, Chard. Hang all the bodies so they can be clearly seen. Burn the buildings.'

'Yes, sir. When you say no prisoners . . . you mean the men?'

'Kill them *all*. I have chosen the men you will have with you. They are mercenaries, scum mostly. They'll have no problem with the task. When they're finished let them loot. They will also – most certainly – keep some of the younger women alive for a while. Let them have their enjoyment, it's good for morale.' The Baron's cold eyes fixed on Chard. 'You have a problem with this?'

Chard wished he had the courage to tell the man just how much a problem he had with butchery. Instead he had swallowed hard and mumbled, 'No, sir.'

'How is your back?'

'Healing, sir.'

'You won't fail me again, will you, Chard?'

'No, sir.'

The sun was high and sweat trickled down on to the whip wounds. Chard groaned. An officer rode alongside as they reached the valley floor.

'Beyond that line of hills, isn't it?' the man asked and Chard turned his head. The officer was thin-faced, with protruding eyes, his face marred by the scars of smallpox. Several white-headed pimples showed around his nostrils and a boil was beginning on the nape of his neck. 'Many women there?' asked the officer, as Chard ignored the first question.

'Set the men in a skirmish line,' Chard ordered.

'What for? It's only a pigging village. There's no fighting men likely to ambush us.'

'Give the order,' said Chard.

'Whatever you say,' answered the officer, with a thinly disguised sneer. Twisting in the saddle, he called out to the men, 'Every second man left skirmish. All others to the right!' He swung back to Chard. 'You have orders for the attack?'

'How many ways are there to attack a helpless village?'

'Depends if they know they're going to be attacked. If they don't, you just ride in and get the head man to call all the people together. When they're all in one place you slaughter 'em. If they do know, then they'll all be locked in their houses, or running for the woods. Lots of different ways, on foot, in a charge. It's up to you.'

'Attacked many villages, have you?'

'Too many to count. It's good practice. I'll tell you, you can learn a lot about your men by the way they conduct themselves in a situation like this. Not everyone can do it, you know. We had a young lad once, fearless and damn good with a sword or lance. But this sort of mission, useless. Blubbed like a baby . . . ran around witlessly. Know what happened? Some young kid ran at him and slashed his throat open with a scythe. It was a damn shame. That boy had potential, you know?'

'Send a scout up to the high ground. He'll see the village from there.'

The officer wheeled his horse and rode to the left. A young mercenary kicked his horse into a run and Chard watched him climb the hill and rein in at the top. The soldier waved them on.

Chard led the men up the hill. The officer came alongside and the two men stared down at the cluster of buildings. A narrow stream cut across the south of Cilfallen, and there were two small bridges. Chard examined the line of water; the horses could cross it with ease. Beyond the stream was a low retaining wall, around two feet high and some thirty feet in length. Beyond that were the homes he had been sent to destroy. As he watched a young woman walked from one of the buildings; she was carrying a wicker basket full of clothes, and she knelt at the stream and began to wash them. Chard sighed, then he spoke. 'Send fifty men around the village to the north to cut them off from the hills. The rest of us will attack from the south.'

The officer gave out his orders and two troops filed off to the north-east. Then he leaned across his saddle. 'Listen, Chard, I'd advise you to wait here. From what I hear your back's in a mess, so you won't be able to fight. And I guess you won't want any . . . pleasures. So leave it to me and my men. You agree?'

Chard longed to agree. Instead he shook his head. 'I will ride in with the attack,' he said. 'When it is over I will leave you to your . . . pleasures.'

'Only trying to be helpful,' said the officer, with a wide grin.

They waited until the fifty horsemen had reached their position to the north of the village, then Chard drew his sword. 'Give the order,' he told the officer.

'No prisoners!' shouted the man. 'And all the looting to be left until the job is done! Forward!'

Chard wondered briefly if God would ever forgive him for this day, then touched spurs to his mount. The beast leapt forward. The soldiers around him drew their weapons and charged. The men were lighter armoured than he, wearing leather breastplates and no helms, and the mercenaries soon outpaced him, forming three attacking lines.

Chard was some fifteen lengths behind the last man when the first line of mercenaries reached the stream. The woman there dropped her washing and, lifting her heavy skirts, ran back towards the buildings. The raucous cries of the mercenaries filled the air and then the horses galloped into the water, sending up glittering fountains that caught the sunlight and shone like diamonds.

The first line had reached the middle of the stream when disaster struck. Horses whinnied in fear and pain as they fell headlong, tipping their riders over their necks. For a moment only Chard was stunned.

Tripwire! staked beneath the water line. My God, they were ready for us!

The riders of the second line dragged on their reins, but they collided with their downed comrades in a confused mass. Chard pulled up his mount. Experienced in battle, he knew that the trip-wire was only the beginning. Swiftly he scanned the buildings. There was no sign of a defensive force . . .

And then they were there!

Rising up from behind the low retaining wall, a score of bowmen sent volley after volley of shafts into the milling men. Wounded mercenaries began to scream and run, but long shafts slashed into them, slicing through their pitiful armour.

'Dismount!' shouted Chard. 'Attack on foot!'

Scum though they were, the mercenaries were not afraid to fight. Leaping from their horses they rushed the bowmen, who stood their ground some thirty feet beyond the stream. More than twenty mercenaries went down, but Chard was confident that once hand-to-hand fighting began they would be swept aside by weight of numbers.

Urging his horse to the edge of the stream, he shouted encouragement to his men.

From behind the buildings came a surging mass of fighting men, armed with claymores, scythes, spears and hammers – and women carrying knives and hatchets. They smote the mercenaries' left flank. Chard saw the baker, Fat Tovi, slash his claymore through the shoulder and chest of a mercenary, and then the white-bearded smith, Grame, grabbed the pox-marked officer by the throat, braining him with his forge hammer.

The mercenaries broke and ran. But there was no escape.

Chard wheeled his horse and galloped along the stream, crossing a small bridge, then riding for the second group. All fifty were waiting as ordered in skirmish formation some twenty yards below the tree line. With these men he could yet turn the battle.

His pain was forgotten as he urged his stallion up the hill.

As Chard came closer he watched with horror as a dozen men pitched from their saddles with arrows jutting from their backs. Horses reared, spilling their riders.

A line of mounted bowmen rode from the trees, shooting as they came: grim, dark men, clothed in black and silver. As they neared the stunned mercenaries they threw aside their bows, drawing shining silver sabres. There were no more than twenty soldiers left. A few of them tried to fight, the others fled.

Chard, his force in ruins, his fragile reputation gone for ever, shouted his defiance and galloped towards the attackers. From their centre, on a jet-black horse, came a red-cloaked rider in silver armour. Chard raised his sword, slamming his spurs into the weary stallion's flanks. The horse leapt forward.

The silver rider swung her horse at the last second and the two beasts collided. Chard was flung from the saddle as his stallion went down. The silver rider sprang from her mount and ran in just as he was trying to rise. Despairingly he swung his broadsword at her

160

legs. She jumped nimbly and, as she landed, lashed her sabre across his face. The blade struck his temple, biting deep and dislodging his helm.

Chard fell, rolled and struggled to rise. The sabre smashed down upon his skull, glancing from the chainmail headguard. The blow stunned him and he sagged to his back. The sabre lanced into his throat. Chard felt pain only briefly, for the sword plunged through his neck and into the cold earth beneath him.

All was quiet now, and he felt a curious sense of relief. No dead children, no raped and murdered women. Perhaps God would forgive him after all.

Perhaps . . .

Sigarni stepped back from the corpse and heard Asmidir order his men into the village to check on casualties. She was breathing heavily, yet her limbs felt light. Asmidir came alongside her. 'How are you feeling?' As he spoke, his hand came down on her shoulder.

'Don't touch me!' she hissed, pulling away and turning to face him. She saw the shock and the dismay, but it was nothing to the roaring panic his contact aroused within her. 'Stay away from me!' she said.

'Sigarni.' His voice was soft, his eyes troubled. 'You are in no danger from me. The battle is over, and I believe we have won. Calm yourself before the others see you.'

The roaring receded and she began to tremble. 'God, what is happening to me?' she said, dropping her sabre and sitting down on the grass.

He moved to sit opposite her. 'I think we should blame it on the reaction to the battle, though we both know that is not the truth,' he said sadly. 'However, let us put that aside for now and enjoy the moment of victory. You risked it all, Sigarni. And I am proud of you. As I told you, I did not believe in the wisdom of this course. It was, in my view, too early for a confrontation. But you proved me wrong. Now perhaps you will explain why you were so confident.'

She smiled and felt some of the tension ease from her. 'It was not confidence. You told me I must have special skills. Whether or not

161

that is true only time will tell. But I knew I could gather no support without a victory. Who would follow me? An untried woman in a world of beaten men.'

'But why here in Cilfallen? How did you know they would come here? There are scores of hamlets and villages throughout the Highlands.'

'Indeed there are, and we won't be able to protect them all. But Cilfallen was *my* village, and from here they took the hostages. It is also on largely open land. No major walls, no defences. Added to this, it is the closest main settlement to Citadel.'

'And why did you believe there would be an attack?'

'I questioned Obrin concerning Outland tactics. He believed they would send between one hundred and two hundred men.'

Asmidir smiled. 'We could have lost it all, my lady. We gambled everything on a single throw of the dice. That is not to be recommended for every occasion, I assure you.'

Sigarni rose, then extended her hand to pull Asmidir to his feet. He looked up and met her eyes, and she knew he could see there her fear at the prospect of his touch. Slowly he reached out and clasped her wrist, rising smoothly and disengaging his grasp. 'That took courage, did it not?' he said.

She nodded. 'I am sorry, Asmidir. You are a dear friend, and will always be so. But they took something from me and I cannot get it back.'

He shook his head. 'I fear they *took* nothing. They *gave* you something . . . something vile, like a poison that eats into your heart. I am your friend, Sigarni. More than that, I love you. I would die for you. But you alone must find a way to defeat the monsters tormenting you.'

'What do you mean *defeat* them? I killed them!'

'You misunderstand me,' he said gently. 'They may be dead, but you hold them to you. They exist in every thought you have; you see their faces on all men – even your friends. I cannot advise you, for I have no . . . no *perception* of what you have been through. But you are now a fortress, barred against those who love you. Yet you have the enemy trapped within also. I think you will have to find a way to raise the portcullis and allow your friends in.'

'Nonsense,' she retorted. 'There is no portcullis.' Before he could speak again, she swung away and walked to her horse. 'Let's get to the village,' she said.

The two of them rode in silence.

The narrow lanes of Cilfallen were strewn with Outland corpses. Sigarni gazed on them dispassionately and guided her horse to the south of the town. The bodies of the mercenaries – stripped of all weapons – were slowly being carted across the bridge to an open field. Fell was sitting on the retaining wall surrounded by several of his foresters; they rose when they saw Sigarni. She dismounted and approached them. 'You did well,' she said. 'Did you suffer any losses?'

'Three men wounded, none seriously. Four of the villagers were killed. Eleven others sustained wounds, most of them minor.' She turned towards the waiting foresters, recognizing them all. Three of them had been casual lovers. The men stood silently, their expressions guarded.

'You have now seen how the Outlanders keep the peace. Know this: In the spring they will come with an army. Their mission will be to annihilate all clansmen, and their families, and their children. I intend to fight them – just like today. I will drench the Highlands in their blood. Today we are few, but that will change. Those who wish to serve me should make their wishes known to Fell. Those who do not should make plans to leave the mountains. There are only two sides now: Outland and Highland. Those not with me will be deemed traitors, and I will hunt them down also. That is all.'

Spinning on her heel, she walked back to where Asmidir waited with the horses. 'I need to see Tovi,' she said. They found him at the bakery, with the ovens heating. He had discarded his sword and was kneading a batch of dough.

'One last time,' he said, with an embarrassed smile. 'I don't know why I wanted to.' He gazed around the long room with its racks of empty shelves. 'This place has been my life.'

'Now you have another life,' she said sternly. 'You were a warrior, Tovi; you understood discipline. You and Grame and Fell will train the Loda men. We will fall back into the forest and there I shall leave you. You will gather fighting men, organize stores for the winter, and put out scouts to watch for any further incursions into our territory. You understand this?'

'We can't win, Sigarni. I understand that.'

'We just did!'

'Aye,' he said, wiping the dough from his hands and moving to stand before her. 'We defeated a band of ill-led mercenaries. We tricked them and trapped them. What happens when the Baron marches with his regular soldiers? I watched your man Obrin fight today. He was deadly. What happens when there are thousands like him against us?'

Sigarni stepped in close, her eyes cold, her voice hard as a blade. 'Has all your courage gone, fat man? Has it melted into the blubber around your belly? I am Sigarni. I am of the Blood. And I wear the Crimson. I do not promise victory. I promise war and death. Now you have two choices. The first is to take your family and run, leave the Highlands. The second is to drop to your knee and pledge yourself to serve me until the day you die. Make that choice now, *Hunt Lord*!'

At the use of his title Tovi stiffened, and Sigarni saw the anger in his eyes. 'You have fought one battle, Sigarni. I have fought many. I know what war is, and I know what it achieves. It is no more than a pestilence. It is a terrible thing – it consumes and destroys, birthing hatreds that last for generations. But I am the Hunt Lord, and I will not leave my people in this desperate hour.'

'Then kneel,' she said, her voice flat and unrelenting.

Tovi stepped forward and dropped to one knee. 'My sword and my life,' he said, solemnly.

'Let it be so,' she told him.

Sigarni left him there and walked from the bakery. Grame was sitting by his forge with a bloody bandage around his upper arm. Gwalchmai was with him. The smith grinned as he saw her. Gwalchmai belched, stood, staggered and sat down. 'He's drunk,' said Grame.

'He always is,' said Sigarni. 'Will you serve me, Grame?'

The smith scratched his thick white beard. 'You've changed, lass. You always had iron in you, but I'd guess it has been run through the fire and moulded into something sharp and deadly. Aye, I'll serve you. What would you have me do?'

'Make the pledge.'

'I gave that pledge once already, and the King ran away and left me and others to rot.'

'I will not run, Grame. Make the pledge.'

He stood and looked into her eyes. Bending his knee, he took a deep breath: 'My sword and my life,' he said.

'Let it be so.'

'Where do I begin?' he asked, rising.

'See Tovi. He will tell you what I require in the coming weeks. For now, gather all weapons and supplies and lead our people deep into Pallides territory. We will speak again when the evacuation is complete. Any man who comes to you, Grame, and wishes to serve, make him speak the pledge. From now on we are Highlanders again. Nothing and no one will ever steal our pride. You understand?'

'Hail to thee, Battle Queen!' shouted Gwalchmai, lifting his jug in salute.

The words chilled Sigarni. 'Be silent, old fool! This is no place for your drunken ramblings.'

'He may be drunk,' said Grame, 'but he is not wrong. Only the sovereign can call for the pledge. And only to a sovereign would I make it. You are the Battle Queen, Sigarni. Nothing can change that.'

Sigarni said nothing. Fell and his foresters came into sight, along with scores of villagers, forming a great semi-circle around the forge. All had heard Gwalchmai's drunken salute, and Sigarni saw both confusion and apprehension on the faces of the people around her.

She walked slowly to her horse and stepped into the saddle. There was no noise now, and she felt their eyes upon her as she rode slowly towards the hills.

8

Like a gift from a merciful god winter came twelve days early, blizzards sweeping across the mountains, heavy snowfalls blocking narrow passes and making treacherous even the best of the roads. Sigarni sat alone on a high ridge, wrapped in a cloak of sheepskin, and stared out over the hills to the south. A mile away she could see three figures making their slow progress through the snow.

The heady days of victory at Cilfallen were weeks behind her now, and all the subsequent news had been bad. Stung by unexpected defeat the Outlanders had reacted savagely, sending three forces deep into the mountains to the east and the west. Three Farlain villages had been attacked, and more than four hundred Highlanders massacred in their homes. In the east a Pallides settlement was razed to the ground, and several Loda hamlets were struck during the same week, bringing the death total to more than five hundred.

Ten days before the slaughter Sigarni had travelled with Fell and Asmidir to the main Farlain town, seeking warriors to join their growing band. The experience had proved a hard lesson. As she sat watching the walkers in the snow, Sigarni steeled herself to recall the day.

More than five hundred people had gathered in the main square as the Hunt Lord, Torgan, waited to greet her. There were no cheers as the trio rode in. Torgan, a tall slender man, with wiry black hair cut short to expose a sharp widow's peak and a bald spot at the crown, was waiting for them. He was sitting on a high seat in the centre of the square, flanked by six warriors carrying ritual ebony staffs, adorned with silver. Sitting at his feet was a white-bearded old man dressed in a long robe of faded grey.

'What do you seek here, Woman of Loda?' asked Torgan, as Sigarni dismounted. He did not rise from his seat, and his words were spoken scornfully.

'Is this the Farlain Gifted One?' countered Sigarni, pointing at the old man.

'It is. What concern is that of yours?'

Sigarni turned away from him, scanning the faces in the crowd. There was hostility there. 'Have his dreams been made known to the people of the Farlain?' she asked, raising her voice so that the crowd could hear her.

Torgan rose. 'Aye, they have. He told us of a troublesome woman who would bring death and destruction upon the clans: a Loda woman of low morals who by murder would enrage the Outlanders. And his dreams were true!'

Despite her anger Sigarni stayed calm. 'He is no Gifted One,' she said. 'He is a fraud and a liar. And I will speak no more of him. Let the Farlain know this: An Outland force raided Cilfallen. We destroyed them. More will come, and they will attack and butcher any in their path, whether they be Loda, Farlain, Pallides or Wingoras. All true Gifted Ones know this. And you will see the truth of my words. I am Sigarni. I am of the Blood of Kings. And I do not lie.'

Torgan laughed. 'Aye, we know who you are, Sigarni. Word of your talent has reached us even here. You will leave the lands of the Farlain, and think yourself fortunate that we do not bind you and deliver you to the Outlanders for a just execution. Go back to your pitiful band and tell the idiots who follow you that the Farlain are not to be fooled.'

'How can I tell them that,' responded Sigarni, 'when it is obvious that they have been fooled already?' Spinning on her heel she strode to her stallion and stepped into the saddle. 'There are other Gifted Ones,' she told the crowd, 'in other clans. Be wise and seek their guidance. For the days of blood are here and if we do not join together we will be slaughtered separately. A leader has been prophesied – one who will unite the clans against the enemy. I am that leader.'

'No whore will ever lead the Farlain,' shouted the Hunt Lord. 'Begone before we stone you!'

Sigarni touched heels to her stallion and rode from the town.

Now, as she sat in the icy cold beneath a darkening sky, her anger remained, hot and compelling. Sigarni had been better received among the Pallides, but even here they had promised no warriors to serve under her leadership. Arriving in the Larn Valley, she had been met outside the township by the blond warrior Loran, who had bowed as she dismounted.

'Well met, lady, and welcome,' he said. 'It is good to see you again.' The memory of their meeting by Ironside's Falls seemed as distant as a dream of another life and she found herself gazing at the handsome Pallides as if he was a stranger. 'Your armour fits you well,' he said. 'I am sorry that the shelters we built for the Loda people are so . . . so humble. But we did not have much time.'

'They will suffice,' she said. From the tree line a huge man ambled into view and waved at Loran. Sigarni watched his approach with undisguised amazement. A little over six feet tall, his shoulders seemed impossibly wide, and his neck was easily as big as her thigh. His head was large, and though beardless he had grown his sideburns long and they merged with his hair line to give him a leonine appearance.

'By God!' she whispered. 'Is *it* real?'

Loran chuckled. 'It is my cousin Mereth. And he's real enough.'

'Is this her?' said Mereth, squinting at Sigarni. His voice was a low rumble like distant thunder.

'Aye, Mereth, this is Sigarni.' He moved his head close to her face. 'Handsome woman,' he said amiably.

'Mereth's vision is weak,' explained Loran. 'It is his only weakness. He's the strongest man I've ever seen.'

'The strongest that ever was,' said Mereth proudly. 'I broke Lennox's record for the caber – and they said that couldn't be done. They said he was a giant. I broke it. Are you the Queen now?'

'This is not the time, Mereth,' said Loran softly, laying his hand on the giant's shoulder.

'I heard the Loda Gifted One named her Queen. I was only asking.'

'The Loda Gifted One is a drunkard. Now look after the lady's horse and I will see you at Fyon's house when you have stabled the mount.'

Mereth smiled. 'I can fight too,' he told Sigarni. 'I fear nothing.'

Loran and Sigarni walked on into the town. 'Poor vision is not his only weakness,' she said, when Mereth was out of earshot.

'Do not misjudge him, Sigarni. I admit he is not the most intelligent of men, but he is no simpleton. It just takes him a long time to work through a problem.'

Fyon Sharp-axe entertained her at his home in the Larn Valley. It was a fine old house, built of stone with a roof of carefully carved slate. Fyon, Loran and Mereth sat around the long table and listened intently as Sigarni told them of the events that had led to the battle of Cilfallen. The Hunt Lord, a squat powerfully built warrior with a square-cut black beard, forked with silver, had waited courteously until she finished her tale. As she concluded he raised a wine cup and toasted her. 'You did well, Sigarni,' he said. 'I applaud you for the way you saved the people of your clan. But I do not yet know if you are the leader who was prophesied. Our Gifted Ones say one is coming who will lead us, but they cannot name him. I know we have no choice now, save to battle for our lives. I will not relinquish this battle to you, for despite your victory at Cilfallen you are untried. And you are a woman. It is not a woman's place to lead men into battle. I do not say this slightingly, Sigarni, for I admire your courage. It is merely common sense. Men are ultimately dispensable. If, in a war, all but ten of a clan's warriors are killed, but the women remain, the clan would survive. But if only ten of the clan women were left it would die. Men are made for hunting and battle, women for gathering and childbirth. This is the way of the world. I cannot see Pallides warriors fighting for a woman – even one as spirited as you.'

Sigarni nodded. 'I understand your fears, Fyon,' she said. 'But I would like to hear the thoughts of Loran.'

The blond warrior leaned back in his chair. He glanced at Sigarni. 'I have waited for a leader – as have we all. And I was surprised when I heard that Gwalchmai had named you. We all here know that you are of the blood of Gandarin, and that he was directly descended from Ironhand. And a boy child of yours would have first claim to the throne. Yet there is no boy child, and never have the clans been led by a woman.'

'What of the Witch Queen?' countered Sigarni.

'Aye, I'll grant that,' admitted Loran, 'but she was from beyond the old Gateways, drawn to our aid by sorcery. And she did not stay to rule, but returned to her own land when the war was won.'

'As I shall,' said Sigarni.

'Be that as it may,' continued Loran, 'I cannot as yet make a judgement. I echo the Hunt Lord's praise for your victory at Cilfallen, and I deplore the treatment of you by the Farlain. Even so, I do not believe we should commit ourselves to you at this time. I ask that you do not judge us too harshly.'

Sigarni rose. 'I do not judge you harshly, Loran. You came to Tovi and warned him of invasion. Because of your arguments he sent enough supplies back into Pallides lands to ensure survival for the people of Loda during the winter. You have given us land, built us homes. For this I am grateful. And I understand your concerns. I did not ask for this role, and would be more than happy to surrender it. But I know now that I am the one prophesied. I know it. What I need to know is what can be done to convince the Pallides. What do you require of me?'

'A good question,' said Fyon, also rising. He rubbed at his silver-forked beard and moved to the fire blazing in the hearth. 'And I wish I had an answer. We need a sign, Sigarni. Until then you must train your own warriors.'

Ten days later Fyon had ridden his horse into the makeshift camp of the Loda, seeking out Sigarni.

'Welcome,' she said, as he ducked into the small log dwelling. It was dark inside, and lit by the flickering fire within a small iron brazier. Fyon seated himself opposite Sigarni and cast a nervous glance at the black man at her side. 'This is Asmidir. He is my general, and a warrior of great skill.' Asmidir held out his hand and Fyon shook it briefly.

'The Outlanders struck several Farlain villages,' said Fyon. 'Hundreds were slaughtered, women and children among them. Torgan led his men on a vengeance strike, but they were surrounded and cut to pieces. Torgan escaped, but he lost more than three hundred warriors. He has blamed you — claims you are a curse upon the people. My scouts tell me the Outlanders are marching towards us. They will be here in less than five days.'

'They will not arrive,' said Sigarni. 'There are blizzards in the wind; they will drive them back.'

'Only until the spring,' said Fyon. 'What then?'

'Let us hope that by then you will have had a sign,' said Sigarni coldly.

High on the mountainside Sigarni wrapped her sheepskin cloak more tightly around her shoulders. Lady padded across the snow and hunkered down by her side. Sigarni pulled off her fur-lined mittens and stroked the dog's head. 'We'll soon be back in the warm, girl,' she said. At the sound of her voice Lady's tail thumped against the snow.

The three walkers were at the foot of the mountain now and Sigarni could see them clearly. The first was Fell. With him were Gwyn Dark-eye and Bakris Tooth-gone. Slowly the three men climbed the flank of the mountain, reaching the ridge just before dusk. Snow was falling again, thick and fast.

Fell was the first to climb to the ridge. Snow was thick upon his hair and shoulders.

'What did you learn?' asked Sigarni.

'They have put a price of one thousand guineas upon your head, lady. And they are expecting another three thousand men by spring.'

'Did you see Cilfallen?'

Fell sighed. 'There is nothing there. Not one stone upon another. As if it never was.'

'Come back to the settlement,' she said. 'You can tell me all.'

'There's one piece of news I'd like to spit out now,' he said, brushing the snow from his hair. 'There was an arrival in Citadel — a wizard from the south. His name is Jakuta Khan. There are many stories about him, so we were told. He conjures demons.'

Sigarni could see the fear in their eyes, and she hoped they could not see the same fear in hers. 'I do not fear him,' she heard herself say.

'He came to our fire last night,' said Gwyn. 'Just appeared out of nowhere, and seemed to stand within the flames. Tell her, Fell.'

'He said for us to tell you he was coming for you. He said you were lucky that night by the Falls, but that this time he would not fail. You would remember him, he said, for the last time you saw him he had your father's heart in his hand. Then he vanished.'

Sigarni staggered back and swung away from the men. Her mouth was dry, her heart beating wildly. Panic welled in her breast, and she felt herself adrift on a current of fear. Her legs were weak and she reached out to grip the trunk of a tree.

The demons were coming again!

For Tovi Long-arm the onset of winter was a nightmare. The people of the Loda were spread now across two valleys, in five encampments. Food was a problem for almost three thousand refugees. Four of the Loda herds had been driven north after the attack on Cilfallen and three had been slaughtered to supply meat for the clan, leaving only breeding stock for the spring. But meat alone was not enough. There was a shortage of vegetables and dried fruit, and dysentery had spread among the old and infirm. Lung infections had begun to show among the old and the very young, and eleven greybeards had died so far in the first month of snow. Worse was to come, for soon the milk cows would go dry and then hunger would border on famine. Blizzards had closed many of the trails and communication was becoming difficult, even between camps. The structures erected by the Pallides were sound enough, but they were spartan and draughty, smoke-filled and dark.

Complaints were growing, and morale was low. Added to this there was resentment about the Outlander Obrin and his training methods. Day after day he would order the young men to engage in punishing routines, running, lifting, working in groups. It was not the Highland way, and Tovi had tried to impress this on the Outlander.

To no avail . . .

It was dawn when Tovi roused himself from his blankets. Beside him his wife groaned in her sleep. It was cold in the cabin and Tovi placed his own blanket over hers. The children were still asleep. Tovi moved to the fire, which had died down to a few smouldering ashes. With a stick he pushed the last few glowing embers together, then blew them into life, adding kindling until the flames licked up. Pulling on his boots and overshirt he tried to open the door of the cabin, but snow had piled up against the door in the night and Tovi had to squeeze through a narrow gap to emerge into the dawn light. Using his hands, he scooped the snow away from the door and then pushed it shut.

Grame was already awake when Tovi called at his small hut. The smith, wrapped in a long sheepskin coat and holding a long-handled felling axe, stepped out to join him. 'The sky's clear,' said Grame, 'and it feels milder.'

'The worst is yet to come,' said Tovi.

'I know that!' snapped Grame. 'God, Tovi, must you stay so gloomy?'

Tovi reddened at the rebuke and glared at the white-bearded smith. 'Give me one good reason to be optimistic and I shall. I will even dance a jig for you! We have nearly three thousand people living in squalor, and what are we waiting for? To face famine or slaughter in the spring. Am I wrong?'

'I do not know if you are wrong, Tovi. That's the truth of it. But you could be. Concentrate on that. We now have five hundred fighting men, hard men, fuelled by anger and the need for revenge. By spring we could have thousands. Then we will see. Why do you need to show such despair? It does no good.'

'I am not skilled at hiding my feelings, Grame,' admitted Tovi. 'I am getting old and I have no fire in my belly. They killed my son, destroyed my village. Now I feel as if I am waiting for the rest of my family to be put to the sword. I find it hard to stomach.'

Grame nodded. 'You are not so old, Tovi. And as for your stomach – well, you look better than you have in years. Felling trees and build-ing cabins has been good for you. Come the spring, that claymore will have no more weight than a goose feather. Then you'll find the fire.'

Tovi forced a smile and scanned the camp. To the south the new community hall was almost half built, the ground levelled, the log walls already around five feet high. Eighty feet long and thirty wide, the structure when finished would allow many people of the encampment to gather together in the evenings. This, Tovi knew, would encourage a greater camaraderie and help lift morale. 'How long now?' he asked pointing at the structure.

'Five days. We'll be felling trees on the north slope today. If there's no fresh snow for a while we might finish in three.'

All around them people were emerging from the huts. Tovi saw the Outlander Obrin. The man was dressed now in borrowed leggings and a leather tunic; he strolled to a tree and urinated against the trunk. 'I don't like the man,' said Tovi.

'Aye, he's iron hard,' Grame agreed.

'It is not that. There is an arrogance about him that slips under my skin like a barbed thorn. Look at the way he walks . . . as if he is a king and all around him are serfs and vassals.'

Grame chuckled. 'You are seeing too much. Fell walks like that. Sigarni too.'

'Aye, but they're Highlanders.'

Grame's chuckle became a full-blooded laugh as he clapped his hand on Tovi's shoulder. 'Listen to yourself! Is that not arrogance? Anyway Obrin is a Highlander – Fell's son.'

'Pah! Put a wolf in a kilt and it is still a wolf!'

Grame shook his head. 'You are not good company today, Hunt Lord,' he said. Tovi watched him stride away through the snow.

He's right, thought Tovi, with a stab of guilt. I am the Hunt Lord and I should be lifting the hearts of my people. He sighed and trudged off towards Obrin. The warrior had removed his shirt and was kneeling and rubbing snow over his upper body. As Tovi came closer he saw the web of scars on Obrin's chest and upper arms. The man looked up at him, his eyes cold.

'Good morning, Hunt Lord.'

'And to you, Obrin. How is the training progressing?'

Obrin rose and pulled on his shirt and tunic. 'Six of the groups are proving adequate. No more than that. The others . . .' he shrugged. 'If they don't want to learn, then I cannot force them.'

'You don't need to teach a Highlander to fight,' said Tovi. Obrin gave a rare smile but it did not soften his face. If anything, Tovi realized, it made him look more deadly.

'That is true, Hunt Lord. They know how to fight, and they know how to die. What they don't comprehend is that war is not about fighting and dying. It is about winning. And no army can win without discipline. A general must know that when he – or in our case *she* – gives an order it will be obeyed without question. We don't have that here. What we have is five hundred arrogant warriors who, upon seeing the enemy, will brandish their claymores and rush down to die. Just like the Farlain.'

Tovi's first response was one of anger, but he swallowed it down. What would this Outlander understand of Highland pride, of the warrior's code? Fighting involved honour and couage. These Outlanders treated it as a trade. Even so, he knew that the man was speaking honestly. Worse, he was not wrong. 'Try to understand, Obrin,' he said, softly. 'Here each man is an individual. Wars between clans always come down to man against man. There was never any question of tactics. Even when we fought . . . your people . . . we did not learn. We charged. We died. You are dealing with a people who have fought this way for generations. I don't even know whether the older warriors can absorb these new ideas. So be patient. Try to find some way to appeal to the younger men. Convince them.'

'I have already told them what is real,' said Obrin stubbornly. 'And if that wasn't enough they have the example of the Farlain.'

'We are a proud people, Obrin. We can be led to the borders of Hell itself, but we cannot be driven. Can you understand that?'

'I'll think on it,' said the Outlander. 'But I never was an officer, and I'm no leader. All I know is what I've learned through seventeen years of bloody war. But I'll think on it.'

A young woman approached them, a heavy woollen shawl wrapped around her slender shoulders. 'By your leave, Hunt Lord,' she said, with a curtsey. 'My grandfather is sick and cannot rise from his bed. Can you come?'

'Aye, lass,' said Tovi wearily.

*   *   *

Obrin watched the Hunt Lord trudge off through the snow, saw the weariness in the man. He wears defeat like a cloak, thought the warrior. The former Outlander wandered away from the camp, climbing high on to the mountainside to the meeting cave. Three men were already present, and they had lit a fire. Their conversation faded away as Obrin entered. He walked slowly to the far side of the fire and sat, glancing down at the two bundles he had left there earlier; they were untouched. Obrin waited in silence until others arrived, some singly, some in pairs, others in small groups until twenty-five were assembled. Obrin rose and looked at their faces. Many of them were scarce more than children. They waited, sullen and wary.

'No work today,' said Obrin, breaking the silence. 'Today we talk. Now I am not a great talker – and even less of a teacher. But at this moment I am all that you have. So open your ears and listen.'

'Why should we listen?' asked a young man in the front row. He was no more, Obrin guessed, than around fourteen years of age. 'You tell us to carry rocks, we carry rocks. You tell us to run and we run. I do not need to hear the words of an Outland traitor. Just give us your orders and we shall obey them.'

'Then I order you to listen,' said Obrin, without trace of anger. His eyes raked the group. 'Your friendship means nothing to me,' he told them. 'It is worth less than a sparrow's droppings. We are not here for friendship. What I am trying to do is give you a chance – a tiny chance – to defend your loved ones against a powerful enemy. Oh, I know you are prepared to die. The Farlain have shown us all how well a Highlander can give up his life. But you don't *win* by dying. You win by causing your enemy to die. Is that so hard to understand? The Hunt Lord says a Highlander cannot be driven. Is he incapable also of learning? If not, how did he acquire the skills to build homes, weave cloth, make bows and swords? What is so different about war? It is a game of skill and daring, of move and counter-move. The Outlanders – as you call them – are masters of war.'

'Masters of slaughter more like!' came a voice from the middle rows.

'Aye, and slaughter,' agreed Obrin. 'But in a battle they hold together. It is called discipline. It is nothing to do with honour, or glory. Yet all victories are based upon it.' Obrin walked to the first of the bundles and flipped back the blanket covering it. Stooping he lifted a dozen sticks, each no thicker than his thumb and no longer than his forearm. Tossing them one by one to the nearest clansmen, he said, 'Break them!'

The first man chuckled and glanced down at the thin length of wood. 'Why?' he asked.

'Just do it.'

The sound of snapping wood echoed in the cave, followed by laughter as someone said, 'The great warrior has certainly taught us to master stick splitting.'

'Easy, was it not?' said Obrin amiably. 'No trouble. A child could do it. And that, my fine clansmen, is how the Outlanders will deal with you. It is not a question of bravery, or honour. You fight as individuals, single sticks. Now, this is how the Outlanders fight.' Taking up the second bundle which was also composed of a dozen sticks, but tightly bound with twine, he tossed it to the jester. 'Come then,' said Obrin, 'show me how you have mastered stick-splitting. Break them!'

The man stood and held the bundle at both ends. Suddenly he bent his knee and brought the sticks down hard across his thigh. Several sticks gave, but the bundle remained intact. Angrily he hurled the sticks on the fire. 'What does it prove?' he snarled. 'But give me a claymore and I'll show you what I can do!'

'Sit down lad,' said Obrin. 'I do not doubt your courage. The lesson is a simple one to absorb. What you saw was two bundles. Each bundle had twelve sticks. One could be broken, the other could not. It is the same with armies. When the clans fought at Colden Moor they fought in the only way they knew, shoulder to shoulder, claymores swinging. They were brought down by archers and slingers, lancers and pikemen, heavy cavalry and armoured swordsmen. They were beaten decisively, but not routed. They stood their ground and died like men. By God, what a waste of courage! Did any here see the Farlain dead?'

Several men spoke up. Obrin nodded and waved them to silence. 'What you saw was easy to read. The Outlanders were in the valley. The Farlain attacked from the high ground, sweeping down on them, their claymores bright in the morning sun. The Outlanders formed a tight shield wall, their spears extending. The Farlain ran upon the spears, trying to beat a path through. Then the cavalry came from the right, from their hiding places in a wood. Archers appeared on the left sending volley after volley into the Highland ranks. How long did the battle last? Not an hour. Not even half that. According to Fell it was probably over in a few short minutes. The Outlanders carried their dead away in a single wagon – ten . . . fifteen . . . twenty bodies at the most. The Farlain lost hundreds. Are the clans too stupid to learn from their errors?' They were listening now, intently, their eyes locked to Obrin's face. 'We all know the animals of the forest, and their ways. When faced with wolves, a stag will run. The wolves lope after him, slowly robbing him of strength. At last he turns at bay, and they come at him from all sides. If he is strong his horns will kill some, then he dies. You are like the stag. The Outlanders are the wolves; only they are worse than wolves. They have the horns of the stag, the stamina and cunning of the wolf pack, the claws of the bear, and the fangs of the lion. To defeat them, we must emulate them.'

'How do we do this?' asked the boy who made the earlier jest.

'Your question is a good beginning,' Obrin told him. 'Understanding is the first key. All war is based on deception. When you are weak, you make the enemy think you are strong; when you are strong, make him think you are weak. When you are far away, make him believe you are near, and when you are near, lead him to think you are far away. The Outlanders did this to the Farlain. Their scouts must have told them the clansmen were near, so they hid their cavalry and archers. The Farlain saw the infantry occupying a weak position and attacked. In doing so, they walked into the iron jaws of the monster. We will not follow their example. We will fight on our own terms, choosing our own ground. If necessary, we will fight and run. We will make them the stag, and we shall be the wolves.

'To fight like this takes great discipline and enormous strength of heart, but it is the only way to win. Go now and talk amongst yourselves. Choose a unit leader from among you; he will be your officer. Pass the word to the other twenty-five groups. Tell them to appoint one man to represent them. Then I want all officers to report to me here at dawn tomorrow.'

As the men stood to leave Obrin lifted his hand. 'One more point, my lads. I am from a Highland people far to the south. We are called the Arekki. I am the only man of my clan within three hundred miles. I am Obrin, and I do not lie, cheat or steal. Not once in my life have I betrayed a friend or comrade, nor have I ever fled from an enemy. The next man to call me a traitor to my face will die on my sword. Go now!'

Sleeting hail beat against the windows as Asmidir sat at his desk with quill pen in hand, poring over maps of the Highlands. Two lanterns were glowing close by, casting gentle light on the sheets of paper littering the desk top. Asmidir stared hard at the lines on the ancient parchment, trying to picture the pass of Duane. Sheer to the east, mildly sloping to the west, it opened out into two box canyons and a long, narrow plain. Dipping his pen into the ink jar he sketched the pass, adding notations concerning distance and height.

Ari entered, still dressed in his armour of silver and black. He bowed. 'Shall I bring your food here, lord?' he asked.

'I'm not hungry. Sit you down.' The tall warrior pulled up a chair and sat. Leaning forward, Ari's dark eyes scanned the lines of the new map Asmidir was creating.

'Duane Pass,' he said. 'A good battle site – if the defenders number more than two thousand. Five hundred could not hold the ridges and would be flanked to the west. Cavalry would encircle them, then no escape would be possible.'

'Aye, it is a problem. We need more men. I'd give half of all I own to see Kalia here with her regiment.'

Ari gave a rare smile. 'Kalia and Sigarni? Panther and hawk. It would be . . . interesting.'

'She is three thousand miles away – if she still lives. But you are right, it would be fascinating to see them together. Now, you know these maps as well as I. Where will the first attack come?'

Ari sifted through the sheets. 'They will bring an army to the first invasion fort. From there I would think they would swing north-east towards the deeper lands of the Farlain. They may even split their force and push north-west into Pallides territory. I think you are right to choose Duane; it is three miles south of their first fort.'

Asmidir leaned back and rubbed his tired eyes. 'Duane is a natural battle site. The enemy trapped below with only one means of escape, the defenders with their backs to the mountains, able to slip away at the first sign of impending defeat. As you say, however, we need at least two thousand. Where else?'

Ari shuffled through the maps. 'With five hundred? Nowhere.'

'Precisely my thoughts. And the Baron is no fool, he will know our approximate number. Son of a whore!' Lifting a detailed sketch of an Outland fort, he passed it to Ari. 'What if we took it before they arrived? They'd have no supplies. How long could we hold them?'

'Four or five days. But they have three supply forts, not one. They will merely send a force around us. And then there would be no escape for the defenders. No prospect of victory either.'

Asmidir pushed himself to his feet and wandered to the window. The snow was falling thick and fast, piling against the base of the leaded panes. 'My head is spinning,' he said. 'Tell me something good. Anything.'

Ari chuckled. 'Our enemy is the Baron. He is hot-headed and reckless. Better yet, he is impatient and will not give us respect in the first battle. That is an advantage.'

'That is true,' agreed Asmidir. 'But it is not enough to give him a bloody nose. The first battle must be decisive.'

'And that means Duane Pass,' said Ari.

'Which the Baron will also be aware of.' Asmidir shook his head and laughed. 'Are we being fools, Ari? Have we waited this long merely to stand and die on a foreign mountain?'

'Perhaps,' agreed the warrior. 'Yet a man has to die somewhere.'

'I'm not ready to die yet. I swore an oath to make the Outlanders pay for the rape of Kushir. I must honour it – or my spirit will walk forever through the Valley of Desolation and Despair.'

'I also swore that oath, lord,' said Ari. 'We all did. Now our hopes rest with the silver woman.'

Asmidir returned to the table and stared into the dark eyes of the man opposite. 'What do you think of her, Ari? Could she truly be the One?'

The warrior shrugged. 'I do not know the answer to the second question. As to the first – I admire her. That is all I can say.'

'It does not bother you that this Chosen One is a woman?'

'Kalia is a woman – and she has fought in many wars. And Sigarni's battle plan at Cilfallen was inspired. Fraught with peril – but inspired.'

Asmidir gathered up the maps and sketches. 'I must be heading back to the mountains tomorrow. I need to see her.'

'It will take around four days now,' said Ari. 'The snows have blocked many passes. Perhaps you should wait for more clement weather.'

'These mountains do not know the meaning of clement weather,' said Asmidir, with a wry smile. 'Even in summer the wind can chill a man to the bone.'

'It is a hard land,' agreed Ari, 'and it breeds hard men. That is another advantage.'

Another warrior entered and bowed. 'There is a man to see you, lord,' he said. 'He came out of the snow.'

'Do we know him?' Asmidir asked.

'I have not seen him before, lord. He is very old, and wears a cloak of feathers.'

'Bring him in.'

The warrior stepped aside and Taliesen entered. He did not pause or bow but strode straight to the table. Snow had gathered on his feathered cloak and his eyebrows and eyelids were tinged with ice.

'She is gone,' he said. 'The demons are coming – and she has gone!'

The blizzard came suddenly, fierce winds slashing across the mountains, sending up flurries of ground snow to mix with biting sleet. Sigarni was on open ground with the temperature dropping fast. Shielding her eyes with a gloved hand, she looked for shelter. Nothing could be seen. To be caught outside was to die, she knew, for already the sleet was penetrating her leggings and soaking into the sheepskin coat she wore; her fur-lined hood was white with ice and her face was burning with pain.

There was no panic in her, and in the distance she saw a huge fir tree, part buried in the snow. Striking out for it she waded through a thick drift, half climbing and half crawling until she reached the lee side of the tree. The branches of such a fir would spread in a radius of at least ten feet from the trunk, she knew, and that meant there was likely to be a natural cave below the buried branches. Lying on her belly, Sigarni began to dig with her hands and arms pushing aside the freezing snow, burrowing down beneath the boughs. Her pack snagged against a branch, and snow cascaded down on her. Digging deeper, she squeezed herself under the bough. Suddenly the snow beneath her gave way and she slid head first into the natural pocket below. The snow cave was around seven feet deep and eight feet across, the fir branches above forming the roof. Out of the biting wind, Sigarni shivered with pleasure. From the side pocket of her pack she took a small tinder-box and the stub of a thick candle. Striking the flint, she ignited the dried bark scrapings, gently blowing them to life, before holding the candle wick over the tiny flames. With the candle lit, she set it on the ground beside her and leaned back against the trunk of the fir.

She was cold, and she stared lovingly at the flickering candle flame. The heat from it would gather in the snow cave – not enough to melt the snow overhead but more than ample to prevent death from cold. Above her she could hear the ferocity of the blizzard raking across the mountains, talons of icy sleet ripping at the land.

Here I am safe, she thought. She closed her eyes. Safe? Only from the blizzard.

She had seen the fear in Fell's eyes as he promised to stand beside her against the wizard and his demons, but more than this she had remembered the awful events of her childhood . . .

They had been enjoying a supper by the fire – when all the lanterns went out, as if struck by a fierce wind. Only there was no wind – only a terrible cold that swept across the room, drowning the heat of the fire under an invisible wave. Mother had not screamed, or shown any sign of panic, though the fear was there on her careworn features. She had leapt to the far wall, dragging down a sabre and tossing it to Father who stood silently in the centre of the room staring at the door. He looked so strong then, with his full red beard glistening in the cold firelight.

'Get under the table, girl,' he told the six-year-old Sigarni. But she had scrambled to be beside her mother, who had drawn two hunting knives from their sheaths. Sigarni tugged her mother's skirt.

'I want a knife,' she said. Her mother forced a smile and looked at her father. Little Sigarni didn't understand the look then, but now viewing it from the distance between adulthood and infancy, she knew they were proud of her.

The door exploded inwards and a tall man stood there, dressed in crimson. Sigarni remembered his face; it was long and lantern-jawed, the eyes deep-set and small, the mouth full-lipped. He was carrying no weapon.

'Ah,' he said, 'everyone ready to die, I see. Let it be so!' In that moment a huge tear appeared in her mother's side, blood gushing from the wound. Father leapt forward, but staggered and shouted in pain as blood welled from talon marks on his neck. Something brushed Sigarni's dress and she saw the tear across her shoulder.

Father swung his claymore. It struck something invisible, black blood appearing in the air. Screaming his battlecry, he swung on his heel and sent the sword out in a second whistling arc. It thudded into another unseen assailant – and stuck there. Blood gushed from Father's mouth and Sigarni saw his chest rip open, his heart explode from the cavity and fly across the room into the outstretched hands of the man in red. Sigarni's mother hurled one of her knives at the man, but it flew by him. Turning she leapt for the window, pushing it open, then swung back into the room and sprang towards Sigarni, grabbing her by her dress and lifting her from her feet. Spinning, she hurled the terrified child through the window.

Sigarni hit hard and rolled, then came upright and looked back at the cabin. Her mother shouted: 'Run!'

Then her head toppled slowly from her shoulders . . .

And Sigarni had run, slipping and sliding down muddy slopes, panic-stricken and lost, until at last she came to the pool by the Falls . . .

Jerking her mind back to the present, she peeled off her gloves and extended her hands to the candle-flame. Fell would be angry that she had left him behind, but he could not fight the demons. The forester would fare no better than her parents. No. If she had to die it would be alone.

No, she decided, not alone. I will find a way to kill some of them at least.

She sat for more than an hour, listening to the storm. Finally it swept by and the silence of the night fell on the mountains. Lifting the candle she blew it out, returning it to her pocket. Then slowly she climbed from the ice cave, and continued on her way to the pool by the Falls.

The journey was not an easy one. Many natural landmarks were hidden under drifts, the very shape of the land subtly altered by wind-sculpted snow. Above her the clouds cleared, the stars shining bright. The temperature plummeted. Sigarni pushed on, careful to move with the minimum of effort, anxious not to waste energy or to become too hot within her winter clothing. Sweat could be deadly, for it formed a sheet of freezing ice on the skin.

It was close to midnight when Sigarni struggled over the last rise. Below her the Falls were silent, frozen in mid-fall, and the pool was a field of snow over thick ice. Sigarni clambered down to the cave where Taliesen had nursed her. There was still some firewood stacked against the far wall. Releasing her pack, she built a blaze. The skin of her face prickled painfully as the heat touched her, and her fingers were thick and clumsy as she added fuel to the fire.

Removing her top-coat, she opened the pack and lifted clear the contents, setting them out in neat rows.

When to begin? Tomorrow? Tonight? Fear made her consider tackling the tasks now – immediately, but she was a Highlander and well understood the perils of fatigue in blizzard conditions.

No. Tonight she would rest, gathering her strength. Tomorrow the work could begin.

Ballistar awoke when he heard one of the warriors walk along the corridor outside and knock quietly at Kollarin's door. The dwarf sat up. He could hear voices, but the words were muffled by the wall. Curious, he scrambled from the bed and ambled to the door. Outside the former servant, Ari, was talking to Kollarin. The Outlander was bare-chested, his dark hair hanging loose. 'The Lord needs you – now,' said Ari.

'In the middle of the night?' queried Kollarin. 'Can it not wait?'

'Now,' repeated Ari. 'It is a matter of great urgency.'

'Does he want me also?' asked Ballistar.

Ari glanced down at the dwarf. 'He did not say so – but I think your counsel would be most welcome. He will meet you in the Long Hall.'

Minutes later, as Ballistar and Kollarin entered the hall, they saw Taliesen and the black man sitting by the fire. Ballistar cursed under his breath. He tugged the hem of Kollarin's green tunic. 'Sorcerer,' he whispered. As the two men approached the fire, Asmidir beckoned them to sit.

'Sigarni has left the encampment,' he said. 'It is imperative that we find her swiftly.'

'Why would she go?' asked Ballistar. Asmidir switched his gaze to Taliesen and the old man took a deep breath.

'How much do you know of her childhood?' he asked.

'Everything.'

'Then you will recall how her . . . parents were killed.'

Ballistar felt his heartbeat quicken, and his mouth was suddenly dry. 'They were killed by . . . by demons.'

'By demons, yes. Summoned by an enchanter who calls himself Jakuta Khan. There is much that I cannot tell you, but you should know this: Jakuta has returned. Twice already he has tried to capture Sigarni. Once as a babe. I thwarted him then, with the help of Caswallon. Then he found where we had hidden her and came again, killing her guardians. I thought he was finished then, but somehow he survived. We must find her.'

'Why does he want to kill her? Is he hired by the Baron?' asked Kollarin.

'No. This goes back a very long way. As I said, I cannot tell you everything. But the heart of the matter is Sigarni's blood, or more accurately her blood line. She is of the blood of kings. Those who understand the mystic arts will know why that is important to Jakuta.'

Kollarin nodded. Ballistar looked from one to the other. 'Well, I don't know,' he said. 'Why?'

'Power,' Kollarin told him. 'It is believed that the soul of a king carries great power. To sacrifice such a man would bestow enormous power on the one who carried out the deed. It is said that the Demon Lord, Salaimun, conquered the world after killing three kings. I don't know whether there be truth in such tales.'

'Some truth,' said Taliesen. 'Salaimun made pacts with the Lords of the pits. He fed them blood and souls in return for power. Jakuta made a similar pact. But he has failed – twice.'

'As far as I understand it,' said Asmidir, 'if you fail then your own soul is consumed. Is that not one of the dangers of necromancy?'

'It should be,' agreed Taliesen. 'I can only surmise that Jakuta used a familiar through which to cast his spells of summoning.'

'A familiar?' echoed Ballistar.

'A conduit,' Kollarin told him. 'The sorcerer uses an apprentice, who is placed in a trance. The spell is then spoken through the apprentice. If it fails, the demons take the soul of the conduit . . . the familiar.'

'Enough of this!' stormed Taliesen. 'We are not here to educate the dwarf! Can you find her, Kollarin?'

Kollarin shook his head. 'Not from here. I must go to where she last slept, then I will pick up her spirit trail.'

'It will take three days in the snow,' said Asmidir. The black man swung to the sorcerer. 'However, it did not take you three days, Taliesen. Do you know another path?'

'Aye, but none of you could walk it,' he said despondently.

'Why do you need to be in the hut, Kollarin?' asked Ballistar. 'Could you not merely track her by using a piece of her clothing?'

'I am not a bloodhound, you idiot! I don't follow the trail with my snout to the snow!'

'Then how do you hone your talent?' asked Asmidir.

'It is hard to explain. But for me a person leaves an essence of themselves in any building. It fades over a period of weeks, but once I hook to it I can follow it anywhere.'

'And where is such an . . . essence . . . most strongly felt?'

'In a bed, or a favourite chair. Sometimes attached to a family member, or a close friend.'

'By going to the hut, could you gain a sense of her ultimate destination?'

'No,' admitted Kollarin. 'I would follow the trail.'

'Damn!' said Asmidir. 'It brings us no closer. What of you, Taliesen? You are a sorcerer. You claim to be able to see the future. How then do you not know her whereabouts?'

'Pah!' said the old man. 'You think in straight lines. You talk of *a* future. There are thousands upon thousands. New futures begin with every heartbeat. Aye, in all of them Sigarni is the Chosen One. In some of them she even succeeds for a while. In most of them she dies, young and unfulfilled. I am seeking the one future among so many. I do not know where she is; I don't know why she has run away. Perhaps in this future she lacks courage.'

'Nonsense,' said Ballistar, reddening. 'She would not flee. If she knew the demons were coming she would try to think of a way of fighting them. I know her — better than any of you. She has gone to choose her ground.'

'Where would that be?' asked Asmidir. 'That is the question. And why did she not come to us to aid her?'

'Her father was a great fighter,' said Ballistar, 'but he was torn to pieces. She would not take her friends into such peril. Who among us could fight demons?'

'I could, but I wasn't here,' said Taliesen. 'My people are fighting a war in another time. They needed me.'

'There was no one she could turn to,' said the dwarf. 'Therefore she will fight alone.'

'Wait!' said Taliesen, his eyes brightening. 'There is one she would turn to. I know where she is!'

'Where?' Asmidir asked.

'The cave by the pool. She has an ally there. I must go!' Taliesen rose.

Ballistar lifted his hand. 'A moment, please,' said the dwarf. 'Do you know what Sigarni took with her when she left?'

'Knives, balls of twine, some food, a bow, arrows. What does it matter?' asked the sorcerer.

'It matters more than you think,' said Ballistar. 'You had better let me come with you.'

9

Sigarni held out her hand to the fire. The warmth was both welcoming and reassuring. When the demons had killed her parents all heat had vanished from the blaze in the hearth. This, she reasoned, would be her only warning that death was close. She stared at her hands. There were blisters on her palms and on the inside joints of her fingers; one had bled profusely and they were painful.

It was the eve of her second day by the frozen Falls and she had worked hard through the hours of daylight. Fear was a constant companion, but somehow that fear was eased merely by being alone. Sigarni the Huntress had no other concerns now save to stay alive. To do that she must somehow defeat a wizard and his demons.

They can be killed, she thought. Father struck one of them and black blood flowed from it. And that which bleeds can die. Banking up the fire, she drew her sabre and honed the edge with a whetstone. Outside the light was failing fast. Sigarni hooked her quiver of arrows over her shoulder and kept the bow close at hand.

Will it be like last time, she wondered? Will the man in red come first? And if he does, how many creatures of the dark will be with him? How many had been back at the cabin on that awful day? One? Two? More? How could she tell? Father had been struck first. Perhaps it was the same creature which slew her mother.

Sigarni had made plans for three.

The wind was building outside, and flurries of snow were blowing into the cave-mouth. A distant wolf howled. The fire crackled and spat and Sigarni knocked a burning cinder from her leggings. Feeling drowsy, she took up her bow and walked to the mouth of the cave, drawing a deep, cold breaths. How long since you slept? Too long, she realized. If they did not come tonight, she would catch a few hours after dawn.

Perhaps they won't find me here, she thought suddenly. Perhaps I am safe.

The moon shone in a cloudless sky, but the wind continued to blow flurries of snow across the frozen pool, rising like a white mist and sparkling in the moonlight. The air was cold against her face, but she could just feel the warmth of the fire behind her.

Alone in the wilderness of white Sigarni found herself thinking of her life, and the great joys she had known. It saddened her that she had not appreciated those joys when she had them; those glorious golden days with Abby and Lady, walking the high country without a care. Recalling them was a strange experience, as if she was looking through a window on to the life of a twin. And she wondered about the white-haired girl she could remember. How could she have lived in such a carefree manner?

Her thoughts roved on, and Bernt's sweet face appeared from nowhere. Sigarni felt a swelling in her throat and her eyes misted. He had loved her. Truly, loved her. How callous she had been. *Is this all a punishment for my treatment of you, Bernt? Is God angry with me?* There was no way of knowing. *If it is, I will bear it.*

A white owl swooped over the trees – silent killer, silent flight. Sigarni remembered the first time she had seen such a creature. After the murder of her parents she had lived with old Gwalchmai. He had walked her through the woods on many a night, educating her to the habits of the nocturnal creatures of the forest. The old drunkard had proved a fine foster-father, restricting his drinking to when Sigarni was asleep.

Sigarni sighed. Only a few short months ago she had been a wilful and selfish woman, revelling in her freedom. Now she was the leader of a fledgling army with little hope of survival.

Survival? She shivered. *Will you survive the night?*

Weariness sat upon her like a boulder, but the bow felt good in her hands. I am not a child now, she thought, running from peril. I am Sigarni the Huntress, and those who come for me do so at the risk of their lives.

Moving back into the cave, she added two large chunks of dead wood to the fire, then returned to the entrance.

190

Doubts blossomed constantly. *Your father was a great fighter, but he lasted only a few heartbeats.*

'He did not know they were coming,' she said, aloud. 'He was not prepared.'

How can you prepare against demons of the dark?

'They have flesh, even if they cannot be seen. Flesh can be cut.'

Fear rose like a fire in her belly, and she allowed the flames to flicker. Fear is life, fear is caution, she told herself.

You are a woman alone!

'I am a Highlander and a hunter. I am of the blood of heroes, and they will not bring me to despair and panic. They will *not*!'

A silver fox moved out into the open and padded across to the poolside. 'Hola!' shouted Sigarni. The noise startled the beast and it leapt out on to the ice and ran across the pool. As it reached the centre it swerved to the left, then raced to the other side. Sigarni's eyes narrowed. Why had it swerved? What did it see? Whatever it was remained invisible within the snow mist. Sigarni ran back to the fire; it was still warm. Notching an arrow to her short hunting bow, she returned to the cave-mouth and waited.

Long minutes passed. Then he appeared, walking with care upon the ice. He was not as tall as she remembered, but then she had only looked upon him with the eyes of a child. Shorter than Fell, he was a stocky man, his belly straining at the red leather coat he wore. His hair was black, close-cropped, silver at the temples, his face fleshy and round. His leggings and boots were red, as was the ankle-length cloak he wore.

Sigarni drew back the bow-string, took careful aim, and waited as he approached. The man saw her, and continued to move closer. Forty feet, thirty. He looked up and smiled. Sigarni let fly and the arrow flashed through the air. He raised his hand and the shaft burst into flame. She notched another.

'Don't waste your energy, child,' he said, his voice surprisingly light and pleasant. 'This is the day you die – and move on to worlds undreamed of. Great adventures await you. Accept your destiny with joy!'

The temperature in the cave plummeted. Something moved behind her . . . instantly Sigarni leapt out and ran to the right, toward a gentle, tree-covered slope. She did not look back, keeping her eyes to the trail. Halfway up the slope she suddenly twisted to the right once more, cutting behind a snow-covered screen of low bushes. The moonlight was bright and she stared at the snow, and the footprints she had left behind.

Alongside them now she saw other footprints, huge and appearing as if by magic. They were moving inexorably towards her at great speed. Drawing back the bow-string, she aimed high and released the shaft. It travelled no more than twenty feet before stopping suddenly, half of its length disappearing. A terrible screech sounded, and she saw dark blood pumping out around the arrow. She loosed a second. This too thudded home into her invisible assailant. 'Come on, you whoreson!' shouted Sigarni. The creature roared and charged, much faster now, smashing aside the screen of bushes. An invisible leg punched against a hidden length of twine, dislodging the slip ring and springing the toggle. Released from tension, a spear-thick sapling whiplashed back into a vertical position. The three sharpened stakes bound to it, each more than a foot long, plunged into the creature's chest. It thrashed and screamed. The sapling was snapped, but the stakes remained embedded in the invisible flesh. Then it fell and the roaring faded to a low moan. This too died away.

Sigarni did not wait for the death throes, and was already running as the trap was sprung. Angling across the fresh-fallen snow she ran up the slope, cutting to the left until she was just below the crest of the hill. There were no trees or bushes close by. Dropping to her knees, she notched an arrow and waited.

No more than a few heartbeats passed before she saw first one, then two sets of footprints being stamped into the snow. Anger flared in her, fuelling her determination. The closest of the creatures struck the first trip-wire. As the trigger bar was dislodged the rough-made long-bow hidden beneath a snow-covered lattice of thin branches released its deadly missile. Four feet long, the sharpened stick had been barbed all along its length. It slammed into the first creature at what to Sigarni appeared to be lower belly height. She had no time to revel in the strike, for the second creature was almost upon her.

The second hidden bow loosed its deadly shaft – and missed!

With no time to shoot, Sigarni dropped the bow and took a running dive down the hill, landing on her shoulder and rolling headlong towards the lake. Halfway down she felt her sabre snap, then belt and scabbard tore free. Sigarni staggered to her feet. There was one more trap, but it was some way to the left of the cave.

Too far.

Spinning round, she saw the terrifying footprints closing in on her right. A low sound came from the left. Sigarni ducked down – just as talons ripped into her shoulder. The silver chainmail she wore stopped her flesh being ripped from her bone, but even so she was picked up and hurled ten feet through the air, landing hard on the snow-covered ice pool.

Both creatures now made their way after her.

Sigarni pushed herself upright and began to run. She had one hope now – perhaps the ice at the pool's centre would not support the weight of the beasts pursuing her.

The creatures were closing on her and Sigarni could hear the pounding of their taloned feet upon the ice. The sabre was gone, but she still had her knife.

Damned if I'll die running, she thought. Skidding to a stop, she drew the hunting knife and spun to face them. The swirling snow highlighted their bulk, plastering against the skin of their chests and bellies. In the moonlight they appeared as hairless bears. Flipping the knife and taking the blade in her hand, 'Bite on this, you ugly bastard!' she yelled, hurling the weapon with all her might. The point lanced home in the belly of the first; she saw its head go back and a terrible cry of pain and rage echoed in the mountains.

The creature took two steps forward, then fell to the ice. The last of them closed in on Sigarni . . . and stopped.

An eerie glow was enveloping it now, faint and golden. It was indeed a hairless bear, though the head was round, the ears and nose humanoid. The beast's eyes were large, and slitted like a great cat. Malevolence shone in the creature's golden gaze as it stood blinking in the strange light.

'Kill her!' shouted the man in red, beginning to run across the ice. 'Kill her!'

The noise caused the creature to jerk its head. It blinked, then focused again on Sigarni. Thin lips drew back to expose a set of sharp teeth. Long arms came up, talons gleaming in the moonlight.

'Step aside, girl,' came a calm voice. Sigarni scrambled back.

The glowing figure of Ironhand was standing before the creature now, a two-handed sword held ready. He was translucent and shimmering, and Sigarni could not believe such an insubstantial figure could hold back the power of the beast. As the creature growled and leapt, the golden-lit sword flashed out, cleaving through the huge chest. There was no blood, and no visible wound. But the demon tottered back and then sank into the ice.

The red-garbed wizard looked horror-struck as the last of the beasts fell. Ironhand swung to him. 'It's been a long time, Jakuta,' he said.

'You can't hurt me. You might be able to slay a demon's soul – but you cannot harm the living!'

'Indeed I cannot. Nor will I have to. Is this not the third time you have tried to steal Sigarni's soul? And where is your familiar?'

The wizard blanched. Slowly he drew a wickedly curved dagger. 'There is still time,' he said. 'She cannot stand against me.'

'There is no time, Jakuta,' Ironhand told him. 'I can see them now!'

The wizard spun. Heavy footprints were thumping down in the snow. Scores of them . . .

Dropping his knife, the wizard began to run. Sigarni saw him make fewer than twenty paces before his body was lifted into the air. His arms and legs were torn from him and his screams were awful to hear. They were cut off abruptly as his head rolled to the ice.

'You should have called upon me,' Ironhand told the stunned woman.

'I needed to fight them alone,' she said.

'I would expect no less from Ironhand's daughter,' he told her.

Just as the dawn light crept over the mountains a tiny pocket of darkness opened like a black teardrop on the hillside overlooking the frozen falls. Taliesen stepped from it, leading a blindfolded

Ballistar. As his feet touched the snow-covered earth Ballistar collapsed to the ground, trembling. Tearing loose the blindfold, he blinked in the light. Taliesen gave a dry chuckle. 'I told you the way would not be to your liking,' he said.

'Sweet Heaven,' whispered the dwarf. 'What kind of beasts made the noises I heard?'

'You do not wish to know,' said Taliesen. 'Now let us find Sigarni, for I am already growing cold.'

'Wait!' ordered the dwarf, pushing himself to his feet and brushing snow from his leggings.

'What now?'

'There are traps set,' Ballistar told him. 'She did not come here to hide – she came to fight. Now give me a moment to gather my wits, and I will lead you to her.'

'There may be no need,' said Taliesen softly, pointing to the ice-covered pool. Ballistar saw the patches of blood smeared across the ice. He and Taliesen moved carefully down the slope. Then the dwarf spotted what appeared to be two boulders close to the centre of the pool. 'Atrolls,' said Taliesen. 'Creatures of the First Pit.'

A severed human leg was half buried in snow. Taliesen tugged it clear. The boot was still in place. 'Not hers,' said the wizard. 'That is promising.' Ballistar backed away from the grisly find – and stepped on a human hand.

'Dear god, what happened here?' he said.

'Aha!' hissed Taliesen, finding the head of Jakuta Khan. Lifting it by the ears, he brought it up until he could look into the grey corpse face. 'Well, well,' he said. 'Come to me, Jakuta!'

The corpse eyes flipped open, and blinked twice. The mouth began to move, but there were no sounds. 'No good trying to speak, my boy,' said Taliesen, with a cruel smile. 'You have no throat. I take it I called you back from your torment. It must be so very terrible. Are they still hunting you? Of course they are.' Ballistar saw tears form in the sunken eyes. 'Well, I can help you there, Jakuta. Would you prefer your spirit to live for a while in this hapless skull, free from terror? You would?' Gently he laid the head upon the ice, then spoke in a harsh tongue unknown to Ballistar.

The ice around the severed head began to melt away. Taliesen knelt by it. 'As long as there is still flesh upon the skull you will be safe here, Jakuta. But when the fishes have stripped it away, you will return to the pit.' The ice gave, the head falling into the cold water beneath as Taliesen stood.

'How was it still alive?' asked Ballistar.

'I called him back. I fear his stay will be brief.'

'It was terribly cruel.'

Taliesen laughed. 'Cruel? You have no idea of what he suffered where he was. He called upon the creatures of the Pit for help – and failed them. Now he dwells with them in perpetual torment. I have given him a short respite from that.'

'At the bottom of an ice lake. How kind you are!' sneered Ballistar.

'I never claimed to be kind. I am certainly not disposed towards mercy for such as he. Jakuta Khan caused the death of Ironhand and destroyed a dynasty that might have changed the course of our history. He did it for profit, for greed. Now he pays. You want me to grieve for him, dwarf?'

Ballistar nodded. 'Yes, that would be good. For in what way are you different from him, Taliesen? You delight in his suffering and you add to his torment. Is that not evil?'

Taliesen's eyes narrowed. 'Who are you, dwarf, to lecture me? I have fought evil for ten times your lifetime. Even now in my own land the ancestors of these Outlanders are waging a war that will see hundreds, perhaps thousands, of my people die. What pity I have is for them. And there is nothing that I would not do to save them. Now, find me the woman!'

Ballistar swung away from him and walked back across the ice. With care he climbed the slope before the cave, feeling his way forward. 'For the sake of Heaven!' hissed Taliesen. 'Why the delay? I am freezing to death out here!' Ballistar ignored him. Some way to the left he halted, his hands burrowing into the snow. 'What now?' asked Taliesen, exasperated.

There was a sharp hiss, then a sapling reared upright, whiplash-ing back and forth. Three sharpened stakes were bound to it. 'It is a pig spear-trap,' said Ballistar, 'but angled to strike high. The twine is connected to a ring at the end of the trip-wire . . .'

'Yes, yes, I need no instruction. Are there more?'

'We will see,' said Ballistar. The cave was no more than forty feet away, yet it took the two men almost half an hour to reach it. Taliesen was the first inside, where Sigarni was sleeping by a dying fire. The wizard sat down beside her.

Satisfied that she was alive, Ballistar walked away. 'Where are you going?'

'There may be more traps. I don't want some unsuspecting traveller to spring one.'

Outside the dwarf took several deep breaths. His relief was almost palpable: Sigarni was alive! Ballistar stood for a moment scanning the area. To the right he could see a huge grey corpse, two arrows in its chest and three stakes in its back. One trap. On the hillside there was another body.

Ballistar trudged out towards it.

For two hours he searched the land around the pool. There were no more traps. Returning to the cave he found Sigarni still asleep, with the wizard dozing beside her. Taliesen awoke as he entered. 'Four creatures were killed,' said the dwarf, squatting by the fire and extending his hands to the heat. One had a dagger in its heart, one was slain by a pig spear-trap, the third by a lance-arrow. There was no mark on the fourth.'

'She did well,' agreed the sorcerer.

'How did she pierce their skin?' asked Ballistar. 'I could not pull her dagger free. It was as if it was embedded in stone.'

'It was,' said Taliesen. 'You have seen the corpses of men stiffen in death?' Ballistar nodded. 'With the Atrolls it is many times as powerful. The corpses turn grey, like rocks, then within a few days they putrefy and disappear. Even the bones rot.'

'Will more come?'

'It is unlikely, though not impossible. Jakuta pursued Sigarni through the Gateways of Time. He had to, for his soul was pledged against her death. I know of no other sorcerer hunting her.'

'Why did he seek her?'

'Perhaps she will tell you that when she wakes,' said Taliesen. 'And now I am tired. I shall sleep. Be so kind as to fetch wood and keep the fire blazing.'

Sigarni stood on the battlements, staring out over the flanks of the mountains and the distant peak of High Druin. Ironhand stood beside her, his huge hand on her shoulder. Moonlight glistened on his braided silver beard, and shone from his silver chainmail and breastplate. She felt power radiating from him, encompassing her, bathing her in its warmth. 'Where are we?' she asked.

'You mean you don't recognize it?' he said, mystified. 'I'm sure that I have created it perfectly. Perhaps you need to see it from the outside?'

'I know this area,' she told him. 'There is nothing here save a few wooded hills.'

'That cannot be!' he said, his hand of red iron sweeping out to encompass the hills. 'This is my stronghold of Al-Druin. It was here that I fought the Four Armies, and slew their champion, Grayle.' Sigarni saw the sadness in his eyes.

'I'm sorry, Ironhand. I have travelled these hills all my life. There are some broken stones that show there was once a large dwelling place here. But it is long gone. And not even the eldest of the Loda know what stood here.'

'Ah well,' he said, turning from the parapet, 'it is . . . was . . . merely stone. And at least you can see it now. Come inside and we will talk. I have a fire prepared; it will offer no heat, but is pretty to look upon.' The scene shimmered and Sigarni found herself in a rectangular room, velvet curtains covering the high windows. A log fire blazed in the hearth but, as Ironhand predicted, it burned without heat.

'How is it done?' she asked, running her hand through the flames.

'Here all is illusion. We are spirits, you and I.' The giant warrior, clad now in a simple tunic of green, with soft leather troos, sat himself down in a deep chair. Sigarni seated herself on the bearskin rug before the fire. 'It took a long time to learn how to do all this,'

198

he said, waving his hand to encompass the room. 'I do not know how long, for there is no sense of the passage of time. To me it was an eternity. Now it is the only home I know – save for the pool by the Falls where my body lies.' Sigarni sat silently, aware that his sorrow was great. 'Ironhand's Falls. It is a beautiful place,' he continued, forcing a smile. 'A man could choose far worse for his death. During the centuries I have watched the trees grow and die in that wondrous cycle of birth, growth and death. People too – hunters, wanderers, tinkers, clansmen, foreign soldiers. And I saw you, Sigarni, diving from the edge of the Falls, straight as an arrow. I was there when you found my bones. But I could not speak, for you were not ready to listen. You can have no idea how good it is to speak to another soul.'

'Are there no others here?' she asked.

'No, not now. This is my world, the silent kingdom of Ironhand. Others have come, demons and evil spirits. I slew them, and now the others avoid my . . . lands.'

'You must be lonely.'

He nodded. 'I hope you will never know how much. I would give anything – accept the darkness and solitude of the true grave for just one hour in your mother's company. It is not yet to be. I can accept that.'

'My mother?' asked Sigarni. 'You knew her?'

'Did you not listen to me back at the pool? You are my daughter, Sigarni. Your mother was my wife, Elarine. I see her in you, the same strength of purpose, the same pride.'

'But you lived hundreds and hundreds of years ago. I can't be your daughter! It is not possible! I knew my mother and father – lived with them until they were slain.'

'For all my faults, Sigarni, I was never a liar. Not in life, and certainly not in death. You were born in the last year of my life, when enemies I thought were friends were meeting in secret with plans to destroy me. When I did learn of their plans I urged Elarine to run, to cross the water. She would not.' He smiled at the memory. '"We will fight them," she said. "We will conquer once more." I tried. My wizards were slain, all mystic protection lost to me. That was the work of Jakuta Khan. I tried to reach Elarine, but the assassins trapped me at the Falls. I died there. Elarine died at Kashar. I learned this from Taliesen, when he summoned my spirit to the Falls. You were a babe then. He and Caswallon carried you through a Gateway and left you with your *new* parents: a fine couple, unable to have children of their own. Taliesen disguised you, changing the colour of your hair.' Reaching out, he stroked her head. 'All our family are born with silver hair. We took it as a sign of greatness. Perhaps that was arrogance. Perhaps not. We did become kings, after all. And not one foreign enemy ever brought us low.'

'How did my mother die?' asked Sigarni. 'Did Taliesen tell you this?'

'Aye, he told me. She had a sabre in her hand, the blood of the enemy staining it. And as she died she cursed them.' He rose and turned away from her, a tall man of immense power and even stronger grief. His head was bowed and Sigarni went to him taking his hand in hers.

'Why are you here?' asked Sigarni tenderly. 'Why not in paradise, or wherever it is that heroes go?'

He smiled. 'I had to wait, Sigarni. I made a promise, a sacred oath, that I would come again when my people needed me. I have felt the desire to quit this place many times, seen the far light shining. But I will not travel the swans' path until the time is right.'

'Perhaps she waits for you there, Elarine.'

'Aye, I have thought of that often. But I never made a promise I did not fight to keep. Now that promise is upon me. For you are the heir to Ironhand, you are the hope of the Highlands.'

'But how can you help me?' she asked. 'You are a spirit, a ghost. What can you do within the world of men?'

'Nothing,' he admitted. 'But you can. And I shall continue to teach you what it means to be a king. I will recreate battles for you, and you shall see how they are fought and won. I will show you my life, the traitors and the friends, the good and the deceitful, the brave and the unmanly. All of this and more you will experience here.'

'How long will this take?'

'As before, you could be with me for what seems like years, yet when you awake only a single night will have passed. Trust me, my daughter. When you return you will be closer to the warrior queen they have longed for.'

'I forgot much of what passed between us before. In the true world all this will seem a hazy dream.'

'The knowledge will be there,' he said. 'As it was at Cilfallen.'

'That was your doing?'

Ironhand shook his head and led her back to the fire. 'Not at all. It was you! What I did was to open your mind to the ways of war. I never lost a battle, Sigarni, for when forced to fight I was always prepared with lines of retreat and secondary plans. And I understood the importance of *speed* – of thought, of action. You have a fast mind, and great courage. You will teach your enemies to fear you.'

'We have a very small army,' said Sigarni. 'The enemy is large, well disciplined, and used to the ways of war.'

'Aye, it was the same with me, at the very beginning. There is, however, an advantage in such a situation. An army is like a man. It needs a head, and a heart, two good arms, two sound legs. It requires a strong belly and a solid backbone. Now, while it is yet small, is the time to lay the foundations of your force.'

'Which is the leader,' asked Sigarni, 'the head or the heart?'

He chuckled. 'Neither. He – or in this case *she* – must be the soul. Take heed, my daughter. Choose your men with great care, for some will be exceptional when commanding small forces, less capable with larger groups. Others will seem too cautious, yet when the swords are drawn will fight like devils.'

'And how do I know which to choose?'

'Honour your instincts, and never cease to be vigilant. You can read a general by the attitudes of his men. They may fear him or love him – that is generally of no consequence. Look at their discipline. See how fast or how badly they react. The men are merely an extension of the captain commanding them.'

'How then does the *soul* operate?'

'The head suggests the plans, the heart gives men spirit, the backbone gives them strength, the belly gives them confidence.

The soul gives them the *cause* to fight for. Men will fight well for loot and plunder, for pride and honour. But when the *cause* is perceived as noble they will fight like demi-gods.'

Sigarni sighed. 'All this I can understand. But when the war starts I cannot keep travelling to the Falls to speak with you, to ask your advice. I will be alone then, and my lack of experience could condemn us all.'

'I cannot be with you always, Sigarni, for this is your world and your time. When the spring comes, dive once more into the pool and swim to where my bones rest. Take one small fragment and keep it with you. Then you may call upon me and I will be with you. Let no one know of this, and never speak to me unless you are alone. Now let us begin with your lessons.'

Fell was tired, his spirits low as he stood in the new long hut, watching Sigarni discussing tactics and strategies with Asmidir, Obrin, Tovi and Grame. The Pallides man, Loran, was present, sitting quietly, offering nothing but listening intently. Beside him was the colossal Mereth. Gwyn Dark-eye, Bakris Tooth-gone and other group leaders were also seated on the floor before Sigarni, who occupied the only chair. In all there were close to forty people present. It seemed to Fell that the meeting was drifting aimlessly, yet Sigarni seemed unperturbed. Some were for storming the three Outland forts, others for sending raiding parties into the Lowlands. Voice after voice was raised in the debate, often resulting in petty arguments.

Fell soon became oblivious to it all, allowing the sound to wash over him. Tired, he sat with his back to the wall, resting his head against the wood. The late summer seemed so far away now, when he had travelled to Sigarni's cabin to have his wound stitched. Her beauty had dazzled him, and left a heaviness in his heart that would not ease. She was so different now, tense as a bow-string, her eyes cold and distant. She no longer laughed, and gone was the lightness of heart and the carefree joy she once exhibited. Now she kept a distance from her followers, allowing no man to come close. A week before Fell had been explaining some of the logistical problems to her and had touched her arm. Sigarni had drawn back as if stung. She had said nothing, but had moved further away from him. Though hurt by it, Fell saw that he was not the only man to affect Sigarni in the same way. No one could approach within touching distance of her, save the dwarf. He would sit at her feet, as he was doing now.

Fell rubbed his bloodshot eyes. Food was running low. There had not been enough salt to preserve all the meat, and much of it was now bad. The only cattle left were breeding stock, and to kill these would cause great grief among the clan, and ensure future famine. It had been bad enough slaughtering all the others. Grown men had wept at the loss. All cattlemen understood the need of the winter cull, for there was not enough fodder gathered to feed all the animals through this hardest of seasons. But to lose all the hay meant the destruction of whole herds, the loss of prize bulls which were the result of generations of breeding.

The period of late midwinter was always a time of hardship, when the milk cows dried and the meat was all but gone. This year would be ten times worse, and it would be followed by a terrible war.

Fell drifted into a troubled sleep, only to be awoken by the sounds of men pushing themselves to their feet. Cold air touched him as the doors were pushed open and the forester struggled to his feet, dizzy and disoriented. Loran, Asmidir, Obrin, Tovi and Grame all remained behind, as did Ballistar. Fell decided to leave them to it and moved to the door, but Sigarni called him back. 'I need some sleep,' he said.

'You can sleep later,' she told him, then turned to the others. Fell walked to where they all sat and joined them. Sigarni stood. 'Obrin has now appointed twenty-five group leaders,' she said. 'It is therefore time for our warriors to know the structure of our leadership. There will be two wings in the army. Grame will lead one, and Fell the other. Obrin will retain responsibility for training, and will also captain a third and smaller force; the role of this third force I will discuss with you later. Tovi, you will relinquish the role of Hunt Lord, passing it to me. From that moment you will remain in charge of all supplies, the gathering of food and its distribution; you will liaise with Loran. Later you will have a second role, and that we will discuss tomorrow.'

Fell glanced at the former baker, and saw that his face had grown pale. Tovi had worked as hard as any during and after the exodus from Loda lands. To lose his role as Hunt Lord was bitterly hard, and would be seen as a humiliation. No one spoke. All waited for Tovi's reaction.

The man pushed himself to his feet and walked slowly from the building. As the door closed Fell spoke. 'That was not right,' he said. 'It was cold cruelty and the man deserved more than that.'

'Deserve?' countered Sigarni. 'Did his son deserve to die? Do the Loda deserve to be living in the mountains as beggars, their homes destroyed? Did I deserve . . . ?' Abruptly Sigarni returned to her seat, and Fell could see her struggling to control her anger. 'The decision is made,' she said at last. 'The left and right wings of the army will be led by you and Grame. Obrin will select your groups tomorrow; discuss the dispositions with him. Once your wings are organized you will work with them, testing your officers, and if necessary promoting others.'

'Does Asmidir have no role?' asked Fell. 'I understood he was once a general.'

'He will advise me. Now the hour is late, and as you said, Fell, you are in need of sleep. We will meet here tomorrow night, and then I will tell you of Obrin's force and what they must do.'

The men rose to their feet and walked from the room, leaving only Obrin with Sigarni.

Fell stepped into the moonlight, Grame beside him. The white-bearded smith clapped him on the shoulder. 'Do not be so down-hearted, general,' he said. 'If Tovi is honest he will admit to his relief. His heart is not in war.'

'It would have been more kind had she spoken to him alone.'

The smith nodded. 'She's been through the fire, boy, and it does tend to burn away softness. And she'll need to be harder yet, if the Loda are to survive.'

'Those words should be chiselled in stone,' said Asmidir softly, from behind them. The two clansmen said nothing. Neither was comfortable in the presence of the black man. He smiled and shook his head, then politely bade them good night and headed for his own small hut.

'I don't like that man,' said Grame.

'He can be trusted,' said Ballistar, from where he was standing unnoticed by the door. 'I'd stake my life on it.'

'I didn't say he couldn't be *trusted*, little man. I just don't like him; there's no heart in him.'

Snow began to fall once more and the bitter wind came down from the north. Fell pulled his cloak around his shoulders. 'I'm for sleep,' he said. 'I feel like I haven't closed my eyes since autumn.'

'I'll stay up for a while yet,' said Grame. 'She gave us much to think about.' He grinned at Ballistar. 'I still have a jug of Gwalchmai's throat burner. You're welcome to a dram.'

Ballistar chuckled. 'Just the one, mind.'

Fell left them and wandered away.

Obrin's anger was hard to contain as he stood before Sigarni. 'If you want me to die, why not just ask one of your soldiers to do it? Or you could cut my throat now!'

'I am not looking for you to die, Outlander.' The coldness of her tone only served to inflame him further.

Obrin forced a laugh. 'Come now, lady, there's no one else here. I see the way you look at me: loathing and hatred. You think I've never seen it before? What I don't understand is why you'd want to send a hundred of your own men to die with me.'

'Are you finished?' stormed Sigarni, rising from her chair. 'Or have you still some whining to do?' She stood directly before him, her eyes blazing. 'You are entirely correct in your assessment of my feelings towards you. Perhaps towards all men, including clansmen. There is no room in my heart for love. No room. In less than twelve weeks an army will descend on these mountains, and I *must* have a force to oppose them. Not only that, but they must be denied supplies. They have three forts built deep into our territory – tell me what they contain?'

'You know the answer.'

'Tell me. *Exactly!*'

'Food and supplies, weapons – bows, arrows, lances, swords, helms. But more importantly they each contain one hundred fighting men, and are impregnable against all but a huge encircling force. The palisade walls are twenty-five feet high, the entrance guarded by drop-gates. Any force approaching would be open to bowshot for one hundred paces all around the fort. Once they arrived they would have to scale the walls. I've done that, lady, and I can tell you that a man with a good sword can kill twenty men scaling. You can't defend yourself when you're scrambling up a rope.'

'I am not asking you to scramble up ropes, Obrin. I did not ask you to *assault* the fort on Farlain land. I said you were to *take* it. Now will you listen to my plan?'

'I'm listening,' he said, 'but I spent half my life building those damned forts. I know what goes into their construction.'

'I want you to ride up to the drop-gate, with your hundred men, and I want you to relieve the defenders of their command.'

Obrin's jaw dropped. 'Relieve? What are you talking about?'

'When we were both at Asmidir's home I asked you about the forts. You said the men who manned them would expect to serve no more than two months, then a relief force would arrive.'

'But the snow? There's no way through those southern passes.'

'They won't know that, will they? You are a former officer . . .'

'Sergeant,' he corrected.

'Whatever!' she snapped. 'Some of them may know you and that is good. They have been trapped in those forts and will have no knowledge of your . . . change of loyalty. We still have the weapons, and what passed for uniforms, of the mercenaries who attacked Cilfallen. We also have the horses. I want you to choose a hundred men and take over the Farlain fort.'

He said nothing for a moment, his mind racing. They *would* be hoping for a relief force. Most of the men would be thinking about the Midwinter celebrations in Citadel, the parties, the dancing, the women. 'It's a fine idea,' he said, 'but I should be carrying sealed orders from the Baron. Without them no officer will turn over his command.'

Sigarni returned to her seat, and he could see her pondering his words. 'Discipline,' she said softly. 'Orders and rules.' She nodded. 'Tell me this, Obrin, what would happen if a *verbal* order reached a commander and, when refusing to obey it, the Baron's plans were thrown into chaos? Would the Baron merely congratulate the commander on holding to the rules?'

'It is not quite that easy,' replied Obrin. 'In that situation the Baron would have the man flogged or hanged for not acting on his own initiative. But if the commander did obey the verbal order, and then failed, he would still be blamed for not holding fast to the regulations.'

'I see,' said Sigarni. 'Then you will ride to the Farlain fort with only . . . say . . . eighty-five men. Get some bandages soaked in cattle blood and disguise some of your men as wounded. You will ride to the fort and tell the commander that your officer was slain, and that you are the relief force. You will say that the Pallides fort is under attack and that the Baron has ordered the commander to reinforce it.'

'But there are no sealed orders!'

'You will tell him that when you were surrounded your officer, thinking all was lost, destroyed the orders so that the enemy would not see them. Then a blizzard broke and you were able to lead your men to safety.'

'He won't relinquish the fort,' said Obrin stubbornly. 'You have to understand the officer mentality.'

'Oh, I think I understand it, Obrin. Hear me out. The commander will be caught on twin horns. If he disobeys an order you tell him was issued by the Baron and the Pallides fort falls, he will be hanged or flogged. If he obeys and everything goes wrong, he will be asked why he did not follow the rules and remain where he was.'

'Exactly,' said Obrin.

'Then, as a good sergeant, you will help him. You will offer to lead the rescue of the Pallides fort. That way he has not disobeyed an order, and he has not left his post.'

'Aye,' said Obrin slowly. 'He might go for such a plan. But where does that leave us? I'll be riding out again with my men.'

'No, *his* men. You will explain that your forces are exhausted, whereas his are fresh.'

'So I ride out with a hundred enemy soldiers behind me? What then?'

'You lead them into an ambush. Grame will tell you where.'

Obrin stared hard at the tall young woman. Her face, though beautiful, was emotionless, the eyes cold now and cruel. 'You are a canny woman, Sigarni,' he said. 'It has a good chance of success.'

'Make it succeed,' she urged him. 'I need those supplies and weapons. More importantly, I need to deny them to the Baron.'

'I can understand that, lady, but why that fort? The Pallides is closer. Even if we do take the Farlain fort we have a great distance to cover carrying the supplies back here, much of it over rough country.'

'You will take all three forts,' she assured him. 'The Farlain will be first. And you will not carry the supplies far – only to Torgan's town. Then you will move on to the others. Now get some rest and be here tomorrow at dawn with Grame and Tovi.'

Obrin bowed and walked out into the night. He could hear the sounds of laughter from Grame's hut, but elsewhere all was quiet.

She was canny all right. Not only would the plan – if it succeeded – ease the food shortage, and rob the Baron of spring supplies, but it would also impress the Farlain, who had lost scores of men in useless assaults on the fortification. And the chances of success, he knew, were high indeed. Sigarni was using the enemy's great strength against them. Discipline. Blind obedience.

Who would have thought that an untutored clans-woman could have such a devious mind?

'All women have devious minds,' he said, aloud. 'It's why I never wed.'

Sigarni rapped on the door of the small hut. 'Who's there?' called Tovi. Stepping inside, she saw the Hunt Lord sitting by an open fire. He glanced up as she entered. 'How did you find me?' he asked.

'Kollarin has a talent for these matters. Why are you not with your family?'

'I need time to think.'

Sigarni sat down opposite the man. 'You are angry.'

'What do you expect? I know I was a better baker than a Hunt Lord, but I have done my best since the attack. I could do no more.'

'I do not ask for more,' said Sigarni. 'I need your skills in other areas.'

'What skills?' he asked bitterly. 'You want me to bake bread for you? I can do that. Just build me an oven.'

'Yes, I want bread,' she said softly. 'I want the people fed. Battles alone will not win us this war, Tovi. Once we have defeated the first Outland army we will need to move from defence to attack and that means invading the Lowlands. The army will need to be supplied with food. We will need mercenaries, and that means we must have gold; a treasury. Our forces will be spread, and that requires lines of communication. You understand? The role I need you for will stretch your talents to the limit. You will have no time for other burdens.'

'Why could you not say this in front of the others? Why did I need to suffer humiliation, Sigarni?'

She looked at the older man, saw the hurt in his eyes. 'They did not need to know my plans. There are hard days coming, Tovi. Some of the men in that room will die in our cause: they may even be captured and tortured. Worse, one or more of them will seek to betray us. What I say to you here is not to be repeated.'

'I may be captured and tortured,' he pointed out.

'It is unlikely, for you will not be fighting.'

'You deny me even that? A chance for revenge, to restore the honour of my family?'

'Listen to me! What is more important, that you drive your claymore into one enemy heart, or your skills bring down a thousand? You are vital to me, Tovi. You have a feel for organization, and a mind that can cope with a score of problems simultaneously. I have seen those talents here, in the four encampments. Few could have achieved what you have. When the war comes I will need your skills.'

He laughed and scratched his beard. 'Here we sit with a tiny force made up of many old men and young lads, and you speak of invading the Lowlands! Better still, I believe you when you speak of it. What has happened to you, Sigarni? From where do these ideas spring?'

'From my blood, Tovi.'

'All these years I have watched you, and never seen you. When you were a child you used to hide behind my bakery and wait until I stepped out at the front for a breath of air. Fast as a hawk, you would sprint inside to steal a cake – just the one from the middle of the tray, then you would push the others together, disguising the gap.'

'You knew?'

'I knew. You hid behind the water barrel.'

'How did you know?'

'Lemon mint. Gwalchmai always loved that scent and you used to rub the leaves over your body when you bathed. Every time I stepped back inside I could smell lemon mint.'

'You never caught me,' she said softly.

He shrugged. 'I never wanted to. You were a child of sorrow, Sigarni. Everyone loved you. And I could spare a morsel on Cake Day.'

Sigarni fed some wood to the fire and they sat in companionable silence for a while. 'I am not that child any longer,' she said.

'I know. Yet she is still there, deep down inside. She will always be there.' He sighed, then smiled. 'I will serve you, Sigarni, in any way that you want me.'

'Thank you, Tovi,' she said, her voice tender. 'For this – and for the cakes.' Rising smoothly, she moved to the door. 'Be at the log hall at dawn.'

'Why?'

'Because I need you there,' she said.

10

Torgan's mood was not enhanced by the news from his scouts that the Loda woman was riding towards the town. At first the people of the Farlain had talked of little else – how strong she was, now noble she looked, how brave. Torgan had fast become heartily sick of it. That was why he had led his rash raid on the Outlanders, to prove that *he* was the natural leader of the clans. It might have worked too, save for the craven tactics of the enemy, drawing back and then loosing cavalry upon him. Had they stood and fought like men he was sure the Farlain warriors would have cut them to pieces. After that he had led two spectacularly unsuccessful attacks on their fort. Another forty men had been struck by arrows; seven had died.

Now the Farlain were talking about Sigarni once more, how she had supposedly killed demons sent against her, and how successful *she* had been against the Outlanders at Cilfallen. God, could they not see what she was? Just a Loda whore in pretty armour! There was little doubt in Torgan's mind that the battle at Cilfallen had been masterminded by the black-skinned bastard who rode with her. Rode with her? Rode her, more like!

Now she was coming here again.

This time I'll make her humiliation complete, he thought.

His wife, Layelia, entered the room, bearing a cup of sweet tisane. He took it without a word and sipped it. Layelia did not depart, but stood staring at him. He looked up into her large, soft brown eyes. 'What?' he asked, gruffly.

'She is coming,' said his wife.

I know that. I'll deal with her.'

'Are you sure you are in the right?'

'What is that supposed to mean?' he snapped. She flinched, which pleased him. A woman should know her place.

I've heard talk that she *is* the chosen one. Carela told me . . .'

'I'm not interested in women's gossip, Layelia. And I've heard enough!'

For a moment he thought she would stand her ground, but she bowed her head and left him alone once more. Torgan ran his hand over his close-cropped back hair. The bald spot was growing on the crown and his widow's peak was becoming more pronounced by the day. He swore softly. Why should he alone of his family lose his hair? His father had a shock of white hair, like a lion's mane, until the day he died at eighty.

Torgan threw his cloak around his shoulders and stepped out into the winter sunlight. It was bright, the day clear and cold. He could see the Loda woman in the distance. The black man was not with her, but there were a dozen or so riders following her as she made her way down the long slope. More people were on the streets than was normal for this time of day. They were making their way to the square, ready to hear the whore's words.

Torgan strode out, looking to neither left nor right. His chair had been set at the centre of the square, his lieutenants were already standing beside it. This time there was no Neren, or Calias, or Pimali. All had fallen in the battle.

I never would have acted so fast had the woman not inflamed my anger, he thought. It's her fault they are dead.

By the time Sigarni and her followers rode into the square, there were more than two hundred Farlain gathered to witness the exchange. She did not dismount, but sat her horse staring at Torgan.

'Well, woman?' he called out. 'What now? Why are you here?'

'Perhaps I just wanted to look at a fool,' she said, her words colder than the wind. 'Perhaps I wondered whether the Outlanders had made you a general in return for the number of clansmen you killed for them.'

Torgan was outraged. 'How dare you?' he shouted, surging to his feet. 'I did not come here to listen to your insults.'

'Where do you normally go?' she said. 'By God, I'd think you'd have to travel far from the Highlands *not* to hear insults. Three hundred men! You led them into a trap that a child could have

212

seen. Or did no one mention cavalry to you? Did your scouts not see their hiding places? Come to that, Torgan, did you even send out scouts?'

'I don't answer to you.'

'That is where you are wrong,' Sigarni told him as, dismounting, she walked towards him. 'You answer to me, Torgan, because you have wasted three hundred Highlanders. Thrown their lives away in a moment of crass stupidity. Aye, you'll answer to me!'

Stepping in close, she slammed a right-hand punch to his chin. The blow shocked him and he stepped back, trying to ready himself. She turned away from him, then spun back and leapt, her boot cannoning against his jaw. Torgan hit the seat and fell heavily, striking his temple against the cold flagstones. Dazed, he heard her carrying on speaking as if nothing had happened. Only she wasn't talking to him, she was addressing the Farlain. 'In eleven weeks,' she said, 'an army will come to these Highlands of ours – a murderous force intent on butchery. If we are to destroy them we need to act together, under a single leader. The fool lying there will lead you to destruction. I think you already know that. Pick him up!'

Torgan felt strong arms lifting him to his feet, then sitting him in his chair. 'The position of Hunt Lord *can* be passed from father to son,' he heard her say, 'but that has not always been the Highland way. We are in a war, and it is up to you to choose a Hunt Lord who can best serve the needs of the people. All the people – Farlain, Loda, Pallides and Wingoras. I do not care who you choose. But whoever it is will serve under my leadership.'

'By what right?' asked a tall, broad-shouldered warrior with a silver moustache. Torgan blinked as Harcanan stepped up to stand before the woman. His uncle would put her in her place. He was a man of iron principles, not one to be fooled by this whore in scarlet.

'By what right?' echoed Sigarni. 'By right of blood and right of battle. By virtue of my sword and my skills.'

He shook his head. 'I do not know of your blood, Sigarni, but your battle was one skirmish fought at Cilfallen. As to your sword and your skills, I have seen no evidence that you can carry a fight

213

with either. I say this with no disrespect, for I applaud your defence of Cilfallen and your determination to fight against the Outlanders. But I need more proof that you are the war leader we should follow.'

'Well said,' she told him. 'And how would you like this proof delivered?'

'I cannot say – but one battle does not convince me. Even now the Outlanders are camped on our land, their position impregnable. A war leader should be able to free us of their presence.'

'What is your name?'

'I am Harcanan.'

'I have heard of you,' she said. 'You fought at Colden Moor. It is said you killed twenty Outlanders, and led the King to safety.'

He smiled grimly. 'An exaggeration, Sigarni. But I was there the last time the clans gathered against the Outlanders and I will be there the next time, God willing.'

'So then, Harcanan, will you follow me?'

'I have already said that I need more proof.'

Sigarni stood silently for a moment. 'I will make a bargain with you, Harcanan,' she said at last. 'Pledge yourself to me, and *then* I will show you proof.'

'Why not the other way round?' he countered.

'Because I require your faith, as well as your sword.'

He smiled. 'I hear you require men to bend the knee to you, as if to a monarch. Is that what you are asking?'

'Aye, Harcanan. Exactly that. As in the old days. But you will not need to lead me to safety; you will live to see the Outlanders crushed and broken, begging for mercy. Now give me your pledge.'

Torgan sat quietly, waiting for the old warrior to laugh in her face. He did not. Instead he walked slowly forward and dropped to one knee before her. 'My sword and my life,' he said.

Sigarni swung to the crowd. Throwing up her arm, she pointed to the line of horse-drawn wagons making their slow way over the crest of the hill. 'Those wagons you see are loaded with the spoils of war, taken from the fort on Farlain land. My forces took that fort two days ago. Even as we speak, the Pallides fort is falling to us.'

Harcanan rose. 'How many men did you lose?' he asked.

'None,' she told him. 'Assemble the council, for I would address them.'

Harcanan bowed, and Sigarni turned to Torgan. 'I could – and probably should – kill you,' she said. 'But you are a Highlander, and not without courage. Be at the council meeting.'

Torgan rose and stumbled away, his mind reeling.

Gwalchmai was sober. It was not an uplifting experience. As he sat in the log hall, surrounded by the younger children of the encampment, he found himself yearning for the sanctuary of the jug. There were several older women present, dishing out the last of the milk to the eager young, and about a dozen younger mothers sitting in a group, holding their babies and talking animatedly. Gwalchmai could not hear their conversation, for most of the smaller children had gathered around him and were asking questions he found it hard to answer. For some weeks now his powers had been waning, and he found himself unable to summon visions. It was ironic, that now of all times his Talent should desert him. He had often prayed to be released from the gift – the curse – and now that it had happened he felt terribly alone, and very frightened.

The clan needed him – and he had nothing more to give.

'Why do they want to kill us all, Gwalchmai?' asked a bright-eyed young boy of around twelve. 'Have we done something wrong?'

'No, nothing wrong,' he grunted, feeling himself hemmed in by the youngsters.

'Then why are we being punished?'

'It's no good asking me to make sense of it, lad. It's a war. There's no sense in war.'

'Then why are we doing it?' questioned another boy.

'We don't have a choice,' said Gwalchmai. There was still a little left in the jug, he remembered. But where had he put it?

'Are we all going to be killed?' asked a girl with long red hair. Gwalchmai cleared his throat. A man's voice cut in and Gwalchmai looked up to see Kollarin, moving through the youngsters. The younger man grinned at Gwalch, patted his shoulder and then sat

215

down beside him. 'When a thief enters your house,' he told the children, 'to take what is yours, then you either allow him to roam unchecked or you stop him. When a wolf pack attacks your cattle, you slay the wolves. That is the way of the hunter. The Outlanders have decided to take all that is yours. Your fathers have decided to stop them.'

'My father is a great hunter,' declared the girl. 'Last year he killed a rogue bear.'

'Not on his own,' said the boy. 'My father was with him. He shot it too.'

'He did not!' A squabble broke out between the two. Kollarin's laughter boomed out.

'Come, come, clansmen, this is no way to behave. I did not have a father – well, not that I recall. I had a mother who could shoot a bow, or wield a sword. Once, when a lioness got in amongst our sheep she strode out to the pasture, carrying only a long staff, and frightened it away. She was a fine woman.'

'You are an Outlander,' said the first boy, his earnest gaze fixed to Kollarin's face. 'Why do you want to kill us?'

'I never wanted to kill anyone,' Kollarin told him. 'There are many . . . Outlanders, as you call them, from many nations. They have built an empire; I am from one part of that empire. They conquered my country a hundred and ten years ago. The Outlanders are not, by nature, evil; they do not eat babies, or make blood sacrifices to vile gods. Their problem is that they believe in their own destiny as masters of the world. They respect strength and courage above all else. Therefore the strongest, the most ruthless, tend to achieve high rank. The Baron is such a man; he is evil, and because he leads in the north his evil spreads through the men under his command.'

'What happened to your father?' asked the red-haired girl.

'He ran away when I was a babe.'

'Why?'

Kollarin shrugged. 'I cannot answer for him. My mother told me he found life on the farm too dull.'

'Did people torment you?' asked a small boy with thick curly hair.

216

Kollarin nodded. 'Aye, they did. A boy without a father becomes, for some reason, an object of scorn.'

'Me too,' said the boy. 'My father ran away before I was born.'

'He didn't run away,' put in another child scornfully. 'Not even your mother could have said who he was.'

The curly-haired boy reddened and started to rise. Kollarin spoke swiftly. 'Let us have no violence here. You are all of the clan, and the clan is in danger; it is no time to argue with another. But there is something else you could think about. How does evil grow? What makes it appear in a human heart, growing like a weed among the blooms? I tell you. It is born from anger and injustice, from resentment and jealousy. You have all witnessed the tiniest seed of it here in this hall. A boy with no father has been insulted for what may – or may not – have been the sin of his mother. That insult, and others like it, will simmer inside him as he grows. And by what right is he treated so unjustly?' Kollarin fixed his eyes on the older boy. 'Has his birth damaged you in some way?'

'Everyone knows his mother is a—'

'Do not say it!' said Kollarin, icily. 'For when you speak thus, you give birth to evil.'

'It's the truth!'

'No, it is a *perception* of the truth. There is a difference. To the Outlander *you* are an untutored barbarian, worth less than a pig. You are not even human: your mother is a whore and your father is a stinking piece of filth who needs to be eradicated. That is their *perception* of the truth. They are wrong – and so are you. I do not say this to you in anger, boy. In fact it saddens me.'

'I will tell my father what you said about him, Outlander!' shouted the boy. 'He will kill you for it!'

'If that is true,' said Kollarin softly, 'there will be one less person to fight the Baron's men. No, I do not think that he will. I think it more likely he will be saddened, as I am, that you should insult a brother at a time like this.'

'He's not my brother! He's the son of a whore!'

'That's enough!' roared Gwalchmai, surging to his feet. 'I am the Clan Dreamer, and I know the truth. Kollarin has spoken it, though

217

perhaps he should not. What festers inside you, young man, is that everyone can see the resemblance between you and Kellin. You *are* brothers, and no amount of harsh words will change that. You have a great deal of growing up to do. Start now.'

The older boy ran from the hall, leaving the door swinging on its canvas hinges. Snow blew in and another child moved to the door, pushing it shut and dropping the latch. The children gathered again around the two men, their faces fearful. 'Sometimes,' said Kollarin, 'life can be needlessly cruel. You have witnessed such a time. Evil does not grow from the head of a devil with horns – if it did we would all run from it. It springs from an angry word, and settles in the ears of the hearers. It can grow almost unnoticed until it flowers in rage and envy, jealousy and greed. The next time you have an angry thought about a clan brother or sister, remember this.'

'He will kill you, you know,' said the curly-haired Kellin. 'Jaren's father has a terrible temper. You should get a sword.'

'I will, should the need arise,' said Kollarin sadly. 'But now I think we should play a game, and change the mood. How many here know Catch the Bear?'

Gwalchmai quietly left the hall with the game still in progress, and the squeals and laughter of the children ringing in his ears. It was bright and cold outside, but the old man could smell the approach of distant spring upon the wind. He shivered.

Kollarin was right. Evil was not an external force waiting to seize upon a wandering heart. It dwelt within the heart, a cocooned maggot waiting for the moment to break out and feed, gorging itself on the darker forces of the human soul. This was well understood by the founders of the clan, who instilled the stories and myths for youngsters to emulate. Heroes *never* oppressed or tormented the weak, *never* lied or stole or used their powers for selfish purposes. Heroes were always subject to such dark desires, but resisted them manfully. All such stories had but one purpose – to encourage the young to battle the demons inside.

Even with his Talent fading, Gwalchmai knew what demons drove young Jaren. Other children whispered that Kellin was his brother . . . this meant that his father had been unfaithful to his mother, and had then betrayed another woman leaving her to bring up a son in shame. Jaren would not have his father slandered in such a way, and had turned his anger towards little Kellin, blaming him for the lies. His anger and his hatred were born of love for his father.

Gwalchmai stood in the cold sunlight, waiting.

It was not long before he saw the boy heading back with a stocky clansman beside him. For a moment he could not remember the man's name, then it came to him – Kars. When Gwalchmai called out to him, the man let go of his son's hand and strode towards the Dreamer. His square, beardless face was pale with anger.

'You lied about me, Dreamer,' he said, his tone icy. 'If you were a younger man I would slay you where you stand. The Outlander is different; he will die for the honour of my family.'

'And will the blood wash away the shame?' asked Gwalchmai, holding to the man's gaze.

Kars stepped in close. 'The woman was any man's for a copper farthing. That was her work and her pleasure. Aye, I rutted with her. Find me a man who did not.'

'That is inconsequential,' said Gwalchmai.' Good God, man, have you not looked at the boy? Every line of his face mirrors yours. Yet even that is beside the point. Why should the child carry the sins of his mother? What has he done, save to serve as a reminder of a night of casual coupling? And as for the Outlander, he spoke only the truth.'

'He called me a piece of filth!' snarled Kars. 'Is that the truth, old man?'

'He did not call you anything, Kars. He was explaining to the children about how the Outlanders perceive us. Jaren became angry and took it all personally.'

'Enough talk!' snapped the man, drawing his claymore and turning away.

'What now, Kars?' asked Gwalchmai softly. 'Will you walk into a children's gathering and slaughter the man who leads them in games? Can you not hear the laughter? The joy? How long since the clan children knew such moments?'

At that instant the doors opened and the children moved out into the light. Kars stood stock-still, his sword in his hand. The laughter of the young faded away, and they stood by silently as Kollarin stepped out and swung his green cloak around his slender shoulders. A small boy moved out to stand beside him. Kars looked at the child, then at his own son, Jaren. No one moved. Kars plunged his sword into the snow and stepped forward to drop on one knee before Kellin. The little boy did not flinch, but stared back at the warrior.

Gwalchmai felt his heart beating erratically, his breathing shallow. For Kars to accept the boy as his own would mean a loss of honour to the proud clansman, causing grief to himself and shame to his family. To reject the evidence of his eyes would bring a different kind of shame, but one that was at least private.

The warrior reached out and placed his hands on Kellin's shoulders. 'You are a fine lad,' he said, his voice choked with emotion. 'A fine lad. Should you wish it, you would be welcome at my fire, and at my home.'

Gwalchmai could scarce believe he had heard the words. Switching his gaze to Jaren, who was standing near to his father, he saw that the boy looked close to tears. Kars glanced up and called to his son and Jaren ran to him. Kars stood, then offered his hand to Kellin. 'Let us walk for a while,' he said. Kellin took his left hand, Jaren his right.

Together they walked away towards the trees.

Kollarin strolled across to where Gwalchmai stood. 'A curious encounter,' observed the younger man.

'There is still nobility within the clan,' said Gwalchmai proudly. 'And I will die happy.'

Kollarin's face showed his sorrow. 'You are going back to your cabin, to meet the soldiers who will kill you. Why? You know that if you stay here you will thwart them.'

'Aye,' agreed Gwalchmai. 'There are magical moments when a man can change the future. But not this time. I still have one small task to perform, one last gift for Sigarni.'

'You will plant a seed,' said Kollarin sadly, 'and you will die for it.'

'Take care of my dogs, young man. I have grown to love them. And now I must go.' Suddenly Gwalchmai chuckled. 'There are two jugs of honey mead liquor hidden in my loft back home. I can hear them calling to me!'

Kollarin put out his hand. 'You are a good man, Gwalchmai, and a brave one. I know you are concerned about Sigarni, and how she will fare without your guidance. I will be her Gifted One . . . and I will never betray her.'

'There is one who will,' said the old man. 'I do not know who.'

'I will watch for him', promised Kollarin.

Leofric's servant banked up the fire and brought in fresh candles which he lit and placed atop the dying stubs. The blond-haired young man did not acknowledge his presence, but remained poring over maps and calculations. Leofric was not a happy man. Much as he enjoyed the logistics of a campaign, he could not divorce himself from the feeling that it was all so unnecessary. The clans had been peaceful for years, and now the Baron was set to bring fire and death into their lands. And for what? A little glory and the chance to rise again in the King's eyes. That and the speculation on land prices south of the border.

It was all so meaningless.

The servant placed a goblet of steaming tisane before him. Leofric lifted it and sipped the brew, which was sweet and spiced with liquor. 'Thank you. Most thoughtful,' he said, looking up at the servant. The man disappeared from his mind instantly.

The army would march in ten weeks. Each of the six thousand men would carry four days' food supply with them. Leofric lifted a quill pen. One pound of oats, eight ounces of dried beef, half an ounce of salt. Seven pennies for each pack, multiplied by six thousand. He shook his head. The Baron would not be pleased at such an outlay.

Sipping his tisane, he leaned back in his chair.

By his reckoning this war would cost twelve thousand four hundred gold pieces in wages, food and materials. But the Baron had budgeted for ten thousand.

Where to make cuts? Salt was expensive, but soldiers would not march without it, and it was common knowledge that an absence of beef in the diet led to cowardly behaviour. But halving the oats ration would mean less bulk food, and besides would save only . . . he scribbled down a calculation, then multiplied it. Three hundred and forty-two gold pieces.

Then he brightened. You have not considered the dead, he thought. The Highlanders will fight, and that means a percentage of the army would not be requiring food or payment. But how many? On a normal campaign with the Baron the losses could be as high as thirty per cent, but that would not be the situation here. Half that? A quarter? Say five per cent: Three hundred men. Once more he bent over his calculations.

Almost there, he decided.

The servant returned. 'Begging your pardon, my lord, but there is a man to see you.'

'What time is it?'

'A little before midnight, sir.'

'An odd time to be calling. Who is it?'

'I do not know him, sir. He is a stranger. He asked for you and said he had information you would find invaluable.'

Leofric sighed; he was tired. 'Very well, show him in. Give us no more than ten minutes, then interrupt me on a matter of importance – you understand?'

'Of course, sir.' The man bowed and departed.

Leofric rubbed his eyes and yawned. Midnight. Dear God, I have been working on these papers for seven hours! Hastily he gathered them together, pushing them into a drawer. The servant returned, ushering in a middle-aged man with a round fleshy face and glittering eyes.

'I trust you will forgive this intrusion,' said the newcomer. 'But the news I have could not wait for the morning.'

'And why is that pray?' countered Leofric, gesturing the man to a seat.

'You were working on the invasion plans,' said the other, with a smile. 'My information will force substantial changes.'

222

'How do you know what I was working on?'

'Let us come back to that, Leofric,' said the man, with a wide smile. 'For now, let me tell you that two of your three forts have fallen to the clansmen, and all the supplies they contain are now being consumed by your enemies.'

Leofric's weariness vanished immediately. 'That's not possible! I supervised the structures myself. They were impregnable!'

'Not from deceit, it appears.'

Leofric sat down. 'Deceit?'

'The woman Sigarni sent the traitor, Obrin, and a hundred men posing as a relief force. Both forts surrendered without a fight.'

'How . . . ? Who are you?'

'I think you can fairly assume that I am a friend, Lord Leofric. I also have information concerning Sigarni and her plans. She is gathering an army, you know.'

'Under whose leadership?'

'Her own, of course. She is of the blood royal, and she master-minded the defeat of your forces at Cilfallen. Fine credentials, don't you think?'

'How many men does she command now?'

'Close to two thousand. The Farlain are with her, and the Pallides will soon follow. Unless she is stopped, that is.'

'We cannot get through until the thaw. All the northern passes are blocked.'

'*You* cannot get through but I can. I have already, in a manner of speaking.'

The servant entered. 'My lord, I think you should . . .'

'Yes, yes, no need for that now. Bring me another tisane, and one for our guest.'

The man nodded and bowed as Leofric returned his attention to his guest. 'I think it is time you declared your interest in this matter,' he said.

'Of course. I am hunting the witch, Sigarni. My reasons are of no concern to you, but it is important to me that I find her. Surrounded as she is now by loyal clansmen, it might be . . .

difficult for me to reach her. You can help me in my quest – as I can help you in yours.'

'You're a magicker?'

The man laughed. 'Nothing so dainty, my lord. I am a sorcerer. Some time ago I was paid to . . . remove the problem Sigarni posed. I failed. Three times. I say this without shame, for my opponents were mighty indeed. Happily, they now believe me to be dead, which leaves me free to enjoy the success I have waited for.'

'Why would they think you dead?'

'A man was torn to pieces by demons. I made sure he resembled me in every way. You wish to hear more?'

Leofric shook his head. 'Absolutely not. What is it you require of me, in return for your information?'

'I find that I am short of funds in Citadel town. I am far from my own bankers, and would be grateful for a gratuity that would enable me to rent a house in Citadel. There is much I must do to prepare for my next attempt. Men and materials, that sort of thing.'

'Of course. Where are you staying at present?'

'A hostelry nearby, the Blue Duck tavern.'

'I will have one of my servants bring you money tomorrow morning. I would also appreciate any further information you can supply concerning the plans of the rebels.'

The man rubbed his fleshy chin. 'I will consider that,' he said. 'It is a delicate business. You see, I don't want you to capture or kill Sigarni. That delight is for me. I'll think on it, and let you know my decision.'

'The Baron will almost certainly want to see you.'

'I don't believe so, Lord Leofric. Tell him you have a spy who brought you this information. That, after all, is the truth. Do not mention me to him. It would displease me.'

'Who shall my servant ask for tomorrow?' Leofric enquired.

'Oh, I am sorry, I did not introduce myself. My name is Jakuta Khan.'

Ballistar's hatred for winter was deep and perfect, for it was the one season designed to highlight his deformity. His short, stumpy legs

224

could not cope with deep snow and he felt a prisoner in Asmidir's house. Ballistar longed to be with Sigarni again, planning for the spring and the coming war.

'You would be useless now,' he said aloud, as he perched on the battlements staring out over the winter landscape. 'Useless.'

Scrambling to his feet, he stood. Yet today there was no enjoyment in being so high. It served only to emphasize how tiny he was. Snow began to fall as Ballistar dropped to his belly and lowered himself to the parapet.

Back inside his upper room, he stoked the fire and sat down on the rug staring into the flames. The chairs were all too tall, and Ari had brought a wooden box to the room so that Ballistar could climb into bed. Why was I born like this? he wondered. What sin could a child be guilty of that a vengeful God would condemn him to a life such as this.

No one understood his torment. How could they? Even Sigarni had once said, 'Perhaps one day you will meet a beautiful dwarf woman and be happy.'

I don't want a dwarf woman, he thought. Just because I am deformed, it does not mean I will find deformity attractive in others.

I want you, Sigarni. I want you to love me, to see me as a *man*.

It won't happen. He remembered the taunts that marked his childhood and adolescence. Bakris Tooth-gone had once caused great merriment with a joke about Ballistar and his inability to find love. 'How could he make love to a woman?' Bakris had said. 'If they were nose to nose, he'd have his toes in it, toes to toes he'd have his nose in it, and if he ever got there he'd have no one to talk to.'

Oh yes, great roars of laughter had greeted the jest. Even Ballistar had chuckled. What other choice was there?

Ballistar left his room and wandered downstairs and out into the stable-yard. The little white pony was in her stall and the dwarf climbed to the rail by her head and stroked her neck. The pony swung her head and nuzzled him. 'Do you worry about being a

225

dwarf horse?' he said. 'Do you look at the tall mares with envy?' The pony returned to munching the straw in her feed box. It was cold in the stable and Ballistar saw that the pony's blanket had slipped from her back. Climbing to the floor he retrieved it, and tried to flip it back into place. It was a large blanket and, as he tried to throw it high, it fell back over Ballistar's head. Three times he tried. On the last it was almost in place, but the pony moved to its right and the blanket fell to the left.

It was the final humiliation for Ballistar. Tears welled in his dark eyes, and he thought again of the high parapet. On the north side, at the base of the wall, there were sharp rocks. If I were to throw myself from the battlements I would die, he thought. No more pain, no more humiliation . . .

Ballistar returned to the house and began to climb the stairs.

The servant-warrior, Ari, moved out of the library and saw him. 'Good morning, Ballistar.'

'Good morning,' mumbled the dwarf, continuing his climb.

'I was wondering if you could assist me.'

Ballistar hesitated, and glanced down through the stair rails at the tall black man.

'Not today,' he said.

'It is important,' said Ari softly. 'I am studying the maps of the Duane Pass, for that is where we believe the first battle will be fought. Do you know it?'

'I know it.'

'Good, then you will be of great assistance.' Ari turned away and re-entered the library. Ballistar stood for a moment, then slowly climbed down the stairs and followed the man. Ari was sitting on the floor with maps all around him. A coal fire was burning in the hearth.

Ballistar slumped down beside the man. 'What do you need?' he asked.

'These woods here,' said Ari, pointing to a green section, 'are they thick and dense, or light and open?'

'Reasonably light. Firs, mostly. You thought to hide men there?'

'It was a possibility.'

226

Ballistar shook his head. 'Not possible. But there is a gully just beyond the woods where a force could be concealed. There!' he said, stabbing his index finger on the map. 'Now I will leave you.'

'Ah, but we have just begun,' said Ari, with a smile. 'Look at this.' He passed Ballistar a sketch and the dwarf took it. Upon it was an outline of Duane Pass and a series of rectangles, some blacked in, others in various colours.

'What are these?'

'The classic Outland battle formation – infantry at the centre, the heavy black blocks. Two divisions. The blue represents the cavalry, the yellow archers and slingers. The cavalry also may be in two divisions, lightly armoured and heavily armoured. But this we do not yet know. Where would you place our forces?'

'I'm not a soldier!' snapped Ballistar.

'Indeed not, but you are a bright, intelligent man. Skills can be learned. Let me give you an example: Where would cavalry be of limited use?'

'In a forest,' answered Ballistar, 'where the trees and undergrowth would restrict a mounted man.'

'And what slows down infantry?'

'Hills, mountains, rivers. Forests again.'

'There, you see?' Ari told him. 'Having established that, then we look for ways to ensure that battles are fought where *we* desire them – in forests, on hills. So, where in Duane would you position our forces?'

Ballistar gazed at the map. 'There is only one good defensive point. There is a flat-topped hill at the northern end of the pass – but it would be surrounded swiftly.'

'Yes,' said Ari, 'it would. How many people could gather there?'

'I don't know. A thousand?'

'I would think two thousand,' said Ari. 'Which is our entire force.'

'What would be the point of such an action?' asked Ballistar. 'Once surrounded there would be no way to retreat, and even the advantage of occupying a hill would be overcome by an Outland army numbering more than five thousand men.'

'Yet it remains the only true defensive position,' insisted Ari. 'Once the Outlanders are through Duane Pass, they can spread out and attack isolated hamlets and villages. Nothing could stop them.'

'I don't know the answer,' Ballistar admitted.

'Nor I, but we will speak of it again. Tonight at dinner.' He looked directly into Ballistar's eyes. 'Or did you have other plans?'

Ballistar took a deep breath. 'No, no other plans.'

'That is good. I will see you later.'

'You really believe I can be of help in this?' asked Ballistar, struggling to his feet.

'Of course. Take the sketches with you, and think about them.'

Ballistar smiled. 'I will, Ari. Thank you.'

The black man shrugged and returned to his studies.

11

'By God, she's some woman,' said Obrin, peeling off his jerkin and sitting by the fire. 'They fell just like she said they would. Like skittles! I could scarce believe it, Fell. When I rode up to that Farlain fort my heart was in my mouth. The officer just ordered the gates opened, listened to my report, then turned over command to me and rode out. What a moment! I even told him the best route through the snow, and he rode his men into Grame's trap.'

'Grame lost no men in that first encounter, yet more than twenty when the Pallides detachment was ambushed,' said Fell.

'That's nothing compared with the two hundred we slew in those engagements,' pointed out Obrin. 'But it's a damn shame the men from the Loda fort escaped. I still don't know what went wrong there.'

'They simply got lost,' said Fell, 'and missed the trap. No one's fault.'

Obrin reached for a pottery jug and pulled the cork. 'The Baron's wine,' he said, with a dry chuckle. 'There were six jugs in each fort. It's a good vintage – try some.'

Fell shook his head. 'I think I'll take a walk,' he said.

'What's wrong, Fell?'

'Nothing. I just need to walk.'

Obrin replaced the cork and looked hard at the handsome forester. 'I'm not the most intuitive of men, Fell. But I've been a sergeant for twelve years and I know when something is eating at a man. What is it? Fear? Apprehension?'

Fell smiled wearily. 'Is it so obvious then?'

'It is to me, but your men must not see it. That is one of the secrets of leadership, Fell. Your confidence becomes their confidence. They feed off you, like wolf cubs suckling at the mother's teats. If you despair, they despair.'

Fell chuckled. 'I've never been compared with a mother wolf before. Pass the jug!' He took several long swallows. 'You're right,' he said, wiping his lips with the back of his hand. 'The wine is good. But I don't fear the Outlanders, Obrin. I am not afraid to die for my people. What gnaws at me is more personal. I shall make sure that my feelings do not show as strongly in the future.'

'Sigarni,' said Obrin, lifting the jug.

'How would you know that?' asked Fell, surprised.

Obrin grinned. 'I listen, Fell. That's another secret of leadership. You were lovers, but now you are not. Don't let it concern you. You're a good-looking lad and there are plenty of women who'd love to warm your bed.'

Fell shook his head. 'That's not the *whole* reason for my sadness. You didn't know her when she was just the huntress. God, man, she was a wonder! Strong and fearless, but more than that she had a love for life and a laugh that was magical. She could make a cold day of drizzle and grey sky suddenly seem beautiful. She was a *woman*. What is she now? Have you ever seen her laugh? Or even smile at a jest? Sweet Heaven, she's become a creature of ice, a winter queen.' Fell drank again, long and deeply.

'There's not been a great deal to laugh about,' observed Obrin, 'but I hear what you say. I once owned a crystal sphere. There was a rose set inside, as if trapped in ice. I've always loved roses, and this was one of the most beautiful blooms, rich and velvet red. It would live for ever. Yet it had no scent, and would not seed.'

'That is it,' said Fell. 'Exactly that! Like the Crown of Alwen – all men can see it, none can touch it.'

Obrin smiled. 'I've often heard Highlanders talk of the lost Crown. Is it a myth?'

Fell shook his head. 'I saw it when I was ten. It appears once every twenty-five years, at the centre of the pool at Ironhand's Falls. It's beautiful, man. It is more a helmet than a crown, and the silver shines like captured moonlight. There are silver wings, flat against the helm like those of a hawk when it dives, and a golden band around the brow inscribed with ancient runes. It has a nasal guard – like an Outland helm – and this is also silver, as are the cheek-guards. I was there with my father. It was the winter before he went down with the plague, my last winter with him. He took me to the Falls and we stood there with the gathered clans. I could not see at first, and he lifted me to his shoulders. A man cursed behind us, but then the Crown appeared. It shimmered for maybe ten, twelve heartbeats. Then it was gone. Man, what a night!'

'Sounds like a conjuring trick to me,' said Obrin. 'I've seen magickers make birds of gold that fly high into the air and explode in showers of coloured sparks.'

'It was no trick,' said Fell, without a hint of anger. 'Alwen was Ironhand's uncle. He had no children, and he hated Ironhand. When he was dying he ordered one of his wizards to hide the Crown where Ironhand would never find it, thus condemning his nephew to a reign fraught with civil war and insurrection. Without it, Ironhand was a King with no credentials. You understand?'

'It makes no sense to me,' said Obrin. 'He had right of blood. Why did he need a piece of metal?'

'The Crown had magical properties. Only a true King could wear it. It was not made by Alwen's order, it was far older. Once, when a usurper killed the King and placed the crown on his head, his skin turned black and fire erupted from his eyes. He melted away like snow in the sunshine.'

'Hmmm,' muttered Obrin, unconvinced. ''Tis a pretty tale. My tribe has many such, the Spear of Goldark, the Sword of Kal-thyn. Maybe one day I'll see this Crown. But you were talking of Sigarni. If you loved her, and she you, why did it end?'

'I was a fool. I wanted sons, Obrin. It's important in the Highlands. I had a need to watch my boys grow, to teach them of forestry and hunting, to instil in them a love of the land. Sigarni is barren – like your rose in crystal. I walked away from her. But not an hour has passed since when her face does not shine in my memories. Even when I lay with my wife, Gwen, all I could see was Sigarni. It was the worst mistake of my life.' Fell drained the last of the wine and lay back on the floor of the hut. 'I'd just like to see her laugh once more . . . to be the way she was.' He closed his eyes.

Obrin sat quietly as Fell's breathing deepened.

You're wrong, Fell, he thought. I know what war is, and I know the pain and terror that is coming. Given a choice I'd keep Sigarni the way she is, the Ice Queen, the cold-hearted warrior woman whose strategies have already seen three enemy forts overcome, and several tons of supplies brought into the encampments.

Obrin pulled on his jerkin and stepped out into the night.

Sigarni was tired. The morning had been a long one, discussing supplies with Tovi, organizing patrols with Grame and Fell, then poring over the battle plans drawn up by Asmidir and Ari, listening to Obrin's tales of woe concerning training.

'We've not the time to train them properly,' said the stocky Outlander. 'I've got them responding to the hunting horn for attack and retreat and re-form. But that is it! Your army will be like a spear, Sigarni. One throw is all you get.'

She felt as if her mind could take not one more ounce of pressure, and had walked with Lady to a hilltop to look upon the ageless beauty of High Druin, hoping to steal a fragment of its eternal peace.

Two of Asmidir's *Al-Jiin* walked twenty paces behind her, never speaking but always present. At first their ceaseless vigilance had been a source of irritation, but now she found their silent presence reassuring. A stand of trees grew across the hilltop, and these gave some shelter from the wind as Sigarni stared out over the winter landscape at the brooding magnificence of High Druin, its sharp peaks spearing the clouds. Down on the slopes leading to the valley she could see Loda children tobogganing, and hear the squeals of their laughter. The sounds were shrill, and echoed in the mountains.

Will they still be laughing in a few weeks, she wondered?

Taliesen had disappeared again, gone to whatever secret place wizards inhabit, and his last words to her echoed constantly in her memory: 'The Pallides will ask for a sign.'

'They already have,' she had told him.

'No, no, listen to me!' They will ask for something specific. When they do, agree to it. Don't hesitate. I will be back when I have prepared the way. Will you trust me?'

232

'You have given me no reason to distrust you. But what if they ask me to supply the moon on a silver salver?'

'Say that you will,' he said, with a dry laugh. He threw his tattered cloak of feathers around his scrawny frame, and his smile faded. 'They will not ask that, but it will seem as difficult. Remember my words, Sigarni. I will be back before the first snowdrops of spring. We will meet by Ironhand's Falls in twelve days.'

Lady brushed against her leg and whined. Sigarni knelt and stroked her long ears. 'I have neglected you, my lovely,' she said. 'I am sorry.' Lady's long nose pushed against Sigarni's cheek and she felt the hound's warm tongue on her face. 'You are so forgiving.' She patted Lady's dark flank.

'She wishes solitude,' she heard one of her guards say. Sigarni turned to see a tall, dark-haired woman standing with the two men.

'Let her through,' she called. The woman gave the black men a wide berth and walked up the hillside. She was thin of face, with a prominent nose, but her large brown eyes gave her face a semblance of beauty. 'You wish to speak with me?' said Sigarni.

'I do. I am Layelia, the wife of Torgan.'

'There is no place for him among my officers,' said Sigarni sternly. 'He is a fool.'

'That is a trait shared by most men I have met,' said Layelia. 'But then war is a foolish game.'

'Have you come to plead for him?'

'No. He will regain his honour – or he will not. That is for him. I came to speak with you. I have questions.'

Sigarni removed her cloak and spread it over the snow. 'Come, sit with me. Why not more questions? That is my life now. Endless questions, each with a hundred answers.'

'You look tired,' said Layelia. 'You should rest more.'

'I will when there is time. Now ask your questions.'

The dark-haired woman was silent for a moment, staring deeply into Sigarni's pale blue eyes. 'What if we win?' she asked, at last.

Sigarni laughed. 'If we lose we die. That is all I know. My God, I certainly have no time to think of the aftermath of a victory that is by no means certain.'

'I think you should,' said Layelia softly. 'If you don't, then you are just like a man, never seeing beyond the end of your nose.'

Sigarni sighed. 'You are correct, I am tired. So let us assume the hare is bagged, and move on to the cooking. What do you want?'

Layelia chuckled. 'I have heard a lot about you, Sigarni. You have lived a life many women – myself included – would envy. But I don't envy you now, trying to adjust to a world of men. I ask about victory for a simple, selfish reason. I have children, and I want those children to grow in the Highland way, with their father beside them, learning about cattle and crops, family, clan and honour. The Outlanders threaten our way of life – not just by their invasion, but by our resist-ance. Tell me this, if you beat the Baron, what then? Is it over?'

'No,' admitted Sigarni. 'They will send another army.'

'And how will you combat them?'

'In whatever way I can,' said Sigarni guardedly.

'You will be forced to attack the Lowland cities, sack their treas-uries and hire mercenaries.'

Sigarni smiled grimly. 'Perhaps.'

'And if you defeat the next army, will that end the war?'

'I don't know!' snapped Sigarni, 'but I doubt it. Where is this leading?'

'It seems to me,' said Layelia sadly, 'that win or lose our way of life is finished. The war will go on and on. The more you win, the further away you will take our men – perhaps all the way to the Outland capital. What then, when the outlying armies of their empire gather? Will you be fighting in Kushir in ten years?'

'If I am, it will not be from choice,' Sigarni told her. 'I hear you, Layelia, and I understand what you are saying. If there is a way I can avoid what you fear, then I will. You have my word on that.'

The dark-haired woman smiled, and laid her hand on Sigarni's arm. 'I believe you. You know, I have always thought the world would be a better place with women as leaders. We wouldn't fight stupid wars over worthless pieces of land; we would talk to one another, and reach compromises that would suit both factions. I know that you have to be a war leader, Sigarni, but I ask that you be a *woman* leader, and not just a pretend man in armour.'

'You are very forthright, Layelia. A shame you were not so forthright with Torgan.'

'I did my best,' said the other, with a wry smile, 'but he was not gifted with a good brain. He is, however, a fine partner in bed, so I will not complain too much.'

Sigarni's laughter rang out. 'I'm glad he is good at something.'

'He is also a good father,' said Layelia. 'The children adore him, and he plays with them constantly.'

'I am sorry,' said Sigarni. 'I have obviously not seen the best of him. Have you been married long?'

'Fourteen years come summer.' She smiled. 'He hasn't changed much in those years, save to lose some of his hair. It's beautiful here, isn't it, the sun gleaming on High Druin?'

'Yes,' Sigarni agreed.

Layelia rose. 'I have taken too much of your time. I will leave you to your thoughts.'

Sigarni stood. 'Thank you, Layelia. I feel refreshed, though I don't know why.'

'You've spent too long in the company of men,' said Layelia. 'Perhaps we should talk again?'

'I would enjoy that.'

Layelia stepped forward and embraced the silver-haired warrior woman, kissing her on both cheeks. Sigarni felt hot tears spill to her face. Abruptly she pulled clear and turned back towards High Druin.

'You shouldn't have brought me,' grumbled Ballistar. 'I'm slowing you down.'

'That's true,' grunted Sigarni, as they faced yet another deep snow-drift. 'But you're such good company!'

Ballistar shifted on her shoulders. 'Put me down and we'll see if we can crawl along the top of it. There should be solid ground about thirty feet ahead. Then it is just one more hill to the Falls.'

Sigarni swivelled and tipped the little man from her shoulders. He fell head-first into the drift, and came up spluttering and spitting snow. 'You are heavy for a small man,' she said laughing.

'And you have the boniest shoulders I ever sat upon,' he told her, brushing snow from his beard. Turning to his stomach, Ballistar began to squirm across the snow. Sigarni followed him, using her arms to force a path. After an hour of effort they reached solid ground and sat for a while, gathering their strength. 'I'm freezing to death,' muttered Ballistar. 'I hope you left enough firewood in the cave. I'm in no mood to go gathering.'

'Enough for a couple of hours,' she reassured him.

The Falls were still frozen at the centre, but at the sides water had begun to trickle through the ice. 'The thaw is coming,' said the dwarf.

'I know,' said Sigarni softly.

Inside the cave Sigarni started a fire and they shrugged out of their soaked outer clothing. 'So why did you bring me?' asked Ballistar.

'I thought you'd enjoy my company,' she told him.

'That's not very convincing.'

She looked at him, and remembered how out of place he had seemed back at the encampment, how lonely and sad. 'I wanted company,' she said, 'and I could think of no one else I would rather have with me.'

He blushed and looked away. 'I'll accept that,' he said brightly. 'Do you remember when we used to play here as children? You, me, Fell and Bernt built a tree house. It fell apart in the big storm. Fell was climbing and the floor gave way. You remember?'

Sigarni nodded. 'Bernt stole the nails from Grame. More nails in that structure than wood.'

'It was fun, wasn't it?'

'Fun? You were always arguing with the others, getting into scrapes and fights.'

'I know,' he said. 'I was young then, and not growing like the rest of you. But I look back on those times as the happiest of my life. Do you think the others would?'

'Bernt no longer looks back,' she said, her voice almost a whisper.

'Oh, I'm sorry, Sigarni. I wasn't thinking.' Reaching out, he took her slender hand in his own, his stubby fingers caressing her wrist. 'It wasn't your fault, not really. I think if you had gone he

236

would still have killed himself had you turned him down. It was his life; he chose to take it.'

Sigarni shook her head. 'I don't think that is the whole truth. Had I known the outcome beforehand I would have acted differently. But now I think about how I was lying in bed with Asmidir, enjoying myself utterly.' She sighed. 'And while I was being pleasured, Bernt was tying a rope around his neck.'

Ballistar looked away and fiddled with the fire, poking small sticks into the flames. 'Now I have embarrassed you,' she said.

'Yes, you have,' he told her, reddening. 'But we are friends, Sigarni. We always will be. I don't want you to feel there are words you cannot say in my presence. When is the wizard due?' he asked, changing the subject.

'Tomorrow.'

'I wish he'd chosen a more hospitable meeting place.'

'It had to be here,' she said. 'He knew what the Pallides would ask of me.'

'Madness!' snapped Ballistar. 'Who do they think they are? Here we sit on the verge of war and they play games. Do they believe they can win without us?'

'No, my friend, they don't think that. Their Dreamers have told them that the leader will wear the Crown of Alwen. If that is true, then I must find it. Taliesen will have a plan.'

'I don't like wizards,' said the dwarf.

'I remember you saying that about Asmidir. A black sorcerer, you called him.'

'I still don't like him. Are you still lovers?'

'No!' Her voice was sharper than she intended and Ballistar gazed at her quizzically.

'Did he wrong you?'

She shook her head. 'I don't want to talk about it. I want your help before dusk. I want you to come with me to the far side of the pool and break the ice.'

'Why?' he asked, mystified.

'I need to swim.'

'That's ridiculous! The cold will kill you.'

237

'You can wait for me with a blanket,' she said.

'There's something you are not telling me. What are you looking for?'

Sigarni stretched out her hand to the fire. The cave was glowing now in the firelight, and the sounds of winter outside only served to make it seem more cosy within. 'I am going to find a small bone,' she said. 'A talisman if you like, a good luck charm.'

'Whose bones?' he asked, wide eyed.

'Ironhand.'

Ballistar's jaw dropped. 'You found his bones? He didn't pass over the Gateway?'

'No. He died here fighting his enemies.'

'How will a bone help you?'

'Enough questions, Balli. Come on, we're warm enough now.'

Together they left the cave and trudged across the snow-covered ice of the pool. Sigarni found the boulder under which the bones lay, and she and Ballistar began to chip away at the surrounding ice with their knives. It was slow work and Ballistar lost his patience. Climbing to the top of the jutting boulder he jumped to the ice, landing hard. Four times more he did so, then on the fifth a large crack appeared. 'Almost there,' he said. Suddenly the ice gave and he fell through into the dark water beneath. Sigarni dived across the ice, her hand snaking out to grab his collar just as he was about to sink. With a great effort she hauled him back.

'You'd better get back to the cave,' she said.

'No, no, I'm all right,' he said, shivering. 'Can you reach the bones from here?'

'I don't know. I'll have to be fast.' Slipping out of her clothes, she slithered into the water.

'Be careful, there's an undertow,' warned Ballistar.

The cold chilled her to the bone, and all was darkness. Holding to the boulder, she released some air and dived deeper. Her hand touched the bottom and she scrabbled around, but could feel nothing but stones. Something sharp cut the palm of her hand. The sudden shock caused her to breathe out and, her lungs aching, she rose towards the surface. Her head thumped against ice.

She had missed the opening.

Holding down panic she rolled to her back, pushing her face towards the ice. There was always a tiny gap between ice and water, and she breathed in deeply. The cold was bitter now and she could not feel her fingers.

You stupid woman! she thought. To come so far and die so stupidly.

A faint glow surrounded her. 'Why do you never call for me, child?' asked Ironhand. 'Dive to the bottom and collect what you came for, then follow me to the surface.'

Filling her lungs with air she rolled and dived, kicking out against the ice to propel herself down. In the glow she saw Ironhand sitting on the pool floor; beside him was a human head but she did not recognize the face. On the other side of the ghostly giant lay his bones. Swiftly she grabbed a finger-bone and rose towards the surface.

As she broke clear Ballistar took hold of her arm and dragged her on to the ice.

'I was worried near to death,' complained the dwarf. Sigarni could not speak; she had begun to shake uncontrollably. 'And look, you've cut your hand,' he said, pointing to the trickle of blood on her palm.

Ballistar took up her clothes and led her back to the cave, where she sat wrapped in a blanket, her face and hands blue. 'I hope that bone was worth it,' he said.

'It . . . was,' she told him. 'He . . . is . . . here.'

'Who is?'

'Ironhand.'

'Ironhand?' he repeated. 'In the cave? With us?' Ballistar gazed around fearfully. 'I don't see him.'

Sigarni shrugged off the blanket and moved a little way from the fire. 'Come and rub my skin,' she said. Ballistar put his hands on her shoulders and began to massage the flesh.

'So now we are dealing with wizards *and* ghosts,' he said.

'Lower. On my back,' she ordered.

Ballistar knelt behind her and rubbed gently at the cold skin. 'You should sit closer to the fire.'

'No. It would do more harm than good. When I am a little warmer . . . That is nice. Now my arms.'

He sat beside her, kneading her flesh, encouraging the blood to flow. He tried not to stare at her breasts, but failed. Sigarni did not seem to notice. Of course she doesn't, he thought. I am not a man to her.

'I am going to sleep now, Balli. Watch over me, and keep the fire going.'

Holding fast to the bone, she lay down by the fire. Ballistar covered her with two blankets. As she closed her eyes, he leaned down and kissed her cheek.

'What was that for?' she asked sleepily.

'I love you,' he said.

'I love you too,' she whispered. And slept.

The fire burned low and Ballistar added the last of the wood. Sigarni's flesh was still cool and the dwarf wandered out into the cold of the night to gather dead wood. The carcasses of the demons still lay where Sigarni had slain them, but they were not rotting; it was too cold for that. They'll smell bad come spring, thought Ballistar as he wandered beneath the trees, kicking at the snow and seeking fuel.

'Over there,' said a voice. 'Beneath the oaks.'

Ballister leapt, turned and fell over. Standing beside him was a glowing figure in ancient armour, his white beard braided into forks. He wore a long, double-handed broadsword in a scabbard of embossed silver – and the hand resting on it was made of red iron. 'By Heaven, you are skittish,' said the ghost. 'Are you going to fetch the wood or not?'

'Yes, lord,' answered Ballistar.

'I'm not your lord, dwarf. I am merely a spirit. Now fetch the wood before she freezes to death.'

Ballistar nodded, and dug around in the snow beneath the oaks, gathering dead wood, then returning to the cave. The glowing figure stayed by him, watching his efforts. 'It cannot be easy to live in such a body,' he said.

'A choice would be pleasant,' muttered Ballistar.

'You've a handsome face, lad. Be thankful for small gifts.'

'All my gifts are small – bar one. And I'll never get to use that,' answered Ballistar, kneeling by the fire and placing two long sticks upon it.

The ghost assumed a sitting position by the fire. 'You can never be sure,' he said. 'I had two dwarfs at my court and they were always in demand. Once I had to adjudicate in a very delicate matter, where a knight cited one of my dwarfs as his wife's secret lover. He wanted the dwarf hanged and his wife burned at the stake.'

'What did you do? Did you kill them?'

'Do I look like a barbarian? I told the knight that he would be laughed out of the kingdom if he sought a public trial. The wife was sent back to her family in disgrace. I had the dwarf castrated. However, that is not the point. Never lose faith, little man.'

'Well, thank you for your advice,' snapped Ballistar. 'However, I have not yet met a woman who would wish to have me clamber all over her.' He told the spirit of Bakris' jest and Ironhand laughed.

'Nose to nose . . . yes, that's very good. How did you respond?'

'I laughed with them – though it broke my heart.'

'Aye, it's the best way.' He leaned forward, peering at Sigarni. 'Is she warming up?' he asked.

Ballistar moved alongside the sleeping woman and touched the flesh of her arm. 'A little. She was seeking your bones. Damn near died for it.'

'I know, I was there. Wilful child.' The ghost smiled. 'She can't help it, it is in her blood. I was wilful myself. How is the war progressing?'

'I would have thought you'd know more about that than a mere dwarf,' said Ballistar. 'Can spirits not fly around the world?'

'I don't know any spirits,' said Ironhand. 'But *I* cannot. I'm trapped here, where I died. Well, until now. Wherever Sigarni goes, I shall go too.'

'That's a comforting thought. I think you'll cause a certain amount of panic back at the encampment.'

Ironhand shook his head. 'No one will see me, boy – not even you. I only showed myself to you since Sigarni was foolish enough to tell you about me. So, what is happening?'

241

Ballistar told the King of the Pallides' request that Sigarni should find the lost Crown. 'We are waiting for Taliesen,' he concluded. 'He'll show us where it is.'

'Oh, I know where it is,' said Ironhand. 'That won't be the problem. Getting there and out again alive is the issue.'

'Where is it?'

'In a dying world of sorcery, a dark malevolent place. Even the air is poisonous with magic. No true man can live there for more than a few months. He would sicken and die. One of my wizards tracked it down and passed through a Gateway to retrieve it; we never saw him again. A second followed him; he came back broken and diseased, not all our medicines and charms could heal him. But while he lived he told us of the world, its beasts, and its wars. I decided then to send no more of my people in search of the Crown.'

'But Sigarni *must* go there,' said Ballistar. 'Without the Crown the Pallides will not accept her leadership. They might believe you, though. You could appear to Fyon Sharp-axe and tell him Sigarni is the chosen one.'

The ghost shook his head. 'It might work, but then Sigarni would rule only through a long-dead king. No Ballistar, she must win the right for herself. When my wizard returned he told me the Crown was in a temple, at the centre of a city at war. He saw it, was even allowed to touch it. I think he believed that to do so would heal him of his afflictions in that world. It didn't.'

'You say *allowed* to touch it. There are people there?'

'Aye, there are people. They cling to life in a world of death.'

'What is killing them?'

'There is no sun to bring life to the land. The city was built inside a forest of dead trees. There is no grass, and no crops grow. The land is in perpetual twilight. The mountains there spew fire and ash, and occasionally rip themselves apart with sounds like a thousand thunders. You can see why I forbade any further ventures into that land.'

'But without cattle and crops, how do they survive?' asked Ballistar.

'On war,' the King told him.

'That makes no sense,' said the dwarf.

'It does, lad, if you have a mind dark enough to examine it.'

Ballistar awoke with a start and sat up blinking and afraid. He had failed Sigarni and slept. Swiftly he rushed to her side. She was warm to the touch and sleeping deeply. Relieved, the dwarf knelt by the fire and blew the coals to glowing life, adding shreds of bark to feed the tiny flames. Once it had flared he placed two small logs atop the coals.

From Sigarni's pack he took a flat-bottomed pot and a sack of dried oats. Filling the pot with snow, he stood it upon the fire. Despite being full of snow it melted to only a tiny amount of water and Ballistar spent some time moving back and forth bringing handfuls of snow from outside the cave. When the pot was half full of water he added oats and a pinch of salt.

The sun was up, the cave-mouth lit with golden light. Birdsong could be heard from the trees outside and the air was fresh with the promise of the coming spring.

Sigarni awoke and stretched. The blanket slid from her naked body. 'Ah, breakfast,' she said. 'What a fine companion you are, Ballistar.'

'I live to serve, my queen,' he said, making an elaborate bow.

'No sign of Taliesen?'

'Not yet, but the dawn has only just arrived.' Using two long sticks, Ballistar lifted the pot from the fire and stirred the contents, which had thickened considerably. 'You brought no honey,' he chided her. 'Porridge is bland and tasteless without it.'

'I had to carry enough food for two. Come to think of it, I had to carry you as well for a while. There was no room for honey. Have you slept?'

'A little,' he admitted.

She smiled. 'The next time I suggest a swim under the ice, be so kind as to remind me of my previous stupidity.'

'I will. How are you feeling?'

'Rested, and at peace for the first time in weeks. No plans to study, no quarrels to adjudicate, no ruffled feathers to smooth. Just breakfast at dawn in a peaceful cave, enjoying good company.'

'I trust you include me in that description?' said Taliesen, stepping into the cave and brushing snow from his tattered cloak of feathers. Sigarni nodded, but her smile had faded.

'Welcome, Taliesen.'

The old man made his way to the fire and sat. 'You have a beautiful body, Sigarni. Fifty years ago it would have inspired me to carnal thoughts. Now, however, I can appreciate its beauty on an entirely different level. I take it the Pallides asked for the Crown?' Sigarni nodded and rose from bed, dressing swiftly. 'It will not be easy – and yet you must not dally,' continued Taliesen. 'I will send you through the Gateway as soon as you are dressed.'

'The world beyond is poisonous,' said Ballistar coldly. 'She could die there.'

Taliesen swung to him. 'It is very rare that I am surprised, dwarf. Yet you have accomplished it. How is it that you know of Yur-vale?'

'I am a creature of legend,' said Ballistar, with a wide grin. 'I know many things.'

'Then perhaps you would like to continue my story?'

'Gladly,' said Ballistar, who then told Sigarni all that Ironhand had confided to him the night before. The dwarf took great pleasure in the look of amazement that Taliesen sought to disguise. When he had finished Ballistar moved to Sigarni's pack, pulling out two shallow bowls. Ladling porridge into each, he passed one to Sigarni. 'You are welcome to eat from the pot,' he told Taliesen.

'I am not hungry!' snapped the wizard. 'Is there anything else you wish to add about Yur-vale?'

'No,' said Ballistar happily. 'Do continue.'

The wizard cast him a baleful glance. 'Yur-vale was once a paradise. There was no physical ugliness there, and no natural disease – at least no disease that affects the inhabitants. It was a land of beauty and light. Now it is the opposite. It is an ocean world, with a very small land mass at the equator. The land mass has two great cities, and these are in a perpetual state of war. The war is necessary, for reasons we do not need to trouble ourselves with. The Crown is in a temple at the centre of the city of Zir-vak. It is a city under siege and you will need to enter it by means of a black river which flows through it. Do not drink the water, it has been polluted by volcanic ash. The city's inhabitants have a way of purifying the water, involving filters. Once inside the city, the water you find will be good to drink. Take food with you, and eat nothing offered to you during your stay – no matter how appetizing it looks.'

'How do I get there?' asked Sigarni.

'There is a Gateway close to the Falls. I will send you through and you will arrive at a point some seven miles south of the city. Since you will not see the sun, you must head for a set of twin peaks you will see to the north. When you return to the Gateway you will make a cut upon your arm and allow blood to drop on each of the six standing stones that make up the circle. I will then bring you back.'

'Bring *us* back,' put in Ballistar.

'I go alone,' said Sigarni. Ballistar was about to argue, when Taliesen cut in.

'I agree with him,' said Taliesen, with a rare smile. 'Take the dwarf. He will be of use.'

Ballistar was surprised. 'Why do you support me, wizard? I know you have no love for me.'

'Perhaps that is why I support you,' said Taliesen. 'Have you brought weapons?'

'Yes,' said Sigarni. 'Bows, knives and my sabre.'

'Good. Now, if you are both ready, we should depart.'

Sigarni took a small pouch from her pack and dropped the finger-bone of Ironhand into it. Looping a thong through the pouch, she tied it around her neck.

'What is that?' asked Taliesen.

'A talisman,' she told him.

Ballistar thought he was about to speak, but Taliesen said nothing. The wizard rose. 'When you have cleaned and stowed your pots, I will be waiting for you on the other side of the pool,' he said, and padded out of the cave.

'Are you sure you want to come with me, Balli?' asked Sigarni.

'Always,' he said.

★　　★　　★

They found Taliesen waiting by a cliff-face some two hundred yards from Ironhand's burial place. Sigarni had played there as a child, and she and her friends had often debated the meaning of the strange symbols carved on the rocks. The area was flat, as if smoothed by man, and deep grooves had been chiselled from the rock in the shape of a tall rectangular door. There was also evidence of an inscription, though wind and rain, snow and hail had long since eroded the greater part of it.

'This is one of the Lesser Gateways,' said Taliesen. 'It does not allow movement through *our* time, but does serve to open time doorways to other realities. Now remember what I said. Do not drink of the water of the black river, nor eat any meat offered to you. This is vital. I knew a sorcerer once who went there and ate a little pork; it swelled inside him and ripped him apart. Yur-vale is a world of great magic, and you are strangers to it. Because of your very *strangeness* its power will be many times greater around you. Bear this in mind. Now, you know where you are heading?'

'Seven miles towards the twin peaks,' said Sigarni.

'Good. Now my bones are freezing here, so let us begin. Are you ready?' Sigarni nodded and Taliesen turned to Ballistar. 'And you, dwarf? There is still time to change your mind. What awaits you is not pleasant. Your worst nightmare is beyond this Gate.'

Ballistar thought he detected a note of concern in the wizard's voice, and felt his fears rise. 'I will travel with Sigarni,' he said stoutly. Reaching up, he took hold of her hand.

'Then let it begin,' said Taliesen. The old wizard closed his eyes and spoke softly in a language unknown to either of the Highlanders. It was soft and fluent, almost musical. Pale light flooded from the rectangular grooves in the rock face, which became translucent, and then transparent, and Sigarni found herself staring through it at a cold, grey landscape. 'Step through quickly,' said Taliesen. 'It will hold for a few seconds only.'

The silver-haired woman and the dwarf stepped through the portal. Sigarni shivered as she passed through, for it was like walking through a waterfall, cold and yet not as refreshing. On the other side they found themselves standing within a circle of six tall granite stones. Sigarni swung round in time to see Taliesen fade away to nothing.

'Well, we are here,' she said, turning back to Ballistar. The dwarf was lying on the ground, his body twitching. 'Balli! Are you ill?'

His body began to writhe.

And stretch.

Dropping her bow and loosing her pack, Sigarni knelt beside him. His limbs were thrashing around, his legs jutting now from his tiny trousers. The small doeskin boots split as his feet grew. His black leather belt snapped. Sigarni moved back from him and waited. Finally the spasmodic twitching eased and she found herself gazing down at a healthy young man in torn clothes and shredded boots. Part of one boot was still around the ankle like an adornment. Ballistar groaned and sat up. 'What happened to me?' he asked. Then he saw his arms, full length and strong, with long, slender fingers, and his legs. He scrambled to his feet and found himself staring into Sigarni's eyes. 'Oh God, dear God,' he said. 'I'm a man!'

Throwing his arms around the stunned Sigarni, he kissed her cheek. 'I'm a man,' he said again. 'Look at me, Sigarni!'

'You look very fine,' she said, with a smile. 'Truly this is a magical place.'

'He said my worst nightmare awaited me. How wrong can a man be? This is everything I dreamt of. Now I will be able to stand with the others and fight the Outlanders. No more jibes and cruel jokes. Oh, Sigarni . . .' Abruptly he sat down and began to weep.

'I brought a spare tunic and leggings,' said Sigarni. 'I think they might fit you. Even if they don't, they'll look better than the rags you are wearing.'

He nodded and moved to her pack. 'I could even get married,' he said, 'and sire sons. Tall sons!'

'You always were handsome, Balli, and you'll make a fine father. Now stop talking and get dressed, we must be moving on.'

Sigarni gazed at the bleak landscape, the sky was slate-grey and the air smelt acrid. Far to the east she could see fires on the horizon as two distant volcanoes spewed hot ash and lava out over the land. 'Not a hospitable place,' she said.

'I think it's wonderful,' said Ballistar.

She turned to see him struggling out of his ruined leggings. 'By Heaven, Balli, has *that* grown also?' He giggled. 'No, it was always this big. Do you like it?' She laughed. 'Just cover it, you fool!'

Ballistar dressed and tied the thongs of his new green leggings. 'They are a little tight,' he said. 'Am I as tall as Fell?'

'No. But you are taller than Bakris and Gwyn. That will have to do.'

Sigarni reached for her bow – and froze. The weapon had rooted itself in the ground and small, slender branches were growing from it. 'Would you look at that!' she said. Roots were spreading out from the bow, delving into the grey, ash-covered ground.

'What about your arrows?' asked Ballistar. Sigarni swung her quiver clear and pulled a shaft from it; it was unmarked. At that moment a single ray of sunshine seared through the ash-grey sky, a pillar of light bathing what had once been a bow and was now a swiftly growing tree. The sudden warmth was welcome and Sigarni glanced up at the sky, enjoying the feeling of sunlight on her skin. Then it was gone.

Something moved against her chest and, startled, Sigarni glanced down. The small leather pouch was bulging now, and writhing, as if a large rat were inside. Swiftly she ripped it from her neck and hurled it to the ground. The leather split and a white bone protruded, others joining to it. As with Ballistar the bones stretched and grew, cartilage and ligaments slithering over them, pulling joints into sockets. At last a huge skeleton lay on the volcanic ash.

For a moment nothing more happened. Then suddenly, in a vivid burst of colour, red muscle and sinew, flesh and veins danced along its frame, covering lungs and liver, heart and kidneys. Skin flowed over the whole, and silver hair sprouted from head and chin.

For a while Ironhand lay naked on the ground, then took a long shuddering breath. His eyes opened, and he saw Sigarni. 'I can feel,' he said. 'The ground beneath me, the air in my lungs. How is this possible?'

'I have no idea,' said Sigarni, removing her green cloak. She cut a hole in the centre and passed it to the naked man.

Ironhand stood and looped it over his head. 'Where are we?'

'In the land of Yur-vale,' Sigarni told him. 'Taliesen sent us through a magical Gateway.'

'It is puzzling,' he said, 'but, by Grievak, it is good to feel again – and to have two good hands of flesh and blood,' he added, clenching his fists. 'Who is this?' he asked turning to the young man at her side.

'It is me, Ballistar the Dwarf. The magic made me grow. Though not as tall as you,' he added, with a frown.

Ironhand chuckled. 'You are tall enough, boy. What now, daughter?'

She pointed to the twin peaks. 'We make for the city and find the Crown.'

Yos-shiel had been a Black River trader for more than two hundred and seventy years, and remembered with great regret the ending of all that was beautiful in Yur-vale. He had been celebrating his twenty-fourth birthday when the first mountain had erupted, spewing molten lava down the hillside, destroying the vineyards and the corn-fields.

It had been a bitter summer. First the war, and then the natural upheavals which hid the sun from the sky. Year by year it had grown steadily worse. Yos-shiel pushed his thin fingers through his thick white hair, and stared out of the window at the quay, where men were loading supplies on to one of the three barges he would send down to Zir-vak after dusk. Smoked fish and timber: the only two items of any worth in Yur-vale. Yos-shiel sold them for gold and water, in the vain hope that one day gold would be a viable currency once more.

The old man rose and stretched. From his window he saw a single ray of sunshine to the south and his heart swelled. How long since there had been a break in the clouds? A year? Two? several of the loaders saw it also, and all ceased their work.

A young man, seeing Yos-shiel at the window, called out, 'Is it a sign, master? Is the sun returning?'

The pillar of light vanished. 'I do not look for signs any more,' he said softly.

Stepping out into the dull light, he counted the barrels of fish. 'There should be fifty,' he said.

A huge man wearing a red shirt embroidered with gold moved into sight. 'Two were spoiled,' he said, his voice low, rumbling like distant thunder. Yos-shiel looked into the man's small, round eyes. He knew Cris-yen was lying, but the man was a thug and, he suspected, a killer. The two guards Yos-shiel had appointed to supervise the loads had mysteriously disappeared. He feared them dead.

'Very well, Cris-yen, carry on.' With a contemptuous smile the big man swung away.

I never should have employed him, thought Yos-shiel. He and his brothers will strip me of all I have. I will be lucky to escape with my life. Glancing up at the iron sky, he suddenly smiled. What is life worth now, he wondered? Would I miss it?

Soldiers manned the ramparts of the stockade and Yos-shiel considered asking them for help in dealing with Cris-yen. The supplies he sent were vital to the city, and his plea deserved to be heard. But then *deserve* has nothing to do with it, he realized. Cris-yen had made friends with the officers, giving them presents. If I go to them and they turn against me my death will come all the sooner, he thought.

Strolling to the edge of the quay, he stared down into the inky depths of the river. No fish swam there now. The fleets were forced to put out far to sea in order to make their catches.

The barge from the city came into sight, its cargo of barrels lashed to the deck. Fresh drinking water, cleaned in the charcoal filters of Zir-vak, and fresh meat for the soldiers.

Yos-shiel wandered back to his small office and continued working on his ledgers.

Just before noon he heard a commotion from outside, and saw his workers moving towards the stockade gates. Yos-shiel closed the books, cleaned the quill pen, and followed them. The gates were open and three people had entered the stockade, two men and a woman. The woman was silver-haired and strikingly beautiful. Beside her was a giant in an ill-fitting green tunic, tied at the waist with what looked like an old bow-string; he too was silver-haired. The last of the trio was a young man, dressed in green troos and a shirt too small for him.

'Where are you from?' asked Cris-yen, pushing to the front of the crowd and standing before the woman, his hands on his hips.

'South,' she said. 'We're looking for passage into the city.'

'And how will you pay me?'

The woman produced a small gold coin and Cris-yen laughed. 'That's no good here, my pretty; it doesn't put food in mouths any longer. I'll tell you what I'll do, you and me will go to the warehouse and we'll arrange something.'

'We'll find passage elsewhere,' she said, turning away. One of Cris-yen's brothers stepped forward, grabbing her arm.

'There's nowhere else, you'd better listen to him,' he said.

'Take your hand off my arm,' said the woman icily.

The man laughed. 'Or what?'

The woman ducked her head, hammering her brow into his nose. The man released her and staggered back but she leapt, her foot cracking against his chin and catapulting him back into the crowd. Yos-shiel saw the soldiers watching from the ramparts but they made no move to interfere.

'That was an assault!' yelled Cris-yen. 'Take her!' Several men rushed forward. The woman downed the first with a straight left. The smaller of her companions rushed in and threw himself at the others; he and several men tumbled to the ground.

'That's enough!' bellowed the silver-bearded giant. The sound boomed around the stockade and all activity ceased as he stepped in close to Cris-yen. 'Well,' he said, 'you seem to be the lead bull of the pox-ridden herd. Perhaps you and I should decide the issue.'

Cris-yen said nothing, but his huge fist hammered into the man's chin. The giant took the blow and did not move. He merely grinned. 'By God, son, if that is the best you have to offer you are in serious trouble,' he said. Cris-yen tried to throw a left, whereupon the giant blocked it with his right and slapped Cris-yen open-handed across the cheek. The sound was like snapping timber. Cris-yen staggered to his right – then, head down, rushed the

251

giant. The charge was met by a right cross that smashed Cris-yen's jaw and spun him from his feet. He hit the ground face down, twitched once and was still.

'A chin like crystal,' muttered the giant. 'Any more for the fray?' No one moved. The man walked to the unconscious Cris-yen and calmly removed the embroidered red shirt. Pulling off his own tunic, he donned the garment. 'A little tight,' he said, 'but it will do.' Without hurry he stripped Cris-yen naked and clothed himself in the man's leather leggings and black boots. 'That feels better,' he said. 'Now who is in charge here?'

Yos-shiel stepped from the crowd. 'I am sir.'

'Then it is with you we should discuss passage?'

'It is. And you are welcome to travel free of any charges.'

'Good. That is most hospitable. I am Ironhand, this is my daughter Sigarni and her friend, Ballistar.'

'I can see why you earned your name,' said Yos-shiel.

Yos-shiel offered his guests wine and food, and if he was offended by their refusal to eat, he did not show it. Ballistar liked the little old man, and listened with relish as he told of his troubles with Cris-yen.

'I don't believe he will cause you more trouble for a while yet,' said Ironhand, 'but if you'll take my advice you'll promote a man to take his place immediately, and then dismiss all of his henchmen.'

'I shall,' said Yos-shiel, 'although I would be grateful if you could stay beside me while I do the deed.'

'Gladly,' promised Ironhand.

'I was amazed that Cris-yen fell so swiftly to you. I have seen him break men's arms, and cudgel them down with hammer blows from his fists.'

'They breed them tough where we come from,' said Ballistar.

'And where is that?' asked Yos-shiel.

'South,' answered Ballistar vaguely, wishing he had kept his mouth shut.

'We are from another world, Yos-shiel,' said Sigarni, moving to sit on the desk opposite the old man. 'We passed through a magical Gateway.'

The trader smiled, waiting for the end of the joke. When it didn't come his smile vanished. 'You . . . are wizards?'

'No,' said Sigarni, 'but a wizard sent us. We have come to reclaim something that was lost in this world, and return it to our own.'

'The sunlight,' said the old man. 'That was you, in the south. What did you do?'

'I don't know what you mean,' said Sigarni. 'You mean the break in the clouds?'

'Yes. It's been years since we've seen the sun. Can you make it come at will?'

'I did nothing, Yos-shiel. It was merely my bow. The wood began to sprout leaves and root itself in the soil. Then the sun shone.'

'We had wizards once – a whole temple of them. They supervised the building of the Great Library in Zir-vak. They were blamed when the sun went away and sacrificed on the high altar. The King promised that with their deaths the mountains would stop spewing fire, but it didn't happen. In the last two hundred years there have been other prophets who claimed that blood sacrifice would appease the gods, and they would relent of their punishment. But they have not. We are a dying people, Sigarni; there is no hope for us.'

'And yet amid all this turmoil you fight a war,' she said. 'Why?'

'It was originally over a woman. The King's grandfather fell in love with a noblewoman from the east, but she was betrothed to the King of Kal-vak. Despite her pleas her father made her honour her promise, and she was sent to Kal-vak. Our King was furious – and swore he would free her. We went to war. Our troops attacked Kal-vak and were repulsed. Then the first of the mountains exploded. Each side blamed the other for the catastrophe, claiming that treachery had alienated the gods against us. At first it wasn't too terrible; the summers got shorter, and less warm, but crops still grew. But gradually the sky turned darker, and fine ash was deposited over the farmlands. Food grew scarce, save for the fish. But even these are swimming far from shore now.'

'Yet the war goes on,' said Ironhand. 'How is it that neither side has won? You said the battle was begun by the King's grandfather. How long ago was that?'

'A little more than two hundred and forty years. Most of the principal players are now dead though the war goes on for other reasons. People need to eat.'

'They eat the corpses!' whispered Ballistar.

'It is a little like pork, I am told,' said Yos-shiel. 'I have not eaten it myself, but when the time comes I don't doubt that I shall. Life is always sweet – even in the Hell of Yur-vale.' The old man sighed. 'But tell me, my friend, what is the object you seek? I may be of some assistance.'

'The Crown of Alwen,' said Sigarni.

'I know of no such object.'

'It is a winged helm, bright silver, embossed with gold.'

'The Paradise Helm,' said Yos-shiel, his eyes widening. 'You cannot take that! It is all that gives the people hope. Every twenty-five years it shows us a vision of Paradise, waterfalls and green trees, and a multitude standing around it, happy and smiling. That is our most prized artefact.'

Sigarni laid her hand on the old man's shoulders. 'What you see is my people standing by the Alwen Falls. Every quarter of a century the Crown reappears there, shimmering over the water. We all gather to see it, and you in turn, it seems, gather to see us. Tell me, Yos-shiel, of the last time the sun shone.'

'It was on the day of the old King's burial. I was there as they laid him on the funeral ship and sent it blazing on the river. The clouds broke and the sun shone for a full day. It was magnificent, there was singing and dancing in the streets.'

'And before that?'

'I don't remember exactly. Wait . . . yes, I do. Twelve years ago, at the Feast of Athling. We saw the dawn on the following day, the sun huge and red. That lasted only minutes.'

'What happened on the next feast day?'

'You don't understand, the Feast of Athling corresponds with the public display of the Paradise Helm. It happens only four times a century.'

254

For some time Sigarni questioned the old man and soon Ballistar became bored with the dialogue. He wandered to the window, leaned on the sill and watched the barges being loaded.

At last the conversation died away and Ironhand broke in. 'Best bring your men in for dismissal, old fellow,' he said, 'for we have a hankering to be on one of those barges when it pulls away.'

'Yes, I will,' said Yos-shiel. 'Thank you.'

An hour later the three sat at the stern of a forty-foot barge as the crew poled it steadily up-river. The vessel was fortified by hinged wooden flaps along both rails, which could be raised to offer protection from an assault. Huge rocks had been left at intervals along both sides of the deck, ready to be hurled down on any boat that sought to impede the barge's progress. Armed men sat at the prow, and all of the barge workers carried long knives.

'So we find the temple and steal the Crown?' said Ballistar. 'It would be best to enter it at night.'

Sigarni rose, stretched and walked away down the port side of the vessel. A soldier smiled at her. 'Stay with your friends,' he said. 'Soon it will be so dark you will not be able to see your hand before your face.'

She thanked him and returned to the others, seating herself on a coil of rope. The light faded fast, and soon the barge was engulfed in a darkness so complete that Sigarni felt an edge of panic.

'It's like being dead,' whispered Ballistar. Sigarni felt his hand brush against her arm; she took hold of it and squeezed his fingers.

'No, it isn't,' said Ironhand. 'Death is not dark; it is bright and vile.'

'How can they see to steer?' Ballistar asked.

'Quiet back there,' came a voice. 'We'll see the city within an hour.'

There was little sensation of movement within the all-encompassing blackness and Sigarni found herself thinking back to her days with Fell, when they had hunted together and made love before the fire. He had been able to read her moods so well. There were times when she had wanted nothing more than to curl up beside him, stroking his skin. On such occasions he would hug her

255

and kiss her fondly. On other nights, when the fey mood was upon her she would desire to make love with passion and fire. Always he responded. I was good for you too, Fell, she thought. I knew you, your thoughts and your dreams.

The first kiss had been shared on the slopes of High Druin, on a bright summer's day. They had raced over the four miles from Goring's Rock to the White Stream. Fell was faster and stronger, but his staying power could not match Sigarni's; she had doggedly clung to his trail, always keeping him in sight until the last, long rise. Then, as he faltered, she drew on her reserves and passed him.

At the White Stream he had sunk back to his haunches and fought for breath. Sigarni brought him water in a hastily made cup of bark.

'You are a wonder, Sigarni,' he said at last, taking her hand and kissing it.

She sat beside him, looping her arm around his neck. 'My poor Fell! Is your pride damaged beyond repair?'

He looked at her quizzically. 'Why would my pride be hurt? I did my best.'

'I liked it when you kissed my hand,' she said, changing the subject.

'Then I shall do it again.'

'I would like it more if you kissed my mouth.'

He smiled then. 'You are very forward for a Highland girl – I shall put it down to Gwalchmai's poor teaching. I don't mind losing a race to a woman like you, but it is not meet for you to do the seducing.'

'Why?'

'Because I sat up through most of the night trying to think of a way to get you to kiss me. It makes a mockery of all my planning.'

Sigarni lay back on the soft grass. 'Not at all. Go ahead. Show me your strategy.'

He chuckled. 'Too late. I think the fox is already in the henhouse.'

'Even so, I would like to hear it.'

Rolling to his elbow he lay beside her, looking down. 'I wanted to tell you that I have never known anyone like you, and that when

256

I am with you I am happier than at any other time. You are the delight in my life, Sigarni. Now and always.'

'You've won me over with your fine words,' she said. 'Now the kiss, if you please.'

Ballistar's voice cut through her thoughts. 'Your hand is very warm,' he whispered.

'I was thinking good thoughts,' she told him, keeping her voice low.

The journey continued, until at last they could see the faint lights of the city ahead. The barge moved on, approaching an arched portcullis gate. The helmsman flashed a signal with his lantern which was answered from above the arch. Then, with a great creaking and groaning, the portcullis rose and the barge passed beneath it.

Lanterns hung from poles all along the quayside and Sigarni heard Ballistar breathe a sigh of relief. 'It was awful,' he said, 'like being blind.'

'It was not awful,' said Sigarni, wistfully.

The barge clanked against the stone quay. Ironhand was the first ashore, followed by Sigarni and Ballistar.

'What now?' asked the warrior.

'We'll find some sheltered place to sleep,' Sigarni told him. 'Tomorrow we'll see the King.'

'For what purpose?' Ballistar asked.

'I shall ask for the Crown to be returned.'

'And he will just give it to you?'

'Of course not, Balli. I shall offer him something in return.'

'It will need to be a very large gift,' Ironhand pointed out.

'It will be,' she promised.

12

The city was unlike anything Sigarni had ever seen. Crammed together, the houses reared like cliff faces, dotted with lighted windows. Narrow alleyways filtered off like veins in the flesh of a stone giant. Arched tunnels led deeper into the city, and these boasted oil-lamps, hung at regular intervals to guide the traveller. There were signs on every alley, giving names to the streets and the wider avenues that led off from them. Sigarni felt hemmed in and dwarfed by the colossal nature of Zir-vak.

Ironhand was less impressed. 'They have structures in Kushir of far greater beauty,' he said, 'and there is evidence at least of planning there. These . . . huge hovels give a man no space to breathe.'

'It is oppressive,' agreed Ballistar. They wandered on aimlessly for a while until they saw the lights of a tavern. Ironhand headed for it. 'Wait!' called Ballistar. 'How will we pay?'

'I'll think of something,' said Ironhand.

The tavern was more than half empty, and few diners sat at the rough-built tables. There was a long, timbered drinking area at which several men stood, downing ale. Ironhand moved to the bar and a serving maid approached him. She was extraordinarily fat, her mouth turned down at the corners, her eyes small and seemingly set in several acres of unnecessary flesh; her enormous breasts sagged over the bar.

'What is there on offer?' asked Ironhand, as Sigarni and Ballistar moved alongside.

'To eat or to drink, or both?' she countered, idly wiping at the counter with a stained rag.

'Just to drink,' said the silver-bearded giant.

'We have ale or water, or if you'd rather something hot we have a dry root tisane.'

'And with what do we pay?'

'What?'

'What currency do we need? We are strangers here and have been told that gold is of no use.'

'You don't pay,' she said, as if talking to someone retarded. 'Everything's free . . . has been for years. So what will it be?'

'Ale,' said Ironhand.

'I'll have water,' said Sigarni. 'Where can we find lodgings for the night?'

'Wherever you choose. There's a room upstairs that you're welcome to. There's no fire, mind – no wood, you see. But the oil-lamps keep the room warm enough. There's only one bed, but it's big enough for the two of you,' she said, gesturing towards Ballistar and Sigarni. 'As for him . . . well.'

'I could always share your bed, my pretty,' said Ironhand. 'I expect it's a large one.'

'The cheek of the man!' said the woman, blushing.

'Those that don't ask never get,' said Ironhand, with a wink. 'And you've no idea how long it has been since I've enjoyed the company of a handsome woman.'

'Handsome, indeed! I *was* a fine-looking young woman, I'll have you know. Men travelled far to court me – and I don't take kindly to being mocked.'

'I would never mock you, my lovely. I've always preferred my women with a little meat on their bones. You think on it, while you fetch us our drinks. I'm a man of considerable patience.'

Ironhand turned away and strode to a nearby table, where Ballistar sat alongside him. 'Good God, man, how could you make love to that . . . that . . . sow?'

'She looks mighty good to me, lad. Now there's your sort of woman,' he added, pointing to another serving maid carrying a tray to the far table. She was slim and dark-haired, no more than seventeen. Ballistar stared at her with undisguised longing. 'I'll call her over,' whispered Ironhand.

'No!' squealed Ballistar.

It was too late, for Ironhand waved at the girl. She finished delivering the dishes to a table by the window, then walked over. 'My friend, here, . . .' began Ironhand.

'For pity's sake!' snapped Ballistar. He smiled sheepishly at the maid. 'I'm . . . er . . . sorry.'

'What he's trying to say, my lovely,' continued Ironhand, 'is that he is smitten by your beauty. If I were a younger man I'd fight him to the death for you. Now we are strangers in this city, and have no understanding of the normal practices. It will have to suffice that he finds you astonishingly attractive and would like to spend a little time with you when you are finished with your work. What do you say?'

The girl smiled and stared hard at Ballistar, who felt he had reddened to his toes.

'He is a handsome boy,' she said, 'And you are an old devil. However, since you've already seduced my mother – and that puts me out for the night – I think I will spend a little time with the young man. The rooms upstairs are all numbered. I shall be in room eleven in an hour or so.' Reaching out, she cupped Ballistar's chin. 'Your beard is soft,' she said. 'I like that.'

Her mother appeared, bearing a wooden tray on which was set a pitcher of ale, a jug of water and three tankards. She set it down carefully and turned to Ironhand. 'Don't you be drinking too much of that,' she said. 'It has a habit of turning hard men to softness, if you take my meaning.'

Ironhand's laughter bellowed out. Grasping the woman round her ample waist, he drew her into his lap. Then taking the pitcher, he raised it to his lips and began to drink. Ballistar and Sigarni watched in amazement as he downed more than half of it. 'By God, that's better,' he said. Then he rose, lifted the astonished woman into the air and began to spin and dance.

'She must weigh a ton,' whispered Ballistar to Sigarni. 'How does he do that?'

Ironhand returned to the table, still carrying the woman. 'It's no good,' he said. 'I can wait not a moment longer. I'll see you both in the morning.' So saying, he carried his conquest from the room.

For a little while Ballistar and Sigarni sat in silence. At last he spoke. 'The woman I'm going to see . . . I don't . . . what should I . . . ?'

Sigarni laughed softly. 'Do whatever comes naturally. Sit with her and talk for a while. My advice would be to tell her that she is your first, and that you are unskilled.'

'I couldn't do that!'

'She will know anyway. Enjoy yourself, Ballistar. And make sure that she too has fond memories of the meeting. Too many men get carried away by their lust, and forget that their partners need loving too.'

'How do I . . . ?'

'This is not a lesson, Balli. Kiss, touch and explore. Make it last. This is the one experience you will never forget.'

He grinned. 'I can't believe this. When we get back I'm going to pick up the little wizard and kiss both his wizened cheeks!'

'He'll turn you into a spider and tread on you.'

'Will you be all right alone?'

Leaning forward, she covered his hand with her own. 'I stood in a cave and waited for demons, Balli. I think I'll probably survive a night in a strange inn, don't you?'

They sat and talked for a while, then the young maid came for Ballistar and Sigarni smiled at the look of sudden panic that flashed across his handsome face. 'Go,' she said, 'enjoy yourself.'

Alone now, she sipped the water and concentrated on the magical events that had overtaken them in Yur-vale. Three separate bursts of magic: the growth of Ballistar, the sprouting of the bow and the rebirth of Ironhand. The dwarf had become a man, strong and straight. Why? And why the bow, and not the arrows? She had tried to discuss it with Ballistar, but he had merely shrugged and said, 'It was magic. Who cares why?'

But there must be laws governing magic, she thought. Ironhand had been reborn through a piece of dried bone. But what of the bone tips on her arrows? Why had they not grown into deer? And the leather of her belt or boots – why had these items remained intact?

Taliesen had warned that this was a world of strong magic, and that it would affect them far more than the inhabitants of Yur-vale. What had he said about his fellow sorcerer? He had eaten pork and

261

it had swelled inside him? Sigarni shuddered. Like the bone of Ironhand, the flesh had reconstituted itself in his belly and he had been ripped to pieces from within by a live and panic-stricken boar.

Reaching for the water goblet, she winced as the cold metal edge pushed at the still healing cut on her palm.

And instantly she had the answer. On the night before the journey she had held Ironhand's bone. On the journey itself through the Gateway she had gripped Ballistar's hand.

My blood touched them. The bow also – but not the arrows!

Sigarni rose from her seat and walked upstairs to her room. The bed was deep and soft, but she did not sleep for several hours. When she awoke Ironhand was sitting beside the bed.

'I hope your dreams were good ones,' he said.

'I had none that I can recall,' she told him. 'You?'

'I didn't sleep a wink,' he said with a grin. 'But I could eat a horse.'

'That would not be advisable. The horse would eat you.'

He looked at her quizzically and she explained about Taliesen's warning. 'Well, then, we had better find the Crown and head back to the Highlands. I want to taste a good steak again, and smell the pines.'

'First we must find the palace, or wherever it is that the King resides.'

'You think he will just give you a national treasure?'

'We'll see.'

The King stared from the window of his eighth-floor study, and watched as the enemy siege engines slowly approached the city's north wall. There were seven of them, each around eighty feet high, clad in sheets of hammered iron and impervious to flame arrows. When they reached the walls, which they would within the hour, the fighting would be hard. Close to the wall the towers would lower their drawbridges, and fighting men would pour out on to the ramparts.

His Guards would meet them, blade to blade, hacking and slaying, buying time for the engineers to hurl fire bombs through the

262

apertures. The iron cladding outside would offer no protection to the scores of men waiting on the siege tower stairs.

You are coming to your doom, he told himself. He glanced to his left, where his ceremonial armour was laid out on a bench of oak. You are getting too old to fight, he thought. And what will happen to Zir-vak when you fall in battle? Neither of his sons had yet reached one hundred – and even if they had, he thought with regret, they could not shoulder the responsibilities of command. Perhaps I have been too easy on them.

Stepping back from the window he moved to his desk, lifting a bronze-rimmed oval mirror. The face that peered back at him was grey with fatigue, the eyes dull. Dropping the mirror, he picked up the letter that had arrived the previous evening from the merchant Yos-shiel. Three strangers had come to the city, intent on stealing the Paradise Helm. They would find a fine surprise waiting for them!

A servant entered the room and bowed deeply. 'Majesty, there is a woman who wishes to see you.'

'Tell her I have no time today. Let her make her entreaty to Pasan-Yol!'

'With respect, Majesty, I feel you may wish to speak with the woman. She says she wishes to see you in connection with the Paradise Helm – and she matches the description you gave to the soldiers.'

The King turned. 'Is she alone?'

'No, her companions are with her, Majesty – a white-haired giant and a young man.'

'Are they armed?'

'They gave their weapons to the Royal Sentries.'

Intrigued, the King moved to his desk. 'Show them in – and fetch Pasan-Yol.'

Bowing once more, the servant departed.

As Yos-shiel had reported, the woman was very beautiful, and moved with a grace that stirred the King's blood. 'I understand you claim to be from another land,' he said. 'Where might that be?'

'I could not say where in relation to Yur-vale,' she told him, her voice deep, almost husky. 'We were sent through a magical Gateway.'

The King picked up the letter. 'So Yos-shiel tells me. I must say I find it hard to believe. Could it be that you are spies, sent by the enemy?'

A squad of guards moved in behind the newcomers. 'You wish them arrested, Majesty?' asked Pasan-Yol.

'Not yet,' the King told the young guardsman. 'They interest me. So tell me, woman, why you are here.'

'To bring back the sun,' she said. The silence in the room grew as the listeners took in her words.

'You are a witch?' asked the King.

'I am.'

'Sorcery has long been considered a crime here, punishable by death.'

The woman smiled. 'Whereas stupidity has obviously not. Do you wish to see the sun shine over Yur-vale?'

The King leaned back in his chair. 'Let us suppose – merely for the sake of argument – that you could achieve this . . . this miracle. What do you desire in return?'

'I think the letter from Yos-shiel will answer that,' she told him.

'You know of that – and yet you come here? Was that wise, witch?'

She shrugged. 'The wisdom of any course can only be judged by the outcome. I offer you the sun for a piece of metal. You make whatever choice seems fitting.'

'What do you think, Pasan?' asked the King.

The young guardsman gave a derisory laugh. 'I think they are spies, Father. Let me interrogate them.'

'Yet another numbskull,' said Ironhand to Sigarni, in the same tone of voice. 'You think they are all victims of in-breeding?' The guardsman's sword snaked from its scabbard. 'Put it away, boy,' said Ironhand, 'before I take it away from you and swat your backside.' The guardsman took a deep breath and dropped into a fighting position with sword extended.

'That's enough!' said the King. 'Put up your blade, Pasan!'

'You heard what he said, Father!'

'Aye, I did,' answered the King, wearily. 'So let us not be too swift to prove his point.'

'I think a little proof would not go amiss,' put in Sigarni to the King. 'Do you have a garden here?'

'Nothing grows in Zir-vak,' he said. 'But, yes, there was a garden. I do not go there now, for the sight of it saddens me.'

'Take me there,' she said, 'and I will show you something to lift your heart.'

The King stood and moved to the window, where the siege towers were inching ever closer. He swung back to the woman. 'Very well, I will humour you. But know this, if there is no miracle I shall not be best pleased – and the charge of sorcery will be laid against you.'

'If there is no miracle,' said the woman, 'then the charge will be hard to prove.'

For the first time the King smiled. 'Let us go to the garden,' he said.

The garden was more than two hundred feet long, and had been designed around a series of winding white-paved pathways. There were three fountains, none of them in use, and the flower-beds were covered with thick grey ash. Scores of dead trees lined the marble walls at the outer edges of the garden, and the area was devoid of any life.

Sigarni felt a moment of fear as she surveyed the landscape. What if her reasoning was flawed?

'I'm looking forward to this,' said Ironhand, with a wink.

'Well,' said the King, 'we are here, and you promised a miracle.' He was standing with his arms folded, his son beside him with hand on sword. The six guards stood nervously by.

Sigarni approached the King. 'May I borrow your dagger, my lord?' she asked.

'What nonsense is this?' stormed the young man at his side.

Sigarni frowned, then raised her arm before him. 'Make a shallow cut, here,' she said, pointing to her forearm.

Pasan-yol drew his dagger, and drew the blade slowly across her skin. Blood welled, and Sigarni walked to a line of dead bushes, kneeling down before the first and holding her arm above the dry branches. Slowly drops of blood dripped to the wood.

Nothing happened. Sigarni stayed where she was, and glanced at Ironhand, who was watching her intently. She had explained her theory to him, and he had listened thoughtfully.

'Well, where is this miracle?' asked the King, his tone hardening.

Ironhand stepped forward and knelt beside Sigarni. 'Touch the bush,' he whispered.

Lowering her arm, her fingers brushed against the wood and she felt her hand grow hot. The blood upon the branches disappeared into the grey wood, which began to swell and grow. Buds appeared, pushing out into new red growth, stretching up towards the iron sky, then darkened to green and finally to brown. Three blooms appeared, opening to roses the colour of Sigarni's blood.

She stood and turned towards the King, ready to present her arguments.

Just then a beam of sunlight pierced the clouds, illuminating the garden. In its bright light the King looked older, more weary, his face lined, dark rings beneath his eyes. 'How have you done this?' he whispered, moving to the rose and kneeling before it to smell the blooms.

'The war must end,' she said. 'That is all that keeps the sun at bay.'

'What are you saying?'

'This is a magical land, Majesty, where the war and the devastation feed the dark side of the magic. Every act of hate, of malice, of bloodlust only serves to fuel the fires beneath the mountains. You are destroying this world with your fighting. Think back to the days before, when the sun shone. The Feast of Athling. There was a three-day truce between the armies; when the fighting stopped the sun shone. It was the same when your father was buried: a day of truce. And before the war Yur-vale was a paradise. Can you not see it? In some way the feelings of the people are magnified by the land itself. All this hatred and violence is reflected by the land which, like the people here, is turning on itself.'

'I told you she was a spy!' roared Pasan-Yol. 'This is all a trick to lull us.'

From some distance away came a series of dull, booming sounds, and the faint clash of steel upon steel. The sunlight faded away.

'The siege towers have reached the walls,' said the King. 'I must go now. But I will give your words serious consideration and we will meet again this afternoon. In the meantime I will ask one of my servants to show you the palace museum. There are many wonders there – including the Helm you seek.'

Sigarni and Ballistar bowed. Ironhand merely inclined his head.

'Your tall friend does not care for the formalities. Does he not know it is wise always to pay respects to a king?'

'He does, my lord,' said Sigarni. 'But he is a king himself, and is unused to bowing before others.'

The King chuckled. 'A monarch should have better dress sense,' he said, pointing to Ironhand's ill-fitting red shirt. 'And you, young lady, should have that wound dressed – unless of course you plan to revive my entire garden.' He swung to the young man. 'You cut too deeply, Pasan. See that the surgeon is sent for, and that our guests are looked after.'

'But, Father . . .'

'Just do it, Pasan. I have no time for further debate.' The King strolled away, followed by four of the guards.

Pasan glared at Sigarni. 'You may have fooled him with your witchery, but not me. You are an enemy – and enemies are to be destroyed. And look at your rose,' he said triumphantly. 'It is already dying.'

'Aye,' she agreed sadly. 'With every death upon the walls. With every mouthful of corpse meat. With every word of hate.'

Summoning Ballistar and Ironhand, Sigarni walked back towards the palace.

Her arm bandaged, the blood still seeping through, Sigarni sat with Ironhand and Ballistar in the main hall of the Palace Museum. There were statues lining the walls, paintings hung in alcoves, but pride of place went to the Crown of Alwen, which sat upon a slim column of gold within a crystal case. The Helm shimmered in the lamplight and Ironhand gazed upon it with undisguised admiration. 'Had I retained the Crown,' he said softly, 'there would have been no civil war. Elarine and I could have enjoyed a peaceful reign and you, Sigarni, would have known great joy.'

'I have known great joy,' she said. 'Gwalchmai was a fine foster-father, and I have lived a free life in the Highlands.'

'Even so, I wish it had been different.'

'It is never wise to long for days past,' she told him. 'They cannot come again. What will you do when we get back? Will you announce yourself and lead the army? You are much more suited to the task than I.'

'I think not,' said the giant. 'You are the new Battle Queen. Let it be so. I will advise – and take an hour or two to smite the enemy,' he added with a grin.

'*If* we get back,' pointed out Ballistar. 'There is no certainty. What if you are wrong about this war, Sigarni? What if the sun does not shine again?'

'I am not wrong,' she said. 'I sensed it from the moment the bow sprouted leaves. This is a land in torment. Everything here is unnatural. When the war ends, so will the upheavals of nature – I am convinced of it.'

'I think you are correct,' said Ironhand, 'but the fact remains that for the war to end, both sides must agree terms. After fighting for this long, such a decision will be hard. There is something else too, daughter. If there is no peace, and the King refuses to give you the Crown, what then?'

'We will leave without it – and fight the Outlanders without the aid of the Pallides.'

'I'm hungry,' said Ballistar. 'Do you think they would allow us a cooking pot? We still have some oats?'

'You could ask,' said Sigarni, gesturing towards the silent guards at the door. But the request was refused, and the trio moved around the museum, studying the various artefacts.

Towards dusk several servants entered, filling the oil-lamps and lighting more. Huge velvet curtains were drawn across the high, arched windows.

At last the King returned. He was wearing armour now, and looked even more weary than he had in the morning. 'Their siege engines were destroyed,' he said, 'but the death toll was very high. I have asked for a truce, and will meet with their King outside the walls in an hour. I want you with me when I speak with him.'

'Gladly, sire,' said Sigarni.

More than fifty lanterns had been set on poles outside the main gates, and a score of chairs were set out in two lines of ten, facing one another. The night was pitch-black, the lanterns barely giving out sufficient light to see more than a few paces. 'Fetch more,' ordered the King, and two officers moved away into the blackness. The King, now dressed in a simple tunic of blue, sat down, with Sigarni on his left and Pasan-Yol on his right.

Twenty more lanterns were set out.

They waited for some time, and then saw a slow-moving column of men walking from the enemy camp, their King in the lead, wearing silver armour embossed with gold. He had no helm and Sigarni saw that his lean face showed the same edge of weariness as that of the man beside her.

He did not look at the waiting party, but strode directly to a chair opposite the King of Zir-vak and sat down.

'Well, Nashan,' he said at last, as his twenty-man escort fanned out behind him, 'for what purpose do you call this meeting?'

The King told him of Sigarni's arrival, and of the miracle in the rose garden. The enemy leader was less than impressed.

'Today you destroyed a few siege towers, but they proved their worth, did they not? You were hard pressed to stop them. I have now ordered fifty to be built, then Zir-vak will fall. You think me a fool, cousin? You seek to stave off defeat with this nonsense?'

'It is all nonsense, Reva. We fight a war our grandfathers began. And for what? For the honour of our Houses. Where is the honour in what we do?'

'I will find honour,' stormed Reva, 'when I have your head impaled on a lance over the gates of Zir-vak.'

'Then you may have it,' said the King. 'You may take it now. If that will end the war and bring the sun back to our lands, I will die gladly. Is that all you desire?'

'The surrender of all your forces, and the opening of the gates,' demanded Reva.

'The gates are already open,' pointed out the King. 'And we will fight no more.'

'No!' screamed Pasan-Yol. 'You cannot betray us all.'

'It is not betrayal, Pasan, it is a new beginning.'

The young man lurched to his feet, a dagger in his hand. Before anyone could stop him he had rammed the blade into his father's breast. The King groaned and fell against Sigarni. Ironhand, standing behind the King, reached over and grabbed Pasan-Yol by the throat, dragging him away. Ballistar threw himself at the young man, wrenching the knife from his grasp.

Sigarni lowered the dying King to the ground. 'Reva!' he called.

The enemy King knelt by his side. 'I spoke the truth, cousin. This war is killing the land and it must end. Not just for you and I, and our Houses, but for the land itself. You now have my head, and my city. Let the hatred pass away with my death.'

For a moment Reva said nothing, then he sighed. 'It will be as you say, Nashan. I too have a need to see the sun.' Pulling off his gauntlet, Reva took Nashan's hand.

A man cried out and pointed upwards. A full moon had appeared in the night sky, and the glimmering of distant stars could be clearly seen. 'It begins,' whispered Nashan.

And he died.

Sigarni closed the King's eyes and stood. 'A sad end to a fine man,' she said, turning and walking away. Ironhand released Pasan-Yol, who stood staring at the moon and stars. Then he ran to his father's body, hurling himself across it and sobbing.

Sigarni, Ballistar and Ironhand returned to the museum. Ironhand thundered his fist against the crystal case, which exploded into fragments. Reaching inside, he drew out the Crown and passed it to Sigarni.

'It is time to go,' she said, opening her pack and stowing the Crown inside.

Vast numbers of people thronged the streets, staring up at the sky as the trio made their slow way down to the river. There were several boats moored there and Sigarni chose a small craft, with two oars. Loosing it from its moorings, they climbed aboard, and set out on the journey downstream.

Sigarni sat staring back at the receding city. Ballistar put his arm around her shoulder. 'Why so sad, Sigarni? You saved them.'

'I liked him,' she said. 'He was a good man.'

'But there is something else, I think?' he probed.

She nodded. 'We stopped one war, and now we have the means to pursue another. Is our land any different from this one? How does High Druin feel about the slaughter that is coming?'

'Our fight is not about honour, or a stolen wife,' said Ballistar. 'We fight for survival against a pitiless enemy. There is a difference.'

'Is there? My hatred is all used up, Balli. When they raped me, I wanted to see every Outlander slain. That is not what I desire any more.'

Later the following day, in bright sunlight, the three stood at the circle of stones. Sigarni unwound the bandage on her forearm and used it to press her blood against each of the six stones. Then the three of them stood at the centre, holding hands and waiting.

'I'm anticipating that steak with great pleasure,' said Ironhand.

'And I can't wait to see their faces when they see what I have become,' said Ballistar happily.

Light grew around them and Sigarni felt dizziness swamp her. Then Taliesen appeared before her, and a cold winter breeze touched her face.

'Did you get it?' the wizard asked.

Sigarni did not answer. In her right hand lay the tiny bone fragment of Ironhand, while clinging to her left was Ballistar the Dwarf, tears flowing from his eyes as he stood, dressed in her outsize leggings.

* * *

271

Like all Highlanders, Gwalchmai loved the spring. Life in the mountains was always harsh, and people lived with the constant knowledge that death waited like a monster beyond the firelight. Winter fell upon the mountains like a mythical beast, robbing the land of crops, of food, sucking the heat from the soil and from the bones of Man.

But spring, with her promise of sunshine and plenty, was a season to be loved. The burst of colour that appeared on the hillsides as the first flowers pushed their way through the cold earth, the singing of birds in the trees, the fragrant blossom on bush and branch – all these things spoke of *life*.

The ache in Gwalchmai's back had faded away in the morning sunlight, as he sat in the old chair on the porch of his cabin. I almost feel young again, he thought happily. A faint touch of regret whispered across his mind, and he opened the parchment he had held folded in his hand. It had been so long since he had written anything that the words seemed spidery and over-large, like a child's. Still, it was legible.

Time for the last of the mead, he thought. Leaning to his right, he lifted the jug and removed the stopper. Tipping it, he filled his mouth with the sweet liquor and rolled it over his tongue. He had hidden the mead the year Sigarni was brought to him, which had been a vintage year. Gwalchmai smiled at the memory. Taliesen had walked into the clearing, leading the child by the hand. In that moment Gwalchmai had seen the vision of his death. That night, as the child slept, he had taken two jugs and hidden them in the loft, ready for this day.

This day . . .

The old man pushed himself to his feet and stretched his back. The joints creaked and cracked like tinder twigs. Drawing in a deep breath, he swirled the last of the liquor in the jug. Less than half a cup left, he realized. Shall I save it until they come? He thought about it for a moment – then drained the jug. Letting out a satisfied sigh, he sank back to the chair.

The sound of horses' hooves on the hard-packed ground made him start and panic flickered within his breast. He had waited so

272

long for this moment – and now he was afraid, fearful of the long journey into the dark. His mouth was dry, and he regretted the last swallow of mead.

'Calm yourself, old fool,' he said, aloud. Rising, he strolled out into the wide yard and waited for the horsemen.

There were six scouts, clad in iron helms and baked leather breastplates. They saw him and drew their weapons, fanning out around him in a semi-circle. 'Good morning, my brave boys!' said Gwalchmai.

The riders edged their horses closer, while scanning the surrounding trees. 'I am alone, boys. I have been waiting for you. I have a message here that you may read,' he added, waving the scrap of parchment.

'Who are you, old man?' asked a rider, heeling his horse forward. Gwalchmai chuckled. 'I am the reader of souls, the speaker of truths, the voice of the slain to come. They found the body, you know, back in your village. Upon your return they intend to hang you. But do not let it concern you – you will not return.'

The man blanched, his jaw hanging slack.

'What's he talking about?' demanded another rider. 'What body?'

Gwalchmai swung to the speaker. 'Ah, Bello, what a delight to see you again! And you, Jeraime,' he added, smiling up at a third rider. 'Neither of you like each other, and yet, together you will stand back to back at the last, and you will die together, and take the long walk into Hell side by side. Is that a comforting thought? I hope not!'

'Give me the message, old man!' demanded the first rider, holding out his hand.

'Not yet, Gaele. There is much to say. You are all riding to your deaths. Sigarni will see you slain.'

'How is it you know my name?' demanded Gaele.

'I know all your names, and your sordid pasts,' sneered Gwalchmai. 'That is my Gift – though when I gaze upon your lives it becomes a curse. You buried her deep, Gaele, by the riverbank – but you never thought that the old willow would one day fall . . . and in so doing expose the grave. Worse yet, you left the ring upon her

273

finger, the topaz ring you brought back from Kushir. All the village knows you killed her. Even now a message is on its way asking that you be returned for trial! Fear not, brave boy, for your belly will be opened at the Duane Pass. No hanging for you!'

'Shut up!' screamed Gaele, spurring his horse forward. His sword lashed down, striking the old man on the crown of his head and smashing him from his feet. Blood gushed from the wound but Gwalchmai struggled to his knees.

'You will all die!' he shouted. 'The whole army. And the crows will feast on your eyes!' The sword slashed down again and Gwalchmai fell to his face in the dirt. All tension eased from his frame, and he did not feel the blades lance into his body.

All these years, he thought, and at the last I lied. I do not know whether Sigarni will win or lose, but these cowards will carry the tale of my prophecy back to the army, and it will rage like a forest fire through their ranks.

As if from a great distance, Gwalchmai heard his name being called.

'I am coming,' he said.

Gaele dragged his sword clear of the old man's back, wiping the blade clean on the dead man's tunic. Stooping, he plucked the parchment from the dead fingers and opened it.

'What does it say?' asked Bello, as the others gathered round the corpse.

'You know I can't read,' snapped Gaele.

Jeraime stepped forward. 'Give it to me,' he said. Gaele passed it over and Jeraime scanned the spidery text.

'Well?' demanded Gaele.

Jeraime was silent for a moment, and when he spoke his voice was trembling. 'It says, *"There will be six. One of them a wife-killer. Gaele will strike me down. Jeraime will read my message."*

Jeraime let the parchment fall and backed away to his horse.

'He was a sorcerer,' whispered Bello. 'He said we were all going to die. The whole army! Dear God, why did we come here?'

The army made camp near the ruins of Cilfallen: seven thousand men, incorporating four thousand heavily armoured footsoldiers, fifteen hundred archers and slingers, five hundred assorted engineers, cooks, foragers and scouts, and a thousand cavalry. The Baron's long black tent was erected near the Cilfallen stream, while the cavalry camped to the north, the footsoldiers to the east and west and other personnel to the south. Leofric set sentry rotas and despatched scouts to the north; then he returned, weary, to his own tent.

Jakuta Khan was sitting on a canvas-backed chair, sipping fine wine. He smiled as Leofric entered the tent. 'Such a long face,' said the sorcerer, 'and here you are on the verge of a glorious expedition.'

'I dislike lying to the Baron,' said Leofric, opening a travel chair and seating himself opposite the red-clad man.

'I told you, it was not a lie. I am a merchant – of sorts. Where do you think the first battle will be fought?'

'The Baron believes they will fortify the Duane Pass. We have several contingency plans for such an eventuality. Can you not tell me what they are planning? The fall of the forts has left me out of favour with the Baron. He blames me!'

Jakuta Khan shook his head and adopted a suitably apologetic expression. 'My dear Leofric, I would dearly love to help you. But to use my powers while Taliesen is nearby would be costly to me – perhaps fatal. The old man is not without talent. When he departs I will reach out and, shall we say, observe them. Relax, my boy. Enjoy the wine. It really is very good.'

Leofric sighed. He knew the wine was good; it had cost a small fortune. Accepting a goblet, he sipped the liquid appreciatively. 'You said you had tried to capture the woman before, and had failed. Is she charmed? Is this Taliesen as powerful as you?'

'Interesting questions,' said Jakuta Khan, his jovial round face now looking serious and thoughtful. 'I have pondered them often. The first attempt was thwarted by Taliesen and a Highlander named Caswallon. They took her as a babe, and hid her . . . here. At that time I did not know of Taliesen's existence, and therefore had no plan to cope with him. By the time I found her hiding place she was a small child; her foster-mother threw her from the cabin

275

window, and she ran to a nearby waterfall. There Caswallon and Taliesen once more intervened, though how they came to be there at that precise time, I do not know. They could not have stopped me, for I was well prepared. Sadly, a third force intervened; I believe it was a spirit. He aided her again – and that cost the life of the dearest of my acolytes. But there it is. That is life and we cannot grumble. But last week I used one of the four great spells. Infallible. Either the victim dies, or the sender. I risked everything. And nothing happened. Curiously, the demon I summoned disappeared as soon as my spell was complete. I can tell you, Leofric, I have spent many a long night since thinking over that problem. I know it is hard for you to imagine, but think of aiming a bow at an enemy and loosing the shaft. As it flies through the air, it disappears. It was like that. The question is, where did the demon go?'

'Did you find an answer?' asked Leofric, intrigued.

'I believe so. I cast the spell just outside Citadel town, inside a circle of ancient stones. They are believed to be Gateways to other worlds. In some way I believe I activated the Gateway. Even so, the creature was completely attuned to Sigarni. Therefore wherever it went, she would have been there also. Mystifying.'

Leofric refilled his goblet. 'Does that mean the creature is still looking for her?'

'It is possible. In fact, it is more than likely. The Gateways operate through time as well as space, and even now he is winging his way towards her. What a cheering prospect – I'll drink to that!'

'Why do you hate her so? Has she done you some harm?'

'Good Heavens, Leofric, I do not hate her. I don't hate anyone. Such a harmful emotion! I rather admire her, don't you? But I need what she has. The blood royal! All the great spells require blood royal. And anything can be achieved with it, lead to gold, immortality – of a kind – physical strength. As limitless as the imagination.'

'She's just a Highland woman, for God's sake. What royal blood does she carry?'

'What blood? How arrogant of you, Leofric. Your own King does not carry the blood royal, though his grandsons might. Sigarni is the daughter of the great King, Ironhand, who was done to death by assassins centuries ago. He had a fortress near here, colossal and impregnable. Only the foundation stones are left.'

'Then how could she be his daughter?'

'She was carried through a Gateway in time. Do you not listen, my boy?'

'I think the wine must be going to my head,' Leofric admitted. 'It all sounds like gibberish.'

'Of course it does,' said Jakuta Khan soothingly, leaning forward and patting the young man's knee. 'But that is the simple answer to your question. Her blood carries power, and I need that power. If there was a way to utilize it without killing her, I would. For I am not fond of death.'

Leofric refilled his glass for the second time. 'You are a strange man, Jakuta. Perhaps you are insane. Have you thought of that?'

'You are full of interesting ideas, Leofric. It makes you a joy to be with. Let us examine the premise. Insanity: not being sane. Yet how do we establish sanity? Would we, for example, look to the majority of people and claim them as normal and sane?'

'That seems reasonable,' agreed Leofric.

'But the King is not normal like them, is he? He is an extraordinary man, as is the Baron. Does that make them insane?'

'Ah, I see what you are saying,' said Leofric, leaning forward and spilling his wine. 'But then normality is not just a question of who farms or who rules. It is surely an ability to discern right from wrong, or good from evil, perhaps.'

'Now the waters become even muddier, my boy. If a farmer sees a neighbour with a bigger section of land, and more wealth, and sets out to murder him, is he evil?'

'Of course.'

'But if a king sets out to destroy his enemy's kingdom in order to swell his own treasury, then he, by that example, is evil also.'

'Not so!' insisted Leofric, aware he was on dangerous ground. 'There may be many reasons why a nation goes to war. Security, for example, protecting one's borders.'

'Of course, of course,' agreed Jakuta. 'And this war? Against an enemy with no army to speak of, a pretend war for the purpose of self-glorification, is this evil?'

'For God's sake keep your voice down!'

'Sanity is not easy to establish, is it, Leofric? All I know is that one man's good is another man's evil. That is the way life works: it favours the rich and the powerful, it always has and I suspect it always will. I am not rich, but I am powerful. I intend to become more powerful.'

'As powerful as this Taliesen?'

'Less and more. He is a curious fellow. He has vast resources, and chooses not to use them. You would like him, I think, Leofric. He knows more about the Gateways than any man alive. Yet he lives like a peasant, and dresses worse. He has a cloak of feathers that has seen better days, and he has allowed his body to become old and wizened. We have not conversed, but I would make a wager that he believes his powers to be a gift from some supreme source, to be used wisely and carefully.'

'Perhaps he is right.'

'Perhaps. I cannot disprove his theories, but I tend towards disbelief. I have conversed with demons who serve a greater demon, and I have known holy men who claim to have spoken with God. Whereas I, more powerful than most, have never felt the need to serve either God or the Devil, and neither of them has seen fit to approach me.'

'How will you know when Taliesen has left the Highlands?'

'Oh, I will know.'

In the morning Leofric felt that he had a caged horse inside his skull, trying to kick its way to freedom. His head pounded and the bright sunlight induced a feeling of nausea. Jakuta Khan, who seemed untouched by the excesses of the night before, sat quietly, watching the dawn. Leofric stumbled from the tent and made his way to the stream, where he stripped off his tunic and bathed in the clear, cold water.

Wet and shivering, he dressed and walked to the Baron's tent. As he had expected the Baron was already awake, and was sitting at his travel desk examining maps. Leofric entered and bowed. 'Good morning, my lord. I trust you slept well?'

The Baron rubbed at the black leather eye-patch he wore. 'I have not slept well since that damned bird tore out my eye. What news?'

'The scouts are not in yet sir. Shall I fetch you breakfast?'

'Not yet. How do you think they will defend the pass?' The Baron spread out a series of maps on the rug at his feet. Leofric crouched down and studied them.

'They have few choices, sir. My spies tell me the Pallides had pledged themselves to Sigarni. That brings the total of her force to just over three thousand – not quite enough, I would imagine, to defend the eastern slope. They would be too thinly stretched and we could outflank them. The western slope is shorter, but that would mean leaving a gap in their eastern defences, through which a force of cavalry could ride, creating havoc in their villages. Of course, they may try to defend both slopes, or they may, if desperate, choose to occupy the flat-topped hill at the north end of the pass. The slopes are steep and a shield-ring would be hard to penetrate.'

'In what way do you see this as a desperate move?' enquired the Baron.

'We would surround them, and there would be no means of escape. They would be gambling all on being able to hold us, wear us down, then counter-attack.'

'I agree,' said the Baron. 'So which do you believe they will choose?'

'I am not a warrior, my lord, and I do not fully understand their mentality. I would, however, think it likely they will try to occupy the western slope. It is wooded, and covered with boulders. We would be forced to attack many times to discover the areas in which they are weak.'

'Aye, they'll try to be canny,' said the Baron. 'That black traitor Asmidir will see to that. Their line will be of varying strength, at its most powerful where an attack is likely.' He stabbed his forefinger at a point on the first map. 'Here, where the slope is not so steep, and

279

here, where the tree line thins. We will attack both simultaneously with the infantry. But the cavalry will strike here!'

'The highest ground? Is that wise, my lord?'

'Asmidir knows the way we fight, Leofric. Therefore we change. If I am wrong we will lose a few score cavalry, but the outcome will remain the same. What of supplies?'

Leofric rubbed at his eyes, praying that his head would stop pounding. 'I commandeered as many wagons as were available, my lord, and they should start arriving by late this afternoon. The men will be on short rations until we take the Pallides villages and the cattle there.'

'We have your negligence to thank for that,' snapped the Baron. 'I shall not swiftly forget the fall of your *impregnable* forts. If you were not my cousin, I would have had you flayed alive.'

'I am very grateful to you, sir,' said Leofric dutifully. The sound of horsemen approaching allowed him to avoid further embarrassment and he rose swiftly and moved outside. The first of the scout troops were returning. Lightly armed on fast horses, they could move swiftly across the countryside. All were veterans of many campaigns, and had travelled with the Census Taker in the autumn in order to accustom themselves to the land.

The lead rider dismounted, the other four riding off towards the cook-fires. The man saluted.

'Your report?' demanded Leofric.

'No sign of the enemy, sir. We killed one old man who ran at us with an ancient broadsword, and we spotted some foresters heading south but, as ordered, we avoided contact. The Loda fort has been plundered and the walls part dismantled. We rode to the Pallides fort, and this has seen similar treatment.'

'Any activity at Duane?'

'None that I could see, sir, and I thought it best not to push too far. We'll head out again after the men have eaten and acquired fresh mounts.'

'Good. We will be moving on to the Loda fort within the hour. When you return, make your report to me there.'

'Yes, sir.'

The Baron appeared and called out to the man as he was about to mount his horse.

'You, how many foresters were heading south?'

'Around a score, sir. Maybe a few more hidden by the trees.'

'Not an attacking force, then?'

'I don't believe so, sir. I think they may have been hunting. I expect food is scarce about now.'

'That's all,' said the Baron, moving alongside Leofric as the man saluted and turned away. 'How many men do you have guarding the supply wagons?'

Two troops, my lord, and a section of infantrymen.'

'Send back another fifty cavalrymen. I don't think they are hunting deer, they are seeking to cut our supply line.'

'Yes, sir. I'll do that immediately.'

'And give the orders to take some of them alive for questioning.'

'Yes, sir.'

'Now you can order me that breakfast,' said the Baron, returning to his tent.

Asmidir fought to keep himself calm. 'Sigarni, listen to me, you cannot continue to risk everything on a single throw of the dice. We have enough men now to hold the western slope. We can wear them down, harry their flanks, disrupt their supply lines. There is simply no need for us to take unnecessary chances.'

'I hear what you say, Asmidir, and I will consider it,' she said. 'Leave me now.'

She watched him depart, knowing his turmoil. He was a soldier, a strategist, and his hatred of the Outlanders had seeped into his bones. He had travelled far to find an enemy capable of inflicting savage defeats on his enemies, and now he felt it was all at risk. As indeed it was . . .

Fell had stood by silently during the exchange, and she turned to him. 'You are slow to offer your opinions, general?'

He laughed. 'I'm no general. I am a forester and proud of it. What he says makes sense to me, but who am I to argue with the great Battle Queen of the Highlands?'

'Stop it, Fell,' she said irritated. 'Just tell me what you think.'

'The man understands war – and he knows the ways of the Outlanders. The western slope must be defended, for it leads into our heartland. He knows it. You know it. The Outlanders know it.'

'Exactly my point,' said Sigarni. 'We all know where the dangers lie – therefore it is time to think of something different. And, by God, I shall!' She sat in silence for a few moments. 'Any sign of Gwalchmai yet?' she asked.

'No. I think he headed home.'

'To die,' she said, softly.

'Aye. His time had come, he said. He told me he was due to die in the spring – even knew the face of the soldier who would do the deed.'

'He did not say goodbye,' she said. 'He took me in when the beasts slew my . . . parents, and he cherished me throughout my childhood. Why would he leave without saying goodbye?'

'He knew the day and the hour, Sigarni. He left soon after you set off for the Crown. He spoke to Taliesen just before he departed; maybe the wizard can tell you more.'

'And what of Ballistar?'

Fell shook his head. 'Nothing yet, but Kollarin is seeking him.'

'It broke his heart, Fell. He wanted you to see him as he was in that other world, strong and straight. He even bedded a woman there. It is often said that what is never had cannot be missed. I think that is true. All his life he has yearned to be like us. Then it happened, and he experienced a joy he could not have dreamed of. The return was a living nightmare for him.'

'You look tired, Sigarni. Perhaps you should rest for a while.'

'No,' she told him, 'I need to see Taliesen before he leaves. Will you fetch him?'

'And then you will rest?'

She nodded. As Fell left the cabin Sigarni felt the truth of his words. Her bones ached with weariness, and her mind seemed to float from problem to problem, never settling. How long since you slept, she asked herself? Three days? Four?

282

Taliesen entered. 'The enemy is six thousand strong,' he said, 'and they will be here in two days. I wish you good fortune, Sigarni. It all rests now on your skill, and the courage of your men.'

'I wish you could stay, Taliesen. Your powers would be more than useful.'

'I shall return when the battle is over.'

'You are assuming that we will conquer?'

'No,' he said sadly. 'I am making no assumptions. I have seen many futures, Sigarni. In some you win, in others you die.'

'They cannot all be true,' she pointed out.

'Oh, they can,' he said softly. 'I long ago learned that there are many worlds identical to our own. When we travel between them, all things are possible. If you are dead when I return I will travel more Gateways, seeking a Sigarni who survived.'

'Why not seek her now – and then tell me how she did it?'

He smiled. 'I like you, Battle Queen. Truly. And now I must go. Have you spoken to Ironhand since he lost his second life?'

'Yes. His hurt is considerable, but he is still with me,' she said, touching the pouch hanging at her throat.

'I am sorry for the dwarf. I did not know that he would be so affected beyond the Gate.'

'Kollarin will find him. Ballistar is strong; he will recover. Go in peace, Taliesen.'

The old man bowed once more and walked to the door. Sigarni stretched herself out on the narrow pallet bed.

And drifted into the bliss of a dreamless sleep.

When she awoke Ironhand was sitting beside her. The old King was clad once more in his silver armour, with a great winged helm upon his head, his beard braided. 'How long have I been asleep?' she asked.

'Three hours. Fell is outside the cabin and is allowing no one in.'

'Now is the time for decisions,' she said, sitting up and rubbing the sand of sleep from her eyes. 'And it frightens me.'

'As it should. A little fear is like yeast to the spirit, encouraging it to grow strong.'

'What if I make a mistake now?'

'Then all die,' he told her bluntly.

She took a deep, calming breath. 'What advice can you offer me?'

'You are the Queen of the Highlands, my daughter, and I am proud of you. But now you must learn the one, terrible lesson of monarchy. That you are alone. The decision is yours. Win or lose, *you* carry the weight. For what it is worth, however, I will offer one thought – seek out the wife of Torgan.'

'You know her?'

'I was with you when you spoke last to her. She made you smile, and she made you cry. Both were good for you.'

'Then you cannot say which defensive plan would be the best for us? I was relying on you, Ironhand. You have fought so many battles. You won them all.'

'No, I didn't. Wish I had. I was always too headstrong. I just won the important ones. Seek out the woman, then make a decision. Stick to it, and be firm in your leadership. If you have doubts, hide them. You are the Battle Queen. They will all look to you, now and always.'

'You will be with me on the battlefield?'

'Aye, then I will seek Elarine and the fields of glory.'

The image shimmered and vanished. Sigarni rose and called out to Fell, who entered the room and knelt beside her. 'You were talking in your sleep,' he said. 'I could not make out the words.'

'I am going for a walk. Will you join me?'

'I am at your command,' he told her.

'I am asking you as a *friend,* Fell,' she told him, holding out her hand. For a moment only he stared at it, then their fingers touched. She looked into his deep brown eyes, and watched his smile grow.

'I love you, Sigarni,' he said, his voice thickening. 'Always did, always will. Welcome home.'

Together they walked from the cabin and down the hillside. The snow was melting fast, and spring flowers were everywhere. 'Is Torgan still here?' she asked.

'As far as I know. He and his wife have taken lodging with Fyon Sharp-axe. Are you going to give him a command?'

'Yes,' she said, 'under you.'

'Why? The man insulted you – and all of us.'

'But he's a Highlander, Fell, and a brave man. He deserves a second chance – for his wife and family if for nothing else.'

'Why the change, Sigarni? What has happened to you?'

'Perhaps it is High Druin,' she said, with a smile. 'Perhaps he spoke to me. When I went through the Gateway to that strange land I could almost feel its emotions. Yet the people there could not. I think it is the same here. The land cannot abide hatred, Fell. And I have no place left in my heart for it. Tomorrow we fight the Outlanders – because we must. We will destroy them if we can – but only because we must. Torgan was wrong, but he believed himself right and acted with the best interests of his clan at heart. Now he suffers shame. I shall end that.'

As they approached the end of the tree line Sigarni turned towards Fell and curled her arms around his neck. 'I hated you when you left me, and when I heard about the death of your wife I was glad. It shames me to admit, and I feel sorrow now.'

Dipping his head he kissed her tenderly. 'This is all I ever wanted, Sigarni. I know that now.'

'Leave me here, Fell. I will see you later – at the meeting hall. There I will announce our battle plan.'

'And after that?'

'We will go home. Together.'

Sigarni walked down the winding lane to the home of Fyon Sharp-axe. Loran, Torgan, and the huge warrior Mereth were sitting in the sunshine with the Hunt Lord. All rose as Sigarni approached.

'You are welcome, lady,' said Fyon, with a short bow.

Loran fetched a chair for her, and they sat. Torgan remained standing, then turned towards the house. 'Wait,' said Sigarni. 'I would value your counsel.'

'Do you wish to shame me again?' he asked, standing tall, his eyes angry.

285

'No. I want you to be at the meeting tonight. Tomorrow you will command the Farlain wing, under Fell's leadership.'

Torgan stood stock-still, and she could see the anger replaced by wariness. 'Why are you doing this?' he asked.

'I need strong men in positions of authority. You may decline if you choose.'

'No! I accept.'

'Good. The meeting begins at dusk. Is Layelia in the house?'

'Yes,' said Torgan, still stunned. 'Shall I fetch her?'

'No. I will find her.' Sigarni rose and left the men to their conversation. As she passed Torgan he called out to her.

'Wait!' Dropping to one knee, he bowed his head. 'My sword and my life,' he said.

It was an hour before dusk as Sigarni set out from the Pallides village. The afternoon was clear and bright, the sun dappling the new leaves on the trees. She felt better than she had in days, her mind cleansed of doubt. Whatever the outcome now, she felt that her plan was the best chance for Highland success.

Breaking into a run, she raced up the track, her body revelling in the exertion. As she ran she noticed a mist spreading out from the undergrowth. At first she ignored it, but it thickened suddenly, swirling around her. Sigarni slowed. The trees were indistinct now, mere faint shadows in the grey. Glancing up she saw that the mist was also above her, blocking the sun.

Unafraid, yet with growing concern, she walked on, heading upward. The trail was no longer beneath her feet, but if she continued climbing she would arrive at the encampment. A line of bushes appeared directly before her and she tried to skirt them, moving to the left. The undergrowth was thicker here, the ground flat.

Her irritation grew, but she pushed on.

After a while she came to a gap in the mist, a small hollow inside a ring of oak trees. The mist clung to the outer ring, and rose up over the dip to form a grey dome. There was a man sitting on the grass at the centre of the hollow, portly and friendly of face. Looking up, he smiled broadly.

'Welcome, Sigarni. At last we meet in perfect circumstances.'

'I saw you die at the Falls, ripped to pieces,' she said, her hand closing around the hilt of her dagger.

'Happily that was an acolyte of mine. I say happily, though I miss him dreadfully. Happily for me, I should have said.'

'You will not find today so happy,' she told him, drawing the blade and advancing towards him. Her legs felt suddenly heavy, as if she was wading through knee-deep mud. The knife was a terrible weight in her hand . . . it dropped slowly towards her side, then tumbled from her trembling fingers.

'You are quite correct,' he said, 'I do not find this a happy experience. You have done well among your barbarian friends and, were you to live, I believe you could cause the Outlanders considerable embarrassment. Sadly you must die – would that it were different.' Pushing himself to his feet, he drew a slender curved blade and advanced towards her. Sigarni fought to move, but could not. The knife came up and he took the neck of her tunic between the pudgy fingers of his left hand and cut away the cloth, exposing her breasts. 'I apologize for this apparently unseemly behaviour,' he said amiably. 'I have no intention of soiling your virtue. It is just that I need to make the correct incision for the removal of your heart.'

'Why are you doing this?' she asked him. 'What have I ever done to you?'

'As I recall, my dear, you used to hunt hares for sport. What had they ever done to you? We are not dealing here in petty squabbles or feuds. I am a sorcerer and a student of the universe. It is well known among my peers that certain sacrifices are considerably more powerful than others. A man, for example, will provide more power than . . . a hare. But the blood royal! Ah now, that is a priceless commodity.' Taking a small chunk of charcoal from his pocket, he drew a line between her breasts and along the rib line on her left side.

'Ironhand!' she cried.

'Ah,' he said, stepping back, 'so he was the mysterious force. Fascinating! Sadly, however, my dear, I have established a mystic wall around this hollow. No spirit can enter here, so save your breath. Your friend will not hear you either, for the mist dampens all sound. Now what I am about to do is remove your heart. There will be no pain. I am not a savage, and your death will be swift.'

'Give me until tomorrow,' she begged him. 'Let me save my people first!'

He chuckled. 'And you, of course, will give me your word to return?'

'Yes, I will. I swear it.'

'Ah, but you know what you hunters say — a hare in the bag is worth ten in the burrow. Let us merely hope that your officers will perform ably without you. Now, do you have a God you wish to make a final prayer to?'

'Yes,' she said, silently praying for the return of Taliesen.

'Then make it brief, my dear, for I wish to return to Leofric's tent. He has a fine stock of wine which I am looking forward to savouring. This country air does not suit me. I was born to exist within well-stocked cities. Let me know when you are finished, Sigarni. And do not waste your time seeking to contact Taliesen. He has gone back to his own time and is too far away to be of assist-ance — even could he hear your thoughts, which he cannot. I am afraid, dear lady, you are all alone. There are no creatures of myth or legend to help you now.'

'Don't be too sure,' she said, with a smile.

'Oh, I am sure,' he said. The knife rose and Jakuta Khan leaned forward, then arched back with a cry. He staggered several paces, his hand scrabbling at his back, where a bone-handled knife jutted from his kidneys. Sigarni felt the spell holding her dissipate and fall away. She lunged for her dagger and sprang at the sorcerer, ramming her blade into his fat belly and ripping it up towards his lungs. His scream was high-pitched and pain-filled as he sank to the ground. 'Oh, you have wounded me!' he cried.

Ballistar ran forward to stand beside Sigarni and Jakuta Khan looked up at him, his eyes already misting in death. 'A dwarf,' he whispered, surprised. 'I have been killed by a dwarf!'

He turned his dying eyes upon Sigarni. 'It is . . . not over. I sent a . . . demon. He is lost somewhere in time. But one day . . . when you look into his eyes ... remember me!' And he slumped face down on the grass.

'Your arrival was most timely,' she said, kneeling beside the dwarf and kissing his bearded cheek.

'Gwalchmai appeared to me. Told me to be here. I was ready to kill myself, but he said I would be needed, that I could help the clans.'

'Oh, Balli, if you had died my heart would have been broken. Come, let us go to the meeting!'

'I suggest you dress yourself first,' he said.

13

Fell lay awake, Sigarni's sleeping body pressed closely against him and her head upon his shoulder. Lady lay at Sigarni's left, her black flanks gleaming in the firelight. The coals in the iron brazier were burning low now, and the cabin was bathed in a gentle red glow.

Fell had stood at the back of the meeting hall and watched the faces of her officers as she outlined her battle plans. At first they had been shocked, but they had listened to her arguments, delivered quietly but forcefully, and had offered no objections. Each of the officers had been given a task – save for Fell.

He had returned to the cabin with Sigarni, and their lovemaking had been tender and joyous. No words spoken throughout, but both experiencing an intensity that led to tears. Fell had never known anything like it; he felt both complete and fulfilled. In all his adult life he had dreamt of moments like this, to be at one with the object of his love.

The night was quiet, and the entire world consisted of nothing more than the four walls he could see and the glowing fire that warmed the cabin. Tomorrow the great battle would begin and, God willing, after that he and Sigarni could begin a new life together. Once the Baron was defeated, they could send emissaries to the Outland King and end a war neither side had truly wanted. Then he and Sigarni could build a home near the Falls.

She moaned in her sleep and he stroked her silver hair. She awoke and smiled sleepily. 'You should be asleep,' she said.

'I am too happy for sleep,' he told her. Her hand stroked down his warm belly and arousal flared instantly.

'Then I shall tire you,' she said, sliding her body over his. Her mouth tasted sweet and he smelt the perfume of her hair, felt the warmth of her body.

At last the passion subsided and he sighed. 'Are you ready for sleep now?' she whispered into his ear.

'You held them, Sigarni,' he said proudly. 'All those warriors and greybeards! They stood and listened and they believed. I believe! It is so hard to think of you now as the huntress who lived alone and sold her furs. It is as if you were always waiting to be a queen. Even Bakris Tooth-gone speaks of you with awe. Where did you send him, by the way?'

'South,' she said.

'Why?'

'To cut their supply lines. God, Fell, I wish this was over. I don't want to be a Battle Queen.'

'We can end it tomorrow,' he said. 'Then we'll build a house. You know the flat land to the west of the Falls? I've often thought that it would make a splendid home. A little back from the pool, so that the noise of the Falls would be filtered by the willows. There's good grazing land close by, and I know Grame will loan me some breed cattle.'

'It sounds . . . wonderful,' she told him.

'There's good hunting too.'

At the sound of their voices Lady awoke and pushed herself between them. Sigarni stroked the hound's ears. 'It is a fine dream,' said Sigarni. 'Now let's get some rest.'

'What do you mean, a dream?' Fell asked.

'The war will not be over with one battle,' she said sadly. 'If we sin, the Outlanders will see it as a blow to their pride. They will have no alternative but to send another army north.'

'But it makes no sense!'

'War makes no sense, Fell. Let's talk about it all tomorrow.'

'Aye, we'll do that,' he said. 'I will be proud to stand beside you.'

'You won't be beside me, Fell. I need you and your men to take up a position away from the battle, on the right. They will break through on the western slope, and head for the encampments. They must be stopped. Destroyed. Hold the right, Fell. Do it for me!'

'Oh, God!' he whispered, his stomach knotting.

'What is it?' she asked, concern in her voice.

'Nothing,' he assured her. 'It is all right, just a little cramp in my leg. You are right, Sigarni. We should sleep now. Come, put your head on my shoulder.'

Sigarni sat up and pushed Lady away. 'Back to your blanket, you hussy!' she said. 'He is mine alone!'

Settling down beside him with her arm across his chest, she fell asleep almost immediately. But for Fell there would be no rest that night. He remembered the night at Gwalchmai's cabin, and the drunken words of the Dreamer.

'But I know what I know, Fell. I know you'll live for her. And I know you'll die for her. "Hold the right, Fell. Do it for me!" she'll say. And they'll fall on you with their swords of fire, and their lances of pain, and their arrows of farewell. Will you hold, Fell, when she asks you?' Gwalch looked up, his eyes bleary. *'I wish I was young again, Fell. I'd stand alongside you. By God, I'd even take that arrow for you.'*

No house by the Falls. No golden future in the sunshine on the mountains. This one night is all there is, he realized. He felt the panic in the pit of his belly, and in the palpitations of his heart. Fell so wanted to wake Sigarni again, to tell her of Gwalchmai's prophecy. Yet he did not.

Instead he held her to him and listened to her soft breathing.

'Will you hold, Fell?'

Aye, he thought, I will hold.

The loss of a group of his scouts was not entirely unexpected, and the Baron had despatched four more men to scout the Duane Pass. Only one returned – and he had an arrow wound high on the right shoulder.

'Well?' asked the Baron.

The man's face was grey, and he was in great pain. 'As you predicted, lord, they have taken up a position on the flat hill. A wall of shields. I estimate there are almost three thousand warriors there.'

'Their full force?' The Baron laughed and turned to his officers. 'See what happens when a woman leads? What fools they are!' Swinging again to the wounded scout, he asked, 'What of the western slope?'

292

'Around a hundred men hidden in the trees. I got pretty close before they saw me.'

'To the east?'

'I saw no one, sir.'

'Good. Go and get that wound seen to.'

'Yes, sir. Thank you, sir.'

The Baron gathered his officers around him. 'You have all studied the maps, and you will realize that their position is a strong one. We must first encircle the hill; that will stretch us thin in places, but it is too high for them to make a swift sally down upon us.' He fixed his attention on a tall, lean cavalryman. 'Chaldis, you will take half the cavalry and a thousand foot. Kill the defenders on the western slope and attack their encampment and the surrounding Pallides villages.'

'Yes, my lord,' Chaldis responded.

'Where is Cheops?' asked the Baron.

'Here, my lord,' answered a short, stocky figure in uniform of brown leather, pushing forward from the back.

'You will take your archers to the eastern slope and pepper them. I will initiate attacks from the western side. Be wary, Cheops. I would sooner your arrows fell a little short than sailed over the defenders and struck our own men. Nothing so demoralizes a fighting man as to fear death from the shafts of his own archers.'

'You can rely on us, my lord.'

'Leofric, you will command the cavalry wing. Skirt the hill and continue sporadic raids from the north side. Use only the heaviest armoured lancers. The enemy will have good bowmen on that hilltop. Do not push too far. Hit hard, then break away. It will be the infantry who apply the hammer blow.'

'Understood, my lord.'

'Gentlemen,' said the Baron, with a rare smile. 'A magnificent opportunity lies ahead of us. In the south there is a great panic concerning these rebel Highlanders, and when we have defeated them the King will make sure you are rewarded for your efforts. But remember this, though they are barbarians and scum they still know how to fight. I want the woman alive; I will send her in chains to the capital. As to the rest, slaughter them to a man. God is with us, gentlemen. Now let us be about our duties.'

The Baron strode to his tent and ducked below the flap. Once inside he turned his attention to the Highlander, sitting flanked by two guards. The man was of medium height, with greasy dark hair and a wide mouth. He did not look the Baron in the eye.

'Your information was correct,' said the Baron. 'The bitch has fortified the hilltop.'

'As I told you, my lord,' said Bakris Tooth-gone, starting to rise from his chair. But a soldier pressed his hand on Bakris' shoulder, easing him back into the seat.

'Treachery always fascinates me,' said the Baron, flicking his fingers and pointing to a jug of wine. A servant filled a goblet and passed it to his lord; the Baron sipped it. 'Why would one of Sigarni's captains betray her?'

'It's a lost cause, my lord,' said Bakris bitterly. 'They're all going to die. And I want to live. What's wrong with that? In this life a man must look out for himself. I've never had nothing. Now by your leave, I'll have some gold and some land.'

'Gold and land,' echoed the Baron. 'I have sworn to see every Highlander slain and you are a Highlander. Why should I not kill you?'

Bakris grinned, showing stained and broken teeth. 'You won't get them all in this one battle, lord. I know all the hiding places. I was a forester; I can lead your soldiers to where they run to. And I'll serve you well, lord.'

'I think you will,' the Baron agreed.

Three servants set about dressing the Baron in his black armour, buckling his breastplate, hooking the gorget into place, attaching his greaves and hinged knee protectors. Accoutred for war, he strode to his black stallion and was helped into the saddle.

Touching heels to the stallion's flanks, he rode to the front of the battle line and lifted his arm.

The army moved on towards the mouth of the Duane Pass.

To the Baron's surprise there were no flights of arrows from the rearing cliff faces on either side, nor any sign of defenders on the gentle slopes to left and right. Ahead the sun glimmered on the shield wall of the defenders, as they ringed the flat-topped hill half a mile distant.

A long time ago the Outlanders themselves had employed the shield-ring defence. It was strong against cavalry, but weak against a concerted attack from infantry, with support from archers. Bowmen could send volley after volley of arrows over the shields, cutting away at the heart of the defenders.

The Baron rode on. Now he could see the tightly packed clansmen, and just make out the silver-armoured figure standing in the front line.

I should be grateful to you, he thought, for you have made my glory all the greater. Swinging in the saddle, he glanced back at his fighting men. If the losses were too light the victory would appear shallow, too high and he would be deemed an incompetent. Around three hundred dead would be perfect, he thought.

Leofric rode past him on the right, leading the cavalry in columns of three. On the left, Chaldis led his fifteen hundred men up the western slope to the enemy's right. 'That's good, Chaldis,' shouted the Baron admiringly. 'Let them see where you are heading; it will give them time to think about the fate of their wives and sons. Fire some buildings as soon as you can. I want them to see the smoke!'

'Aye, my lord,' the captain replied.

The Baron rode on, leading his infantry to the foot of the hill but remaining out of bowshot. Custom demanded that he give the enemy the opportunity to surrender, but today was not a time to consider custom. Good God, they might accept!

Glancing to his right, he saw Cheops and his fifteen hundred lightly armoured archers toiling up the slope. Each man carried thirty shafts. Four thousand five hundred sharp missiles to rain down upon the unprotected defenders!

The Baron ordered the encirclement of the hill and the three thousand remaining infantrymen, holding tightly to their formations, spread out to obey.

There was no movement from the defenders, and no sound. No harsh, boastful challenges, no jeering. It was unusual. The Baron could see the woman, Sigarni, moving among the men. The helm she wore was truly magnificent and would make a fine trophy.

Dark storm-clouds obscured the sun, and a rumble of distant thunder could be heard from the north. 'The Gods of War are preparing for the feast!' he shouted. 'Let us not disappoint them.'

Fell waited behind the cover of the trees, Torgan beside him. They could not yet see the lancers, but they could hear the thundering of their hooves on the hard-packed earth of the hill. Fell glanced to his right, and saw the Highlanders notching arrows to their bows. To his left the swordsmen waited, their two-handed claymores held ready. Five hundred fighting men, ready to defend their homes, their families and their clans.

The first of the lancers breasted the hill: tall men on high horses, their breastplates shining like silver in the sunlight, their long lances glittering. Each man carried a figure-of-eight shield on his left arm. They were still travelling in a column of fours, but as they reached open ground they spread out. The officer drew rein, shading his eyes to study the tree line.

Fifty Highlanders moved out on to open ground and loosed their longbows. Some of the shafts struck home, and several men and half a dozen horses fell, but most were blocked by the shields of the lancers. Levelling their lances, the riders charged.

'Now?' whispered Torgan.

'No,' Fell told him. 'Wait until they are closer.'

The fifty exposed Highland bowmen continued to loose shaft after shaft at the oncoming riders. Horses tumbled under the deadly volleys, but the lancers rode on. The distance closed between them, until no more than thirty paces separated the two groups.

'Now!' said Fell. Torgan lifted his hunting horn to his lips and blew two short blasts. Another hundred bowmen ran from the trees to stand beside their comrades. Hundreds of shafts tore into the lancers; the charging line faltered as the missiles slashed home into unprotected horseflesh. Horses reared and fell, bringing down following riders. Amid the sudden confusion the Highland swordsmen charged from cover, screaming their battle-cries. The lancers panicked, though many tried to swing to meet this unexpected attack. Horses reared, throwing their riders, then the Highlanders were among the lancers, dragging riders from their saddles and hacking them to death upon the ground.

Among the first to die was the enemy officer, hit by four shafts, one taking him through his right eye. The horsemen at the rear pulled back, galloping towards the safety of open ground. Torgan blew three blasts on his horn, and a chasing group of Highlanders reluctantly halted and jogged back to the tree line.

Over the hilltop marched a thousand Outland infantry, flanked by a score of archers. They drew up and surveyed the scene of carnage, then locked shields and advanced in broad battle formation, one hundred shields wide, ten deep.

'More than we thought would come,' said Torgan.

'They can't hold that formation within the woods,' said Fell. 'Fall back fifty paces.'

Torgan's hunting horn sounded once more, in one long baleful note.

Highland archers continued to shoot into the advancing mass of men, but to little effect. Some fell, but the infantry held their long rectangular shields high and most of the shafts bounced from them.

The lancers had re-formed now, and galloped forward to try an encircling sweep of the woods. Obrin and two hundred riders counter-charged them from the left, cleaving into their flank, hacking and cutting. The lances of the Outland riders were useless in such close quarters and they frantically threw aside their long weapons, drawing their sabres. But this second attack demoralized them, and they were pushed steadily back.

The Outland infantry slowed its advance, their leader unsure whether to push into the trees or swing and defend the beleaguered cavalry.

'Come on, you bastard!' whispered Fell. 'Come to us!'

The line began to move once more, the formation breaking into a skirmish line as each of the soldiers increased the distance between himself and his fellows by around three feet. Fell was forced to admire the smoothness of the switch from tight ranks to open formation.

These were enemies to respect.

Less able to protect one another in this new formation, however, the Outlanders began to take heavy losses from the retreating archers.

'This is it,' Fell told Torgan. 'By God, we'd better get it right!' Torgan gave a wide grin, and sprinted off to the left where his hundred men waited. With a harsh battlecry Torgan led his warriors in a frenzied assault on the enemy's right flank, just as they crossed the tree line. Fell saw the Farlain leader push himself deep into the fray, his claymore rising and falling with deadly skill.

Drawing his own sword, Fell signalled his own hundred and they crept through the undergrowth towards the enemy's left flank. Outnumbered ten to one, Torgan's men were being driven back as the wings of the Outland force pushed out to encircle the defenders.

With all attention on the right Fell charged the left, his claymore smashing through a soldier's helm and scattering his brains over his comrades. The Outlanders fell back but re-formed smoothly, trying to close ranks. The thick undergrowth and the trunks of tall trees prevented them re-forming into a tight single unit and the Highlanders, unencumbered by heavy armour, tore at them like wolves around a stag at bay.

A sword flashed for Fell's face. Swaying aside, he swept up a vicious two-handed cut that glanced from the tip of the soldier's shield and smashed into his cheekbone. The soldier was punched from his feet by the blow.

On the right Torgan had pulled back his men. Some Outlanders had given chase, but Torgan swung back his group and cut them down.

Out on open ground the lancers broke into a full retreat. Obrin made no attempt to give chase, but gathered his men and galloped for the woods. Leaping from their horses, the Highlanders ran to the aid of their comrades. Torgan saw them coming and blew on his horn. Highland archers dropped their bows, drew their swords and joined him.

Again he charged the enemy right, and such was the ferocity of the charge that the Outlanders buckled and broke, losing formation. Beside him the giant Mereth, wielding a club of oak reinforced with iron studs, hammered his way forward with Loran beside him.

'Pallides! Pallides!' roared Mereth.

Torgan hurdled a fallen tree and shoulder-charged an Outland soldier. The man staggered back, falling into his comrades. Torgan's claymore sang through the air as three men hurled themselves at him. He blocked the lunge of the first, all but decapitating him with a reverse cut. The second man's sword cut into Torgan's side, the third aimed a blow at his face. It was blocked by an upraised sword, and Torgan saw Obrin smash the man from his feet.

Ignoring his own wound, Torgan leapt once more into the action. To his right Mereth was surrounded by swordsmen, but was holding them at bay with great sweeps of his murderous club. 'Farlain!' shouted Torgan, rushing to his aid. Several men followed him, including Loran. An arrow sliced by Torgan's cheek, taking Loran in the side of the neck; the handsome Pallides staggered to his right and fell. Ignoring the bowmen Torgan raced into the fray, ducking beneath a wild sweep and slashing his sword through the knee of the wielder; the leg broke with a sickening snap and the swordsman fell, screaming. Mereth bellowed a war-cry and ran at a second group of men. One of them rammed a spear through the giant's belly and Mereth staggered to a stop. Then his club swept up and across to smash the skull of the spear-wielder. A sword clove into Mereth's bull neck. Blood spurted from the severed jugular as Torgan stabbed his own sword into the killer's belly.

On the left Fell was battling furiously. Here the Outlanders retained at least a semblance of order, and were pulling back towards open ground. Again and again Fell led his men in increasingly desperate charges.

But there were fewer of them now. Obrin and twenty Highlanders ran to his aid. Fell had been cut on the right cheek, and blood was flowing from a deep wound in his thigh. His claymore, though, felt light in his hand as he charged again, Obrin beside him.

'Don't let them re-form!' he bellowed.

The archer captain Cheops reached the crest of the eastern slope and glanced across at the enemy defensive wall. Beyond that he could see the cavalry charging the woods. It was all going well; the range from his position to the enemy was less than two hundred yards, well within killing distance. It was hot, and today would be thirsty work. Glancing behind him he saw a heavy stand of gorse, and beyond it a grove of trees.

'You!' he shouted to a young recruit. 'Go back into the trees and see if there's a stream or a pond. If there is, you can refill our canteens.'

'Yes, sir!' the boy called out, setting off at a run.

Cheops strung his longbow. He had made it himself five years ago, a splendid weapon tipped with horn. Pulling his shafts from his quiver, he pushed them point first into the earth. For some reason that Cheops had never been able to fathom, arrowheads with a little clay stuck to them pierced armour all the better.

Selecting his first shaft, he notched it to the bow. There was little point in trying to select a target, since he would have to arc the arrow over the shield-wall. Still, the Highlanders were densely packed on the hilltop, and any hit would be an advantage. Cheops drew back on the string and sent the shaft in a long, looping flight.

This was going to be a good day. No sign of rain, to warp the arrows. Not much wind.

His archers gathered on both sides of him, selecting their arrows and removing their cloaks.

It was all so easy.

Idly he wondered why the Highland bitch had decided to make a stand here.

Cheops did not have long to wait for an answer. From behind there came a scream and he swung round to see the boy he had sent looking for water, running for all he was worth. The lad had discarded his longbow, which amazed Cheops, for the loss of a weapon meant a thirty-lash flogging. What had he seen? A bear?

The boy glanced back as he ran and tripped, rolling headlong. Gripped by panic, he scrambled to his feet. From the gorse and the undergrowth came thousands of Highland warriors.

Cheops stood transfixed. It was not possible. They had an army of three thousand – and there were at least that many on the hilltop opposite.

Impossible or not, they were here!

'Back! Back!' yelled Cheops. His men hardly needed the order. Lightly armed with bow and knife, they were no match for sword-wielding warriors and began to stream back down the hill, leaving their arrows stuck in the soft earth. The Highlanders poured after them.

Cheops hurled aside his longbow and pumped his arms for extra speed. Ahead he could see the Baron, directing an attack on the western side of the hilltop.

The Baron swung round, and stood open-mouthed as his archers hurtled down into the pass. The thin circle of soldiers around the hill also glanced up. Cheops knew that his dignity was fleeing ahead of him, but he didn't care. Dignity could be regained. Life was another matter entirely. He reached the foot of the pass just ahead of the fastest of his men, and slipped through the infantry to what appeared the relative safety behind the infantry lines.

There he stopped and looked back.

The Highlanders were pouring down the hillside, screaming some incomprehensible battlecry. They struck the infantry like a hammer. Then they were through.

With nowhere left to run, Cheops drew his dagger. As a burly white-bearded warrior carrying a battle-axe charged him, Cheops ducked under the swinging blade and thrust his knife at the man. The blade was turned by a breastplate and Cheops stumbled and fell. The axe clove him between the shoulder-blades.

On the hillside the Baron shouted orders to the infantry to form a defensive square and retreat down the pass. With fine discipline they gathered, the Baron at the centre.

The Highlanders beat ineffectually against the shield-wall, and the withdrawal began.

Leofric had never wanted to be a soldier, or any kind of fighting man. His loves were numbers, logistics and organization. As he sat his gelding on the north side of the hill he found himself contemplating his future. Never having seen a battle, he was unprepared for the ferocity, the screams and the cries. It was all so . . . barbaric, he realized.

Once it is over I will return to the capital, he decided. The University had offered him a teaching post in languages. I will accept it, he thought.

'Do we attack, sir?' asked the lieutenant at his side. The man had drawn his sword, and seemed eager to lead the five hundred cavalrymen up the steep slope. Leofric glanced up at the shield-wall above.

'I suppose so,' he said. 'The Baron ordered us to make probing assaults.'

'I understand,' said the officer. 'Wasp formation, sting and run. How many should I take, sir?'

Leofric swung in the saddle and gazed at his five centuries. 'Take three,' he said. 'Harry them!'

'Yes, sir.'

The remnants of Chaldis' cavalry came galloping down the western slope – no more than thirty men, some of them wounded. An officer rode up to Leofric. 'We were ambushed, sir. More than a thousand Highlanders were waiting for us in the woods. They are cutting the infantry to pieces.'

At that moment the archers led by the sprinting Cheops came racing down the slope – pursued by, Leofric gauged, some two thousand Highlanders.

'Son of a whore!' hissed the officer. 'Where in Hell did they come from?'

Leofric was momentarily stunned. He had an eye for numbers, and had already estimated there to be around three thousand on the hilltop. Now from nowhere the number of the enemy had risen to six thousand, which was not even within the bounds of possibility.

'God's blood!' said the lieutenant. 'What now, sir!'

Leofric needed a moment to think. Looking up at the shield-wall above him, the answer came like a blinding revelation. 'There are no men on the hilltop,' he said. 'We are besieging the Highland women!'

All around them the infantry were falling back around the Baron. Raising his arm, Leofric led his cavalry in a charge against the enemy's left cutting through to where the Baron stood, Leofric leapt from his mount and ran to him. Swiftly he told him of the Highland deception.

The Baron swore. 'How many do we have left?' he asked.

Leofric cast his eyes at the sea of fighting men. 'Two thousand. Perhaps less.'

'Advance on the hill!' shouted the Baron. 'Formation One!'

'What is the point!' screamed Leofric. 'It is over!'

'It will be over when I've killed the bitch!'

With a discipline gained during decades of warfare, the Outland troops re-formed into a fighting square one hundred shields wide and ten deep. 'Double time!' shouted the Baron, and the men began to run. Leofric, caught in the centre, had no choice but to run alongside the Baron. On the outer edges of the battle his cavalry were being cut to pieces trying to protect the exposed right flank of the square. Even so, inexorably the phalanx moved up the hill towards the waiting women.

'I'm coming for you, you whore!' bellowed the Baron, his voice rising above the clashing swords and the screams of the wounded and dying.

A black cloud of arrows slashed into the advancing line and Leofric could see scores of women loosing their shafts. He felt sickened by it all. The finest soldiers in the empire were now charging a force of wives and mothers.

Behind them the Highlanders were assaulting the troops at the rear of the phalanx, slashing their swords at unprotected backs. Many men turned to face the enemy, and this thinned the square. The Baron seemed unconcerned.

The enemy archers fell back behind the shield-wall and a volley of iron-tipped spears sliced down into the advancing men. The

303

Highlanders were all around them now, a pack of wolves ripping at their flesh. The square began to break up but the Baron ignored the threat, urging his front line on and up.

The shield-wall opened and Leofric saw Asmidir charge out, with a group of men in black and silver armour. They came in a tight wedge that clove through the advancing line. Behind them, bearing spears and swords, the Highland women rushed at the attackers.

The sight of thousands of fighters streaming from the hilltop finally unnerved the advancing men. They broke and ran.

Asmidir leapt at the Baron, his two-handed sword slashing towards the Baron's neck. The Baron blocked it with his shield and gave a return blow that crashed against Asmidir's shoulder-plate, dislodging it. The black man dropped to one knee and sent a wild cut that thundered against the Baron's calf, smashing his greave to shards and knocking him to the ground. Rolling to his left, the Baron clambered to his feet and threw aside his shield. Holding his own blade two-handed, he rushed the black man. 'You treacherous bastard!' he screamed.

Their swords clashed again and again. A blow from Asmidir smashed the links on the Baron's neck protector and slashed up to open his cheek. Blood streamed from the cut.

Suddenly weary, Leofric sat down and watched the duel. All around him men were dying, but no one attacked the slightly-built spectator who sat quietly with his hands hugging his knees.

Both men were strong and the fight continued at a savage pace. Asmidir was bleeding from wounds in both arms and a cut on his temple. The Baron blocked an overhead cut and, as Asmidir pressed in close, headbutted the black man, sending him staggering back. Dropping his sword, the Baron hurled himself at his half-stunned opponent and both men fell to the ground. The Baron drew his dagger and raised it high.

An arrow punched through his leather eye-patch, slicing deep into his brain. Leofric glanced to his right and saw the warrior queen, Sigarni, in armour of bright silver, a winged helm upon her head, a short hunting bow in her hand. The Baron gave a choking cry, and toppled from Asmidir.

Leofric stood and walked over to the black man, kneeling beside him. 'Are you all right?' he enquired.

'How is it that you live?' asked Asmidir, surprised.

Leofric shrugged. 'Forgot to draw my sword.' He helped Asmidir to his feet and the two men approached Sigarni.

Handing the bow to a dark-haired woman on her right, she surveyed the battlefield. There were still isolated pockets of fighting, but the battle was over.

She swung to Leofric and Asmidir introduced them. 'You have a charmed life, Leofric,' she said. 'Thousands of men died today, and you have not even been scratched.'

'I'm not much of a soldier,' he said. 'I've been offered a teaching post at the capital's University. With your leave, I think I'll accept it.'

She nodded. 'There has been enough blood-letting today. Go from here, Leofric, ride south to your King. Tell him the truth about all that happened here. I fear it will make little difference.'

'It won't, lady. He'll come with an army ten times the size of the one you defeated here. It will never end.'

Stepping forward, she placed her hands upon his shoulders and brought her face close to his. 'Look into my eyes, Leofric, and hear me well. It *will* end, for I will end it. Tell him these words from Sigarni, the Queen of the North: Advance against me and I will destroy you. I will bring fire and death into your kingdom, and I will snatch you from your throne and throw your body to the dogs.'

Sigarni turned away from him and walked down the hillside. Asmidir took the young man's arm and led him down into the pass. They found a horse and Leofric climbed into the saddle. 'Your strategy was masterful,' he said. 'I congratulate you.'

Asmidir smiled. 'Not my strategy, boy. Hers. All war is based on deception and she learned that lesson well. Go in peace, Leofric, and be sure never to cross my path again.'

'I wish you well, Asmidir,' said the young man, 'but I fear there will be no happy ending here.'

'The man who ripped the heart from my country is dead. That is a good enough ending for today. Now ride!'

Leofric touched spurs to the stallion and cantered from the battlefield.

High in the skies above, the crows were already gathering for the feast.

Bakris was dragged before Sigarni. 'They captured me,' he said, 'but I told them nothing.'

Sigarni sighed. 'You told them everything that you were supposed to,' she said. 'Kollarin warned me that you were a treacherous cur, who would sell your people for a handful of gold. But know this, Bakris, your treachery helped us. Without it the Baron might have sent out more scouts, and found our hidden forces. As the rope settles around your neck, think on that. Now get him from my sight – and hang him from the nearest tree!'

Fell sat quietly with his back against the tree-trunk, Obrin and Torgan beside him. 'It was a good day,' he said. 'We broke them. By God, we broke them!'

'Aye,' said Obrin softly, his eyes drawn to the black-feathered arrow jutting from Fell's chest. The clansman's face was pale, there were dark rings beneath his eyes, and his lips had a bluish tinge that Obrin had seen all too often before.

'Fetch Sigarni,' Obrin told Torgan. The Farlain leader nodded, and loped away. 'Maybe if I removed the arrow you would have a chance,' said Obrin, but Fell shook his head.

'I can feel the life draining from me. Nothing will stop it now. We won, though, didn't we?'

'Aye, we won.'

Fell looked up at the sky and watched the crows swooping and diving. It was a beautiful day. High Druin wore a crown of clouds and the sun was bright behind them.

'It is a Highland custom,' said Fell, 'that a man's son sends him on the swans' path. I have no children of my blood, Obrin.' He smiled. 'But I used the *Cormaach* to save you, and that means you are my son. I want my best bow beside me, and two knives. Some bread and some wine should be wrapped in leaves. Lastly, two coins should be placed . . . upon my eyes. The coins are for

306

the gatekeeper, who will usher me through. Will you do this for me?'

'I will, man.'

'I want to be buried on the flanks of High Druin. Sigarni will know where. I want to sleep for ever beneath the spot where we became lovers. And if I must walk as a spirit, and be chained to any part of the land, it should be there.'

'God's eyes, Fell, I thought we had made it through together. One cursed archer hiding in the undergrowth.'

'It's done now. It cannot be undone. I have often said that a man should never dwell on regrets, but I find that hard to maintain now, Obrin. You will need a sword-bearer at my funeral. Choose a good one.'

'I shall.'

Fell closed his eyes. 'She's a wonder, isn't she? A hilltop defended by women. Who would have considered it?'

'Aye, she's a wonder, Fell. She'll be here soon. Hang on, man.'

'I don't think I can. I can hear the cry of gulls. Can you?'

'No, just the crows.'

Fell opened his eyes and looked past Obrin. He smiled, as if in greeting, but when Obrin glanced back there was no one there. 'Come to walk with me, you old drunkard?' said Fell. 'Ah, but it is good to see you, man. Give me your hand, for my strength is all but gone.'

Fell reached out, then his hand fell limply into his lap and his head sagged back against the tree. Obrin leaned in and closed Fell's eyes. 'You were a fine man,' he said, 'and a true friend. I hope you find what you deserve.'

Obrin rose and turned towards the battlefield as Sigarni came running, with Torgan alongside her. She sped past Obrin and knelt by Fell's body. Torgan paused beside Obrin and the two men moved away to a respectful distance.

Sigarni had knelt down at Fell's side. She was holding his hand, and speaking to him. Obrin saw the tears on her face and, taking Torgan's arm, drew the Farlain warrior away from the scene. 'You ought to get that wound stitched,' said Obrin, pointing to the congealed blood on Torgan's side.

'It'll mend,' said the Highlander. 'A shame he had no sons to speak his name on High Druin.'

'I'll do that,' said Obrin.

'Ah yes, the *Carmaach*. I had forgotten. Do you know the ritual?'

'I can learn it.'

'I would be proud to teach you,' said Torgan. 'And, if you choose, I will stand beside you on High Druin as Fell's sword-bearer.'

The two men reached the crest of the western slope and looked down over the battlefield. The Outlanders lay dead in their thousands, but many also of the Highland were slain. Women were moving around the pass, tending to the wounded. Later they would strip the Outland dead of their weapons. To the South Obrin could see Grame's warriors marching to capture the enemy's supply wagons. 'What now, do you think?' asked Torgan. 'Will the Outlanders listen to reason?'

Obrin shook his head. 'No, they'll send Jastey and twenty thousand men. They'll be here by summer's end.'

'Well,' said Torgan grimly, 'we'll be here to meet them!'

It was dusk when Asmidir and Kollarin found Sigarni. She was sitting alone on a distant hilltop, her red cloak wrapped tight around her.

'Thank you, my friend,' said Asmidir. 'I would be grateful if you would leave us alone now.' Kollarin nodded and trudged away back to the encampment as Asmidir moved alongside Sigarni and sat down with his arm across her shoulder, drawing her in to him.

'Dear God, I am so sorry,' he said.

'He was gone when I arrived,' she told him. 'Not even a farewell.'

Asmidir said nothing, but held her tightly. 'One arrow,' she continued. 'A piece of wood and a chunk of iron. And Fell is no more. Why him? Why not me, or you, or a thousand others?'

'In my land we believe in fate, Sigarni. It was his time . . . it was not yours, or mine.'

'I can't believe that he's gone. I try to concentrate on it, but I see his face smiling at me. I find myself thinking that if I walk back to the encampment he will be waiting for me. It is so unreal.'

'I never really spoke to Fell,' said Asmidir. 'I think he saw me as a rival, and he was jealous of our . . . friendship. But he was a man I was proud to fight alongside. I do not know whether there is a paradise, or a hall of heroes, or a field of glory. But I hope there is, for his sake.'

'There is,' she told him. 'Fell will be there now, with Gwalchmai, and Fyon Sharp-axe, and Loran and Mereth, and hundreds of others who died today. But that is of little comfort to the widows they left behind, and the children who now sit crying. I never saw a battle before. It is the most evil sight. Why do men lust after it so?'

'Few soldiers do,' he told her. 'They know the reality of it. But your warriors will grow old, and they will remember this day above all others. The sun shining, the enemy defeated. They will remember it as a golden day, and they will tell their children of it, and their children will long to know a day like it. That is the way of things, Sigarni. I wish Fell had lived, for I can feel your sorrow and it pains me. But he did not, and you must put off your tears for another day. Your men are waiting for you. They wish to cheer you, and to celebrate their victory.'

She pulled away from him. 'It is not over, Asmidir; you know that. What is there to celebrate? We have won a reprieve until the summer. Before that we will have to take Citadel town, and establish strongholds in the Lowlands.'

'But not tonight. Come, this is your moment, Sigarni. You are their queen, their promised one, their saviour. You must walk among them like a queen.'

Sigarni glanced up and saw the shimmering figure of Ironhand standing before her. Asmidir was oblivious to his presence.

'The black man is right,' said Ironhand.

Sigarni leaned in to Asmidir and kissed his cheek. 'Go back and tell them I am coming,' she said.

'I will walk with you.'

'No, I will come alone. Soon.'

Asmidir rose and as he walked away, Ironhand's spirit settled down beside her. 'Fell died,' she said.

'I know. I saw him walk the path towards the Light. The old man, Gwalchmai, was beside him. I tried to follow but the way was closed to me. I stayed too long, Sigarni. Now I am trapped.'

'That is so unfair,' she told him.

He smiled. 'In all my dealings in life – and subsequently in death – fairness has never seemed apparent. It is not important. My spirit lived to see your day, and to know that my blood, and Elarine's, ran true in our daughter. The future is fraught with peril, but you will lead your people well. I know this, and my pride soars higher than High Druin. Now it is time for you to meet with your generals. To thank them, and praise them, and promote others to take the place of those who lie dead.'

'I cannot think of that now!'

'You can and you *must*! You restored Torgan's pride, and he fought like a lion for you. He should take Fell's place.'

'He is too headstrong. Harcanan would be better.'

Ironhand chuckled. 'You see, you *can* think of it! Go now, my daughter. And think of me once in a while.'

'You're not leaving me?'

'It is time. The Path of Light is closed to me, but perhaps there are other paths. Who knows?'

'I've lost Fell, and now I am losing you.'

'You will find others, Sigarni. You will never be short of friends and advisors. I wish that I could hug you, but such pleasures are not for the dead. Go back now, my daughter.'

Without a word more of farewell, he faded away.

Sigarni stood for a moment, then turned and strode back towards the victory fires at the encampment.

EPILOGUE

The summer had just begun when Sigarni the Queen rode with her retainers to Ironhand's Falls. Taliesen was waiting at the cave, as he had promised. The Queen dismounted and walked through to where he sat, a small fire taking the chill from the damp air within the cave.

'Well met, Taliesen.'

'And you, Battle Queen. Are you ready for the next battle?'

'Time will tell, Taliesen. What of you? Are you ready to tell me why you gave me your aid?'

'Not yet,' he said, with a smile. 'But my land is also at war, and I cannot dally here long. I have a queen to meet; she is old, but iron-hard, and she has faced her enemies all her life, and now waits to meet the last of them – a demon sent through time to hunt her.'

'Sent by Jakuta Khan,' she said. 'I know; he told me just before he died.'

'I have no doubt you will kill it, my lady,' he said solemnly.

'I have much to do, Taliesen. You asked me to meet you here, and now I ask you to tell me why.'

'I thought you might wish to say goodbye to a friend.'

'Are we friends, sorcerer?'

'I hope so, but I was not speaking of myself. The dwarf Ballistar came to me, and asked a favour. I said I would grant it and by your leave I shall.'

Sigarni sighed.'He wants to go back to Yur-vale?'

'That is what he requested.'

'But he will die there.'

'I think so. But, in his own words, he will die as a whole man. He will stand tall again before the end. It could even be that, with the new order there, the air will not be as poisonous or the food so deadly. I do not know. What I do know is that without your blessing, and a drop of your blood, he will be a dwarf on the other side also.'

'You are asking me to send a friend to his death.'

'No, my lady, I am asking you to give him a chance at a life he desperately desires.'

Sigarni sat down by the fire. 'I love that man,' she said, 'and I would do anything in my power to make him happy. If that is what he wants, then of course I shall grant it.'

'It is what he wants. Are you ready?'

'I am.'

Together the Queen and the sorcerer left the cave and began the long walk around the pool to the engravings on the cliff-face. Ballistar was waiting there, a large pack beside him. He stood as she approached.

'Will you forgive me for leaving you?' he asked, reaching up to take hold of her hand.

'There is nothing to forgive, Balli. You are my dearest friend.'

'There may be some magic beyond the Gate that will allow me to come back – and still be tall,' he said.

'Yes,' she said. Drawing her dagger, she made a small cut in the palm of her hand, then gripped his pudgy fingers. Reaching into the pouch that hung from her neck, she drew out a small bone, pressing this against the trickling wound. Passing it to Ballistar, she smiled. 'You may need a friend on the road,' she told him, 'and I think Ironhand would welcome a second tilt at the fat tavern woman.'

Holding tightly to the bone he looked up at her, tears spilling to his cheeks.

'I will always love you,' he said.

'And I you. Go now, Balli. And know joy.'

The Gateway shimmered and the dwarf hoisted his pack and stepped through.

The Hawk Eternal

The Hawk Eternal is dedicated to the memory of Matthew Newman, a young writer from Birmingham who never had the chance to see his name in print. He should have. He was talented, dedicated, and gifted with great determination. But he was also one of the many haemophiliacs whose lives were further blighted by HIV-contaminated blood products. In the short time I knew him I gained a great insight into his courage and his amazing lack of outward bitterness.

He desperately wanted to finish his book and see it in print before he died. He didn't make it.

But his effort was truly heroic.

Prologue

The young priest was sitting in the sunshine, studying an ancient manuscript. Slowly he ran his index finger over the symbols upon it, mouthing each one. It was cold up here by these ancient stones, but Garvis had wrapped himself in a hooded sheepskin cloak, and had found a niche in the rocks away from the wind. He loved the solitude of these high, lonely peaks, and the distant roar of the mighty Falls of Attafoss was a far-away whisper upon the wind. *'All the works of Man are as dust upon a flat rock,'* he read. *'When the winds of time blow across them they are lost to history. Nothing built of stone will endure.'* Garvis sat back. Surely this was nonsense? These mountains had existed since the dawn of time and they would be here long after he was dead. He glanced up at the old stone circle. The symbols upon each standing stone had weathered almost to nothing. Yet still they stood, exactly where the ancients had placed them a thousand years ago. The sun was high now, but there was little warmth in the rays. Gaunt shadows stretched out from the stones. Garvis pulled his cloak more tightly about him.

According to the Lord Taliesen, this was once one of the Great Gates. From here a man could travel across time and space. Garvis rubbed a slender hand over his pockmarked face. Time and Space: the legends fascinated him. He had asked Lord Taliesen about the Ancient Gates and had been rewarded with extra study. The Lesser Gates still allowed a man to move through space. He himself had travelled with Lord Taliesen from the mountains to the outskirts of Ateris – that was more than sixty miles of space, but the journey had taken less than a heartbeat. According to Metas, the Lesser Gates could carry a man all over the land. So why were the Great Gates special?

Garvis' attention was distracted momentarily, as his fingers found a ripe spot upon his chin. Idly he squeezed it. It was not ready to burst, and pain flared across his face. Garvis gave a low curse and rubbed at the wounded skin. A hawk landed on the tallest of the standing stones, then flew away. Garvis watched it until it rose high on the thermals and was lost to him. 'I would like to have been a hawk,' he said, aloud.

Lightning flashed across the stones, a blaze of brightness that caused Garvis to fall backwards from the rock on which he sat. Rolling to his knees, he blinked and tried to focus. The stones seemed darker now. Violet light blazed out, and pale blue lightning forked up from the tallest stone. More lights flared, gossamer threads of light forming a glittering web around the stones. It seemed to Garvis as if tiny stars were caught in a pale blue net, gleaming like diamonds. It was the most beautiful sight. At the centre of the light storm one diamond grew larger and brighter than all the others, swelling until it was the size of a boulder. Then it flattened, spreading out like a sheet upon a wash-line, moving from circle to square, its four corners fastening to the top and bottom of two standing stones. The wind increased, howling over the crags, and for less than a heartbeat two suns hung in the sky.

All was silent as Garvis knelt, mouth open, shocked beyond words. Standing between the central stones was a tall warrior in bloodstained armour. He was supporting a woman, also attired for war; blood was flowing from a wound in her side. Garvis had never seen armour quite like that worn by this fearsome pair. The man's helm was full-faced, and boasted a white horsehair plume. His bronze breastplate had been fashioned in the shape of a human chest, complete with pectorals and a rippling solar plexus. He wore a leather kilt reinforced with bronze, and high, thigh-length riding boots. With a start Garvis realised that the warrior was looking at him. 'You!' he called. 'Help me.'

Garvis scrambled to his feet and ran forward as the man lowered the warrior woman to the ground. Her face was grey, and blood had stained her silver hair. Garvis gazed down upon her. Old she was, but once she had been beautiful.

'Where is Taliesen?' asked the warrior.

'Back at the Falls, sir.'

'We must take her to shelter. You understand, boy?'

'Shelter. Yes.'

The woman stirred. Reaching up, she gripped the warrior's arm. 'You must go back. It is not over. Leave me with the boy. I will . . . be fine.'

'I shall not leave you, my Lady. I have served you these thirty years. I cannot go now.' Reaching up, he made to remove his helm.

'Leave it,' she said, her voice ringing with authority. 'Listen to me, my dear friend. You must go back, or all may be lost. You are my heir; you are the son I never had; you are the light in my life. Go back. Set a lantern for me in the window.'

'We should have killed the bitch all those years ago,' he said bitterly. 'She was warped beyond evil.'

'No regrets, my general. Not ever. We win, we lose. The mountains do not care. Go now, for I can feel the air of the Enchanted Realm healing my wounds even as we speak. Go!'

Taking her hand, he kissed it. Rising, he gazed around at the mountains. With a sigh he drew his sword and ran back to the stones. Lightning flickered once more. Then he was gone.

Garvis ran into Taliesen's chambers, his face flushed, eyes wide with excitement. 'A warrior woman has appeared by the Ancient Gate,' he said. 'She is wounded, and nigh to death.'

The old man rose and gathered up his cloak of feathers. 'The Ancient Gate, you say?'

'Yes, Lord Taliesen.'

'Where have you taken her?'

'I helped her to the supply cave on High Druin. It was the closest shelter I could find. Metas was there and he has stitched her wounds, but I fear there is internal bleeding.'

Taliesen took a deep breath. 'Has she spoken of herself?'

'Not a word, Lord. Metas is still with her.'

'That is as it should be. Go now and rest. Make sure that not one word is spoken of this – not even to a brother druid. You understand me?'

'Of course, Lord.'

319

'Be sure that you do, for if I hear any whisper of it I shall turn your bones to stone, your blood to dust.'

Taliesen swung the cloak of feathers about his skinny shoulders and strode from his rooms.

Two hours later, having activated one of the Lesser Gates, he was climbing the eastern face of High Druin and feeling the bitter wind biting through his cloak. The cave was deep, and stacked with supplies to help wandering clansmen through the worst of the winter – sacks of dried oats and dried fruit, salt and sugar, salted meat and even a barrel of smoked fish. It was a haven for crofters and other travellers who needed to tackle the high passes in the winter months. There was a man-made hearth in the far corner, and two pallet beds; also a bench table, rudely fashioned from a split log, and two log rounds which served as seats.

The druid Metas was seated upon one of the rounds, which he had placed beside a pallet bed. Upon it lay an old woman, bandages encasing her chest and shoulder. As Taliesen approached the bed, Metas rose and bowed. Talisen praised him for his skill in administering to the woman, then repeated the warning he had given to the young druid when in his chambers.

'All will be as you order, Lord,' said Metas, bowing once more. Taliesen sent him back to Vallon and seated himself beside the sleeping woman.

Even now, so close to death, her face radiated strength of purpose. 'You were a queen without peer, Sigarni,' whispered Taliesen, taking hold of her hand and squeezing the fingers. 'But are you the one who will save my people?'

Her eyes opened. They were the grey of a winter sky, and the look she gave him was piercing. 'Again we meet,' she whispered, with a smile. The smile changed her face, returning to it the memory of youth and beauty he recalled so well. 'I fought the last battle, Taliesen . . .' He held up his hand.

'Tell me nothing,' he said. 'Already the strands of time are so interwoven that I find it hard to know when – or where – I am. I would dearly love to know how the Ancient Gate was opened, but

I dare not ask. I will only assume that I did it. For now you must rest, and regain your strength. Then we will talk.'

'I am so tired,' she said. 'Forty years of war and loss, victory and pain. So tired. And yet it is good to be back in the Enchanted Realm.'

'Say nothing more,' he urged her. 'We stand at a delicate place on the crossroads of time. Let me say only this. Two days ago you urged me to hunt down Caracis, and return to you the sword, Skallivar. You remember asking me this?'

She closed her eyes. 'I remember. It was almost thirty years ago. And you did.'

'Yes,' he said, his gaze drawn to the fabled sword that stood now against the far wall beside the fire.

'You sent the goddess walking on the water of the pool below the Falls. All my generals saw the miracle, and when word spread of it men came flocking to my banner. I owe you much for that, Taliesen.' Her words faded away, and she fell into a deep sleep.

Taliesen stood and walked to the sword, his thin fingers stroking the ruby pommel. He sighed and moved back into the sunlight. 'The goddess upon the water,' he repeated. What did she mean? Taliesen had spent the last two days desperately trying to think of a way to achieve what the Queen told him he already had!

And he remembered the words of his master, Astole, many centuries before. 'Treat the Gates with respect, Taliesen, lest you lose your mind. They are not merely doorways through time. You must understand that!'

Oh, how he understood! He glanced back at the sleeping Queen. How many times had he seen her die? Thirty? Fifty? Again the words of Astole drifted back to haunt him.

'Hold always to a Line, my boy. A single thread. Never move between the threads, for that way lies madness and despair. For every moment that the past can conjure gives birth to an infinity of futures. Cross them at your peril.'

The sun was hot upon Taliesen's face, though the wind remained cool. 'I crossed them, Astole,' he said, 'and now I am trapped in a future I cannot unravel. Why is she here? How was the Gate opened? How was it that I returned her sword? Help me, Astole, for I am lost, and my people face annihilation.'

No answer came, and with a heavy heart Taliesen returned to the cave.

1

Caswallon watched the murderous assault on Ateris, a strange sense of unreality gripping him. The clansman sat down on a boulder and gazed from the mountainside at the gleaming city below, white and glorious, like a child's castle set on a carpet of green.

The enemy had surprised the city dwellers some three hours before, and black smoke billowed now from the turrets and homes. The distant sound of screaming floated to his ears, disembodied, like the echo of a nightmare upon awakening.

The clansman's sea-green eyes narrowed as he watched the enemy hacking and slaying. He shook his head, sadness and anger competing within him. He had no love for these doomed lowlanders and their duplicitous ways. But, equally, this wanton slaughter filled him with sorrow.

The enemy warriors were new to Caswallon. Never had he seen the horned helms of the Aenir, the double-headed axes, nor the oval shields painted with hideous faces of crimson and black. He had heard of them, of course, butchering and killing far to the south, but of their war against the lowlanders he knew little until now.

But then, why should he? He was a clansman of the Farlain, and they had little time for lowland politics. His was a mountain race, tough and hardy and more than solitary. The mountains were forbidden ground for any lowlander and the clans mixed not at all with other races.

Save for trade. Clan beef and woven cloth for lowland sugar, fruits and iron.

In the distance Caswallon saw a young girl speared and lifted into the air, thrashing and screaming. This is war no longer, he thought, this is merely blood sport.

Tearing his gaze from the murderous scene he glanced back at the mountains rearing like spearpoints towards the sky, snow-capped and proud, jagged and powerful. At their centre the cloud-wreathed magnificence of High Druin towered above the land. Caswallon shivered, drawing his brown leather cloak about his shoulders. It was said that the clans were vicious and hostile to outsiders, and so they were. Any lowlander found hunting clan lands was sent home minus the fingers of his right hand. But such punishments were intended to deter poachers. The scenes of carnage on the plain below had nothing to do with such practices; this was lust of the most vile kind.

The clansman looked back at the city. Old men in white robes were being nailed to the black gates. Even at this distance Caswallon recognised Bacheron, the chief elder, a man of little honesty. Even so, he did not deserve such a death.

By all the gods, no one deserved such a death!

On the plain three horsemen rode into sight, the leader pulling a young boy who was tied to a rope behind his mount. Caswallon recognised the boy as Gaelen, a thief and an orphan who lived on scraps and stolen fruit. The clansman's fingers curled around the hilt of his hunting dagger as he watched the boy straining at the rope.

The lead rider, a man in shining breastplate and raven-winged helm, cut the rope and the boy began to run towards the mountains. The riders set off after him, lances levelled.

Caswallon took a deep breath, releasing it slowly. The flame-haired boy ducked and weaved, stopping to pick up a stone and hurl it at the nearest horse. The beast shied, pitching its rider.

'Good for you, Gaelen,' whispered Caswallon.

A rider in a white cloak wheeled his mount, cutting across the boy's path. The youngster turned to sprint away and the lance took him deep in the back, lifting him from his feet and hurling him to the ground. He struggled to rise and a second rider ended his torment, slashing a sword-blade to his face. The riders cantered back to the city.

Caswallon found his hands shaking uncontrollably, and his heart pounded, reflecting his anger and shame.

How could men do such a thing to a youth?

Caswallon recalled his last visit to Ateris three weeks before, when he had driven in twenty long-horned highland cattle to the market stalls in the west of the city. He had stolen the beasts from the pastures of the Pallides two days before. At the market he had seen a crowd chasing the red-haired youngster as he sprinted through the streets, his skinny legs pounding the marble walkway, his arms pumping furiously.

Gaelen had shinned up a trellis by the side of the inn and leapt across the rooftops, stopping only to make an obscene gesture to his pursuers. Spotting Caswallon watching, he drew back his shoulders and swaggered across the rooftops. Caswallon had grinned then. He liked the boy; he had style.

The fat butcher Leon had chuckled beside him. 'He's a character, is Gaelen. Every city needs one.'

'Parents?' asked Caswallon.

'Dead. He's been alone five years – since he was nine or ten.'

'How does he survive?'

'He steals. I let him get away with a chicken now and then. He sneaks up on me and I chase him for a while, shouting curses.'

'You like him, Leon?'

'Yes. As I like you, Caswallon, you rascal. But then he reminds me of you. You are both thieves and you are both good at what you do – and there is no evil in either of you.'

'Nice of you to say so,' said Caswallon, grinning. 'Now, how much for the Pallides cattle?'

'Why do you do it?'

'What?' asked Caswallon innocently.

'Steal cattle. By all accounts you are one of the richest clansmen in the Farlain. It doesn't make any sense.'

'Tradition,' answered Caswallon. 'I'm a great believer in it.'

Leon shook his head. 'One of these days you'll be caught and hanged – or worse, knowing the Pallides. You baffle me.'

'No, I don't. I make you rich. Yours is the cheapest beef in Ateris.'

'True. How is the lovely Maeg?'

'She's well.'

'And Donal?'

325

'Lungs like bellows.'

'Keeping you awake at nights, is he?'

'When I'm not out hunting,' said Caswallon with a wink.

Leon chuckled. 'I'm going to be sorry when they catch you, clansman. Truly.'

For an hour they haggled over the prices until Leon parted with a small pouch of gold, which Caswallon handed to his man Arcis, a taciturn clan crofter who accompanied him on his raids.

Now Caswallon stood on the mountainside soaking in the horror of Aenir warfare. Arcis moved alongside him. Both men had heard tales of war in the south and the awful atrocities committed by the Aenir. Foremost among these was the blood-eagle: Aenir victims were nailed to trees, their ribs splayed like tiny wings, their innards held in place with wooden strips.

Caswallon had only half-believed these tales. Now the evidence hung on the blood-drenched gates of Ateris.

'Go back to the valley, my friend,' Caswallon told Arcis.

'What about the cattle?'

'Drive them back into the mountains. There are no buyers today.'

'Gods, Caswallon! Why do they go on killing? There's no one fighting them.'

'I don't know. Tell Cambil what we have seen today.'

'What about you?'

'I'll stay for a while.'

Arcis nodded and set off across the slopes, running smoothly.

After a while the Aenir warriors drifted into the city. The plain before the gates was littered with corpses. Caswallon moved closer, stopping when he neared the tree-line. Now he could see the full scale of the horror and his anger settled, cold and malignant. The cattle-dealer, Leon, lay in a pool of blood, his throat torn open. Near him was the boy thief Gaelen.

Caswallon swung away and moved back towards the trees.

I am dying. There was no doubt in Gaelen's mind. The pain from his lower back was close to unbearable, his head ached, the blood was seeping from his left eye. For a long while he lay still, not knowing if the enemy was close by; whether indeed an Aenir warrior was at this moment poised above him with a spear or a sharp-edged sword.

Fear cut through his pain but he quelled it savagely. He could feel the soft, dusty clay against his face and smell the smoke from the burning city. He tried to open his eyes, but blood had congealed on the lashes. I have been unconscious for some time, he thought.

An hour? Less? Carefully, he moved his right arm, bringing his hand to his face, rubbing his right eye with his knuckle to free the lashes. The pain from his left eye intensified and he left it alone, sealed shut. He was facing the shuttered gates and the ghastly ornaments they now carried. Around him the crows were already settling, their sharp beaks ripping at moist flesh. Two of them had landed on the chest of Leon. Gaelen looked away. There were no Aenir in sight. Gingerly he probed the wound above his left hip, remembering the lance that had cut through him as he ran. The wound still bled on both sides, and the flesh was angry and raw to the touch.

Turning his head towards the mountains, and the tall pine trees on the nearest slope, he tried to estimate the time it would take him to reach the safety of the woods. He made an effort to stand, but a roaring began in his ears, like an angry sea. Dizziness swamped him and he lost consciousness.

When he awoke it was close to dusk. His side was still bleeding, though it had slowed to a trickle and once again he had to clear his eye of blood. When he had done so he saw that he had crawled twenty paces. He couldn't remember doing it, but the trail of blood and scored dust could not lie.

Behind him the city burned. It would not be long before the Aenir returned to the plain. If he was found he would be hauled back and blood-eagled like the elders.

The boy began to crawl, not daring to look up lest the distance demoralise him, forcing him to give in.

Twice he passed out for short periods. After the last he cursed himself for a fool and rolled to his back, ripping two strips of cloth from his ragged tunic. These he pressed into the wounds on his hip, grunting as the pain tore into him. They should slow the bleeding, he thought. He crawled on. The journey, begun in pain and weakness, became a torment. Delirious, Gaelen lived again the horror of the attack. He had stolen a chicken from Leon and was racing through the market when the sound of screaming women and pounding hooves made him forget the burly butcher. Hundreds of horsemen came in sight, slashing at the crowd with long swords and plunging lances.

All was chaos and the boy had been petrified. He had hidden in a barn for several hours, but then had been discovered by three Aenir soldiers. Gaelen had run through the alleys, outpacing them, but had emerged into the city square where a rider looped a rope over his shoulders, dragging him out through the broken gates. All around him were fierce-eyed warriors with horned helms, screaming and chanting, their faces bestial.

The rider with the rope hailed two others at the city gates.

'Sport, Father!' yelled the man, his voice muffled by his helm.

'From that wretch?' answered the other contemptuously, leaning across the neck of his horse. The helm he wore carried curved horns, and a face-mask in bronze fashioned into a leering demon. Through the upper slits Gaelen could see a glint of ice-blue eyes, and fear turned to terror within him.

The rider who had roped Gaelen laughed. 'I saw this boy on my last scouting visit. He was running from a crowd. He's fast. I'll wager I land him before you.'

'You couldn't land a fish from a bowl,' said the third rider, a tall wide-shouldered warrior with an open helm. His face was broad and flat, the eyes small and glittering like blue beads. His beard was yellow and grimy, his teeth crooked and broken. 'But I'll get him, by Vatan!'

'Always the first to boast and the last to do, Tostig,' sneered the first rider.

'Be silent, Ongist,' ordered the older man in the horned helm. 'All right, I'll wager ten gold pieces I gut him.'

'Done!' The rider leaned over towards the boy, slicing the dagger through the rope. 'Go on, boy, run.'

Gaelen heard the horse start after him and, throwing himself to the ground, he grabbed a rock and hurled it. The yellow-bearded warrior – Tostig? – pitched from his rearing mount.

Then the lance struck him. He tried to rise, only to see a sword-blade flash down.

'Well ridden, Father!' were the last words he heard before the darkness engulfed him.

Now as he crawled all sense of time and place deserted him. He was a turtle on a beach of hot coals, slowing burning; a spider within an enamel bowl of pain, circling; a lobster within a pan as the heat rose.

But still he crawled.

Behind him walked the yellow-bearded warrior he had pitched to the ground. In his hand was a sword and upon his lips a smile.

Tostig was growing bored now. At first he had been intrigued by the wounded boy, wondering how far he could crawl, and imagining the horror and despair when he discovered the effort was for nothing. But now the boy was obviously delirious, and there was little point in wasting time. He raised the sword, pointing downward above the boy's back.

'Kill him, my bonny, and you will follow him.'

Tostig leapt back a pace, his sword flashing up to point towards the shadow-haunted trees as a figure stepped out into the fading light. He was tall, wearing a leather cloak and carrying an iron-tipped quarterstaff. Two daggers hung from a black leather baldrick across his chest, and a long hunting-knife dangled by his hip. He was green-eyed, and a dark trident beard gave him a sardonic appearance.

Tostig looked beyond the man, straining to pierce the gathering darkness of the undergrowth. The warrior seemed to be alone.

The clansman stepped forward and stopped just out of reach of the Aenir's sword. Then he leaned on his staff and smiled. 'You're on Farlain land,' he said.

'The Aenir walk where they will,' Tostig replied.

'Not here, my bonny. Not ever. Now, what's it to be? Do you leave or die?'

Tostig pondered a moment. His father Asbidag had warned the army not to alienate the clans. Not yet. One mouthful at a time, that was Asbidag's way.

And yet this clansman had robbed Tostig of his prey.

'Who are you?' Tostig countered.

'Your heart has about five beats of life left in it, barbarian,' said Caswallon.

Tostig stared deeply into the sea-green eyes. Had he been sure the man was alone, he would have risked battle. But he was not sure. The man was too confident, too relaxed. No clansman alive would face an armed Aenir in such a way. Unless he had an edge. Tostig glanced once more at the trees. Archers no doubt had him in range at this moment.

'We will meet again,' he said, backing away down the slope.

Caswallon ignored him, and knelt by the bleeding youngster.

Gently he turned him to his back, checking his wounds. Satisfied they were plugged, he lifted the boy to his shoulder, gathered up his staff, entered the shadows and was gone from the sight of the Aenir.

Gaelen turned in his bed and groaned as the stitches front and back pulled at tender, bruised flesh. He opened his eyes and found himself staring at a grey cave wall. The smell of burning beech-wood was in his nostrils. Carefully he moved on to his good side. He was lying on a broad bed, crafted from pine and expertly joined; over his body were two woollen blankets and a bearskin cloak. The cave was large, maybe twenty paces wide and thirty deep, and at the far end it curved into a corridor. Looking back, the boy saw that the entrance was covered with a hide curtain. Gingerly he sat up. Sombody had bandaged his side and his injured eye. Gently he probed both areas. The pain was still there, but more of a throbbing reminder of the acute agony he remembered from his long crawl.

Across from the bed, beyond a table and some chairs rough-cut from logs, was a man-made hearth skilfully chipped away at the base of a natural chimney in the cave wall. A fire was burning brightly. Beside it were chunks of beechwood, a long iron rod, and a copper shovel.

Bright sunlight shafted past the edges of the curtain and the boy's gaze was drawn to the cave entrance. Groaning as he rose, he limped across the cave, lifting the flap and looking out over the mountains beyond. He found himself gazing down into a green and gold valley dotted with stone buildings and wooden barns, sectioned fields and ribbon streams. Away to his left was a herd of shaggy long-horned cattle, and elsewhere he could see sheep and goats, and even a few horses in a paddock by a small wood. His legs began to tremble and he dropped the curtain.

Slowly he made his way to the table and sat down. Upon it was an oatmeal loaf and a jug of spring water. His stomach tightened, hunger surging within him as he tore a chunk from the loaf and poured a little water into a clay goblet.

Gaelen was confused. He had never been this far into the highlands. No lowlander had. This was forbidden territory. The clansmen were not a friendly people, and though they occasionally came into Ateris to trade, it was well-known to be folly for any city-dweller to attempt a return visit.

He tried to remember how he had come here. He seemed to recall voices as he struggled to reach the trees, but the memory was elusive and there had been so many dreams.

At the back of the cave the man called Oracle watched the boy eating and smiled. The lad was strong and wolf-tough. For the five days he had been here he had battled grimly against his wounds, never crying – even when, in his delirium, he had re-lived fear-filled moments of his young life. He had regained consciousness only twice in that time, accepting silently the warm broth that Oracle held to his lips.

'I see you are feeling better,' said the old man, stepping from the shadows.

The boy jumped and winced as the stitches pulled. Looking round, he saw a tall, frail, white-bearded man dressed in grey robes, belted at the waist with a goat-hair rope.

'Yes. Thank you.'

'What is your name?'

'Gaelen. And you?'

'I no longer use my name, but it pleases the Farlain to call me Oracle. If you are hungry I shall warm some broth; it is made from the liver of pigs and will give you strength.'

Oracle moved to the fire, stooping to lift a covered pot to the flames. 'It will be ready soon. How are your wounds?'

'Better.'

The old man nodded. 'The eye caused me the most trouble. But I think it will serve you. You will not be blind, I think. The wound in your side is not serious, the lance piercing just above the flesh of the hip. No vital organ was cut.'

'Did you bring me here?'

'No.' Using the iron rod, Oracle lifted the lid from the pot. Taking a long-handled wooden spoon from a shelf, he stirred the contents. Gaelen watched him in silence. In his youth he must have been a mighty man, thought the boy. Oracle's arms were bony now, but the wrists were thick and his frame broad. The old man's eyes were light blue under thick brows, and they glittered like water on ice. Seeing the boy staring at him, he chuckled. 'I was the Farlain Hunt Lord,' he said, grinning. 'And I was strong. I carried the Whorl boulder for forty-two paces. No man has bettered that in thirty years.'

'Were my thoughts so obvious?' Gaelen asked.

'Yes,' answered the Oracle. 'The broth is ready.'

They ate in silence, spooning the thick soup from wooden bowls and dipping chunks of oatmeal loaf into the steaming liquid.

Gaelen could not finish the broth. He apologised, but the old man shrugged.

'You've hardly eaten at all in five days, and though you are ravenous your stomach has shrunk. Give it a few moments, then try a little more.'

'Thank you.'

'You ask few questions, young Gaelen. Is it that you lack curiosity?'

The boy smiled for the first time. 'No, I just don't want any answers yet.'

Oracle nodded. 'You are safe here. No one will send you back to the Aenir. You are welcome, free to do as you wish. You are not a prisoner. Now, do you have any questions?'

'How did I get here?'

'Caswallon brought you. He is a clansman, a Hunt Master.'

'Why did he save me?'

'Why does Caswallon do the things he does? I don't know. Caswallon doesn't know. He is a man of impulse. A good friend, a terrible enemy, and a fine clansman – but still a man of impulse. When he was a youth he went tracking deer. He was following a doe when he came upon it caught in a Pallides snare. Now the Farlain have no love for the Pallides, so Caswallon cut the deer loose – only to find it had an injured leg. He brought the little beast home upon his back and nursed it to health; then he released it. There's no accounting for Caswallon. Had the beast been fit he would have slain it for meat and hide.'

'And I am like that injured doe,' said Gaelen. 'Had I run into the trees unharmed, Caswallon might have killed me.'

'Yes, you are sharp, Gaelen. I like quick wits in a boy. How old are you?'

The boy shrugged. 'I don't know. Fourteen, fifteen . . .'

'I'd say nearer fourteen, but it doesn't matter. A man is judged here by how he lives and not by the weight of his years.'

'Will I be allowed to stay, then? I thought only clansmen could live in the Druin mountains?'

'Indeed you can, for indeed you are,' said Oracle.

'I don't understand.'

'You are a clansman, Gaelen. Of the Farlain. You see, Caswallon invoked the *Cormaach*. He has made you his son.'

'Why?'

'Because he had no choice. As you said yourself, only a clansman can live here and Caswallon – like all other clansmen – cannot bring strangers into the Farlain. Therefore in the very act of rescuing you he became your guardian, responsible in law for everything you do.'

'I don't want a father,' said Gaelen. 'I get by on my own.'

'Then you will leave,' agreed Oracle, amiably. 'And Caswallon will give you a cloak, a dagger, and two gold coins for the road.'

'And if I stay?'

'Then you will move into Caswallon's house.'

Needing time to think, Gaelen broke off a piece of bread and dipped it into the now lukewarm broth.

Become a clansman? A wild warrior of the mountains? And what would it be like to have a father? Caswallon, whoever he was, wouldn't care for him. Why should he? He was just a wounded doe brought home on a whim. 'When must I decide?'

'When your wounds are fully healed.'

'How long will that be?'

'When you say they are,' said the old man.

'I don't know if I want to be a clansman.'

'Reserve your judgement, Gaelen, until you know what it entails.'

That night Gaelen awoke in a cold sweat, screaming.

The old man ran from the back of the cave, where he slept on a narrow pallet bed, and sat down beside the boy. 'What is it?' he asked, stroking Gaelen's brow, pushing back the sweat-drenched hair from the boy's eyes.

'The Aenir! I dreamed they had come for me and I couldn't get away.'

'Do not fear, Gaelen. They have conquered the lowlands, but they will not come here. Not yet. Believe me. You are safe.'

'They took the city,' said Gaelen, 'and the militia were overrun. They didn't even hold for a day.'

'You have much to learn, boy. About war. About warriors. Aye, the city fell, and before it other cities. But we don't have cities here, and we need no walls. The mountains are like a fortress, with walls that pierce the clouds. And the clansmen don't wear bright breastplates and parade at festivals, they don't march in unison. Stand a clansman against a lowlander and you will see two men, but you will not be seeing clearly. The one is like a dog, well-trained and well-fed. It looks good and it barks loud. The other is like a wolf, lean and deadly. It barks not at all. It kills. The Aenir will not come here yet. Trust me.'

When he woke Gaelen found a fresh-baked honey malt loaf, a jug of goat's milk and a bowl containing oats, dried apple and ground hazelnuts awaiting him at the table. There was no sign of Oracle.

Gaelen's side was sore and fresh blood had seeped through the linen bandages around his waist, but he pushed the pain from his mind and ate. The oats were bland and unappealing, but he found that if he crushed the honey-cake and sprinkled it over the mixture the effect was more appetising.

His stomach full, he made his way outside the cave and knelt by a slender stream that trickled over white rocks on its journey to the valley below. Scooping water to his face, he washed, careful to avoid dampening the bandage over his injured eye. He had thought to take a short walk, but even the stroll to the stream had tired him and he sat back against a smooth rock and gazed down into the valley.

It was so calm here. Set against the tranquillity of these mountain valleys the events at Ateris seemed even more horrifying. Gaelen saw again the crows settling on fat Leon, squabbling and fighting over a strip of red flesh.

The boy was not surprised by the Aenir savagery. It seemed a culmination of all that life had taught him about people. In the main, they were cruel, callous and uncaring, filled with greed and petty malice. The boy knew all about suffering. It was life. It was being frozen in winter, parched in summer, cold-soaked and trembling when it rained. It was being thrashed for the sin of hunger, abused for the curse of loneliness, tormented for being a bastard, and despised for being an orphan.

Life was not a gift to be enjoyed, it was an enemy to be battled, grimly, unremittingly.

The old man had been kind to him, but he has his reasons, thought Gaelen sourly. This Caswallon is probably paying him for his time.

Gaelen sighed. When he was strong enough he would run away to the north and find a city the Aenir had not sacked, and he would pick up his life again – stealing food and scraping a living until he was big enough, or strong enough, to take life by the throat and force it to do his bidding.

Still dreaming of the future, he fell asleep in the sunshine. Oracle found him there at noon and gently carried him inside, laying him upon the broad bed and covering him with the bearskin cloak. The fur was still thick and luxuriant, yet it was thirty years since Oracle had killed the bear. An epic battle fought on a spring day such as this . . . The old man chuckled at the memory. In those days he had been Caracis, Hunt Lord of the Farlain, and a force to be considered. He had killed the bear with a short sword and dagger, suffering terrible wounds from the beast's claws. He never knew why it had attacked him; the large bears of the mountains usually avoided man, but perhaps he had strayed too close to its den, or maybe it was sick and hurting.

Whatever the cause it had reared up from the bushes, towering above him. In one flowing motion he had hurled his hunting-knife into its breast, drawn sword and dagger and leapt forward, plunging both blades through the matted fur and into the flesh beyond. The battle had been brief and bloody. The beast's great arms encircled him, its claws ripping into his back. He had released the sword and twisted at the dagger with both hands, seeking the mighty heart within the ribcage.

And he had found it.

Now the bear, the lord of the high lonely forest, was a child's blanket, and the greatest of the Farlain warriors was a dry-boned ancient, known only as Oracle.

'Time makes fools of us all,' he whispered.

He looked down at the boy's face. He was a handsome lad, with good bones and a strong chin, and his flame-red hair contained a glint of gold, matching the tawny flecks in his dark eyes.

'You will break hearts in years to come, Gaelen, my lad.'

'Hearts . . . ?' said Gaelen, yawning and sitting up. 'I'm sorry. Were you talking to me?'

'No. Old men talk to themselves. How are you feeling?'

'Good.'

'Sleep is the remedy for many of life's ills. Especially loss of blood.'

'It's peaceful here,' said Gaelen. 'I don't normally sleep so much, even when I've been hurt. Is there anything I can do to help you? I don't want to be a burden.'

'Young man, you are not a burden. You are a guest. Do you know what that means?'

'No.'

'It means you are a friend who has come to stay for a while,' the old man told him, laying his hand on the boy's arm. 'It means you owe me nothing.'

'Caswallon pays you to look after me,' said Gaelen, pulling his arm away from Oracle's touch.

'No, he does not. Nor will he. Though he may bring a joint of venison, or a sack of vegetables the next time he comes.' Oracle left the bedside to add several chunks of wood to the fire. 'It's so wasteful,' he called back, 'keeping a fire here in spring. But the cave gets cold and my blood is running thin.'

'It's nice,' said Gaelen. 'I like to see a fire burning.'

'Chopping wood keeps my body from seizing up,' said the old man, returning to the bedside. 'Now, what would you like to know?'

Gaelen shrugged. 'About what?'

'About anything.'

'You could tell me about the clans. Where did they come from?'

'A wise choice,' said Oracle, sitting at the bedside. 'There are more than thirty clans, but originally there was one: the Farlain. Under their leader, Farla the First, they journeyed to Druin more than six hundred years ago, escaping some war in their homeland. The Farlain settled in the valley below here, and two neighbouring valleys to the east. They prospered and multiplied. But, as the years passed, there was discord and several families broke from the clan. There was a little trouble and some fighting, but the new clan formed their own settlements and began calling themselves Pallides, which in the old tongue meant Seekers of New Trails. In the decades that followed other splits developed, giving birth to the Haesten, the Loda, the Dunilds and many more. There have been several wars between the clans. In the last, more than one hundred years ago, six thousand men lost their lives. Then the mighty king Ironhand put an end to it. He gave us wisdom – and the Games.'

'What are the Games?' asked Gaelen.

337

'Tests of skill in a score of disciplines. Archery, swordsmanship, racing, jumping, wrestling . . . many, many events. All the clans take part. It lasts two weeks from Midsummer's Night, and concludes with the Whorl Feast. You will see it this year – and you will never forget it.'

'What are the prizes?'

'Pride is the prize – and always has been.' The old man's blue eyes twinkled. 'Well, pride and a small sack of gold. Caswallon took gold in the archery last year. A better bowman has never been seen in these mountains.'

'Tell me of him.'

The old man chuckled and shook his head. 'Caswallon. Always the children seek stories of Caswallon. If Caswallon were a swallow he would stay north for the winter, just to see how cold it gets. What can any man tell you of Caswallon?'

'Is he a warrior?'

'He is certainly that, but then most clansmen are. He is good with sword and knife, though others are better. He is an expert hunter and a good provider.'

'You like him?' asked Gaelen.

'Like him? He infuriates me. But I love him. I don't know how his wife puts up with him. But then Maeg's a spirited lass.' Oracle rose from the bedside and moved to the table, filling two clay goblets with water. Passing one to Gaelen, he sat down once more. 'Aye, that's the story to give you a taste of young Caswallon.'

'Three years ago at the Games, he saw and fell in love with a maid of the Pallides, the daughter of their Hunt Lord Maggrig. Now, Maggrig is a formidable warrior and a man of hasty and uncertain temper. Above all things on this earth he hates and despises the Farlain. Mention the clan name and his blood boils and his face darkens.

'So imagine his fury when Caswallon approaches him and asks for his daughter's hand. Men close by swore his veins almost burst at the temples. And Maeg herself took one look at him and dismissed him for an arrogant fool. Caswallon took the insults they heaped on him, bowed, and departed to the archery tourney, which

338

he won an hour later. Most of us thought that would be the last of the affair.' Oracle rose and stretched his back, then moved to the fire and added two thick logs. He sighed and refilled his goblet.

'Well, what happened?' urged Gaelen.

'Happened? Oh, yes. I'm sorry, my boy, but the mind wanders sometimes. Where was I? Caswallon's courting of Maeg.' Returning to the bedside, he sat down again. 'Many of the Farlain enjoyed the jest for such it had to be. Maeg was almost twenty and unmarried and it was considered she was a frosty maiden with little interest in men.

'Two months later, in dead of night, Caswallon slipped into the Pallides lands, past their scouts and into the heart of Maggrig's own village. He scaled the stone wall of the old man's house and entered Maeg's room unseen. Just before dawn he awoke Maeg, stifled her scream with a kiss, climbed from the window and was gone into the timberline. Oh, they chased him all right. Fifty of the fleetest Pallides runners, but Caswallon was the racer to beat them all, and he made it home without a scratch.

'Now, back at Maggrig's house there was rare fury, for the young Farlain hunter had left a pair of torn breeches, a worn shirt, and the hide cut out in the shape of a new pair of shoes. Soon the entire highlands chuckled at the tale and Maggrig was beside himself with fury. You have to understand the symbolism, Gaelen. The trousers, shirt and hide were what you'd leave a wife to mend and make. And the fact that he'd spent the night alone in her bedroom made sure no other man would marry her.

'Maggrig swore he'd have his head. Pallides hunters spent their days hoping Caswallon of the Farlain would darken their territory with his shadow. Finally, some three months later, as winter took its hold making the mountains impassable, the Pallides withdrew to their homes. On this night in the long hall, where the clan chiefs were celebrating the Longest Night, the doors opened and there, covered in snow and with ice in his beard, stood Caswallon.

'He walked slowly down the centre of the hall, between the tables, until he stood before Maggrig and his daughter. Then he smiled and said, "Have you finished my breeches and shirt, woman?"

"'I have," she told him. "And where have you been these last months?"

"'Where else should I be?" he answered her. "I've been building our house."

'I tell you, Gaelen, I would have given much to see Maggrig's face that night. The wedding took place the following morning and the two of them stayed most of the winter with the Pallides. Caswallon would not hear of taking Maeg back the way he had come, for he had scaled the east flank of High Druin – no easy task in summer, but in winter fraught with peril.

'Now, does that help you understand Caswallon of the Farlain?'

'No,' answered Gaelen.

The old man laughed aloud. 'No more should it, I suppose. But keep it in your mind and the passing years may explain it to you. Now strip off that shirt and let me check that wound.'

Oracle carefully cut away the bandages and knelt before the bed, his long fingers prising away the linen from the blood-encrusted stitches. Gaelen gritted his teeth, making no sound. As the last piece of linen pulled clear Gaelen looked down. A huge blue and yellow bruise had spread from his hip to his ribs and round to the small of his back. The wound itself had closed well, but was seeping at the edges with yellow pus.

'Don't worry about that, boy,' said Oracle. 'That's just the body expelling the rubbish. The wound's clean and healing well. By midsummer you'll be running with the other lads at the Games.'

'The wound seems wider than I remember,' said Gaelen. 'I thought it was just a round hole.'

'Aye it was – on both sides,' Oracle told him. 'But round wounds take an age to heal, Gaelen. They close up in a circle until there is just a bright tender spot at the centre which never seems to close. I cut a wider gash across it. Trust me; I know wounds, boy. I have seen enough of them, and suffered enough of them. You are healing well.'

'What about my eye?' asked Gaelen, tenderly fingering the bandage.

'We'll know soon, lad.'

* * *

Maeg placed the babe in his crib and covered him with a white woollen blanket. She ran her fingers over the soft, dark down on his head and whispered a blessing to protect him as he slept. He was a beautiful child, with his father's sea-green eyes and his mother's dimpled chin. Tomorrow his grandfather would arrive, and Maeg was secretly delighted that the child had Maggrig's wide cheek-bones and round head. She knew it would please the fiery Hunt Lord of the Pallides. For all that he was a warrior and a man to be respected, Maeg knew that within the crusty shell was a soft-hearted man who had always doted on children.

Men walked warily round the old bull, but children clambered over him, shrieking with mock terror at his blood-curdling threats and tugging at his rust-red beard. He was a man who had always wanted sons, and yet had never made his daughter feel guilty, nor blamed his wife for becoming barren thereafter.

And Maeg loved him.

The sound of the axe thudding into logs drew her to the thin north-facing window. In the yard beyond, stripped to the waist, Caswallon was preparing the winter fuel. An hour a day through spring and summer and the logs would be stacked against the side of the house three paces deep, thirty paces long and the height of a tall man. In this way the wood performed a double service, keeping the fire fed and the northwind away from the wall, insulating their home against the ferocity of the winter.

Caswallon's long hair was swept back from his face and tied at the nape of the neck in a short ponytail. The muscles of his arms and shoulders stretched and swelled with each smooth stroke of the axe. Maeg grinned as she watched him, and rested her elbows on the sill. Caswallon was a natural showman, imbuing even such a simple task as chopping wood with a sense of living poetry. His movements were smooth and yet, every now and then, as he swung the axe, he twisted the handle flashing the blade in a complete turn before allowing it to hammer home in the log set on an oak round. It was almost theatrical and well worth the watching. It was the same with everything he did, Maeg knew; it wasn't that he needed to impress an audience, he was merely creative and easily bored, and amused himself by adding intricacy and often beauty to the most mundane of chores.

'You will win no prizes at the Games with such pretty strokes,' she called as the last log split.

He grinned at her. 'So this is why my breakfast's late, is it? You're too busy gawking and admiring my fine style? It was a sad day, woman, when you bewitched me away from the fine Farlain ladies.'

'The truth of it is, Caswallon, my lad, that only a foreign woman would take you – one who hadn't heard the terrible tales of your youth.'

'You've a sharp tongue in your head, but then I could expect no more from Maggrig's daughter. Do you think he'll find the house?'

'And why shouldn't he?'

'It's a well-known fact the Pallides need a map to get from bed to table.'

'You tell that to Maggrig when he gets here and he'll pin both your ears to the bedposts,' she said.

'Maybe I will, at that,' he told her, stooping to lift his doeskin shirt from the fence.

'You will not!' she shouted. 'You promised you'd not aggravate the man. Did you not?'

'Hush, woman. I always keep my promises.'

'That's a nonsense. You promised you'd seal the draught from this very window.'

'You've a tongue like a willow switch and the memory of an injured hound. I'll do it after breakfast – that is, if the food ever sees the inside of a platter.'

'Do the two of you never stop arguing?' asked Oracle, leaning on his quarterstaff at the corner of the house. 'It's just as well you built your house so far from the rest.'

'Why is it,' asked Maeg, smiling, 'that you always arrive as the food is ready?'

'The natural timing of an old hunter,' he told her.

Maeg dished up hot oats in wooden platters, cut half a dozen slices of thick black bread and broke some salt on to a small side dish, placing it before the two men. From the larder she took a dish of fresh-made butter and a jar of thick, berry preserve. Then she sat in her own chair by the fire, taking up the tiny tunic she was knitting for the babe.

The men ate in silence until at last Caswallon pushed away his plate and asked, 'How is the boy?'

Maeg stopped her knitting and looked up, her grey eyes fixed on the old man's face. The story of Caswallon's rescue of the lad had spread among the Farlain. It hadn't surprised them, they knew Caswallon. Similarly it hadn't surprised Maeg, but it worried her. Donal was Caswallon's son and he was barely four months old. Now the impulsive clansman had acquired another son, many years older and this disturbed her.

'He is a strong boy, and he improves daily,' said Oracle. 'But life has not been good to him and he is suspicious.'

'Of what?' Caswallon asked.

'Of everything. He was a thief in Ateris, an orphan, unloved and unwanted. A hard thing for a child, Caswallon.'

'A hard thing for anyone,' said the clansman. 'You know he crawled for almost two hours with those wounds. He's tough. He deserves a second chance at life.'

'He is still frightened of the Aenir,' said Oracle.

'So should he be,' answered Caswallon gravely. 'I am frightened of them. They are a bloodthirsty people and once they have conquered the lowlands they will look to the clans.'

'I know,' said the old man, meeting Caswallon's eye. 'They will outnumber us greatly. And they're fighters. Killers all.'

'Mountain war is a different thing altogether,' said Caswallon. 'The Aenir are fine warriors but they are still lowlanders. Their horses will be useless in the bracken, or on the scree slopes. Their long swords and axes will hamper them.'

'True, but what of the valleys where our homes are?'

'We must do our best to keep them out of the valleys,' answered Caswallon with a shrug.

'Are you so sure they'll attack?' asked Maeg. 'What could they possibly want here?'

'Like all conquerors,' Oracle answered her. 'They fear all men think as they do. They will see the clans as a threat, never knowing when we will pour out of the mountains on to their towns, and so they will seek to destroy us. But we have time yet. There are still lowland armies and cities to be taken, and then they must bring their families over from the south land and build their own farms and towns. We have three years, maybe a little less.'

'Were you always so gloomy, old man?' asked Maeg, growing angry as her good humour evaporated.

'Not always, young Maeg. Once I was as strong as a bull and feared nothing. Now my bones are like dry sticks, my muscles wet parchment. Now I worry. There was a time when the Farlain could gather an army to terrify the world, when no one would dare invade the highlands. But the world moves on . . .'

'Let tomorrow look after itself, my friend,' said Caswallon, resting a hand on the old man's shoulder. 'We'll not make a jot of difference by worrying about it. As Maeg says, we are growing gloomy. Come, we'll walk aways and talk. It will help the food to settle, and I know Maeg will not want us under her feet.'

Both men rose and Oracle walked round the table to stand over Maeg. Then he bowed and kissed her cheek. 'I am sorry,' he said. 'I promise I'll not bring gloom to this house – for a while, at least.'

'Away with you,' she said, rising and throwing her arms around his neck. 'You're always welcome here – just bear in mind I've a young babe, and I don't want to hear such melancholy fear for his future.'

Maeg watched them leave on the short walk through the pasture towards the mountain woods beyond. Then she gathered up the dishes and scrubbed them clean in the water bucket by the hearth. Completing her chores the clanswoman checked on the babe, once more stroking his brow and rearranging his blanket. At her touch he awoke, stretching one pudgy arm with fist clenched, screwing up his face and yawning. Sitting beside him, Maeg opened her tunic and held him to her breast. As he fed she began to sing a soft, lilting lullaby. The babe suckled for several minutes, then, when he had finished she lifted him to her shoulder. His head sagged against her face. Gently she rubbed his back; he gave a loud burp which brought a peal of laughter from his mother. Kissing his cheek, she told him, 'We'll need to improve your table manners before long, little one.' Carefully she laid him back in his cot and Donal fell asleep almost instantly.

Returning to the kitchen, Maeg found Kareen had arrived with the morning milk and was busy transferring it to the stone jug by the wall. Kareen was a child of the mountains, orphaned during the last winter. Only fifteen, it would be a year before she could be lawfully wed and she had been sent by the Hunt Lord, Cambil, to serve Maeg in the difficult early months following the birth of Donal. In the strictest sense Kareen was a servant under indenture, but in the highlands she was a 'child of the house', a short-term daughter to be loved and cared for after the fashion of the clans. Kareen was a bright, lively girl, not attractive but strong and willing. Her face was long and her jaw square, but she had a pretty smile and wore it often. Maeg liked her.

'Beth's yield is down again,' said Kareen. 'I think it's that damned hound of Bolan's. It nipped her leg, you know. Caswallon should chide him about it.'

'I'm sure that he will,' said Maeg. 'Would you mind seeing to Donal if he wakes? I've a mind to collect some herbs for the pot.'

'Would I mind? I'd be delighted. Has he been fed?'

'He has, but I don't doubt he'll enjoy the warmed oats you'll be tempting him with,' said Maeg, winking.

Kareen grinned. 'He's a healthy eater, to be sure. How is the lowland boy?'

'Healing,' Maeg told her. 'I'll be back soon.' Lifting her shawl cloak from the hook by the door, Maeg swung it about her shoulders and stepped out into the yard.

Kareen placed the last of the stone jugs by the wall, hefted the empty bucket and walked out to the well to wash it clean.

She watched Maeg strolling towards the pasture woods, admiring the proud almost regal movements and rare animal grace that could not be disguised by the heavy woollen skirt and shawl. Maeg was beautiful. From her night-dark hair to her slender ankles she was everything Kareen would never be. And yet she was unconscious of her beauty and that, more than anything, led Kareen to love her.

Maeg enjoyed walking alone in the woods, listening to the bird-song and revelling in the solitude. It was here that she found tranquility. Caswallon, despite being the love of her life, was also the cause of great turmoil. His turbulent spirit would never be content with the simple life of a farmer and cattle-breeder. He needed the excitement and the danger that came from raiding the herds of neighbouring clans, stealing into their lands, ghosting past their sentries. One day they would catch and hang him.

You'll not change him, Maeg, she thought.

Caswallon had been a child of the mountains, born out of wedlock to a flighty maid named Mira who had died soon after childbirth — supposedly of internal bleeding, though clan legend had it that her father poisoned her. She had never divulged the name of her lover. Caswallon had been raised in the house of the Hunt Lord, Padris, as foster-brother to Cambil. The two boys had never become friends.

At seventeen Caswallon left the home of Padris with a dagger, a cloak, and two gold pieces. Everyone had assumed he would become a crofter, eking out a slender existence to the north. Instead he had gone alone to Pallides land and stolen a bull and four cows. From the Haesten he stole six cows, selling three in Ateris. Within a year every out-clan huntsman watched for Caswallon of the Farlain.

Maggrig, the Pallides Hunt Lord, offered two prize bulls to the man who could kill him. Caswallon stole the bulls.

At first his fellow clansmen had been amused by his exploits. But as his wealth grew, so too did the jealousy. The women, Maeg knew, adored Caswallon. The men, quite naturally, detested him. Three years ago, following the death of Padris, Cambil was elected as Hunt Lord and Caswallon's stock amongst the men plunged to fresh depths. For Cambil despised him, and many were those seeking favour with the new Lord.

This year, Caswallon had even declined to take part in the Games, though as defending champion he could have earned points for the clan. What was worse, he had given as his reason that he wished to stay home with his lady, who had a showing of blood in her pregnancy. He had put her to bed and undertaken the household chores himself – an unmanly action.

Yet, as his stock had fallen with the men, so it climbed in direct proportion with the women.

Now there was the business of the lowland boy, and the almost perverse use of clan law to accommodate the act. How could he invoke *Cormaach* for such a one? The old law – crafted to allow for the children of a fallen warrior to be adopted by relatives of the hero – had never been invoked to bring a lowlander into the clans.

Cambil had refused to speak publicly against Caswallon, but privately he had voiced his disgust in the Council. Yet Caswallon, as always, was impervious to criticism.

It was the same when he caught two Haesten hunters on Farlain lands. He had thrashed them with his quarterstaff, but he had not cut off their fingers. That and his marriage to Maeg had left the Council furious: a slight, they called it, on every Farlain maiden.

Against their fury Caswallon adopted indifference. And in some quarters this fanned the fury to hatred.

All of this Maeg knew, for there were few secrets among the Farlain, and yet Caswallon never spoke of it. Always he was courteous, even to his enemies, and rarely had anyone in the three valleys seen him lose his temper. This was read by many as a sign of weakness, but among the women, who often display greater insights in these matters, there was no doubt as to Caswallon's manhood.

If he didn't maim the hunters, there was a reason that had naught to do with cowardice. And Caswallon's reasons, whatever they were, were good enough for his friends. Since no answer would justify his actions to those who hated him, Caswallon offered them exactly that – no answer.

It was a matter of sadness for Maeg that the result of the hatred would be the letting of blood and a death feud between Farlain houses. But that was a worry for tomorrow, and there were always more pressing problems of today to concern the women of the mountains.

2

Unaware of the controversy, of which he was now a part, the boy Gaelen sat in the cave slowly unwinding the bandage around his head, gently easing it from the line of stitches on his brow and cheek.

With infinite care he rubbed away the clotted blood sealing the eyelid and gently prised the eye open. At first his vision was blurred, but slowly it cleared and perspective returned, though a pink haze disturbed him. By the hearth was a silver mirror. Gaelen picked it up and gazed at his reflection. No expression crossed his face as he looked upon his scars, but something cold settled on his heart as he saw the eye.

It was totally red, suffused with blood, giving him a demonic appearance. The top of his head had been shaved to allow the stitches to be inserted, though now the hair was growing again. But it was growing white around the scar.

A change came over him then, for he felt the fear of the Aenir drift away like morning mist, making way for something far stronger than fear.

Hatred filled him, instilling in his soul a terrible desire for vengeance.

For three weeks Gaelen stayed in or around the cave, watching the rain and the sunshine that followed it turn the mountain gorse to gold. He saw the snow recede from the mountain peaks and the young deer emerge from the woods to the fast-flowing streams. In the distance he saw a great brown bear stretching to claw his territorial mark on the trunk of a wiry elm, and the rabbits hopping in the long grass of the meadow in the pink light of dawn.

At night he talked to Oracle, the two of them sitting on a rug before the fire. He heard the history of the clans, and began to learn the names of the legendary heroes – Cubril, the man known as

Blacklatch, who first carried the Whorl stone; Grigor, the Flame-dancer who fought the enemy even as his house burned around him; Ironhand and Dunbar. Strong men. Clansmen.

Not all of them were from the Farlain, that was the strange thing to Gaelen. The clansmen hated each other, yet would glory in tales of heroes from other clans. 'It's no use trying to understand it yet, Gaelen,' the old man told him. 'It's hard enough for us to understand ourselves.'

On the last evening of the month Oracle removed the boy's stitches and pronounced him fit to rejoin the world of the living.

'Tomorrow Caswallon will come, and you'll meet with him and make your decisions. Either you'll stay or you'll go. Either way, you and I will part friends,' said Oracle gravely.

Gaelen's stomach tightened. 'Couldn't I just stay here with you for a while?'

Oracle cupped the boy's chin in his hand. 'No, lad. Much as I've enjoyed your company it cannot be. Be ready at dawn, for Caswallon will come early.'

For much of the night Gaelen was unable to sleep, and when he did he dreamed of the morning, saw himself looking foolish before this great clansman whose face he couldn't quite see. The man told him to run, but his legs were sunk in mud; the man lost his temper and stabbed him with a spear. He awoke exhausted and sweat-drenched and rose instantly, making his way to the stream to bathe.

'Good morning to you.'

Gaelen swung to see a tall man sitting on a granite boulder. He wore a cloak of leaf-green and a brown leather tunic. Slung across his chest was a baldric bearing two slim daggers in leather sheaths, and by his side a hunting-knife. Upon his long legs were leggings of green wool, laced with leather thongs criss-crossed to the knee. His hair was long and dark, his eyes sea-green. He seemed to be about thirty years of age, though he could have been older.

'Are you Caswallon?'

'I am indeed,' said the man, standing. He stretched out his hand. Gaelen shook it and released it swiftly. 'Walk with me and we'll talk about things to interest you.'

Without waiting for a reply Caswallon turned and walked slowly through the trees. Gaelen stood for a moment, then grabbed his shirt from beside the stream and followed him. Caswallon halted beside a fallen oak and lifted a pack he had stowed there. Opening it he pulled clear some clothing; then he sat upon the vine-covered trunk, waiting for the boy to catch up.

Caswallon watched him closely as he approached. The boy was tall for his age, showing the promise of the man he would become. His hair was the red of a dying fire, though the slanted sunlight highlighted traces of gold, and there was a streak of silver above the wound on his brow. The scar on his cheek still looked angry and swollen, and the eye itself was a nightmare. But Caswallon liked the look of the lad, the set of his jaw, the straight-backed walk, and the fact that the boy looked him in the eye at all times.

'I have some clothes for you.'

'My own are fine, thank you.'

'Indeed they are, Gaelen, but a grey, threadbare tunic will not suit you, and bare legs will be cut by the brambles and gorse, as naked feet will be slashed by sharp or jagged stones. And you've no belt to carry a knife. Without a blade you'll be hard-pressed to survive.'

'Thank you then. But I will pay you for them when I can.'

'As you will. Try them.' Caswallon threw him a green woollen shirt edged with brown leather and reinforced at the elbows and shoulders with hide. Gaelen slipped off his own dirty grey tunic and pulled on the garment. It fitted snugly, and his heart swelled; it was, in truth, the finest thing he had ever worn. The green woollen leggings were baggy but he tied them at the waist and joined Caswallon at the tree to learn how to lace them. Lastly a pair of moccasins were produced from Caswallon's sack, along with a wide black belt bearing a bone-handled knife in a long sheath. The moccasins were a little too tight, but Caswallon promised him they would stretch into comfort. Gaelen drew the knife from its scabbard; it was double-edged, one side ending in a half-moon.

'The first side is for cutting wood, shaving or cleaning skins; the second edge is for skinning. It is a useful weapon also. Keep it sharp at all times. Every night before you sleep, apply yourself to maintaining it.'

Reluctantly the boy returned the blade to its sheath and strapped the belt to his waist.

'Why are you doing this for me?'

'A good question, Gaelen, and I'm glad you asked it early. But I've no answer to give you. I watched you crawl and I admired you for the way you overcame your pain and your weakness. Also you made it to the timberline, and became a child of the mountains. As I interpreted clan law, that made you clan responsibility. I took it one stage further, that is all, and invited you into my home.'

'I don't want a father. I never did.'

'And I already have a son of my blood. But that is neither here nor there. In clan law I am called your father, because you are my responsibility. In terms of lowland law – such as the Aenir will not obliterate – I suppose I would be called your guardian. All this means is that I must teach you to live like a man. After that you are alone – should you so desire to be.'

'What would you teach me?'

'I'd teach you to hunt, and to plant, to read signs; I'd teach you to read the seasons and read men; I'd teach you to fight and, more importantly, when to fight. Most vital of all, though, I'd teach you how to think.'

'I know how to think,' said Gaelen.

'You know how to think like an Ateris thief, like a lowland orphan. Look around and tell me what you see.'

'Mountains and trees,' answered the boy without looking round.

'No. Each mountain has a name and reputation, but together they combine to be only one thing. Home.'

'It's not my home,' said Gaelen, feeling suddenly ill-at-ease in his new finery. 'I'm a lowlander. I don't know if I can learn to be a clansman. I'm not even sure I want to try.'

'What *are* you sure of?'

'I hate the Aenir. I'd like to kill them all.'

'Would you like to be tall and strong and to attack one of their villages, riding a black stallion?'

'Yes.'

'Would you kill everyone?'

'Yes.'

'Would you chase a young boy, and tell him to run so that you could plunge a lance into his back?'

'NO!' he shouted. 'No, I wouldn't.'

'I'm glad of that. No more would any clansman. If you stay among us, Gaelen, you will get to fight the Aenir. But by then I will have shown you how. This is your first lesson, lad, put aside your hate. It clouds the mind.'

'Nothing will stop me hating the Aenir. They are vile killers. There is no good in them.'

'I'll not argue with you, for you have seen their atrocities. What I will say is this: A fighter needs to think clearly, swiftly. His actions are always measured. Controlled rage is good, for it makes us stronger, but hatred swamps the emotions – it is like a runaway horse, fast but running aimlessly. But enough of this. Let's walk awhile.'

As they strolled through the woods Caswallon talked of the Farlain, and of Maeg.

'Why did you go to another clan for a wife?' asked Gaelen, as they halted by a rippling stream. 'Oracle told me about it. He said it would show what kind of man you are. But I didn't understand why you did it.'

'I'll tell you a secret,' said the older man, leaning in close and whispering. 'I've no idea myself. I fell in love with the woman the very first moment she stepped from her tent into the line of my sight. She pierced me like an arrow, and my legs felt weak and my heart flew like an eagle.'

'She cast a spell on you?' whispered Gaelen, eyes widening.

'She did indeed.'

'Is she a witch?'

'All women are witches, Gaelen, for all are capable of such a spell if the time is right.'

'They'll not bewitch me,' said the boy.

'Indeed, they won't,' Caswallon agreed. 'For you've a strong mind and a stout heart. I could tell that as soon as I saw you.'

352

'Are you mocking me?'

'Not at all,' he answered, his face serious. 'This is not a joking matter.'

'Good. Now that you know she bewitched you, why do you keep her with you?'

'Well, I've grown to like her. And she's a good cook, and a fine clothes-maker. She made those clothes you are wearing. A man would be a fool not to keep her. I'm no hand with the needles myself.'

'That's true,' said Gaelen. 'I hadn't thought of that. Will she try to bewitch me, do you think?'

'No. She'll see straight away the strength in you.'

'Good. Then I'll stay with you . . . for a while.'

'Very well. Place your hand upon your heart and say your name.'

'Gaelen,' said the boy.

'Your full name.'

'That is my full name.'

'No. From this moment, until you say otherwise, you are Gaelen of the Farlain, the son of Caswallon. Now say it.'

The boy reddened. 'Why are you doing this? You already have a son, you said that. You don't know me. I'm . . . not good at anything. I don't know how to be a clansman.'

'I'll teach you. Now say it.'

'Gaelen of the Farlain, the . . . son of Caswallon.'

'Now say, "I am a clansman." '

Gaelen licked his lips. 'I am a clansman.'

'Gaelen of the Farlain, I welcome you into my house.'

'Thank you,' Gaelen answered lamely.

'Now, I have many things to do today, so I will leave you to explore the mountains. Tomorrow I shall return and we'll take to the heather for a few days and get to know one another. Then we'll go home.' Without another word Caswallon was up and walking off down the slope towards the houses below.

Gaelen watched until he was out of sight, then drew his dagger and held it up before him like a slender mirror. Joy surged in him. He replaced the blade and ran back towards the cave to show Oracle his finery. On the way he stopped at a jutting boulder ten feet high. On impulse he climbed it and looked about him, gazing with new eyes on the mountains rearing in the distance.

Lifting his arms to the sky he shouted at the top of his voice. Echoes drifted back to him, and tears coursed from his eyes. He had never heard an echo, and he felt the mountains were calling to him.

'I am going home!' he had shouted.

And they had answered him.

'HOME! HOME! HOME!'

Far down the slopes Caswallon heard the echoes and smiled. The boy had a lot of learning to do, and even more problems to overcome. If he thought it was hard to be a thief in Ateris, just wait until he tried to walk among the youths of the Farlain!

A lowlander in highland clothing . . .

A sheep to be sheared . . .

And being the son of Caswallon would make life no more easy. Caswallon shrugged. That was a worry for tomorrow.

For three days the new father and son wandered the Farlain mountains and woods, into the high country where the golden eagle soared, and on into the timberline where bears had clawed their territorial marks deep into the trunks of young trees.

'Why do they do that?' asked Gaelen, staring up at the deeply-scored gashes.

'It's very practical,' Caswallon answered him, loosening his leather pack and easing it to the ground. 'They rear up to their full height and make their mark. Any other bear in the vicinity will, upon finding the mark, rise to reach it. If he can't he leaves the woods – for the other bear is obviously bigger, and therefore stronger, than he is. Mind you, the bear that lives here is a canny beast. And he can't reach his own mark; in fact he's quite small.'

'I don't understand,' said Gaelen. 'How then did he make the gashes?'

'Think about it for a while. Go and gather some wood for a fire and I'll skin the rabbit.'

354

Gaelen scoured the clearing for dead wood, snapping each stick as Caswallon had taught him, discarding any that retained sap. Every now and again he glanced back at the tree. Could the bear have rolled a boulder against the trunk? He didn't know. How clever were bears? As he and Caswallon sat by the fire he told the older man his theory about the boulder. Caswallon listened seriously.

'A good theory,' he said at last, 'but not true. Now look around you and describe your setting.'

'We are in a hollow where our fire cannot be seen, and there is protection from the wind.'

'But exactly where in the hollow are we?'

Taking his bearings from the mountains, as Caswallon had taught him, the boy answered with confidence, 'We are at the north end.'

'And the tree, how is it placed?'

'It is growing ten paces into the hollow.'

'Where does the wind come from in the winter – the freezing wind?'

'From the north,' answered Gaelen.

'Picture the hollow in winter,' prompted the clansman.

'It would be cold, though sheltered, and snow-covered.'

'How then did the bear make his mark?'

'I see it!' yelled Gaelen. 'The wind whipped the snow into the hollow, but it built up against the bole of the tree like a huge step and the bear climbed up the snow.'

'Very good.'

'But was that just luck? Did the bear intend to fool other bears?'

'I like to think so,' said Caswallon. 'You see bears tend to sleep through the winter. They don't hibernate as other animals; they just sleep a lot. Mostly a bear will only come out in winter if it's hungry, and then it wouldn't be thinking about territorial marks.

'But the lesson for you, Gaelen my lad, is not about the bear – it's about how to tackle a problem. Think it through, all the way. A question about the land involves all four seasons.'

As Gaelen rolled into his blankets that night, beneath the hide roof Caswallon had made, his mind overflowed with the knowledge he had gained. A horse always kicks the grass back in the direction from which it has come, but the cow pushes it down in the direction it is facing. Deer avoid the depths of the forest, for they live on saplings and young shoots which only grow in strong sunlight, never in the darkened depths. Never kill a deer on the run, for in its terror its juices flood the muscles making it tough and hard to chew. Always build your fire against a cliff wall, or fallen tree, for the reflected heat will double its warmth. That, and the names of all the mountains, floated through his mind and his sleep was light, his dreams many.

He awoke twice in the night – once as it began to rain, and the second time when a large fox brushed against his foot. In the moonlight the beast's face seemed to glow like some hellish demon of the dark. Gaelen screamed and the fox fled.

Caswallon did not stir, though in the morning as he packed their makeshift tent he told Gaelen grimly, 'In the mountains a man can pay with his life for a moment's panic. That was a good lesson for you. In future, make no noise when faced by a threat. You could have been hiding from the Aenir, and felt a snake upon your leg. One scream, one sudden movement – and you would face death from both.'

'I'm sorry. It won't happen again.'

Caswallon ruffled the boy's hair and grinned. 'It's not a criticism, Gaelen. As I said, it's a valuable lesson.'

Throughout the morning the companions followed the mountain paths and trails. Gaelen listened to the older man's stories of the clans and learned. He learned of the Farlain march to the island of Vallon and the mysterious Gates, and their entry to the mountains. He learned of the structure of the society and how no kings were permitted within the clans, but that in times of war a High King would be elected: a man like the legendary Ironhand. But most of all he learned of Caswallon of the Farlain. He noticed the smooth, confident manner in which he moved and spoke, the gentle humour in his words, the authority in his statements. He learned that Caswallon was a man of infinite patience and understanding, a man who loved the high country and its people, despite lacking the harsh cruel quality of the former and the volatile, often violent passions of the latter.

Towards the afternoon Caswallon led the way into a small pine-wood nestling against the base of a towering rock face. As they entered the trees the clansman stopped and Gaelen started to speak, but Caswallon waved him to silence. They could hear the wind swishing the leaves above them, and the rustle of small animals in the dry bracken. But inlaid into the sounds was an occasional squealing cry, soft and muted by the trees, like an echo.

Caswallon led the boy to the left, pushing his way through inter-twined bushes until they reached a larger clearing at the base of the cliff.

Here, before the cave-mouth, lay the evidence of a mighty strug-gle. A dead mountain lion was locked in a grotesque embrace with a huge dog, the like of which Gaelen had never seen. The dog's jaws were clamped together in the throat of the lion which in its death throes had disembowelled the hound with the terrible claws of its hind legs. The dead animals had already begun to putrefy, the lion's belly bloated with gases.

'What kind of hound is that?' asked Gaelen.

'The best there is,' answered Caswallon. 'That is Nabara, the War Hound, she who belonged at one time to Cambil, the Farlain Hunt Lord. But she was a vicious beast and she ran away to the hills the day before she was to be slain.'

Gaelen walked close to the bodies. 'Her jaws are huge, and her body is long. She must have been formidable,' he said.

'There are few war hounds left now. I don't know why. Maybe because we don't have the old-style wars. But yes, they are formi-dable. Terrifying, in fact. As you see, they can even be a match for a lion.'

The squealing began again from within the cave.

'Her cubs are inside,' said Caswallon. 'That is why she fought to the death. Little good it will do them.'

'Are you going to kill them?'

'Yes.'

'But why?'

357

'She's been living in the mountains for over a year. The only animal she's likely to have mated with is a wolf. But we'll see.'

The cave ceiling was low and the companions entered warily on hands and knees. Inside, the cave narrowed into a short tunnel bearing right. Beyond that was a deep cleft in which the hound had left her pups. There were five small bodies and a sixth struggling to stand on shaking legs. Caswallon reached over, lifted the black and grey pup and passed it back to the boy. Then he checked the bodies. All were dead.

Once back in the sunlight Caswallon retrieved the pup, tucking it half into his tunic where his body heat would warm it.

'Build a fire over there, Gaelen, and we'll see if the beast is worth saving.'

Gaelen built a small circle of stones, laid his tinder and struck sparks from his dagger and a small flint block. The tinder began to smoke. He blew on it softly until the first tongue of flame rose, then he added small twigs and finally thinner sticks. Caswallon eased his pack from his shoulders, pulling out the strips of dried meat packed by Maeg.

'We need a pot to boil some thick broth,' he said. 'And here is another lesson for you. Cut me a long strip of bark from that tree over there.'

Gaelen did as he was bid and watched amazed as Caswallon shaped the edges and then twisted the bark into the shape of a deep bowl. Half filling it with water from the canteen, he laid the pot on the small fire.

'But it will burn away,' said Gaelen. 'It is wood.'

'It will not burn as long as water is in it and the flames stay below the waterline.' Taking his dagger, Caswallon sliced the dried meat into chunks and added them to the pot.

Before long the stew began to bubble and steam, the meat expanding. Caswallon added more meat, stirring the contents with his dagger. Gaelen moved beside him, reaching to stroke the small dark head poking out from Caswallon's tunic.

As the sun sank behind crimson clouds, bathing the mountain peaks in glowing copper, Caswallon ordered the lad to remove the bowl and allow the stew to cool. As they waited, the clansman opened his tunic and lifted the pup to his lap. Then he cut a section of the dried beef and began to chew it. 'Can you give some to the pup?' pleaded Gaelen. 'He is starving!'

'That's what I am doing, boy. It's too tough for him. I am doing what his mother would do.'

Removing the half-chewed meat from his mouth, Caswallon shredded it and offered a small amount to the pup. Its tiny tongue snaked out, nose wrinkling at the smell of the meat. The tiny beast ate a little, then its head sank against Caswallon's hand. 'Still too tough for him,' said the clansman. 'But see the size of his paws? He will be big, this one. Here, hold him.'

The pup began to whine as Caswallon passed him over, but he settled down as Gaelen stroked behind his floppy ears.

'As I thought, he is half wolf,' said the clansman. 'But there's enough dog in him to be trained, I think. Would you like to keep him?'

Gaelen lifted the pup to his face, staring into the tiny brown eyes. Like him, the helpless beast was an orphan, and he remembered his own long crawl to the high ground.

'He is a child of the mountains,' said Gaelen. 'I shall adopt him. Is it my right?'

'It is,' said Caswallon gravely. 'But first he must live.'

After a while Caswallon tested the stew. When it had reached blood heat he passed it to Gaelen. 'Dip your smallest finger into it and get the beast to lick it. He's obviously too young to take it any other way.' The stew was thick and dark and Gaelen followed the instructions. The pup's nose wrinkled again at the smell, but its tongue licked out. The boy continued to feed the animal until at last it fell asleep in his arms.

'Do you think it will live?'

'I don't know. Tomorrow we will have a better idea.'

'I hope it does, Caswallon.'

'Hope is akin to prayer,' said the clansman, 'so perhaps it will.' He rose to his feet. 'Wait here, there's something I must check. I should not be long.' With that he was gone into the undergrowth. The sun had set, but the moon was high and bright in the clear sky, and Gaelen sat with his back against a tree, staring into the flickering coals of the fire.

This was life, this was a peace he had never known. The little pup moved in its sleep and he stroked it absently. In the distance the mountains made a jagged line against the sky like a wall against the world – deeply comforting and immensely reassuring.

Caswallon returned silently and sat beside the boy.

'We have a small problem Gaelen,' he said. 'I saw a couple of footprints at the edge of the woods as we entered, but I was intent on finding the cub. I have followed the track to softer ground where the prints are clearer. There is no doubt they are made with iron-studded boots. Clansmen all wear moccasins.'

'Who made the footprints then?'

'The Aenir. They are in the mountains.'

In the morning as Gaelen fed the pup the remains of the stew which had been warmed on the glowing coals of the fire, his mind was clear, the terror of the night condensed and controlled into a manageable apprehension.

'How many are there?' he asked the clansman.

'Somewhere in the region of twenty. I think they're just scouring, but they're headed into Farlain lands and that could prove troublesome. We will walk warily today, avoiding the skylines. Have no fear, though, Gaelen, for these are my mountains and they shall not surprise us.'

Gaelen took a deep breath, and his gaze was steady as he met Caswallon's eyes. 'I am not afraid today,' he told the clansman. 'Last night I was trembling. Today I am ready.'

'Good,' said Caswallon, gathering up his quarterstaff and looping the straps of the pack across his shoulders. 'Then let us put the Aenir from our minds and I will show you something of rare grandeur.'

'What is it?'

'Do not be impatient. I'll not spoil it with words.'

The clansman set off towards the west, and Gaelen gathered up the pup and followed him.

Throughout the morning they climbed through the timberline, over rocky scree slopes, down into verdant vales, and finally up into a sandstone pass. A sound like distant thunder growled in muted majesty and Gaelen's heart hammered.

'Is it a beast?' he asked.

'No. Though legends have it otherwise. What you are about to see is the birthplace of many myths. The Rainbow bridge to the home of the gods is but one that springs from Attafoss.'

Once through the pass, Caswallon led the way along a grassy track, the thunder growing below and to the right. Finally they climbed down towards the noise, clambering over rocks and warily walk-sliding down scree slopes, until Caswallon heaved the pack from his shoulders and beckoned the boy to him. Caswallon was standing on the lip of a slab-like ledge. As Gaelen approached he saw for the first time the glory of Attafoss, and he knew deep in his heart that he would never forget the moment.

There were three huge falls, the water split by two towering boulders before plunging three hundred feet to a foaming pool beneath, and on to one great waterfall whose roar deafened the watchers. Sunlight reflected from black, basaltic rock, forming rainbows in the spray, one of which spanned the falls and disappeared high in the air above the mountains. The falls were immense, almost half a mile wide. Gaelen stood open-mouthed and stared at the Rainbow bridge. Even in Ateris he had heard stories of it.

Caswallon lifted his arms to the sky and began to speak, but the words were whipped from his mouth by the roaring voice of Attafoss. The clansman turned to the boy and grinned, 'Come on,' he bellowed.

Slowly they worked their way above the falls to sit beside the surging water in the lea of a rock face that deadened the cacophonous noise.

Caswallon pointed to a tear-shaped island in the centre of the lake. It was heavily wooded, and from here the boy could see the mouths of deep caves in the rocky hills above the tree-line.

'That is Vallon,' he said, 'and upon it lies one of the magic Gates through which the Farlain passed hundreds of years ago. We came in winter when the water was frozen solid, and we walked upon the ice.'

They stayed the night above the falls, and Gaelen fed the pup with dried meat which he had first chewed to softness; this time the hound ate with relish. The following day Caswallon led them south towards the Farlain. The boy saw that Caswallon moved more cautiously, scanning the surrounding countryside and waiting in the cover of woods, checking carefully, before moving out into open country.

Twice they came upon Aenir tracks, and once the remains of a camp-fire. Caswallon worked his fingers into the grey ash, and down into the earth beneath.

'This morning,' he said. 'Be watchful.'

That night they made camp in a narrow cave and lit no fire. At first light they moved on. Caswallon was uneasy.

'They are close,' he said. 'I can almost smell them. To be honest, Gaelen, I am worried. I may have underestimated these Aenir. For all that there are twenty of them they leave little spoor, and they avoid the skylines in their march. They are woodsmen and good scouts. And that concerns me; it could mean the Aenir are preparing to march upon us far more early than I anticipated.'

By dusk Caswallon's unease had become alarm. He didn't talk at all but checked the trail many times, occasionally climbing trees to scan the horizon.

'What is wrong?' Gaelen asked him as he pored over a near-invisible series of scuffs and marks on the track.

'They have split up into small parties. Three have gone ahead, the rest have moved into the woods. My guess is that they know we are close and they have formed a circle round us.'

'What can we do?'

'We do not have many choices,' said the clansman. 'Let's find a place to make camp.'

Caswallon chose a spot near a stream, where he built a small fire against a fallen trunk and the two of them ate the last of the food Maeg had prepared. Once again the night sky was cloudless, the moon bright. Gaelen snuggled into his blankets with the pup curled against his chest, and slept deep and dreamlessly until about two hours before dawn when Caswallon gently shook him awake. Gaelen opened his eyes. Above him knelt Caswallon, a finger held to his lips, commanding silence. Gaelen rose swiftly. Caswallon pointed to the pup and the boy picked it up, tucking it into his tunic. The clansman filled Gaelen's bed with brush and covered it with a blanket. Then he added fuel to the fire before moving into the darkness of the woods. He stopped by a low, dense bush in sight of the clearing and the flickering fire.

Putting his face close to Gaelen's ear, he whispered, 'Crawl into the bush and curl up. Make no sound and move not at all. If the pup stirs–kill it!'

'I am willing to fight,' whispered Gaelen.

'Willing – but not yet ready,' said Caswallon. 'Now do as I bid.'

Dropping to his knees Gaelen crawled into the bush, pushing aside the branches and wrapping himself in the cloak Caswallon had given him. He waited with heart hammering, his breath seeming as loud as the Attafoss thunder.

Caswallon had disappeared.

For more than an hour there was no sign of hostile movement in the woods. Gaelen was cramped and stiff, and the pup did stir against him. Gently he stroked the black and grey head. The tiny hound yawned and fell asleep. Gaelen smiled – then froze.

A dark shadow had detached itself from the trees not ten paces from the bush. Moonlight glistened on an iron-rimmed helm and flashed from a sword-blade in the man's hand.

The warrior crept to the edge of the clearing, lifted his sword and waved it, signalling his companions. His view partly screened by leaves and branches, Gaelen could just make out the assault on the camp. Three warriors ran across the clearing, slashing their swords into the built-up blankets.

As the boy watched the Aenir drew back, realising they had been fooled. No word passed between them, but they began to search the surrounding trees.

Gaelen was terrified. The bush stood alone, out in the open, plainly in sight of the three hunters. Why did Caswallon leave him

363

in such an exposed place? He toyed with the idea of crawling clear and running, but they were too close.

One of the warriors began to search at the far side of the clearing, stepping into the screen of gorse. Gaelen's eyes opened wide as Caswallon rose from the ground behind the warrior, clamped a hand over his mouth, and sliced his dagger across the man's throat. Releasing the body, he turned and ducked back into the gorse.

Unsuspecting, the remaining hunters checked to the west and east. Finding nothing, they moved towards the bush where Gaelen sat rigid with fear.

The first warrior, a burly man in bearskin tunic and leather breeches, turned to the second, a tall, lean figure with braided black hair.

'Fetch Karis,' said the first. The warrior moved back towards the clearing, while the leader walked towards Gaelen's hiding place. The boy watched in amazement. The man never once looked down; it was as if he and the bush were invisible.

The warrior was so close that Gaelen could see only his leather-clad legs and the high, laced boots he wore. He did not dare look up. Suddenly the man's body slumped beside the bush. Gaelen started violently, but stopped himself from screaming. The Aenir lay facing him, his dead eyes open, his neck leaking blood on the soft earth.

The dead man began to move like a snake, only backwards. Gaelen looked up. Caswallon had the man by the feet and was pulling him into the undergrowth. Then, dropping the body, the clansman vanished once more into the trees.

The last Aenir warrior, sword in hand, stepped back into the clearing. 'Asta!' he called. 'Karis is dead. Come back here.'

Caswallon's voice sounded, the words spoken coldly. 'You're all alone, my bonny.'

The warrior spun and leapt to the attack, longs word raised. Leaning back, Caswallon swivelled his quarterstaff stabbing it forward like a spear. It hammered into the warrior's belly and with a grunt he doubled over, his head speeding down to meet the other end of the ironcapped staff. Hurled from his feet, he hit the ground hard. Groggy, he tried to rise. Strong fingers lifted him by his hair, ramming his face into the rough bark of an old oak. He sank to the ground once more, semi-conscious.

Ongist could feel his hands being tied, but could find no strength to resist. He passed out then, returning to consciousness some hours later for the sun had risen. His head ached and he could taste blood in his mouth. He tried to move but he was bound to a tree trunk.

Several paces before him sat the two he had been tracking, the man and the boy. Both were obviously clan, but there was something familiar about the lad although the warrior couldn't place him.

'I see you are back with us,' said the clansman. 'What is your name?'

'Ongist, son of Asbidag.'

'I am Caswallon of the Farlain. This is my son Gaelen.'

'Why have you not killed me?'

'I like a man who makes his point swiftly,' said Caswallon. 'You are alive by my whim. You are here to scout Farlain lands. Your instructions were probably to remain unseen, or kill any who discovered you – in which case you have failed twice. You had us encircled, and the circle is now tightening. Therefore if I leave you here you will be found, and you can give this message to your leaders: leave now, for I shall summon the Farlain hunters before the day is out and then not one of you will live to report to your lord.'

'Strong words,' muttered the Aenir.

'Indeed they are, my friend. But understand this, I am known among the Farlain as a mild-mannered man and the least of warriors. And yet two of your men are slain and you are trussed like a water fowl. Think what would happen if I loosed two hundred warcarles upon you.'

'What are your two hundred?' spat the warrior. 'What are your two *thousand*, compared to the might of the Aenir? You will be like dry leaves before a forest fire. The Farlain? A motley crew of semi-savages with no king and no army. Let me advise you now. Send your emissaries to the Lord Asbidag in Ateris and make your peace. But bring presents, mind. The Lord Asbidag appreciates presents.'

Caswallon smiled. 'I shall carry the words of your wisdom to the Farlain Council. Perhaps they will agree with you. When your men find you, tell them to head south. It is the fastest way from the Farlain.'

The warrior hawked and spat.

'Look at him, Gaelen. That is the Aenir, that is the race that has terrorised the world. But for all that he is merely a man who smells strong, whose hair is covered in lice, and whose empire is built on the blood of innocents. Warriors? As you saw last night they are just men, with little skill – except in the murder of women, or the lancing of children.'

Ongist's eyes flashed in recognition. The boy was the lad Asbidag had speared at the gates of Ateris. He bit his lip and said nothing. His brother Tostig had told them all how the boy had crawled to the mountains and been rescued by twenty clansmen. It had worried Asbidag.

'Would you like to kill him, Gaelen?'

Ongist felt the hatred in the boy's gaze, and he stared back without fear. 'I see we made our mark upon you boy,' he sneered. 'Do they call you Blood-eye, or Scar-face?'

The boy said nothing, but the cold gaze remained. 'Did someone cut your tongue out?' hissed Ongist.

Gaelen turned to his father. 'Yes, I want to kill him,' he said. 'But not today.'

The man and the boy left the clearing without a backward glance and Ongist settled back to wait for his brother and the others. It was nearing midday when the Aenir found him; they cut him loose and hauled him to his feet. His brothers Tostig and Drada supported him, for his head was dizzy and his vision blurred as he stood.

'What happened?' asked Drada, his elder by three years.

'The clansman tricked us. He killed Karis and Asta.'

'I know. We found the bodies.'

'He told me to leave Farlain lands. He says he will alert their hunters.'

'Good advice,' said Drada.

'Asbidag will be angry,' muttered Tostig. Ongist rubbed at his bruised temple and scowled. Tostig was the largest of the brothers, a towering brute of a man with braided yellow hair and broken teeth. But he was also the most cautious – some would say cowardly. Ongist despised him.

'What was he like?' asked Drada.

Ongist shrugged. 'Tall. Moved well. Fought well. Confident.'

'Then we'll take his advice. Did you talk to him, try to bait him?'

'Yes.'

'And?'

'No reaction, he just smiled. I told him the Aenir would sweep his people away. I advised him to come to Asbidag and beg for peace. He just said he would take my words of wisdom to the Council.'

'Damn,' said Drada. 'I don't like the sound of that. Men who don't get angry make the worst enemies.'

Ongist grinned, draping his arm over Drada's shoulder. 'Always the thinker, brother. By the way, the boy he claimed was his son is the same lad Father speared at the city gates.'

Drada swore. 'And still he didn't get angry? That does make me shiver.'

'I thought you'd enjoy that,' said Ongist. 'By the way, Tostig, how many men did you say rescued the boy?'

'I couldn't see them all. They were hidden in the bushes.'

'How many could you see?' asked Drada, his interest caught by Ongist's question.

'I could see only the leader clearly. Why? How many men did he say he had?'

'He didn't say,' answered Ongist, 'but I know.'

'A curse on you!' shouted Tostig, storming to the other side of the clearing.

Drada took Ongist by the arm and led him to the fallen trunk where Caswallon had made their fire. The two men sat down and Drada rubbed his eyes. 'What was the point of all that?' he asked.

367

'There were no twenty clansmen,' sneered Ongist. 'Just the one – the same man, I'd stake my life on it.'

'You are probably right,' Drada agreed. 'Did he give a name?'

'Caswallon of the Farlain.'

'Caswallon. Let's hope there are not too many like him among the clans.'

'It won't matter if there are. Who can stand against thirty thousand Aenir warriors?'

'That is true,' agreed Drada, 'but they remain an unknown quantity. Who knows how many there are? Our estimate is less than seven thousand fighting men if all the clans muster. But suppose we are wrong?'

'What do you suggest?'

'I think we ought to deal with them gently. Trade first and earn a welcome among them. Then we'll see.'

'You think they'll be foolish enough to allow us into the mountains?' asked Ongist.

'Why not? Every other conquered nation has given us the same facility. And there must be those among the clans who are disenchanted, overlooked or despised. They will come to us, and they will learn.'

'I thought Father wanted to attack in the summer?'

'He does, but I'll talk him out of it. There are three main lowland areas still to fall, and they'll yield richer pickings than these mountains.'

'I like the mountains. I'd like to build a home here,' said Ongist.

'You will soon, my brother. I promise you.'

Oracle sat alone, gazing into the fire, lost in yesterday's dreams when armies swept across the land with their lances gleaming and banners raised.

A red Hawk on a field of black. The Outlanders streaming from the battlefield, broken and demoralised. Sigarni raising her sword in the sunset, the Battle Queen triumphant.

Such had been the glory of youth when Oracle crossed the Gate to the kingdom beyond. The old man drew his grey cloak about his shoulders, stretching his legs forward, soaking in the heat from the burning beech in the hearth. He stared down at the backs of his hands, wrinkled and spotted with the drab brown specks of age.

But once upon a time . . .

'Dreaming of glory?' asked Taliesen.

Oracle jerked up as if struck, twisting in his seat. He cursed softly as he recognised the ancient druid. 'Pull up a chair,' he said.

The druid was small, and skeletally thin, his white hair and beard sparse and wispy, clinging to his face and head like remnants of winter mist. But his eyes were strangely youthful and humorous, antelope-brown and set close together under sharp brows. From his skinny shoulders hung a cloak of birds' feathers, many-hued, the blue of the kingfisher flashing against raven black, soft pale plover and eagle's quill.

He leaned his long staff against the cave wall and seated himself beside the Oracle. 'The boy came then,' said the druid, his voice soft and deep.

'You know he did.'

'Yes. And so it begins: the destruction of all that we love.'

'So you believe.'

'Do you doubt me, Oracle?'

'The future is like soft clay to be moulded. I cannot believe it is already set and decided.'

The druid gave a low curse. 'You of all men should know that the past, present and future exist together, woven like a cloth, interweaving. You crossed the Gate. Did you learn nothing?'

'I learned the error of pride. That was enough for me.'

'You look old and tired,' said the druid.

'I am both. How is it that you still live, Taliesen? You were old when I was a babe at the breast.'

'I was old when your grandfather was a babe at the breast.'

For a while both men sat in silence staring into the flames, then Oracle sighed and shifted in his seat. 'Why have you come here?' he whispered.

'Sigarni has crossed the Gate. She is at the cave on High Druin.'

Oracle licked his lips, his mouth suddenly dry. 'How is the girl?'

Taliesen gave a dry laugh. 'Girl? She is a woman near as old as you. As I said, you do not understand the intricacies of the Gateways.'

'Well, how is she anyway, damn you?'

'Gravely wounded, but I will heal her.'

'May I see her?'

The druid shook his head. 'It would not be wise.'

'Then why come to me at all?'

'It may be that you can help me.'

'In what way?'

'What happened to the sword you stole from her?'

Oracle reddened. 'It was payment for all I had done for her.'

'Do not seek to justify yourself, Caracis. Your sin led to more wars. You cost Sigarni far more than you were worth; then you stole Skallivar. You told me you lost it in the fight that brought you back to us, but I no longer believe you. What happened to it?'

Oracle rose and walked to the rear of the cave. He returned carrying a long bundle wrapped in cloth. Placing it on the table, he untied the binding and opened the bundle. There lay a shining sword of silver steel. 'You want it?' Oracle asked.

Taliesen sighed, and flipped the cloth back over the blade. 'No. Damn you, man! You crossed the Lines of Time. You will die and never know the chaos you gave birth to. I have tried to put it right, and have only succeeded in creating fresh paradoxes.'

'What are you talking about?'

'Without the sword Sigarni was crushed, defeated and slain.'

'But you said she was here!'

'As she is. I tried to help her, Caracis, but she died. I crossed the Lines finding another Sigarni, in another world. She died. Time and time again I travelled the Gates. Always she died. I gave up for a long while, then I returned to my quest and found another Sigarni who was fated to die young. She defeated her first enemy, and then the second, Earl Jastey. She did it with the help of Caracis. You remember that, do you not?' Oracle looked away. 'And Caracis, once again, stole her sword. But this time she asked *me* to return it to her. That had never happened before. I did not know what to do. And now – suddenly – she is here. A victorious Queen carrying *this* sword.'

'I did not want to part with it,' whispered the man who had been Caracis.

'You had such talents, Caracis,' said Taliesen softly. 'How was it that you became such a wretch?'

'I wanted to be a king, a hero. I wanted songs sung about me, and legends written. Is that so shameful? Tell me, did she rule well?'

'She won the final battle, and held the clans together for forty years. She is a true legend and will remain so.'

Oracle grinned. 'Forty years, you say? And she won.' Hauling himself to his feet, the old man fetched a jug of honey mead and two goblets. 'Will you join me?'

'I think I will.'

'Forty years,' said Oracle again. 'I could not have done it. Forty years!'

'Tell me of the boy Gaelen.'

Oracle dragged his mind back to the present. 'Gaelen? He's a good lad, bright and quick. He has courage. I like him. He will be good for Caswallon.'

'How does Caswallon fare?'

'As always, he walks his own path. He has been good to me . . . like a son. And he eases my shame and helps me forget . . .'

'Have you told him of your past?' inquired Taliesen, leaning forward and staring hard at Oracle.

'No, I kept my promises. I've told no one of the worlds beyond. Do you doubt me?'

'I do not. You are a wilful man and proud, but no one ever accused you of oath-breaking.'

'Then why ask?'

'Because men change. They grow weak. Senile.'

'I am not senile yet,' snapped Oracle.

'Indeed you are not.'

'What will happen to the Queen?'

Taliesen shrugged. 'She will die, as all die. She is old and tired; her day is gone. A sorcerer long ago sent a demon to kill her. He made a mistake and cast his spell too close to a Gateway. The beast is almost upon her.'

'Can we not save her?'

'We are talking of destiny, man!' snapped Taliesen. 'The beast must find her.' His stern expression relaxed. 'Even should the demon fail, she will die soon. Her heart is old and worn out.'

'At least she achieved something with her life. She saved her people. I've destroyed mine.'

'I cannot make it easier, for you speak the truth. But it is done now.'

'Is there truly no hope?' Oracle pleaded.

The druid sighed and stood, gathering his long staff. 'There is always hope, no matter how slender or unrealistic. Do not think that you are the only one to feel regret. The Farlain are my people, in a way you could never comprehend. When they are destroyed my life goes with them. And all the works of my life. You! You are just a man who made a mistake. I must bear the cost. Hope? I'll tell you what hope there is. Imagine a man standing in Atta Forest at the birth of autumn. Imagine all the leaves are ready to fall. That man must reach out and catch one leaf, one special leaf. But he doesn't know which tree it is on. That is the hope for the Farlain. You think the idiot Cambil will catch the leaf?'

'Caswallon might,' said Oracle.

'Caswallon is not Hunt Lord,' said Taliesen softly. 'And if he were . . . the clans are sundered, and widely spread. They will not turn back an enemy as strong as the Aenir.'

'Did you come here to punish me, druid?'

'Punish you? I sometimes wish I had killed you,' said Taliesen sadly. 'Damn you, mortal! Why did I ever show you the Gate?'

Oracle turned away from him then, leaning forward to add fuel to the fire. When he looked back the druid had gone.

And he had taken the sword . . .

*   *   *

'You are a little unfair on Caswallon,' Maeg told her father as he sat in the wide leather chair, chuckling as the infant Donal tugged at his beard. Maggrig was well into middle age, but he was still powerful and his thick red beard showed no grey. Donal yawned, and the Pallides Hunt Lord brought the babe to his chest, resting him in the crook of his arm.

'Unfair to him?' he said, keeping his voice low. 'He married my only daughter, and still he raids my herds.'

'He does not.'

'I'll grant you he's stayed out of Pallides lands recently – but only because the Aenir have cut off his market.'

'It is tradition, Father,' argued Maeg. 'Other clans have always been fair game; and Caswallon is Farlain.'

'Don't give me that, girl. That tradition died out years ago. By God, he doesn't need to raid my cattle. Or Laric's. And sooner or later someone will catch him. Do you think I want to hang my own son-in-law?'

Maeg lifted the sleeping child from Maggrig's arms, laying him in his crib and covering him.

'He needs excitement, he does it because he enjoys it.' The words sounded lame, even to Maeg. For all his intelligence and quick wit, Caswallon refused to grow up.

'He used to enjoy taking other men's wives, I hear,' said Maggrig.

Maeg turned on him, eyes flashing. 'Enough of that!' she snapped. 'He's not looked at another woman since we wed ... well, he's looked, but that's all.'

'I can't think why you married him. Did you know he's got my prize bull in the meadow behind the house? Now there's a sight to greet a visitor, his own stolen bull!'

'Take it with you when you go,' said Maeg, smiling.

'And be seen by all the men of the Farlain? I'd sooner they thought it was a present.' He shook his head. 'I thought you'd change him, Maeg. I thought marriage would settle him.'

'It has. He's a wonderful husband, he cares for me.'

'I don't want to kill him,' admitted Maggrig. 'Damn it all, I like the boy. There must be other ways to get excitement.'

'I'll talk to him again. Are you sure that's your bull?'

'Sure? Of course I'm sure. The night he took it, Intosh and seven others chased him for hours – only he and that damn crofter Arcis had split up. Caswallon led Intosh a merry run.'

'He must have been furious,' said Maeg, keeping the smile from her face.

'He's promised to have Caswallon's ears for a necklace.'

'That wasn't because of the bull,' said his daughter. 'It is said that when Intosh came back to his house he found his bed had been slept in and his best sword stolen.'

'The man is unreasonable,' said Maggrig, unable to suppress a grin. 'I gave Intosh that sword after he won the Games.'

'Shall I get it for you, Father? I'm sure Intosh would like it back.'

'He'd bury it in pig's droppings rather than use it now.'

'Caswallon plans to wear it at the Games.'

'Ye gods, woman! Has he no shame?'

'None that I've noticed.'

From the hearth room below they heard a door open and close, and the sound of whistling floated up the stairs.

'Well, I suppose I'd better see him,' said Maggrig, pushing himself to his feet.

'Be nice,' said Maeg, linking her arm with his.

'Be nice, she says. What should I say? "Been on any good raids lately?"'

Maeg chuckled, looped her arm round his neck and kissed his bearded cheek, 'I love you,' she told him.

He grinned at her. 'I was too soft in the raising of you, child. You always had what you wanted.'

The two of them walked downstairs where Caswallon was standing before the hearth, hands stretched out to the flames. He turned and smiled, green eyes twinkling. 'How are you Father?' he asked.

'Not a great deal better for seeing you, you thieving swine,' snapped Maggrig. Maeg sighed and left them together.

'Is that any way to talk to the husband of your daughter?' Caswallon asked.

'It was a miserable day when you crossed my doorway,' said Maggrig, walking to the far table and pouring a goblet of honey mead. It was full-flavoured and rich, and he savoured the taste. 'This has a familiar feel to it,' he said. 'It is not unlike the special mead that Intosh brews.'

'Really?' said Caswallon.

Maggrig closed his eyes. 'That is all I need to complete my day – my own bull grazing in your meadow, while I drink mead stolen from my comrade.'

'You must give him my compliments. It is the finest mead I've tasted.'

'I'll do that. Where is Gaelen?'

'I've sent him out to meet the other lads.'

'Was that wise?'

The smile faded from Caswallon's mouth as he moved to Maggrig's side and poured himself a goblet of mead. 'It had to happen sooner or later,' he said, gesturing Maggrig to a chair. Sitting opposite him, Caswallon gazed at the golden liquid, then sipped at it slowly. 'He's a good boy, Maggrig, but he's been through much. I think they'll make him suffer. Agwaine will lead them.'

'Then why send him?'

'Because he has to learn. That's what life is – learning how to survive. All his life he has done that. Now he must find out that life in the mountains is no different.'

'You sound bitter. It is not like you.'

'Well, the world is changing,' said Caswallon. 'I watched the Aenir sack Ateris and it was vile. They kill like foxes in a hen-house.'

'I hear you had words with them in the mountains?'

Caswallon grinned. 'Yes.'

'You killed two.'

'I did. I had no choice.'

'Will they attack the clans, do you think?'

'It is inevitable.'

'I agree with you. Have you spoken to Cambil?'

Caswallon laughed aloud. 'The man hates me. If I said good-day he would take it as an insult.'

'Then talk to Leofas. Make plans.'

'I think I will. He's a good man. Strong.'

'More than that,' said Maggrig, 'he's canny.'

'He sounds like you, Maggrig.'

'He is.'

'Then I'll see him. And you needn't worry about your herds. Those days are behind me. After watching Ateris I lost my appetite for the game.'

'I'm glad to hear it.'

Caswallon refilled their goblets. 'Of course I might just sneak back for some more of Intosh's mead.'

'I wouldn't advise it,' said Maggrig.

3

Gwalchmai listened as Agwaine planned the downfall of the lowlander. Around the Hunt Lord's son, in a wide circle, sat fifteen other youngsters – the sons of councilmen, who would one day be councillors themselves. They listened as Agwaine spoke, and offered no objections. Gwalchmai wasn't happy with such conversation. An orphan child of the mountains, he knew what loneliness was, the pain it brought, and the inner chill. He had always been popular, but then he worked at it – jesting and joking, seeking approval from his peers. He ran errands for the older boys, always willing to help in any chore, but in his heart his fears were great. His father had died when he was seven – killed while poaching Pallides lands. His mother contracted lung fever the following year and her passing had been painful. Little Gwalchmai had been sent to live with Badraig and his son, and they had made him welcome. But Gwalchmai had loved his parents deeply, and their loss hurt him beyond his ability to cope.

He was not a big child and, though he approached fifteen, he was by far the smallest of his group. He excelled in two things: running and bowmanship. But his lack of strength held him back in both. At short distances he could outpace even Agwaine, and with a child's bow at twenty paces he could outshoot the Farlain's best archers. But he had not the strength to draw a man's bow, and failed in tourneys when the distance grew beyond thirty paces.

Agwaine was talking now about humiliating Caswallon's new son. Gwalchmai sat and stared at the Hunt Lord's son. He was tall and graceful, with a quick and dazzling smile, and normally there was little malice in him. But not today. Agwaine's dark eyes glittered, and his handsome face was marred as he spoke of tormenting the lowlander. Gwalchmai found it hard to understand, and he longed to find the courage to speak out. But when he looked inside

377

himself he knew that his nerve would fail him. Nervously his eyes sought out Layne. While all others would follow Agwaine blindly, Layne would always go his own way. At the moment the son of Leofas was saying nothing, his aquiline face showing no emotion. Beside him his giant brother Lennox was also silent. Layne's grey eyes met Gwalchmai's gaze and the orphan boy willed Layne to speak out; as if in answer to prayer Layne smiled at Gwalchmai, then spoke.

'I think this Gaelen has already been harshly treated, Agwaine,' said Layne. 'Why make it worse for him?' Gwalchmai felt relief flow through him, but Agwaine was not to be persuaded.

'We are talking about a jest,' said Agwaine smoothly, 'I'm not suggesting we *kill* him. Where's the harm?'

Layne ran a hand through his long, dark hair, his eyes holding Agwaine's gaze. 'Where is the good in it?' he countered. 'Such an action is beneath you, cousin. It is well known that your father has no love for Caswallon, but that is a matter for the two of them.'

'This is nothing to do with my father,' said Agwaine angrily. He swung to Lennox. 'What about you?' he asked. 'Do you side with your brother?'

Lennox shrugged his huge shoulders. 'Always,' he said, his voice deep as distant thunder.

'Do you never think for yourself, you ugly ox?' snapped Agwaine.

'Sometimes,' answered Lennox amiably.

'What about the rest of you?'

'Oh, let's have a little fun with him,' said Draig, Gwalchmai's foster-brother. 'Where's the harm? What do you think, Gwal?'

All eyes turned to Gwalchmai and his heart sank. He spent his life avoiding argument, and now whatever he said would hurt him. Layne and Lennox were his friends. Layne was stern of nature but a loyal youth, and his brother Lennox, though strong as an ox, was a gentle companion. But Agwaine was Cambil's son and the accepted leader of the Farlain youth, and Draig was Gwalchmai's foster-brother and a boy given to hot temper and malice-bearing. Of the other five, all were larger than Gwalchmai.

'Well, what do you think?' urged Draig.

378

'I don't mind,' mumbled Gwalchmai. 'Whatever you think best.' He tried not to look at Layne, but his eyes were drawn to the other's gaze. Layne merely smiled at him, and he felt the pity in that smile; it hurt him more than he could bear.

'Then let's do it!' said Agwaine, grinning.

The plan was a simple one. Kareen had innocently told them that Caswallon planned to send his son to the meadow that morning to meet the other boys of the village. Agwaine had suggested they take his clothes and chase him back to his house, lashing him the while with birch sticks.

Now Layne and Lennox moved away from the group to lounge on the grass. Gwalchmai sat miserably on a fallen tree, wishing he had stayed at home.

He looked up as the conversation died. Coming towards them was a slender boy in a green woollen tunic edged with brown leather; his hair was red, with a white flash above the jagged scar which ran down the left side of his face. He wore a wide belt and from it hung a hunting-knife. There was no swagger in his walk, but he seemed nervous. Layne and Lennox ignored him as he passed, and Gwalchmai saw the boy's jaw was clamped tight.

He approached the group with eyes fixed on Agwaine. Gwalchmai saw that his left eye was filled with blood and he shivered.

'I am Gaelen,' said the boy, addressing Agwaine.

Agwain nodded. "Why tell me?'

'I see from the way your friends are grouped around you that you are the leader.'

'How observant of you, lowlander.'

'Will you tell me your name?'

'To what purpose? You will never address us directly, you are like the wolf pup you brought home — of no account to those with pedigree.'

Gaelen said nothing but his mind raced. In Ateris there had been many thieves and many gangs, but he had always been alone. This scene was no different from many in his life. There would be a little more talk, then tempers would grow and the violence would begin. The difference was that in Ateris he always had somewhere to run; he knew every alley and tall building, every rooftop and hiding place. As he had approached the group he had scanned them, making judgements, deciding which were the boys to be feared, which to be ignored. Two were lounging on the grass away from their comrades; one of these was slender, but athletically built, his face strong. Beside him was a veritable giant, bigger than most clansmen Gaelen had seen. But since they were apart from the group Gaelen ignored them. His eyes had been drawn to a small boy sitting with the others. Slight of build, with short-cropped ginger hair, he had seemed nervous, frightened. Gaelen put this one from his mind. The others had gathered around the young man now facing him. These would not act — only react. Therefore everything depended on the outcome of this confrontation with the leader. Gaelen took stock of him. His face was strong, the eyes dark, the gaze steady. And he was proud. In that instant Gaelen knew that he was facing no cowardly bully who could be browbeaten, or dominated by words. His heart sank.

Still, one thing he had learned early was that you never allow the enemy to dictate the pace of the game. 'Well, don't just stand there,' he told Agwaine, forcing a grin, 'Teach this wolf pup the lesson you have planned.'

'What?' said Agwaine, momentarily taken aback.

'It's obvious that you and your mongrel playmates have already decided how this game is going to be played, so let's be at it. Here, I'll make it easy for you.' Casually he stepped forward and then, with a lack of speed that dulled Agwaine's reflexes, punched the other boy full in the face, toppling him backwards to the grass.

Gaelen drew his knife and leaped back as the other youths surged to their feet. Agwaine shook his head and slowly rose, eyes glittering. He too drew a knife.

'I'll kill you for that, outlander,' he said. His face was set and he moved forward, perfectly in balance. The other youths drew their blades, spreading out in a half-circle.

'That's enough!' said the tall young man Gaelen had seen sitting apart from the others. Walking forward, he stood by Gaelen. 'In fact it is more than enough. The joke has soured, Agwaine.' Another figure moved to the other side of Gaelen; he was enormous, towering above all the other youths.

'Do not interfere,' Agwaine warned them. 'I mean to cut his heart out.'

'Move behind me,' Layne told Gaelen.

'I'm not afraid of him.'

'Move behind me!' The voice was not raised, and yet had great authority. Even so, Gaelen's anger was so great now that he was ready to refuse. Then the giant laid a massive hand on his shoulder and Gaelen felt the power in the grip.

'Best do as he says,' said the huge youth softly. 'Layne's usually right.'

Gaelen obeyed and Layne stepped forward until his stomach pressed against Agwaine's dagger.

'Do you really want to kill me, cousin?' he asked.

'You know I will not.'

'Then think on it. The boy did well. He knew you planned to thrash him and he took you all on; he has courage. It would not be fitting to punish him now – would it?'

Agwaine sheathed his blade. 'He is a lowlander, and I will never accept him. Neither will my friends. He will be shunned by all who follow me.'

'I'll not shun him, Agwaine. Neither will Lennox.'

'Then you are my friend no longer. Let's go!' he told the others. As they trooped away Gwalchmai hung back, but Draig spotted him and called out.

'I'll see you later,' Gwalchmai replied.

Draig trotted back to his side. 'You can't stay here,' he said. 'You heard what Agwaine said.'

'I stay with my friends,' said Gwalchmai.

'You're a fool, Gwal. No good will come of it.' Draig strode off.

Gaelen slid the knife back in its sheath. The tall youth with the dark hair and grey eyes turned to him, holding out his hand.

'I am Layne, son of Leofas,' he said. 'This is my brother Lennox and my cousin Gwalchmai.'

Gaelen shook hands with them all. 'Why did you do this for me?' he asked.

'It wasn't for you, it was for Agwaine,' Layne told him.

'I don't understand.'

'Agwaine is a fine friend and a brave one,' said Layne. 'He acted in anger and would have regretted slaying you. He is not evil, not malicious. But he has the conceit of his father and he loves to lead.'

'I have caused you trouble. For that I am sorry.'

Layne shook his head. 'You caused nothing. It was not you they were seeking to humble, but your father. Caswallon is not liked.'

'Why?'

'It is not for me to prattle on with gossip. I like Caswallon but others do not, and among the clans such matters usually end in bloodshed and family feuds. We are a violent race, Gaelen, as you have discovered.'

'Caswallon is not violent.'

'Indeed he is not. But he has the capacity for it, as you saw in the mountains with the Aenir.'

'You heard of that?'

'Who has not? My father led the hunters that escorted them from the Farlain.'

The lads settled themselves on the grass, enjoying the sunshine. Lennox and the ginger-haired Gwalchmai said little.

Layne asked Gaelen about life in Ateris, and the Aenir invasion. Gaelen found the memories too painful and switched the conversation back to Caswallon. 'I know you don't want to gossip,' he said, 'but I am a stranger here, and I need to know how my . . . father earned such dislike.'

'Caswallon is the richest man in the valley. He has the largest herds and his fields carry more wheat than any save Cambil's. But he holds himself apart from other clansmen, and the Hunt Lord hates him.'

'He doesn't appear rich,' said Gaelen. 'In Ateris rich men have . . . had . . . marble palaces and carriages of gold. And many servants. They wore rings and necklets, bracelets and brooches.'

382

'We have no use for such finery,' Layne told him. 'We live free. Caswallon supports more than one hundred crofters. If he desired, he could start a new clan. That is rich – believe me.'

'Then why doesn't he? I mean, if he's so disliked it would seem to be good sense. Then he would be his own Hunt Lord.'

'He would have to surrender his valley land and find somewhere else to live, and that is no longer easy. To the north-east the Haesten control the land bordering the lowlands. North of them are the Pallides. The rest of the land for a six-day march is all Farlain, and beyond that the minor clans – the Loda, the Dunilds, and the Irelas – fight over territory. Anyway, Caswallon is Farlain and always will be.'

'I'm damned hungry,' said Lennox suddenly.

Gaelen fished in his leather hip-pouch and produced a thick slice of cold meat-pie. He passed it to Lennox. Thanking him, the huge youth wolfed the pie down at speed.

'My father would also be rich,' said Layne dryly, 'were it not for my brother's appetite.'

'He's big,' said Gaelen. 'I don't think I've seen anyone his age bigger.' Lennox was already more than six feet tall, with a bull-like neck and an enormous frame. His face was broad, his eyes deep-set and brown. His chin and cheeks were already darkening with the promise of a beard.

'And he's as strong as he looks. Also, despite what you will hear, he's no fool. He just says little. Isn't that right, brother?'

'Whatever you say,' said Lennox, grinning.

'I don't know why, but he likes to play the fool,' said Layne. 'He lets people think he has no brains.'

'It does no harm,' said Lennox mildly.

'No, but it irritates me,' replied his brother, scowling. Gaelen would not have guessed them to be brothers. Layne, though tall, was of more slender build, his face fine-boned.

'I can't think why it should, Layne,' said Lennox, smiling. 'You are the thinker in the family.'

'Nonsense.' Layne swung to Gwalchmai. 'Why so silent, little one?'

383

'I was thinking about Agwaine,' answered Gwalchmai. 'I don't like to make anyone angry.'

'He won't be angry with you for long. And besides, I'm proud of you. What do you think, Lennox?'

'I think it took nerve to stay with us. You'll not regret it, Gwal, my lad.'

'Do you think they'll attack Gaelen again?' Gwal asked.

'No,' replied Layne. 'When he has had time to think on it, Agwaine will realise that Gaelen acted like . . .' he grinned '. . . like a highlander,' he said. 'He will respect that.'

Gaelen blushed and said nothing.

'Well,' said Layne. 'I think it's time we told Gaelen about the Hunt.'

Caswallon stood nervously outside the door biting his lip, a habit he thought he had left behind in childhood. But then standing before the door of Leofas brought back memories, none of them pleasant.

When Caswallon was a child he had stolen a dagger from the home of the Sword Champion, Leofas. His foster-father, Padris, had been furious when Cambil informed him of Caswallon's misbehaviour, and had sent the boy to Leofas to confess.

Caswallon had stood before the door then as now, on edge and fearful. The clansman chuckled. 'You fool,' he told himself. But it didn't help.

Rapping the door with his knuckles, he took a deep breath.

Leofas let him in without a word of greeting and pointed to a chair before the hearth. Removing his cloak, Caswallon sat down. The room was large, strewn with rugs of goatskin and wolf-hide, and on the far wall hung a bearskin, dust-covered and patchy with age.

Caswallon stretched out his legs before the fire. 'The last time I was here, you thrashed me with your belt,' he remarked.

'I recall that you deserved it,' said Leofas. He was a big man, not tall, but wide in the shoulder with a thick neck and heavy beard streaked with grey. But his blue eyes were keen, the stare forbidding.

'Indeed I did.'

'State your business, Caswallon,' snapped the older man.

Caswallon pushed himself to his feet, a knot of anger deep within him. 'I don't think that I will,' he said softly. 'I am not the child who stole your knife, I am a man. I came here because Maggrig advised it, and it seemed sensible, but I'll not sit here swallowing your discourtesies.'

Leofas raised his eyebrows, waiting as Caswallon reached for his cloak.

'Would you like a drink, boy?' he asked.

Caswallon hesitated for a moment, then dropped his cloak across the back of a chair and turned to the older man. 'That would be pleasant,' he said.

Leofas left the room, returning with two jugs of ale. Then he sat opposite Caswallon. 'Now will you state your business?'

'Before I do, let's clear the air. When you were young you raided all over the druin to build your herds. So why are you set against me?'

'That's easy answered, and I like a man who states his grievance swiftly. When I was a lad there was open warfare between the clans. No man knew what it was like to be rich. Raiding was often the difference between starvation and small comfort. But times changed and clans prospered. I applauded you when you began, I thought you were spirited and cunning. But then you grew rich, and yet the raids continued. And then I knew that the raids were not a means to an end but the end itself.

'Sometimes in life a man must risk death for the sake of his family, but you risk it merely for pleasure. Most men in the mountains value their clan, for it is like a great family and we depend on one another to survive. Children of the mountains are cared for; no one man starves while another gluts himself. But you, Caswallon, you don't care. You avoid responsibility, and your very existence eats away at what makes the clan strong. Children imitate you. They tell tales of your exploits and they want to be like you, for you are exciting, like a clansman out of time. A myth from the past.

'Cuckoo Caswallon they used to call you, because of your amorous exploits. Women yearn for you and I can understand that and don't begrudge it. But when you creep into the bed of another man's wife, and sire him a son, all you have done is destroy that man's life. He cared for his wife deeply, loved her and cherished her. She surrenders all that for a few nights of passion with you. You don't stick by her, so she despairs. And her life is ruined too.

'As for your raids . . . you encourage other clans to copy you. Last autumn I caught three Pallides poachers making off with my prize bull. I had to mutilate them, it was the law. But why did they do it? Why? Because Caswallon had stolen *their* bull. Now state your business.'

Caswallon leaned back in his chair, his heart heavy for he could not refute a word of Leofas's damning indictment.

'Not yet, Leofas. First let me say this: Everything you accuse me of is correct and I cannot gainsay it. But I never intended evil. Cuckoo Caswallon? Sometimes a man gives in to selfishness, telling himself there is a nobler reason – he is bringing a little happiness into a dull life. But since I married Maeg I have been faithful, for I learned by my mistakes.

'As for the raids, they too were selfish, but I don't regret them for I enjoyed every moment. If men suffered by imitating me, then it is on their heads, for my risk was as great as theirs. But that too is now a thing of the past.

'I came to you because of the Aenir; that is my *business* with you. I seek not your friendship nor your approval. I care for neither. The Aenir are killers and they will invade the clans.'

'Cambil is Hunt Lord,' said Leofas guardedly. 'Have you seen him?'

'You know I have not. Nor will I. If I told Cambil that sheep ate grass he would deny it and feed his flock on beef.'

The older man nodded. That is true enough. And I agree with you about the Aenir, but Cambil thinks differently. He seeks new trade agreements, and he has invited an Aenir captain to watch the Hunt.'

386

'He didn't see the sack of Ateris,' said Caswallon.

'No. But you did and it changed you.'

'I won't deny that.'

'How is the boy you brought home?'

'He is well. Your lads helped him, I think, though he has not spoken of it.'

'Neither have they, but I heard. They're good boys. Layne would not allow Agwaine to harm him and Lennox stood by him. That made me proud, for it's hard bringing up boys without a mother. And they've turned out well.'

'They are a credit to you.'

'As is Gaelen to you,' said Leofas, 'for he took them all on.'

'He is a credit to himself. Will you argue against Cambil on the Council?'

'On the question of the Aenir, I will.'

'Then I'll take up no more of your time.'

'Man, you haven't finished your ale. Sit and be comfortable for a while. I don't get many visitors.'

For an hour or more the men sat, drinking ale and swapping stories. It came to Caswallon that the older man was lonely; his wife had died six years before and he had never taken another. On the death of Padris three years ago Leofas had refused to stand for Hunt Lord, claiming it was a young man's duty. But he remained on the Hunt Council, and his words were heeded.

'How long do you think we have – before they invade?' asked Leofas suddenly, his eyes clear despite the jugs of ale.

Caswallon fought to clear his mind. 'I'd say a year, maybe two. But I could be wrong.'

'I don't think so. They're still fighting in the lowlands. Several cities are holding out.'

'We need a plan of our own,' said Caswallon. 'The valley is indefensible.'

'Seek out Taliesen,' Leofas advised, 'I know these druids raise the hairs on a man's neck, but he is wise, and he knows much about events outside Druin.'

*   *   *

387

For two months Caswallon took Gaelen with him on every hunt, teaching him more of the land and the creatures of the land. He taught him to fight hand-to-hand, and to wrestle and to box, to roll with the punches, and to counter swiftly. The lessons were sometimes painful, and Gaelen was quick to anger. Caswallon taught him to hold his fury and use it coolly.

'Anger can strengthen a man or destroy him,' he told the youth as they sat on the hillside above the house. 'When you fight, you stay cool. Think with your hands. When you strike a blow it should surprise you as well as your opponent. Now pad your hands and we will see what you have understood.' Warily the two circled one another. Caswallon stabbed a straight left to Gaelen's face. Gaelen blocked it, hurling a right. Caswallon leaned out of reach, the punch whistling past his chin. He countered with a swift left that glanced from the boy's jaw. Off-balance, Gaelen hit the ground hard, rolled and rose to his feet with eyes blazing. Caswallon stepped in to meet him, throwing a right cross. It never landed, for Gaelen ducked inside the punch and caught the taller man with an upper-cut that sent him reeling in the grass.

'Good. That was good,' said Caswallon, rubbing his jaw. 'You are beginning to move well. A little too well.' Reaching up, he took Gaelen's hand and the younger man pulled him to his feet. 'Let's sit for a while,' he said. 'My head is still spinning, I think you've shaken all my teeth.'

'I'm sorry.'

Caswallon laughed. 'Don't be. You were angry, but you kept it under control and used the power of your anger in your punch. That was excellent.' The two sat together beneath the shade of an elm.

'There is something I have been meaning to ask you,' said Gaelen, 'about the bush you hid me in when the Aenir were close.'

'It was a good hiding place.'

'But it wasn't,' insisted Gaelen. 'It was out in the open, and had they looked down they would surely have seen me.'

'That's *why* it was good. When they attacked their blood was up. They were moving fast, thinking fast, seeing fast. You understand?

388

They didn't examine the clearing, they scanned it swiftly, making judgements at speed. The bush was small and, as you say, in plain sight. It offered little cover and was the last place, so they believed, that anyone would choose as a hiding place. Therefore they ignored it. Similarly that made it the best place to hide in.'

'I see that,' said Gaelen, 'but what if they had stopped to examine the clearing?'

'Then you would probably have been slain,' said Caswallon. 'It could have happened – but the odds were vastly against it. Most men react to situations of violence – or threatened violence – by animal instinct. Understanding that instinct allows an intelligent man to win nine times out of ten.'

Gaelen grinned. 'I do understand,' he said. 'That's why when you raided the Pallides you chose to hide in the village itself. You knew they would expect you to flee their lands at speed, and so they raced from their village to catch you.'

'Ah, you've been listening to the tales of my wicked youth. I hope you learn from them.'

'I am learning,' agreed Gaelen. 'But why did you choose the house of Intosh to hide in? He is the Sword Champion of the Pallides, and everyone says he is a fearsome opponent.'

'He is also a widower with no children. No one would be in the house.'

'So you had it planned even before you did it. You must have scouted the village first.'

'Always have a plan, Gaelen, *always.*'

Later, as they sat on the hillside above Caswallon's house, awaiting the call to the midday meal, Caswallon asked the boy how he was settling in with the other lads in the small village.

'Very well,' Gaelen told him guardedly.

'No problems?'

'None that I can't handle.'

'Of that I have no doubt. How do they compare with the boys of Ateris?'

Gaelen smiled, 'In the city I used to watch them play games: Hunt-seek, Spider's folly, Shadowman. Here they play nothing.

They are so serious. I like that . . . but I always wanted to join in back in Ateris.'

Caswallon nodded. 'You joined us a little late for children's games, Gaelen. Here in the mountains a boy becomes a man at sixteen, free to wed and make his own life. It is not easy. Two in five babes die before their first birthday, and few are the men who reach fifty years of age. Childhood passes more swiftly here. Have you teamed yet for the Hunt next week?'

'Yes, I travel with Gwalchmai, Lennox and Layne.'

'Fine boys,' said Caswallon, 'although Gwalchmai is a little timid, I think. Are you content with the teaming?'

'Yes. We are meeting today to plan the Run.'

'What problems will you face?'

'Lennox is strong, but no runner. We may not beat Agwaine's team to the first tree.'

'Speed is not everything,' said Caswallon.

'I know.'

'Which of you will lead?'

'We're deciding that this afternoon – but I think it will be Layne.'

'Logical. Layne is a bright fellow.'

'Not as bright as Agwaine,' said Gaelen.

'No, but you are. You should enjoy yourselves.'

'Did you lead when you ran in the Hunt?'

'No. Cambil led.'

'Did you win?'

'Yes.'

'Was Cambil a good leader?'

'In his way. He still is. And he has been a good Hunt Lord for the Farlain.'

'But he doesn't like you, Caswallon. Everyone knows that.'

'You shouldn't listen to idle chatter. But you are right. He doesn't like me – but then he has good cause. Three years ago I robbed him of something. I didn't mean to, but it worked out that way, and he has not forgotten.'

'What did you steal?' asked Gaelen.

'I didn't actually steal anything. I just refused to stand against him for the position of Hunt Lord. I didn't want the role. So he was voted to it by the elders.'

'I don't understand. How can he hold that against you?'

'That's a difficult question, Gaelen. Many people assumed I would try for Hunt Lord. In truth I would have lost, for Cambil is – and always was – worthy of the role. But had I stood and lost, he would have known he was considered the better man. Because I did not stand he will never know.'

'Is that why Agwaine doesn't like me?' asked Gaelen. 'Because his father doesn't like you?'

'Perhaps. I have been very selfish in my life, doing only that which I enjoyed. I should have acted differently. If I am nominated for the Council again I shall accept. But that is not likely.'

From the house below they heard Kareen calling. Gaelen waved at her, but Caswallon remained where he was.

'Go and eat,' he said. 'I will be down soon.'

He watched the boy running down the hillside and smiled, remembering his own Hunt Day fifteen years before. Every lad in the Farlain over the age of fourteen, and not yet a man, was teamed with three others and sent out into the mountains to recover a 'treasure'. Skilful hunters would lay trails, hide clues and signs, and the teams would track them down until at last one team returned with the prize. For Caswallon the prize they had sought was a dagger, hidden in a tree. Often it was an arrow, or a lance, or a helm, or a shield. This year it was a sword, though none of the lads knew it.

Every year Caswallon helped lay the trails and delighted in his work. But this year was special for him, for Gaelen would be taking part.

He removed from his pouch the strip of parchment Taliesen had given him and he re-read the words written there.

Seek the Beast that no one finds,
always roaring,
never silent,

beneath his skin,
by silver wings,
bring forth the
long lost
dream of kings.

After the meal Caswallon would read the verse to his new son, even as, all over the Farlain, fathers would be doing likewise. There were times, Caswallon considered, when tradition was a wholesome thing.

In the wide kitchen Caswallon's young son Donal lay on a woollen blanket by the hearth. Beside him slept the pup Gaelen had brought home; it had grown apace in the last two months, showing signs of the formidable beast it would be in the years ahead. Kareen sat beside Maeg opposite Gaelen, and they were all laughing as Caswallon entered.

'And what is amusing you?' he asked.

'Rest your poor bones at the table,' Maeg told him, 'and tell us, gently, how Gaelen here dumped you to the earth.'

'It was a wicked blow and I was unprepared,' he answered, seating himself beside the boy who was blushing furiously.

'Have you been bragging, young Gaelen?' he asked.

'He has not,' said Maeg. 'Kareen herself saw the deed done as she fed the chickens.'

'Fed the chickens, indeed,' said Caswallon. 'It could not be seen from the yard. The lazy child climbed the hill and spied on us, for a certainty.' Now Kareen began to blush, casting a guilty glance at Maeg. 'In fact,' said Caswallon, smiling broadly, 'on my way back here I saw two sets of tracks. One had the dainty footprints of young Kareen, the other I could not make out except to say the feet must have been uncommonly large.'

'So!' said Maeg. 'It's back to jibes about my feet, is it?'

'You have beautiful feet, Maeg, my love. There isn't a woman in the Farlain who could match them for beauty – or length.'

Throughout the meal they good-naturedly sniped at each other, and only when she began to list Caswallon's faults did he open his arms in surrender and beg her forgiveness.

'Woman,' he said, 'you're full of venom.'

After the meal he gave leave to Gaelen to seek his friends, and read him the druid's parchment. 'Do not be late home. We've an early start tomorrow.'

Later, as Maeg and Caswallon lay arm in arm in the broad bed, she leaned over him and kissed him gently on the lips. 'What troubles you, my love?' she asked him, stroking his dark hair back from his eyes.

His arm circled her back, pulling her to him. 'What makes you think I am troubled?'

'No games, Caswallon,' she said seriously. She rolled from him and he sat up, bunching a pillow behind him.

'The Council have voted to resume trade with Aterís, and allow an Aenir group to visit the Farlain.'

'But we had to trade with them,' said Maeg. 'We always have dealt with Aterís, for iron, seed-corn, seasoned timbers, leather.'

'We didn't always, Maeg. We used to do these things ourselves. We're no longer dealing with merchant lowlanders; this is a warrior race.'

'What harm can it do to allow a few of them to visit us? We might become friends.'

'You don't make friends with a wolf by inviting it to sleep with the sheep.'

'But we are not sheep, Caswallon. We are the clans.'

'I think the decision is short-sighted and we may live to rue it.'

'I love you,' she said, the words cutting through his thoughts.

'I can't think why,' he said, chuckling. Then he reached for her and they lay silently enjoying the warmth of each other's bodies and the closeness of their spirits.

'I cannot begin to tell you what you mean to me,' he whispered.

'You don't have to,' she said.

One moment the mountainside was clear, rolling green slopes, the occasional tree, two streams meeting and foaming over white boulders. Sheep grazed quietly near a small herd of wild ponies.

Suddenly the air reeked with an acrid smell none of the animals recognised. Their heads came up. Blue light replaced the gold of the sun. Rainbows danced on the grass and a great noise, like locust wings, covered the mountainside. The ponies reared and wheeled, the sheep scattering in all directions.

For a fraction of a second two suns hung in the sky, then they merged and the golden sunlight bathed the mountain. But all was not as it had been . . .

In the shadow of a great boulder stood a towering figure, six-inch fangs curving from a wide snout, massive shoulders covered in black fur, huge arms ending in taloned fingers. The eyes were black and round, the brows deep, and it blinked as its new surroundings came into focus.

Lifting its shaggy head, the beast sniffed the air. The sweet smell of living flesh flooded its senses. The creature leaned forward, dipping its colossal shoulders until its talons brushed the earth. Its eyes focused on a three-year-old ewe, which stood trembling on the hillside.

Dropping fully to all fours, the beast bunched the muscles of its hind legs and leaped forward, bearing down on the sheep with terrible speed. Startled, the ewe turned to run. It had made only three running jumps before the weight of the hunter smashed its spine into jagged shards.

Taloned fingers tore aside the ewe's flesh and the blood ran.

The beast ate swiftly, lifting its shaggy black head often, peering short-sightedly around the mountainside, ready for any enemy that might chance upon it. It was uncomfortable out in the open, unused to shimmering horizons and bright light. But the blood was good upon its tongue, the flesh rich and greasy. Casually it ripped out the ewe's entrails, hurling them far from body, concentrating instead on the flesh of the loins. Slowly, methodically the giant creature fed, snapping bones and sucking out the marrow, splitting the skull with one blow and devouring the brains.

Hunger satisfied, the beast sank back to its haunches. It blinked in the sunlight as an image fashioned itself in its mind. A bright image. Grunting, it shook its head, then gave a low growl. Dimly it remembered the circle of stones and the red-clad sorcerer whose fingers danced with fire. The fire had entered the creature's breast, settling there without pain. The beast howled as hunger returned.

It would always be hungry – until it devoured the image-woman. Angrily the beast slammed its hands against the ground.

Away to the left it saw the line of trees that merged into the forest above Vallon. Hunger returning, it began to lope towards them, stopping at a stream to drink. The trees were smaller than the ones it had known and climbed, less closely packed and strangely silent. No chittering monkeys swung from the vines, few birds sang, and there was no sign of fruit upon the boughs.

The wind shifted and a new smell filtered to the beast's flaring nostrils. The black eyes glittered with the memory of salty-sweet flesh and marrow-filled bones. The sorcerer had implanted a soul scent upon its senses – and this creature was not the victim ordained. Nor was the spell scent close by. Yet it could almost taste the sweet meat of the approaching man-beast.

Saliva dripped from its maw and its dark tongue licked out over its fangs. The smell was growing stronger. There was no need to stalk, for the simple-minded creature was moving this way.

A hundred paces to the west Erlik of the Pallides, a tall young hunter from the house of Maggrig, leaned on his staff. Beside him his war hound Askar growled deep in his throat. Erlik was puzzled. An hour ago he had seen the blue haze across the mountains, and the two suns appear in the sky. And despite this being Farlain land he had ventured here, led by the curiosity of the young. Less than a year before Erlik had gained his manhood in the Hunt, and was now a contender for the Games.

And where a more seasoned veteran would hesitate, Erlik, with all the confidence of youth, had crossed the border and ventured into the lands of the enemy. He did not fear Farlain hunters, for he knew he could outrun them, but he had to know why the air burned blue. He sensed it would be a fine tale to tell his comrades at the evening feast.

He leaned down and stroked Askar, whispering it to silence. The hound obeyed unwillingly. It didn't like the idea of moving with the direction of the breeze, and it sensed danger ahead which made the fur on its shoulders rise. With the natural cunning of the canine it began to edge left, but Erlik called it back.

The young hunter moved forward towards an area of thick bracken and gorse. Askar growled once more and this time the dog's unease filtered through to the man. Carefully he laid down his quarterstaff, then swung his bow from his shoulder, hastily notching an arrow to the string.

The gorse exploded as a vast black creature reared up from the ground at Erlik's feet. A taloned arm flashed out, half-severing the hunter's left arm and hurling him to the ground. The war hound leaped for the beast's throat, but was brutally swatted aside. Erlik drew his hunting-knife and struggled to rise, but the talons flashed once more and his head toppled from his shoulders.

Minutes later the war hound came to its senses, pain gnawing at its broken ribs. The great head came up slowly, ears pricking at the sounds of crunching bones.

With infinite care the hound inched its way to the west, away from the feeding beast.

In the valley of the Farlain fourteen teams of youngsters were packing shoulder sacks with provisions ready for the hunt. Families and kin thronged the Market Field.

The brothers Layne and Lennox were seated side by side on a fallen oak while Gaelen lay on his back, eyes closed, nearby. Beside him sat the slender Gwalchmai, whittling with a short dagger.

'I wish they would announce the start,' said Layne. 'What are they waiting for?'

Gaelen sat up. 'Caswallon said the druid must give his blessing.'

'I know that,' snapped Layne. 'I meant why the delay?' Gaelen lay back on the grass and said nothing. Layne was not normally this edgy.

'Are you looking forward to it?' asked Gwalchmai. Gaelen could see that the ginger-haired youth was worried by Layne's tension and seeking to change the mood.

'Yes, I am,' said Gaelen.

'Do you understand the meaning of the riddle?'

'No. Have you deciphered it?'

Gwalchmai shrugged. 'Maybe it will be clearer when we find the second clue.'

In the house of Cambil, beyond the field and the waiting teams, sat the Druid Lord, Taliesen. Opposite him, pacing before the hearth, was the tall Hunt Lord Cambil, a golden-haired handsome young man wearing a leaf-green tunic and a red cloak.

By the hearth sat a stranger clad in leather shirt and breeches, his long blond hair braided beneath a round leather helm. He too was handsome but, unlike Cambil, there was no softness in him. His eyes were the cold blue of the winter sky, and upon his mouth was a mocking half-smile. That the druid disliked him was obvious and seemed to amuse the Aenir; but for Cambil the meeting was a monstrous embarrassment.

The druid was angry, though he showed nothing of it as he sipped water from a clay goblet. Cambil was uneasy and pulled at his golden beard. The stranger sat back in the leather-covered chair, his face expressionless.

'It is rare,' the druid said at last, 'for a stranger to be present at the Youth's Hunt – though it is not without precedent. There shall be no blessing today, for the words of power cannot be spoken in the presence of lowlanders. In this there is no disrespect intended for your guest, Cambil, it is merely the weight of tradition which forbids it.'

Cambil bit his lip and nodded.

'May I ask,' continued the druid, 'that we speak privately?'

Cambil turned to the man beside him. 'My apologies, Lord Drada, but please feel free to join the men at the food table beyond and refresh yourself.'

Drada stood and bowed to Cambil, then he turned to the druid. 'I am sorry to have caused you problems. Had I known my presence would disrupt the ceremony I would have turned down the invitation.' Neither Taliesen nor Cambil missed the stress he placed on the word invitation, and the Hunt Lord felt himself blushing.

The Aenir warrior carefully hung his black cloak upon his broad shoulders and left the room, closing the door quietly behind him.

The ancient druid turned his dark eyes on the Hunt Lord and leaned forward across the table. 'It was not wise to invite him into Farlain lands,' he said.

'He is friendly enough,' insisted Cambil.

'He is the Enemy to Come,' snapped the druid.

'So you say, old man, but I am the Hunt Lord of the Farlain, and I alone decide whether a man is a friend or enemy. You are a druid and as such are to be respected in religious matters, but do not exceed your authority.'

'Are you blind, Cambil, or merely stupid?'

Anger shone in the Hunt Lord's eyes, but his response was calm. 'I am not blind, druid. And I make no great claims to be wiser than any other clansman. What I do know is that war brings no advantage to either side. If the Aenir can be convinced that we offer them no threat, and that there is no wealth to be found in the mountains, I see no reason why we cannot exist together – if not as friends, then at least as good neighbours. Keeping them out will only cause suspicion, and make war more likely.'

Cambil walked to the door, wrenching it open. 'Now, the boys are waiting and I shall send them off, and I don't doubt the lack of your words of power will affect them not at all.'

At the edge of the field Caswallon sat with Maeg and Kareen, watching the boys line up for the first race to the trees. Once there, they would find a leather pouch hanging from the branch of the central pine. Within the pouch were four clues, written on parchment. The first team to reach the tree would be able to read all the clues, and remove one. The next team would find three clues, and remove one. And so on until the fourth team would find only one remaining.

Gaelen, who could not yet read, would be useless to his team on this first run, but they had chosen Gwalchmai to lead the sprint, and he was almost as fast as Cambil's son Agwaine.

The teams sprinted away at Cambil's command and Caswallon watched as Gwalchmai and Agwaine forged a lead over the rest, with Gaelen loping beside the lumbering Lennox at the rear.

At that moment Caswallon caught sight of the black-coated

Aenir warrior standing by the grey house. Leaving Maeg and Kareen, he walked the short distance to the building. As he walked he gauged the man. The Aenir was tall and well-built, but slim of hip. He looked what he was – a warrior. As Caswallon approached the man turned and the clansman knew he was undergoing the same appraisal.

'The lads move well,' said the Aenir, pointing towards the youngsters who were now halfway up the hillside.

'I see your men took my advice,' said Caswallon. 'That was wise.'

Drada smiled. 'Yes, I always listen to wise counsel. But I saw no sign of the Farlain hunters you promised to send after us.'

'They were there.'

'I was surprised to find you are not a councillor, Caswallon.'

'Why so?'

'I gained the impression that you were a man of influence but Cambil tells me this is not so. He says you are a thief and a bandit.'

'What do you think of the Farlain mountains?' Caswallon countered.

'They are beautiful. Most especially this valley.'

'There are many valleys in the Farlain, and a vast number more in the Druin range,' said the clansman.

'I have no doubt I shall see them all eventually,' Drada told him, with a wolfish smile.

'Travel alone when you do so.'

'Really, why?'

'The mountains can be tranquil and a man alone can best enjoy their harmony.'

'And if he is not alone?' asked Drada.

'If he travels with many, then the mountains can be hostile, even deadly. Why, even now two Aenir corpses are rotting in the mountains. And there is room for many more.'

'That is no talk for new friends, Caswallon.'

Caswallon laughed with genuine humour; then the smile faded. 'But then I am not your friend, my bonny. Nor ever shall be.'

★　　★　　★

399

More than fifty youngsters pounded up the slope, feet drumming on the hard-packed grass-covered clay of the hillside. Gwalchmai tucked himself in behind Agwaine, fastening his eyes on the other boy's pack and running on grimly. After forty paces he loosened the straps of his own heavy pack and let it fall to the ground behind him. Then, as Gaelen had instructed him, he once more moved up behind Agwaine.

Here the hillside was at its steepest and the young Agwaine was breathing heavily, his legs began to burn as the body's waste acids settled to the muscles of his calves. He did not look back. He could afford no wasted energy. And besides he was the fastest runner for his years in the Farlain.

Back down the slope, Lennox scooped up Gwalchmai's pack and continued to lope alongside Gaelen, way to the rear of the other runners.

'I hope this is allowed,' shouted Lennox.

Gaelen said nothing. Caswallon had told him that the rules were specific. All runners had to start the race carrying their own provisions. Well, Gwalchmai had done that.

Layne had not been easy to convince, for he was a youth who lived on traditions of honour and would sooner lose than cheat. But Gaelen had called a vote, as was his right, and had won the day. Layne seemed to harbour no grudge.

Gwalchmai and Agwaine had now increased their lead over the following pack to fifty paces, and it was obvious that they would reach the trees well ahead of their rivals.

As the timberline neared Gwalchmai sped past his astonished opponent. Agwaine was furious. Sweat-soaked and near-exhausted, he released his pack and set off after the sprinting youth. Fury pumped fresh adrenalin to his tired legs and against all the odds he began to close the gap.

Fifty paces from the trees Agwaine was running in Gwalchmai's shadow, but the canny youngster had one more ploy. As Agwaine came abreast of him Gwalchmai kicked again, releasing the energy he had held in reserve. Agwaine had nothing more to offer. In an agonising effort to match his opponent, he stumbled against a stone and pitched to the earth.

Gwalchmai ran ahead, eyes flickering from tree to tree, seeking the pouch. It was in plain view, fastened to a low branch. He pulled it clear, removing the small pieces of paper it contained. Reading them all, he selected one and tucked it in his belt. Then he re-hung the pouch and wandered back towards Agwaine.

The Hunt Lord's son ignored him, racing past to tear the pouch clear. He read the three remaining strips, took one and replaced two. Then he turned after Gwalchmai.

'You dog!' he shouted, his breathing laboured. 'You . . . cheating . . . cur!'

Frightened, Gwalchmai backed and opened his hands. 'The rules did not forbid it, Agwaine.'

Other runners came between them in the last frantic dash for clues, and Agwaine turned away to sit in the shade of a spreading elm.

Gwalchmai was grinning broadly as Layne reached him and he handed the parchment over. Layne read it, nodded, then walked over to where Agwaine was sitting.

'Well run, cousin,' he said, squatting beside him.

'Thank you. That was a devious strategy. But, as Gwalchmai says, it was within the rules and therefore I can have no complaint.' Layne offered Agwaine the parchment. 'What is this? What are you doing?'

'There may be nothing in the rules against our tactic,' said Layne, 'but I am not happy with it. Here. Read the line, and from now we start level.'

'No, cousin,' said Agwaine, gripping the other's shoulder, 'though I thank you for your courtesy. I must confess that were I not the fastest runner it is likely I would have used the tactic myself. I take it the lowlander conceived it?'

'Yes.'

'He has quick wits, I'll give him that.'

Layne nodded. Then he stood and returned to the others, who had been watching the scene, puzzled. 'Let's find a place out of earshot and discuss our next move,' he said, walking past them to the trees. Gaelen bit back his anger and followed. He had seen

Layne offer the clue to Agwaine and noted the other's refusal. It was confusing and deeply irritating.

In a deep hollow, away from the crowds, the four squatted in a huddled circle. Layne nodded to Gwalchmai, who began to speak in a hushed whisper. They were all aware that those teams without clues would now seek to follow and spy on the leading four.

'The clues were simple to understand,' whispered Gwalchmai. 'The one we have is the simplest: "That which Earis lost." So, it is a sword we seek. The other clues confirm it: "A King's Sorrow", "The Light that brings Darkness", and "The Bane of Eska". The question now is, where is it hidden?'

'It's hidden at, or near, Attafoss,' whispered Gaelen.

'What?' said Layne, astonished. 'How do you know?'

'The rhyme: "Seek the beast that no one finds, always roaring, never silent . . ." When Caswallon took me to Attafoss it sounded like a great monster, but when we arrived there was no monster, merely a roaring fall of water.'

'It could be,' said Layne. 'What do you think, Gwal?'

'I agree with Gaelen.'

'Lennox?'

The youth raised his shoulders in a non-committal shrug.

'So,' said Layne, 'we are agreed. Well done, Gaelen. If we look at the rest of the verse it becomes even more obvious. "Beneath its skin, by silver wings, bring forth the long-lost dream of kings." The blade is hidden under the water, guarded by fishes. But where? Attafoss is huge.'

'There will be other clues,' said Gwalchmai. 'We must follow the right tracks.'

'True,' said Layne. 'All right. We'll make camp higher up in the trees, then slip away before dawn and strike for Vallon.'

Dawn found the four of them miles from the first timber and well on their way. Layne led them down rocky slopes and over difficult terrain, constantly checking on what tracks they were leaving. By mid-morning he was content. Even the most skilful hunters would have difficulty finding them and, above all, the task would be time-consuming.

As they strolled through patches of yellow-gold gorse and across meadows bedecked with blooms, Gaelen rediscovered the strange sense of joy he first felt when Caswallon formally adopted him. He was home. Truly home.

Beside him Gwalchmai was whistling a merry tune and ahead Layne and Lennox were deep in conversation. Gaelen rubbed at his scarred eye, for it itched now and then, usually when he was tired.

'Is it troubling you?' asked Gwalchmai. Gaelen shook his head and Gwalchmai resumed whistling, but his thoughts remained on the youngster beside him. Gwalchmai had liked Gaelen from the first. He didn't know why, but then he rarely rationalised such things; he relied on his emotions to steer him and they rarely played him false. He remembered his shock when he first saw the boy, his red hair streaked with a white slash, his left eye filled with blood – for all the world like a ruby set in his skull.

He had been prepared to dislike the lowlander, having listened to Agwaine speak sneeringly of Caswallon's rescue. But there had been something about the way Gaelen carried himself – like a clansman, tall and proud. Gwalchmai stopped whistling as he noticed a track some ten paces from the trail.

'Layne!' he called. 'Hold on.' Gwalchmai stepped from the trail and knelt by the soft earth beside the gorse. The three companions gathered around him, staring in wonder at the footprint

'It's as long as my forearm,' said Gwalchmai. 'And look, the thing has six toes.' All four lads scouted back along the line of tracks, but they found nothing. The earth by the gorse was soft, but the surrounding ground was rocky and firm.

'What do you think it is?' asked Gaelen, whose knowledge of mountain animals was still sparse.

'It isn't anything I've ever seen,' said Gwalchmai. 'Layne?'

The leader grinned suddenly. 'It's perfectly obvious, my friends. It's a hunter's joke. When they were laying the trails for our Hunt they made a jest of the rhyme "Seek the Beast . . ." the footprint points towards Vallon and the print was created to show we're on the right track.'

Gwalchmai's freckled face split into a grin. 'Yes, of course,' he said.

An hour before nightfall Layne scouted a small hollow where they could build a fire against a towering granite stone. The tiny blaze could not be seen from any distance and the four travellers unrolled their blankets and settled down for a light meal of oatcakes and water.

As the night closed in and the stars shone bright, Lennox curled up like a dozing bear and slept, leaving the others seated by the fire talking in low voices.

'Who was Earis?' Gaelen asked as he fed the fire with dry sticks.

'The first High King,' Layne told him. 'Hundreds of years ago the Farlain lived in another land, beyond the Gates. There was a great war and the clans were nigh obliterated. Earis gathered the remains of the defeated army and launched one last desperate assault on the enemy, smashing their army and killing their leader, Eska. But it was only one of several armies facing him. The druids told the King of a way to save his people. But it was hazardous: they had to pass a Gate between worlds. I don't know much about that side of it, but the legends are many. Anyway, Earis brought the Farlain here and we named the mountains Druin.

'During the journey a strange thing happened. As Earis stepped through the Gate of Vallon, into the bitter cold of winter, his sword disappeared from his hand. Earis took his crown and hurled it back through the Gate. The sword, he said, was the symbol of kingship, and since it had gone so too would his position. From henceforth there would be no King for the Farlain. The Council voted him to the position of Hunt Lord and so it has remained.'

'I see,' said Gaelen. 'So "the Bane of Eska;" that is a clue I can understand. But why the light that brings darkness?'

'The sword was called Skallivar, meaning Starlight on the Mountain,' said Gwalchmai. 'But in battle whoever it touched found only the darkness of death.'

'And that is what we seek? Skallivar?'

Layne laughed. 'No. Just a sword. It makes the clues more poetic, that's all.'

Gaelen nodded. 'There is much still to learn.'

'But you will learn, cousin,' said Layne. Gaelen felt a surge of warmth and comradeship within him as Layne spoke, but it was shattered by a sound that ripped through the night. An eerie, inhuman howling echoed through the mountains.

Lennox awoke with a start. 'What was that?' he asked, rolling to his knees.

Gaelen shuddered and said nothing.

'I've no idea,' said Layne. 'Perhaps it's a wolf and the sound is distorted.'

'If it's a wolf,' muttered Gwalchmai, 'it must be as big as a horse.'

For several minutes they sat in silence, straining to hear any more sounds in the blackness of the night. But there was nothing. Lennox went back to sleep. Layne exchanged glances with Gwalchmai.

'It wasn't a wolf, Layne.'

'No, but it could have been a hunter trying to frighten us.'

'I hope so,' said Gwalchmai. 'I think we should stand watches tonight, though.'

4

Gaelen awoke at Gwalchmai's touch, his eyes flaring open, his troubled dreams fragmented and instantly forgotten.

'I can't keep my eyes open any longer,' whispered Gwalchmai. 'I don't think there's anything out there. I saw a fox that's all.'

Gaelen sat up and yawned, 'It's chilly,' he whispered. Gwalchmai rolled himself swiftly into his blanket, laying his head on his pack. Within seconds he was asleep. Gaelen stretched, then crept to the fire, easing himself past Lennox. Taking a dry stick he poked around the embers of the dying fire, gently blowing it to life. Adding more sticks, he watched the flames flicker and billow. Then he looked away. Caswallon had told him never to stare into a fire, for the brightness made the pupils contract, and when you looked away into darkness you would be blind.

Gaelen wrapped his blanket round his shoulders and leaned back against the granite boulder. An owl hooted and the boy's fingers curled around the hilt of his hunting-knife. You fool, he told himself. You've never been afraid of the dark. Calm down. These are your mountains, there is nothing to harm you.

Except wolves, bears, lions and whatever made that bestial howling . . .

Gaelen shuddered, and fed more sticks to the fire. The supply was growing short and he didn't relish the prospect of entering the menacing darkness of the surrounding trees to replenish the store.

Slowly the fire died and Gaelen cursed softly. He had hoped it would last until first light, when the woods would become merely trees and not the frightening sentinels they now appeared. He stood up, loosening the dagger in its sheath, and walked carefully toward a fallen elm at the edge of the woods. Swiftly he collected dead wood and thicker branches. Back at the fire, relief washed over him. He was comforted by the sound of Lennox snoring and the sight of his other two friends sleeping soundly.

It was ridiculous. If danger was upon them they would be no use to him, sleeping as they were. And yet he felt at ease.

Layne muttered in his sleep and turned onto his back. Gaelen gazed down at his square, honest face. He looked so much younger asleep, his mouth half-open and childlike.

Gaelen turned his gaze to Lennox. Where Layne was clean-cut and athletic, Lennox was all bulk, with sloping shoulders of tremendous power, barrel-chested, thick-waisted. His hands were huge and the strength in them awesome. A year before he had straightened a horseshoe at the Games, having seen it done in the Strength Test. Too young to be entered, he had shamed several of the contestants and caused great merriment among the Farlain clan.

Later that day a dozen youths of the Haesten clan, having seen their man shamed, lay in wait for Lennox as he strode home. They came at him out of the darkness bearing cudgels and thick branches. As the first blow rapped home against his thick skull Lennox had bellowed in anger and lashed out, sending one luckless youngster through a bush. Two others followed him as Lennox charged amongst them; the rest fled.

Gaelen had heard the story and chuckled. He believed it. He wished he had seen it.

To the east the sky was brightening and Gaelen stood and wandered through the trees, on and up, scrambling over the lip of the hollow to stare at the distant mountains. In the trees around him birds began to sing, and the eldritch menace of the night disappeared. The boy watched as the snow-capped peaks to the west began to burn like glowing coals, as the sun cleared the eastern horizon. Fields below were bathed in glorious colours as blooms opened to the golden light.

Gaelen breathed deeply, filling his lungs with the sweet mountain air. He slid back down the slope and burrowed into Lennox's large pack, more than twice the weight of his own, and produced a copper bowl. Stoking up the fire, he placed the bowl upon it, filling it with water and adding the dry oats Maeg had wrapped for him.

407

Layne was the first to wake. He grinned at Gaelen. 'No monsters of the night, then?'

Gaelen grinned back and shook his head.

Had he remained on the rim of the hollow for a minute more he would have seen a Farlain hunter racing back towards Cambil's village, his cloak streaming behind him.

Badraig was a skilful huntsman whose task it was to set the trails for those of the boys travelling towards Vallon. He enjoyed his role. It was good to see tomorrow's generation of clansmen testing their mettle, and his son Draig and foster-son Gwalchmai were among them.

But today his mind was on other matters. During the night, as he made cold camp by a narrow stream, he had heard the howling that so disturbed Gaelen and his companions. They had half-dismissed it as a hunter's prank; Badraig knew it was not, for he was the only hunter in the area.

Being a cautious man, with over twenty years' experience, Badraig waited until near dawn before checking the source of the cry. With infinite patience he had worked his way through the wood, keeping the breeze in his face. As it shifted, so too did he.

And he found the butchered, broken remains of Erlik of the Pallides. In truth he didn't know it was Erlik, though he had seen the man many times at the Games. But no one could have recognised the bloody meat strewn across the track. Badraig lifted a torn section of tunic, recognising the edging as Pallides weave. In the bushes to the left he found part of a foot.

At first he thought it was the work of a bear, but he scouted for tracks and found six-toed footprints the like of which he had never seen. There were also the tracks of foxes and other small carrion creatures, but they had obviously arrived long after the killing beast had departed.

The prints were enormous, as long as a short sword. Badraig measured the stride. He was not a tall man, neither was he the shortest clansman in the Farlain, but he could not match the stride except by leaping. He gauged the height of the beast as half that again of a tall man. And it walked upright. The deepest impression was at the heel. He followed the track for a little way until he reached the foot of the slope. Here the spoor changed. The creature dropped to all fours and scrambled up at speed, gouging great tears in the clay. Badraig dug his fingers into the earth with all his strength, then compared his efforts with those of the killer. He could barely scratch the surface.

So it was big, bigger than a bear, and much faster. It could run on all fours or walk upright like a man. Its jaws were enormous — the fang-marks in the leg he had found proved that. He considered following the beast up the slope, but dismissed the idea.

From the remains he could see that the Pallides hunter had been carrying his bow with the arrow notched. He had been given no time to shoot. Badraig was confident of his own skills, but his strength lay also in the understanding of his weaknesses. Armed with only a hunting-knife and a quarterstaff, he was no match for whatever had wreaked this carnage. His one duty was to carry the news to Cambil and clear the mountain of youngsters.

Luckily, so he believed, no teams had passed his vantage point, so he would be able to stop any he came across as he returned. By mid-afternoon every village in the Farlain had the message and by nightfall six hundred clansmen, in groups of six, were scouring the mountains. By noon the next day forty-eight puzzled and disappointed youngsters had been shepherded back to their villages.

Only two teams remained to be found, those led by Layne and Agwaine. At dusk on the second day Cambil sat with his advisers round a camp fire half a day's march into the mountains.

'They've just vanished,' said Leofas. 'Layne's group made camp near the elm grove, and then moved north-east. After that the tracks cease.'

'It was a cunning ploy,' said Badraig. They obviously thought they had a clue and didn't wish to be followed. It doesn't make it any easier for us, though — except that we know they didn't head for Vallon.'

'I disagree,' said Caswallon.

'A pox on you, Caswallon,' snapped Badraig. That was my area. Are you saying I'm that poor a huntsman that I could have missed eight callow boys?'

'What I am saying is that we've searched everywhere and found no sign,' answered Caswallon softly.

Badraig snorted. 'Then maybe it's you who've missed the trail.'

'Enough of this quarrelling,' ordered Cambil. 'What shall we do now?'

'Look in Vallon,' said Caswallon. 'We have two missing teams. Both are led by the brightest, most able of our young men. The rhyme was not easy, but the answer was there for those with the wits to work at it. Agwaine I am sure would have deciphered it. Do you not agree, Cambil?'

Cambil bit his lip and stared into the fire. 'Yes, he misses little.'

'Now, all the boys who headed west say they saw no sign of Agwaine. Or Layne. In fact, after the first night they just dropped from sight. No team headed for Vallon, because none of the others deciphered the rhyme. To my mind the conclusion is inescapable.'

'So you *are* saying I'm lacking in skill!' stormed Badraig.

'Please be calm, cousin,' said Caswallon. 'We are talking about two teams who travelled carefully so that no rivals would spot them. It doesn't mean you lacked skill because you missed them.'

'I still say they headed west.'

'Then go west and find them,' said Caswallon. 'I'm heading for Vallon.'

Badraig swore, but Cambil cut across him. 'Hold your tongue, man! In this I think Caswallon is right. Now we have men hunting the west, and we'll lose nothing by visiting Attafoss. I just wish that druid would get here. I'd like to know what Hell spawn we're facing.'

'Well, "that druid" can help you,' said Taliesen, moving out of the tree shadows and seating himself among them. 'The beast crossed a Gateway and it is following the youngsters towards Attafoss. Caswallon is right. Let these arguments cease.'

'Are you sure, Lord Druid?' asked Badraig.

'As sure as death,' answered Taliesen. 'You had best move now, for there is tragedy in the air, and more blood to be spilt before you find them.'

'A curse on your prophecies,' said Cambil, lurching to his feet. 'Is this beast more of your magic?'

'None of mine, Hunt Lord.'

'Have you seen who will die?' asked Badraig. 'Can you tell us that?'

'No, I cannot tell you.'

'But my son is with Agwaine.'

'I know. Go now, for time is short.'

The men rolled their blankets and set off without a backward glance at the druid, whose dark eyes followed them seemingly without emotion. Taliesen watched them go, his heart heavy, a great sadness growing within him. The threads were beginning to come together now. In another time the sorcerer Jakuta Khan had sent a beast to kill the young Sigarni. That beast had vanished into the mists of time. Now it was here, in the Farlain, and being drawn inexorably toward the frail and wounded queen. And between the hunter and his victim were the boys of the Farlain. Taliesen longed to intervene. He remembered the long nights sitting at the Queen's bedside, in the cave on Druin's flanks. He had told her to say nothing of events in her own world, lest the knowledge cause even more fractures in the Time Lines. But when she became delirious with fever she had spoken in her sleep, and Taliesen had felt the weight of sorrow bear down on him like a huge rock.

He longed to rescue the boys. And he could not. 'It rests with you now, Gaelen,' he whispered.

And with the Hawk Eternal, he thought.

The four men walked for most of the night, stopping only to snatch an hour's sleep before dawn. Then they moved on, crossing hills, running across narrow valleys, scaling tree-lined slopes. During the afternoon they were joined by six hunters cutting in from the east. A hurried conference was held. One man was sent back to the village to fetch more bowmen, and the remaining nine hoisted their packs and ran single-file towards the towering peaks of the north-east.

They drove themselves hard, calling on reserves of endurance built during years of tough mountain living. Only Leofas, the oldest of them, struggled to maintain the pace; but maintain it he did, giving no sign of the pain from his swollen knee.

Just before nightfall Badraig halted the column, spotting something to the right of the track; it was a half-eaten oatcake. Badraig picked it up, breaking it into crumbs. At the centre it was still dry.

'Yesterday,' he said. Then he scouted carefully around the area. Rather than destroy any faint traces of spoor, the other hunters squatted down to wait for Badraig's report. Within minutes he returned.

'Four lads,' he said. 'One is very large and can only be Lennox. You were right, Caswallon; they passed me.'

The group pushed on into the mountains and, as the sun sank, Caswallon found the hollow Layne had chosen for their camp. The men gathered round.

'Tomorrow should be easier going,' said Cambil, stretching his long legs in front of him and resting his back against the granite boulder. 'The tracks will be easy to find.' His strong fingers kneaded the muscles of his thigh, and he grunted as the pain flowed.

Leofas sank to the ground, his face grey, his eyes sunken. With great effort he slipped his pack from his shoulders and unrolled his blanket. Wrapping himself against the night chill, he fell asleep instantly.

Badraig took two huntsmen and began to scour the area. The moon was bright and three quarters full and the tracks left by the boys could be clearly seen. Badraig followed them halfway up the north slope of the hollow. Here he stopped.

Overlapping Lennox's large footprint was another print twice as long. Badraig swore, the sound hissing between clenched teeth. Swiftly he returned to the men in the hollow.

'The beast is hunting them,' he told Cambil. 'We must move on.'

'That might not be wise,' the Hunt Lord replied. 'We could miss vital signs in the darkness. Worse, we could stumble on the beast itself.'

'I agree,' said Caswallon. 'How close behind them is it, Badraig?'

'Hard to say. Several hours, perhaps less.'

'Damn all druids!' said Cambil, his broad face flushed and angry. 'Damn them and their Gates.'

Caswallon said nothing. Wrapping himself in his blanket, he leaned back, closed his eyes. He thought of Gaelen and wondered if Fate could be so cruel as to save the boy on one day, only to have him brutally slain thereafter. He knew that it could. All life was chance.

But the Gates were a mystery he had never been able to fathom.

The elders had a story of a time just before Caswallon was born, when a leather-winged flying creature had appeared in the mountains, killing sheep and even calves. That had been slain by the then Hunt Lord, a strong proud man who sought to be the first High King since Earis. But the people had voted against him. Embittered, he had taken thirty of his followers and somehow found a way to cross the churning waters of Attafoss to the Island of Vallon. There he had overpowered the druids and led his men through the Forbidden Gate.

Twenty years later he returned alone, gravely wounded. Taliesen had asked for his death, but the Druid Council denied him and the man was returned to the Farlain. No longer Hunt Lord, he would tell no man of his adventures, saying only that a terrible vision had been revealed to him.

Many thought him mad. They mocked him and the once-proud lord took it all, making his home in a mountain cave where he lived like a hermit. Caswallon had befriended him, but even with Caswallon the man would not speak of the world beyond the Druid's Gate. But of the Gates themselves he spoke, and Caswallon had listened.

'The feeling as you pass through,' Oracle had told him, 'is unlike any other experience life can offer. For a moment only you lose all sense of self, and experience a great calm. Then there is another moment of sense-numbing speed, and the mind is full of colours, all different, moving past and through you. Then the cold strikes marrow-deep and you are human again on the other side.'

'But where did you go?' Caswallon asked.

'I cannot tell you.'

413

The wonder of it, Caswallon knew, was that Oracle had returned at all. There were many stories of people disappearing in the mountains, and even rare occasions when strange animals or birds appeared.

But Oracle was the only man he had heard of – save for Taliesen – to pass through and return. There were so many questions Oracle could have answered. So many mysteries he could lay to rest.

'Why can you not tell me?' Caswallon asked.

'I promised the druids I would not.'

Caswallon asked no more. A promise was a thing of steel and ice and no clansman would expect to break such an oath.

'All will be revealed to you, Caswallon. I promise you,' Oracle had told him cryptically.

Now as the young clansman sat beneath a moon-lit sky his mind harked back to that conversation. He wasn't at all sure he desired such knowledge. All he wanted was to find the boys and return them safely to the valley.

Badraig prepared a fire and the men gathered round it silently, fishing in their packs for food. Only Leofas slept.

Cambil pushed back the locks of blond hair from his forehead and wiped sweat from his face. He was tired, filled with the exhaustion only fear can produce. Agwaine was his only son, and he loved him more than anything else the world could provide. The thought of the lad being hunted by a beast from beyond the Gates filled him with terror; he could not face the possibility that Agwaine might die.

'We will find them,' said Caswallon softly.

'Yes,' answered the Hunt Lord. 'But alive?'

Caswallon saw the man's angular, honest face twist, as if a sudden pain had struck him. Beneath the wiry yellow-gold beard Cambil was biting his lip hard, seeking to prevent the collapse into tears of frustration.

'What did you think of the pack incident?' asked Caswallon suddenly.

'What?'

'Gwalchmai dropping his pack and outstripping Agwaine.'

'Oh, that. Clever move. Agwaine did not give up, though. He ran him to the end.'

'Bear that in mind, Cambil. The boy is a fighter. Given half an opportunity he will survive.'

'The thing will probably seek to avoid Man,' said Badraig. 'It is the way with animals of the wild, is it not? They know Man is a killer. They walk warily round him.'

'It didn't walk too warily around the Pallides scout,' said a balding bearded clansman from the west.

'True, Beric – but then, from the tracks, the Pallides was stalking it, though I can't see why. Still, it is well-known the Pallides are long on nerve and short on brain.'

Slowly, as the night passed, the men drifted off to sleep until at last only Cambil and Caswallon remained sitting side by side before the fire.

'It's been a long time since we sat like this, cousin,' said Cambil, breaking a lengthy silence.

'Yes. But we walk different paths now. You have responsibility.'

'It could have been yours.'

'No,' said Caswallon.

'Many would have voted for you.'

'They would have been wrong.'

'If Agwaine is taken I shall take my daughter and leave the Farlain,' said Cambil, staring into the glowing ashes of the dying blaze.

'Now is not the time to think of it,' Caswallon told him. Tomorrow we will talk as we walk the boys home.'

Cambil said nothing more. He unrolled his blanket, curled it round his shoulders and settled down against his pack.

Caswallon stood and made his way slowly up the farthest slope into the deep, cool pine-woods beyond. From the tallest point he gazed to the north-east, seeking sign of a camp-fire, yet knowing he would see nothing. The boys were too well-trained.

Sixteen miles north-east the four companions were arguing over the choicest morsels of a freshly-cooked rabbit. Lennox, who had cooked the cony and served it, was protesting innocence, despite his plate bearing twice as much meat as any other.

'But I am bigger,' he said seriously. 'My pack carries all the cooking equipment. And it was my snare.'

Gwalchmai broke from the argument for long enough to pop a small piece of meat in his mouth and begin chewing. He dropped from the discussion instantly, tugging surreptitiously at Gaelen's cloak. Gaelen saw the expression on his face. He tried his own meat, chewed for a moment, then removed the offending gobbet. Lennox and Layne were still arguing furiously. 'I think Lennox is right,' said Gaelen suddenly. 'He is the largest and he has the greatest burden. Here, take mine too, my friend.'

'I couldn't,' said Lennox, his eyes betraying his greed.

'No, truly. One small rabbit is scarce enough to build your strength.' Gaelen tipped the contents of his plate on Lennox's own. In the meantime Gwalchmai had whispered to Layne.

'I'm sorry, brother,' said Layne, smiling. 'Gaelen has made me realise how selfish I am. Take my portion too.'

'And mine,' added Gwalchmai eagerly.

Lennox sat back on his haunches. 'You are all true friends,' he said, gazing dreamily at his plate. Discarding his knife he scooped a handful of meat into his mouth. For several seconds he chewed in silence, then his face froze. His three companions waited in nerve-tingling silence until he doggedly finished the mouthful and swallowed.

'Is it good?' asked Layne, his face set and serious.

'Yes, it is,' said Lennox. 'But look, I feel bad about taking it all.'

'Think nothing of it,' said Gwalchmai swiftly. 'Your need is the greatest.'

'Yes, but . . .'

'And you cooked it,' put in Gaelen.

'I know, but . . .'

'Eat on, brother,' said Layne. 'See, it grows cold and . . . congeals.'

The dam burst and all three broke into giggling laughter. Realisation struck Lennox and he hurled the diseased meat into the bushes. 'Swine!' he said.

A hundred paces above them, on the edge of the trees, the beast squatted on its haunches glaring down at the fire. The laughter puzzled it, for the sound was similar to the screeching of the small apes of its homeland. Its black nostrils flared, catching the aroma of scorched flesh – rancid-smelling sickly flesh.

The beast snorted, blowing the scent away. It stretched its powerful legs, moving several paces left. Here the flesh scent was different, warm-blooded, salty and alive. The creature's eyes glittered. Hunger urged it to charge the camp and take the meat. Instinct made it fear the fire.

The beast settled down to wait.

Gaelen's dreams were troubled. Once more the Aenir killers pursued him, the pounding of their horses' hooves drumming fear into him as he ran. His legs were heavy, his movements sluggish. Suddenly a calming blue light filled his mind and the warriors faded. A face appeared, wrinkled and ancient, only the dark eyes giving a hint of life.

'The fire,' said a deep melodious voice, though the lips did not move. 'The fire is dying. Awake!'

Gaelen groaned and rolled over, trying to force the man from his mind.

'The fire, fool! Your life is in danger! Awake!'

The calming light disappeared, to be replaced by a red haze. Within the haze was a monster, black and menacing. Its huge jaws slavered, and its taloned hands reached for him.

Gaelen awoke with a jolt, eyes opening to the bright moonlight and the glittering stars in the velvet-dark sky. He glanced at the fire. As the dream had told him, it was failing fast, the last flickering twigs turning to ash and glowing embers.

The boy did not want to leave the warmth of his blanket, but the dream left an edge of fear in him. He sat up, running his fingers through his hair, scratching at the scar beneath the blaze of white above his left eye. Swiftly he broke twigs and small branches, feeding them to the tiny blaze and blowing life back into the fire. He felt better as the flames danced.

A rustling to his right made him turn. A large bush quivered and a low growl reverberated in the clearing. Gaelen drew his hunting-knife and narrowed his eyes, trying to pierce the darkness. He felt a fool. Had Caswallon not warned him endlessly about staring into fires? Now he could not see clearly. A giant shadow rose above the bush and Gaelen screamed a warning to the others.

Layne rolled from his blanket with knife in hand, standing in a half-crouch beside Gaelen. 'What is it?' Gaelen pointed at the thing beyond the bush. It was at least eight feet high, its head round like a man's except that the jaws were huge and rimmed with curving fangs. Gwalchmai and Lennox had left their beds and were staring horror-struck at the creature.

Gaelen pushed his trembling hand towards the fire, grasping the last of the branches they had stacked. It had not been stripped of its dry leaves for they would be good tinder for the morning blaze. Lifting the branch, Gaelen held it over the flames. The leaves caught instantly, flaring and crackling. On trembling legs, Gaelen advanced towards the beast holding the torch before him.

Layne and Lennox exchanged glances, then followed behind him. Gwalchmai swallowed hard, but he could not force his legs to propel him forward and stood rooted to the spot, watching his friends slowly advance on the nightmarish beast. It was colossal, near nine feet in height, and the light from the blazing branch glinted on its dagger-length talons.

Gaelen's legs were trembling as he approached the monstrosity. It reared up and tensed to leap at the youth but he drew back his arm and flung the blazing brand straight at the creature's face. Flames licked at the shaggy fur around its eyes, flaring up into tongues of fire on its right cheek. A fearful howl tore the silence of the night and the beast turned and sprang away into the night. The boys watched until it blended into the dark woods. Layne placed his hand on Gaelen's shoulder. 'Well done, cousin,' he said, his voice unsteady. 'I'm glad you woke.'

'What in the seven hells was that?' asked Gwalchmai, as they returned to the comfort of the fire.

'I don't know,' said Layne grimly. 'But from the look of those jaws it's not after berries and grubs.'

Gwalchmai retrieved the blazing torch and examined the beast's tracks. Returning to the fire he told Layne, 'It's the same track we saw in the valley. And we know no hunter made it. Congratulations, Gaelen, you saved our lives. There is no doubt of that.'

'I had a dream,' Gaelen told him. 'An old man appeared to me, warning me.'

'Did you recognise him?' asked Layne.

'I think he was the druid with Cambil on Hunt Day.'

'Taliesen,' whispered Gwalchmai, glancing at Layne.

'What are we going to do,' asked Lennox. 'Go back?'

'I don't see that we need to,' said Layne. 'We turned the beast away easily enough. And most animals avoid Man anyway. Also we will be at Attafoss in the morning, so we might just as well see it through.'

'I'm not sure,' said Gwalchmai. 'That thing was big. I wouldn't want to face it without fire.'

'If it's hunting us,' said Gaelen, 'it can do so equally well whether we go forward or back.'

'Are we all agreed, then?' Layne asked them. Gwalchmai longed to hear Lennox suggest a swift retreat back to the valley, but Lennox merely shrugged and donned his pack.

Dawn found the companions on the last leg of their journey, climbing the steep scree-covered slopes of the last mountain before Attafoss. As they crossed the skyline the distant roar of the falls could be heard some miles ahead.

'Always roaring, never silent,' quoted Gwalchmai. 'Whenever I hear it I feel the hairs rise on the back of my neck.'

Layne hitched his pack into a more comfortable position. 'No sign of the beast, anyway,' he said, leading them on down the slope to cross a narrow stone bridge and on to a winding trail through gorse-covered countryside. Layne bore right down a rock-strewn slope and on, at last, to a narrow strip of black sand nestling in a cove below the falls. Here they loosened their packs and settled down for breakfast. The jutting wall of rock deadened the thunder of the falls, but the wind carried the spray high into the air before them, and the sun made rainbows dance above the camp.

'It occurs to me,' said Gwalchmai as they ate, 'that we have not come across a single clue. No pouches. No stones marking the trail. It is an unpleasant thought, but we might be wrong.'

'I've been thinking that,' said Layne, 'but then the rhyme is clear. Perhaps the clues are all at the falls.'

After the meal they gathered at the water's edge to indulge in the age-old sport of stone-skimming, at which Gwalchmai excelled, beating Layne by three jumps. Refilling their water canteens, the boys picked their way up the slope and into the timberline above the falls.

Lennox prepared a fire in the afternoon and Layne suggested a quick search of the woods for clues. Leaving their packs by the fire they set off to scout, travelling in pairs – Lennox and Layne moving south, Gaelen and Gwalchmai north.

From a highpoint on the hillside Gaelen glazed once more at the majesty of Attafoss, watching the churning white water thunder to the river below.

'That, my friend, is the soul of the Farlain,' said Gwalchmai.

Gaelen turned to his comrade and grinned. 'I can believe it.'

Gwalchmai's face shone with pride and his green eyes glittered. 'Everything we are is contained there,' he said. 'All the poetry, the grandeur, and the strength that is Clan.'

Gaelen watched him as he soaked in the sight. Gwalchmai was not built on the same powerful lines as Lennox or Layne – he was slight and bird-boned, his face almost delicate. But in his eyes shone the same strength Gaelen had come to see in all clansmen – a sense of belonging that rooted them to the land, allowing them to draw on its power.

'Come on, Gwal, let's find the clues,' he said at last, and the two of them re-entered the timberline.

By mid-afternoon they had found nothing, and then Gwalchmai discovered a set of tracks that set him cursing loudly.

'What is it?' asked Gaelen. 'Hunters?'

'No,' snapped Gwalchmai. 'It's Agwaine. They reached here this morning. That's why there are no clues; he's taken them. Curse it!'

'Let's follow them,' said Gaelen. 'We have nothing to lose.'

The trail led south and was easy to follow. After less than an hour they reached a gentle slope, masked by thick bushes. Here Gwalchmai stopped.

'Oh, my soul!' he whispered. 'Look!'

Overlaid upon the moccasin tracks was a huge print, six-toed, and as long as a man's forearm.

Pale-faced, Gwalchmai looked at Gaelen. 'Are we going up the slope?'

'I don't want to,' answered his friend. 'But is there a choice?' He licked dry lips with a dry tongue.

Slowly they made their way to the top of the slope and entered a grove of pine. The sun was sinking slowly and long shadows stretched away from them.

'The beast was upon them here,' hissed Gwalchmai. 'Oh, Gods, I think it killed them all. Look at the tracks. See, they scattered to run, but not before one was downed. Look there! The blood. Oh, God.'

Gaelen could feel his heart racing and his breathing becoming shallow: the beginning of panic. Caswallon had told him to breathe deeply and slowly at such times, and now he did so, calming himself gradually. Gwalchmai was inching his way into the bushes, where he stood and covered his face with his hands at what he saw lying there. Gaelen joined him.

His stomach turned and bile filled his throat. He swallowed hard. Inside the screen of bushes were the remains of three bodies, mutilated beyond recognition. A leg was half-buried in rotting leaves, and a split skull lay open and drained beside it.

Everywhere was drenched in blood.

Gwalchmai stumbled back from the sight, and vomited on to the grass. Gaelen forced himself to look once more, then he rejoined Gwalchmai who was shivering uncontrollably.

'Gwal, listen to me. We must know where the beast has gone. Check the tracks. Please.'

There was no indication that Gwalchmai had heard him.

Gaelen took him by the shoulders and shook him gently. 'Gwal, listen to me. We must find out; then we'll tell Layne. Can you hear me?'

Gwalchmai began to weep, slumping forward against Gaelen, who put his arms around him, patting his back as with a child. 'It's all right,' he whispered.

After a few moments Gwalchmai pulled away, breathing deeply. 'I'm sorry,' he said, drying his eyes on his sleeve.

'That's all right, cousin,' said Gaelen. 'They were your friends.'

'Yes. All right. Let's see where the swine went.'

For several minutes Gwalchmai circled the scene of the massacre, then he returned.

'The beast waited for them, hidden at the top of the slope. It reared up and killed the first as he cleared the top. The second, it was Ectas I think, turned to run and he too was slain. The other two ran west. The beast overtook one of them, but the fourth – Agwaine – got clear. The beast has followed him now. But first it . . . it ate.'

'So,' said Gaelen, 'the creature is in the west. Now let's find Layne.'

Gwalchmai nodded and set off north in a loping run, his green eyes fixed to the trail. Gaelen ran just behind him, eyes flickering to the undergrowth around them. Fate was with them and they found the brothers within the hour. They were sitting by a stream. Swiftly Gaelen explained about the slaughter.

'How long ago did this happen?' Layne asked Gwalchmai.

'This morning, while we sat on the beach. I think the beast was following us, but when we cut away down to the waterside it picked up Agwaine's trail.'

'Do you think Agwaine survived?'

'He certainly survived the first attack, for the beast returned to the bodies. But then it set out after him once more. What kind of creature is it, anyway? I mean, it's fed. Why hunt Agwaine?'

'I don't know, but we must help our cousin.'

'We will not help him by dying, brother,' observed Lennox. 'Gwal says the beast has gone west. If we follow the wind will be behind us, carrying our scent forward. And we will be walking straight towards it.'

'I know that's true,' said Layne. 'Yet we cannot leave Agwaine.'

'Would you mind a suggestion from a lowlander?' Gaelen asked.

Layne turned to him. 'You're not a lowlander, cousin. Speak on.'

'Thank you. But I am not as wise in these things as the rest of you, so my plan may be flawed. But I think we should find a hiding place where we can watch the . . . food store. Once the beast has returned, unless the wind changes we should then be able to travel west without it picking up the scent. What do you think?'

'I think you are more clan than you realize,' said Layne.

They left the stream at a brisk run and headed for the line of hills less than half a mile distant – Layne leading, Gaelen and Gwalchmai just behind, and Lennox at the rear.

Once on the hillside they settled down on their bellies to watch the trail. From their vantage point they could see clearly all the way to the lake above the falls and beyond, while to the north-west a range of rocky hills cut the skyline. Above them the sky was red as blood as the sun sank to the level of the western mountain peaks.

'I hope it comes back before nightfall,' said Layne.

Luck was with them for, in the last rays of the dying sun, Gwalchmai spotted the beast ambling on all fours along the trail. It moved carefully, hugging the shadows before disappearing into the bushes where the corpses lay.

The companions wormed their way back down the slope, cutting a wide circle round the beast's lair before picking up its trail and beginning the long process of back-tracking it to the west. They ran through the timberline and on towards the rocky hills. The moon had risen before they arrived, but the night sky was clear and Gwalchmai pointed up to the boulder-covered hillside.

'I think Agwaine sought refuge in the caves,' he said, and they climbed the slope, seeking sign.

'We must bear in mind,' said Layne, 'that the beast will come back tonight after it has fed.'

It was Gaelen who found the boy, wedged deep in a narrow cleft in the rocks halfway up the slope. 'Agwaine, are you all right?' he called.

'Sweet Gods, I thought it was the beast come back,' said Agwaine. Tears rolled down his cheeks and he gritted his teeth to strangle the sobs he knew were close to the surface. Gaelen reached down as Agwaine climbed closer and he pulled him clear as the others gathered round. Agwaine was unhurt, but his face showed the strain he had endured. His eyes seemed sunken and blue rings stained the sockets.

'It came at us from nowhere,' he said. 'It beheaded Cael. Ectas was next; as he turned to run, the beast opened his back with one sweep of its talons. There was nothing to do but run. I was at the back and I turned and sprinted away. Draig was right behind me. I heard his screaming, but it was cut short and I knew I was the only one left. I could hear it chasing me and I ran as never before. It found me here, but it couldn't reach me.'

'We must get away, cousin,' put in Layne.

'Yes. No! First I must get something. I threw it away as we ran.'

'We can't go back in those woods,' hissed Gwalchmai.

'We must. It's not far; I threw it as I saw the slope.'

'What can be that important?' asked Layne. 'Even now the beast may be coming.'

'You set off then and I'll catch up,' said Agwaine.

'Damn you, cousin, you know we cannot do that.'

'Let's find the cursed thing,' said Gaelen. 'I don't want to spend all night discussing this.'

Agwaine led them back to the woods. Gaelen was furious, but he held himself in check. He knew what Agwaine was seeking. The sword. Agwaine had found the sword.

The woods loomed dark and threatening and the boys drew their knives. Little good would they be, thought Gaelen. He glanced at Gwalchmai. His friend's face was pinched and ashen in the moonlight. Only Lennox seemed unconcerned.

Agwaine held up his arm and then stopped. The Hunt Lord's son disappeared into the bushes, returning quickly with a long closely-tied package.

'Let's go,' he said, and led them away down towards the falls. The shifting wind made them take wide detours to avoid their scent being carried to the beast, and dawn found them below Attafoss with the river to the left, a section of woods before them. They were tired, but the fear of the beast was upon them and they hesitated before entering the wood.

Daggers held firm, they walked warily, but as they moved under the overhanging branches a voice jolted them. Gwalchmai dropped his dagger in fright, then scooped it up swiftly.

'Good morning, boys.'

To their right, in a circular clearing, a woman was sitting on a fallen oak. At her feet was a blanket on which was laid a breakfast of black bread and cold meat.

She was dressed in a manner they had never seen before. Upon her shoulders was a mail scarf of closely-linked silver rings. Beneath this she wore a fitted breast-plate of silver, embossed with a copper hawk, its wings spread wide, disappearing beneath the mail scarf. About her waist was a leather kilt, studded with copper and split into sections for ease of movement. She wore dark leggings and silver greaves over riding boots. Her arms were bare save for a thick bracelet of silver on her right wrist; on her left was a wrist-guard of black leather.

And she was old. Thick silver hair swept back from a face lined with wisdom and sorrow. But her eyes were bright, ice-blue, and her bearing straight and unbending.

Gaelen watched her closely, noting the way she looked at them all. She must have been beautiful when young, he thought. But there was something in her expression he could not pinpoint; it seemed a mixture of wonder and regret.

'Will you join me for breakfast?' she invited.

'Who are you?' asked Agwaine.

The woman smiled, 'I am Sigarni – the Queen,' she said.

'We have no queens in the Farlain,' said Layne.

'I am the Queen Beyond,' she said, with a slow smile.

'You are on Farlain land,' Agwaine told her sternly. 'No stranger is allowed here. Are you from the Aenir?'

'No, Agwaine. I am a guest of the Lord Taliesen.'

'Can you prove this?'

425

'I don't feel the need to. You boys are here on the Hunt. Taliesen asked if he could borrow my sword for it. If you open the package you will find it – a beautiful weapon of metal which one of you will have seen. The hilt is of ebony, and shaped for a warrior to hold with both hands, while the guard is of iron decorated with gold and silver thread. The scabbard is embossed with a hawk, even as on my breastplate. Now open the package and return what is mine.'

'Open it,' said Layne. 'If it is true, then the sword must be returned to its rightful owner.'

'No, it is mine,' said Agwaine, flushing. 'I won the Hunt and this is my proof.'

'You don't need proof,' said Gaelen. 'We know you won, the sword is only a symbol. Open the package.'

Agwaine drew his dagger and sliced the leather thongs binding the oilskins. As the woman had predicted, the sword was indeed a wondrous weapon. Reluctantly Agwaine handed it over. The woman swiftly buckled the scabbard to her waist. Had there been any doubt as to the ownership, it was laid to rest as she placed it at her side. It was like watching a picture completed, thought Gaelen.

The sword in place, she returned to her seat on the tree. She gestured at the food. 'Come. Eat your fill,' she said, 'I was expecting eight of you. Where are the others?'

The boys exchanged glances.

'They are dead,' said Gaelen.

'Dead?' asked the Queen, rising to her feet gracefully. 'How so?'

Gaelen told of the beast and their flight from the mountains.

'Damn!' she said. 'Taliesen came to me in a dream yester-eve. He told me you were lost upon the mountain and that I should seek you here. He said nothing of a beast.'

'He came to me also,' said Gaelen. 'And he said nothing of a queen.'

She smiled without humour. 'So be it, then. The ways of wizards are a mystery to me and I pray they'll stay that way. Now, describe this creature.'

All of them started to speak at once, but she waved them to silence and pointed to Agwaine. 'You saw it closely. You speak.'

426

Agwaine did as he was bid, recalling vividly the power of the brute and its awesome size, its speed and its semi-human appearance.

'You are right to consider running,' said the woman when he had finished, 'I have seen the like of the beast before in my own kingdom. More than once. They are terrible – and hard to slay. Although it kills to eat, once it has fixed on a prey it will pursue it damn near for ever. This beast has – in a way – been hunting me for forty years.'

'Why you?' whispered Gaelen.

'It was sent a long time ago by a sorcerer named Jakuta Khan. But that is a story for another day, Gaelen.'

'What can we do?' asked Layne.

'You can eat breakfast and put some strength in your limbs. Then we will plan for battle.'

The companions seated themselves at her feet and dug into the loaves and meat. The bread tasted fresh-baked and the beef was tender and pink. They ate without gusto, except for Lennox who tore great chunks of bread and crammed them into his mouth.

The Queen watched him, eyebrows raised. 'You were perhaps expecting a famine?'

'Either that or he's going to cause one,' observed Gwalchmai.

Agwaine said nothing. The appearance of this strange woman had angered him, and he was loath to hand over the great sword – their only real defence against the beast – to a woman.

'How will we fight this beast?' asked Layne.

'How indeed?' she replied, her pale eyes showing sorrow.

'We could make spears,' suggested Gaelen, 'by fastening our daggers to poles.'

'Come to that, I could make a bow,' said Gwal. 'It wouldn't be a great weapon, or very accurate. But it might serve at close range.'

'Then do it swiftly,' said the Queen, 'and we will talk again.'

The boys rose and spread out nervously into the woods, searching for saplings or stout straight branches. Gaelen and Agwaine selected an infant elm and began to hack at it with their daggers.

'What do you think of her, lowlander?' Agwaine asked as the sapling snapped.

'I think she is what she says she is,' snapped Gaelen. 'And if you call me lowlander again, you'll answer for it.'

Agwaine grinned. 'I don't like you, Gaelen, but you are right. Whatever your pedigree, you are now a clansman. But I'll never call you cousin.'

'I don't care about that,' Gaelen told him. 'You are nothing to me.'

'So be it.'

They stripped the sapling of twigs and leaves and shortened it to a manageable five feet. Then Gaelen unwound the thongs of his right legging and bound his knife to the wood. He hefted it for balance and hurled it at a nearby tree. The spear hammered home with a dull thud. Gaelen tugged it loose and examined the binding; it remained firm.

It seemed a formidable weapon, but he summoned the image of the beast to mind and then the spear seemed puny indeed.

'Were you surprised I found the sword?' Agwaine asked him.

'No, disappointed.'

'That was a good trick with the pack.'

'I'm glad you enjoyed it.'

'I didn't, but it was good anyway.' Gaelen nodded. He waited while Agwaine fashioned his spear, then wandered away; he didn't enjoy Agwaine's company and he knew the feeling was reciprocated.

He made his way back to the clearing where the old woman sat. She was deep in thought and Gaelen watched her for some time from the edge of the woods. It was easy to believe she was a queen, for her bearing was proud and confident and she was clearly used to being obeyed. But there was more to her than that: a kind of innate nobility, an inner strength, which shone through.

'Are you going to stand there all day, Gaelen?' she asked without moving her head.

Gaelen stepped forward. 'How did you know I was here? And how do you know my name?'

'Let's leave it at the first question. I heard you. Come and join me for a while, and eat something. To work efficiently the body must be fed.'

'Are you no longer a queen?' asked Gaelen, seating himself cross-legged before her.

The woman chuckled and shook her head. 'A queen is always a queen. Only death can change that. But I am, at present, without a realm. Yet I hope to return soon. I promised my people I would – just as my father did before me.'

'Why did you leave your land?' Gaelen asked.

'I was wounded, and likely to die. And so the prophecy was fulfilled and . . . my captain . . . sought the Gate and passed me through. Taliesen healed me.'

'How were you wounded?'

'In a battle.' She looked away, her eyes distant.

'Did you win?'

'I always win, Gaelen,' she said sadly. 'My friends die and yet I win. Winning is a hard habit to break; we can come to feed on it to the exclusion of all else.'

'Is that a bad thing?'

'Not when you're young,' she said, smiling again.

'Why have you stayed up here and not in the village?'

'As I told you, I am a guest of the Lord Taliesen. He felt it would be wiser to remain near Vallon. Now, enough of questions. Look around you. Is this a good place to face the beast?'

'Is there a good place?' countered Gaelen.

'There are places you should avoid, like open ground.'

'Is here a good place?'

'Not bad. You have the trees to shield you, and yet there is no dense undergrowth so it cannot creep up on you unnoticed.'

'Except at night,' said Gaelen.

'Indeed. But it will be over, for good or ill, long before then.'

'What about you? You have no spear.'

The queen smiled, 'I have my sword; it has been with me these forty years. I thought it had been left behind when I passed through the Gateway, but Taliesen brought it to me. It is a fine weapon.'

Lennox came into view carrying an enormous club of oak. 'I found this,' he said. 'It will do for me.'

The Queen laughed loud. 'There is nothing subtle about you, Lennox, my lad. Nor ever will be. Indeed it is a fine weapon.'

Gwalchmai had fashioned a short bow and had found six pieces of wood straight enough to slice into shafts for it. 'It's a clumsy thing,' he said, 'and the range will be no greater than twenty paces.' Squatting down, he began to shape pieces of bark into flights for his arrows.

By noon they had completed their preparations and they sat waiting for the woman's instructions. But she said nothing, merely sitting among them slowly chewing the last of the bread. Gaelen caught the Queen's eye and she smiled, raising an eyebrow questioningly. He turned to Gwalchmai. 'You are the lightest of us, Gwal. Why don't you climb that tree and keep a watch for the creature?'

Gwalchmai nodded. 'Wouldn't the oak be better? It's more sturdy.'

'The beast might be able to climb,' said Gaelen. 'The elm would never support its weight.'

'How will you tackle it when it comes?' asked the Queen, staring at Gaelen.

'We must confuse it,' he said, his mind racing. He had no idea how five boys and an old woman should tackle a creature of such speed and strength, but the Queen asked him a question and seemed to expect a rational reply. 'If we spread out, the beast must attack us one at a time. Each time it does, one or all the others must stab at it, turning the creature all ways. Gwal, you will stay in the tree,' he called to the climbing boy. 'Shoot when you have a clear target.'

'That is all good thinking,' said the Queen, 'but, even so, to confuse the beast you must surprise it. Once it is sighted, and we know which direction it is coming from, you must hide yourselves, forming a rough circle. But one of you must act as bait and stay in plain sight. With luck the beast will charge; I've seen that before. Ideally we must make it charge on to a spear. That way its weight will carry the point home far more powerfully than any thrust of yours.'

'I will be the bait,' said Gaelen, surprising himself.

'Why you?' asked Agwaine. 'I am the fastest here, and I've outrun it before.'

'Speed is not usually required of bait,' Gaelen told him.

Agwaine chuckled and shook his head. 'All right. I will stay on your right, Lennox and Layne can take the left. And may God give us luck.'

'Do not ask for luck, ask for courage,' said the Queen.

'How will you fight?' Agwaine asked her.

'With my sword,' she replied softly. 'As I always have, against man and beast. Don't worry about me, boy.'

'Why should you fight for us at all?'

'That is a mystery you will one day understand, but it is not for me to explain to you.'

'It's coming!' called Gwalchmai from high in the elm. They could all see where he was pointing; the beast was moving from the northwest.

'Take up positions,' said the woman. Lennox and Layne ran to the left, crouching behind a large bush. Agwaine moved to the right, spear held before him, and squatted behind the bole of an oak. High in the elm Gwalchmai strung his bow, hooked his leg round a thick branch and wedged himself in position, notching an arrow to the string.

The Queen drew her sword and held the blade to her lips. Then she smiled at Gaelen. 'This should be something to tell your five children,' she said.

Gaelen did not reply. Some fifty paces ahead the beast had come into view. This close it seemed even more colossal. Seeing Gaelen, the creature reared up to its full height and bellowed a bloodcurdling howl. Then it dropped to all fours and charged.

The boy glanced to his left, seeking assurance from the warrior.

But the Queen had gone.

The ground beneath Gaelen's feet shook as the beast thundered towards him. He gripped his spear and waited, all fear vanishing like mist in a breeze. In that moment a strange euphoria gripped

431

him. All his life he had been alone, afraid and unhappy. Now he was part of something; he belonged. Even if his life had to end in the next moments nothing could take away the joy he had known in these last few precious months.

He was no longer alone.

He was Clan.

The beast slowed, rearing to its full height with arms spread, fangs gleaming in the morning sun. Gaelen gripped his spear firmly, muscles tensed for the thrust. The beast came on, drawing abreast of the hidden Agwaine. Fear swept over the Hunt Lord's son, shrouding him in a tidal wave of panic. He wanted to run. To hide.

But he too was Clan.

Rising up from his hiding place as the creature's shadow fell across him, Agwaine rammed the spear into the beast's side. A blood-chilling scream filled the clearing. Agwaine vainly tried to pull his weapon clear. A taloned arm swept backhanded, punching the boy from his feet; he hit the ground on his face and rolled to his back. The beast stepped over him, jaws slavering and talons reaching out. Agwaine screamed.

At that moment Layne raced from the left, hurling his spear with all his strength. The weapon flashed through the air to bury itself in the beast's broad back. It came upright, swinging to meet the new attack. Behind it Agwaine tried to stand, but his legs gave way and he pitched to the earth, nausea filling his throat. Layne, weaponless, stood transfixed as the beast bore down on him. Lennox grabbed him by the shirt and hauled him aside, then stood waiting for the creature, his club raised, his eyes defiant.

Gaelen ran in to attack, screaming at the top of his voice. The beast's black eyes flickered toward the charging boy and in that moment Lennox struck, stepping forward to thunder the oak club against the creature's head. It staggered, but blocked Lennox's next blow with a raised arm. Gaelen's spear sliced into the flesh above its hip, then broke, pitching the boy to the ground at the monster's feet.

Now only Lennox remained in the fight. The young giant hit once more, but his time the beast was ready – it parried the blow

432

with its paw and a taloned hand gripped the youth's upper arm, smashing the bone and ripping the flesh from the shoulder. Lennox staggered back but did not fall. Transferring the club to his right hand, he waited for the beast's next attack.

An arrow cut deep into the monster's thigh, causing it to bellow in pain and rage. A second glanced from its thick skull. Lennox crashed his club into the creature's mouth, but a backhanded blow hurled him from his feet.

Injured though the beast was, none of the wounds were mortal, and the battle had turned. From his precarious position in the tree, Gwalchmai fired a third shaft which buried itself in the ground by the beast's right foot. Leaning out for the fourth shot, the young archer toppled from the branch, landing on his back.

Running behind the beast, Gaelen grabbed Layne's spear and plucked it from the creature's back. As it turned he stabbed at its face, the point slashing a jagged line up and into the sensitive nostrils. To Gaelen's right Layne gathered up Lennox's club and tried to help, but the monster turned on him, slashing the boy's chest. The talons snaked out again. Gaelen leaped backwards, tumbling to the earth.

The beast's jaws opened and another terrifying howl pierced the air.

The boys were finished.

'Ho, Hell spawn!' shouted the Queen. The beast swung ponderously, glittering black eyes picking out the tall, armoured figure at the centre of the clearing. 'Now face me!'

She stood with feet apart, her silver sword before her.

The beast reared to its full height – eight feet of black, merciless destruction. Before its power the woman seemed to Gaelen a frail, tiny figure. The monster moved forward slowly – then charged, dropping to all fours. The Queen sidestepped, her silver sword swung arcing down to rebound from the creature's skull, slicing its scalp and sending a blood spray into the air. The beast twisted, launching itself in a mighty spring, but the woman leaped to the right, the sword cutting across the creature's chest to open a shallow wound.

Agwaine crawled to where Gaelen crouched.

'She cannot win,' whispered the Hunt Lord's son.

'Run, boys!' yelled the Queen.

But they did not. Gaelen scooped up the broken spear, while Layne helped Lennox to his feet and gathered once more the club of oak.

The old woman was breathing hard now. Taliesen had stitched her wounds, but her strength was not what it was. Under the breastplate stitches had parted and blood oozed down her belly. Sweat bathed her face and her mouth was set in a grim line.

Once more the beast reared above her. Once more she hammered the sword in its face. The creature shook its head, blood spraying into the air.

The woman knew she could last but a little longer, while the creature was only maddened by the cuts it had received. A plan formed in her mind and weighed down her heart. It had been her hope to return to her realm and lead it out of the darkness of war. Now there would be no going home. No future. No golden days of peace watching the nation prosper.

In that final moment, as the creature prepared to attack once more, it was as if time slowed. Sigarni could smell the forest, the musky brown earth, the freshness of the breeze. Images leapt to her mind and she saw again the handsome forester, Fell, the first great love of her life. He had died in the battle against the Baron, cut down by the last arrow loosed in that fateful battle. Faces from the past glittered in her memory: Ballistar the dwarf, who had sought a new life in a new world; Asmidir, the black battle captain; Obrin, the renegade Outlander; and Redhawk – above them all, Redhawk.

'I will never see you again,' she thought, 'though you promised to be with me at the end. You gave me your word, my love. You promised!'

Talons lashed towards her. Ducking beneath them she leapt back, lifting her sword towards the beast. It sprang forward, but this time the Queen did not side-step. With a savage battlecry she launched herself into its path, driving the blade deep into the creature's huge chest. The silver steel slid between its ribs, plunging through its lungs and cleaving the heart.

As it screamed in its death throes its great arms encircled the woman. The breastplate buckled under the immense pressure and the Queen's ribs snapped, jagged bone ripping into her. Then the beast released her and toppled to the earth. The woman staggered back, then fell. She struggled to rise, but agony lanced her.

The boys ran to her side, Gaelen kneeling by her and raising her head to lay it on his lap. Gently he stroked the silver hair from her eyes.

'Give the sword to Taliesen,' whispered the Queen, blood staining her lips. She coughed weakly and swallowed. 'We did it, lads,' she said. 'You did well, as I knew you would.'

Agwaine knelt on her right, taking her hand.

'You saved us; you killed it,' said Gaelen.

'Listen to me, for I am dying now, but remember my words. I shall return to the Farlain. You will be older then. Men. Warriors. You will have suffered much and I will aid you again.'

Agwaine glanced at Gaelen. 'What does she mean?'

Gaelen shrugged. The sound of running feet echoed in the clearing as Caswallon, Cambil and the clansmen raced into view. Caswallon knelt by Gaelen. 'Are you all right?'

'Yes. She saved us. She slew the beast.'

'Who is she?' asked Caswallon.

The Queen's eyes opened. 'Ah, it is you,' she whispered, smiling. 'Now the circle is complete, for you told me you would be with me at my death. How well you look. How young. How handsome! No . . . silver in your beard.'

Caswallon gazed down into the bright blue eyes and saw that the woman was fading fast. Her hand lifted towards him and he took it, holding it firm.

'Did I do well, Caswallon? Tell me truly?'

'You did well,' answered Caswallon. 'You saved the boys.'

'But my kingdom? Was I . . . truly the Queen you desired me to be?'

'Yes,' answered Caswallon, nonplussed.

She smiled once more, then a tear formed and slowly fell to her pale cheek. 'Poor Caswallon,' she whispered. 'You do not know whose hand you hold, but you will.' Tears filled her eyes. Lifting her hand to his lips, he kissed the fingers, 'I know you are brave beyond words,' he said, 'and I do not doubt you were a Queen beyond compare.'

Her eyes closed and a long broken sigh hissed from her throat. Caswallon sat for a moment, still holding onto the hand. Then he laid it gently across the Queen's chest.

Cambil knelt beside him. 'Who was she?' asked the Hunt Lord.

Caswallon stared down at the dead warrior woman. 'Whoever she was, I mourn her passing.'

'She was the Queen Beyond,' said Gaelen, 'and she always won.' Then he began to weep.

5

Lennox sat with his back against a tree as they stitched his shoulder and strapped his broken arm. His face was grey with pain, but he uttered no groan, merely squeezed his eyes shut and gritted his teeth.

His father Leofas said nothing, but pride shone in his eyes. Layne lay beside his brother, enduring the stitches in his chest in the same stoic fashion. Away from the others sat Badraig, tears flowing and head in hands. His son Draig had been killed the day before.

Even through his own immense relief Cambil felt the other man's sorrow and, leaving his son Agwaine, he walked over to sit beside the hunter. He put his hand on Badraig's shoulder.

'I am sorry, my friend. Truly.'

The man nodded, but neither lifted his head nor answered.

Caswallon stood with the other clansmen looking down on the beast. Even in death it was a terrifying sight, its great jaws drawn back in a last snarl, its fangs, as long as a man's fingers, bared and bloody.

'I have never seen the like,' muttered Caswallon, 'and I pray I never shall again.'

They buried the Queen deep, marking the grave with flat white stones. Cambil promised to have a headstone carved. Then the men split into two groups, Badraig leading the five hunters back to the falls and burying what was left of the bodies; Cambil, Leofas and Caswallon staying with the boys. It was decided they would rest in the clearing until morning and then attempt the long walk back to the village.

The main worry was Lennox, who had lost a great deal of blood. Gwalchmai, though stunned by his fall, was back on his feet and unhurt. He alone of the boys had missed the Queen's last battle.

That night around the camp-fire the boys were unnaturally silent. Lennox, in great pain, sought refuge in sleep, but the others sat together staring at the flames. Agwaine had lost friends and suffered the terror of being hunted; Layne had seen the leadership of the group taken quietly from him by the former lowlander; and Gaelen had discovered in his heart a strength he had not known existed. Only Gwalchmai was untouched by the drama, but he remained silent, for he sensed his friends' needs.

Caswallon prepared a strong broth for them all. His own thoughts were many. Through his sorrow at the death of the three lads he felt a surging pride at the way the others had tackled the beast, and a sense of joy at the manner in which Gaelen had conducted himself. Thinking back, he did not know if he could have duplicated the feat at Gaelen's age. But overriding these thoughts he could not help but remember the words of the Queen. At first he had thought the woman delirious, but her eyes had been clear.

Caswallon had always enjoyed an ability to read character truly, and he knew instinctively that the dying warrior was a great woman, a woman of courage, nobility of spirit and great inner strength. That she was a queen was no surprise.

But Queen of where? And how did she know him?

Beyond the Gate. What was beyond the Gate?

Only Oracle knew. And Taliesen.

The night wore on and Caswallon strolled away from the fire, seeking solitude and a place to think. But Cambil joined him and they sat together on a high hillside under the clear sky.

'Badraig is a broken man,' said Cambil softly, gathering his green cloak about his broad shoulders.

'Yes. What can one say?'

'I feel a burden of guilt for it,' said Cambil. 'Last night I prayed that Agwaine would survive. I would willingly have exchanged any life for his. When I saw he was alive I didn't care anything for Badraig's loss; it only struck me later.'

'That is understandable.'

'Don't patronise me, Caswallon!' snapped the Hunt Lord, eyes blazing.

'I was not trying to. How do you think I felt when I saw Gaelen?'

'It's not the same thing, is it? You may be fond of the boy, but he's not of your blood. You didn't watch him take his first faltering steps, hear his first words, take him on his first hunt.'

'No, that is true,' admitted Caswallon, realising the futility of the arguement.

'Still Gaelen did well,' said Cambil. 'He proved his right to be a clansman.'

'Yes.'

'But he can never be Hunt Lord.'

Caswallon turned then, catching Cambil's eye, but the Hunt Lord looked away, staring into the woods. At once Caswallon understood the man's meaning. Gaelen had planned the battle with the beast, had taken over leadership from Layne. Agwaine had done his bidding. On such talents were future Hunt Lords built. Cambil's dream was that Agwaine would succeed him, but now he was unsure.

'Be content that your son is alive,' said Caswallon. 'The future will look to itself.'

'But you agree it would not be fitting for a lowlander to lead the clan?'

'The Council can decide on the day you step down.'

'So, it is your plan to supplant Agwaine with this boy?' accused Cambil, face reddening.

Caswallon sighed. 'Nothing could have been further from my mind.'

'It was Agwaine who found the sword.'

'Indeed it was.'

A long silence enveloped them, until at last Cambil stood to leave. 'We will never be friends, Caswallon,' he said sadly.

'You see ogres where there are none,' Caswallon told him. 'I have no ambition, cousin – not for myself, nor my sons. They will be what they desire to be, and what they are able to be. I want to see them happy, married well, and content. All else is dross, for we all die and there is no evidence we take anything with us when we go.'

Cambil nodded, 'I wish I could believe you, but I see a different Caswallon. I see a man who could have been Hunt Lord. Children imitate your walk, tales are told about you around the campfires. And yet what have you done? You steal other men's cattle. What is it about you, Caswallon?'

'I have no idea. I never listen to the stories.'

Caswallon watched as Cambil walked slowly down the slope towards the fire. Gathering his own cloak about him, he stared at the stars, mind wandering.

After about an hour he felt a cold wind blow against his neck, but the leaves about him did not stir. He turned. Behind him stood Taliesen, wrapped in his cloak of shimmering feathers and holding a staff of oak entwined with mistletoe.

'Three boys are dead,' he told the druid, gesturing to a place beside him on the flat boulder. The druid sat, leaning forward on his staff.

'I know. The Queen also.'

'Who was she?'

'Sigarni the Hawk Queen. Did she say anything before she died?'

'She said she would come again, so the boys tell me. And she thought I was someone she once knew.'

'The old man you know as Oracle brought this upon us,' said Taliesen. 'I only hope I can make it right.'

'What are you talking about?'

'Seek Oracle and tell him you have spoken to me. Tell him that it pleases me for you to know his story. But when you have heard it, promise me you will repeat it to no one. Do you agree to this?'

'I do.'

Maeg ran from the house, Kareen beside her, as the men appeared on the far hill. Other women streamed from crofts and homes. Men working in the fields dropped their tools and joined the rush.

Within minutes the hunters and the boys were surrounded. Cambil answered all questions and Caswallon led Gaelen through the throng to where Maeg waited. She moved forward, cupping Gaelen's face with her hands.

'Are you well, my bonny lad?'

'Yes.'

440

She read the sorrow in his eyes and linked her arm in his for the long walk to the house. He had suffered so much in his life and now it was obvious that he had endured more pain. Her heart ached for him.

At the house the crofter Durk was waiting for Kareen. He asked after Gaelen and then left, taking the girl with him to walk up the hillside.

Gaelen was exhausted and stumbled to his bed while Caswallon and Maeg sat together by the hearth. The clansman told her of the ordeal in the mountains and how well the boys had handled themselves.

'He is a lad to be proud of, Caswallon,' she said.

He grinned sheepishly, 'I know. I was close to tears as he told me the tale.'

'He'll be a fine man.'

'Sooner than you think,' said Caswallon.

'And how did you fare with Cambil for so many days?'

He shrugged. 'The man fears me, Maeg. He thinks I plan to supplant Agwaine with Gaelen. Is it not madness? His doubts must sit on his shoulders like a mountain.'

'He is a sad, lonely man. I'm glad you harbour no ill-will.'

'How can I hate him? I grew up with him. He was always the same; he believed his father liked me more than him. Always he strived to beat me, and he never did. Had I been wiser, I would have lost at least once.'

'It's not in you to lose,' she said. 'You are a clansman. And a proud man – too proud, I think.'

'Can a man be too proud? It harms no one. I have never insulted another man, nor abused my strength by destroying a weaker opponent. I do not parade my talents, but I am aware of them.'

'Nonsense. You're as vain as a flamingo. I've seen you trimming your beard by the silver mirror and using my brush to comb it flat.'

'Spying on me now, is it?'

'Yes, it is. And why shouldn't I? Am I not your wife?'

He pulled her to his lap and kissed her. 'Indeed, you are the best thing I ever stole from the Pallides. Except for that bull of your father's.'

'When I think that Intosh proposed to me,' said Maeg, tugging his beard, 'and instead I ended with you, I wonder if the gods hold a grudge against my family.'

'Intosh? He was my rival? You'd have hated it, Maeg. The man has ticks in his bed. I was scratching for days after I stole his sword.'

'You dog! So that's where they came from.'

'Now, now, Maeg my love,' he said as she pulled from his grasp, eyes blazing. 'Let's not have a row. The boy needs his sleep, he's been through much.'

'You've not heard the last of this, my fine Farlain,' she said softly.

'And now, while you're quiet for a moment,' he said, pulling her to him once more, 'perhaps you'll welcome me home. It's been a tiring journey.'

'Then you'll be wanting to sleep?'

'Indeed I do. Will you join me?'

'You can bathe first. I'll have no more of your ticks.'

'Is there any heated water?'

'There is not.'

'You'd not expect me to bathe in the yard in the cold?'

'Of course not. You can sleep down here and bathe tomorrow in the warm water.'

'Sleep here?' Their eyes met and there was no give in her. 'It's the yard then,' he said.

Later, as Caswallon slept, Maeg heard Gaelen moaning in his sleep in the next room. She rose quickly, wrapping a blanket around her naked body, and made her way to his bedside. It was a familiar nightmare and she knew he was once more running from the Aenir, his legs leaden, his wounds bleeding.

She sat beside him stroking his hair. 'It's all right, Gaelen,' she whispered. 'You're here with Maeg. You're safe. Safe.'

He groaned and rolled to his back. 'Maeg?'

'I'm here.'

'Dreaming,' he whispered and his eyes closed once more.

She remembered the first time Caswallon had brought him home. He had been nervous then, and his eyes had flickered from

442

wall to wall as if the house was a prison. And he had avoided her. When she showed him his room, his delight had stunned her.

'This is my room?'

'Yes.'

'My very own? To share with no one?'

'Your very own.'

'It's wonderful. Thank you.'

'You are very welcome.'

'You cannot bewitch me,' he said suddenly.

'I see,' she said, smiling. 'Caswallon has told you about my spells?'

'Yes.'

'But he didn't tell you my powers faded soon after we were wed?'

'No.'

'It happens to women once they've snared their men.'

'I see,' he said.

'So let us be friends. How does that sit with you?'

'I'd like to be friends,' he said, grinning. 'I've never had friends.'

'It'll be nice to have someone to talk to,' she told him.

'I don't talk very much,' he said, 'I never had anyone to practise with. I'm not terribly clever at it.'

'It's not clever that counts, Gaelen. Clever comes from the mind, truth from the heart. Now I will begin our friendship by telling you the truth. When Caswallon first rescued you I was worried, for we have a son. But I have thought long about it, and now I am glad. For I like you, and I know you will be happy with us. For our part, we will teach you to be a clansman.'

'I may not be very good at that either,' admitted the boy.

'It's not a matter of being good at it. Merely *being* is enough. It will not be easy for you, for Caswallon is not a popular man, and some will make it hard – perhaps even unpleasant – for you.'

'Why is he not popular?'

'That is a complex question. He is independent, and it has made him all that he has. He holds to the old ways of raiding and stealing from other clans. But there are other reasons that I think it best you find out for yourself.'

'He is a thief?'

443

She chuckled. 'Yes. Just like you.'

'Well, I like him. I don't care about the others.'

She laid a hand on his shoulder. 'Here is a first lesson for you, Gaelen: Care. That is what the clan is. We care. For one another. Even if we dispute matters, we still care. I tell you this. If Caswallon's house burned to the ground, even those who disliked him would gather round and help rebuild. If Caswallon died, I would be cared for should I need it. If Caswallon and I both died, little Donal would be taken in by another family – perhaps one that disliked us both – and raised with love.'

He had been hard to convince, especially after the early trouble with Agwaine. But at least he had found friends. Maeg sat by the bedside for a while, then moved to the window.

The moon was high, the mountains silver, the valley at peace. Behind her, Gaelen stirred and opened his eyes, seeing her silhouetted against the sky. 'Maeg,' he whispered.

She returned to the bedside. 'Yes?'

'Thank you.'

'For what?'

'For caring.'

Leaning down, she kissed his brow. 'Sleep well, young warrior,' she said.

Caswallon strolled up towards the cave, aware that the old man was watching him. Oracle's sunken blue eyes looked hard at the clansman. 'You look tired, man,' said Oracle as Caswallon sat beside him in the cave mouth.

'Aye, I am tired. And hurt by the suffering of those poor boys.'

'A bad day,' agreed the older man. For a time they sat in silence, then Oracle spoke again, 'It is always good to see you, my boy. But I sense there is something on your mind, so spit it out.'

Caswallon chuckled. 'As always, you miss little. Taliesen told me to speak to you; he said it would please him for you to tell the story of what happened beyond the Gate.'

'Aye, please him and shame me.' Oracle stood and wandered back into the cave, sitting beside the glowing fire. Caswallon joined him. Oracle filled two clay cups with watered wine, passing one to the younger man. 'I have told no one else this tale in twenty-five years. I trust you not to repeat it while I live.'

'You have my word on it,' Caswallon assured him.

'I wanted to be High King,' said Oracle, 'I felt it was my right after the battles I had led – and won. But the people rejected me. This much you know already. I took my followers and we overpowered the druids guarding the Vallon Gate. We passed through. At first it seemed that nothing had changed; the mountains remained the same, High Druin still stood sentinel over the lands of the clans. But it was different, Caswallon. In a land beset by war, a woman had become High Queen. Her name was Sigarni. For reasons which I cannot explain now – but which you will understand later – I shall say no more about her, save that my men and I helped her in her battles with the Outland army. We stayed for two years. I still wanted to be a king, to found my own dynasty. I returned, with the survivors of my men, to the Vallon Gate, and passed through once more. It was the biggest mistake of my life.'

The old man drained his wine and refilled the cup, this time adding no water. Looking at Caswallon, he smiled grimly. 'Cursed is the man who achieves his dreams. In this new land – after ten blood-drenched years – I did become King. I led my armies to victory after victory. Great victories, Caswallon. Great victories . . .' he fell silent.

'What happened?' asked the clansman.

'Failure and flight,' responded Oracle, with a sad smile. 'I was betrayed – but then I deserved to be. Just because a man desires to be a king, it does not necessarily follow that he will make a good one.' He sighed. 'But this is not what Taliesen wanted me to tell you. While I was fighting for my kingdom I made an alliance with a butchering killer named Agrist. I told him the secrets of the Gateways. After he had betrayed me, and plundered his way across my kingdom, he led his army through another Gate.' Oracle licked his lips. 'They arrived here forty years ago; they are the Aenir, Caswallon. I brought the Aenir to destroy us all.'

'They haven't destroyed us yet,' Caswallon pointed out.

'They are demons, Caswallon, unsurpassed in violence and terror. I have seen them fight. I told Gaelen the clans were strong, like wolves. It's true. But the Aenir will outnumber us by twenty to one. They live to conquer and kill.' Oracle looked up. 'Did Sigarni speak to you before she died? Did she mention me?'

'No, but she knew me, Oracle. Can you tell me how?'

Oracle shook his head. 'I could – but I won't. Trust me, Caswallon. All will be revealed to you. I can say no more.'

During the months that followed the horror in the mountains the five survivors found their lives had changed substantially. They were now young men, accepted as clansmen, but more than this they were the 'Five Beast Slayers'. A Farlain bard named Mesric had immortalised them in song and their deeds were the envy of the young boys of all clans.

The mystery of the Queen was much discussed, but upon that theme the druids remained silent. Taliesen had questioned the boys at length on their conversation with the woman, but he gave them no further hint as to her history. All five spent a great deal of time thinking back over the Hunt, and the changes it forced on them.

Layne, the deepest thinker, saw Gaelen with new eyes, seeking his company often and recognising in the scarred youngster the signs of a natural leader.

Lennox drove himself hard once his broken arm had mended. He hauled logs, lifted rocks, spent all his spare time building up his strength. The huge frame gathered power and added muscle and still he drove himself on. His strength had been something he could rely on in a world where his wits were not as keen as his brother's. The beast had been stronger and Lennox was determined no enemy would best him again.

Gwalchmai no longer feared being unpopular, born as this had been from a sense of inferiority. He had always known Gaelen was a leader, and been happy to follow. But he watched Lennox pushing himself to greater limits and recognised in the young giant the kind of fear he once had himself.

For Gaelen the world had changed. He realised now that his life of loneliness in the city had been, by a freak of chance, the perfect apprenticeship. He had learned early that a man had to rely on himself. More than this – that such a man was stronger than his companions. And yet, having tasted the chilling emptiness of a life alone, he could value the clan as no other clansman ever would.

There was a natural arrogance now about the tall young man with the white blaze in his red hair. He ran like the wind, revelling in his speed. And though his bowmanship was merely average, he threw a spear with more accuracy than many tried warriors. He boxed well, emotions in check as Caswallon had taught him, and his sword-work was dazzling. Yet the arrogance he showed in his skills was missing in his life, and this made him popular without effort on his part.

The wise men among the Farlain marked him well, watching his progress with increasing interest. All of which hurt Agwaine, who saw in Gaelen a rival for the ultimate prize.

The Hunt had changed Agwaine more than any of them. He had been schooled to believe he was more than special, a talented natural leader to follow his father. And nothing that had transpired in the mountains had changed that. All that had changed was that Agwaine feared Gaelen was the better man. Before the encounter with the beast he would have hated Gaelen for bringing home such a truth. Now he could not.

They took part in their first Games together in the five-mile run, Gaelen beating Agwaine by forty paces, the boys arriving home in ninth and tenth place.

Cambil had been furious. 'He is faster, Father,' said Agwaine, towelling the sweat from his face. 'There is nothing more to it.'

'You must work harder: drive yourself. You must not let him beat you ever again.'

Agwaine was stricken, and for the first time he saw his father in a fresh light. 'I will work harder,' he said.

Layne and Gwalchmai delighted the younger clansmen by competing to the finals of their events, Layne in the spear tourney and Gwalchmai in the bow. Layne took third prize, beating the

Loda champion into fourth place; Gwalchmai finished last of the eight finalists, but was satisfied, for by next year he would have added height and strength to his frame and believed he could win. For Lennox the Games were a sad affair, for his injured arm robbed him of the chance to lift the Whorl Stone.

Summer drifted into a mild autumn and on into a vicious winter.

Caswallon and Gaelen spent their time forking hay to the cattle and journeying high into the mountains to rescue sheep trapped in snowdrifts. It was a desperately hard time for all the clans, yet Gaelen absorbed the knowledge Caswallon imparted readily.

In winter, Caswallon told him as they sheltered from a fierce blizzard high on the eastern range, it is vital not to sweat. For sweat turns to ice beneath the clothing and a man can freeze to death in minutes. All movement should be slow and sure, and all camps prepared hours before dusk.

That afternoon, trapped by a fierce snow-squall, Caswallon had led them to a wooded ridge. Here he had pulled four saplings together, tying them with thongs. Then he carefully threaded branches between them and built a fire in the centre. As the snow continued it piled against the branches, creating a round shelter with thick white walls. The fire within heated the walls to solid ice and the two men were snug and safe.

'Make the storm work for you,' said Caswallon, stripping off his sheepskin jerkin and allowing the fire's heat to reach his skin. 'Take off your outer clothes, Gaelen.'

'I'll freeze,' answered the young man, rubbing his cold hands together.

'Clothes keep heat in, but similarly they can keep heat out. Remove your coat.'

Gaelen did as he was told, grinning sheepishly as the heat in the shelter struck him.

Later Gaelen found himself staring into the glowing coals, his mind wandering. He rubbed his eyes and scratched at the jagged scar above.

'What are you thinking?' Caswallon asked.

'I was thinking of the Queen.'

448

'What about her?'

'About her coming again.'

'She is dead, Gaelen. Dead and buried.'

'I know. But she seemed so sure. I wonder who she was.'

'A Queen – and I would guess a great one,' said Caswallon. Silence settled around them, until Caswallon suddenly grinned. 'What's this I hear about you and Deva?'

At the mention of Agwaine's sister Gaelen began to blush.

'Aha!' said Caswallon, sitting up. 'There is more to this business than rumour.'

'There's nothing,' protested Gaelen. 'Really, there's nothing. I've hardly even spoken to her. And when I do, my tongue gets caught in my teeth and I seem to have three feet.'

'That bad?'

'It's not anything. I just . . .' Glancing up, he saw Caswallon raise his right eyebrow, his face mock-serious. Gaelen began to giggle. 'You swine. You're mocking me.'

'Not at all. I've never been one to mock young love,' said Caswallon.

'I'm not in love. And if I was, there would be no point. Cambil cannot stand me.'

'Do not let that worry you, Gaelen. Cambil is afraid of many things, but if young Deva wants you he will agree. But then it's a little early to think of marriage. Another year.'

'I know that. And I was not talking about marriage . . . or love. A man can like a girl, you know.'

'Very true,' admitted Caswallon. 'I liked Maeg the first moment I saw her.'

'It is not the same thing at all.'

'You'll make a fine couple.'

'Will you stop this? I'm going to sleep,' said Gaelen, curling his blanket around him. After a few moments he opened his eyes to see Caswallon was still sitting by the fire looking down at him.

Gaelen grinned. 'She's very tall – for a girl, I mean.'

'She certainly is,' agreed Caswallon, 'and pretty.'

'Yes. Do you really think we'd make a good couple?'

'No doubt of it.'

'Why is it that whenever I talk to her the words all tumble out as if they've been poured from a sack?'

'Witchcraft,' said Caswallon.

'A pox on you,' snorted Gaelen. 'I'm definitely going to sleep.'

The winter passed like a painful memory. Losses had been high among the sheep and calves, but spring was warm and dry, promising good harvests in summer.

Cambil accepted an invitation from Asbidag, leader of the Northern Aenir, to visit Ateris, now called Aesgard. Cambil took with him twenty clansmen. He was treated royally and responded by inviting Asbidag and twenty of his followers to the Summer Games.

Caswallon's fury stunned Maeg, who had never seem him lose control. His face had turned chalk-white, his hands sweeping across the pine table top and smashing pottery to shards.

'The fool!' he hissed. 'How could he do such a thing?'

'You think the danger is that great from twenty men?' Maeg asked softly, ignoring the ruined jugs and goblets.

Caswallon said nothing. Taking his cloak and staff, he left the house and set off in a loping run towards the hills and the cave of Oracle.

Taliesen sealed shut the door to his private chambers and opened a small, hidden recess in the wall. Reaching in he touched a sensor and light bathed the small room, radiating from panels set in the four walls. With another touch he activated the viewer. The oak veneer of his crudely carved desk-top slid back and revealed a dark screen, which rose into a vertical position. Taliesen moved to the rear wall. Scores of paper sheets were pinned to the panelling here, each covered in lines and scrawled with symbols. To the unskilled eye the drawings would appear to be of winter trees, with hundreds of tiny, leafless branches. Taliesen stared at them, remembering the perilous journeys through the Gateways that each represented. Here and there, on every sheet a branch would end with a single stroke drawn through it. By each was a hastily drawn star. Taliesen counted them. Forty-eight. On the desk-top, beside the dark screen, was a newly drawn tree which showed no stars. Taliesen pinned it to the wall.

This was the tree of the Hawk Eternal.

The tree where Sigarni regained her sword that was stolen. Where she did not die in some last despairing battle, but survived to reach the Farlain and save the children. Taliesen gazed at the drawing. 'Simple to see,' he said, 'but where are you? Which of the Time Lines will bring me to you?'

Seating himself before the screen, he opened the right-hand desk drawer and removed a round earring with a spring clip. It was in the shape of a star. Clipping it to his ear, he closed his eyes. The screen flickered, then brightened. Taliesen took a deep, calming breath and opened his eyes.

'Be careful,' he warned himself. 'Do not seek to see too much. Concentrate on the minutiae.' The screen darkened, and with a soft curse Taliesen reached up and touched the star upon his ear, pressing it firmly. The screen leapt to life, and the old druid stared hard at the scene which appeared there.

For more than an hour he watched, occasionally scribbling short notes to aid his memory. Then he removed the earring, touched a button below the desk-top and stood. The screen folded down, the oak veneer covered it once more.

Taliesen studied the notes, adding a line here and there. Rising, he moved to the wall, pinning the notes alongside the tree of the Hawk Eternal. He shook his head. 'Somewhere there is a rogue element,' he said, 'and it has not yet shown its face. What, where and when?' A thought struck him and his mouth tightened. 'Or perhaps I should be asking: Who?' he mused.

'Pah! Do not be so foolish,' he told himself. There is no one. You are the Master of the Gates, and the rogue element is a figment of your paranoia. If there was someone you would have found him by now. Or seen greater evidence to point towards him. You are an old fool! The secret lies with the Hawk Eternal – and you will teach him.'

His eyes were drawn to the stars scrawled on the sheets. Focusing on each, he dragged the painful memories from the depths of his mind. The most galling of them was the last. Having defeated Earl Jastey, Sigarni contracted a fever and died in the night. By Heaven, that was hard to take. Taliesen had all but given up then.

For several months he had made no attempt to scan the Lines, in order to find a new Sigarni. The quest felt hopeless. Yet as he gazed down on the valleys of the Farlain, and at the butchery taking place in the lowlands, he knew he had to struggle on.

Intending to make more notes now, Taliesen returned to his desk. Weariness swamped him as he sat, and his laid his head on his arms. Sleep took him instantly.

What had once been the gleaming marble hall of the Ateris Council was now strewn with straw and misty with the smoke from the blazing log-fire set in a crudely built hearth by the western wall. A massive pine table was set across the hall, around which sat the new Aenir nobility. At their feet, rolling in the straw and scratching at fleas, were the war hounds of Asbidag – seven sleek black fierce-eyed dogs, trained in the hunt.

Asbidag himself sat at the centre of the table facing the double doors of bronze-studded oak. Around him were his seven sons, their wives, and a score of war councillors. Beside the huge Aenir lord sat a woman dressed in black. Slim she was, and the gown of velvet seemed more of a pelt than a garment. Her jet-black hair hung to her pale shoulders and gleamed as if oiled; her eyes were slanted and, against the sombre garb, seemed to glitter like blue jewels, bright and cold; her mouth was full-lipped and wide, and only the mocking half-smile robbed it of beauty.

Asbidag casually laid his hand on her thigh, watching her closely, a gap-toothed grin showing above his blood-red beard.

'Are you anxious for the entertainment to begin?' he asked her.

'When it pleases you, my lord,' she said, her voice husky and deep.

Asbidag heaved himself to his feet. 'Bring in the prisoner,' he bellowed.

'By Vatan, I've waited a long time for this,' whispered Ongist, swinging round on his stool to face the door.

Drada said nothing. He had never cared much for torture, though it would have been sheer stupidity to mention it. The way of the Grey God was the way of the Aenir, and no one questioned either.

Drada's eyes flickered to his other brothers as they waited for the prisoner to be dragged forth. Tostig, large and cruel, a man well-known for his bestial appetites. Ongist, the second youngest, a clever lad with the morals of a timber-wolf. Aeslang, Barsa and Jostig, sons of Asbidag's long-time mistress Swangild. They remained in favour despite Asbidag's murder of their mother – in fact they seemed unmoved by the tragedy – but then Swangild had been a ruthless woman as devoid of emotion as the black-garbed bitch who had replaced her. Lastly there was Orsa the Baresark, dim-witted and dull, but in battle a terrible opponent who screeched with laughter as he slew.

The sons of Asbidag . . .

The great doors swung open, admitting two warriors who half-dragged, half-carried a shambling ruin of a man. His clothes were in rags, his body covered in weeping sores and fresh switch-scars which oozed blood. His hands were misshapen and swollen, the fingers broken and useless, but even so, his wrists were tied together. The guards released the man and he sank to the floor, groaning as his weight fell on his injured hands.

Drada stole a glance at his father's mistress. Morgase was watching the crippled man closely. Her eyes shone, her white cheeks were flushed and her tongue darted out over her stained red lips. He shuddered and returned his gaze to the man who had commanded the lowland army. He had met him once at court; a strong, proud warrior who had risen through the ranks to command the northern legions. Now he lay weeping like a babe at the feet of his conquerors.

'Now that is how an enemy should look,' said Asbidag. Dutiful laughter rose around him as he left the table to stand over the prisoner. 'I have good news for you, Martellus,' he said, turning the man over with his foot, 'I'm going to kill you at last.'

The man's swollen eyes fought to focus and his mouth sagged open, showing the remains of his teeth, black and broken.

'Are you not going to thank me, man?'

Just for that one moment Drada saw a glint of anger in the man's eyes. For a fleeting second manhood returned to the ruined warrior. Then it passed and tears reformed.

'How should we kill him, Morgase?' asked Asbidag, swinging his body to face the table.

'Let the dogs have him,' she whispered.

'Poison my dogs? No. Another way.'

'Hang him in a cage outside the city walls until he rots,' shouted Tostig.

'Impale him,' said Ongist.

Drada shifted in his seat, forcing his mind from the spectacle. For more than a year one task had filled his waking hours: planning the defeat of the clans.

The problems were many. The clans had the advantage of terrain but, on the other hand, they lacked any form of military discipline and their villages were widely spaced and built without walls. Each clan mistrusted the others and that was an advantage for the Aenir. They could pick them off one by one.

But it would be a massive operation, needing colossal planning.

Drada had worked for months to be allowed to enter the Farlain with a small company of men. Always his requests had been politely refused. Now, at last, Cambil had agreed they should be guests at the Games. It was a gift from the Grey God.

All the clans gathered in one place, a chance to meet every chieftain and Hunt Lord. An opportunity for the Aenir to scout valleys, passes and future battlegrounds.

Drada was hauled back to the present, even as the hapless prisoner was dragged from the hall. Asbidag's shadow fell across him. 'Well, Drada, what do you think?'

'Of what, Father?'

'Of my decision with Martellus?'

'Very fitting.'

'How would you know that?' snapped Asbidag. 'You were not listening.'

'True, father, but then you have planned his death for so long that I knew you would have something special for him.'

'But it doesn't interest you?'

'It does, sire, but I was thinking about that problem you set me today, and I have a plan that may please you.'

'We will talk later,' said Asbidag, returning to his place beside Morgase.

'They're going to skin him,' whispered Ongist to Drada.

'Thank you.'

'Why must you take such risks?'

'I don't know. I was thinking about something else.'

'It is good you are a thinker, brother. For you know Father cannot stand you.'

'I know – but then I think he likes none of us.'

Ongist laughed aloud. 'You could be right,' he whispered, 'but he raised us to be like him, and we are. If I thought I'd get away with it I'd gut the bloated old toad. But you and my other dear brothers would turn on me. Wouldn't you?'

'Of course. We are a family built on hatred.'

'And yet we thrive,' said Ongist, pouring mead into his cup and raising it to toast his brother.

'Indeed, we do, brother.'

'This plan of yours, it concerns the clans?'

'Yes.'

'I hope you suggest invasion. Boredom sits ill with me.'

'Wait and see, Ongist.'

'We've waited a year already. How much longer?'

'Not long. Have patience.'

The following afternoon Drada made his way to the ruins of the Garden of the Senses, a half-acre of blooms, trees and shrubs that had once been a place of meditation for the Ateris intellectuals. Many of the winding paths had disappeared now, along with a hundred or so delicate flowers choked by weeds and man's indifference.

And yet, so far, the roses thrived. Of all things Drada had yet encountered on this cruel world, the rose alone found a place in his

455

feelings. He could sit and gaze at them for hours, their beauty calming his mind and allowing him to focus on his problems and plans.

As he had on so many such afternoons, Drada pushed his way through the trailing undergrowth to a rock-pool fringed with wooden benches. Unclipping the brooch which fastened his red cloak, he chose the west-facing bench and sat in the sunshine.

Unwilling to incur Asbidag's displeasure, he had spent the morning watching the flaying of Martellus. The scene had been an unpleasant distraction to the young Aenir warrior; he had seen men flayed before, indeed had witnessed more barbarous acts. And they bored him. But then most of what life had to offer ultimately left Drada bored. It seemed to the young warrior that the journey from birth screech to death rattle was no more than a meaningless series of transient pleasures and pain, culminating at last in the frustration of missed moments and lost opportunities.

He thought of his father and grinned wolfishly. Asbidag, the destroyer of nations, the bringer of blood. The most brutish warrior of a generation of warriors. He had nothing to offer the world, save ceaseless agony and destruction. He had no genuine thoughts of empire, for it was alien to him to consider building anything of worth. He lived to fight and kill, dreaming only of the day when at last he would be summoned to the hall of the Grey God to recite the litany of his conquests.

Drada shivered, though the sun was warm.

Asbidag had sired eleven sons. Three had died in other wars, one had been strangled by Asbidag soon after birth during a row with the mother. She had died less easily.

Now seven sons remained. And what a brood, cast as they were in the image of their father.

Of them all Drada hated Tostig the most. A vile man of immense power, Tostig possessed all the innate cruelty of the natural coward. A pederast who could only gratify himself by killing the victims of his lust. One day I will kill you, thought Drada. When Father is dead. I will kill you all. No, he thought. Not all. I will spare Orsa

456

the Baresark, for he has no ambition, and despite his frenzy in battle, carries no hate.

Drada leaned his head back, closing his eyes against the bright sunlight.

'So this is where you plan your campaigns.'

Drada opened his eyes. 'Welcome, lady. Please join me.' He didn't like to be disturbed here, but with Morgase he was careful to mask his feelings.

As always she was dressed in black, this time a shimmering gown of silk and satin. Her dark hair was braided, hanging over one marble-white shoulder. She sat beside him, draping her arm along the back of the bench, her fingers hovering near his neck. 'Always so courteous, Drada. A rare thing among the Aenir.'

'My father sent me away as a child to the court of Rhias. I was brought up there.'

'You were a hostage?'

'More a viper in the bosom of a future enemy.'

'I see.' Her hand dropped to his shoulder, squeezing the firm flesh of his upper arm. 'Why do you not like me?' she asked, her bright eyes mocking him.

'I do not dislike you,' he countered, with an easy lie. 'But let us assume that I made love to you here and now. By tonight my bloody corpse would be alongside the unfortunate Martellus.'

'Perhaps,' she said, interest fading from her eyes. She took her hand from his shoulder and glanced around the garden. 'A pretty place.'

'Yes.'

'Are you planning a war against the clans?'

'They are not the enemy.'

'Come now, Drada, do you think I never talk with your father? Do you see me merely as a mistress? Someone who shares only his bed?'

'No, Lady.'

'Then tell me.'

'I am planning for our visit to the Farlain. We have been invited to view the Games.'

457

'How dull.'

'Indeed it is,' he agreed.

'Tell me, then, if you *were* planning a war against the clans, how would you go about it?'

'This is a game?'

'Why not?'

'Very well. First tell me how *you* would plan it, Lady, and then I shall add my own refinements.'

'Are you always this cautious?'

'Always,' he said, smiling.

She leaned back, closing her eyes as she relaxed in thought. She was beautiful but Drada instantly quelled the desire that surged within him. It confused him momentarily, for in the six months she had been with Asbidag Drada had never been attracted to her. Her eyes flickered open and the answer came to him. There was something reptilian in those eyes. He shuddered.

'Extermination,' she said triumphantly.

'Explain,' he whispered.

'Conquering a city can be considered in a number of ways. You may desire to take over the existing enterprise of that city; therefore you would take it with a minimum loss of life and make the inhabitants your servants. In this way you would merely transfer ownership of the enterprise. But with the clans it is a different matter. The Aenir desire only the land, and obviously the livestock. But not the people. They are a wild race, they would not tolerate serfdom. Therefore an invasion against the Farlain would be a prelude to the extermination of the people.'

'You would not advocate taking the women as slaves?' asked Drada.

'No. Use them by all means to satisfy the lusts of the warriors, but then kill them. Kill all the clans. Then the land is truly Aenir.'

'That is fine as the object of the war. How would you go about invasion?'

'I don't know the terrain, and therefore could not supply answers to logistical problems,' said Morgase.

'Neither do I.'

458

'And that is why you plan so carefully for your visit to their Games?'

'You speak of logistical problems, Morgase. You have been involved in the planning of war?'

'Are you surprised?'

He considered the question for a moment. 'No, I am not.'

'Good. We should be friends, Drada, for we have much in common.'

'It would appear so, Lady.'

'Tell me then, as a friend, what do you think of me.'

'I think you are intelligent and beautiful.'

'Don't speak the obvious,' she snapped. 'Speak the truth.'

'I do not know enough about you to form a stronger opinion. Before today I thought you were merely an attractive woman, bright enough, who had seduced my father. Now I must think again.'

'Indeed you must. For I have plans of my own – great plans. And you can help me.'

'How so?'

'First the Aenir must take the Farlain. Then we will talk.'

'Why is that so important? You have no dealings with the clans; they can mean nothing to you.'

'But then, my dear Drada, you do not know all that I know. There is a prize within the Farlain beyond the understanding of lesser mortals: the gateway to empires beyond counting.'

'How do you know this?'

'It is enough that I know.'

'What do you seek, Morgase?'

Her eyes glittered and she laughed, reaching out to stroke his bearded face, 'I seek revenge, my handsome thinker. Simply that, for now.'

'On whom?'

'On a woman who murdered my father and ordered my mother raped. A woman who stole an empire that ought to have been mine – that *would* have been mine.' Her reptilian eyes glittered as she spoke, and her tongue darted over her lips. Drada hid his distaste. 'Will you be my friend, Drada? Will you aid me in my quest?'

459

'I serve my father, Lady. But I will be your friend.'

'I admire caution, Drada,' she said, rising. Her fingers stroked the skin of his throat and he was amazed to find arousal once more stirring his blood, 'I admire it – as long as it is accompanied by ambition. Are you ambitious?'

'I am the son of Asbidag,' he said softly.

As he watched her leave, the fear began. He had underestimated her. She was chilling, clever and utterly ruthless. Yet another viper in our basket, he thought.

Caswallon was gone for three days, returning just after dawn as Maeg administered to the infant, Donal. He stood silently in the doorway, listening to the gentle words she crooned as she cleaned and oiled him. Caswallon closed his eyes for a moment, his emotions rising and threatening to unman him. He cleared his throat. She turned, her hair falling across her face, then she swept it back and smiled.

He knelt beside her. The child reached for him, giggling. Caswallon lifted the boy and patted his back as his son's small chubby arms tried to encircle his neck.

Caswallon returned Donal to his mother, who dressed him in a woollen undershirt and a light tunic, and they moved downstairs to the kitchen where Kareen was preparing breakfast. Leaving Donal with the girl, Caswallon took Maeg by the hand and they left the house to watch sunrise over Druin. Maeg said nothing as they walked, sensing the weight of sadness Caswallon carried.

They reached the crest of a hill and sat beneath a spreading oak. 'I am so sorry, Maeg, my love,' said Caswallon, taking her hand and kissing it.

'For what? A man will give way to anger now and again.'

'I know. But you are the one person in the world I'd never seek to hurt.'

'Foolish man, do you think you can hurt me with a little broken crockery?'

'Why did you marry me?' he asked suddenly.

'Why are men so foolish?' she countered.

'No, I mean it. Why?'

She looked at him closely and then, seeing the sorrow in his green eyes, sensed the burden he was bearing. Reaching up, she stroked his beard and then curled her arm about his neck and pulled him down to kiss her.

'No one can answer such a question. I didn't like you when you approached me at the Games; I saw you as an arrogant Farlain raider. But after Maggrig sent you away I found myself thinking about you often. Then, when I awoke that day and found you in my room, I hated you. I wanted you slain. But as the days passed thoughts of you grew in my mind. And when you walked into the Long Hall on that winter's night, your beard stiff with ice, I knew that I loved you. But now tell me why you risked your life to wed me.'

Gently he eased her from him, cupping her face in his hands. 'Because before I saw you I had no life to lose,' he said simply.

For a long time they sat beneath the tree, saying nothing, enjoying the warmth of the risen sun, until at last Maeg spoke. 'Now tell me truly, Caswallon, what is troubling you?'

'I cannot. I have given a promise. But I can say this: the old days are finished, and what we have here is perhaps the last golden summer of the Farlain. I know this, and the knowledge destroys me.'

'The Aenir?' she asked.

'And our own stupidity.'

'No one lives for ever, Caswallon. A man, or a woman, may die at any time. That is why today is so important.'

'I know.'

'Yes, you do. But you've not lived it. Suppose you are right, and the Aenir destroy us next month, or next year. Suppose, further, that they kill us both . . .'

'No! I'll not even think of that!'

'Think of it!' she commanded, pulling away from him. 'What difference all this heartache? For the Aenir are not here today. On this morning we have each other. We have Donal and Gaelen. We have peace, we have love. How often have you said that tomorrow's problems can be dealt with tomorrow?'

'But I could have changed it.'

'And that is the real reason for your sorrow. You refused to be considered for Hunt *Lord,* and denied yourself a place on the Council. Now you suffer for it. But one man will not thwart a race like the Aenir. They are killers all. What do they seek? War and death. Conquest and bloodshed. They will pass, for they build nothing.'

'I have made you angry,' he said.

'Yes, you have, for you have allowed fear to find a place in your heart. And there it has grown to fill you with defeat. And that is not what I expect from you, Caswallon of the Farlain.'

'What do you expect?' he asked, smiling.

'I expect you to be a man always. You are angry because Cambil has allowed an Aenir company to attend the Games.'

'Yes.'

'Why?'

'Because they will scout our lands and learn that which should have cost them blood.'

'Then see they are escorted here. Surround them with Scouts.'

'I cannot do that. The Council . . .'

'A pox on the Council! You are one of the richest men in the three valleys. As such, you are a man of influence. There are others who agree with you: Leofas, for example. Find a hundred men to do your bidding. And one more thing. Kareen was walking on the east hills yesterday and she saw men running round the walls of Ateris. Others were practising with the bow and spear.'

'So? The Aenir have Games of their own.'

'We've not seen such a practice before.'

'What are you suggesting?'

'The Aenir are bringing twenty men. I think they will ask to be allowed to take part in the Games.'

'For what purpose?'

'To win.'

'It would never be allowed.'

'Cambil is Games Lord this year,' she said.

'It is unthinkable,' he whispered. 'But there could be many advantages. If they could prove themselves superior it would boost the morale of their warriors and, equally, diminish our own. And they would earn the right to travel the mountains.'

'That is better. That is the Caswallon I know.'

'Indeed it is. I should have spoken to you before, Maeg.'

Caswallon took Gaelen and Gwalchmai with him to observe the strange antics of the Aenir. It seemed that half of Asbidag's army at Aesgard was at play. The plain before the city was sectioned off by tents, stalls and ropes, creating a running track, an archery field, a series of spear lanes, and a vast circle at the centre of which men wrestled and boxed, or fought with sword and shield. Strength events were also under way.

'It is like the Games,' said Gwalchmai. 'How long have they been doing this?'

Caswallon shrugged. 'Kareen saw them yesterday.'

'They have some fine athletes,' observed Gaelen. 'Look at that white-haired runner leading the pack. He moves like the wind.'

On the plain below Drada and Ongist were watching the foot races with interest. Ongist had wagered ten pieces of gold on Snorri Wolfson to beat Drada's favourite, the ash-blond Borak. Snorri was trailing by thirty paces when they reached the last lap.

'A curse on the man!' snarled Ongist.

'He is a sprinter,' said Drada, grinning. 'He's not built for distance.'

'What about a wager against Orsa?'

Drada shook his head. 'No one will beat him in the strength events.' The brothers wandered across the running track to the twelve men contesting the weights. They were drawing lots to decide which man would first attempt the hurling and Drada and Ongist settled on the grass as the draw was decided.

One man approached a cart on which was set a block of marble. It was shaped as a ball and carefully inscribed with the names of Ateris' greatest poets. Before today it had rested on a velvet-covered stand in the city library.

It weighed over sixty pounds.

The man placed his hand on either side of the sphere, bent his knees and lifted it to his chest. He approached the marker stake, hoisted the sphere above his head and, with a grunt of effort, threw it forward. With a dull thud it buried itself in the ground some five paces ahead. Three officials prised it loose with spears and rolled it back to the marker stake, lifting it for the next thrower.

Drada and Ongist watched with scant interest as the men took their turns until, at last, Orsa stripped himself of his shirt and stood grinning by the stake. He waved to his brothers.

Two officials lifted the sphere into his arms. Even before they were clear Orsa shifted the weight to his right hand, dipped his shoulder and hurled the sphere into the air. It sailed over the other marks by some three paces; as it landed it shattered into a score of pieces.

'Must have hit a buried rock,' muttered Ongist.

Orsa ambled across to them. 'Easy,' he said, pointing at the ruined marble.

Drada nodded. 'You are still the strongest, brother.'

'No need for proof,' said Orsa. 'Waste of time.'

'True,' Drada agreed.

'I'm hungry,' said Orsa, wandering away without another word. Drada watched him go, marvelling anew at the sheer size of the man. His upper arms were as large as most men's thighs.

'By Vatan, he's a monster,' said Ongist.

Drada looked away. In a family of monsters it seemed ironic that Ongist should so describe the only one among them who hated no one.

High on the hillside the three clansmen stood to depart. They had seen enough. 'I think Maeg is right,' said Caswallon. Tell me, Gaelen, do you think you could beat that white-haired runner?'

'I fear we will find out next month,' said Gaelen. 'I think I can. But he wasn't stretched today; he set his own pace. Still, if they do bring a team I hope that giant comes with them. I'd love to see him against Lennox.'

6

Deva awoke in the first moments of dawn, as the sun lanced its light through the slats of her window. She yawned and stretched, rolling to her side to watch the dust-motes dance in the sunbeams. Kicking aside the down-filled quilt, she opened the shutters and leaned on the stone sill, breathing deeply.

The cool early-morning breeze held the promise of autumn, and already the leaves on the distant trees were dappled with rusty gold. Mountain ash and copper beech glistened and their leaves looked like coins, rich and freshly minted.

Deva was always first to rise. She could hear her brother Agwaine snoring in the next room. Stripping her woollen nightdress from her slender body, she poured water into a clay bowl and washed her face. She was a tall girl, willowy and narrow-hipped. Her features were clean-cut, not beautiful, but her large, grey eyes with traces of tawny gold gave her magnificence. Most of the young men of the Farlain had paid court to her and she rejected them all. The mother of kings! That's what the old tinker-woman had predicted at her birth. And Deva was determined to fulfil her destiny. She would not do that by marrying a Highland boy! Over the door hung a silvered mirror. Wiping the water from her face and neck she walked over to it, looking deep into her own eyes. Grey they were, but not the colour of arctic clouds, nor winter seas. They were the soft grey of a rabbit's pelt, and the glints of gold made them warm and welcoming. She smiled at herself, tilting her head.

She knew she was attractive. She combed her fingers through her corn-gold hair, shaking her head to untangle the knots. Then she remembered the visitors her father Cambil had welcomed the night before.

Asbidag, Lord of the Aenir! She shivered, crossing her arms. The Aenir was a large man with powerful shoulders and a spreading gut.

His face was broad, his mouth cruel and his eyes evil. Deva didn't like him.

No more did she like the woman he brought with him — Morgase, he called her. Her skin was white as any Ateris statue and she seemed just as cold.

Deva had heard much talk during the last few months about the dangers of the Aenir, and had dismissed it from her mind, believing as she did in the wisdom of her father. Last night she had thought afresh.

Asbidag brought two of his sons to the house. Both were handsome, and had they been Farlain Deva might have considered allowing them to join her at the Whorl Dance. The dark-haired Ongist had smiled at her, but his eyes betrayed his lust and she had lost interest in him. The other, Drada, had merely bowed and kissed her hand. Him she had seen before. His voice was deep, yet soft, and in his eyes she saw only a hint of mockery.

Now *he* was interesting . . .

Deva had been looking forward to the Games all summer. As the Games Maiden, elected by the Council, she would preside over the Whorl Dance and be the only woman to choose her dancing companions. No man could refuse the Games Maiden.

In her mind's eye she could see herself walking the lines of waiting men, stopping momentarily, lifting a hand. She would halt by Gaelen and smile. As he stepped forward, she would walk on and choose Layne.

She giggled. Perhaps she would choose Gaelen . . .

The thoughts were delicious.

She dressed quickly in a flowing, skirt of leaf-green and a russet shirt with billowing sleeves. Then she walked downstairs.

The woman Morgase was in the kitchen, talking to Drada. Their conversation ceased as she entered. 'Good morning,' she said as they turned.

They nodded at her and she felt uncomfortable, as if she had blundered in on a secret assignation. Moving past them, she opened the kitchen door and walked into the yard beyond.

The Games fields in the valley below were ablaze with colour. Tents of every shade and hue had sprouted overnight like immense flowers. Ropes had been staked, creating tracks and lanes, and enormous trestle tables were ready for the barter of goods. Several cooking-pits had been dug in preparation for the barbecue and the barrels of mead were set in the centre of the field where the Whorl Stone had been placed on a bulging hill.

Already the clans were gathering. Her eyes scanned the surrounding hillsides. Everywhere was movement. They came from the Pallides, the Haesten, the Loda, the Irelas, the Dunilds, the Clouds – from every clan, large and small.

Today they would muster and pitch their tents. Tomorrow Cambil, the Games Lord, would announce the order of events. And then Deva would start the first race.

Movement to her left caught her eye. She turned and watched as the Druid Lord approached her. 'Good morning, Taliesen,' she said, smiling to hide her apprehension. She didn't like the old man; he made her skin crawl and she had often heard her father speak of his eldritch magic.

'Good morning, Deva. How is the Games Maiden?'

'I am well, my Lord. And you?'

'I am as you see me.'

'You never seem to change.'

'All men change. You cannot fight the years. I wondered if you might do me a small service?'

'Of course.'

'Thank you. Will you walk with me a way?'

'Where?' she asked, fear taking the place of apprehension.

'Do not worry. I shall not harm you. Come.'

The old man moved away towards the western woods and Deva followed some paces behind. Once in the trees Taliesen stopped and retrieved a long bundle lying behind a fallen trunk. Unwrapping it, he removed the sword found by Agwaine.

'What are you doing?' asked Deva, stepping back.

'This must be returned to its owner,' he told her.

'I thought the old woman was dead.'

'She is – and she is not.'

Deva felt the colour ooze from her face. 'You're not going to conjure her ghost?'

'No, not her ghost.' He smiled gently. 'Trust me, little one. Take the sword in your hands.' He offered it to her, hilt forward. She took it; it was heavy but she was strong and held it firmly.

Taliesen closed his eyes and started to whisper sibilantly in a language Deva had never heard. The air about her began to crackle and a strange odour pervaded the wood. She wanted to run, but was frozen in fear.

The druid's eyes opened and he leaned towards Deva. 'Walk into the mist,' he said. Deva blinked and stepping back she saw a thick grey mist seeping up from the ground, billowing like smoke some ten paces before her. There is no danger, girl,' snapped Taliesen.

Deva hesitated. 'What is waiting there?'

'You will see. Trust me.' Still she did not move and Taliesen's patience snapped. 'By God, are you a Farlain woman or some lowland wench afraid of her own shadow?'

Deva steeled herself and walked forward, holding the sword two-handed, the blade pointing the way. The mist closed around her. Ahead she saw flickering lights. Her feet were cold now. She glanced down and saw, to her amazement, that she was walking in water. No, not in. Upon! Momentarily she stopped as a large silver fish swam beneath her. 'Go on!' came the voice of Taliesen in her mind.

To her right she heard the sound of a waterfall but it was strangely muted, muffled. Looking straight ahead she walked across the lake pool, and saw a crowd of armed men at the poolside carrying torches. At their centre stood a young woman. She was beautiful, though her hair was bright silver, and she wore dark armour.

'Stop now!' came Taliesen's voice. Deva waited, the sword heavy in her hands. The warrior woman waded out into the pool. The water was thigh-deep as she approached where Deva stood.

'Who are you?' the armoured woman asked.

'Say nothing!' ordered Taliesen. 'Give her the sword.'

Obediently Deva reversed the blade, offering it to the woman.

For a moment their eyes met, and Deva felt chilled by the power in the other's gaze. 'Can you read the future, spirit?' asked the Queen. Taliesen whispered another order and Deva turned away, walking slowly back across the surface of the pool and re-entering the mist.

The old druid waited for her in the sunshine. He was sitting on the grass, his cloak of feathers wrapped around his scrawny shoulders, his face grey with exhaustion.

Deva knelt beside him. 'Who was she?' she asked.

'A Queen in another time,' he answered. 'Tell no one of what passed here today.'

The following day almost four thousand clansmen, women and children thronged the fields, gathering round the Whorl Hill on which was set the legendary stone of Earis, by which he had pledged to lead the Farlain to safety beyond the Gate. The stone itself was black, but studded with clusters of pearl-white deposits which caught the sunlight and sparkled like tiny gems. Although a man could encompass it with his arms, it weighed more than two hundred pounds.

Around the stone stood the Hunt Lords of the clans, and in their midst Asbidag of the Aenir. The clan lords were clearly uncomfortable.

Maggrig of the Pallides was furious. The Games were a clan affair, yet last night Cambil had sprung upon them his invitation for the Aenir to enter a team. The argument had raged for over an hour.

'Are you mad?' Maggrig had stormed. 'Has the addled Farlain mind finally betrayed you?'

'I am the Games Lord this year. They are on Farlain land; it is my decision,' Cambil answered, fighting to control his anger.

'Be that as it may, Cambil,' put in the white haired Laric, Hunt Lord of the Haesten, 'but should any one man be allowed to set a precedent others will be forced to follow?' He was known to be a man rarely aroused to anger. Yet his thin face was flushed now, his fists clenched.

'It is my decision,' Cambil repeated stonily.

Laric bit back his anger. 'The Aenir have no friends – only vassals. They have tried to scout all our lands and been turned back.

You realise that if they win outright we are obliged to allow them access? The Games Champions can travel and hunt where they will.'

'They will not win,' said Cambil. 'They are not clansmen.'

'Calling you a fool serves nothing,' said Laric, 'for you have proven that beyond my speculation. What breaks my heart is that one man's foolishness could bring about the ruin of the clans.' There was a gasp from the assembled Hunt Lords and Cambil sat very still, his face ashen.

Maggrig rose. 'I am tempted to take the Pallides home, away from this stupidity, yet I cannot,' he said, 'for without them the Aenir would have a greater chance of victory. I suspect it is the same for every lord here. But I tell you this, Cambil. Until now I have had scant respect from you. From today even that is a thing of the past. It matters not a whit to me if the Farlain are run by a fool; that hurts only the Farlain. But when you put the Pallides at risk I cannot forgive you.'

Colour drained from Cambil's face. 'How dare you! You think I care what some pot-bellied out-clan thinks of me? Take your ragbag carles home. With or without the Aenir your Pallides would win nothing, only humiliation.'

'Hark, the Aenir lapdog can still bark,' snapped Maggrig.

'Enough of this!' stormed Laric, as Maggrig and Cambil moved towards one another. 'Listen to me. I have no love for the Farlain, nor for the Pallides. But we are clansmen and no man will violate the spirit of the Games. There will be no violence among the Hunt Lords. The thing has been done and long will it be argued over. But it is *done*. Now let us consider the order of events, or we'll be here all night.'

Later, as Maggrig and Laric walked back to their tents in the moonlight, the taller Haesten lord was deep in thought. Maggrig also kept silent. Laric – the oldest Hunt Lord in Druin, approaching sixty years of age – was also by far the wisest. Maggrig liked him, though he'd swallow live coals rather than tell him so.

They reached Laric's tent first and the older man turned to Maggrig, resting a hand on his shoulder. 'Cambil is a fool. He cannot see that which should be clear to every clansman. The Aenir are tomorrow's enemy. My land borders yours, Maggrig, and we have had many disputes ere now, but if the Aenir cross Pallides land I shall bring my clansmen to your aid.'

Maggrig smiled. It was a nice ploy, but the fact remained that for the Aenir to cross Pallides borders they must march through either Farlain land or Haesten – and the Haesten were less powerful than the Farlain. Laric was asking for an ally.

'Between us we have perhaps two thousand fighting men,' said Maggrig. 'Do you think they could stop an Aenir army?'

'Perhaps.'

'Agreed, then. We will be allies. I would expect, of course, to be War Lord.'

'Of course,' said Laric. 'Good night.'

The following morning Maggrig stood alongside Asbidag, biting back his anger. The two men could have been brothers. Both had striking red beards flecked with silver, both were powerfully built. Deva watched them with anxiety. They were so similar – until you looked into their eyes. There was no evil in Maggrig. Deva looked away.

Cambil's opening speech of welcome was short, and he quickly outlined the order of the Games. The first event would be the mountain run, five miles on a twisting circuit through woods and valleys. Three hundred men were entered and the Hunt Lords had decided on six qualifying races. The first five in each race would contest two semi-finals, and fifteen of the fastest, strongest clansmen would run the final on the last day.

Other qualifying events were outlined and then it was left to Deva, in a flowing dress of white linen garlanded with flowers, to signal the start of the first race. The named atheletes, Gaelen and Agwaine among them, jostled for position as Deva's arm swept up, hovered momentarily, then flashed down and the race began.

Caswallon watched the start, saw Gaelen running smoothly in the centre of the pack and, knowing the youth would qualify easily, strolled to the market stalls on the edge of the field.

The stalls were doing brisk business in brooches, daggers, trinkets and tools, cloth, furs, blankets and shoes, meats, cheeses, fruit and vegetables. Caswallon eased through the massed crowds seeking a necklace for Maeg. Finding nothing to his taste, he bought a jug of mead and an oatmeal loaf. There were still one or two empty tables at the edge of the field and he chose a place away from the crowd where he would be alone with his thoughts. Since his talk with Maeg he had been less obsessed with the Aenir threat but now, as was his way, he thought the problem through, examining every angle.

Morgase and Drada were sitting less than thirty paces away, but hidden by the crowd Caswallon did not see them. Morgase was bored, and her eyes flickered over the mass of people seeking something of even passing interest. She saw the tall man walking to the empty table and her gaze lingered, her eyes widening in alarm. He wore a leaf-green cloak and a tunic of polished brown leather, while across his chest hung a baldric bearing two slim daggers. By his side was a long hunting-knife. His trews were green laced with leather thongs. Morgase stared intently at the face. The short trident beard confused her, but the eyes were the same deep green she remembered so well.

And with such hatred . . .

She stood and walked over to where he sat. 'Good morning,' she said, her throat tight, her anger barely controlled.

Caswallon looked up. Before him was a woman dressed in black, a sleek-fitting gown that hid nothing of her slender figure. Her dark hair was braided and curled like a crown on her head and pinned with gold. He rose. 'Good morning, Lady.' He gestured for her to be seated and asked if he could bring her refreshments. Then she saw Drada approaching, carrying two goblets of wine.

'How are you, Caswallon?' asked Drada.

'Well. Will you introduce me to the lady?'

'You do not know me then?' asked Morgase, surprised.

'I have been known to be forgetful, Lady, but not insane. Such beauty as yours is unforgettable.'

472

She seemed confused, uncertain. 'You are very like someone I once knew. Uncannily like.'

'I hope he was a friend,' said Caswallon.

'He was not.'

'Then allow me to make up for it,' he said, smiling. 'Will you join me?'

'No, I must go. But please, since you two know each other, why don't you finish your drinks together?'

The men watched her walk away. 'A strange woman,' said Drada.

'Who is she?'

'Morgase, my father's consort. Beautiful but humourless.'

'She thought she knew me.'

'Yes. Are you taking part in the Games?'

'I am.'

'In what event?' asked Drada.

'Short sword.'

'I thought you were a runner?'

'I was. You are well-informed. And you?'

'No, I'm afraid I excel at very little.'

'You seem to excel in the field of selection,' said Caswallon. 'Rarely have I seen men train as hard.'

Drada smiled. 'The Aenir like to win.'

'I wonder why?'

'What does that mean? No man likes to lose.'

'True. But no clansman trains for the Games; they are an extension of his life and his natural skills. If he loses, he shrugs. It is not the end of the world for him.'

'Perhaps that is why you are clansmen, living a quiet life in these beautiful mountains, while the Aenir conquer the continent.'

'Yes, that is what I was thinking,' said Caswallon.

'Was it your idea to have us escorted here?'

'I was afraid you might get lost.'

'That was kind of you.'

'I am a kind man,' said Caswallon. 'I shall also see that you are escorted back.'

473

'Cambil assured us that would not be necessary. Or is he not the Hunt Lord?'

'Indeed he is, but we are a free people and the Hunt Lord is not omnipotent.'

'You take a great deal on yourself, Caswallon. Why can we not be friends? As you have seen, the Aenir have respected your borders. We trade. We are neighbours.'

'It is not necessary for you and me to play these games, Drada. I know what is in your heart. Like all killers, you fear that a greater killer will stalk you as you stalk others. You cannot exist with a free people on your borders. You must always be at war with someone. And one day, if you ever achieve your ambition, and the Aenir rule from sea to sea in every direction, even then it will not end. You will turn on yourselves like rabid wolves. Today you strike fear into men's hearts. But tomorrow? Then you will be thought of as a boil on the neck of history.'

The words were spoken without heat. Drada sipped his wine, then he looked up to meet Caswallon's gaze. 'I can see why you think as you do, but you are wrong. All new civilisations begin with bloodshed and horror, but as the years pass they settle down to prosper, to wax and to grow fat. Then, as they reach their splendid peak, a new enemy slips over the horizon and the bloodshed begins anew.'

'The Farlain will be your undoing,' said Caswallon. 'You are like the man poised to stamp on the worm beneath his feet – too far above it to see it is a viper.'

'Even so, when the man stamps the viper dies,' said Drada.

'And the man with it.'

Drada shrugged. 'All men die at some time.'

'Indeed they do, my bonny. But some die harder than others.'

For ten days the Games progressed and the fear of the Hunt Lords grew. The Aenir competed ferociously, bring new edge to the competitions. Gone was any semblance of friendly rivalry – the foreigners battled as if their lives depended on the result.

By the evening before the last day an overall Aenir victory had moved from possibility to probability. Only the athletes of the

Farlain could overhaul them. The Aenir had won all but two of the short sprint finals, had defeated Gwalchmai in the archery tourney, but lost to Layne in the spear. Caswallon had beaten the Aenir challenger in the short sword, but lost the final to Intosh, the Pallides swordsman. Gaelen and Agwaine had fought their way to the final five-mile race planned for the morrow, though Agwaine had only reached it when a Haesten runner twisted his ankle hurdling a fallen tree. His disappointment in qualifying in such a manner was deepened by the fact that the Aenir athlete, the white-haired Borak, had beaten Gaelen into second place in their semi-final.

Lennox, in an awesome display of sheer power, had strolled comfortably to the final of the strength event, but here he was to face the fearsome might of the giant Orsa, himself unbeaten. The Aenir had won grudging respect from the clansmen, but all the same the Games had been spoiled.

Cambil remained withdrawn throughout the tournament, knowing in his heart the scale of his error. The unthinkable was on the verge of reality. The Aenir were two events from victory. He had summoned Gaelen and Agwaine to him and the trio sat before the broad empty hearth of Cambil's home.

'Are you confident of beating this Borak, Gaelen?' Cambil asked, knowing now that his own son could not compete at their level.

Gaelen rubbed his eye, choosing his answer carefully, 'I saw no point in making a push yesterday; it would only show him the limit of my speed. But, on the other hand, he concealed from me his own reserves. No, I am not confident. But I think I can beat him.'

'What do you think, Agwaine?'

'I can only agree with Gaelen, Father. They are superbly matched. I would not be surprised either way.'

'You have both performed well and been a credit to the Farlain. Though you are adopted, Gaelen, you have the heart of a clansman. I wish you well.'

'Thank you, Hunt Lord.'

'Go home and rest. Do not eat too heavy a breakfast.'

Gaelen left the house and wandered to the pine fence before the yard. Turning, he looked up at Deva's window hoping to see a light. There was none. Disappointed, he opened the gate and began the short walk through the woods to Caswallon's house in the valley.

The night was bright, the moon full, and a light breeze whispered in the branches overhead. He thought about the race and its implications. It was true that he was not confident of victory, but he would be surprised if the Aenir beat him. He thought he had detected an edge of fatigue in the blond runner as he came off the mountain on the last circuit of the field. Gaelen hadn't pressed then, but had watched his opponent carefully. The man's head had been bobbing during the last two hundred paces, and his arms pumped erratically.

Gaelen had finished all of thirty paces adrift and it would be closer tomorrow. Caswallon had pointed out one encouraging thought; no one had yet tested Borak. Did he have the heart to match his speed?

A dark shadow leapt at Gaelen from the left, another from the right. He ducked and twisted, using his forearm to block a blow from a wooden club. He hammered his fist into the belly of the nearest man, following it with a swift hook to the jaw. The attacker dropped as if poleaxed. As he hurled himself to the right, Gaelen's shoulder cannoned into the midriff of the second man. The grunting whoosh of his opponent's breath showed he was badly winded. Scrambling to his feet, Gaelen kicked the fallen man in the face. More men ran from the trees; in the darkness Gaelen could not recognise faces, but they were dressed like clansmen.

He caught an attacker with a right cross to the chin, but then a wooden club thudded against his temple. Gaelen reeled to the left, vainly holding up his arm to protect his head. The club hammered into his thigh and agony lanced him. Another blow to the calf and he collapsed to the ground, struggling to rise as a booted foot crashed into his face. Twice more he felt blows to his right leg, and he passed out.

It was dawn before he was found. Caswallon came across the unconscious body as he made his way to Cambil's home. The clansman had been worried about Gaelen staying out all night

476

before the race, but had assumed he was sleeping at the house of the Hunt Lord. Carefully he turned Gaelen to his back, checking his heartbeat and breathing. He probed the dried blood on the youth's temple; the skull was not cracked. With a grunt of effort, he lifted Gaelen to his shoulder and stumbled on towards the house.

Deva was the first to be awakened by Caswallon kicking at the door. She ran downstairs, pulled back the bolts and let him in. Walking past her, Caswallon eased Gaelen down into a leather chair. Deva brought some water from the kitchen and a towel to bathe Gaelen's head.

Cambil, barechested and barely awake, joined them. 'What has happened?' he asked, bending over the unconscious youth.

'From the tracks, I'd say five men set on him after he left here last night,' Caswallon told him.

'Why?'

Caswallon glanced at him, green eyes blazing. 'Why do you think? I was a fool not to consider it myself.'

'You think the Aenir . . . ?'

'You want further proof?' Caswallon carefully unlaced the thongs of Gaelen's leggings, pulling them clear. His right leg was mottled blue, the knee swollen and pulpy. He groaned as Caswallon checked the bones for breaks. 'Skilfully done, wouldn't you say?'

'I shall cancel the race,' said Cambil.

'And what reason will you give?' snapped Caswallon. 'And what purpose would it serve? We need to win both of today's events. Cancelling one will only give the trophy to the Aenir.'

Agwaine stood at the foot of the stairs watching the exchange. He said nothing, moving past his father and making his way to the yard. From here he gazed out over the Games field and the mountains beyond. Deva joined him, a woollen shawl across her shoulders, her white nightdress billowing in the morning breeze. Curling her arm about his waist, she rested her head on his shoulder.

'What are you thinking?' she asked.

'I was thinking of Father.'

'In what way?'

477

'Oh, I don't know. Many ways. He's wrong, I know that now. The Games were ruined from the moment he allowed Drada to honey-talk him into allowing an Aenir team. But they flattered him so.'

'You are disappointed?'

'Yes, I suppose I am. Do not misunderstand me, Deva. I love Father dearly, and I would give anything for him to be respected as he desires to be. But, like all men, he has limits, he makes mistakes.'

'Gaelen's waking up.'

'Yes, but he won't run today.'

'No, but you will, brother.'

'Yes,' he answered, sighing. 'Yes, I will.'

The field was packed, the stalls deserted as three thousand clansmen thronged the start of the Mountain Race. The fifteen runners, dressed only in kilted loincloths and moccasins, were separated from the crowd by a lane of corded ropes staking the first two hundred paces, before the long climb into the timberline.

Agwaine eased his way through the athletes to stand beside the tall Borak. The man looked to neither right nor left, his eyes fixed ahead, ears tuned for the command to run.

As Games Lord it was Cambil's duty to start the race. Beside him stood Asbidag and Morgase, Maggrig, Laric and the other Hunt Lords of minor clans.

Cambil lifted his arm. 'Ready yourselves,' he shouted. The crowd fell silent, the runners tensing for the race. 'Race!' yelled Cambil and the athletes tore away, jostling for position in the narrow roped lane.

Agwaine settled in behind Borak, and was pulled to the front of the pack as the lean Aenir surged ahead. Gaelen, walking with the aid of a staff, watched, feeling sick with disappointment. Beside him, Lennox and Layne were cheering their cousin.

The runners neared the base of the mountain, Agwaine and the Aenir some twenty paces ahead of the pack. Borak shortened his step, leaning forward into the hill, his long legs pounding rhythmically against the packed clay. A thin film of sweat shone on his body

478

and his white-gold hair glistened in the sunlight. Agwaine, his gaze pinned on his opponent's back, was breathing easily, knowing the testing time would come before the third mile. It was at this point that he had been broken in the semi-final, the Aenir increasing his pace and burning off his opponents. He had learned in that moment the strength-sapping power of despair.

The crowd below watched them climb and Asbidag leaned over to Cambil. 'Your son runs well,' he said.

'Thank you.'

'But where is the boy with the white flash in his hair?'

Cambil met his gaze. 'He was injured last night in a brawl.'

'I'm sorry to hear that,' said Asbidag smoothly. 'Some trouble between the clans, perhaps?'

'Yes, perhaps,' answered Cambil.

The runners reached the two-mile mark and swung along the top of the slope, past a towering cliff of chalk, and into the trees on the long curve towards home. Agwaine could no longer hear the following runners, only his heart hammering in his chest and the rasping of his breath. But still he kept within three paces of the man before him.

Just before the three-mile mark Borak increased the length of his stride, forging a ten-pace lead before Agwaine responded.

Caswallon had pulled the young Farlain aside earlier that day, after Gaelen's wounds had been tended. 'I know we don't see eye to eye on many things, cousin,' Caswallon had told him. 'But force yourself to believe what I am going to tell you. You know that I won the Mountain Race three years ago. The way I did it was to destroy the field just after halfway – the same method the Aenir used in the semi-final. So I know how his mind works. He has no finish sprint, his one gamble is to kill off his opponents. When he breaks away, it will hurt him. His legs, just like yours, will burn and his lungs will be on fire. Keep that in mind. Each pain you feel, he feels. Stay with him.'

Agwaine didn't know how the Aenir felt at this moment, but as he fought to haul back the distance between them the pain in his legs increased and his breathing grew hot and ragged. But step by step he gained, until at last he was nestled in behind the warrior.

Twice more Borak fought to dislodge the dogged clansman. Twice more Agwaine closed the gap.

Up ahead, hidden behind a screen of bushes, knelt an Aenir warrior. In his hand was a leather sling, in the pouch of which hung a round black stone. He glimpsed the runners and readied himself. He could see the shorter clansman was close to Borak, and he cursed. Difficult enough to fell a running man, without having the risk of striking his comrade. Still, Borak knew he was here. He would pull ahead.

The runners were nearer now and the Aenir lifted his sling . . .

'Are you lost, my bonny?'

The warrior swung round, dropping the sling hurriedly.

'No. I was watching the race.'

'You picked a good position,' said Caswallon, smiling.

'Yes.'

'Shall we walk back together and observe the finish?'

'I'll walk alone,' snapped the Aenir, glancing away down the trail in time to see the runners leave the woods on the last stretch of slope before the final circuit.

'As you please,' said Caswallon.

Borak was worried now. He could hear the cursed clansman behind him and within moments he would be clear of the trees. What in Vatan's name was Snorri waiting for?

Just before they came in sight of the crowds below, Borak chopped his pace. As Agwaine drew abreast of him, Borak's elbow flashed back, the point smashing Agwaine's lips and snapping his head back. At that moment Borak sprinted away out of the trees, on to the gentle slope and down to the valley.

Agwaine stumbled, recovered his balance, and set off in pursuit. Anger flooded him, swamping the pain of his tired legs.

In the field below, three thousand voices rose in a howling cheer that echoed through the mountains. Cambil couldn't believe it. As Games Lord it behoved him to stay neutral, but it was impossible. Surging to his feet he leaped from the platform and joined the crowd, cheering at the top of his voice.

Borak hurtled headlong into the wall of sound, which panicked him for he could no longer hear the man behind him. He knew it

480

was senseless to glance back, for it would cost him speed, but he couldn't help himself. His head turned and there, just behind him, was Agwaine, blood streaming from his injured mouth. Borak tried to increase his pace – the finishing line was only fifty paces away – but the distance stretched out before him like an eternity. Agwaine drew abreast of him once more – and then was past.

The crowd was delirious. The rope lanes were trampled down and Agwaine swallowed by the mass, only to be hoisted aloft on the shoulders of two Farlain men. Borak stumbled away, head bowed, then stopped and sought out his master.

Asbidag stood silently gazing down from the Hunt Lord's platform. Borak met his gaze and turned away.

'There is still Orsa,' said Drada.

His father nodded, then watched the broken Borak walking away from the tents of the Aenir.

'I don't want to see his face again.'

'I'll send him south,' said Drada.

'I don't want *anyone* to see his face again.'

Clan fervour, which had seemed to reach a peak following Agwaine's unexpected and courageous victory, hit new heights during the long afternoon. No one toured the stalls, nor sat in comfort at the tables sipping mead or wine. The entire crowd thronged the central field where Lennox and Orsa battled for the Whorl Trophy, awarded to the strongest man of the mountains.

That the two men were splendidly matched had been obvious from the culling events, when both had moved comfortably to the final. Both towered over six feet. In physique they were near identical, their huge frames swollen with thick, corded muscle. Deva thought them equally ugly, though the male watchers gazed in frank admiration.

The event had five sections. The first man to win three of them would be the Whorl Champion.

The first saw Orsa win easily. A sphere of lead weighing twenty pounds had to be hurled, one-handed. Orsa's first throw measured eighteen and a half paces. Lennox managed only thirteen. But the clansman drew level in the next event, straightening a horseshoe.

Watching the contest with Gaelen and Maeg, Caswallon was concerned. 'The Aenir is more supple, and therefore his speed is greater. That's why he won the hurling so easily, and it must make him the favourite for the open wrestling.'

The third event involved lifting the Whorl Stone and carrying it along a roped lane. Lennox was first to make the attempt.

The black boulder had been carried to a wooden platform at the head of the lane. Two hundred pounds of slippery stone. Lennox approached it, breathing deeply, and the crowd fell silent, allowing him to concentrate on the task ahead. The weight was not the problem. Set the boulder on a harness and Lennox could carry it across the Druin range. But held across the chest, every step loosened the grip. A strong man could carry it ten paces; a very strong man might make twenty; but only those with colossal power carried it beyond thirty. The man now known as Oracle had, in his youth, made forty-two paces. Men still spoke of it.

Lennox bent his knees and curled his mighty arms around the stone, tensing the muscles of his shoulders and back. Straightening his legs with a grunt of effort, he slowly turned and began to walk the lane.

At fifteen paces the stone slipped, but he held it more firmly and walked on. At thirty paces the steps became smaller. Gone was the slow, measured stride. His head strained back, the muscles and tendons of his neck stood out like bars of iron.

At forty paces his face was crimson, the veins on his temples writhing, his eyes squeezed shut.

At forty-five paces Lennox stumbled, made one more step, then jumped back as he was forced to release the weight. Three men prised the stone clear, while a fourth marked the spot with a white stake.

Sucking in great gasps of air, Lennox sought out his opponent, reading his face for signs of concern. Orsa ran his hand through his thick yellow hair, sweeping it back from his eyes. He grinned at Lennox, a friendly, open smile. Lennox's heart sank.

To the stunned amazement of the crowd, Orsa carried the Whorl Stone easily past the stake, releasing it at fifty-seven paces. It was an incredible feat, and even the clansmen applauded it. Men's eyes switched to Lennox, knowing the blow to his morale would be great. He was sitting on the grass watching his opponent, his face set, features stern.

Cambil called for a halt to allow the contestants to recover their strength before the rope haul, and the crowd broke away to the mead tables and the barbecue pits.

Caswallon and Gaelen made their way to Lennox, along with Agwaine, Cambil and Layne. 'Can you beat him?' asked Cambil.

'Not now, cousin,' snapped Caswallon. 'Let him rest.' Cambil's eyes flashed angrily and he turned away. Agwaine hesitated, then followed his father.

'How do you feel?' asked Caswallon, sitting down. Lennox grinned and shrugged.

'I feel broken. How could any man carry that stone for almost sixty paces? It's inhuman.'

'I thought the same when you carried it for forty-six.'

'I don't think I can beat him.'

'You can.'

'You've not been watching very closely, cousin.'

'Ah, but I have, Lennox, and that's how I know. He took a lower grip, and kept his head down. Your head went back. That shortened your steps. You could have matched him; you still can.'

'Don't misunderstand me, Caswallon. I shall do my best. But he is stronger, there's no doubt of that.'

'I know.'

'But he's not Farlain,' said Gaelen. 'You are.'

Lennox grinned. 'So speaks our limping cousin, who allowed a mere five Aenir to remove him from the race.'

Gaelen chuckled, 'I meant it, though. I don't think he can beat you, Lennox. I don't think there's a man alive to beat you. You'll see.'

'That's a comforting thought, Gaelen. And I thank you for it.' Lennox grunted as he stretched his back.

'Roll on your stomach,' commanded Layne. 'I'll knead that muscle for you.'

Caswallon helped Gaelen to his feet, for his leg stiffened as he sat. 'Let's get some food. How do you feel?'

'I ache. Damn, Caswallon, I wish I'd run in that race.'

'Why?'

'I wanted to do something for the clan. Be someone.'

'You *are* someone. And we all know you would have won. But it was better for Agwaine to do it.'

'Why?'

'Because Agwaine needed to do it. Today he learned something about himself. In some ways he's like his father, full of doubts. Today he lost a lot of them.'

'That may be good for Agwaine, but it doesn't help me.'

'How true,' said Caswallon, ruffling Gaelen's hair. 'But there is always next year.'

That afternoon began with the rope haul, a supreme test of a man's strength and stamina. The contestant looped a rope around his body and braced himself. On the other end three men sought to tug him from his feet. After ten heartbeats a fourth man could be added to the team, ten beats later another man, and so on.

This time Orsa went first. The men trying to dislodge him were Farlain clansmen. Bracing his foot against a deeply-embedded rock, he held the first three men with ease, taunting them and exhorting them to pull harder. By the time six men were pulling against him he had run out of jeers, saving his breath for the task in hand. The seventh man proved too much for him and he fell forward, hitting the ground hard. He was up in an instant, grinning, and complaining that the rock beneath his foot had slipped.

Lennox stepped up to the mark, a blanket rolled across his shoulders to prevent rope burn. Swiftly he coiled the rope, hooking it over his shoulder and back. Then he checked the stone; it was firm. He braced himself and three Aenir warriors took up the slack.

A fourth man was sent forward, then a fifth. Lennox wasted no energy taunting them; he closed his mind to his opponents. He was a rock set in the mountain, immovable. A tree, deeply-rooted and strong. His eyes closed, his concentration intense, he felt the building of power against him and absorbed it.

At last the pressure grew too great and he gave way, opening his eyes to count his opponents.

Nine men!

Dropping the rope, he turned to Orsa. The Aenir warrior met his gaze and nodded slowly. He was not smiling now as he walked forward to stand before the dark-haired clansman. Blue eyes met grey. Orsa was in his late twenties, a seasoned warrior who had never been beaten and never would be. His confidence was born of knowledge, experience and the pain borne by others. Lennox was nearing eighteen, untried in war and combat, but he had faced the Beast and stood his ground.

Now he faced the Aenir and his gaze remained cool and steady. Orsa nodded once and turned away.

With two events each, the Whorl Championship would be decided in the open wrestling, a cultured euphemism for a fight where the only rule was that there were no rules. It was held in a rope circle six paces in diameter, and the first to be thrown from the ring was the loser. As they prepared, Caswallon approached Lennox and whispered in his ear. The huge clansman nodded, then stepped into the circle.

Orsa stepped in to join him and the two men shook hands, acknowledging the cheers of the crowd. Then they backed away and began to circle, hands extended.

Suddenly Lennox stepped inside and lightly slapped Orsa's face. Expecting a punch, the Aenir ducked and stepped back. Lennox flicked his hand out again, this time slapping Orsa's arm. Someone in the crowd began to laugh and others joined in. Lennox dummied a right, then slapped Orsa once more, this time with his left hand. The laughter swelled.

Orsa's blue eyes glittered strangely and he began to tremble. With a piercing scream he charged his tormentor. No more did he seek merely to throw him from the circle. Now only death would avenge the insult.

Orsa was once again a Baresark!

Lennox met the charge head-on, swivelling to thunder a right hook to Orsa's bearded chin. The Aenir shrugged off the blow and charged again. This time Lennox hit him with both hands, but a wildly swinging punch from Orsa exploded against his ear. Lennox staggered. A left-hand punch broke Lennox's nose, blood spattering to his chin. Warding off the attack with a desperate push, the clansman moved back to the edge of the circle. Orsa charged once more, screaming an Aenir battlecry. At the last moment Lennox dropped to his knees, then surged upright as Orsa loomed over him. The speed of the rush carried Orsa on, flying headlong over his opponent to crash into the crowd beyond the circle.

The fight was over and Lennox had won. But Orsa in his berserk rage knew nothing of tournaments and petty victories. Hurling aside the men who helped him to his feet, he leaped back into the circle where Lennox was standing with arms raised in triumph.

'Look out!' shouted Gaelen and a score of others.

Lennox swung round. Orsa's massive hand encircled the clansman's throat. Instinctively Lennox tensed the muscles of his neck against the crushing strength of the man's fingers. His own hands clamped down on Orsa's throat, blocking his demonic snarling.

The crowd fell silent as the two men strained and swayed in the centre of the circle.

Then the tall red-caped figure of Drada appeared, pushing through the mass. In his right hand he carried a wooden club which he hammered to the back of his brother's skull. Orsa's eyes glazed and his grip loosened. Drada hit him once more and he fell. Lennox stepped back, rubbing his bruised throat.

Orsa staggered to his feet, turning to his brother. 'Sorry,' he said, and shrugged. He walked to Lennox, gripping his hand. 'Good contest,' he said. 'You're strong.'

'I don't think any man will ever carry the Whorl Stone as far as you did,' Lennox told him.

'Maybe so. Why did you slap me?' The question was asked so simply and directly that Lennox laughed nervously, unable at first to marshal his thoughts. But Orsa waited patiently, no sign of emotion on his broad face.

'I did it to make you angry, so you would lose control.'

'Thought so. Beat myself – that's not good.' Still nodding, he walked away. Lennox watched him, puzzled, then the crowd swamped him, slapping his back and leading him on to the Hunt Lord's platform to receive the congratulations of the Games Lord.

As the crowd moved away, Drada approached Caswallon. 'It was your advice, was it not, to make my brother baresark?'

'Yes.'

'You are proving to be troublesome, Caswallon.'

'I'm glad to hear it.'

'No sensible man should be glad to make an enemy.'

'I haven't made an enemy, Drada. I've recognised one. There is a difference.'

The Whorl Dance had begun around a dozen blazing fires, and the eligible maidens of the Farlain chose dancing companions from the waiting ranks of clansmen. There was music from the pipes, harsh and powerful; from the flute, wistful and melodic; and horn the harp, enchanting and fey. It was mountain music, and stronger than wine upon the senses of the men and women of the clans.

Deva danced with Layne, the Spear Champion, while Gaelen sat alone, fighting a losing battle against self-pity. His leg ached and he eased it forward under the table, rubbing at the swollen thigh.

Gwalchmai found him there just before midnight. The young archer was dressed in his finest clothes, a cloak of soft brown leather over a green embroiderd tunic. 'No one should be alone on Whorl Night,' said Gwal, easing in to sit opposite his comrade.

'I was just waiting for a girl with a swollen left leg, then we could hobble away together,' said Gaelen, pouring more mead wine into his goblet.

'I have two legs, but have not found a partner,' said Gwal, helping himself to Gaelen's wine.

'Come now, Gwal, there must be five hundred maidens here.'

'They are not what I want,' said Gwalchmai sadly. Gaelen glanced at his friend. Gwal's hair was flame-red in the firelight, his face no longer boyish but lean and handsome.

'So what do you want . . . a princess?'

Gwalchmai shrugged. 'That is hard to answer, Gaelen. But I know I shall never wed.'

Gaelen said nothing. He had known for some time, as had Layne and Lennox, that Gwalchmai had no interest in the young maidens of the Farlain. The boys did not understand it, but only Gaelen suspected the truth. In Ateris he had seen many who shared Gwalchmai's secret longings. 'You know what I am, don't you?' said Gwalchmai, suddenly.

'I know,' Gaelen told him. 'You are Gwalchmai, one of the Beast Slayers. You are a clansman, and I am proud to have you for my friend.'

'Then you don't think . . . ?'

'I have told you what I think, cousin,' said Gaelen, reaching forward to grip Gwalchmai's shoulder.

'True enough. Thank you, my friend.' Gwalchmai sighed – and changed the subject. 'Where is Caswallon?'

'Escorting the Aenir back to Aesgard.'

'I am not sorry to see them go,' said Gwal.

'No. Did you hear about Borak?'

The runner? What about him?'

'He was found this evening hanging from a tree on the west hill.'

'He killed himself?'

'It seems so,' said Gaelen.

They're a strange people, these Aenir. I hope they don't come back next year.'

'I think they will, but not for the Games,' said Gaelen.

'You're not another of those war-bores?'

'I'm afraid so.'

'What could they gain? There are no riches in Druin.'

'War is a prize in itself for the Aenir. They live for it.'

Gwalchmai leaned forward on his elbows, shaking his head. 'What a night! First I lose in the archery, then I get maudlin, and now I'm sitting with a man who prophesies war and death.'

Gaelen chuckled. 'You were unlucky in the tourney. The wind died as the Aenir took his mark, and it gave him an edge.'

'A thousand blessings on you for noticing,' said Gwal, grinning. 'Have you ever been drunk?'

'No.'

'Well, it seems the only enjoyment left to us.'

'I agree. Fetch another jug.'

Within an hour their raucous songs had attracted a small following. Lennox and Agwaine joined them, bringing fresh supplies, then Layne arrived with Deva.

The drink ran out just before dawn and the party moved to sit beside a dying fire. The songs faded away, the laughter eased, and the talk switched to the Games and the possible aftermath. Deva fell asleep against Layne; he settled her to the ground, covering her with his cloak.

Gaelen watched him gently tuck the garment around her and his heart ached. He looked away, trying to focus on the conversation once more. But he could not. His gaze swept up over the mountains, along the reddening skyline. Caswallon had told him his theory of the Aenir plan to demoralise the clans. The scale of their error was enormous. By the end they achieved only the opposite. Men of every clan had cheered Agwaine and Lennox against a common enemy; they had united the clans in a way no one had in a hundred years.

He heard someone mention his name and dragged his mind back to the present.

'I'm sorry you missed the race,' said Agwaine.

'Don't be. You were magnificent.'

'Caswallon advised me.'

'It was obviously good advice.'

'Yes. I'm sorry he and my father are not friends.'

'And you?'

'What about me?'

'How do you feel now . . . about Caswallon, I mean?'

'I am grateful. But I am my father's son.'

'I understand.'

'I hope that you do, cousin.' Their eyes met and Agwaine held out his hand. Gaelen took it.

'Now this is good to see,' said Lennox, leaning forward to lay his hand upon theirs. Layne and Gwalchmai followed suit.

'We are all Farlain,' said Layne solemnly. 'Brothers of the spirit. Let it long remain so.'

'The Five Beast Slayers,' said Agwaine, grinning, 'It is fitting we should be friends.'

Deva opened her eyes and saw the five young men sitting silently together. The sun cleared the mountains, bathing them in golden light. She blinked and sat up. Just for a moment she seemed to see a sixth figure standing beyond them – tall, she was, and beautiful, silver-haired and strong. By her side hung a mighty sword and upon her head was a crown of gold. Deva shivered and blinked again. The Queen was gone.

7

Gaelen stood on the lip of a precipice looking down on Vallon from the north, listening to the faint sounds of the falls echoing up through the mountains. Spring had finally arrived after yet another bitter winter, and Gaelen had been anxious to leave the valley to stretch his legs and open his heart to the music of the mountains. He had grown during the winter, and constant work with axe and saw had added weight to his arms and shoulders. His hair was long, hanging to his shoulders, and held back from his eyes by a black leather circle around his brow. Kareen – before her marriage to the west valley crofter, Durk – had made it for him, as well as a tunic of softest leather, polished to a sheen, and calf-length moccasin boots from the same hide. His winter cape was a gift from Caswallon, a heavy sheepskin that doubled as a blanket. During the cold winter months he had allowed his beard to grow, shutting his ears to jibes about goose-down from Maeg and Kareen. It had taken long enough but now, as he stood on the mountainside in the early morning sunshine, it gave him that which he desired above all else – the look of manhood.

Gone was the frightened, wounded boy brought home by Caswallon two years before. In his place stood a man, tall and strong, hardened by toil, strengthened by experience. The only reminders left of the hunted boy were the blood-filled left eye, and the white streak in his hair above the jagged scar on his forehead and cheek.

The black and grey war hound by his side growled and rubbed against him. Gaelen dropped his hand to pat its massive head. 'You don't like these high places, do you, boy?' said Gaelen, squatting beside the animal. It lifted its head, licking his face until he pushed it away laughing.

'We've changed, you and I,' he said, holding the dog at bay. It had the wide jaws of its dam and the heavy shoulders of its breed, but added to this it also had the rangy power of the wolf that had sired it.

The wolf in it had caused problems with training, and both Caswallon and Gaelen had despaired at times. But slowly it had come round to their patient handling, until at last Gaelen had walked it unleashed among a flock of sheep. He told it to sit, and it obeyed him. But its eyes lingered over the fat, slow ewes and its jaws salivated. After a while it had hunkered down on its haunches and closed its eyes, unable to bear such mouth-watering sights any longer.

Under Caswallon's guidance, Gaelen taught the hound to obey increasingly complex instructions, beginning with simple commands such as 'sit', 'heel' and 'stay'. After that it was taught to wait in silence if Gaelen lifted his hand palm outward. Finally Caswallon built a dummy of wood and straw, dressed it in old clothes, and the hound was taught to attack it on Gaelen's command of 'kill'. This training was further refined with the call, 'hold,' at which command the dog would lunge for the dummy's arm.

Painstakingly they honed the dog's skills. Once it attacked, only one call would stop it: *Home*. Any other call, even from Gaelen, would be ignored.

'This,' said Caswallon, 'is your safeguard. For a dog is a creature of instinct. You may order it to attack, but another voice may call it back. "Home" should remain a secret command. Share it not even with your friends.'

Gaelen called the beast Render. The hound's nature was good, especially with Caswallon's son Donal, now a blond toddler who followed Render – or Wenna, as he called it – about the house, pulling its ears and struggling to climb on its back. Attempts to stop him would be followed by floods of tears and the difficult-to-answer assertion, 'Wenna like it!'

Maeg was hard to convince that Render was a worthy addition to the household, but one afternoon in late winter it won her over. Kareen had ventured into the yard to fetch wood for the fire, but had not secured the kitchen door on her return. Donal had sneaked out to play in the snow, an adventure of rare magic.

He was gone for more than half an hour before his absence was noted. Maeg was beside herself. Caswallon and Gaelen were at the Long Hall where Caswallon was being elected to the Council in

492

place of an elderly clansman who had collapsed and died soon after the Games. Maeg wrapped a woollen shawl about her shoulders and stepped out into the storm. Within minutes it had grown dark and as she called Donal's name the wind whipped her words from her mouth. His track had been covered by fresh snow.

Kareen joined her. 'He'll die in this,' yelled Maeg.

Render padded from the house. Seeing the hound, Maeg ran to it and knelt by its side.

'Donal!' she shouted, pushing the dog and pointing out past the yard. Render tilted his head and licked her face. 'Fetch!' she shouted. Render looked around. There was nothing to fetch. 'Donal! Fetch Donal!' Render looked back towards the house and the open door that led to the warm hearth. The hound didn't know what the women were doing out in the cold. Then its ears came up as a wolf howled in the distance. Another sound came, thin and piping. Recognising instantly the pup-child of Caswallon, Render padded off into the snow.

Maeg's hands and feet were freezing, but she had no idea if the dog had understood her and she had not heard the faint cry, so she continued to search, terror growing within her and panic welling in her mind.

Render loped away into a small hollow hidden from the house. Here it found the toddler who had slipped and rolled down on to a patch of ice and was unable to get up. Beyond him sat two wolves, tongues lolling.

Render padded towards the boy, growling deep in his throat. The wolves stood, then backed away as the warhound advanced. Canny killers were the grey wolves, but they knew a better killer when they saw him.

'I cold, Wenna,' said Donal, sniffing. 'I cold.'

Render stopped by the boy, watching the wolves carefully.

They backed away still further, and, satisfied, Render nuzzled Donal, but the boy could not stand on the ice. Render ducked his head, taking the boy's woollen tunic in his teeth. Donal was lifted clear of the ice and the huge dog bounded up the slope and back towards the house.

Maeg saw them and waded through the snow towards them, but Render loped past her and into the kitchen. He was cold and missed the fire. When Maeg and Kareen arrived Donal and Render were sitting before the hearth. Maeg swept Donal into her arms.

'Wolfs, mama. Wenna scare 'em away.'

Maeg shuddered. Wolves! And her child had been alone. She sat down hurriedly.

Neither of the women told Caswallon of the adventure, but he knew something was amiss when Maeg explained she had given his own cold meat supper to the hound.

Caswallon's activities during the summer and winter puzzled many of the clansmen. He drove no cattle to Aesgard, nor delivered grain and oats. The fruit of his orchards disappeared, and no man knew where, though the carts were driven into the mountains by trusted workers. There, it was said, they were delivered to the druids.

In the meantime, Caswallon gathered round him more than a hundred clansmen, and several of these he paid to scout around Aesgard and report on Aenir movement.

Cambil had been furious, accusing Caswallon of amassing a private army. 'Can you not understand, Caswallon, that such deeds make war more likely?' said the Hunt Lord. 'You think me foolish for trying to forge friendships among the Aenir, I know that. As I know they are a warlike people, harsh and cruel. But as Hunt Lord I must consider the long-term well-being of my people. We could not win a war with the Aenir; they would swamp us. What I have tried – and will continue to try – to do is to make Asbidag aware of the futility of war in the highlands. We have no gold, no iron. There are no riches here. This he understands. What is more important is that he must feel no threat from us. It is in the Aenir nature to see enemies all around. If we can make them our friends, there will be no war.'

Caswallon listened in silence until Cambil had finished speaking. Under different circumstances I would agree with every word, cousin,' he said at last. 'War is the last beast an intelligent man would let loose. Where I think you are wrong is in believing that the

Aenir see war as a means to an end. For them it is the end in itself. They live to fight, they lust for slaughter and blood. Even their religion is based on the glory of combat. They believe that only if they die in battle will their souls be blessed with an eternity of pleasure. Now that their war with the lowlanders is over where else can they turn for war, save with us? I respect you, cousin – and I mean that truly. You have acted with honour. Yet now is the time to open your eyes and see that your efforts have been in vain. The Aenir are massing troops on the southern borders.'

Cambil shook his head. 'Asbidag assures me that the troops are being gathered in order for the majority of them to be disbanded and offered land to farm, as a reward for loyal service. You are wrong, Caswallon. And the wisdom of my course will be appreciated in the years to come.'

Despite Cambil's assurances Caswallon advised the Council to marshal a militia against a spring invasion. They refused, agreeing with the Hunt Lord that there were no indications the Aenir nursed any hostile intent towards the clan. The feeling was not unanimous. Badraig and Leofas supported Caswallon openly. Beric, a tall balding warrior from the northern valley, voted with them, but said nothing.

'You have a hundred men, Caswallon,' said Leofas as the four met after the spring banquet, 'I can muster eighty crofters. Badraig and Beric the same between them. When the Aenir come it will be like a sudden storm. Three hundred men will not stop them.'

'Let us be honest,' said Badraig. 'The Farlain united could not stop them. If every man took up his sword and bow we would have . . . what? . . . five thousand. Against a force five times as great.' Badraig had changed since the beast killed his son. His hair was grey and he had lost weight, growing haggard and lean.

'That is true,' agreed Caswallon, 'but we can wear them down. We'll fight no pitched battles; we'll harry them, cutting and running. Soon they'll tire and return to Aesgard.'

'That will depend on why they're here,' said Beric. 'If they take the valleys we'll have no way to support ourselves. We'll die in the mountains, come winter.'

'Not necessarily,' said Caswallon. 'But that debate can wait for a better time. What worries me is not the long-drawn-out campaign, but the first strike. If they hit the valleys unawares, the slaughter will be horrific.'

'There is not a day we do not have a scout watching them,' said Leofas. 'We should get at least an hour's warning.'

Six hours' march to the east, the crofter Arcis breathed his last. His arms had been nailed to the broad trunk of an oak and his ribs had been opened, splaying out from his body like tiny tattered wings.

The blood-eagle had arrived in the Farlain.

One Aenir army burst upon the villages and crofts of the Haesten, bringing fire and death into the darkest part of the night. Homes blazed and swords ran with blood. The Aenir swept into the valley of Laric, hacking and slaying, burning and looting. The Haesten had not time to group a defence, and the survivors streamed into the mountains, broken and panic-stricken.

A Pallides hunter, camped on the hillside inside Haesten territory, watched stunned as the Aenir charged into the valley. As if in a dream he saw the warriors in the garish armour and winged helms race down to the homes of the Haesten, thrusting burning brands through open windows. And he viewed with growing horror the massacre of the clan. He saw women dragged forth, raped and then murdered; he saw babies speared; he saw small pockets of Haesten resistance swallowed up in rings of steel.

Then he rose and began to run, stumbling over tree roots and rocks in the darkness.

He reached the grey house of Maggrig two hours before dawn. Within minutes the war-horn of the Pallides sounded. Women and children hastily packed clothing and food and were led into the mountains. Thinking there was only one Aenir army, Maggrig miscalculated, and the evacuation was still under way as a second Aenir force, led by Ongist, fell upon them.

Maggrig had eight hundred warriors at his back, with messengers sent for perhaps five hundred more. As he stood on the hillside, watching the Aenir pour into the valley, he reckoned their numbers were in excess of five thousand. Beside him the grim-eyed swordsman Intosh, the Games Champion, cursed and spat. The two men exchanged glances. Whatever decision they made now would lead to tragedy.

The enemy were sweeping down towards the last file of women and children. If Maggrig did nothing they would die. If the Pallides counter-charged they would be cut to pieces. In his heart Maggrig knew it was sensible to leave the stragglers and fight a defensive retreat, protecting the majority.

But he was Clan, and these stragglers were his people.

He lifted his sword, shifted his shield into place and began to run down the hillside towards the Aenir. Eight hundred Pallides warriors followed him without hesitation. Seeing them come, the Aenir turned from the line of women and children. Their deaths would come later.

The two forces collided. Swords clashed against iron shields, against close-set mail rings, against soft flesh and brittle bones. The clansmen wore little or no armour and yet the speed and ferocity of their assault made up for it. Intosh, fighting with two swords and no shield, cut a bloody swathe through the Aenir, while Maggrig's power and cunning sword-craft protected his right flank.

For some minutes the clan held, but then the weight of the Aenir pushed them back. Maggrig parried a wild cut from an axe-wielding warrior, countering with a swift thrust to the belly.

He glanced back at the mountainside. It was clear. With no way of estimating the losses amongst the warriors, Maggrig bellowed, 'Pallides away!' The survivors turned instantly, sprinting for the mountainside. Screaming their triumph, the Aenir swept after them. Halfway to the trees, Maggrig glanced left and right. There were five hundred still with him.

'Cut! Cut! Cut!' he roared. At the sound of their battlecry the Pallides swung about and flung themselves on the pursuing warriors. In their eagerness to overhaul their enemy, the Aenir had lost the close-compacted formation of the battle in the valley. The swiftest of them had outdistanced their comrades and they paid with their lives.

'Pallides away!' shouted Maggrig once more, and the clansmen turned, racing for the relative haven of the trees.

The Aenir surged after them. A leading warrior screamed suddenly, his fingers scrabbling at a black-shafted arrow that hammered into his throat. Another died, and another. The Aenir fell back as death hissed at them from the darkness of the woods.

Within minutes, Maggrig sent his men forward to catch up with the clan, then beckoned Intosh to join him. Together they eased their way through to the women archers hidden by the timberline.

'Well done, Adugga,' said Maggrig as a dark-haired woman rose up before him, bow in hand, 'It was good thinking.'

'It will not stop them for long. They'll outflank us.'

'We'll be long gone by the time they do. They may be fine warriors, but they'll not catch us.'

'That may be true, Hunt Lord. But where will we go?' asked Adugga.

'To the Farlain.'

'You think we'll get a friendly welcome?' asked Intosh.

'Unless I am mistaken, the Aenir will be upon them before we arrive.'

'Then why go there?'

'My son Caswallon has a plan. We've spoken of it often, and at this moment it seems to be the best hope we have. We are making for Attafoss.'

Maggrig stepped forward, parted the bush screen and gazed down upon the burning valley. The Aenir were sitting on the hillside just out of bowshot. They're waiting for dawn,' said Maggrig, 'and that will not be long in coming. Let's away!'

In the first valley of the Farlain, Caswallon was awakened before dawn by a frenzied hammering at his door. He rolled from the bed and ran downstairs.

Outside was Taliesen. The old man, red-faced and wheezing, leaned on his oak staff. Catching his breath, he gripped Caswallon by the arm.

'The Aenir are upon us! We must move now.'

Caswallon nodded and shouted for Maeg to dress Donal, then he helped the druid into the kitchen, seating him by the hearth. Leaving him there, Caswallon lifted his war-horn from its place on the wall and stepped into the yard.

Three times its eerie notes echoed through the valley. Then it was answered from a score of homes and the clarion call was taken up, at last reaching the crofts of the outer valleys. Men and women streamed from their homes towards the Games field, the men carrying bows, their swords strapped to their sides, the women ready with provision and blankets.

Caswallon opened the wooden chest that sat against the far wall of the kitchen. From it he took a mail-shirt and a short sword. Swiftly he pulled the mail-shirt over his tunic and strapped the sword to his side. Taking the war-horn, he tied its thong to his baldric and settled it in place.

'How long do we have, Taliesen?'

'Perhaps an hour. Perhaps less.'

Caswallon nodded. Maeg came downstairs carrying Donal, and the four of the them left the house. Caswallon ran on ahead to where hundreds of mystified clansmen were gathering.

Leofas saw him and waved as Caswallon made his way to him. 'What is happening, Caswallon?'

'The Aenir are close. They've crossed the Farlain.'

'How do you know this?'

'Taliesen. He's back there with Maeg.'

Caswallon helped the druid push through the crowd to make his way to the top of the small hill at the meadow known as Centre Field. The old man raised his arms for silence.

'The Aenir have tonight attacked the Haesten and the Pallides,' he said. 'Soon they will be here.'

'How do you know this, old man?' asked Cambil, striding up the hillside, his face crimson with anger. 'A dream perhaps? A druid's vision?'

'I know, Hunt Lord. That is enough.'

'Enough? Enough that you can tell us that two days' march away a battle is taking place. Are you mad?'

'I don't care *how* he knows,' said Caswallon. 'We have less than an hour to move our people into the mountains. Are we going to stand here talking all night?'

'It is sheer nonsense,' shouted Cambil, turning to the crowd. 'Why would the Aenir attack? Are we expected to believe this old man? Can any of us see here what is happening to the Pallides? And what if the Aenir have attacked them? That is Pallides business. I warned Maggrig not to be bull-headed in his dealings with Asbidag. Now enough of this foolishness, let's away to home and bed.'

'Wait!' shouted Caswallon, as men began to stir and move. 'If the druid is wrong, we will know by morning; all we will have lost is one night on a damp mountainside. If he is right, we cannot defend this valley. If Maggrig and Laric have been crushed as Taliesen says, then the Aenir *must* attack the Farlain.'

'I'm with you, Caswallon,' shouted Leofas.

'And I,' called Badraig. Others took up the shout, but not all.

Debates sprung up, arguments followed. In despair Caswallon once more sounded his war-horn. In the silence that followed he told them, 'There is no more time to talk. I am leaving now for the mountains. Those who wish to follow me, let them do so. To those who do not, let me say only that I pray you are right.'

Cambil had already begun the long walk back to his home and a score of others followed him. Caswallon led Maeg and Taliesen down from the hill and through the crowd. Behind him came Leofas, Layne, Lennox, Badraig and many more.

'Ah, well, what's a night on the mountains?' he heard someone say, and the following crowd swelled. He did not look back, but his heart was heavy as he reached the trees. Of the three thousand people in the first valley more than two thousand had followed him. Many of the rest still stood arguing in Centre Field; others were returning to their homes.

It was at that moment that a ring of blazing torches flared up on the eastern skyline.

Cambil, who was almost home, stopped and stared. The eastern mountainside was alive with armed men. His eyes scanned them.

At the centre on a black horse sat a man in heavy armour and horned helm. Cambil recognised the Aenir lord and cursed him.

'May the gods preserve us,' whispered Agwaine, who had run to join his father.

Cambil turned to him. 'Get away from here. Now! Join Caswallon. Tell him I am sorry.'

'Not without you, Father.'

Cambil slapped his face viciously. 'Am I not Hunt Lord? Obey me. Look after your sister.'

On the hill above Asbidag raised his arm and the Aenir charged, filling the night air with strident screams that pushed their hatred before them like an invisible wall. It struck Cambil to the heart and he blanched. 'Get away!' he yelled, pushing Agwaine from him.

Agwaine fell back a step. There were so many things he wanted to say. But his father had drawn his sword and was running into the valley towards the Aenir. Agwaine turned away and ran towards the west, tears filling his eyes.

In Centre Field hundreds of stragglers drew swords ready to charge to the aid of their beleaguered kin, but Caswallon's warhorn stopped them 'You can do nothing for them!' he yelled in desperation. 'Join us!'

The valley beyond was filled with Aenir warriors. Fires sprang up in the nearby houses. The clansmen in the Centre Field were torn between their desire to aid their comrades and their need to protect their wives and children beside them. The more immediate love-tie took hold and the crowd surged up the hillside.

Cambil raced down the slope, sword in hand, blinking away the tears of shame filling his eyes. Memories forced their pictures to his mind – unkind, ugly pictures. Maggrig, calling him a fool at the Games. Taliesen's eyes radiating contempt. And, way back, the cruellest of all, his father Padris telling him he wasn't fit to clean Caswallon's cloak.

His feet pounded on the grass-covered slope. The Aenir force had swung ponderously round, like a giant horseshoe, to begin the encirclement of the defenders who waited, grim-faced, swords in hand.

Cambil increased his speed. Another hundred paces and he could die among the people he loved, the people he had betrayed with his stupidity. At least the enemy had not yet seen the exodus led by Caswallon.

Breathless and near to exhaustion, Cambil joined the circle, standing beside the councillor Tesk. 'I am so . . . sorry,' said the Hunt Lord.

Tesk shrugged. 'We all make mistakes, Cambil, my lad. But be warned – I might not vote for you again.' The older man gently pushed Cambil back into the circle. 'Get your breath back and join me in a little while.'

Grinning, Tesk shifted his shield into place, transferring his gaze to the screaming horde almost upon them. He could see their faces now, feel their bloodlust strike him like a malignant breeze.

'The stars are out, Farlain!' he yelled, 'It's a fine night for dying.'

The Aenir broke upon them like waves upon a rock, and the slaughter began. But at first it was the flashing blades of the Farlain that ripped and tore at the enemy, and many were the screams of the Aenir wounded and dying as they fell beneath the boots of their comrades.

Cambil forced himself alongside Tesk and all fear left the Hunt Lord. Doubts fled, shredding like summer clouds. He was calm at last and the noise of the battle receded from him. A strange sense of detachment came upon him and he seemed to be watching himself cutting and slaying, and he heard the laughter from his own lips as if from a stranger.

All his life he had known the inner pain of uncertainty. Inadequacy hugged him like a shadow. Now he was free. An axe clove his chest, but there was no pain. He killed the axeman, and two others, before his legs gave way and he fell. He rolled to his back, feeling the warmth of life draining from the wound.

He had finally succeeded, he knew that now. Without his sacrifice Caswallon would never have had the time to escape.

'I did something right, Father,' he whispered.

'Bowmen to me!' shouted Caswallon. Beside him the silver-haired warrior, Leofas, stood with his sons Layne and Lennox. 'Leofas, lead the clan towards Attafoss. Throw out a wide screen of scouts, for before long the Aenir will be hunting us. Go now!'

The clan began to move on into the trees, just as the sun cleared the eastern peaks. Many were the backward glances at the small knot of fighting men ringed by the enemy, and the eyes that saw them burned with guilt and shame.

Three hundred bowmen grouped themselves around Caswallon. Each bore two quivers containing forty shafts. They spread out along the timberline, screened by bushes, thick gorse and heather.

As the light strengthened Caswallon watched the last gallant struggle of the encircled clansmen. He could see Cambil in with them, battling bravely, and some of the women had taken up swords and daggers. And then it was over. The sword-ring fell apart and the Aenir swarmed over them, hacking and slashing, until at last there was no movement from the defenders.

Asbidag rode down the valley and removed his helm. He summoned his captains.

Caswallon could not hear the commands he issued, but he could guess, for the eyes of the Aenir turned west and the army took up its weapons and ran towards the mountainside.

'Do not shoot until I do,' he called to the hidden archers. Caswallon notched a shaft to the string as the Aenir spread out along the foot of the slope. They advanced cautiously, many of them lifting the face-guards of their helms the better to see the enemy. Caswallon grinned. He singled out a lean, wolfish warrior at the centre of the advancing line. At fifty paces he stood, in plain sight of the Aenir, and drew back on the string. The shaft hissed through the air, hammering home in the forehead of the lead warrior.

The Aenir charged . . .

Into a black-shafted wall of death. Hundreds fell within a few paces, and the charge faltered and failed, the enemy warriors sprinting back out of bowshot.

Caswallon walked out into the open and sat down. Laying his bow beside him he opened his hip pouch, removing a hunk of dark bread. This he began to eat, staring down at the milling warriors.

Stung by the silent taunt of his presence, they charged once more. Calmly Caswallon replaced the bread in his pouch, notched an arrow to his bow, loosed the shaft, and grinned as it brought down a stocky warrior in full cry, the arrow jutting from his chest.

The Aenir raced headlong into a second storm of shafts that culled their ranks and halted them. Caswallon, still shooting carefully, eased his way back into the bushes, out of sight. The Aenir fled once more, leaving a mound of their dead behind them.

A young archer named Onic crept through the gorse to where Caswallon knelt. 'We've all but exhausted our shafts,' he whispered.

'Pass the word to fall back,' said Caswallon.

In the valley Asbidag walked among the bodies, stopping to stare down at Cambil's mutilated corpse. 'Remove the head and set it on a spear by his house,' he told his son Tostig. The Aenir lord unbuckled his breastplate, handing it to a grim-faced warrior beside him. Then he looked around him, eyes raking the timber and the gaunt snow-covered peaks in the distance.

'I like this place,' he said, 'It has a good feeling to it.'

'But most of the Farlain escaped, Father,' said Tostig.

'Escaped? To where? All that's out there is wilderness. By tonight Drada will be here, having finished off the Haesten. Ongist will be harrying the Pallides, driving the survivors west into our arms. Once they are destroyed we will take our men into the wilderness and finish the task — that's if Barsa doesn't do it before we arrive.'

'Barsa?'

'He is already in the west with two thousand forest-trained warriors from the south. They call themselves Timber-Wolves, and by Vatan they're a match for any motley rag-bag of stinking clansmen.'

'We took no women,' complained Tostig. 'Most of the young ones killed themselves. Bitches!'

'Drada will bring women. Do not fret.'

Asbidag began to move among the bodies once more, turning over the women and the young girls. Finally he stood up and walked towards the house of Cambil.

'Who are you seeking?' asked Tostig, walking beside him.

504

'Cambil's daughter. Hair like gold, and a spirited girl. Unspoiled. I didn't like the way she looked at me. And I told you to set Cambil's head on a spear!'

Tostig blanched and fell back. 'At once, Father,' he stammered, running back to the bodies and drawing his sword.

Durk of the Farlain was known as a morose, solitary man. He had no friends and had chosen to spend his life in the high country west of the valley, where he built a small house of timber and grey stone and settled down to a life of expected loneliness. Durk had always been a loner, and even as a child had kept himself apart from his fellows. It was not, he knew, that he disliked people, more that he was not good with words. He had never learned how to engage in light conversation. Crowds unnerved him, always had, and he avoided the dance and the feasts. Girls found him surly and uncommunicative, men thought him stand-offish and aloof. Year by year the young clansman felt himself to be more and more remote from his fellows. Durk found this hurtful, but knew that the blame lay within his own shy heart.

But that first winter alone had almost starved him out until his neighbour Onic introduced him to Caswallon's night raids on bordering territories.

In the beginning Durk had disliked Caswallon. It was easy to see why: they were night and day, winter and summer. Where Caswallon smiled easily and joked often, Durk remained sullen with strangers and merely silent with companions.

Yet, for his part, Caswallon seemed to enjoy Durk's company and little by little his easy-going, friendly nature wore away the crofter's tough shell.

Through Caswallon Durk met Kareen, the gentle child of the house and, in spite of himself, had fallen in love with her. In the most incredible slice of good fortune ever to befall the dark-bearded highlander, Kareen had agreed to marry him.

She transformed his dingy house into a comfortable home and made his joy complete by falling pregnant in the first month of their marriage. With her Durk learned to laugh at his own failings, and his shyness retreated. At their marriage he even danced with several of Kareen's friends. Laughter and joy covered him, drawing him back into the bosom of the clan, filling the empty places in his heart.

Four days ago, in her eighth month, Kareen had returned to the valley to have the babe in the home of Larcia, wife of the councillor Tesk and midwife to the Farlain.

But last night Durk had heard the war-horns blaring and he had set out for the valley, filled with apprehension. In the first light of dawn he had met the column of fleeing clansmen.

Tesk was not amongst them.

Caswallon had run forward to meet him, leading him away from the column. There Durk heard the news that clove his heart like an axe-blade. Tesk had died with Cambil and almost eight hundred others. With them was Kareen. Caswallen had seen her in the circle at the last, a hunting-knife in her hand, as the Aenir swept over them.

Durk did not ask why the rest of the clan had not raced back to die with them, although he dearly desired to.

'Come with us,' said Caswallon.

'I don't think that I will, my friend,' Durk replied.

Caswallon bowed his head, his green eyes sorrowful. 'Do what you must, Durk. The gods go with you.'

'And with you, Caswallon. You are the leader at last.'

'I didn't want it.'

'No, but you are suited to it. You always were.'

Now Durk stood at the timberline, gazing down into the valley, past the gutted homes and the Aenir tents, and on to the mounds of bodies in the centre of the field.

He left the trees and began the long walk to his wife.

Two Aenir warriors watched him come. They stood, discarding their food, and moved to intercept him. He was walking so casually, as if on a morning stroll. Could he be a messenger, seeking peace? Or one of Barsa's Timber-Wolves, dressed like a clansman.

'You there!' called the first, holding up his hand. 'Wait!'

The hand vanished in a crimson spray as Durk's sword flashed through the air. The return cut clove the man's neck. As he crumpled to the grass the second drew his sword and leaped forward. Durk ducked under a whistling sweep to gut the man.

He walked on. Kareen had been no beauty but her eyes were soft and gentle, and her mouth seemed always to be smiling, as if life held some secret enchantment and she alone knew the mystery of it.

In the valley Aenir warriors were moving about, eating, drinking and swapping stories. The invasion had gone well and their losses had been few, save for the night before against the ferocious clan sword-ring. Who would have believed that a few hundred men and women could have put up such a struggle?

Durk moved on.

No one stopped him or even seemed to notice him as he walked to the mound of bodies and began to search for Kareen. He found her at the centre, lying beneath the headless corpse of Cambil. Gently he pulled her clear and tried to wipe the blood from her face, but it was dried hard and did not move.

By now his actions had aroused the interest of five warriors who wandered forward to watch him. Durk felt their eyes upon him and he laid Kareen to the ground. He stood and walked towards them, his face expressionless, his dark eyes scanning them.

They made no move towards their swords until he was almost upon them. It was as if his calm, casual movements cast an eldritch spell.

Durk's sword whispered from the scabbard . . .

The spell broke.

The Aenir scrabbled for their blades as Durk's sword licked into them. The first fell screaming; the second tumbled back, his throat spraying blood into the air. The third died as he knelt staring at the gushing stump of his sword arm. The fourth hammered his sword into Durk's side, then reeled away dying as the clansman shrugged off the mortal wound and backhanded a return cut to the man's throat. The fifth backed away, shouting for help.

Durk staggered and gazed down at the wound in his side. Blood flowed there, soaking his leggings and pooling at his feet. More Aenir warriors ran forward, stopping to stare at the dying clansman.

'Come on then, you woman-killers! Face a man!' he snarled.

A warrior ran forward with sword raised. Durk contemptuously batted aside his wild slash and reversed his own blade into the man's belly.

The clansman began to laugh, then suddenly he choked and staggered. Blood welled in his throat and he spat it clear.

'You miserable whoresons,' he said. 'Warriors? You're like a flock of sheep with fangs.'

Dropping his sword, he turned and staggered back to Kareen's body, slumping beside her. He lifted her head.

A spear smashed through his back and he arched upward violently.

His vision swam, his last sight was Kareen's face.

'I'm so sorry,' he said, 'I should have been here.'

Orsa gazed down at the body, then tore the spear from the clansman's back.

'He was a madman,' muttered a warrior behind him.

'He was a *man*,' said Orsa, turning and pushing his way through the throng.

The Aenir milled round the corpses for a while, then drifted back to their forgotten meals.

'He was a fine swordsman,' said a lean, wolfish warrior, dusting off the chicken leg he'd dropped in the dirt.

'It was stupid,' offered a second man, gathering up a bulging wineskin.

'He was baresark,' said the first.

'Nonsense. We all know what happens to a berserker – he goes mad and attacks in a blind frenzy.'

'No, that's what we do. The clansmen are different. They go cold and deadly, where we are hot. But the effect is the same. They don't care.'

'Taken to thinking now, Snorri?'

'This place makes you think,' said Snorri. 'Just look around you. Wouldn't you be willing to die for a land like this?'

'I don't want to die for any piece of land. A woman, maybe. Not dirt, though.'

'Did you enjoy the clan woman you took last night?'

'Shut your stinking mouth!'

'Killed herself, I hear.'

'I said shut it!'

'Easy, Bemar! There's no need to lose your temper.'

'It's this place, it gets under my skin. I knew it wouldn't be easy. I felt it in my bones. Did you see the look in that clansman's eyes? Like he thought we were nothing. A flock of sheep with fangs! You could laugh, but he had just slain seven men. Seven!'

'I know,' said Snorri. 'It was the same last night with their swording-ring. It was like hurling yourself against a cliff-face. There was no give in them at all; no fear. That scout Ongist caught and blood-eagled – he didn't make a sound, just glared at us as we opened his ribs. Maybe they're not people at all.'

'What does that mean?' asked Bemar, dropping his voice to a whisper.

'The witch woman, Agnetha. She can turn men into animals. Maybe the clans are all animals turned into men.'

'That's stupid.'

'They don't act like men,' argued Snorri. 'Have you heard one clansman beg? Have you heard any tales of such a thing?'

'They die like men,' said Bemar.

'I think they are more. You've heard Asbidag's order. Not one man, woman or child to be left alive. No slaves. All dead. Doesn't it strike you as strange?'

'I don't want to think about it. And I don't want to talk about it,' muttered Bemar, hurling aside the wineskin.

'Wolf men, that's what they are,' whispered Snorri.

Caswallon watched helplessly as Durk walked back towards the valley. He knew the clansman was seeking death, and he could not blame him for it. Kareen had been his life, his joy. Even as Maeg meant everything to Caswallon.

The clan column moved on and Caswallon took his place at the head alongside Leofas. Crofters from outlying areas joined the exodus as the day wore on, and many were the questions levelled at the new lord.

Where were they going? What would they do? What had happened to one man's sister? Another's brother? Why did they not turn and fight? Why had the Aenir attacked? Where was Cambil? Who elected Caswallon?

The clansman lost his temper before dusk, storming away from the column and running quickly to the top of a nearby hill. Around him the dying sun lit the valleys of the Farlain, bathing them in blood. Caswallon sank to the ground, staring out over the distant peaks of High Druin.

'It's all a lie,' he said softly. Then he began to chuckle. 'You've lived a damn lie.'

Poor Cambil. Poor, lonely Cambil.

'You should not have feared me, cousin,' Caswallon told the gathering darkness. 'Your father knew; he was wiser than you.'

The night before the young Caswallon had left his foster-father's house for the last time, Padris had taken him to the northern meadow and there presented him with a cloak, a dagger and two gold pieces.

'I will not lie to you, Caswallon,' Padris had told him, his keen eyes sorrowful. 'You have been a disappointment to me. I have raised you like my own son and you have great talents. But you are not worthy. You have a sharp mind, a good brain and a strong body. You will prosper. But you are not worthy. There is in you a fear that I cannot fathom. Outwardly you are brave enough, and you take your beatings like a man. But you are not clan. You don't care. What is it that you fear?'

'I fear nothing,' Caswallon had told him.

'Wrong. Now I see two fears. The one that you hide, and now the fear of showing it. Go in peace, Caswallon of the Farlain.'

'You were right, Padris,' Caswallon whispered to the sky. 'This is what I feared. Chains. Questions. Responsibilities.'

Giving judgements over land disputes, settling rows over cattle or sheep, or thefts, or wayward wives and wandering husbands. Sentencing poachers, granting titles, deciding on the suitability of couples in love, and granting them the right to wed. Every petty problem a double-edged dagger.

And so he avoided the elections.

But what had it gained? The Farlain invaded and thousands dead throughout Druin. And what price the future?

He swore as he heard footsteps approaching. Leofas slumped down beside him, breathing hard. 'No sign of pursuit,' said the old warrior.

'Good.'

'Talk, boy. Shed the burden.'

'It would shed the burden if you agreed to lead.'

'We've been over that before. I'm not the man for it.'

'Neither am I.'

'Whisht, lad! Don't talk nonsense. You're doing fine. So far we've saved the greater number of our cousins, and with luck there's another two thousand crofters who would have heard the horns and taken to the hills.'

'Damn you, old man. I never gave you much of an argument before, and I should have. You've been on the Council since before I was born. You're respected, everyone would follow you. You're the natural choice. What right have you to shirk your responsibility?'

'None whatsoever, Caswallon. And I cannot be accused of it. A man needs to know his strengths if he is to prosper, and his weaknesses if he is to survive. I know what you are going through but, believe me, you are the best man we have. I'll grant that you would make a bad Hunt Lord; you don't have the application. But this is war. With luck it will be a short, sharp exercise, and you're the man to plan it. Think of it as a giant raid. Ye gods, man, you were good enough at that.'

'But it isn't a raid,' snapped Caswallon. 'One mistake and we lose everything.'

'I didn't say it was easy.'

'That's true enough.'

'You have faith in Taliesen, do you not?'

'Yes.'

'Well, he said you were the only man capable of pulling a victory from this catastrophic beginning. And I believe him.'

'I wish I had your faith.'

'It's because you don't that convinces me,' said Leofas, slapping him on the shoulder, 'I'm going to say this once, boy, for I'm not given to compliments. There's a nobility in you, and a strength you've not began to touch. Rescuing Gaelen showed it to me. It was a fine, bonny thing. But more than that, I remember when we hunted the beast. You lifted Cambil that night when his fear for his son threatened to unman him, and among men who despised you it was you they followed when you walked to the north. When the Queen was dying and delirious you gave her words of comfort. You it was who planned the victory at the Games, and you again who brought us out of the valley.

'So don't sit here bemoaning your fate. You are where you should be: War Lord of Farlain. Do I make myself clear?'

'I should have spoken to you ten years ago,' said Caswallon. 'Maybe I would have been different.'

'Ten years ago you wouldn't have listened. Whoring and stealing filled your mind.'

'Good days, though,' said Caswallon, grinning.

'Don't say it as though you're letting me into a secret. I was whoring and stealing before you were born. And probably making a better job of it!'

Gaelen awoke, rolling to his back and rubbing his eyes. The night was silent, save for the movement of bats in the trees above him and the skittering sound of badgers in the undergrowth off to the left. These were sounds he knew well. But something else had pierced his dreams, bringing him to wakefulness. His mind was hazy, confused. It had seemed as if horns were blowing far away, whispering in the night breeze.

But now there was silence as Gaelen sat up and looked around him. Render was gone, hunting his supper, and the fire had died down within its circle of rocks. Gaelen added fuel, more for light than heat. As the blaze flared he pushed back his blanket and stood up, stretching the muscles of his back. He was hungry. The sky was lightening and the dawn was not far off. Gathering his bow and quiver, he made his way to the edge of the wood, looking down on to a gently sloping field, silver in the waning moonlight. Upon it were scores of rabbits nibbling at grass and clover. Gaelen settled down on his knees and strung the bow; he then selected an arrow and notched it to the string. Spotting a buck some twenty paces distant, he drew and loosed the shaft. As the buck fell, the other rabbits disappeared at speed. Returning to the fire he skinned the beast, gutting and slicing it for the pot. Render loped through the bushes, jaws bloody, and squatted down beside him, waiting expectantly for the remains.

Gaelen threw the offal to the hound, who set to work on his second meal of the night. As dawn light seeped into the sky, Gaelen found himself thinking of the Queen Beyond. Often her face would come to him, sometimes in dreams but more often as he went about the chores of the day. She had died for him – for them – and Gaelen wished, with all his heart, that he could have repaid her. And what did she mean when she promised to come again?

By mid-morning Gaelen and Render were picking their way down a wooded slope alongside a tumbling stream. Every forty or fifty paces the water hissed over rocky falls, gushing at ever-increasing speed towards the valley below. Birds sang in the trees, and crimson flowers bloomed by the water. Every now and then, as they came to a break in the trees, Gaelen stopped and gazed on the mountains, still snow-capped, like old men in a line. Gaelen knew he should be feeling guilty about his leisurely pace and the wide western swing he was making, for there was plenty of spring work back home. But after the winter cooped up in the valley, he needed the solitude.

A woman's scream pierced the glade. Render's head came up, a deep growl starting in his throat. Gaelen flashed his hand up, palm outwards, and the dog fell silent. The scream came from the right, beyond a thicket of gorse. Gaelen eased his hunting-knife into his hand, released his pack and bow from his shoulders and moved forward silently. Render padded beside him.

Once in the thicket other noises came to them – the rending of cloth, and slapping sounds as if open-handed blows were being struck. Creeping forward, bent double, Gaelen came to the edge of the thicket. Three Aenir warriors had pinned a young girl to the ground. Two held her arms, the third crouched over her, slashing her clothes with a knife and ripping them from her.

Gaelen calmed the dog and waited. He couldn't see the girl's face, but from the clothes she was Farlain. The Aenir stripped her naked, then one forced her legs apart, dropping his hand to loosen his breeches. As he did so Gaelen pointed to the warrior holding the girl.

'Kill!' he hissed. Render leaped forward, covering the ground in three bounds, snarling ferociously. The three whirled at the sound, dragging their knives clear. Render's great jaws closed upon the throat of his victim, the Aenir's neck snapping with a hideous crack. Gaelen, long hunting-knife in hand, was just behind the dog. He hurdled the beast, batting aside a wild slash from the second Aenir, then himself backhanded a cut across the man's face. The warrior's cheek blossomed red and he fell back, dropping his knife. Gaelen threw himself forward to plunge his own blade through the man's leather jerkin, up under the ribs, seeking the heart. The man's eyes opened in shock and pain. Gaelen twisted the blade to free it from the suction of the man's body and tore it loose, kicking him away. Spinning, he was just in time to parry a thrust from the third warrior who aimed a vicious cut at his head. Gaelen ducked beneath it, stepping inside to hammer the knife into the man's groin. The Aenir screamed and fell. Gaelen dragged the knife clear, punching it to the man's throat and cutting off his screams. Render, still growling, tore at his victim, though the man was long dead.

'Home!' hissed Gaelen. In the following silence he listened intently. Satisfied the Aenir were alone, he ran to the girl.

It was Deva, her face bruised and swollen, her lips cut and bleeding. She was unconscious. Gaelen gathered what remained of her clothes and lifted the girl to his shoulder. Then he made his way back through the thicket to his pack and laboured on up the slope, keeping to the rocky paths and firmer areas that would leave less sign of his passing.

His breathing was ragged as he reached the highest point of the slope, cutting into a sheltered glade where he lowered Deva to the ground. She was breathing evenly. Her shirt was in tatters and he threw it to one side. Her skirt had been ripped in half. Removing it, he spread the cloth and sliced an opening in the centre. Sheathing his knife he lifted the girl to a sitting position and put the skirt over her head, widening the slash until the garment settled over her shoulders like a cape that fell to her knees. He tore her shirt into strips and fashioned a belt which he tied round her waist, then he laid her back.

'Stay!' he ordered Render and the hound settled down beside the girl. Gaelen gathered up his bow and quiver and retraced his steps to the slope, crouching in the undergrowth, eyes searching the trail.

There were so many questions. Why were the Aenir so far into the Farlain? What was Deva doing alone in the wilderness? What manner of men were these warriors who dressed like foresters and carried hunting-knives like the clans? Had the war begun, or were they merely scouts? How many more were searching these woods? He could answer none of the questions.

He had been lucky today, waiting until the men's lust was at its height before launching an attack. But once the enemy discovered the bodies they would be on his trail like wolves after a wounded deer. More than luck would be needed to survive from now on, he knew.

He was at least two days from the valley, but if the war had begun there was no point going east. If it had not, there was little point heading for Attafoss, a day or more to the north-east.

Down the slope he saw a flash of movement and drew back into the bushes. A man appeared, then another, then a file of warriors bearing bows. They did not seem to be hunting a trail, but if they kept moving along the track they would find the bodies. Gaelen waited until the file had passed, counting them, despair growing as the figure topped one hundred.

This was no scouting party.

Pulling back out of sight he ran to the glade, kneeling over Deva, lifting her head and lightly stroking her face. She came awake with a start, a scream beginning as his hand clamped over her mouth.

'Be silent, Deva, it is Gaelen!' he hissed. Her eyes swivelled to him and she blinked and nodded. He removed his hand.

'The Aenir?' she whispered.

'Dead. But more are coming and we must move. Can you run?'

She nodded and he helped her to her feet. Hoisting his pack, he gathered up the remains of her clothing and bade her wait for him. He moved east for two hundred paces, crossing the stream, leaving his track on a muddy bank, and looping a torn fragment of Deva's shirt over a gorse bush. Satisfied with the false trail, he turned west again, moving more carefully over the rocks and firm ground until he rejoined Deva in the glade.

'Let's go,' he said, heading for Attafoss.

They made almost half a mile when the horns sounded, echoing eerily in the mountains around them. 'They've found the bodies,' he said grimly. 'Let's push on.'

Throughout the long afternoon Gaelen led them ever higher into the mountains, stopping often to study the back-trail and keeping ever under cover. Deva stumbled after him, still in shock after her narrow escape, and yet awed by the authoritative manner in which Gaelen was leading. There was no panic in him, nor yet any sign of fear. He was, she realised not without shock, a clansman.

And he had killed three Aenir warriors. She was sorry to have missed that event.

Towards dusk Gaelen found a secluded hollow off the trail and he dumped his pack and sat down. He stayed there silently for some minutes, ignoring the girl; then he stood and returned to the trail, crouching to scan the mountainside. There was no sign of pursuit. He waited until it was too dark to see any distance, then returned to the hollow. Deva was bathing her face with water from his canteen and he squatted beside her.

'How are you faring?' he asked.

'Well. Are they close?'

'I can see no one, but that tells us nothing. They are woodsmen, they could be anywhere.'

'Yes.'

'What were you doing in the mountains?' he asked her.

'I had to visit my uncle Lars, who has a croft cabin south of here. I went with Larain. We were coming home when we saw the Aenir and we both ran. I hid in the woods, I don't know what happened to Larain. Most of the night I listened for them, but I heard nothing. This morning I tried to get back to the valley, but they were waiting for me. I got away once but they caught me back there, where you found me.'

'It's an invasion,' said Gaelen.

'But why would they do such a thing?'

'I don't know, Deva. I don't believe they need a reason to fight. Rest now.'

'Thank you for my tunic,' she whispered, leaning in to kiss his cheek.

'I could do no better,' he stammered. Reaching past her, he pulled his blanket roll from the pack. 'Wrap yourself. It will be a chill night and we can afford no fire.'

'Gaelen?'

'Yes.'

'I . . . I thank you for saving my life.'

'Thank me when we reach safety. If there is such a place still . . .'

She watched the darkness swallow him, knowing he would spend the night on the edge of the trail. Render settled down beside her and she snuggled in to his warm body.

Gaelen awoke just before dawn, coming out of a light doze in his hiding place by the trail's edge. He yawned and stretched. The path below was still clear. Rounding the bushes he stopped, jolted by a heel print on the track not ten paces from where he had slept.

The track was fresh. Swiftly he searched the ground. He found another print, and a third alongside it. Two men. And they were ahead of him.

Ducking once more, he re-entered the glade, waking Deva and rolling his blanket. Taking up his pack, he unstrapped his bow and strung it.

Glancing round, he saw that Render had gone a-hunting.

'We have a problem,' he told the girl.

517

'They are ahead of us?'

He nodded. 'Only two of them. Scouts. They passed in the night.'

'Then give me a bow. My marksmanship is good, and you'll need your hands clear for knife work.'

He handed her the weapon without hesitation. All clanswomen were practised with the bow and Deva had the reputation of being better than most.

Slowly they made their way north and east, wary of open ground, until at last the trees thinned and a gorse-covered slope beckoned beyond. It stretched for some four hundred paces.

'You could hide an army down there,' whispered Deva, crouching beside him in the last of the undergrowth before the slope.

'I know. But we have little choice. The main force is behind us. They have sent these scouts ahead to cut us off. If we remain here the main body will come upon us. We must go on.'

'You go first. I'll wait here. If I spot movement I'll signal.'

'Very well. But don't shoot until you are sure of a hit.'

Biting back an angry retort, she nodded. What did he think she was going to do? Shoot at shadows? Gaelen left the cover of the trees and moved slowly down the slope, tense and expectant. Deva scanned the gorse, trying not to focus on any one point. Her father had taught her that movement was best seen peripherally.

A bush to the right moved, as if a man was easing through it. Then her attention was jerked away by a noise from behind and she turned. A hundred paces back along the trail, a man had fallen and his comrades were laughing at him. They were not yet in sight, but would be in a matter of moments. She was trapped! Fighting down panic, she notched an arrow to the bow. Gaelen reached the bottom of the slope and glanced back. Deva lifted both hands, pointing one index finger left, the other right. Then she jerked her thumb over her shoulder.

Gaelen cursed and moved. He broke into a lunging run for the gorse, angling to the right, his knife in his hand. Surprised by the sudden sprint, the hidden archer had to step into the open. His bow was already bent.

Deva drew back the bow-string to nestle against her cheek. Releasing her breath slowly, she calmed her mind and sighted on the motionless archer. Gaelen threw himself forward in a tumbler's roll as the man released his shaft. It whistled over his head. Deva let fly, the arrow flashing down to thud into the archer's chest. The man dropped his bow and fell to his knees, clutching at the shaft; then he toppled sideways to the earth.

Coming out of his roll, Gaelen saw the man fall. The second Aenir, a huge man with a braided yellow beard, hurled his bow aside and drew his own hunting-knife. He leapt at the clansman, his knife plunging towards Gaelen's belly. Gaelen dived to the left – and the Aenir's blade raked his ribs. Rolling to his feet Gaelen launched himself at the warrior, his shoulder cannoning into the man's chest. Off-balance, the Aenir fell, Gaelen on top of him. The blond warrior tried to rise but Gaelen slammed his forehead against the Aenir's nose, blinding him momentarily. As the man fell back Gaelen rolled on to the warrior's knife-arm and sliced his own blade across the bearded throat. Blood bubbled and surged from the gaping wound, drenching the clansman. Pushing the body under thick gorse, Gaelen rolled to his feet and ran back to the first man. Deva was already there, struggling to pull the body out of sight into the bushes. Together they made it with scant moments to spare.

Huddled together over the corpse, Gaelen put his arm round Deva, drawing her close as the Aenir force breasted the slope. 'If they find the other body we're finished,' he said. His knife was in his hand and he knew with bleak certainty that he would cut her throat rather than let them take her.

The enemy moved down the slope. Grim men they were, and they moved cautiously, many notching arrows to bow-strings, their eyes flickering over the gorse. Gaelen took a deep breath, fighting to stay calm; his heart was thudding against his chest like a drum. He closed his eyes, Deva leaned against him and he could smell the perfume of her hair.

The Aenir entered the gorse, pushing on towards the east. Two men passed within ten paces of where they lay. They were talking and joking now, content that the open ground was behind them.

The last of the Aenir moved away out of earshot. Gaelen felt cramped, but still he did not move. It was hard to stay so still, for hiding was a passive, negative thing that leached a man's courage.

'You can let go of me now, clansman,' whispered Deva.

He nodded, but did not move. Deva looked up into his face, seeing the tension and fear. Raising her hand, she stroked his cheek. 'Help me get this swine's jerkin,' she said.

Gaelen released her, smiling sheepishly. He pulled her arrow from the man's ribs and they worked the brown leather jerkin clear. Deva slipped it on over her tunic. It was too large by far and Gaelen trimmed the shoulders with his knife.

'How do I look?' she asked him.

'Beautiful,' he said.

'If this is beautiful, you should have been struck dumb at the Whorl Dance.'

'I was.'

Deva giggled. She looped the man's knife-belt round her waist. 'You were so forlorn, Gaelen. I felt quite sorry for you, with your swollen leg.'

'I felt quite sorry for myself.'

'What are your plans now? Why are we heading north?'

'With luck the clan will be there.'

'Why should they be?'

'I believe the war has begun. The Aenir will have raided the valleys. But Caswallon has a plan.'

'Caswallon!' she snapped. 'Caswallon is not Hunt Lord!'

'No, but he should be,' hissed Gaelen. A sound in the bushes jolted them, but relief swept over Gaelen as Render's great black and grey head appeared. Kneeling, he patted the dog affectionately, using the time to let the angry moment pass.

'I'm sorry,' he said at last, 'I did not mean that.'

'You meant it. Let's talk no more of it. We've a long way to go.'

8

Drada arrived in Farlain valleys on the second day of the invasion, having completed his attack on the Haesten. Throughout the day his men had been scouring the mountains, hunting down clansmen and their families, killing the men and older women, taking the young girls alive. So far they had killed more than a thousand highlanders.

Leaving a third of his force behind to harry the remnants of Laric's people, he moved on to join his father. There was no word from Ongist and his force, apart from the first message that told of Maggrig's flight into the mountains.

With twenty men Drada rode ahead of the marching army, reigning his mount on the high slope above the first valley. Below him were a dozen or so gutted houses; the rest had been taken over by the Aenir, whose tents also dotted the field. Drada was discontented. The assault had not been a complete success. The Haesten were all but wiped out, but the Pallides and the Farlain were still at large.

Barsa's Timber-Wolves would harry them in the north-west, but Drada did not share his father's scant regard for the clans' fighting abilities. And he had heard of Cambil's death with regret.

Not that he liked the man, more that he was easy to read, and if the Farlain had to escape Drada would have rested more easily knowing Cambil was Hunt Lord. He didn't need to be a prophet to predict the next leader:

Caswallon!

The viper beneath the Aenir heel.

Spurring his mount he rode down into the valley, past the field where cattle and sheep grazed contentedly. His brother Tostig saw him coming and walked out to meet him, standing before the cairn which housed the combined dead of the first assault.

'Greetings, brother,' said Tostig as Drada dismounted, handing the reins to a following rider, 'I told you the war would be short and sweet.'

Drada stared into his brother's ugly face, 'It is not over yet,' he said evenly.

Tostig spat. There's no real fight in these mountain dogs. They'll give us sport for a few weeks, that's all.'

'We'll see,' said Drada, pushing past him. He entered the house of Cambil, seeking his father. Asbidag sat in the wide leather chair before the hearth, drinking from a silver goblet. Beside him was a jug of mead and a half-eaten loaf. Drada pulled up a chair opposite and removed his cloak. Asbidag was drunk; ale dribbled to his red beard at every swallow, flowing over the crumbs of bread lodged there. His bloodshot eyes turned to Drada and he belched and leaned forward.

'Well?' he snarled.

'The Haesten are finished.'

Asbidag began to laugh. He drained the last of the ale and then lifted the silver goblet, crushing it suddenly, the muscles of his forearm writhing as his powerful fingers pressed the metal out of shape.

'Finished? What about the Farlain? Your plan was a disaster.' The words were slurred but the eyes gleamed with malevolent intelligence.

'We have the valleys and the Farlain have nowhere to go, and no food supply.'

'So you say.'

Morgase entered the room and Drada stood and bowed. Ignoring him, she moved to Asbidag and knelt by the chair, stroking the bread from his beard. Asbidag's eyes softened as he gazed on her cool beauty. He lumbered to his feet, pulling her up beside him, his huge hand sliding down her flank. He leered at her and left the room, stumbling on the stairs.

'Wait here,' said Morgase. 'I shall see you presently.'

'I think not, Lady. I fear you will be preoccupied for some little while.'

'We shall see.'

Drada moved from the hard seat to the wide leather chair his father had vacated, easing himself back and lifting his feet to a small table. He closed his eyes, enjoying the comfort. He was tired, he hadn't realised quite how tired. The light was fading. He cursed softly and pushed himself upright, gathering candles from the kitchen. Taking a steel tinder-box from his pouch he struck a flame and lit a candle, placing it in a brass holder on the wall above the hearth. Near the door was a crystal lantern which he also trimmed and lit. Returning to the chair, he tried once more to relax but he could not. He was over-tired and filled with the tension only the planning of war could produce.

Morgase slipped silently into the room wearing only a dark silken robe. She knelt by him as she had knelt by his father. He looked down into her cold blue eyes; her cheeks were flushed, her lips swollen and red. By candlelight her face looked younger, softer.

'He is sleeping,' she whispered.

'Good. I wish I was.'

'Soon, Drada. Soon. Listen to me. I promised you the Gateway to empires. Do you still desire it?'

'Of course.' Leaning forward, he rubbed his tired eyes.

'The druids guard the Gateway. They have a hiding place near the great falls called Attafoss. You must lead an army to the north.'

'What is this Gateway?'

'I don't know what it is, only what it does. It is an entrance to my own world – a land full of riches and ripe for conquest.'

'What do you mean? There is no world to the north, only mountains and sea.'

'You are wrong. I was raised in a far land, not of this world. My father was an Earl. He was killed in a rebellion when I was seven years old. The land is ruled now by a warrior Queen but her armies have fought many battles and they are tired, weary to the bone.'

'I have heard of no Queen . . .' Drada began.

'Listen to me, you fool,' she hissed, her eyes angry. 'My brothers and I fought her for six long years, but our army was crushed. I fled north with two trusted servants; they brought me to a druid who lived in the eastern mountains and he told me of a Gate I could pass

523

that would lead to safety. The entrance was marked by a carving at the mouth of the cave, where someone long ago had chipped out the shape of a goblet. He took me there and we entered the cave, which was shallow and dripping with water. He spoke some words by the far wall, and it shimmered and disappeared. Then he beckoned me to follow him and stepped through where the wall had been. I followed and found myself in the mountains near a great waterfall.

'It was like a dream. The old man stepped one pace back – and disappeared. I tried to follow him but there was no way back. I walked south for many days until I reached the city of Ateris in the distance. There I met your father.'

Drada was awake now. 'You say the Farlain druids control this Gateway?'

'Yes.'

'And they can transport men *wherever* they wish to go?'

'Yes. Now do you see?'

'I do indeed.'

'The druid who helped me told me that if ever I wished to return I should seek a man named Taliesen.'

'I've met him,' said Drada.

'He guards the Gate, and controls its power.'

Drada leaned back in his chair, the tension easing from him, his weariness slipping away. 'Such a Gateway allowed the Aenir to invade these lands,' he said. 'But once we were through it closed behind us, becoming solid rock. For years we sought sorcerers and witches to open them but none succeeded. What are these Gates? Who made them?'

'I don't know. The old druid told me they had existed for centuries. In my land we have legends of trolls and giants, beasts and dragons. The druid said these were all creatures which had passed through random Gates.'

Drada sat back, saying nothing. This was a prize greater than any before. Dreams of empire grew in his mind. Suppose the Gates could send a man *wherever* he wished? Who could resist an army that appeared *within* a walled city? But was it possible? He looked down at Morgase, taking her chin in his hand. 'Have you told my father?'

Her hand came down to rest on his thigh. 'No, you are the man to lead the Aenir.' At her touch he stiffened, his eyes flickering to the darkened doorway.

'Have no fear, Drada. I slipped him a sleeping potion. He will not wake for hours.'

He lifted her to his lap and kissed her, his hand slipping beneath her robe.

'Are you worth dying for?' he asked, his voice husky, his face flushed.

'Find out,' she told him.

Gaelen and Deva spent their second night in a shallow cave, the entrance hidden by a hastily-erected screen of bushes. The day had been fraught, and their trail had been picked up by a second band of Aenir foresters. At one stage they had been sighted and chased for almost a mile before slipping their pursuers. Deva was exhausted, her feet grazed and blistered. Gaelen sliced strips of leather from her jerkin and she set to work shaping them into moccasins; but the leather was soft and they would not last long in the mountains.

They could light no fire and the night was cold. They spent it together, wrapped in Gaelen's blanket.

Gaelen was desperately worried now. The enemy were all around them and there was still open ground to cross. They would never make it. Deva slept on, her head resting on his shoulder. His back was cramped and sore, but he did not move. She was more tired than he, and needed the rest.

What would Caswallon do, he wondered? There must be a way to escape the Aenir net. Closing his eyes, he pictured the route to Attafoss. There were four sections of open ground, where the land dipped away into broad valleys with little or no cover. There was no way to avoid crossing at least one of them. Travelling by day would be suicidal. By night it would be almost as hazardous for, up to now, Gaelen had seen no sign of the Aenir camp-fires. They could blunder straight into an enemy camp.

In two days Gaelen had killed five enemy warriors. He had often dreamed of the day when he would pay them back for his terror and his wounds. But now he realised there was no joy, or satisfaction to be found. He wished they had never come to the Farlain. Wished it with all his heart.

Render stirred beside him, his great head coming up with ears pricked. Gaelen gestured the hound to silence and woke Deva gently, his hand over her mouth.

'Someone's coming,' he whispered. Carefully he crept to the mouth of the cave, easing aside the leaves and branches masking the entrance.

The Aenir had returned and were once more scouring the hillside for tracks.

With infinite care Gaelen withdrew his hand, allowing the branches to settle back. Then he drew his knife and waited. Render moved to him, laying his head on Gaelen's shoulder, nostrils quivering as he scented the Aenir. The cave was marginally below ground level, the entrance only three feet high, and Gaelen had uprooted two thick bushes, pulling them into the cave roots first. From outside they would appear to be growing at the base of the cliff.

For an hour or more the Aenir continued their search, then they moved further down the mountainside out of sight. Gaelen relaxed and crept back to Deva, putting his mouth close to her ear.

'We must wait until nightfall,' he whispered. She nodded. Outside the sun shone brightly, but its warmth could not penetrate the chill of the cave and they sat wrapped in Gaelen's blanket throughout the long afternoon.

Just after dusk Gaelen pushed aside the bushes and climbed from the cave, eyes searching the mountainside. The Aenir had moved on. Deva passed out his pack and bow, then joined him in the open. Gaelen pushed the bush screen back in place.

'We may need to get back here,' he said, 'It leaves us one hiding place.'

They set off in silence, threading a path through the trees towards the first valley. The night was brighter than Gaelen would have liked, a three-quarter moon shining in the clear sky. They stopped at the timberline, wary of leaving the sanctuary of the trees, and remembering the hidden Aenir scouts of the day before.

Stepping out into the open, Gaelen started the long walk to the shadow-shrouded valley. Deva, an arrow notched to the bow, walked just behind him, while Render loped out in a wide circle, content merely to be free of the narrow confines of the cave. The wind was in Gaelen's face and that pleased him, for Render would pick up any scent. Frequently Gaelen glanced at the hound, seeking sign of alarm. But there was none.

It took them an hour to cross the valley and climb the steep slope beyond. With one danger past, the next took its place.

They could not see anything within the trees; overhanging branches shut out the moonlight, creating a wall of darkness. Within the wood could be a hundred, a thousand, Aenir waiting for them.

They had no choice. Hand on knife, Gaelen walked into the darkness, leaning against a broad trunk and allowing his eyes to become accustomed to the stygian gloom. They moved on, carefully. It was uncannily still among the trees, not a sound whispered in the night. The breeze had fallen away and above them the branches hung together forming an archway, the trees like colonnaded pillars. No bats skittered in the trees. No animals disturbed the undergrowth. It was like passing through a Hall of the Dead, murky and silent, pregnant with menace.

Render's head came up and he sniffed the air. He made no sound but looked away to the left. Gaelen patted him softly. About twenty paces away he could just make out the silhouette of a seated man. Gaelen stood statue-still. As he stared he could see more men lying on the ground, wrapped in blankets.

An Aenir camp!

Gesturing to Deva, he dropped to his hands and knees and began to crawl. The sentry coughed and spat. Gaelen froze. They eased their way past the group and into the forest beyond. They were climbing now and it became more difficult to move quietly. Sweat ran down Gaelen's face and his breathing grew ragged. He knew that stress was sapping his strength as much as the flight itself. Deva was bearing up well. He smiled grimly. But then she was clan!

They climbed a steep slope and Gaelen peered over the rim, dropping back almost immediately. Beyond were another twenty Aenir asleep. A sentry was seated on a boulder on the far side. He had – thank God – been looking away when Gaelen appeared. Gaelen edged some thirty paces further along the slope. Carefully he raised his head over the rim. There was a screen of trees now between them and the Aenir sentry. Swiftly he levered himself over the rim. Render scrambled up after him. Deva handed Gaelen the bow, then smoothly climbed to join them.

Once more in the trees, they breasted the rise and pushed on into the second valley. There was more gorse here and Gaelen felt his confidence rising. Then the breeze picked up once more – and saved their lives.

Render growled, hurtling forward into the gorse. A man's scream rent the night. Deva dropped to one knee, drawing the bow-string back to her cheek. Gaelen ran left, dropping his pack and drawing his knife. Three men ran from the bushes towards them. The first fell, Deva's arrow jutting from his right eye. Gaelen leaped feet-first at the second, kicking him in the face; the man fell back. Gaelen hit the ground and rolled as the third Aenir raced past him towards Deva. The girl had no time to draw fully and let fly on half string. The arrow struck the man in the face, ripping open his cheek, but he tore it loose and kept coming. Deva hurled her bow aside as the man leaped upon her, bearing her to the ground.

'I have you now, you bitch!' he shouted, his knife poised above her throat. But a black shadow loomed, and Render's huge jaws clamped down on the man's face, fangs ripping away skin and flesh. Blood sprayed over Deva as the Aenir toppled from her. Weakly he tried to stab the hound, but then came the sound of crunching bones – and his skull shattered.

Gaelen rolled to his feet and hurled himself across the body of the second Aenir, who had been stunned by the kick and was struggling to rise when the young clansman dived upon him. Gaelen's knife plunged into his back. He screamed and thrashed his

528

arms as Gaelen ripped the knife loose, whipping the blade across the man's throat.

Render padded towards him, jaws bloody. The silence that followed was broken by sounds of running men.

Grabbing his pack and bow Gaelen signalled to Deva and began to run, steering away from the pursuers and then cutting north. Beside him Deva ran easily, the bow looped over her left shoulder. Gaelen pushed the pace as hard as he dared, and Deva courageously matched him, though her lungs were burning and her legs aching.

They reached the trees ahead of their pursuers. What they needed now was somewhere to hide. The problem was that in the dark Gaelen had no way of knowing what sort of tracks they were leaving. He halted and grabbed Deva's arm. 'Give them something to think about,' he said. As the Aenir reached the bottom of the slope she sent a shaft into their ranks, catching a man high in the shoulder. The man cursed loudly, the rest diving to the ground. There were only ten men in the pursuing group, and none of them wanted to rush uphill towards a hidden archer.

'Now, let's go,' said Gaelen.

Deva shook her head, still fighting to catch her breath. 'Need . . . a . . . moment,' she said. Taking the bow, he crouched at the edge of the trees, trying to spot any attempt to outflank them.

After a few moments Deva tapped his shoulder. 'I'm ready,' she told him. He nodded and they slipped away into the trees.

As dawn lit the valleys Gaelen took a desperate gamble. Believing them clear of the Aenir he decided to push on through the day, reaching Attafoss before dark. He knew the risks were great, for there could well be enemy soldiers ahead. But, he thought, they would certainly catch up should he hide all day waiting for darkness. And he had no desire to repeat last night's adventures.

They crossed the open ground and found no sign of the enemy. Render loped out ahead of them, cutting off to chase a hare, but it ducked out of sight and the hound padded back to his master. High in the mountains now, the pursuit far behind them, Gaelen relaxed. Deva also felt tension easing from her.

'You don't say much, Gaelen,' she said.

'No. I'm not very good with words.'

'Is that true? Or are you just anxious around women?'

'That, too.'

'Do you like Layne?'

'Yes, he's a good friend.'

'He wants to marry me.'

Gaelen felt a knot of tension growing within him. Angry and uncertain, he said nothing.

'Well, speak, clansman.'

'What is there to say? You did not ask a question. You know that I feel . . . that I would like . . . damn! As I said, I am not good with words. I lived alone for many years as a child. I talked to few people; I never learned the art of conversation. I am dull though I would prefer not to be. It would be nice to make people laugh with a witty jest, but it's not the way I am.'

'You are fine the way you are,' she said, feeling guilty and a little ashamed, 'I'm sorry. I should not have teased you.'

'You could have picked a better time,' he said, smiling.

'Yes. Do you think the clan will be at Attafoss?'

'I hope so.'

'You are a fine man, Gaelen. Truly fine.'

'I am glad that you think so. Will you wed Layne?'

'No,' she told him sorely. 'When I was born an old tinker-woman make a prediction for me. She said I would be the mother of kings.'

'What does that mean? There are no kings.'

'Not here in the highlands,' she said, 'but there are tales of fara-way lands where kings and princes rule. One day a man will come – and I will wed him.'

'I don't begin to understand,' he said. 'What is so important about wedding a king? Or being the mother of one, for that matter? What about love, Deva? Happiness?'

'How could you understand?' she said. 'You were an orphan and a thief. It wasn't your fault. But I shall live in a palace, and my name will be known throughout the world. Perhaps for ever.'

530

He stood silently for a moment, 'I would marry you,' he said, 'and spend my life making you happy. It is a dream I have had since first I saw you. But I cannot give you a palace, Deva.'

She looked up at him and, for a single heartbeat, felt like taking him in her arms and turning her back on the dream she had nurtured. But the dream was too strong and Deva shook her head, 'I know that I love you, Gaelen. Truly. But you must find another,' she said softly, surprised that the words left her feeling empty and more than a little frightened.

Taking her hand he kissed it. 'I'll not ask again,' he told her. 'I wish you well in your quest, Deva. I hope your king comes for you.'

Caswallon pushed his people hard throughout the days following the invasion. He sent a screen of warriors to the north-east and west, led by Badraig and Onic. Then he chose five hundred men and held them back to form a rearguard against any force the Aenir should send against them. He was desperate for news of Laric and Maggrig. Had the Pallides survived as a clan, or were they sundered throughout the mountains, leaderless? He needed to know. He called for volunteers from among the single men, skilled hunters and trackers, to journey back to the south-east and gather information. Among those who came forward were Layne, Gwalchmai and Agwaine. Caswallon chose five men, Agwaine among them.

He took them aside, briefing each one, until at last only Agwaine was left. Caswallon placed both hands on the young man's shoulders, 'I am truly sorry about what happened to your father,' he said. 'He was a fine man, a man of honour and great nobility.'

'He was a fool, Caswallon. But I loved him well. Better than he knew.'

'I doubt that. You meant everything to him. When we tracked you, as you fought the beast, he told me he would leave the Farlain if you did not survive. You were his joy. And as to his being a fool, I want you to think on this: he was made to look foolish by the brutal stupidity of the Aenir. Cambil was right in his philosophy, Agwaine. Sensible men will go to great lengths to avoid the vileness of war. Yet it is also a tragic truth that when war is inevitable, there is no place for sensible men. Intelligence can be a double-edged weapon. One of the blessings of a fine mind is that it allows a man to see both sides of a problem, therefore preventing him from acting in a blind or blinkered way. Your father was such a man. He believed that the Aenir would also see the wisdom of his view. That they did not is not a reflection on him, but a judgement upon them.'

Agwaine shook his head, 'I would like to believe all that. But you are an intelligent man – and the Aenir did not fool you, did they?'

'No,' answered Caswallon slowly, 'but then I did not have thousands of lives resting on my deeds, colouring my thoughts, feeding my hopes. Cambil knew that war would mean colossal loss of life. It does make a difference, Agwaine.'

'Thank you, cousin, for your words. As you advise, I will think on them. Now what do you want me to do?'

'Find Maggrig and gather as many of the Pallides as you can. Then make for the eastern shore of the lake above Attafoss. There we will plan the destruction of the enemy.'

'Do you believe we can win?'

'Be certain of it, Agwaine of the Farlain.'

Agwaine grinned, 'It would be nice to be certain.'

Caswallon took the young man by the arm and led him away from the column. They sat down on the hillside, the stars gleaming above them like gems on a velvet cloak.

'Your father and I grew up together, you know that. You also know we were never friends,' said Caswallon softly, meeting Agwaine's glance and noting, with sadness, the man's resemblance to Cambil. 'He did not like me, but I don't blame him for that. I never did. He saw in me everything that could destroy the clan: selfishness; disregard for the customs that bound us together. I see that clearly now, and I wish he was here so that I could tell him. Instead, I tell his son.

'The clan thrives because we care for one another. Being clan is as much a state of mind as a racial fact. Without it we are no different from the Aenir. Cambil understood this. Caring makes us strong, gives us courage.'

'Why are you telling me this?' asked Agwaine.

'Have you noticed?' countered Caswallon, 'how nature gives and takes? The weakest dog in the litter is always the most cunning, the short man often more competitive, the ugly woman given the disposition of an angel. So it is with character. You saw it at the Games. Borak was faster than you, stronger. He even had an accomplice in the woods to ensure victory. And yet he lost, as his kind will always lose. For courage is born of caring. Evil has no depth of character to call on. You want certainty, Agwaine? I give it to you. They cannot conquer the clan.'

Agwaine bowed his head. 'At this moment,' he said, 'we are in flight. They outnumber us and they have killed thousands.'

'Yes, and many more clansmen will die,' said Caswallon, 'but we shall not lose. Do not think of their numbers. It means nothing if the terrain is right. Think of your father, and his few hundred men. Aye, and women. Think of how the Aenir broke upon that sword-ring. I would wager three Aenir died for every clansman. Think on it. For the Aenir will.

'Deep in their hearts they know the truth. Let you know it too. We are the Farlain and, though we may be ill-suited to it, we carry the torch of Light in this war. And the Aenir darkness will not extinguish it.'

Agwaine chuckled suddenly, leaning back to rest on his elbows. 'Caswallon, you've only been with the Council for a few months and already you're spouting rhetoric.'

'I know, and it surprises me. But what is more surprising, perhaps, is that I believe it. With all my soul.'

'You believe the force of good will always defeat the force of evil?'

'I do – ultimately.'

'Why?'

'I can't argue it, for it springs from the heart and not the mind. Why did the Queen come when you needed her?'

'Chance?'

'From where did you get the strength to beat the faster man?'

'I don't know. But why did the lowlanders fall? They were not evil.'

'I don't say that darkness does not have small triumphs. But we are not lowlanders, we are the Farlain.'

'Now *that* I will agree on,' said Agwaine. 'And now I'd better be heading for Maggrig.'

'Are you more certain?'

'I don't know, but I feel the better for talking.'

'Then that must be enough,' said Caswallon, rising.

'Take care, Caswallon – and look out for Deva. She should be clear of them. She was visiting Lars with her friend Larain.'

'I will send out scouts.'

The clan had made camp on the northern slope of a group of hills, where their campfires could not be seen from the south. As night stole over the countryside Caswallon ordered the fires doused, lest the glow be seen against the sky. He sought out Taliesen and together they walked to the hilltop, the old druid leaning heavily on his oak staff. He wore his birds'-feather cloak over a white robe. Caswallon thought him dangerously tired.

'How are you faring?' he asked as they sat together under the bright stars.

Taliesen's eyes gleamed and he smiled, 'I will not die on you, Caswallon.'

'That does not answer my question.'

'I am exhausted. But then I am old.' He looked at the young warrior beside him, his eyes full of guile. 'Do you know how old?'

'Seventy? Eighty?'

'If I told you my age, would you believe me?'

'Yes. Why would you lie?'

'I will not lie, Caswallon. I am over a thousand years old.'

'I was wrong,' said Caswallon, grinning. 'I do not believe you.'

'And yet I speak the truth. It was I who brought Earis here so many centuries ago. On this very hill, he and I looked down on the Farlain and knew joy.'

'Stop this jest, Taliesen . . .'

'It is no jest, Caswallon, and I am not speaking to impress you. Of all the clansmen, you alone have the capacity to understand what I am going to tell you. You have an open, enquiring mind and

534

a rare intelligence. You are not prey to superstitions. You make your own judgements. I am more than one thousand years old. I was born out there!' The old man's bony hand flashed out, pointing to the stars. 'You've heard tales of the elder race, the vanished people. I am the last of those elders; the last true-blooded anyway. We made the Gates, Caswallon, and we journeyed across distances so great I could not impress on you the scale of it. Think of an ant crossing the Farlain and multiply it a thousand times, and you would have but the first step of my journeys.

'We came here, and from here we spread across the Universe. We were the Star Walkers. We birthed religions and created mythologies wherever man saw us. But then came catastrophe.' The druid bowed his head, staring at his hands.

'What happened?' asked Caswallon.

'The Great Gates closed. Suddenly, without warning. Our links with home and distant empires were severed, gone without trace. All that remained were the Lesser Gates: playthings created for students like myself who wished to study the evolution of primitive societies in a controlled environment.'

'I do not understand any of this,' said Caswallon. 'But I read men well, and I believe what you say. Why are you telling me now?'

'Because I need you. Because you are the catalyst. Because the future of the Farlain – my chosen people – rests with you. And because you will see great wonders in the days to come and your mind must be prepared. I cannot explain to you the nature of the skills that created the Gates. So think of it as magic, impossibility made reality. You know that I have a hiding place for the clan. I am going to tell you now where that hiding place is: Golfallin, the first valley of the Farlain.'

'What nonsense is this? You will take us back where we have come from?'

'Yes. But there will be no Aenir, no crofts and homes, only virgin land.'

'How so?'

'As I did with Earis,' said the old man. The Gates do not merely link different lands, Caswallon. I shall take you all through time itself. We are going back ten thousand years, to a time before the clan, before the Aenir.'

'That would be magic indeed.'

'You, however, will not be going back. There is a task you must perform.'

'Name it.'

'You must find the Queen who died and bring her to the Farlain with her army. Only then can you hope to crush the Aenir.'

'You want me to find a dead woman?'

'Time, Caswallon. Where I will send you she is still young.'

'Why should she aid us?'

The old druid shrugged. 'There are some questions I will not answer. But let me say this: The chaos we are enduring was caused – in part – by one selfish man. I am doing all in my power to reverse it.'

'Oracle?'

'Yes.'

'He told me of his journey,' said Caswallon, 'and that is why I believe you. He said he took his men through the Gate and came to a realm torn by war. He chose to serve the Queen and gained prominence. He told he fought many battles until at last he crossed the Gateway once more and became a king in a far land, with an army of thousands at his back. But then he suffered betrayal and fled back to the Gate.'

'He did not tell you all, Caswallon. Men rarely do when speaking of their mistakes. He became a king, even as he said, but to do so he made alliances with evil men. One such was Agrist, a rare brute. In return for Agrist's services Oracle gave him the secret of the Gate, and Agrist led his people through in search of riches and plunder. They thrived in their new world and grew strong. They became the Aenir, who now pillage the Farlain. For the Gate Oracle gave them brought them to the recent past of our world.'

'He did tell me,' said Caswallon.

The druid gave a thin smile. 'Did he also tell you of the night after Sigarni's great battle when he found the enemy general's widow and her daughter hiding in a cave? Did he describe how he raped the mother in front of the daughter, and of how the noble lady slew herself?'

'No,' replied the clansman.

'No,' echoed Taliesen. 'Nor did he say how he stole the legendary Sword of Ironhand from the Queen, and used its power to build his own kingdom from the blood of innocence. As I said men rarely tell the whole truth of their iniquities. I have spent years, Caswallon, trying to repair the damage his pride and ambition caused.'

Caswallon turned away to gaze out over the silhouetted mountains, black against a grey sky. 'I feel like a child taught to scrawl his name, who is given a book and told to read it. I can make out some of the letters, but the words are lost to me. Gateways, journeys through time.' He glanced at the old man, holding his gaze, 'If we can make such journeys, why can we not merely go back a few days and save all the people? We could hit the Aenir *before* they invade.'

Taliesen nodded. 'What if I told you that we did? And that it failed and the Farlain were destroyed?'

'Now you have lost me utterly.'

'That is what makes the chaos so terrible,' said Taliesen. There are so many alternative realities. If I told you now how many times I have tried to prevent an Aenir victory you would think me mad. The complexities and paradoxes created are legion. Armies out of their time, dead men who were destined to live and achieve greatness, women who should have borne proud sons murdered in their childhood. Destiny thwarted, changed – the Gateways themselves trembling under the weight of the chaos.' Taliesen sighed. 'Do you know how many times you and I have had this conversation? Of course you don't, but it runs into scores, Caswallon. And how many times have I seen the clans destroyed, the Aenir triumphant? Hundreds. Now I grow older and more frail, and the task is as great as ever it was.'

Caswallon smiled grimly, 'I doubt that I can learn what you have to teach, old man. You are taking the clan back to before they were born, and then I shall seek help from a Queen already dead. Do you hold more surprises for me, Taliesen?'

The Druid Lord did not answer. He leaned back, gazing at the stars, naming them in his mind until he fastened on the furthest, its light flickering like a guttering candle.

Taliesen pushed himself to his feet, his heart heavy, his mind tired. 'Aye, I have more surprises, War Lord,' he said. 'If we are to win, Caswallon, which is not likely, then you will change and suffer as no Farlain has before you.' Taliesen sighed, 'I do not yet know how all this will come to pass, but I know that it will, for I have seen the Hawk Eternal.'

Caswallon was about to speak, but Taliesen raised his hand for silence. 'No more words tonight, War Lord. For I am weary unto death.'

Oracle watched the Aenir in the valley below. They had slaughtered three prime steers and were preparing a feast. Since the invasion three days before not one enemy warrior had approached the cave. Heavy of heart, Oracle walked back to the entrance and on into the small room at the rear of the cave. He had seen the death of Durk, and now from beneath his narrow cot bed he pulled an oak chest, brass-edged and finely-worked. From it he took a rusting mail-shirt and helm and an old broadsword wrapped in oiled cloth. He donned the mail-shirt noting, with a wry grin, that it no longer hung well on his bony frame. Man aged less well than iron. Pushing back his white hair, he placed the helm firmly on his head. Looping sword and scabbard about his waist, he moved back into the sunlight and began the long walk into the valley.

Many were the thoughts as he strode down towards the feast. He remembered his childhood, and the first Hunt, his glory at the Games when he carried the Whorl Stone farther than any man before him. He remembered his love, Astel, a spirited lass from among the Haesten, and how she had sickened and died during their first winter together. The sense of loss crippled him still, though she remained young in his memory while he withered in reality.

The trees thinned out and he walked on.

Then had come the day when he approached the Council following his success in the war against the lowland raiders. Great days, when his name was sung throughout the Farlain. He believed they would make him King. Instead they had rejected him, and in his fury he had sworn never to return to the clan.

With a few valiant followers he had risked everything sailing to Vallon. There he overpowered the druids who manned the Gate, and journeyed to the world beyond. For two years he fought alongside the Battle Queen, Sigarni. Regret touched him as the long-suppressed memory of his shame rose to his mind. Sigarni had dismissed him, stripping him of rank. Oracle and his followers had then crossed the Gate once more to a distant land.

And what a land it was, green and fertile, with rolling hills and verdant valleys, broad plains and tall cities of glowing marble. It was a country riven by civil war, petty chieftains and robber princes vying with one another for control. Oracle had arrived in a world made for his talents. Within two years he was a general. Within five he led an army of three thousand men against Vashinu, the Prince of Foxes, and smashed him in a battle near Duncarnin. Five years later he crowned himself King and was acclaimed from northern mountains to southern seas as the undisputed Lord of the Isles, High King.

Had he been possessed of compassion, or even foresight, he might have changed that troubled land, bringing peace and prosperity to his subjects. But he had been a man of war, and had learned nothing of diplomacy, nor forgiveness. He persecuted his enemies, creating greater hatreds and thus more enemies. Two rebellions he crushed, but the third saw his army broken.

Wounded and alone, his few close friends dead or captured, he fled north and there vainly attempted to gather a force. For three years he fought minor campaigns, but always the great victories slipped away until at last he was betrayed by his lieutenants and turned over to his enemies. Sentenced to death, he had broken from his prison, killing two guards, stolen a horse and made his way south-east to the Gateway once more. Twice they almost caught him, an arrow piercing his back. But he had been strong then, and he carried the wound to the druid's cave – the cave he had stumbled from so many years before, when first he laid eyes on the Land of Isles.

There had been a druid there, who had gazed upon him, shocked and bewildered. He had been one of the men Oracle had overpowered long before on Vallon. Oracle, weak from loss of blood, asked the man to send him back home. He had done so without argument.

Now the old man gazed down on the fruits of his ambition, and bitter was the taste. The valley was scarred by the invasion, burnt-out homes black against the greenery, enemy soldiers trampling the wheat in the fields. By the long hall were the guards, and within were the captured women of three clans, kept in chains to endure the lusts of the conquerors.

Men looked up from their work as the old man came in sight, then began to gather and point at him. Laughter began and sped as warriors came running to watch him. The laughter touched Oracle's mind like acid. In his day men had quailed to see him thus attired. Now he was a figure of fun. He drew his sword, and the laughter subsided.

Then someone called, 'Run, lads. It's the entire clan army!'

And they mocked him, spreading out in a circle about him.

'Where is your leader?' he asked.

'Hark, it speaks! You can talk to me, old man. Tell *me* your business.'

'I seek the dog, not its droppings,' said Oracle. The man's face reddened as he heard the laughter and felt the acid. He drew his sword and leaped forward. Oracle parried his thrust, reversing a cut that half-severed the man's neck.

The laughter died, replaced by the sharp, sliding hiss of swords being drawn.

'Leave him. He interests me,' said Asbidag, striding through the crowd – Drada to his right side, Tostig at his left. He halted some five paces from Oracle, grinning as he noticed the rusted mail-shirt.

'I am the leader. Say what you must.'

'I have nothing to say, spawn of Agrist. I came here to die. Will you join me?'

'You want to fight me, old man?'

'Have you the stomach for it?'

'Yes. But first tell me where your clan has gone. Where are they hiding, and what do they plan?'

Oracle grinned. 'They are hiding all around you, and they plan your destruction.'

'I think you can tell me more than that. Take him!'

The men surged forward. Oracle's sword flashed twice and men fell screaming. The old man reversed his blade, driving it deep into the belly of the nearest warrior. In his pain and rage the Aenir lashed back with his own sword, cleaving Oracle's ribs and piercing his lungs. He doubled over and fell, blood gushing from the wound.

'Get back, you fools!' shouted Asbidag, punching men aside. Oracle struggled to rise, but the Aenir War Lord pushed him back to the earth, kneeling beside him.

'You got your wish, old man. But you'll be blind in Valhalla, for I'll cut out your eyes unless you tell me what I wish to know.'

Oracle heard his voice as from a great distance, and then another sound burst upon his mind: a woman's voice, screaming in hatred. He thought he recognised it, but his vision swam and he did not feel the knife-blade that pierced his throat.

Asbidag turned as Morgase plunged the knife again and again into the old man's neck. Tears were falling from her eyes and her sobbing screams unsettled the warriors around her. Asbidag hauled her to her feet, slapping her face; she calmed down then, her eyes misting over as she exerted her will, blanketing down the hatred that had overwhelmed her.

'You knew this man?' asked Asbidag softly.

'Yes. He was a general in the army that saw my father slain. He raped my mother and after that she killed herself. He was Caracis, Sigarni's general.'

'I don't know these names,' said Asbidag. 'You told me your land was ten thousand leagues from here. You must be mistaken. This old man was a clansman.'

'Do you think I would forget such a man?'

'No, I do not. But there is something you have left out, my little dark lady. How is he here?'

'I thought he was dead. He . . . vanished twenty-five years ago.'

Asbidag grunted, then kicked the corpse. 'Well, whatever he was, he's dead now,' said Asbidag, but his gaze rested on Morgase as she walked back to the house.

Drada wandered to his father's side. 'Do you really think she would remember? She must have been a small child twenty-five years ago.'

'It worries me,' answered Asbidag, still watching the woman, 'I've never heard of her realm. I think she's bewitched.'

'What will you do?'

'What I choose. I think she's lying about something, but it can wait. She's far too good a bed partner to spoil now.'

'And the Farlain, Father?'

'We'll set after them tomorrow. Ongist has driven the Pallides west and outflanked them, driving them back towards the east, and Barsa's Timber-Wolves. Tomorrow we march, and if Vatan favours us we'll arrive while there is still a little sport.'

The journey deep into the mountains was difficult, for many of the clan folk were old, while others struggled to carry babies and infants. Even among the young and strong, the defeat and the flight that followed it brought a strength-sapping sense of despair. Rain made the slopes slippery and treacherous, but the straggling column moved on, ever closer to Attafoss. Maeg passed the sleeping Donal to a clansman, who grinned as he settled the boy's head on his shoulder. Then she walked away from the column to where Caswallon was issuing orders to a group of warriors. He saw her coming and waved the men away. Maeg thought he looked tired; there was little spring in his step and his eyes were dull. He smiled and took her hand.

'You're not resting enough,' she said.

'Soon, Maeg.'

Together they watched the clan make their way towards the last slope of the mountains before Attafoss. Already in the distance they could hear the roaring of the great falls. Day by day more stragglers joined the exodus and now almost six thousand people followed

Caswallon. The long column of men, women and children was moving slowly, suffering from the frenzied pace of three days' marching. The old and the very young were placed at the centre of the column. Behind these came the rearguard, while young women strode at the head armed with bows and knives. There was little conversation. The young men were desperate to leave their families in safety on Vallon, so that they could turn back and rend the enemy. The old men were lost in thoughts of youth, regretting their inability to wreak vengeance on the Aenir and ashamed of their faltering pace. The women, young and old, thought of homes lost behind them and the danger their men would face in the days ahead.

Warriors took it in turns to carry the younger children. These tasks were done in good heart, for they were all clan. All one in the spirit of the Farlain.

'You saved the clan, Caswallon,' said Maeg, slipping her arm around her husband's waist and smiling up at him, noting the lines of tension on his face, the dark circles beneath his green eyes.

He kissed her hair, 'I don't need lifting, lovely lady, but thank you for saying it. I seem to be clinging by my fingertips to an icy cliff. There are so many problems. A messenger from Badraig says there is a force in the east. We know the Aenir are also following in the south. I am frightened by all of it. There is no room for a wrong decision now.'

'You will do what is best,' she said, 'I have faith in you.'

'Oh, I have faith in myself, Maeg. But all men make mistakes.'

'Maggrig always said you were as cunning as a fox, and trying to out-think you was like catching wood-smoke with your fingers.'

He grinned and the tension fell from him, though the fatigue remained.

'I will feel better when the clan women and children are safe and my thoughts can turn once more to simple tasks – like killing the Aenir.'

'You think that will be more simple?'

'Indeed it will. They think they have won, they see us running and believe us broken. But we will turn and they will find themselves staring into the tawny eye of the killing wolf.'

She turned to him, staring up into his angry eyes. 'You will not let hate enter your soul?'

'No. Do not fear for me in that way. I do not hate the Aenir; they are what they are. No more do I hate the mountain lion who hunts my cattle. And yet I will fight and kill the lion.'

'Good. Hate would not sit well with you, Caswallon of the Farlain.'

'How could I hold you in my heart and find room for hate?' he said, kissing her lips. 'Now you must go, for I have much to do.'

Hitching up her skirt she ran along the column, found the warrior holding Donal and thanked him for his help. The child was still sleeping and she took him back in her arms and walked on.

Caswallon wandered to the rear of the column where Leofas walked with the rearguard. Surrounded by younger men the burly warrior seemed grizzled and ancient, but his eyes shone as Caswallon approached.

'Well, we made it without incident,' he said.

'It looks that way,' Caswallon agreed.

Leofas scratched his beard. There was more grey than red in the hair, and Caswallon thought it had the look of rust on iron. Leofas was old, but he was tough and canny, and the day had not dawned when an enemy could take him lightly. He wore a glistening mail-shirt of iron rings sewn to a leather base with silver thread. By his side were two short swords and in his hand an iron-capped quarterstaff.

'Did you mean what you said, Caswallon? About sending out people through the Druid's Gate?'

'Yes.'

'Will they be safe?'

'Safer than here, my friend, believe me. A hundred of the older men will go with them, to help with the hunting and building.'

'And then what?'

'Then you and I will hunt a different game.'

The older man's eyes gleamed and he grinned wolfishly. 'It's about time. I do not feel right heading away from the devils. My legs keep turning me about. I never thought the day would come when I'd care about what happened to the Pallides,' Leofas went on, 'but I hope that old wolf Maggrig is safe.'

'He's not a man to be surprised by a sudden attack. He would have had scouts out.'

'Yes, but so did we, Caswallon.'

Forty miles to the south and east Maggrig's anger was mounting. He was tired of being herded towards the west, tired of skulking away from the enemy, and filled with a sense of dread. The Aenir had caught up with them on the afternoon of the day following the attack, but Pallides scouts had hit them with a storm of arrows and slowed their pursuit. Since then they had outflanked the clan to the east and the two groups were seemingly engaged in a deadly race, the Aenir endeavouring to outrun them and prevent the northward exodus. Rare cunning and an intimate knowledge of the land enabled Maggrig to stay ahead, but always the angle of the march was being shifted and the wily Pallides Hunt Lord had begun to suspect they were being herded west for a reason other than the obvious. It had seemed at first that the Aenir commander wanted to force a direct battle by cutting off their flight, but he had spurned two opportunities so to do. Once could have been put down to ignorance, or lack of thought.

Twice was a different tale.

As the swordsman Intosh had pointed out, it could still be stupidity. Maggrig had grunted, dismissing the idea. 'Any general who needs to rely on his opponent being an idiot is in sore trouble. No, I don't think he wants a confrontation yet. I think there's another Aenir force to the west of us. We are between a hammer and a hard rock.'

'We have limited choices,' said Intosh, squatting to the earth and sketching a rough map of the terrain ahead. 'All we can do is react. We are hampered by the presence of our women and children.'

'According to our scouts,' said Maggrig, 'the enemy has two thousand men. We have eight hundred who can fight, and seven hundred women. With older children who can handle a bow, we could muster sixteen hundred fighters.'

'To what purpose?' said Intosh. 'We cannot take them on.'

'We must,' said Maggrig sadly. 'Yes, we can continue to run, but each mile brings us closer to disaster. We must take the initiative.'

'We cannot win.'

'Then we'll die, my friend, and we'll take as many of the swine along the path as we can.'

Intosh's eyes focused on Maggrig. The swordsman was also tired of running. 'It is your decision and I will stand by you. But where do we make this stand?'

Maggrig knelt beside him and together they selected the battle site, tracing the lines of the land in the soft earth.

Dawn found the Aenir under Ongist marching through a wide valley. Ahead was a range of hills, thickly wooded with ancient oaks on the left slope, and to the east a higher hill clear of trees. Upon that hill was the shield-ring of the Pallides, the rising sun glistening on the swords, spears and helms of the clan, and shining into the eyes of the Aenir.

Ongist called his scouts to him. 'How long before Barsa reaches us?'

'Another day,' said a lean, rangy forester. 'Do we wait?'

Ongist considered it. To wait would mean sharing the glory – and the women. Shading his eyes he scanned the hill, making a rapid count. 'How many, would you think?'

The forester shrugged his shoulders. 'Fifteen hundred, maybe two thousand. But half of them must be women. Vatan's balls, Ongist, we outnumber them by three to one!'

Drada had been insistant that no major battle should be joined until Barsa's troops had linked with his, but what would Father say if Aenir warriors merely waited, apparently fearful of attacking a hill defended by women, old men, children and a handful of warriors?

Calling his captains forward, Ongist ordered the advance.

The Aenir swept forward, screaming their battle-cries and racing towards the hill. The slope was steep and arrows and spears hurtled amongst them, but the charge continued.

On the hilltop Maggrig drew his sword, settling his shield firmly in place on his left arm. The Aenir were halfway up the hill, the last of their warriors on the lower slopes, when Maggrig gave the signal to the warrior beside him. The man lifted his horn to his lips and let sound the war call of the Pallides.

In the woods behind the Aenir, eight hundred women dropped from the trees, notching arrows to the bow-strings. Silently they ran from cover, kneeling at the foot of the slope and bending their bows. The Aenir warriors running with their shields before them were struck down in their scores as black-shafted death hissed from behind. Ongist, at the centre of the mass, turned as the screams began.

Hundreds of his men were down. Others had turned to protect themselves from this new assault. These only succeeded in showing their backs to the archers above.

Ongist cursed and ducked as an arrow flew by him to bury itself in the neck of his nearest companion. The charge had faltered. He had but one chance of victory, and that lay in charging the women archers below. He bellowed for his men to follow him and he began to run.

But at that moment Maggrig sounded the horn once more and the shield-ring split as he led his fighters in a reckless attack on the enemy rear. Intosh beside him, the burly Hunt Lord cut and thrust his way into the Aenir pack. A sword nicked his cheek before the wielder fell with his throat opened, to be trampled by the milling mass.

Shaft upon shaft hammered into the Aenir ranks. Death was ahead of them – and behind they could hear the shrill battle cry of the Pallides: 'Cut! Cut! Cut!' Faced with a hail of missiles many of the Aenir broke to the left, streaming away towards the safety of the trees, desperate to be clear of the rain of death. Ongist was furious. With a hard core of his personal carles he stood his ground, but the battle was lost. Arrows tore into his men, opening a gap in the shield wall, exposing Ongist to the enemy. Two shafts pierced the air, ripping into Ongist's chest. With a grunt of pain he broke off the jutting shafts. Turning, Ongist saw Maggrig before him, his beard dark with blood, his eyes gleaming and his lips drawn back from his teeth in a feral snarl.

Ongist lashed out weakly. Maggrig parried the blow with ease, lifting his hand for the archers to cease shooting. Ongist, the last Aenir alive, staggered, then gazed on the enemy with new eyes. His legs buckled and he fell to the ground, pushing himself to his knees with great effort.

'Bring him,' muttered Maggrig, walking past the dying Aenir general and on towards the trees.

Within the hour the Pallides were once more marching north and west. Behind them the crows settled on the Aenir dead – more than eleven hundred bodies stripped of armour and weapons littered the hillside. And nailed to a tree hung the body of Ongist, his ribs splayed grotesquely, his innards held in place with strips of wood. His eyes had been put out and his tongue torn from his mouth.

Maggrig also knew of the Aenir dream of Valhalla.

Ongist's shade would neither speak nor see as it was led to the Grey God's hall.

Gaelen and Deva scrambled over the last skyline before Attafoss, staring out at the great falls and the spreading forests, the wide valleys and the narrow rocky passes beyond.

In the distance he could just make out the moving column, like ants crawling across a green blanket. He sank to the ground beside Deva. He was tired now but she was exhausted, her moccasins cut to rags by the flinty rock and the scree slopes. Her feet were bleeding and her face was grey with fatigue; her golden hair, once so beautiful, hung in greasy rats' tails to her grimy neck.

She laid her head against his neck, 'I did not think we would get here safely,' she said.

He stroked her hair, saying nothing. Beside them Render spread himself out, resting his head on his paws. He had not eaten for two days, and gone was the sleek shine of his fur. Three times they had dodged their pursuers, hiding in caves and beneath thick bushes, and once sheltering in the branches of a broad oak as the Aenir searched beneath.

Twice they had stumbled on the tortured bodies of clansmen nailed to trees and splayed in the horrifying blood-eagle. Deva had wanted the bodies cut down, but Gaelen refused, pointing out that such an action would only alert the trackers.

Now they were clear, with only an hour's gentle downhill stroll to meet with the clan. Gaelen rubbed his sweat-streaked face, scratching idly at the jagged white scar above the blood-filled left eye. He scanned the falls and the rushing white water, then transferred his gaze to the column as it moved with painful lack of speed towards the woods. Suddenly Gaelen jerked as if stung. From his vantage point he could see into the trees and, just for a moment, he caught a glimpse of a warrior, running bent over. The man had been wearing the horned helm of the Aenir.

'Oh, no!' he whispered. 'Oh, Gods, no!'

'What is it?' asked Deva, swinging her head to glance back down the trail, expecting to see their pursuers close by.

'The Aenir are in the woods,' he said. 'They're waiting to hit the clan – and I can't warn them.'

Deva shaded her eyes, searching the timberline.

'I see nothing.'

'It was only one man. But I know there were more.'

Despair washed over the young man. 'Let's move,' he said, and they began to run down the grassy slopes, angling away from the woods.

Far below them Caswallon halted the column. Ahead was the forest of Atta, the dark and holy place of the druids. Beyond that, according to Taliesen, was the invisible bridge to Vallon. Caswallon called Leofas to him – and Badraig, who had returned from the west with news that the Aenir had split into several forces, the majority racing east at speed, the others vanishing into the mountains in small groups.

The scouting party had cornered twenty Aenir warriors and destroyed them, taking one alive whom they questioned at length. He would tell them little, save that they had been pursuing a man and a girl. Badraig killed the man swiftly and led his party back to Caswallon.

549

'What do you think?' asked Badraig. 'Gaelen?'

'It could be. The girl might be Deva. Dirak's scouts found the mutilated body of a clan girl they thought was Larain, and Agwaine said the two girls were together.'

'Why should the Aenir split their forces,' Leofas asked.

'I would bet it is Maggrig. The wily old fox is probably leading them a merry dance.'

Taliesen joined them, leaning on his oak staff, his long white hair billowing in the morning breeze. 'Can we move on, War Lord? I am anxious to be on safe ground.'

'Not yet,' said Caswallon. 'I am concerned about the second force you mentioned, Badraig. Why did they split up, do you think?'

'To re-form elsewhere. Why else?'

'Then where are they? We've searched the west.'

'They could have returned to the south.'

'Or come north,' said Leofas.

'My thoughts exactly,' said Caswallon, switching his gaze to the dark trees of Atta.

'How many would you say were in this second force?' Leofas asked.

Badraig shrugged, 'It could be anything from two hundred to a thousand. Not more, though.'

'Then for once we are not outnumbered,' said Caswallon. 'I think we'll camp here, and tonight we'll set fires. We know no force from the south can be on us before tomorrow past the noon.'

Badraig and Leofas spread the word and the women of the column cast around for firewood, though none approached the trees.

Within the forest Barsa waited patiently with his seven hundred and fifty archers, watching the Farlain make camp.

Unlike his half-brother Ongist, Barsa was not a reckless man. Though neither was he intuitive, as his half-brother Drada. Barsa was simply a trained killer of men who relied on his experience more than his intellect. Experience told him the Farlain did not know of his presence; he had avoided their scouts and taken only the best of his men, breaking into small parties and heading north, re-forming at the falls. He had been guessing as to the line of the clan march and was secretly pleased at the accuracy of his guess. He had no idea where they were ultimately heading, for the north was a mystery to the Aenir save that men said the sea was not far off. And when he had received the message from Ongist saying the Pallides were also racing north he had acted at once, dispatching three thousand to join his brother and taking eight hundred with him to this place.

It would please his father, and Barsa looked forward to basking in his praise. He could decimate the Farlain with his first volley. They would break and run and his men would have their pick of the clan maidens. Sadly they would then have to kill them. It was the one order that made no sense to Barsa; always the Aenir had taken captured women as house slaves and concubines – even wives. But in the mountains Asbidag's orders had been specific.

Kill all the clansmen, women and children.

An Aenir forester crept to Barsa's side. 'They are making camp. Should we attack tonight?'

It was a thought, but Barsa was loath to commit his men in the open for the clans outnumbered him. 'No. We'll wait for morning, as they enter.' The man nodded and moved silently back into the deeper darkness.

Beyond the line of campfires flickering on the open ground, Caswallon silently led a thousand warriors south and then east, circling toward the blackness of Atta forest. Once in the east the Farlain split into three forces, one led by Caswallon, the others led by Leofas and Badraig. Armed only with short swords and hunting-knives the men entered the trees, moving silently forward. It was slow progress.

The moon was bright above the mountains, but its light was diffused by the overhanging branches of the ancient oaks that made up the bulk of the forest. Every three or four steps Caswallon closed his eyes, focusing on the sounds around him, listening for movement in the bushes ahead. The hoarse rasp of cloth on wood came to him and Caswallon raised a hand. The men behind him stopped.

He pointed to the bushes; a clansman crept forward with knife in hand.

In the bushes the Aenir archer dozed – and died without waking as the razor-sharp hunting-knife slid across his throat. Beyond him slept scores of warriors. With bright knives the clansmen moved in among them, killing them as they slept.

The night hunters moved on. Leofas and his group crept deep into the forest to the north, continuing their silent slaughter before working their way down the western side while Badraig, reaching the northernmost point, turned south.

An hour before dawn a cry split the night silence as a clansman's blade slit open an Aenir throat. The man awoke as the knife cut into him, screaming a warning before dying as six inches of iron slashed through his neck.

Barsa leapt to his feet, knowing instantly that he had been tricked. He bellowed a warning to those nearest and drew his sword. Aenir foresters ran to him and then he saw the clansmen bearing down in the gloom. He glanced right and left. He had fewer than a hundred men with him. But if the men of the clan had entered the forest, that left the women alone on open ground. Barsa turned and sprinted south. If they could only hack their way past the women and old men they would be clear.

The Aenir ran from the trees and Barsa's heart sank. A line of women kneeling in the grass, bows bent. He threw himself to the ground as the shafts whistled home.

A second volley hammered into their ranks and then the clansmen were upon them. Barsa leaped to his feet and parried a thrust from a short sword, sweeping a double-handed blow to the clansman's unprotected head and caving in the skull. A second man fell to his sword, and a third, as he roared his defiance at them. Then the clansmen fell back, and a warrior strode through their ranks. The man was tall, his long black hair tied at the nape of the neck, a trident beard giving him a sardonic appearance. His eyes were green and in his hand he carried a short sword. Beside Barsa the last of the Aenir foresters died with an arrow in his ribs. Barsa was not afraid of death. He had earned his place in the Grey God's hall.

Leaning on his sword, he grinned at the blood-drenched clansman.

'Come on then, mountain dung. I'll see your corpse before you see mine.'

The clansman stepped forward as Barsa's sword flashed in the air. He parried it, ducking beneath the swing to thrust at the Aenir's groin. Barsa leaped back, his blade plunging downwards. The clansman blocked the blow, iron clashing on iron as the men circled. The Aenir had the advantage of the longsword, but the clansman moved swiftly, his green eyes probing for weaknesses in the Aenir's defence.

'Frightened, clansman?' sneered Barsa. The man did not reply, but leaped forward with a sword raised. Barsa slashed wildly. The man parried, then spun on his heel to hammer his elbow into Barsa's face. The Aenir staggered back, then felt the searing agony of a sword-blade buried deep in his belly. An awful cry tore from his throat and he pitched to the ground, writhing and straining to free the blade. Then the pain faded, washed from his body by the rushing blood. He rolled to his back, looking up at the sky above him, waiting to see the Valkyrie ride down for his soul.

He wondered if Asbidag would mourn for him. 'I'll cut out his eyes,' he heard someone say. Barsa knew panic; he did not want to be blind in the Hall of Heroes.

'Leave him be,' said the clansman who had cut him.

Relief and release came together, and the light faded.

9

In the early-morning sunlight the clan women stripped the Aenir dead of all weapons and despatched those warriors still clinging to life. Caswallon walked into the forest with many others of the attacking party, stopping at a fast-moving stream and removing his blood-covered clothes.

The night's work had appalled the new War Lord. More than six hundred Aenir warriors had been butchered in their sleep; it was no way for a man to die.

Caswallon stepped into the stream, shivering as the icy mountain water touched his skin. Swiftly he washed, then returned to the bank, sprawling out alongside Leofas and the young raven-haired warrior Onic, the finest quarterstaff fighter in the mountains.

'A fine night,' said Leofas, grinning. Stripped of his clothing, the old warrior looked even more powerful. His barrel chest and muscular shoulders gave evidence of his great strength, yet his belly was flat and taut, the muscles of the solar plexus sharp and clean.

'It was a victory, anyway,' said Caswallon wearily.

'You're a strange man, Caswallon,' said Leofas, sitting up and slapping the younger man between the shoulder-blades. These swine have come upon us with murder and rape and now, I sense, you regret last night's slaughter.'

'I do regret it. I regret it was necessary.'

'Well, I enjoyed it. Especially watching you gut that tall son of a whore.'

A group of clan women, led by Maeg, came to the stream carrying clean clothes for the men. Caswallon dressed, and spotted Taliesen sitting on a fallen tree; the War Lord joined him in the sunshine.

'There is the smell of death in this forest,' said Taliesen. 'It reeks of it.' The druid looked impossibly old, his face ashen, the skin dry.

His cloak of feathers hung limply on his skeletal shoulders, the colours faded and dust-covered. 'But still, you did well, War Lord.'

Caswallon sat beside the old man. 'Who are you, druid? What are you?'

'I am a man, Caswallon. No more, no less. I was a student centuries ago and I joined the trek from the stars to see more of life. I wanted to learn the origins of man. The Gates were a means to an end.'

'And what are the origins of man?'

Taliesen chuckled, his tired eyes showing a glint of humour, 'I don't know. I never will. My teacher was a great man. He knew the secrets of the stars, the mysteries of the planets, and the structure of the Gates. And yet, he never learned the origins. Together we journeyed and studied, and ever the great mystery eluded us. I sometimes fear the cosmic force I cannot see, and he laughs at me in my vanity.

'My teacher, Astole, became a mystic in a far land. It happened soon after the Prime Gate failed. You see, we could never travel back far enough, anywhere, to find the first man. The Gates would always be pushed back. Wherever we went, there was a man, developed to some degree. Several hundred years ago I developed a theory of my own, and I left Astole in the deserts of his world and journeyed to a northern land, a highland kingdom. The people there were under threat, even as you are, and I led them to the Farlain to watch them grow and to see how they would develop. I thought the development would assist my studies.'

'And did it?' asked Caswallon.

'No. Man is a singularly irritating creature. All that happened was that I grew to love the people of the Farlain. My studies were ruined anyway two hundred years ago, when the last of my people wed into the race. We had no women, you see, and every man needs companionship. I recruited many of their children, and so the order survives, but many of those now practising the skill do not appreciate any longer the . . . arts behind the machines.

'You, Caswallon, are of my race. You are the great-grandson of the daughter of Nerist. A bright man, was Nerist. He alone of all

555

my pupils said we would never re-open the Great Gates. You cannot understand the awful sense of separation and loss we experienced when those Gates closed. You see, what happened was an impossibility.'

'Why should it be impossible?' asked Caswallon. 'All things have a beginning and an ending.'

'Indeed they do. But when you play with time, Caswallon, you create circles. Think of this: today you will see the last of the Middle Gates. Today. *Now.* You will gaze upon it, and your people – our people – will pass through it. But tomorrow, let us say, the Gate disappears. We are worried at first, but then we think: It was there yesterday. Therefore we step through a Lesser Gate into yesterday. What should we find?'

'The other Gate should once again be there,' said Caswallon.

'Aye, it should – for we saw it yesterday . . . passed through it. But that is the mystery, my boy. For when the Great Gates disappeared, they vanished *throughout* time. Impossible, for it does not correspond with reality.'

'You told me,' said Caswallon, 'that magic was impossibility made reality. If that is true, there should be no problem accepting the reverse. What happened to your Gates was simply reality made impossibility.'

'But who made it happen?'

'Perhaps someone is studying you, even as you study us,' said Caswallon, smiling.

Taliesen's eyes gleamed. 'Astole believed just such a thing. I do not.'

At that moment Gaelen entered the clearing, calling Caswallon's name. The War Lord leaped to his feet, opening his arms as the young man ran to him. They stood there for several moments, hugging one another. Then Caswallon took hold of Gaelen's shoulders and gently pushed him away.

'Now you're a sight to ease my mind,' said Caswallon.

'And you. Deva and I thought find you cut to pieces by the Aenir. We saw you from the peaks yonder.'

'Just for once we out-thought them. You look tired, and there is dried blood on your tunic.'

'We've been chased over the mountains for three days.'

'But you came through.'

'You taught me well.'

Caswallon grinned. 'Where is Deva?'

'Upstream, washing the grime from herself.'

'Then you do the same. Much as I am glad to see you, you smell like a dead fish. Away with you!'

Caswallon watched the young man walk to the stream and his eyes glowed with pride. Taliesen stood beside him. 'He is a fine young man. A credit to you.'

'A credit to himself. You know, Taliesen, as I carried him on my back from the destruction of Ateris I wondered if I was being foolish. His wounds were grievous – and he was all skin and bone anyway. My legs ached, and my back burned through every step. But I'm glad I didn't leave him.'

'He is tough,' agreed the druid. 'Oracle did well to heal him.'

'Yes. I hope the old man survived the assault.'

'He did not,' said Taliesen.

'How do you know?'

'Let us leave it that I know. He was a strong man, but vain.'

'That is not much of an epitaph,' said Caswallon.

'It is the best I can offer. Now get the clan ready. We must cross the bridge before dusk.'

Almost six thousand people thronged the shoreline as the sun cleared noon. Silence fell upon them as a druid appeared on the island's shore, some forty yards across the foaming water. He tied a slender line to a sturdy pine, then looped the long coil over his shoulder and stepped out on the water. A gasp rose from the watchers, for the man was walking several feet above the torrent. After some twenty paces he stopped, reaching down, and stroked the air in a vertical line by his feet. Then he looped the twine around the invisible post and walked on. This he did every twenty paces, and amazingly the twine hung in the air behind him. Slowly the man made his way to the waiting clan, stopping to tie the end of the twine to a small tree. Then he approached Taliesen and bowed.

557

'Welcome, Lord, it is good to see you again. How many of the clan survived?'

'Just under six thousand. But there could be more hidden in the mountains.'

'And the Pallides?'

'No one knows. But the Haesten were crushed, and I don't doubt many lesser clans were annihilated.'

'Sad news, Lord.'

The druid, who seemed almost as ancient as Taliesen, turned to Caswallon. 'You will instruct your people to hold on to the twine and follow it. There is no danger, and the path is wide enough to take a line of five men. Let them approach slowly. All children to be carried. If anyone falls they are dead. They will be carried over Attafoss within seconds. Instruct your people.'

Caswallon was the first to cross, the clan filing slowly behind him. It was an uncanny sensation, placing weight upon solid air. He soon found it inadvisable to look down, for his sense of balance threatened to betray him.

Behind him the clan followed in silence and there were no mishaps.

Once on the island the clan spread out and pitched their camps. They found dried meat and fruit waiting for them, sacks of grain and oats, bags of salt, and huge tubs of honey, warm blankets and soft hides: all the product of Caswallon's land that had so mysteriously disappeared the previous autumn.

Caswallon himself called a War Council and they met in a cavern beneath Vallon's highest hill.

At the centre of the cavern was a long table of pine, around which were fifty chairs. These were soon filled. Caswallon took his place at the head of the table, flanked by Leofas and his sons Lennox and Layne; beside them sat Gwalchmai and Gaelen, and beyond them Onic and the pick of the Farlain warriors.

'Before we begin,' Caswallon told them, there is a matter to settle. It is our custom to elect our leaders. Most of the Council were slain with Cambil in the valley. We here now constitute a new Council. I offer myself as War Lord, but if there is any here with a hankering to lead, let him speak.'

No one stirred.

'It is accepted then that I lead the Farlain until this war is concluded?'

'Of course it is, Caswallon. Do you think us fools?' said Leofas.

'Very well. Then let us begin the real business of the day. How best can we hurt the enemy?'

Asbidag gazed at the ruin that had been his son. Maggots writhed in the dead flesh, and the sharp beaks of crows had torn at the body, but still it was recognisable as Ongist. In full armour, his helm held in his hands, Asbidag stood before the tree soaking in the sight, feeding his fury and his hatred. Behind him stood Drada and Tostig and beyond them twenty-five thousand Aenir warriors.

Asbidag felt no remorse, no sadness at the death of his child. He had not liked Ongist, he liked none of his offspring. But the boy had been his: blood of his blood. He could hear him praying for vengeance at the door of the Grey God's hall.

Through his anger he felt frustration. How could he wreak vengeance upon the clans? Already his armies had slain four thousand. Many were the blood-eagles decorating the countryside. But he wanted – needed – more.

The clans feared him now, but terror was his desire.

He turned to Tostig.

'Fetch Agnetha from Aesgard. Do it now.'

The colour drained from the warrior's face and he thought of asking his father to send another. But Asbidag's eyes were cold and distant and Tostig knew from experience that he was on the edge of a killing frenzy. He nodded and backed away to his horse.

Drada stood silently as his brother departed. He had scouted the hill where Maggrig made his stand, and had received reports from the foresters as to the ploy the Pallides used. It was a clever plan, but it would have failed against any captain less impetuous than Ongist. Maggrig had gambled the lives of his people on one perilous venture, and he had succeeded. But it proved the measure of the man, and Drada knew he could best him when next they met.

559

Two serious errors had been made by Maggrig. On the night of the first attack he had led his warriors on a suicidal charge to protect a few women and children, and now he had staked everything on one battle. He was obviously a man ruled by his heart.

Drada hoped his success would make him bold.

Asbidag stalked from the tree, and several warriors moved forward to cut down the body, preparing it for the funeral pyre on the hillside.

Drada joined his father in the black tent at the base of the hill. Asbidag was drinking heavily, and Morgase sat in the background saying nothing. 'We will not catch the Pallides before they link with the Farlain,' said Drada.

'Good,' said Asbidag. 'I want them all together.'

'Do you want to press on today?'

'No, we will wait for Agnetha.'

Drada left his father and wandered through the camp to where his own tent had been pitched. Once inside, he stripped his armour and spread his blankets upon the ground. It was early yet, but weariness was upon him and he slept through the afternoon. He awoke to the smell of cooking meat. One of his carles brought him a platter of beef and some bread and he joined the men outside.

For the first time in many years these fierce warriors were fighting not for gold, nor women, nor glory but for land. And he sensed the difference in them.

'It will not be easy,' said his carle-captain Briga, a swarthy black-haired veteran who had been Drada's first Aenir tutor.

'Nothing worth having comes easy,' Drada told him.

The man grinned. 'They fight well, these clansmen.'

'Did you expect less?' Drada asked him.

'Not after the Games.'

'No.' Drada finished his meal and returned to his tent. Briga watched him go. He had been Drada's carle-captain for five years, and before that his sword-master. He liked the boy; he was unlike his brothers, but then he had been brought up as a hostage in a foreign city and upon his return was less Aenir than foreigner. He was soft, and his learning sat heavily upon him. Asbidag had made him Briga's charge.

In the years that followed Drada had learned of battle and death, horror and hate. But blood had run true and he had become, outwardly at least, as much an Aenir as his brothers. Only Briga knew of the lack.

Drada did not love war. He loved the *planning* of war.

Briga did not care. He sensed that Drada would one day rule the Aenir, and he waited patiently for the day to come.

The Aenir warriors were anxious to push on, but Asbidag gave no orders to move. For ten days they remained in camp until, on the morning of the eleventh day, Tostig rode in alone, reining his lathered mount outside his father's tent. Asbidag hauled him from the saddle, eyes blazing.

'Where is the witch-woman?' he stormed. 'If you have failed me I'll kill you! Your body will hang on the same tree as your brother.'

'She is coming, Father, I swear it. She refused to ride, said she would come in her own way.'

Asbidag hauled him to his feet. 'She had better,' he hissed.

At midnight, as the fires burned low, a bitter wind blew up, flashing sparks from the coals. Men shivered as dark clouds obscured the stars and Asbidag, sitting alone before his tent, drew his red cloak around him. A shadow fell across him and, glancing up, he saw the old woman standing before him leaning on a staff. She was as grotesque as ever – almost bald, the remaining greasy white patches of hair hanging like serpents to her emaciated shoulders. Her teeth were broken and black, and her face adorned with wrinkled, leathery skin, as if her skull had shrunk to half its size, leaving the flesh around it to sag monstrously. She wore a matted cloak of human scalps and her tattered gown was said to have been made from the skins of flayed maidens. Asbidag believed it to be true.

'What do you want of me?' she asked, her voice a sibilant hiss.

'Terror among the clans.'

'You have brought terror to the clans. What do you want of me?'

'I want your sorcery.'

'And what will you offer the Grey God?'

561

'Whatever he asks.'

Her eyes gleamed. 'Whatever?'

'Is your hearing going, woman? Whatever!'

'A hundred virgins slain by midsummer.'

'You shall have it.'

'And seven of your strongest men slain tonight.'

'My men?'

'Yours. And I'll need your war-dogs. Bring them to the woods in an hour.'

Asbidag's carles roamed the camp until the seven men had been chosen, bound and gagged. Together with the Aenir Lord's Hunt Master Donic, and his seven hounds, they were taken to a circular clearing within the woods. Asbidag was waiting there with Drada, Morgase and Tostig; the woman, Agnetha, sat close by on a round boulder.

The bound men were forced to kneel before the woman and she waved away Asbidag's carles who returned, relieved, to the camp. Agnetha called Donic forward, ordering him to set each dog before a bound man. He did so, then ran back to his blankets and the guttering fire behind Asbidag's tent.

In the clearing the kneeling men were sweating freely as they stared into the eyes of Asbidag's hounds. Agnetha glanced at the Aenir lord and nodded.

'Kill!' he shouted.

The hounds lunged forward, ripping at the exposed throats before them.

Agnetha ran along the line of dying men, hurling a grey misty powder over them and chanting. One by one the dogs sank to the earth, their teeth embedded in the flesh of the slain men. The witch-woman lifted her arms to the night sky, screaming the name of the Grey God over and over again.

'Vatan! Vatan! Vatan!'

By her feet the hounds began to writhe and swell, while the Aenir corpses twisted and shrivelled. Morgase turned away. Drada swallowed hard, flicking a glance at his father. Asbidag was grinning. Tostig squeezed shut his eyes.

Within seconds the dead warriors were bone-filled husks, while the hounds had grown to treble their size. Their front paws had stretched into taloned fingers, and their dark fur-covered forms parodied men – long muscular legs, deep powerful chests and round heads ending in elongated maws and sharp fangs.

Agnetha danced around them, bidding them rise. Releasing the empty husks, the beasts pushed themselves to their feet, red eyes scanning the clearing. Their gaze fell upon Asbidag and their howling rent the night. Tostig stepped backward in terror and fell. Morgase gripped Drada's arm.

'Is this what you wanted, Asbidag?' said Agnetha.

'Yes.'

'Once unleashed they can never be brought back. They will follow no one. They are created out of hate and they will kill any man they find, be he Aenir or clan. Is this what you want?'

'Yes, curse you! Just send them north.'

'They will go where they will. But I will send them north. Have you done with me now?'

'I have.'

'Remember your promise, Asbidag. One hundred maidens by midsummer. Or the Werehounds will hunt *you*.'

'Don't threaten me, hag,' thundered Asbidag.

The woman cackled and turned to the silent beasts. Lifting her arm, she pointed north and the ghastly pack loped away into the darkness.

Asbidag walked forward, pushing his boot against a shrivelled corpse. A dried bone split the skin and fell to the grass. He shook his head and began to laugh.

Agnetha stopped him, placing her bony hand upon his arm. 'What is so amusing?'

'This,' he answered, pushing the corpse once more. 'This was Anias, son of my brother Casta. Only yesterday I told him he was empty-headed. Now his body matches his head.'

Drada approached Agnetha. 'How can those things live?'

'In the same way as you, Lord Drada. They breathe and they eat. It is an old spell, and a fine one, taught to me by a Nadir shaman in another age.'

'But what are they now, hounds or men?'

'They are both – and neither.'

'Do they have souls?'

'Do you?'

'Not any more,' said Drada, gazing down at the corpses.

The pack made their first kill that night, drifting silently through the pine forests in the north-west. The leader's head came up, nostrils flaring in the breeze. His red eyes turned to the north-east and he led the group deeper into the trees.

A young Haesten clansman and his two daughters were hidden in a cave. Having escaped the assault on their valley, they had met a Farlain scout who told them to head for Vallon. The clansman travelled by night carrying his youngest child, a girl of six years. His other daughter was eleven and she walked beside them. On this night, exhausted and hungry, they had made an early camp in the pine woods after spotting the Aenir army to the south.

The man had fallen into a light sleep when the werebeasts struck and he died without a struggle, his eyes flaring open to see wide jaws lined with fangs flashing towards his face. He had no time to scream.

His elder daughter, Jarka, took hold of her little sister and sped from the cave – only for talons to lance into her back, dragging her to a stop. In the last moment of her young life, Jarka hurled her sister into the undergrowth. The child screamed as she crashed through the bushes; then she was up and running, the awful sound of howling echoing behind her.

For an hour or more the beasts fed, then they slept by the remains of their kill. At dawn they left the cave, their hunger not totally appeased.

The leader dropped to all fours, sniffing at the earth around the cave. His head came up as the breeze shifted. And they set off in pursuit of the child.

Maggrig was angry. An hour before he had been furious. Caswallon had calmly told him that the clans would fight as one, and the one would be led by Caswallon. Maggrig could not believe his ears. The two men had been alone in a tiny cell, the bedchamber of a druid. Caswallon sat beside Maggrig on the narrow cot outlining his plans.

'I have plans of my own,' said the Pallides chieftain. Caswallon had been dreading this moment and he took a deep breath.

'I know it is hard for you, but think about it deeply. The death toll among the clans has been enormous. I have perhaps four thousand fighting men, you have eight hundred. Even together we are no match for one fighting wing of the Aenir army.'

'I accept that, Caswallon. But why should you lead? What experience do you offer? Great gods, man, you've turned down responsibility all your life! Granted you've led us here, and our women and children are safe. But to lead in war calls for more than that.'

'It calls for a cool head,' said Caswallon.

Maggrig grunted. 'You'll not lead the Pallides.'

'Let me make this clear to you. You are on Farlain land, under the protection of the Farlain clan. If you do not accept me then I will require you, and all your people, to leave tomorrow.'

'And where would we go?'

'Wherever you choose. Those that remain will follow me without question.'

'You would really do this thing? Turn out women and children to be slaughtered by the Aenir?'

'I would.'

'What have you become, Caswallon? I mean, I've always liked you, boy. You were different yes; but you were a clansman. Now you sit here and calmly say you would sacrifice my people for your ambition?'

'No, that is what *you* are saying,' Caswallon told him. 'During the Games you made an agreement with Laric that you would support him in any war — as long as you became War Lord. You reached that decision on the grounds that your men outnumbered the Haesten. That argument should surely still apply, can you not see it? If I were to agree that you lead, then most of the Farlain men would quit and go; they would not follow you.'

'You think the Pallides would follow *you?*'

'Yes.'

'Why? What makes you so different?'

'I am your son by law, for I wed your daughter. That gives me the rights of a Pallides warrior. They cannot argue.'

'All right,' said Maggrig at last, 'I will follow you. But only as long as I think you are right.'

'No,' said Caswallon. 'You will take my hand and swear allegiance to me as War Lord. You will offer me your life, as your carles have done for you.'

'Never!'

'Then prepare your people to move.'

Maggrig had stormed from the room seeking Intosh and together they walked among the trees of Vallon, avoiding the dark entrance to the Druids' Hall. Maggrig emptied himself of fury, his words tumbling over one another as he poured scorn on his son-in-law, the Farlain, the Druids, and the One Angry God for bringing him to this pass.

Intosh remained silent, merely walking beside his lord and absorbing his words. Finally exhausted, Maggrig stopped and sat by the water's edge, staring into the torrent. 'Well, what do you think?' he asked.

'Of what?' answered the swordsman.

'Where can we go?'

'There is nowhere.'

'We could go north,' said Maggrig.

'And fight the Dunilds, the Loda and the Sea Clans?'

'Then what do you suggest?'

'Agree to serve Caswallon.'

'Are you serious?'

'He has done well.'

'I know that – and all credit to him. But to serve my own son-in-law . . .'

'He has the power,' said Intosh, shrugging, 'It makes sense.'

'He demanded I swear the vassal oath.'

'You would have done the same.'

566

'That's not the point,' snapped Maggrig.

'No, Hunt Lord?'

An hour later Maggrig swore the vassal oath and was amazed his tongue did not fall out.

That same afternoon Caswallon and Maggrig led the women and children of the Pallides into the Druids' Hall entrance and down into the broad underground chamber housing the Middle Gate.

Maggrig blinked. At the end of the hall was a black marble archway. Yesterday a solid wall of stone had stretched between the pillars. Now that wall was gone and the Pallides Hunt Lord gazed down on the first valley of the Farlain, where already men and women were pitching tents and felling trees for shelter. The archway was twice the height of a man and ten paces across. The two men stood in the Gateway looking down on the valley. Within paces of them a tall pine was waving in the breeze, but no breath of wind touched their faces.

'Where are the Aenir? asked Maggrig as his people bunched behind him, looking down in wonder.

'That is the Farlain ten thousand years ago,' said Caswallon.

Maggrig's eyes widened. 'This is sorcery, then?'

'It most certainly is,' Caswallon told him.

Maggrig stepped through the Gateway, flinching as rushing colours blinded him momentarily. Caswallon walked through behind him, waving the women to follow.

On the other side the breeze was cool, the sunlight warm and welcoming.

'It is not possible,' whispered Maggrig, watching his people materialise from the air. From this side there was no sign of the Gate, only the rolling green countryside.

Caswallon led the Pallides down into the meadow where Leofas was supervising the building work, 'I'm glad to see he survived,' said Maggrig. 'He always was the best of the Farlain.' The old warrior grinned as he saw Maggrig, stepping forward to grip the Hunt Lord by the hand.

'So you got here, you dog,' said Leofas.

'Did you expect a few lowlanders to stop me?'

'Certainly not. I expected you to chase the swine from our lands, leaving nothing for the Farlain to do.'

'I was tempted,' said Maggrig with a broad grin.

Caswallon left the men talking and sought out Gaelen; he found him chatting to Deva by the river's edge. Apologising for disturbing them, Caswallon led Gaelen up into the timberline and they sat beneath the pines.

'I want you to do something for me,' said Caswallon, 'but it is hazardous.'

'Name it,' said Gaelen.

'Don't make hasty judgements. I want you to take some men and head back into the Haesten, gathering as many warriors as you can. I want you to bring them to Axta Glen in three weeks.'

'Why the Glen?'

'It is there we will tackle the Aenir.'

'But that is open ground.'

'I know. Have faith in me. I am hoping there will be upwards of a thousand clansmen still in hiding. I have sent messages to the Dunilds, the Loda, and many other smaller clans, but I don't know if they will come to our aid. But we must get more men; you must find them.'

'I'll do the best I can.'

'I know that, Gaelen.'

'Why me?'

'Because you are known as an outsider. You are accepted within the Farlain, there is no doubt about that. But similarly you are not Farlain; the Haesten may follow you.'

'Even if I did add a thousand to our army, we would still be outnumbered five to one. And on open ground . . .'

'I am also going on a journey,' said Caswallon. 'If it is successful, we will have another ally.'

'Where will you go?'

'Through the Gate. I am seeking help from the Queen Beyond.'

Gaelen shivered. 'You mean the daughter of the woman who saved us from the beast?'

'No, the woman herself.'

'She is dead.'

'As we sit here in this valley, Gaelen, neither of us is born. Our birth cries are ten thousand years in the future. Is it so strange then to think of seeking a dead Queen?'

'Why would she come?'

'I don't know. I only pray that she does – and that her strength will be sufficient.'

'What if she does not?'

'Then the clans will face a difficult day in Axta Glen.'

'What are our chances?'

'Taliesen says they are minimal.'

'What do *you* say?'

'I'd say Taliesen was being wildly optimistic.'

Gaelen returned to Deva at the stream and told her of his mission. She listed quietly, her grey eyes grave. 'It will be dangerous for you. Take care,' she said.

'I would be the more careful,' he said tenderly, 'if I knew you would be waiting for me when I returned.' She looked away then, but he took her hand. 'I have loved you for such a long time,' he told her.

Gently she pulled her hand clear of his. 'I love you too, Gaelen. Not just because you saved my life. But I can't promise to wait for you, nor for any Farlain warrior. I know you think me foolish to believe in the prophecy – but Taliesen confirmed it; it is my destiny.'

Gaelen said nothing more. Rising, he moved away and Deva returned to the waterside. Her thoughts were confused as she sat, trailing her hand in the stream. It was senseless to refuse love when all she had was a distant promise, Deva knew that. Worse, her feelings for Gaelen had grown stronger during the time they spent together, being hunted by the Aenir. All her doubts surfaced anew, and she remembered confiding in Agwaine. He had not scoffed, but he had been brutally realistic.

'Suppose this father of kings never comes? Or worse. Suppose he does, and he does not desire you? Will you spend your life as a spinster?'

'No, I am not a fool, brother. I will wait one more year, then I will choose either Layne or Gaelen.'

'I am sure they will be glad to hear it,' he said.

'Don't be cruel.'

'It is not I who am being cruel, Deva. Suppose they don't wait? There are other maidens.'

'Then I will marry someone else.'

'I hope your dream comes true, but I fear it will not. You sadden me, Deva, and I want to see you happy.'

'A year is not such a long time,' she had said. But that had been before the Aenir invasions, and already it seemed an eternity had passed. Her father was dead, the clan in hiding, the future dark and gloom-laden.

Gaelen chose six companions for the journey south – Agwaine, Lennox, Layne, Gwalchmai, plus Onic and Ridan. Onic was a quiet clansman, with deep-set eyes and a quick smile. Almost ten years older than Gaelen, he was known as a fine fighting man with quarterstaff or knife. He wore his black hair close-cropped in the style of the lowland clans, and around his brow sported a black leather circlet set with a pale grey moonstone. His half-brother, Ridan, was shorter and stockier; he said little, but he had also fought well in the retreat from the valley. Both men had been chosen for their knowledge of the Haesten, gained from the fact that their mother had come from that clan.

Taking only light provisions and armed with bows, short swords and hunting-knives, the seven left Vallon before dawn. A druid guided them over the invisible bridge, for the twine had been removed lest the Aenir march to the island.

Gaelen had mixed feelings about the trip. The responsibility placed upon him weighed heavily. He loved Caswallon, and trusted him implicitly, but to battle the Aenir on the gentle slopes of Axta Glen? Surely that was madness. During the last two years Gaelen had enjoyed many conversations with Oracle about battles and tactics, and he had learned of the importance of terrain. A large, well-armed force could not be met head-on by a smaller group.

The object should be a score of skirmishes to whittle down the enemy, disrupting his supply lines and weakening his morale. Oracle had likened such war to disease invading the body.

Agwaine was content. For him the mission provided an outlet for his grief over the death of his father and a chance to achieve victory for the Farlain. He didn't know if a Haesten force survived. But if it did, he would find it.

The group moved through Atta forest, past the swelling Aenir corpses and on into the first valley. They moved warily, knowing the Aenir could be close. Only in the high passes, where the woods were thick and welcoming and they trusted their skills above those of the enemy, did they relax.

Towards dusk Lennox scouted out a hollow where they made camp. It was set within a pine wood and circled by boulders and thick bushes. There was a stream nearby and Gaelen lit a small fire. It was a good campsite and the fire could not be seen outside the ring of trees. Lennox, as always, was hungry, having devoured his three-day rations by noon. The others mocked him as he sat brooding by the fire watching them eat.

Lennox had grown even larger in the last year, his shoulders and arms heavy with muscle, and he now sported a dark beard close-cropped to his chin. Coupled with the brown goatskin jerkin, it created the appearance of a large, amiable bear.

'We are comrades,' he pleaded. 'We should share a little.'

'I saw some berries on a bush back there,' said Gwalchmai. 'I am sure they will prove very tasty.' He bit into a chunk of oatcake, and swung to Agwaine. 'I think the honey in these cakes is better this year, don't you, Agwaine? Thicker. It makes the cakes so succulent.'

'Decidedly so. It gives them extra flavour.'

'You're a bunch of swine,' said Lennox, pushing himself to his feet.

Laughter followed him as he walked into the darkness in search of berries. The woods were quiet, moon shadows dappling the silver grass. Lennox found the bush and plucked a handful of berries. They served only to heighten his hunger, and he toyed once more with the idea of appealing to his comrades. His stomach rumbled and he cursed softly.

A movement to his right made him turn, dropping into a half-crouch with arms spread. He saw a flash of white cloth disappear beneath a bush, and a tiny leg hastily withdrawn.

Lennox ate some more berries and then ambled towards the bush, as if to walk past. As he came abreast of it he lunged down, pulling the child clear. Her mouth opened and her face showed her terror, but no sound came out. Lennox took her in his arms, whispering gentle words and stroking her hair. She clung to the goat-skin tunic with her tiny hands clenched tight, the knuckles white as polished ivory.

'There, there, little dove. You're safe. I didn't mean to frighten you. There, there. Don't worry about Lennox. He's big, but he's not bad. He won't hurt you, little dove. You're safe.' All the while he stroked her head. She burrowed her face into his jerkin, saying nothing.

Lennox made his way back to the camp. Instantly his companions gathered around, plying him with questions. He shushed them to silence. 'She's terrified,' he said, keeping his voice low and gentle. 'She must have lost her parents in the woods.' Looking at his comrades, he silently mouthed the words. 'Probably killed by the Aenir.'

Gwalchmai, always a favourite with children, tried to get the girl to speak, but she pushed her face deeper into Lennox's jerkin.

'I have never seen a child so frightened,' said Agwaine.

'Where are you from?' whispered Lennox, kissing her head. 'Tell your uncle Lennox.' But the child remained silent.

'I don't recognise the girl,' he said. 'Do you, Gwal?'

'No. She could be Pallides, or Haesten, or even Farlain. Or even a crofter's daughter from the Outlands.'

'Well, we can't take her with us,' said Ridan. 'One of us must take her back to Vallon.'

'I'll do it in the morning,' Lennox agreed.

The fire burned low and the companions took to their blankets, ready for an early rise. Lennox sat with his back to a boulder, cuddling the child who had fallen into a deep sleep. He felt good sitting there. Children had never been easy around him – Layne said his great size frightened them – but whatever the reason, it had always hurt Lennox, who loved the young.

In sleep the child's face relaxed, but her left hand still clutched his tunic. He pushed her yellow hair back from her eyes, gazing down into her face. She was a pretty little thing, like a doll stuffed with straw. As the night grew chill Lennox wrapped his blanket around her.

A strange thought struck him.

This was probably the most important moment of his life.

He was not normally a man given to abstract thoughts, but he couldn't help thinking about the child. Here she was, tiny and helpless and full of fear. She had been suffering the worst days of her young life. And now she slept safe in the arms of a powerful man, content that he would look after her. With no more action than a gentle embrace Lennox had ended her terror. What in life, he wondered, could be more important to her?

If her parents were still alive and making for Vallon they must be sick with worry, he thought. But what if – as was likely – they were dead?

Lennox chewed the problem over for a while. He would take her to Maerie; she was a fine lass with only one child, who would take the girl in and love her into the bargain.

The girl's eyes opened, she blinked and yawned. Lennox felt her move and glanced down, stroking her hair. Her eyes were brown and he smiled at her.

'Are you feeling better?' he asked.

'You're not my papa.'

'No, little dove. I'm your uncle Lennox.'

'My papa's gone. Wolfs et him up,' she said, tears glistening. She blinked. 'Et up Jarka too.'

'Wolves?' asked Lennox.

'Big wolfs. Big as you. Et him up.'

'You've been dreaming, little one. There's no wolves, and certainly none as big as me.'

573

'Lots of wolfs,' she persisted. 'They chased me, to eat me up.'

'Uncle Lennox won't let them. You're safe now. Go back to sleep, we'll talk in the morning.'

'Did you know my papa?'

'No. Was he nice?'

'He played games.'

'He sounds a good man. Where is your mama?'

'Men with swords took her away. She was all bleeding.'

'Well, it's over now. You're with your uncle Lennox, and he's the strongest man in all the world. Nothing will harm you.'

'Are you stronger than the wolfs?' she asked.

'Aye, lass. And I swear upon my soul no harm will come to you while you're with me. You believe me?' She smiled, closed her eyes and put her thumb in her mouth.

In the bushes beyond the firelight, blood-red eyes watched for the flames to die down.

Taliesen took Caswallon deep underground to a small chamber set with walls of shining silver and gold. Soft light filled the room, but Caswallon could not see the source. The druid beckoned him to a tall chair of white leather, then sat upon an oak-topped table.

'This is my inner sactum,' he told the warrior. 'Here I observe the Farlain and I keep my notes – notes no one will read in my lifetime.' He gestured to the shelves, but there were no books there, only small silver cylinders neatly stacked from floor to ceiling. The far wall was covered with sheets of paper, upon which were curious drawings and symbols.

Caswallon studied them. 'What do these represent?' he asked.

Taliesen joined him. 'They are Time Lines, and chart my attempts to aid Sigarni.'

Caswallon ran his eyes over the symbols. 'And the stars?'

'Each time Sigarni dies I mark the spot and pursue a new Time Line – a different reality. It is very complex, Caswallon. Do not seek to stretch your mind around it.'

'When must I seek the Queen?'

'As soon as you are ready.'

'I'm ready now.'

'Then observe,' said the druid. Turning, he walked to the wall by the door and opened a hidden panel. The desk-top slid back and a screen rose silently from it. Lights blazed from the screen, forming the image of a walled city.

'That is Citadel town, where the Queen currently resides — currently being a relative term,' added the druid with a dry chuckle.

'How is this done?' whispered Caswallon.

'It is merely an image. It is summer and Sigarni has won a great battle. She has returned to the north to celebrate with her captains. The enemy has been pushed back . . . for now. But the Outland King is gathering a huge force against her. Now, before I send you through, you must understand this, Caswallon: We will meet again on the other side of the Gate. Ask me nothing of the events that are transpiring now. Do not speak of the Aenir invasion.'

'I don't understand.'

Taliesen sighed. Trust me, Caswallon. In other . . . realities . . . our meeting beyond the Gate has already taken place. Many times. And I have found it disadvantageous to view the possible futures. It all becomes too confusing.'

Caswallon stood silently for a moment, then his green gaze fastened on the druid's dark eyes. 'And I have died in these other realities?' he asked.

'Yes,' admitted Taliesen. 'Do you still wish to go?'

'Can we win if I do not?'

'No.'

Then let us go.'

Taliesen pressed a button on the screen and the image of the city disappeared. He stood and led Caswallon back to the Druids' Hall and the black-arched Gate.

Maeg was waiting there. She stood as he approached, opening her arms, and Caswallon walked into her embrace.

She kissed him, her eyes wet with tears. The world has changed, as you said it would,' she told him.

'We'll change it back.'

'I don't think so,' she said sadly. 'Even if you beat the Aenir, nothing will ever be quite the way it was.'

He did not argue. Instead he kissed her. 'There is one constant fact, Maeg. I love you. I always have. I always will.'

'I have something for you,' she said, pulling away from him. Turning, she lifted a buckskin shirt from the back of a chair. The skin was soft and beige while on the chest, in crimson-stained leather, was a cunningly-crafted hawk with wings spreading to each shoulder. 'If you are to meet a Queen, it is fitting you look your best,' she said.

Caswallon slipped out of his woollen shirt, donning the bucksin. The fit was perfect.

Leofas stepped from the shadows with Maggrig.

'Are you sure about this plan, Caswallon?' he asked.

'No,' admitted the War Lord. 'But Taliesen is, and I can think of no other.'

'Then may the gods guide you.' The two men shook hands.

Taliesen walked to the archway, lifted his hands and began to chant. The view of the Farlain vanished, to be replaced instantly by a sloping plain and a distant city.

Maggrig curled his arm around Maeg's shoulder. 'He will come back,' he said.

Caswallon stepped into the archway – and vanished.

Suddenly the view from the Gate disappeared, a blank grey wall replacing it. Maeg moved forward and touched the cold stone.

Caswallon found himself in a forest glade in the last hour before dusk. Shafts of sunlight lanced the branches of mighty oaks and birds sang in every tree.

But there was no city in sight. Perplexed, he stepped back to where the Gate had been.

It was gone . . .

Cursing he drew his short sword and started prodding the air, seeking the entrance. After a few minutes he gave up and sat back on a jutting tree root. He was loath to leave the spot, and had no idea what plan to pursue.

His thoughts were broken by the sounds of shouting. Looking around him, he marked the spot in his mind and set off towards the sound. Perhaps the Gate had merely sent him too far, and he had come out on the other side of the city. He seemed to recall seeing a wood there.

The shouts became triumphant, and Caswallon guessed the men to be hunters who had cornered their prey. Then a voice cried out. 'Lord of Heaven, aid your servant!'

Caswallon broke into a run. Ahead of him three men had surrounded a bald, elderly man in robes of grey who was holding a tightly-wrapped bundle in his arms.

'Surrender it, priest,' ordered a tall man in a red cape.

'You cannot do this,' said the old man. 'It is against the laws of man and God.'

The red-caped warrior stepped forward, a bright sword in his hand. The sword flashed forward. The old man twisted the bundle away from the blade, which lanced into his belly. He screamed and fell.

Caswallon hurdled a fallen tree, his own short sword glinting in the dying light. 'What vileness do we have here, my bonnies?'

The three spun round and the leader walked forward, his sword dripping blood to the grass.

'It is none of your concern, stranger. Begone.'

'Frightened as I am to face three heroes who can so valiantly tackle old men, I feel I must debate the point,' said Caswallon.

'Then die,' shouted the man, leaping forward. Caswallon parried the lunging blade, his own sword flashing through the man's neck. The remaining warriors ran forward. Caswallon blocked the first thrust, hammering a punch to an unprotected chin, and the attacker staggered.

Pushing past him Caswallon engaged the third, slipping his hunting-knife into his left hand. He ducked beneath a vicious swipe, slicing his sword behind the man's knee; with a scream he fell. Caswallon whirled as the second man was almost upon him, sword plunging for his chest, but Caswallon parried the blow, punching his hunting-knife through the man's tunic. The blade slid between the man's ribs, cleaving the heart. Dragging the knife free, he saw the third man crawling towards the bushes, leaving a trail of blood behind him. Ignoring him, Caswallon ran to the old man, gently turning him.

'Thank the Source,' said the priest. 'For He has sent you in my hour of need.' Blood was seeping fast, drenching the old man's clothes.

'Why did they attack you?'

'It wasn't me, my son; they wanted the babe.' The old man pointed to the bundle by his side. Caswallon lifted the blanket and there lay a sleeping infant no more than a week old. She was tiny and naked, her downy hair pure white.

'Lie still,' urged Caswallon, ripping open the priest's robes, seeking to stem the outflow of blood from the wound. The assassin's sword had ripped down through the man's lower belly, opening the artery in his groin. There was no hope for him, and his face was already losing colour.

'Where are you from?' whispered the dying man.

'Another world,' said Caswallon. 'And I am lost.'

The old man's eyes gleamed. 'You passed through a Gate?'

'Yes.'

'Was it Mordic sent you?'

'No.'

'Cateris, Blean, Taliesen . . .'

'Yes, Taliesen.'

'Take the babe back through the Chalice Gate.'

'I do not know where it is.'

'Close by. North. I opened it myself. Look for a cave on the hillside; it has a goblet fashioned in the rock of the entrance. But . . . beware . . . Jakuta Khan will . . . follow.'

'Who are you?'

'Astole. I was Taliesen's teacher.' Horns sounded in the forest to the south. 'They are coming for the child. Take her and run. Go now! I beg you.' The old man slumped back.

Sheathing his sword and knife, Caswallon scooped the bundle into his arms and began to run. Behind him he could hear the barking of dogs and the shrill call of hunting-horns. He was angry now. Thwarted from his quest, he was being hunted by an enemy he did not know, in a forest which was strange to him.

Dropping his pace to a gentle jog, eyes scanning the undergrowth, he searched for a way to lose his pursuers. He could hear running water away to the left and he cut towards it. A small stream gurgled over rocks. Splashing into it, Caswallon followed it upstream for about thirty paces and then left it on the same side, walking through soft mud to stop before a massive oak.

Without turning he looked down and walked backwards, placing his feet in his own prints. Slowly he backtracked to the stream, then carried on walking through the water. It was an old trick, which in daylight would fool no skilled tracker, but with dusk approaching fast it could hold up the pursuit.

The child opened her eyes, pushing her tiny fist into her mouth. Caswallon cursed. She was hungry and that meant there were scant moments left before she began to cry for food.

Turning again towards the north, he scanned the hillside for the cave the old man had spoken of. The babe in his arms gave out a thin piercing wail and Caswallon cursed again. The sun was slowly sinking behind the western peaks. As it fell below the clouds a shaft of bright light lit the hillside, and Caswallon saw the dark shadow of the cave entrance, some thirty paces above him and to the right.

The barking of hounds was closer. Twisting, he saw four sleek black shapes emerge from the tree-line below, no more than fifty paces behind him. Holding firm to the child, Caswallon sprinted up the slope and into the cave. It was like a short tunnel. Behind him the dying sun was bright against the rocks, yet ahead was a forest bathed in moonlight.

Caswallon spun, for the first of the hounds had reached the cave. As it leapt his sword slashed down across its neck, smashing through flesh and bone. Turning again, he saw the moonlit forest begin to fade. Taking two running steps he hurled himself through the Gateway. He fell heavily, bracing his arm and shoulder so that the babe would be protected.

Rolling to his feet he swung to face his enemies – and found himself staring at a solid wall of grey stone. The sound of a waterfall came to him and he sheathed his sword and walked towards it. I know this place, he thought. But the trees are different. This was Ironhand's Pool, and if he climbed above the falls he would see High Druin in the distance. The wind shifted, bringing the smell of wood-smoke to his nostrils. Moving to his left into the wind, the smell grew stronger. Ahead was a cottage of stone, with a thatched roof, and a cleared yard containing a small flower garden and a coop for chickens. Caswallon ran to the cottage, tapping softly at the door. It was opened by a young woman with long fair hair. 'What do you want?' she asked, her eyes wide with fear.

'Food for a babe,' he answered, handing her the child. Her eyes changed as she gazed at the small face.

'Come inside.'

Caswallon followed her. At a pine table sat a large man with a heavy beard of red-gold.

'Welcome,' said the man. Caswallon noticed that one of his hands was below the table, and guessed a blade was hidden there.

'I found the babe in the forest,' he said lamely.

The man and woman exchanged glances. 'Do you know whose child it is?' the man asked.

'I know nothing of her,' said Caswallon.

'We lost our own daughter three days ago,' said the man. 'That is her crib there, in the corner. You can leave the child with us, if you will. My wife is still milk-swelled – as you can see.' The woman had opened her shirt and was feeding the babe.

Caswallon pulled up a chair and seated himself opposite the man, looking deep into his clear grey eyes, 'If I leave her with you, will you care for her as you would your own?'

'Aye,' said the man. 'Walk with me awhile.' He rose, sheathing the hunting-knife he had held below the table. He was taller than Caswallon, and broader in the shoulder. Stepping out into the night he walked to the far side of the cabin, seating himself on a bench crafted from pine. Caswallon sat beside him. 'Who are you?' he asked. 'Your clothes are clan, but you are not Loda.'

'I am Caswallon of the Farlain.'

'I have dealings with the Farlain. How is it I have never heard of you?'

Caswallon let out a sigh and leaned back against the bench, is there a town near here, on the edge of the Lowlands, called Ateris?'

The man shook his head. 'There is Citadel town. The Outlanders control it now. And I ask you again – who are you?'

'I am a clansman, as I have said.' He laughed suddenly. 'Were our positions reversed, my friend, and you were to tell me the story of how you found the babe, I would think you mad.'

'I am not you,' said the man. 'So speak.'

Quietly Caswallon told him of the Aenir invasion and of his journey through the Gateway, of the dying priest, and the men and hounds who had sought the death of the child. The man did not interrupt, but listened intently. As he finished Caswallon stood and looked down into the man's deep-set grey eyes, awaiting a response.

At that moment the ground trembled. Thrown off-balance, Caswallon lurched to the right. The moonlight brightened and gazing up, both men saw two moons shining in the sky. For moments only the land was bathed in silver brilliance, then the second moon faded.

As it did so the figure of Taliesen appeared beside them. The old man stumbled and fell to his knees as the crofter leapt to his feet, his knife snaking into his hand. 'No!' shouted Caswallon. 'He is the druid I told you of.'

Taliesen tried to stand, failed, and sat glumly on the ground, 'I think the journey almost killed me,' he grumbled. As Caswallon helped him to his feet, the little sorcerer sighed. 'You have no idea of the energy I have expended to arrive here. Who is this?'

'I am Cei,' said the crofter.

'I must see the child,' said Taliesen, shaking himself free of Caswallon's support and moving off to the cabin.

Cei approached Caswallon. 'You were wrong. I did not think you mad. Yesterday an old man came to us as we were mourning the death of our babe. He told us he would come, and that he would bring us joy – and sorrow.'

581

'This man, he was bald and wearing grey robes?' Cei nodded. Both men returned to the cabin, to find Taliesen kneeling beside the crib where the baby was sleeping. When Caswallon and Cei looked closely they saw that the child's silver hair was now corn-gold.

Taliesen stood and turned towards the crofter. 'Enemies will come after this babe,' he said. 'Be warned. I have changed the colour of her hair. As I have told your wife, you must raise her as your own; no one must know how she came here. Your wife says the death of your child is not known among your friends in the clan. Keep it that way.'

'Who is she?' asked Cei. 'Why is she in danger?'

'She is your daughter. You need know no more than that — save that she is of the blood royal,' said Taliesen. 'Now we must go.'

Lennox added fuel to the fire and the flames leapt and twisted. He wasn't cold, he merely wanted to see the child's face in sleep. Her thumb had slipped from her open mouth and she was breathing evenly. Lennox carefully hitched her into the crook of his right arm, stretching his back.

Gaelen yawned and stretched, sitting up and rubbing his eyes. Seeing Lennox still awake, he moved round the fire to join him. 'How is she?'

'She is all right now. She says her father was eaten by wolves . . . and her sister.'

'It's unlikely,' said Gaelen. 'She would not have escaped a pack. A dream, do you think?'

'I don't know. She said the wolves were as big as me.'

'Wolves attack at night and they move fast. A child that small might think them over-large?'

'I agree, Gaelen, but she's clan; her father was clan. How could he be surprised by wolves? It makes no sense. I can't remember a clansman ever being killed by a pack. Wolves don't attack men. I've never heard of such a thing.'

'Perhaps he had no fire, or had been forced to flee without weapons. Perhaps the wolves were starving.'

The two men sat in silence for a while, then Gaelen spoke. 'More likely it was the Aenir and the child was confused. Many of them wear wolfskin cloaks. And at the Games I saw a man with a wolf's head for a helm. An attack at night?'

'She says her mother was killed by men with swords. I don't think she's that confused. I think you should walk warily tomorrow,' said Lennox.

'We'll miss you on the trip,' said Gaelen, gripping Lennox's shoulder.

'Yes, but you don't need me. She does. I'll get her to the island and then join my father. We'll see you in Axta Glen.'

'I hope so. I pray there is an army of highlanders ready to be gathered. But if not I shall still see you there, Lennox. Even if I am alone. I promise you.'

'I know you will, cousin. I'll look forward to it.'

Soon after dawn the companions bade farewell to Lennox and the child and set off to the south. Lennox hoisted the girl to his shoulder and headed north.

As they walked he discovered that her name was Plessie and her clan Haesten; she was the niece of Laric, the Hunt Lord. He was tempted to run back and find the others, for Laric would be well disposed towards a group which had rescued his niece. But Plessie's fearful glances behind them forced him to dismiss the idea.

Whatever had happened to her had left a terrible scar.

Throughout the morning he climbed through the timberline, and they stopped to eat at a rock pool below a small falls. The companions had given Lennox some oatcakes and these he shared with Plessie. The child sat upon a rock dangling her feet in the water, giggling at its icy touch. Lennox smiled – and froze. He slowly climbed to his feet, aware suddenly that he was being watched. Fear grew in his heart – not fear for himself, but for the child. He had promised she would be safe and a promise was a sacred thing among the clans.

Casually he glanced around at the thick undergrowth. He spotted a patch of darkness beyond a blossoming heather, but allowed his eyes to skip over the bush. He had the feeling the dark patch was fur, and if that was so the thing was either a bear or a wolf.

Plessie was sitting in the shade of a tall pine, and a long branch extended above the water. Lennox scooped her into his arms and lifted her high on to the branch.

'Sit there for a moment, little dove,' he said.

'Don't want to,' she wailed.

'Do it for your uncle Lennox. And be careful now.'

Even as he spoke a werebeast charged from the undergrowth, jaws wide, taloned fingers reaching for the clansman. As it leapt it gave a terrifying howl. Beasts of the wild always roar or screech on attacking their prey. The sound freezes the victim.

But Lennox was not a hunted animal. Nor even an ordinary man.

He was the most powerful warrior in the long history of the Farlain.

As the beast broke cover Lennox whirled, bellowing his own scream of fury. He charged it, smashing a right cross to its open jaws. Fangs snapped, the jawbone disintegrating under the impact. The beast screamed and fell, rolling to all fours and howling in pain. A second creature leapt forward and, twisting to meet it, Lennox charged again. Talons lashed across his shoulder, scoring deep through the flesh. The jaws lunged for his face and, throwing up his hand, he fastened his fingers to the furry throat. The downward lunge was halted, the fangs inches from his face. Lennox could feel hot, rancid breath on his skin. The power of the beast was immense. He threw a left-hand blow which thundered against the werebeast's ear; the creature fell back, then leapt again. This time Lennox stood his ground until the beast was almost upon him. As it rushed forward he caught it by the throat and groin, and hurled it with all his strength against the trunk of a pine. It hit with a sickening thud – spine exploding into shards, ribs splitting and piercing the great lungs beneath. Blood flowing from his wounds, Lennox drew his sword. The first beast attacked again, its jaw hanging slack. As its talons lashed out, Lennox ducked beneath the swinging arm and hammered his sword into its unprotected belly.

The creature writhed in agony, then crumpled to the earth, thrashing in its death throes. Lennox dragged his sword loose and drew his hunting-knife, eyes scanning the bushes. There was no movement there. But he had to be sure.

'Stay in the tree, Plessie. Uncle Lennox won't be a moment.'

'No,' she wailed. 'Don't leave me. Wolfs eat me up!' Her tears cut through him, but he moved on, searching the tracks within the undergrowth. Satisfied there were only two of the creatures he returned to the weeping child, lifting her down and cuddling her.

'There, there! You see, I was only a moment or two.'

'Don't leave me again, Uncle Lennox.'

'I won't. Now, you are going to have to be a brave girl and help me to stop this bleeding. Can you do that?' With a grunt of pain Lennox removed his ripped shirt. There were four deep slashes across his right shoulder-blade, but he could reach none of them.

'There's lots of blood, Uncle Lennox.'

'The bleeding will clean the wounds,' he said, moving to his pack. 'Can you sew?'

'Mother taught me,' said Plessie.

'That's good, little one.' Rummaging into his pack, he found needle and thread. 'I want you to close these little scratches for me. Then we'll move on. Will you do that for me?'

'I don't know how.' Lennox could see the fear returning to her.

'It's easy,' he told her, forcing a smile. 'Trust me. I'll show you. First thread the needle. My hands are too big and clumsy for it.' Plessie took the thread, licked the end and carefully inserted it into the eye of the needle. She looked up expectantly at Lennox. Twisting his head, he could see the ragged red line of the first cut on the top of his shoulder. Taking the needle, he pricked it through the skin. 'You do it like this,' he told her, as a wave of nausea hit him. 'Just like this.'

Plessie began to cry. 'You're not going to die, are you, Uncle Lennox?'

'From little scratches like this? No. Now come round to my back and show me your sewing.'

*   *   *

585

Taliesen led Caswallon away from the cabin, and on into the trees. It was not cold, but the breeze brought a promise of autumn in the air. 'The child will be the future Queen – if she lives,' said the druid.

Caswallon stopped. 'What do you mean, if she lives? We know she lives. I watched her die after the killing the Beast.'

Taliesen gave a dry laugh. 'My boy, you saw *one* Sigarni. But it would take too long to explain the infinite possibilities when one deals in time, the paradoxes created. Merely hold to the concept of impossibility made reality. This child is in great danger. First and foremost is the sorcerer Jakuta Khan. He was hired to bring about the fall of the King, Sigarni's real father, and in exchange he was offered wealth – and the life of the King's daughter. He is a gifted magicker, Caswallon. He will track her down; the crofter cannot stand against him.'

Caswallon sat down on a fallen tree. The thought fills me with sorrow, Taliesen, but what can we do? My people need me. I cannot stay here and protect the babe. Nor can you. We do not have the time.'

'That word again – time,' responded Taliesen, sitting beside the taller man. 'It matters not how long we wait here, for when you return no *time* will have passed in the world you know. There is a small settlement close by; we will rest there, and be offered food. Then we will journey back to the falls and make camp by the rock face where the Gateway opened. There you will see in one day what few mortals will ever see.'

The following evening Caswallon built a small fire by the rock face, and the two men sat eating a meal of honey biscuits and watching the fragmented moon dance upon the rippling water of the falls pools.

'How long do we wait?' asked Caswallon.

'Until I feel the magic of Jakuta Khan,' said Taliesen. 'But now there is someone I must summon.' Rising, the little sorcerer moved to the poolside. As Caswallon watched, Taliesen began to chant in a low voice. The wind died down and a mist formed above two boulders close to the pool's edge. Caswallon's eyes widened as the mist rose into an arch some ten paces in front of the sorcerer. Tiny lights, like fireflies, glittered in the archway, and then a man appeared, tall, impossibly broad-shouldered, wearing a silver breast-plate and a shining mail-shirt of silver steel. His hair was moon-white, his beard braided.

'Who calls Ironhand?' he asked, his voice low and deep like distant thunder. Caswallon rose and walked to stand beside Taliesen.

'I call upon you, High King,' said the sorcerer, 'I, Taliesen, the Druid Lord. Your daughter lives, but she is in peril.'

'They killed me here,' said the ghostly warrior. 'My body lies beneath those boulders. They killed my wife, and I cannot find her spirit.'

'But you daughter lives: the babe sleeps in a cabin close by. And the hunters will come for her, the demons will stalk her.'

'What can I do, Taliesen? I am a spirit now.'

'You can do nothing against men of flesh, Ironhand. But I have planted a seed in the child's mind. When the demons materialise she will flee here. The creatures, though flesh, are also summoned through spirit spells. You can fight them.'

'When you need me, call upon me,' said the Ghost King. The archway shimmered and vanished, and Caswallon once more felt the night breeze upon his skin.

'She is Ironhand's daughter? Sweet Heaven!'

'Aye,' whispered Taliesen, 'she is of the blood most royal. Now let us return to the fire. There is a spell I must cast before I leave you.' The druid banked up the fire, and once more began to chant. Caswallon sat silently until he had finished, then Taliesen took a deep breath. 'There is a man I must see. He is a dreamer and a drunkard, but we will need him before long. Stay here, and do not for any reason venture from the fire.' He smiled. 'I think what you are about to see will keep you well entertained until I return.'

Rising, he ambled away along the line of the pool. Caswallon leaned back against the rock face. Suddenly the moon sped across the sky, the sun flashing up to bathe the pool in brilliant light. Then as suddenly as it had come the sun fell away, and the moon reappeared. Astonished, Caswallon gazed around the pool. There was no sound now, but night and day appeared and disappeared in seconds. Beyond the firelight the grass grew long, withered and dried, died and was replaced. Trees sprouted branches before his eyes. Leaves opened, glistened, withered and fell. Within the space of a moment snow appeared beyond the fire, thick and deep. Then it was gone, instantly replaced by the flowers of spring.

He watched the seasons pass by in heartbeats, in blazes of colour and streams of light.

When the snow had appeared for the sixth time, the rushing of time began to slow. The moon reared up and stopped in mid-heaven.

The cold of winter now whispered past Taliesen's spell and Caswallon shivered. Movement to his right caught his eye and he saw Taliesen trudging through the snow towards him. The old man was carrying a short hunting-bow and a quiver of arrows. 'How did you make the seasons move so fast?' asked Caswallon.

'Not even I can do that,' answered Taliesen wearily. 'You are sitting beside a Gateway. I merely activated it. It flickered *you* through the years.'

'It is a memory I shall long treasure,' said the clansman.

'Sadly, we have no time to dwell upon it,' Taliesen told him, 'for the evil is almost upon us.' He squatted down by the fire, holding out his long thin fingers to the flames, 'I am so cold,' he said, 'and tired.' He handed Caswallon the bow and arrows.

'What are we facing?' asked the clansman, stringing the bow and testing the pull. It was a sturdy weapon.

'Men would call them demons, and so they are, but they are also flesh and blood from another dimension . . . another land, if you will. They are huge beasts, Caswallon, some reaching eight feet tall. In build they are much like great bears, but they move with greater speed, and are upright, like men. Their fingers are taloned, each talon the length of your hunting-knife. They have fangs also, and short, curved tusks. They do not use the tusks in combat; these are for ripping flesh from the leather-skinned beasts they have hunted in their own world.'

'Should we not make our way to Cei's cabin? He cannot face them alone.'

Taliesen shook his head. 'Cei's life is over, boy. It was over the moment he agreed to take the babe. The beasts will materialise there.'

'What?'

'They will be conjured there,' snapped Taliesen. 'Jakuta Khan is a spellmaster; he has located Sigarni and will cause the beasts to appear inside the cabin. I have observed him, Caswallon. He has used these beasts before; he makes them invisible to the human eye. The first moment the victim knows of their existence is when the talons rip out his heart. Trust me, we do not want to be inside the cabin when that happens.'

'How then do we save the babe?'

'She is no longer a babe. You have seen the seasons fly by and she is six now. And she will make her way here. I planted a seed in her mind, and that of her mother. As soon as the terror manifests itself, both will act instinctively. The child will run here.'

Caswallon rose and tied the quiver to his belt. 'And how am I to fight these invisible beasts?' he asked softly.

'As best you can, clansman. Come, kneel by me, and I will give you all that I can.'

Dropping to one knee, Caswallon looked into the old man's eyes. The druid was more than tired. His eyes were dull and purple-ringed, his skin dry. Lifting his hand, Taliesen covered Caswallon's eyes and began to chant. Heat emanated from his fingers, lancing into Caswallon's brain like an arrow of fire. The clansman groaned but Taliesen's voice whispered to him: 'Hold on, boy, it will not last much longer.'

The hand fell away and Caswallon opened his eyes. 'What have you done?' he whispered. The trees by the pool had changed now, becoming sharp and unreal, like a charcoal sketch upon virgin paper. Taliesen's features could no longer be seen; he was merely a glowing form of many colours, red in the belly and eyes, purple over the heart, the rest a shifting mix of orange, yellow and white.

'Now you will see them, Caswallon,' said the shimmering druid. 'They will come from the south, hard on the heels of the child. Best you find a place to smite them.'

'How many will come?'

'I would guess at two. It needs a mighty spell to summon just one. Jakuta Khan will expect little resistance from a crofter. But there might be more; he is young and arrogant in his strength.'

Caswallon moved out on to the frozen pool and headed south, moving high into the tree-line. An old oak stood beside the trail, its two main branches – some ten feet high – spreading out like the arms of a supplicant. Caswallon climbed to the right-hand branch and sat with his back to the tree bole.

His thoughts were many as he waited for the beasts. He had never lacked physical courage – in fact, he had often courted danger merely for the thrill of it. But now? The Farlain were under threat, and his wife and child were in peril in another world. No longer able to afford the luxury of danger, he felt fear rise within him. What if he died here? What would become of the Farlain, or Maeg, and Donal? His mouth was dry. His thoughts swung to the child, Sigarni: an innocent hunted by demons. Yet what was her life when set against his entire clan?

'I will fight, but I cannot die for you,' he said softly, 'I cannot risk that.'

His decision made, he relaxed. Looking down at the glimmering colours that were his hands, he realised that the fingers had become difficult to see, and they were cold. He rubbed his palms together and looked again. For a few heartbeats they shone with a dull red light, then faded once more. Tugging his fleece-lined gloves from his belt, he pulled them on. Ice formed in his beard as he waited in the tree. Glancing back, he saw the shimmering colours he recognised as Taliesen moving across the ice. The old man must be frozen, he thought. The cloak of feathers would do little to keep out the bitter cold.

A bestial scream tore through the silence of the night. Caswallon removed his gloves and notched an arrow to the bow-string. For some moments there was no movement, then a small figure ran into sight, the colours glowing around her bright and rich. The figure stumbled and rolled in the snow.

Pulling his gaze from her, Caswallon looked back up the trail. Something huge loomed over the hillside, then another. To his left was a third, moving through the trees. Caswallon cursed, gauging the beasts to be around eight feet tall. The first of the creatures lumbered down the slope. Its colours were strong, mostly purple, orange and red; the purple area spread from the neck to the belly in two vertical circles joined by a red ridge. Caswallon drew back on the bow-string until it touched his right cheek, then he let fly. The arrow hammered home in the upper circle of purple and instantly the colour changed, flowing from the wound as golden light. Caswallon loosed a second shaft that punched through the lower circle. The creature gave a terrifying shriek, tottered to the left and fell heavily.

Twisting round, Caswallon saw that the child had reached the pool-side. Two beasts were converging on her. Of Taliesen there was no sign. Dropping from the tree, Caswallon notched an arrow and raced down the icy slope. His foot struck a tree-root hidden by snow and he was pitched forward. Releasing the bow, he tried to roll over and stop his slide, his hands scrabbling at the snow. Another tree-root saved him, his fingers curling round it. Scrambling to his feet he saw the first of the beasts almost upon the helpless child. His bow was some twenty paces up the slope. Drawing his short sword and hunting-knife Caswallon ran forward. As the beast reared up, he ducked under a sweeping slash from a taloned paw and stabbed his knife hilt deep into the creature's belly. A backhanded blow took him high on the shoulder, lifting him from his feet and hurling him through the air. Falling hard, he struck his left shoulder against a tree-trunk, paralysing his arm. The mortally wounded beast staggered and fell, but the third demon reared up and advanced on the clansman.

With an angry curse Caswallon rose, eyes glittering.

'Run, you fool!' shouted Taliesen, as the beast loomed before the clansman. Deep in his heart Caswallon knew that he should take that advice. There was so much to live for, so much still to be achieved.

The beast turned away from him – towards the child at the water's edge. In that moment Caswallon felt relief flood over him. He was safe! I live and she dies, he thought suddenly.

Without further thought he took three running steps and hurled himself at the beast, plunging his sword into its broad back. The creature screamed and spun. The sword was ripped from the clansman's hand, but remained jutting from the beast's rainbow flesh. Talons ripped into Caswallon's shoulder, pain searing through him as he was thrown to the ground.

In that moment a bright light blazed and Caswallon saw the massive, shimmering figure of Ironhand standing over the child, sword held two-handed and raised high. The beast gave a low growl and sprang at the ghost. The dead King stepped forward to meet it, his silver sword slashing through the air in a glittering arc; it passed through the creature seemingly without leaving a wound.

But the demon froze, tottered, and toppled backwards to the snow.

Taliesen emerged from his hiding place in the undergrowth and ran to the child. Caswallon's vision blurred, the spell placed over his eyes fading. He blinked and saw the druid kneeling beside Sigarni. The girl was sitting silently, her eyes wide open and unblinking. Taliesen placed his hands on the child's head. 'Is she hurt?' asked the Ghost King.

Taliesen shook his head. 'Her body is safe, her spirit scarred,' he said.

With a groan Caswallon pushed himself to his feet. Blood was flowing freely from the gash to his shoulder. 'What will happen to her now?'

'There is one coming who will look after her. His name is Gwalch; he is a mystic,' Taliesen told him.

'I hope this is an end to her adventures with demons,' said Caswallon.

'It is not,' whispered Taliesen. 'But the next time she must fight them alone.'

'Not alone,' said the King. 'For I shall be here.'

With time against him, Gaelen led the companions over the most hazardous terrain, skirting the Aenir army on the third day of travel.

From their hiding place on a wooded hillside, the companions gazed down on the horde moving through the valley.

The size of the enemy force dismayed the clansmen. It seemed to stretch and swell across the valley, filling it. There were few horsemen, the mass of fighting men striding together, bearing round shields painted black and red, and carrying long swords or vicious double-headed axes.

Gaelen was worried. For the last day he had been convinced that the companions were being followed. Agwaine shared his view, though when Gwalchmai and Layne scouted the surrounding woods they found only animal tracks. Onic and Ridan, anxious to push on, accused Gaelen of needless caution.

That night they made late camp on open ground and lit a fire. The moon was hidden by a dark screen of storm cloud and the night covered them like a black fog. Gaelen was glad of the darkness and curled into his blanket. Onic had suggested they head for Carduil, a jagged, unwelcoming series of peaks to the east, and Gaelen had agreed. The companions had moved south at first, hugging the timberline, gradually veering towards the distant mountains. Tomorrow they would head into the rising sun over the most dangerous stretch, wide valleys with little cover. Making a cold camp in a hidden hollow, Gaelen took the first watch. After an hour Layne moved through the darkness to sit beside him.

'Can't you sleep?' asked Gaelen.

'No, cousin. I wish you had brought Render with you. I feel uneasy.'

'He's well trained,' said Gaelen, 'but he's still a hound, and his hunting might have alerted the Aenir.'

'It is not the Aenir that concern me,' whispered Layne.

'You are still thinking about the wolves?'

'Aye – and the beast which killed the Queen.' The moon cleared the clouds and Gaelen looked at his friend. Layne's hair glinted silver in the moonlight.

Gaelen shivered. 'You think they might be demons?'

'I hope not,' said Layne. 'But if they are – and they continued to follow the child – then I fear for Lennox.'

Gaelen put his arm around his friend's shoulder. 'If any man can survive against such beasts, Lennox will. I have no fears for him.'

Layne smiled. 'He is uncommonly strong.' For a time they sat together in silence, then Layne spoke again. 'Did you propose to Deva?'

'Yes. She spurned me.'

'Me too. Some nonsense about birthing kings. I think she'll grow out of it. Will you continue to court her?'

'No, Layne.'

'I shall. Once we have crushed the Aenir, I shall pursue her with such ardour that she will melt into my arms.' He grinned, looking suddenly boyish again.

Gaelen smiled. 'I wish you good fortune, my friend.'

'I think I'll get some sleep now,' said Layne.

'Layne!' whispered Gaelen, as his friend rose.

'What?'

'I never really thanked you for standing up for me on that first day, when Agwaine drew his knife. You made me feel welcome among the Farlain and I'll not forget it. And if ever you need me, I will be there for you.'

Layne said nothing, but he smiled and then moved back to his blanket. Gaelen kept watch for another two hours, then he woke Ridan.

'You've have ruined a fine dream,' muttered the clansman, sitting up and yawning.

Gaelen crossed the clearing and lay down. Sleep came instantly, but a faint rustling brought him awake. Was one of the others moving around? He took a deep breath, releasing it slowly, and listened again.

Silence.

No! There was the sound again, away to the right.

An animal? A bird?

Gaelen curled his hand around the short sword lying next to him, gently easing it from the leather scabbard. He felt foolish, thinking back to the first night he had spent in the open with Caswallon, when the fox had terrified him.

A crunching noise, followed by a bubbling gurgle, brought him to his feet and the clouds above moved away from the moon. A scene of horror met his eyes. Five huge beasts were crouching in the camp. Ridan lay dead, his throat ripped apart, while another body was being dragged towards a screen of bushes.

Gaelen froze.

One beast, red eyes glinting, reared up on its hind legs and ran silently towards him. Gaelen shouted a warning and Onic rolled to his feet, his arm flashing back and then forward. His hunting-knife shot across the camp to plunge deep into the beast's back; it howled then, rending the night silence. Gaelen leaped forward, ramming his sword into the beast's chest. Talons lashed at him and he jumped back, releasing the blade. Then Gwalchmai ran forward and hurled his knife which thudded into the creature's neck.

And the clouds closed, darkness blinding them all.

Gaelen dived for his pack, scrabbling at the canvas lip. Delving inside, he produced his tinder-box. There were only a few shredded leaves inside, but he was desperate for light. Twice the sparks jumped and then a tiny flame licked out. Holding up the box like a flickering candle, Gaelen turned. He could see Agwaine, Onic and Gwalchmai standing together with swords in hand. On the ground nearby lay the hideous corpse of the dead beast. Elsewhere there was no sign of the pack.

The others joined him, gathering twigs and branches, and they built a fire, heedless of any danger from the Aenir. Agwaine took a burning branch and moved to the spot where Layne had slept. The ground was wet with blood, and his body was lying some twenty feet away. Ridan's corpse was nowhere in sight.

Gaelen moved to where Layne lay and with trembling hands turned over the corpse. Layne's throat had been ripped away, but his face was untouched and his grey eyes were open, staring at nothing. Gaelen sank back. Gwalchmai knelt by the body and reached out, his fingers tenderly brushing the skin of Layne's face. 'Oh, God,' said Gwalchmai. Gaelen lifted Layne's hand, picturing him as he had been only a few hours before – tall, handsome, and in love.

'I promised to be there for you, and I wasn't,' he said. 'I am so sorry, Layne.'

'We must bury him – deep,' said Agwaine.

'We can't,' said Gaelen. The fire will have alerted the Aenir, and the beasts could return at any time. We must push on.'

'I'll not have him devoured by those creatures!' stormed Agwaine.

Gaelen rose, tears shining in his eyes. 'You think I do not feel exactly the same, Agwaine? But Layne is gone. His spirit has fled; all that is left is dead flesh which, even if we bury it, will be devoured by maggots. The Farlain need us, Layne does not. Now let us move.'

'But we don't know where those creatures are,' objected Gwalchmai. 'We could run right into them.'

'And if we don't,' snapped Gaelen, 'then by morning we'll all be blood-eagled to the trees.'

'Gaelen is right. It's time to move,' said Agwaine. 'Kill the fire.'

Donning their packs they set off towards the east, where the dark line of the Carduil range could be seen against the sky. They walked with swords in hand, saying little, and the journey was fraught with fear. The storm clouds passed over them, lightning flashing to the south, and the moon shone bright.

'By the gods, look!' exclaimed Gwalchmai.

On either side of them, some twenty paces distant, dark shadows could be seen moving from bush to bush.

'How many?' hissed Agwaine.

'Four,' answered Onic.

Swiftly they doffed their packs, stringing the short hunting-bows.

'Wait! said Gaelen. 'Let us each pick a target, for once they learn the power of the bow they will be more wary.'

Gwalchmai eased back on the string. 'All right. I'll take the one on the left at the rear.'

Choosing their targets they waited patiently, Gwalchmai and Onic kneeling, Agwaine and Gaelen facing right with bows half drawn.

★   ★   ★

The werebeasts crouched in the bushes, confused and uncertain. They could not see the shining talons that had cut down their comrade, only long sticks of wood. But they were wary. The leader edged forward, raising his head. The scent of warm flesh caused his stomach to tighten and saliva dripped from his maw. He moved into the open on all fours, edging still closer. A second followed him. On the other side a third beast was in view.

More clouds bunched above them, the sky darkening.

Gaelen cursed. 'Let fly . . . NOW!'

Shafts hissed through the night air. The leader howled as the missile sliced into his chest, spearing his lungs. Blood filled his throat and the howling ceased. Behind him the second thrashed about in the bushes, an arrow through his eye.

To the left Gwalchmai's target had dropped without a sound, shot through the heart. Only Onic had not let fly. His target had remained in the bushes. Alone and frightened, it sprinted away to the west.

10

Taliesen led Caswallon to a long room beneath the Vallon caves. The walls were lined with shelves of old oak, some of them twisted and cracked with age. Upon some of them were parchment scrolls, leather-bound books, and sheafs of paper bound with twine. Others were stacked with metal cylinders or small glass bottles sealed with wax. On the far side of the hall two druids were sitting at one of the many tables, poring over scrolls and scribbling notes with quill pens.

Maggrig, Leofas and Maeg were waiting there when the druid and the clansman arrived. While Maeg examined the shallow wound in her husband's shoulder, Maggrig pressed Caswallon about his journey through the Gateway. He told them of the baby, and the old man who had been carrying her.

As she spoke the old man's name Taliesen sank to a chair, eyes wide, mouth agape. It was the first time Caswallon had seen him so surprised. 'You did not tell me it was Astole,' he whispered. 'Still alive!'

'He's not alive now,' said Caswallon. 'He died there in that forest.'

Taliesen shook his head. 'Unlikely. He had remarkable powers of recuperation,' said the druid. 'He is twice as old as I am. And I once saw a spear pierce his chest, the point emerging alongside his spine. He made me draw it from him; I did, and watched the wound heal within seconds.'

'Alive or dead, he cannot help us now,' said Caswallon. 'So what do we do?'

'We try again – if you feel strong enough. Do you?'

'Is there a choice, druid?'

Taliesen shook his head. Maggrig loomed over the druid. 'Except that after the last mistake,' he said, 'you might now waft him away to the centre of the Aenir camp, and he can demand their surrender.'

'It was not a mistake,' snapped the druid. 'It was destiny.'

'Well, if there is a moment of *destiny*,' promised Maggrig, 'I'll pierce your scrawny ears with your teeth!'

'That will be hard to do – after I've turned you to a toad!' Taliesen countered.

'Enough!' said Maeg sharply. 'Go back to the Gate – all of you. I need to speak to my husband.' Maggrig swallowed his anger and followed Taliesen and the old warrior Leofas from the room.

When they had gone, Maeg took Caswallon's hand and looked deep into his sea-green eyes, 'I love you, husband,' she said, 'more than life. I want so much to ask you – to beg you – to refuse Taliesen. Yet I will not . . . even though my heart is filled with fears for you.'

He nodded, then lifted her hand to his lips. 'You are mine, and I am yours,' he said. 'You are the finest of women, and I have not the words to tell you what you mean to me.' He fell silent as a single tear rolled to Maeg's cheek, 'I love you, Maeg. But I must do what I can to save my people.'

The clansman stood, and hand in hand he and Maeg walked to the Gate. It stood open, the bright sunshine of another world blazing down upon hills and mountains. Taliesen stood waiting on the other side. Maeg kissed Caswallon and he felt the wetness of her tears on his cheek. Maggrig gripped his hand. 'Take care, boy,' he said gruffly.

Recovering his sword, Caswallon stepped through the archway on to the hillside above Citadel town.

'Remember, Caswallon,' said Taliesen, 'the Queen must have her army assembled within ten days. Take her to the Falls where we fought the demons. Tell her Taliesen needs her help.'

'You think she will remember you – after all these years?'

'She saw me only yesterday,' said Taliesen. 'Well . . . yesterday to her. And now it is time to go. Come back here at dawn in four days and report on your progress.'

Leaving the druid behind him, Caswallon set off down the slope towards the city. There were sentries at the gates, but many people were passing through and the clansman was not challenged. As he walked Caswallon gazed at the buildings; they were not like the houses of Ateris, being higher and more closely packed, built of red brick and stone, the windows small.

There were narrow, open sewage channels on both sides of the street, and the stench from them filled the nostrils. Crowds of revellers were gathering on every side, drunken clansmen and mercenaries, many singing, others dancing to the tune of the pipes. Caswallon threaded his way through them, heading for the Citadel above the town.

At the gates he was stopped by two guards wearing bronze breastplates and leather kilts. Both carried lances. 'What is your business here?' asked the shorter of the two.

'I seek the Queen,' replied Caswallon.

'Many men seek the Queen. Not all are allowed to find her.'

'It is a matter of importance,' said Caswallon.

'Do I know you?' asked the guard. 'You seem familiar.'

'My business is urgent,' said Caswallon. The man nodded once more, then called a young soldier from the ramparts. 'Take this man to the city hall. Ask for Obrin.'

The soldier saluted and walked away. Caswallon followed. The man stopped before a wide flight of marble steps, at the top of which were double doors of bronze-studded oak. Before the doors were four more guards in bronze breastplates, each of these wore crimson cloaks and leather breeches cut short at the calf. The soldier led the way up the stairs and whispered to one of the sentries; the man tapped at the door and passed a message inside. After a wait of several more minutes the door opened once more and an officer came out. He was tall and of middle years, his beard iron-grey, his eyes a frosty blue. He looked at Caswallon and smiled. Taking the clansman by the arm, he led him inside the hall. The Queen is holding a victory banquet,' he said, 'but you will not find her in a good mood.'

The hall was vast, with ten high-arched windows. A huge curved table was set at the centre, around which sat more than two hundred men and women feasting on roast pig, swan, goose, chicken and sundry other meats and pastries. The noise was incredible and

Caswallon found himself longing for the open mountains. Swallowing down his distaste, he followed the officer forward.

At the far end of the hall, where the table curved like an upturned horseshoe, sat the Queen. She was a tall woman, silver-haired and yet young, and she wore a plain dress of white wool. Caswallon had seen this woman die in the Farlain three years before. Then she had been handsome but old; now she was a beauty, proud and strong, her clear grey eyes sparkling with life and energy. The eyes turned on Caswallon and Sigarni rose from her seat, a delighted smile on her face.

She hesitated, as if not believing what she saw. Then she was running to meet Caswallon. 'Redhawk!' she shouted joyously. 'You've returned!'

Caswallon returned the Queen's embrace, his mind racing as Sigarni gripped his shoulders.

'Let me look at you, Redhawk. By Heaven, how is it you have become young again? Have you dyed that beard? It was almost pure silver the last time we met.'

'I hear you have done well,' countered Caswallon, his mind racing.

'Well? Now that is an understatement. The Outland King is slain, his army in ruins. The war may not be won, but we have gained valuable time. Time! Morgase is defeated – but she has vanished. Not one word of her in six months. But enough of that. Where have you been these last two years? I needed you.'

'I have been in my own land, amongst my own people.'

'You are ill at ease, my friend. What ails you?'

'I am merely tired, my Lady.'

She smiled. 'Join us at table. We'll eat and hear a few songs,' said Sigarni, leading him forward. 'Later we'll talk.'

The feast seemed to last an eternity, and great was his relief when eventually it ended. A servant led him to an upper bedchamber. It was small, with a single window and a long, pallet bed. A fire was burning in the hearth. Moving to the window, Caswallon pushed it open and gazed out over the mountains. Confused, he remembered again the Queen's death near Attafoss, and her last words.

'Now the circle is complete,' the Queen had said. 'For you told me you would be with me at my death.' And then at the last she had asked, 'Was I truly the Queen you desired me to be?' The cold winds of approaching winter made him shiver. Closing the window, he crossed the room to sit on the rug before the fire. He thought he had been prepared for anything, but the sight of the Queen had shaken him. She was stunningly beautiful and, despite his love for Maeg, he found in himself a yearning for Sigarni which he would not have believed possible.

For some time he sat there, then felt the draught on his back as the door opened.

Sigarni entered. She was dressed now in a simple woollen shirt of white that showed the curve of her breasts and dark brown leggings which highlighted her long, slim legs. She sat down on the bed. No more the Queen, she looked now like a clanswoman – tall and strong, fearless and free. Her mouth was astonishingly inviting, and Caswallon found his heart beating wildly.

'What are you thinking, my wizard?' she asked, her voice more husky than he recalled from her greeting in the hall.

'You are very beautiful, Lady.'

'And you are changed,' she said softly, her grey eyes holding to his gaze.

'In what way?' he countered.

Sigarni slid off the bed to sit next to him by the fire. 'When I greeted you I saw the surprise in your eyes. And now I am here beside you – and yet you do not seek to hold me. What has happened to you, Redhawk? Have you forsaken me for another? I will understand if that is true. By Heaven, I have said my share of farewells to lovers. I would hope to have the strength to accept similar treatment. Is that what is happening here?'

'No,' he said, his mind reeling. Moving back from her, he stood and returned to the window. The moon was high over the mountains and he stared up at the sky, fighting to make sense of her words. They were lovers! How could this be? For Caswallon loyalty was not like a cloak, to be worn or discarded, but an iron code to live by. And yet . . .

'Talk to me, Redhawk,' said Sigarni.

He swung to face her. Once more her beauty struck him like an arrow. 'Taliesen told me that you understood the Gateways. You know, therefore, that they allow us to move through time as well as to other lands?'

'Of course,' she told him. 'What has that to do with you and me?'

He took a deep breath, 'In all my life I have seen you only four times. Once as a babe in the forest, the second time by Ironhand's Falls, the third . . .' he hesitated and looked away '. . . in my own realm . . . and the fourth tonight in the great hall. Everything you say to me – about us – is . . . new and strange. If we are to be lovers, it is not now but in a time – for me – that is yet to be. As I stand here I have a wife, Maeg, whom I adore, and a small child, Donal.' He saw she was about to speak and raised his hand. 'Please say nothing, for I know I would never betray Maeg while she lived. And I do not want to know what the future holds for her.'

Sigarni rose, her face thoughtful. 'You are a good man, Redhawk, and I love you. I will say nothing of Maeg . . .' She smiled. 'Just as you hesitated about our meeting in your own realm. I will leave you now. We will talk in the morning.'

'Wait!' he called out, as she opened the door. 'There is something I must ask of you.'

'The debt,' she said. Then, noting his incomprehension, she smiled softly. 'You always said there would come a time when you would ask me a great favour. Whatever it is, I will grant it. Good night, Redhawk.'

'You are a rare woman, Sigarni.'

Turning back, she nodded. 'You will one day say that to me with even more feeling,' she promised.

Taliesen sat alone in the semi-darkness of his viewing chamber. It was cold, and idly he touched a switch to his right. Warm air flowed through hidden steels vents in the floor and he removed his cloak. Leaning back against the head-rest of the padded leather chair, he stared at the panelled ceiling, his mind tired, his thoughts fragmented.

He transferred his gaze to the gleaming files. Eight hundred years of notes, discoveries, failures and triumphs.

Useless.

All of it . . .

How could the Great Gates have closed?

And why were the Middle Gates shrinking year by year?

The Infinity Code had been broken a century before his birth by the scientist Astole. The first Gate – a window really – had been set up the following year. It had seemed then that the Universe itself had shrunk to the size of a small room.

By the time Taliesen was a student his people had seen every star, every minor planet. Gates had been erected on thousands of sites from Sirius to Saptatua. Linear time had snapped back into a Gordian knot of interwoven strands. It was a time of soaring arrogance and interstellar jests. Taliesen himself had walked upon many planets as a god, enjoying immensely the worship of the planet-bound humanoids. But as he grew older such cheap entertainment palled and he became fascinated by the development of Man.

Astole, his revered teacher, had fallen from grace, becoming convinced of some mystic force outside human reality. Mocked and derided, he had left the order and vanished from the outer world. Yet it was *he* who had first saved the baby, Sigarni. Taliesen felt a sense of relief. For years he had feared a rogue element amid the complexities of his plans. Now that fear vanished.

He understood now the riddle of the Hawk Eternal.

'You and I will teach him, Astole,' he said, 'and we will save my people.' A nagging pain flared in his left arm and, rubbing his bicep, he rose from the chair. 'Now I must find you, old friend,' he said, 'I shall begin by re-visiting the last place Caswallon saw you.' His fingers spasmed as a new pain lanced into his chest. Taliesen staggered to his chair, fear welling within him. He scrabbled for a box on the desk-top, spilling its contents. Tiny capsules rolled to the floor . . . with trembling fingers he reached for them. There was a time when he would have needed no crudely manufactured remedies, no digitalis derived from foxglove. In the days of the Great Gates he could have travelled to places where his weakened heart would have been regenerated within an hour. Youth within a day! But not now. His vision swam. The fear became a tidal wave of panic that circled his chest with a band of fire. Oh, please, he begged. Not now!

The floor rose to strike his head, pain swamping him.

'Just one more . . . day,' he groaned.

His fingers clenched into a fist as a fresh spasm of agony ripped into him.

And as he died the Gates vanished.

During the week that followed Caswallon's departure Maggrig led his Pallides warriors on a series of killing raids, hitting the Aenir at night, peppering them with arrows from woods and forests. Leofas, with four hundred Farlain clansmen, circled the Aenir force and attacked from the south.

Whenever the Aenir mustered for a counter-attack the clans melted away, splitting their groups to re-form at agreed meeting places.

The raids were no more than a growing irritation to Asbidag, despite the disruption of his supply lines and the loss of some three hundred warriors. The main battle was what counted, and the clans could not run for ever.

But where was Barsa? Nothing had been heard of his son and the Timber-Wolves he led.

Drada trapped a raiding party of twenty Pallides warriors in a wood twelve miles from Attafoss, and these — bar one — were summarily butchered. The prisoner was tortured for seven hours, but revealed nothing. He had been blood-eagled on a wide tree. But the main force, led by Maggrig, escaped to the north, cutting through the ring of steel Drada had thrown around the wood. Still twenty of the enemy had been slain, and Drada was not displeased.

In the south-east Gaelen and his companions had found more than eighty Pallides warriors in the caves of Pataron, a day's march from Caduil. These he had persuaded to march with him on his return. It was a start.

On the fifth day of travel Gaelen and his group entered the thick pines below Carduil, and as they climbed they felt the chill of the wind blowing down from the snow-capped peaks. As they neared the opening to a narrow pass, a tall woman in leather breeches and a hooded sheepskin jerkin stepped out from the trees, a bow half-drawn in her hands.

'Halt where you stand,' she commanded.

'We are seeking Laric,' Gaelen told the clanswoman.

'Who are you?'

'Gaelen of the Farlain. I come with a message from the War Lord Caswallon and his friend Maggrig of the Pallides.'

The warrior woman eased down the bow-string, returned the shaft to the quiver and moved forward, 'I am Lara,' she said, holding out her hand. 'Laric's daughter. My father is dead. He led the men on a raid to Aesgard; they were taken and slain to the last man.'

'All dead?' asked Agwaine, pushing forward.

'Yes. The Haesten are finished.'

'I am sorry,' said Gaelen, his heart sinking.

'No more than we are,' said Lara. 'We are camped within Carduil. Join us.'

The companions followed her into the pass, and up to the winding trail below the caves. Once within the twisted caverns Lara pushed back her hood, shaking loose her dark hair. Leaving the companions at a fire where food was being prepared, she took Gaelen to a small rough-cut chamber in which lay a bed and a table of pine.

'There used to be a group of druids here,' she said, stripping off her jerkin. Tossing it to the bed, she pulled a chair from beneath the table and sat.

Gaelen sat on the bed, his misery evident. 'You thought you'd find an army?' she asked softly.

'Yes.'

'How many Farlain warriors escaped?'

'Close to four thousand.'

'And Pallides?'

'Less than a thousand.'

'They'll fight well,' said the girl. 'Would you like something to drink?' Gaelen nodded. She stood and crossed the chamber, bending to lift a jug and two goblets from behind a wooden chest. The soft leather of her breeches stretched across her hips. Gaelen blinked and looked away, suddenly uncomfortable.

She passed him a goblet of honeyed wine. 'Are you warm?' she asked.

'A little.'

'Your face is flushed. Take your jerkin off.'

She really was quite striking, he realised, as he removed the garment. Her eyes were the blue of an evening sky, her mouth wide and full-lipped.

'Why are you staring?'

'I'm sorry,' he stammered.

'I saw you run in the Games,' she said. 'You were unlucky to miss the final.'

'Luck had little to do with it,' he said, happier to be on firmer ground.

'I heard – you were attacked. Still, the clans won.'

'Yes.'

'They will win again.'

'At this moment I don't see how,' said Gaelen. 'Nothing has gone right for us. We have lost thousands and the Aenir are hardly touched.'

'I have eight hundred warriors at my command,' she said.

'What? Where are you hiding them?'

'They are not hidden. They are here, with me.'

'You mean the women?'

'If that patronising look does not fade soon, you Farlain pig-swill, then you'll be leaving here faster than you came.'

'I . . . apologise,' he said.

'Well, stop apologising!' she snapped. 'It seems you've done nothing else since you arrived. You're the lowlander Caswallon brought home, are you not?'

'I am.'

'Then, this once, I will forgive you for not thinking like a clansman. All our women are skilled with the bow. We can also use

607

knives, though swords are a little unwieldy. Our men are dead and our clan finished. We none of us have any reason to go on living like beasts in the mountains. Even if we survive and smash the Aenir, there will be no Haesten. Our day is gone. The best we can hope for is to find husbands from other clans. Believe me, Gaelen, that is not a happy thought.'

'Let us start again, Lara,' he said, 'I did not wish to insult you. And, though I was once a lowlander, I am well aware of the skill of clan women. I will accept your offer, if you still hold to it. You must forgive me. It has been a long spring and much has happened; I have been hunted, attacked, and seen my closest friend slain. The enemy that destroyed your people did this to me when I was a child in Ateris,' he told her, pointing to the blood-red eye and the jagged white scar above. 'I had few friends in that city, but those were brutally murdered. Youngsters I grew to like among the Farlain are now rotting corpses. I was sent here to gather an army that could descend upon the enemy and, perhaps, turn the tide of battle. I do not patronise you, I admire you. But still I am disappointed.'

'That I can understand,' she said, her voice softening. 'You were one of the Beast Slayers, were you not?'

'That seems so long ago now. There were five of us – and one of those lies dead back in the forest . . . or at least he would, had he not been devoured by another demon beast.'

'Who died?' she asked.

'Layne.'

'The handsome brother of the mighty Lennox,' she said. That is indeed a loss. You say there are more of these creatures still roaming the mountains?'

'One only. We slew the others.'

'Good,' she said, with a smile. 'You know you are now part of clan myths.'

He nodded. 'A small part.'

'The lowlander and the ghost Queen.'

'Is that what they call her?'

'Yes. The story is that she was the daughter of Earis returned from the grave.'

'I don't know about that,' he told her. 'Her name was Sigarni, and she was a mighty warrior Queen – the sort of woman you would follow into the caverns of the damned.'

'I like the sound of her. I'll get us something to eat,' she said, rising and taking his empty goblet.

'Tell me,' he asked suddenly, 'was your man killed?'

'I had no man.'

'Why?'

'What business is it of yours?'

'I . . .'

'And don't apologise!'

He watched her leave the chamber, too aware for comfort of her sensual grace and the sleek lines of her body.

Maggrig was horrified when the young druid, Metas, brought him the news of Taliesen's death. The Pallides leader was still reeling from the trap that had been sprung on him that morning when the Aenir encircled his force. He had escaped, but only by good fortune.

Now he was thunderstruck. He sent a message to Leofas and retired with Intosh to the forest caves to await him. It was late afternoon when Leofas was led to him; with the old warrior was his giant son, Lennox.

'You have heard?' asked Maggrig, rising and gripping the old man's hand.

'Yes.' Leofas was grey with fatigue and he slumped to the ground beside the crackling fire. 'How could it happen?' he asked.

'Damned if I know. Druid magic. Taliesen was found dead in his chambers; they'd run to him to report the disappearance of the Gates. Metas tells me they've tried all the words of power, but none work any more.'

'All our women and children gone. Caswallon trapped in another land. Gods, it's hopeless,' said Leofas.

'The druids are searching through Taliesen's records. So far they've achieved nothing.'

Leofas rubbed his face, scratching at his iron-streaked beard. 'It seems as if the gods are riding with the Aenir.'

'Let them,' said Maggrig. 'I've never had a lot of time for them. A man stands alone in his life; if he stops to rely on some invisible spirit, then he'll fail.'

'Luck has a way of changing,' said Intosh. 'I don't believe we should do anything rash. We must proceed with the original plan.'

'And commit suicide?' asked Maggrig. 'The whole point of the Axta strategy was so that Caswallon could bring the Queen's army down on the enemy. Without that we will be wiped out within the morning.'

'They could still re-open the Gates,' said Lennox.

'I wouldn't trust those druids to open a pouch,' snapped Maggrig. 'It's hard to have faith in a group so prone to panic. Metas doesn't know his buttocks from a lump of cheese. And as for the rest, they're running around like headless chickens, so I'm told. If they re-open them in time, we'll stay with Caswallon's plan. If not – we must think again.'

'There's worse news,' said Lennox. The three men turned to him. 'We caught an Aenir scout last night. He told us that Laric and his Haesten launched an attack on Aesgard. They were repulsed and trapped in Southwood by Orsa and two thousand Aenir, and were all slain. Lane's head was left on a spear. There will be no help from the south.'

'Well, that's about it,' said Maggrig. 'All we need is a plague in our ranks and the day will be complete.'

The four sat in silence round the fire, the burden of despair weighing them down.

A young Pallides warrior entered the cave. 'The Loda Hunt Lord has arrived,' he said.

'Bring him to me.'

'I need no *bringing!*' said Dunild, pushing past the young warrior. The newcomer was short, but powerfully built. He had no beard, and his yellow hair hung to his shoulders beneath a woollen bonnet edged with leather and decorated with an eagle's feather.

Maggrig stood and forced a smile. 'Well met, you poaching rascal!'

Dunild laid his round shield on the ground and gripped Maggrig's wrist. 'You look fat and old, Maggrig,' said the Loda Hunt Lord.

'That's because I *am* old and fat. But still a match for most men – including you. How many follow you?'

'Three hundred.'

'Good news.'

'I hear you've been suffering.'

'I've had better days,' admitted Maggrig. 'What of Grigor?'

'I know nothing of the thieving louse,' hissed Dunild.

'Now that is not the whole truth, my friend,' said Maggrig, 'for you'd not have brought your clan and left your own valley unprotected.'

Dunild grinned. 'He says he will come and fight alongside *you* – as long as he doesn't have to fight alongside *me*!'

'How many will he bring?'

'He'll match me man for man, so I told him five hundred.'

'I trust neither of you will leave any behind to raid each other's lands?'

'On the contrary. We've both done just that.'

'I think you might be right, Intosh,' said Maggrig. 'Perhaps our luck is changing.' The swordsman grinned and the newcomer joined them round the fire.

The discussion carried on into the night, and the men were joined by Patris Grigor, a skeletally-lean, balding warrior and Hunt Lord to the Grigor clan. There were few better sword-killers in the mountains than this taciturn clansman. He sat as far from Dunild as he could, and the two men exchanged not a word during the discussion, all comments directed at Leofas or Maggrig. The atmosphere was tense.

At dawn they received a report from the druid Metas. There had been no success with the Gates, and Taliesen's files had offered no solution. The Gates, he said, were closed for ever.

For a time none of the leaders spoke. Their families gone, their hopes dashed, they sat in the silence of despair. Finally Leofas said, 'All we have left now is to die – and take as many of the enemy with us as we can. Now is the time for a decision, Maggrig. Axta Glen is out of the question. So where do we make a stand?'

His words hung in the air. Maggrig, forcing his mind from thoughts of Maeg and his grandson, lost in time, glanced at Dunild and Grigor. These men had brought their warriors to fight alongside the other clans – not to throw their lives away. Maggrig saw the concern on their faces, and he knew what other thoughts would be stirring in their cunning minds. The Farlain and the Pallides had lost all their women and children. If, by some chance, they were able to destroy the Aenir they would then be forced to raid for women from other clans.

'We will find a way to open the Gates,' he said, surprised at the confidence in his voice.' And more than that. I don't intend to merely lash out like a dying bear. I want to win. By the gods, we're all clansmen here. Brothers and cousins. Together we will destroy Asbidag and his rag-tag band of killers.'

'A pretty speech, Maggrig,' said Dunild softly. 'But how – and where – will this be achieved?'

'That is for us to decide at this meeting,' answered Maggrig. 'Who will begin?'

An hour of discussion followed as the clan leaders suggested various possible battle sites, mostly occupying high ground. None of the sites offered even the possibility of a victory. Then Intosh suggested a mountain pass some twenty miles east. It was known as Icairn's Folly, following a battle there hundreds of years ago when a young chieftain had followed his enemy into the pass and been destroyed.

'We could man the pass walls with archers and lure the Aenir in upon us,' said Intosh. The mountain walls narrow in to two hundred and fifty paces apart at the centre, and a small force could hold a larger.'

'And what when we are pushed back? The pass is blocked and we would be like cattle in a slaughter pen,' said Maggrig.

'Let's *not* be pushed back,' said Intosh.

'But can we win there?' asked Grigor. 'I don't like the idea of hurling my clan to doom on one battle.'

'Can we win anywhere?' asked Leofas.

'The Folly does have one advantage,' offered Maggrig. 'Our archers will wreak a terrible slaughter among the enemy. The Aenir could break and run. They've done it before – when the Pallides crushed them.'

'Even so, is it wise,' asked Dunild, 'to choose a battle site with no avenue of retreat?'

'All other areas are ruled out,' said Intosh. 'Although we cannot retreat, they cannot encircle us.'

'We could continue to hit and run,' suggested Lennox, who had remained silent for much of the planning.

'But we can't win that way,' said his father, 'I hate to admit it, but it seems we have run out of choices. I vote for Icairn's Folly.'

The other leaders nodded, then Grigor spoke. 'This is your war, Maggrig, not mine. I have come because we are all clan. But I'll not watch my men cut to pieces. My archers will man the left-hand slope of the pass. If you are crushed, we can still escape.'

'What more could be expected from the Grigors?' snapped Dunild.

Patris Grigor started to rise, reaching for his sword, but Maggrig stopped him with a raised hand.

'Enough!' he said. 'Patris is entirely correct. Dunild, you and your Loda warriors will hold the right-hand slopes, Patris the left. The Pallides and the Farlain will stand together at the centre. If we are pushed back or scattered, the rest of you must get away with as many men as you can. Take to your own lands. But for the sake of all clansmen, do not go back to war with one another. For your lands will be next, I think.'

'We are decided then?' asked Leofas.

'It seems so,' said Maggrig.

Caswallon's first realisation that anything was wrong came early on the fourth morning of his stay in Citadel. Borrowing a horse, he rode into the hills seeking Taliesen and the Gate. He was anxious to hear of the Aenir advance.

When he arrived at the slope he found no entrance. At first he was unconcerned and returned to the city, spending the day with

Sigarni, listening as she talked warmly of her youth and the early days of her rule — days of bloody war and treachery, and close encounters with disaster. Through the conversations Caswallon's appreciation of the Queen grew. She was a natural tactician but, more than this, knew men, their strengths and weaknesses and what drove them.

She had a close-knit band of followers, fanatically loyal, led by the powerful Obrin, the Queen's Captain, a man of iron strength and innate cunning. Sigarni talked of a black general called Asmidir, who had died holding the rearguard against the Earl of Jastey and his army, and of a dwarf named Ballistar who had journeyed through a Gateway in the company of Ironhand's ghost. But of the Redhawk she had known she said little, save that he had appeared following the death of Asmidir and had helped her to train her men, leading the left wing against Jastey and his thousands.

'Do I have friends here?' he asked.

'Apart from me?' she countered, with a quick smile. 'Who would need more? But yes, there is Obrin. You and he became sword brothers. I think he is a little hurt that you have spent so little time with him.'

The Queen had agreed to lead her warriors into the Farlain, but said she could gather only four thousand. The call went out, and the muster began.

At dawn Caswallon tried again to find the Gate. This time an edge of anger pricked him.

What was Taliesen doing, closing the Gate at such a time?

Taking supplies for three days, he rode north to the great Falls of Attafoss. Leaving the horse tethered on a grassy meadow he swam across to the isle of Vallon and entered the deep honeycomb of caves beneath the hill. Near the entrance he was met by an elderly druid he had seen with Taliesen.

'Why has the Gate been closed?' asked Caswallon. The man wrung his hands. His face was pinched and tight as if he had not slept for days.

'I don't know,' he wailed. 'Nothing works any more. Not one word of power.'

'What does this mean?'

'The Middle and Lesser Gates have vanished – just like the Great Gates of yesteryear. We are trapped here. For ever.'

'I will not accept that!' said Caswallon, fighting down the panic threatening to overwhelm him. 'Now be calm and tell me about the words of power.'

The man nodded and sank back on his narrow cot-bed, staring at his hands. Caswallon's enforced calm soothed his own panic and he took a deep breath.

'The words themselves are meaningless, it is the *sound* of the words. The sounds activate devices set within the hillside here. It is not dissimilar to whistling for a hunting-dog, which responds to sounds and reacts as it has been trained to do. Only here we are dealing with something vastly more complex, and infinitely beyond our comprehension.'

'Something is . . . broken,' said Caswallon, lamely.

'Indeed it is. But we are talking about a device created aeons ago by a superior race, whose skills we can scarce guess at. I myself have seen devices no bigger than the palm of my hand, inside which are a thousand separate working parts. We do not even have the tools to work upon these devices, and if we did we would not know where to start.'

'So we cannot contact Taliesen?' asked Caswallon.

'No. I just pray he is working towards a solution on the other side.'

'Are you one of the original druids?'

The man laughed. 'No, my grandfather was. I am Sestra of the Haesten.'

'Are there any of the elder race on this side of the Gate?'

'None that I know of.'

Caswallon thanked him and returned to the mare. Two days later, weary to the inner depths of his soul, he rode back into Citadel town. Not to see Maeg again, and feel the touch of her lips on his. Not to see Donal grow into a fine man. Never to know the fate of his people. Doomed to walk the rest of his life in a foreign land under strange stars.

He sought the Queen, finding her in her private rooms at the east wing of the hall. He told her nothing of the disappearance of the Gates, but questioned her about the priest who had first brought her to the forest as a babe.

'What of him?' asked Sigarni.

'Did he survive?'

'You know that he did.'

'I am tired, my Lady, and my brain is weary. Forgive me. Does he still live, is what I meant.'

'Only just, my love. He is the Abbot of the Dark Woods, a day's journey to the east. But the last I heard he was blind and losing his wits.'

'Can you spare a man to take me to him?'

'Of course. Is it important?'

'More important than I want to think about,' said Caswallon.

With two horses each, Caswallon and a rider named Bedwyr rode through the day, reaching the Dark Woods an hour after dark. Both men reeled from their saddles and Bedwyr hammered at the door of the monastery. It was opened by a sleepy monk, whose eyes filled with fear as he saw the armour worn by the riders.

'Be at peace, man,' said Bedwyr. 'We're not raiders, we ride for the Queen. Does the Abbot live?'

The man nodded and led them through narrow corridors of cold stone to a small cell facing west. He did not tap upon the door but opened it quietly, leading them inside. A lantern flickered upon the far wall, throwing shadows to a wide bed in which lay a man of great age, his eyes open, seeming to stare at the rough-cut ceiling.

'Leave us,' ordered Caswallon. Bedwyr escorted the monk from the room and Caswallon heard the rider asking for food, and the monk's promise that he would find bread and honey. Caswallon walked forward and sat beside the Abbot. He had changed much since Caswallon first saw him; his face was webbed with age and his sightless eyes seemed preternaturally bright.

'Can you hear me, Astole?' asked Caswallon.

The man stirred, 'I hear you, Redhawk, my friend. There is fear in your voice.'

'Yes. Great fear. I need your help now, as once you needed mine in the forest.'

The man chuckled weakly. 'There is no magic left, Redhawk. With all the wonders my mind encompassed I can now no longer lift this pitiful frame from the bed, nor see the brightest sunset. By tomorrow I shall have joined my Lord.'

'The Gates have closed.'

'That is ancient history.'

'The Middle Gates.'

'Again? That is not possible.'

'Believe me, Astole, they have closed. How may I re-open them?'

'Wait a moment,' said the old man. 'When last did you see me?'

'You were in the forest with the infant Queen.'

'Ah, I understand,' said Astole. 'It is so long since I played with time, and my mind is growing addled.' His head sank back on the pillow and he closed his sightless eyes. 'Yes, it is becoming clear. The Farlain is still under threat, the Queen has not yet passed the Gate and you have yet to learn the mysteries. I have it now.'

'Then help me,' urged Caswallon. 'Tell me how to re-open the Gate. I must lead the Queen through, or my people will perish.'

'I cannot tell you, my boy. I can only show you, teach you. It will take many years – eleven, if I remember correctly.'

'I don't have years,' said Caswallon, hope draining from him. The old man was senile and making no sense. As if reading his mind Astole reached out a hand and gripped Caswallon's arm, and when he spoke his voice was strong with authority.

'Do not despair, my friend. There is much that you cannot understand. I made the Gates in my youth and arrogance. I discovered the lines of power that link the myriad pasts, the parallel worlds, and I made the machines to track them and ride them. It was I who allowed the Great Gates to close. My race were using the universe as an enormous whorehouse. I re-routed the prime power source to feed the Lesser and Middle Gates. But all power sources are finite – even those that flow from collapsed stars and make up the Sipstrassi. It is – in the *Now* that you inhabit – running to its finish. There are other sources, and I will teach you to find and re-align them, and then the Gates will return. The man you see now is but the last fading spark of a bright fire. He will die tonight, and yet he will not be dead. We will meet again and he shall teach you.

'There is a cave behind this abbey; a chalice is carved upon the entrance. Let the muster of the Queen's men continue, and on the appointed day walk into the Chalice Cave and approach the far wall. It will appear as solid rock, but you will pass through it, for this Gate has not vanished but only shifted. On the other side, I shall be waiting.'

'But you are dying!'

'We are speaking of events which have already happened, my boy. I was working upon a complex formula in my study when the Gateway flickered and you appeared. You told me that I had sent you, and you told me why. More I cannot say.' The old man sighed, then gave a weak smile. 'We are to be great friends, you and I. Closer than father and son. And yet I must say farewell to a stranger who is yet to be my friend. Ah, the tricks time plays.'

The old man fell silent and his eyes closed. Caswallon sat beside him, his mind tired, his burdens heavy. Was the Abbot to be trusted? How could he tell? The future of his people rested with the promise of a dying monk. He sat with Astole until dawn's first light seeped through the wooden shutters of the window, then he lifted the Abbot's hand from his arm.

Caswallon stood and gazed down at the old man. He was dead. The clansman lifted the blanket and pulled it over the Abbot's face, pausing to study the man's expression. A faint smile was on the lips and a great feeling of peace swept over Caswallon.

He walked to the window, pulling open the shutters. The woods beyond shone in the early morning light. Behind him the door opened and the lancer Bedwyr stepped into the room.

'Did you find what you hoped for, Redhawk?'

'Time will tell.'

'The old man died then,' said the lancer, glancing at the bed.

'Yes. Peacefully.'

618

'They say he knew great magic. Does that mean his spirit will return to haunt us?'

'I certainly hope so,' said Caswallon.

Unaware of the growing drama, Gaelen led the Haesten women north-west, stopping only to meet the Pallides warriors. The eighty-man force had now swelled to one hundred and ten, as other warriors crept in from the mountains and woods where they had hidden their families in derelict crofts or well-disguised caves. Ten men were to be left behind, to hunt and gather food for the hidden children, but the others were set to follow Gaelen.

The young clansman was truly concerned now, for he had never led such a force and was worried about the route. He conferred with Agwaine, Onic and Gwalchmai. It was one thing for a small party to thread its way through the Aenir lines, quite another for an army numbering almost a thousand.

'We know,' said Onic, 'that the main army is before us, pushing north. We should have no real trouble for at least two days.'

'You are forgetting Orsa,' said Gaelen. 'His force destroyed Laric in the south. We don't know if he will head north now and join his father. If he does, we will be trapped between them.'

'Ifs and buts, cousin,' said Agwaine. 'We will solve nothing by such discussion. We are expected at Axta Glen and one way or another we must move on. We cannot eliminate all risks.'

'True,' admitted Gaelen, 'but it is as well to examine them. So be it, we will head due north, and then cut west to Atta, and then on to the Glen. That way we should avoid Orsa. But we'll push out a screen of scouts west and east, and you, Gwal, shall go ahead of us in the north with five men to scout.'

The self-appointed leader of the Pallides, a burly clansman named Telor, caused Gaelen's first problem. 'Why should you lead, and make such decisions?' he asked when Gaelen told him of the plan.

'I lead because I was appointed to lead.'

'I follow Maggrig.'

'Maggrig follows Caswallon.'

'So you say, Blood-eye.'

Gaelen breathed deeply, pushing aside his anger. He rubbed his scarred eye, aware that Lara and the others were watching this encounter with detached fascination. Such was the way of warriors among the clans. Telor had now implied that Gaelen was a liar, and the two men were hovering on the verge of combat.

'Your land,' said Gaelen at last, 'has been overrun by an enemy. Your people are sundered and preparing to fight alongside the Farlain in a last desperate battle for survival. If they lose, we lose. Everything. And yet here you are debating a point of no importance. Now I will say this only once: I lead because I was chosen to lead. There is no more to discuss. Either draw your sword or obey me.'

'Very well,' said Telor. 'I will follow you north, but once the battle is sighted I will lead the Pallides.'

'No,' said Gaelen.

The man's sword hissed from his scabbard. Then fight me, Farlain.'

The onlookers backed away, forming a circle around the two men.

'I do not desire to kill you,' said Gaelen hopelessly.

Then I lead.'

'No,' said Gaelen softly, drawing his sword. 'You die.'

'Wait!' shouted Lara, stepping forward with hands on hips, it is well-known that the Farlain are arrogant numbskulls, and that the Pallides have too long interbred with their cattle, but this is sheer stupidity. If you must fight, then fight, but let it be clear that if Gaelen conquers then he leads ALL.'

'What if Telor wins?' asked a young Pallides warrior.

'Then he leads the Pallides alone,' said Lara. 'I'll not follow a man with the brain of a turnip.'

'You miserable Haesten bitch,' snapped Telor. 'You seek to rob the contest of any merit.'

'It has no merit,' said Gaelen. 'Thousands of clansmen and their wives lie butchered by invaders, and you seek to add more clan blood to the soil.'

Telor gave a harsh laugh. 'Frightened, are you, Farlain?'

Gaelen shook his head. 'Terrified,' he said, dropping his sword and stepping forward, his forehead thundering against Telor's nose. The Pallides warrior staggered back, blood drenching his yellow beard, as Gaelen moved in with a left cross exploding against Telor's unprotected chin. The Pallides warrior pitched to his left, hitting the ground hard. Gaelen rolled the man to his back and drew his hunting-knife, touching the point to Telor's throat. 'Make a choice, live or die,' he said coldly.

Telor lay very still. 'Live,' he whispered.

'The first wise choice you've made,' said Gaelen. Rising, he gripped the man's right arm, hauling him to his feet. Telor staggered, but remained upright, blood dripping from his ruined nose. 'Now, pick twenty Pallides to follow Agwaine and Onic. I want scouts east and west of us. Then you go, with three of your choosing, to the north to make sure our route is clear. Is that understood?'

Telor nodded.

Turning on his heel Gaelen set off, and the small army followed him. Lara moved up alongside him, grinning. 'That was close,' she said.

'Yes. Thank you for your help; it took away his concentration.'

'It was nothing. I didn't want Telor to cut your ears off; he's second only to Intosh with a blade.'

'Then I thank you again – with even more feeling.'

'Are you a good swordsman?'

'I've recently learned to tell the point from the hilt.'

'No, truly?'

'I am as good as most men.'

'Have you killed any Aenir?'

'Yes.'

'How many?'

'Gods, woman! What does it matter?'

'I like to know who I am following.'

'I've killed five and wounded another.'

'Five? That's not bad. Hand to hand, or with the bow?'

'Hand to hand. The wounded man I hit with an arrow.'

'Marksmanship's not your strong point, then?'

'No. And you?'

'What about me?'

'Well, we seem to be talking about numbers killed, so I am asking you the same question.'

'I see. Why?'

'Because I like to know the calibre of my followers,' said Gaelen, grinning.

'I haven't killed any. But I will.'

'I don't doubt it.'

'Do you have a woman?' she asked suddenly.

'No.'

'Why?'

'She refused me.'

'I see,' said Lara.

'What do you see?'

'I see why you are so nervous around women.'

'I am not nervous around women, I am nervous with you,' he said.

'Why is that?'

Gaelen was growing hot and beginning to feel like a hunted rabbit.

'Well?' she pressed.

'I have no idea, and I don't wish to discuss it,' he said primly. She laughed then, the sound deep and throaty, which only added to his discomfort.

On the first night of camp Gaelen avoided her, talking long into the night with Gwalchmai, who had returned from his scouting trip with Telor. Telor and his companions had remained in the north, and Gwal was due to rejoin them at first light.

'It was an uncomfortable day,' said Gwalchmai. 'I think we only exchanged three words.'

'I'm sorry, Gwal. How does it look?'

'So far the route is clear. That Telor gives me cold chills, though.'

622

'Yes. Let's hope he saves his anger for the Aenir.'

'Let's hope they cut his damned heart out,' muttered Agwaine, joining them.

Gaelen shook his head. 'No wonder the clans are always at war,' he said.

'How are you getting on with Lara?' asked Agwaine, his mouth spreading in a lecherous grin.

'What does that mean?' snapped Gaelen.

'She likes you, man. It's obvious.'

'I don't want to talk about it.'

'She's gorgeous, isn't she? Not beautiful exactly, but gorgeous. And those breeches . . .'

'Will you stop this?'

'I wish she liked me.'

'I cannot believe this conversation is taking place. We are marching towards a battle, I'm trying to think about tactics, and all you can think about is . . . is . . . breeches.'

'What about breeches?' asked Lara, moving up to sit with them.

'Yes, Gaelen, tell her about the breeches tactic,' said Gwalchmai.

Gaelen closed his eyes.

'Well?' she said.

'You're the authority, Gwal. You explain it.'

Gwalchmai chuckled. 'No. If I'm to be with Telor by dawn, I'd best tuck up in my blankets. Excuse me.'

Gwal moved off to fashion a bed below an overhanging pine. Agwaine grinned and also moved away – despite Gaelen's imploring gaze. 'So?' said Lara. 'What about breeches?'

'It was a jest. The clouds are bunching – there could be rain tomorrow.'

'Come with me,' she said, taking his hand. He followed her into the trees and they stopped some forty paces away in a circular clearing, screened by dense bushes. She led him to where she had placed her blankets and pulled him down beside her. The clansman was supremely ill at ease.

'What did you want to talk about?' he asked huskily.

623

'I don't want to talk, Gaelen.' Leaning forward, she curled an arm around his neck and kissed him.

Thoughts of Deva vanished like ice on fire.

Leofas and Maggrig walked the length of the Folly as darkness gathered around them. The slopes on either side were steep and pitted with rocks and boulders, while the pass itself showed a steady incline towards the narrow centre. The Aenir would be charging uphill and that would slow them. But not by much.

The two men were joined by Paths Grigor and a dozen of his archers. 'It's a magnificent killing ground,' said Grigor. 'They'll lose hundreds before they reach you – if they come in, that is. What if they bottle up the mouth of the pass?'

'We attack them,' declared Maggrig.

'That's not much of a plan,' said Grigor, grinning.

'I'm not much of a planner,' admitted Maggrig, 'but I think they'll come at us. They've yet to learn fear.'

'When your arrows are exhausted, we leave. If we can,' said Grigor.

'Understood,' said Maggrig, walking back towards the campfires in the wide pass beyond.

The walls of the box canyon rose sheer, reflecting the red light from hundreds of small fires. Leofas, who had remained silent on the long walk, sat back on a boulder, staring out over the clan army as they rested. Some men were already sleeping, others were sharpening sword-blades. Many were laughing and talking.

'What's wrong, my friend?' Maggrig asked.

Leofas glanced up. In the flickering firelight Maggrig's beard shone like flames, his blue eyes glittering, his face a mask of bronze.

'I'm tired,' said Leofas, resting his chin in his hands and staring out over the campfires.

'Nonsense! You'll be leading the victory dance tomorrow like a first-year huntsman.'

The Farlain warrior looked up, eyes blazing. 'Will you stop for a moment. I'm not a first-year huntsman, and I don't need you trying to lift me. I'm old. Experienced. I've seen war and death. Anyone who can tell a sword-point from a hole in the ground knows we have little chance tomorrow.'

'Then leave!' snapped Maggrig.

'And where would I go, Maggrig? No, I don't mind dying alongside you. In fact I don't mind dying. My hope is that we cull their ranks enough for the other clans to have a chance of defeating them.'

'You think I've been foolish?' asked Maggrig, slumping beside him.

'No. We ran out of choices, that's all.'

For a time they sat in silence, then Maggrig turned to his companion. 'Do you mind if I ask you a personal question?'

'I don't mind if you ask,' said Leofas. 'I may not answer.'

'Why did you never re-marry? You were only a young man when Maerie died.'

Leofas switched his gaze to the stars and the years slipped away like falling dreams. He shook his head. Finally he spoke, his voice soft, his eyes distant.

'I miss her most at sunset, when we'd go to the ridge behind the house. There was an old elm there. I built a seat around the base and we'd sit there and watch the sun die. I'd wrap us both in my cloak and she'd rest her head on my shoulder. It was so peaceful, you could believe there was not another living being in the world. I felt alive then. I never have since.'

'So why not re-marry?'

'I didn't want anyone else. And you?'

'No one else would have me,' said Maggrig.

'That's not true.'

'No, it's not,' admitted Maggrig. 'But then Rhianna and I didn't watch many sunsets. In truth we spent most of our life together squabbling and rowing. But she was a good lass for all that. Maeg was four when Rhianna died, she wouldn't have taken to another mother.'

'We're a pair of fools,' said Leofas again. 'Do you regret not having sons?'

'No,' lied Maggrig. 'And we're getting maudlin.'

'Old men are allowed to get maudlin. It's a rule of life.'

'We're not that old. I'm as strong as ever.'

'I'm ten years older than you, Maggrig, and, according to tradition, that makes me wise. Between us we muster a century or more. That's old.'

'I never used to be old,' said Maggrig, grinning. 'Strange how it creeps up on a man.'

They let the silence grow, each drifting on a river of memories. It was, they believed, their last night alive under the stars and neither wanted to talk about tomorrow.

Drada was angry, more angry than he could ever recall. The clans had mounted a series of raids, retreating always to the east. He sensed a plan behind the attacks and now it had become clear.

That morning Aenir scouts had reported a movement of the clans towards a pass six miles east. Drada, who had scouted the land personally some days before, knew that the pass was blocked and impassable to the north. Surely the clans would not consider a battle there? But they had, and now the Aenir force was waiting in the mouth of Icairn's Folly – and Drada was crimson with rage.

'But why attack, Father? It is unnecessary. There is no way out for them; if we wait they must attack us.'

'I command here!' thundered Asbidag. 'Why do you plead caution when we have them where we want them?'

'Listen to me, Father. The slopes within could hold a thousand archers. They will take a huge toll. The main army will be near the centre of the pass, where the mountain walls narrow, which means our weight of numbers will be lessened. We will be fighting one to one. Of course we'll win – but we could lose thousands in there.'

'They brought me Barsa's rotting corpse this morning,' said Asbidag. 'Now I have two sons calling for vengeance. And you want me to sit and wait.'

'The clans have made a terrible mistake,' said Drada. They are hoping we will do exactly what you are planning. It is their *only* hope.'

'What are you, a prophet now? How do you know what they are planning? I believe we have surprised them in their lair. Get the men ready to charge.'

Drada swallowed his anger, and it tasted of bile. He turned away from his father then, so that he would not see the burning hatred in his eyes.

You are dead, Asbidag, Drada decided. After the battle, I will kill you.

The Aenir line assembled in the mouth of the pass, shield-straps being tightened, sword hands rubbed in dust for better grip. Twenty-five thousand men peered at the rock-strewn slopes and the towering mountain walls beyond. There was no enemy in sight.

The war-horns of the Aenir sounded and the armour-clad mass began to move slowly forward, Drada and Tostig together at the centre, Asbidag's other sons to the left and right of them. Asbidag himself stayed at the mouth of the pass surrounded by his forty huscarles. Morgase stood beside him, her eyes bright, her heart hammering as she waited for the killing to begin.

The Aenir army moved on warily, with shields held high, scanning the slopes. Ahead of them the pass narrowed and still there was no sign of the enemy . . .

Suddenly the Folly was alive with noise as the Farlain and the Pallides moved into sight to man the narrow centre. A great roar went up from the Aenir as they surged forward, beating shields with their sword-blades. On either side of them rose archers from the Dunilds and the Loda. Goose-feathered shafts filled the air. The screams of wounded men rose above the war-cries and now the clans roared out their own battlecry which echoed in the mountains, booming and growing.

Dark clouds of hissing death flashed into the Aenir horde in a series of withering volleys. Some warriors broke from the ranks to charge the archers, but these were cut down by scores of shafts. The charge slowed, but did not stop.

At the front of the Aenir line the giant Orsa felt the baresark rage upon him. Hurling aside his shield, he raced ahead of his men bellowing his anger and swinging his broadsword above his head. An arrow sliced into his thigh but he ignored it.

Lennox leaped from the line to meet him, holding a long-handled mace of lead and iron. He too threw aside his shield as Orsa ran forward slashing his blade towards the clansman's head. Lennox made no move to avoid the blow but lashed the mace into the blade, smashing it to shards. Orsa crashed into him and both men fell to the ground, Orsa's hands closing about Lennox's throat. Releasing the mace, Lennox reached up to cup his hand under Orsa's chin; then punching his arm forward, he snapped the Aenir's head back, tearing the man's grip from his neck. Rolling, Lennox came up with the mace and delivered a terrible blow to Orsa's skull, crushing the bones to shards and powder.

With scant seconds to spare Lennox rejoined the line, standing beside his father Leofas and the Pallides War Lord Maggrig. The front line of the Aenir bore down on the waiting clans. Maggrig lifted his sword, grinned at Intosh, then screamed the battlecry of the Pallides.

'Cut! Cut! Cut!'

The chant was taken up and the clans surged into the charging Aenir. After four years of war in the lowlands the Aenir believed they were the finest fighters under the sky, but never had they met the fierce-eyed, blood-hungry wolves of the mountains. Now they learned the terrible truth, and as the blades of the clans slashed and cut their first line to shreds, the charge faltered.

Maggrig powered his way into the Aenir ranks, cleaving and killing, an awful fury upon him. Many were the Pallides dead whose faces he would never forget, whose souls hungered for vengeance. The War Lord forgot the plan to hold the centre and forged ever deeper into the enemy. Intosh and the Pallides had no choice but to follow him.

Leofas gutted one warrior and parried a blow from a second, back-handing his shield into the man's face. Lennox aided him, braining the man with his mace.

'Sound the horn!' yelled Leofas. 'Maggrig's gone mad!'

Lennox stepped back from the fray, allowing Farlain warriors to shield him from the enemy. Lifting his war-horn to his lips, he blew three sharp blasts. The sound filtered through Maggrig's rage and he slowed in his attack, allowing the Pallides to form around him. The weight of the Aenir numbers was beginning to tell and the clans were pushed back, inch by murderous inch.

The deadly storm of arrows had slowed now, for the archers on the slopes were running short of shafts.

Dunild hurled aside his bow, lifting his shield and drawing his sword. His men followed suit. Now was the time to withdraw, for the battle could not be won; the Aenir had not broken.

Three hundred clansmen joined him, swords in hand. Looking across the slopes to where his enemy Patris Grigor had also drawn his sword, Dunild felt a strange calm settle on him. He lifted his sword in silent farewell to his enemy. There would never be peace while they both lived, for their hatred was stronger than any desire to beat a common foe.

'Cut! Cut! Cut!' yelled Dunild and led his three hundred down the slope to reinforce the Farlain.

Patris Grigor could not believe his eyes. His enemy of twenty years had just surrendered his lands. Patris was now the undisputed lord of the north-west.

'What does he think he's doing?' yelled a man on his left. Grigor shrugged. Twenty years of hatred, and now Dunild was hurling his life away on a futile charge in a doomed battle. Grigor shook his head and dropped his bow.

'Do we leave now?' asked a clansman.

Grigor laughed. 'You know what's happening down there?'

'The Aenir are about to win through. It's all over.'

'That's right. And that brainless idiot Dunild has gone down there to die.'

'Then we are leaving?'

'What do *you* think?'

The man grinned. 'If we charge now we might just be able to hack our way through to Dunild and then, while no one's looking, I'll cut his throat.'

Grigor chuckled and hitched his shield to his arm. 'Yes, by damn. Let's do something noble for a change!' Raising his sword, he began to run down the slope. Five hundred Grigor warriors took up their swords and followed him.

The front line of the Aenir slipped and slithered over blood-covered rocks and sprawled bodies, only to be cut down by the slashing iron blades of the clansmen. Leofas, his cold blue eyes glinting with battle fever, stood at the centre of the defenders, Maggrig and Lennox on either side. Again and again the Aenir swarmed forward, only to be turned back by the sharp blades and steadfast courage of the defenders.

Drada alone among the Aenir was not surprised by the resolute defence, but he had been a part of many battles and knew what must happen now. The clans would fall back, there was no choice. Their strength was failing fast and their losses were enormous. The two at the centre were both old men and their stamina suspect. Once they had fallen, the line would break.

Beside him Briga was poised for the final rush. He had been a warrior for more than twenty years and always, he knew, there came a point where the fight could be read like a game, where the ebb and flow could be charted like a steady current. They had reached that point now.

And the clans were ready to break . . .

The feeling swept among the Aenir and the battle-cries began again. Once more the forces clashed. The clansmen fought silently now, leaden-legged and heavy of arm, and inch by inexorable inch they were forced back towards the open pass beyond.

Briga felt joy surge in his veins. No army in the world could hold now. It was over. The clans were finished!

Maggrig felt it too, and he cursed aloud as he clove his sword through an Aenir neck and ducked under a slashing blade. Well, if he had to die he was damned if it would be in the open ground he had fought so hard to defend. Dropping to his haunches he hurled himself forward into the Aenir, cutting and stabbing. Caught up in the frenzy of the moment, Leofas joined him, with Lennox and Intosh.

And the clans rallied, surging forward to join their leaders. The ferocity of the assault stunned the leading Aenir warriors and they fought to pull back. Briga, just behind the front line, turned to Drada. 'It's impossible!' he shouted. Drada shrugged.

As the Aenir front line backed away from him, Maggrig raised his sword defiantly. 'Come on, you Outland scum. We're still standing!'

A huge warrior in a wolfs head helm leaped from the Aenir ranks, sword raised. Maggrig parried the blow and reversed a cut to the warrior's neck. The blade hammered into the mail-shirt – and snapped. Dropping the useless hilt, Maggrig grabbed the man by his mail-shirt and hauled him forward, butting him savagely and crashing his fist into the man's belly. The warrior doubled over, his head snapping back as Maggrig's knee came up to explode against his face.

Intosh threw Maggrig a sword, Maggrig caught it by the hilt and sliced the blade through the back of the wolfs head helm. The Aenir died without a sound.

'You lice-ridden sons of bitches,' shouted Maggrig. 'Is that the best you can do?'

A roar rose from the Aenir and the line lunged forward.

The battle raged once more and now there were no bloodcurdling battle-cries – only the screams of the dying and the grim determination of the living to survive. The clansmen had been forced back, but their enemies had to climb a wall of their own dead to force a path to the dwindling band of defenders.

Asbidag had climbed into the saddle, the better to see the battle. His trained eye knew it had reached its final stage. A carle beside him screamed suddenly, pitching forward to the ground with a black-feathered shaft in his back. Arrows hissed through the air around him. Asbidag swung in the saddle, tearing his shield from the saddle-horn.

At the mouth of the pass Gaelen lifted his war-horn and blew three blasts. Eight hundred bows were bent and a dark cloud of shafts ripped into the horde.

Maggrig crashed his shield into the face of an attacker, hurling him from his feet, lancing his blade into a second man and dragging it clear.

631

'It's Gaelen!' shouted Lennox. 'He must have a thousand men with him.'

Maggrig staggered as an axe-blade shattered his shield. He hammered his fist into the axe-man's face, feeling the man's teeth break under the impact. A lean Aenir swordsman pushed himself past Maggrig. Leofas blocked his blow, but lost his grip on the sword. Grabbing the man by the neck and groin, he hoisted him into the air and hurled him back amongst his comrades. The man vanished into the mass. Leofas recovered his blade, wincing as a sword cut into his shoulder. Lennox leaped to the rescue, his blood-covered club smashing the swordsman's spine.

At the mouth of the pass Gaelen signalled for the women to scale the slopes on either side of the fighting men. Lara set off to the right with four hundred Haesten women behind her. As she climbed, Gaelen turned to Telor.

'Now let's see what you can do with that blade,' he said.

Hitching his shield into place Gaelen ran at Asbidag's carles, a hundred Pallides warriors yelling their war-cry behind him.

His horse rearing and kicking, Asbidag saw death running at him. An arrow knocked his helm from his head, another thudded into his shield. Panic overwhelmed him. Kicking his heels to his horse's side he rode through his own men, smashing their line, than veered away from the advancing clansmen. Arrows hissed around him and he ducked low over the horse's neck.

Lara saw his flight and notched an arrow to the string, drawing smoothly and sighting on Asbidag's broad back. The shaft sang through the air, punching through the Aenir's mail-shirt at the shoulder. Then he was through and clear and riding south. His horse carried him for a mile before collapsing and pitching him to the earth. He rolled to his feet. Three arrows had pierced the beast's chest and belly; leaving it to die, Asbidag began the long walk south.

In the Folly, Asbidag's panicked flight had opened the way for Gaelen and his warriors to smash the shield-wall and engage the carles. Gaelen ducked under a two-handed cut and drove his sword home into the man's chest. Beside him Telor leaped and twisted, his sword flashing in the sunlight, cleaving and killing. Two men ran at Gaelen. He blocked a blow from the first, gutting the man with a reverse stroke; his sword stuck in his opponent's belly, he saw the second warrior's sword arcing towards his head. Telor parried the blow, chopping his blade through the man's neck.

The burly Pallides grinned. 'Be more careful, Farlain. I can't be watching out for both of us.'

In the valley all was chaos as Drada fought to hold the Aenir steady. Arrows rained upon them from both sides of the pass and the clans were fighting like men possessed. But it was a losing battle. Drada could feel that success was but a matter of moments ahead. Once they pushed the enemy back into the wider pass beyond, nothing could prevent an Aenir victory.

Glancing about him, the young Aenir warrior was horrified at the losses his force had suffered. Considerably more than half his warriors were down: twelve thousand men sacrificed to Asbidag's stupidity!

But against this Drada had seen his father's flight and it filled him with joy. No need to kill him now, and risk death from his carles. No Aenir would follow him ever again. He would be a wolfshead, disowned and disregarded.

Now Drada would have it all: the army, the land, and the magic Gates. He would build the greatest empire the world had ever seen.

'On! On!' he yelled. 'The last yard!'

And it was true. The Aenir pushed forward once more.

Maggrig fell, slashed across the thigh. From the ground he stabbed upward, gutting his attacker. A blow sliced towards his head but Intosh blocked it – and died, an axe cleaving his skull. Maggrig staggered to his feet, plunging his blade through the axeman's chest. A sword lanced his side and he stepped back, lashing out weakly. Lennox bludgeoned a path to stand alongside him, mace dripping blood.

Above the noise of battle came the sound of distant horns. Then they felt the ground beneath their feet tremble, and the rolling thunder of galloping hooves echoed in the mountains. For a moment all battle ceased as men craned to see the mouth of the pass. A huge dust cloud swirled there, and out of it rode four thousand fighting men with lances levelled.

At the centre was a warrior in silver armour. In her hand was a mighty sword of shimmering steel.

'The Queen comes!' yelled Leofas.

Maggrig could not believe his eyes. Blood streamed from the wound in his side and his injured leg, and he stepped back from the fray, allowing two Pallides warriors to join shields before him. Slowly he climbed to the top of a pitted boulder, narrowing his eyes to see the horsemen.

The Aenir moved back from the clan line, straining to identify the new foe. Drada was stunned. What he was seeing was an impossibility; there were no cavalry forces on this part of the continent. But it was no illusion. The thunder of hooves grew and the Aenir warriors facing the charge scrambled towards the rocky slopes on either side of the pass. Their comrades behind them threw aside their weapons and tried to run.

Other more stout-hearted fighters gripped their swords more tightly and raised their shields. It mattered not whether they ran or stood. The terrible lances bore down upon them, splintering shields and lifting men from their feet, dashing them bloody and broken to the dusty ground. Horses reared, iron-shod hooves thrashing down, crashing skulls and trampling the wounded.

The Aenir broke, streaming up on to the slopes into the flashing shafts of the Haesten women.

Leofas urged the Farlain forward, shearing his sword into the confused mass before him. The battle became a rout. Aenir warriors threw down their weapons, begging for mercy, but there was none. With swords in their hand or without, the Aenir were cut to pieces.

Dunild and Grigor fought side by side now – the remnants of their clans, blood-covered and battle-crazed, hacking and slashing their way forward.

The Aenir struggled to re-form. Drada sounded the war-horn and the shield-ring grew around him. An arrow punched through Tostig's helm to skewer his skull. With a bellow of rage and pain he slumped to the ground beside his brother. Drada raised his shield.

Sigarni, her silver-steel blade dripping crimson, wheeled her grey stallion and led her men back down the pass. The Aenir watched them go, sick with horror. At the mouth of the Folly the Queen turned again, and the thunder of charging hooves drowned the despairing cries of the enemy.

Thrice more she charged and the shield-ring shattered.

A lean Aenir warrior ran forward, ducking under Sigarni's plunging sword, stabbing his own blade into the horse's belly. It screamed and fell, rolling across the man who had ended its life, killing him as it died. Sigarni was thrown to the ground in the midst of the Aenir. She came up swinging the double-handed sword, beheading the first warrior to leap to the attack.

The Aenir closed around her. Gaelen and Telor, fighting side by side, saw the Queen go down.

'No!' screamed Gaelen. He cut his opponent from him and raced into the mass. Telor followed him, with Agwaine and Onic and a dozen Pallides.

'Hold on, my Lady!' yelled Gaelen. Sigarni flashed a glance towards him, momentarily puzzled, then blocked a slashing attack from a longsword. Twisting her wrists and returning the blow, she clove the man from collarbone to belly. But the Aenir were all around her now. She swung and twisted and, too late, saw a blade slashing towards her neck. Gaelen's sword flashed up, parrying the death blow, 'I am here, my Lady!' he shouted above the clash of iron on iron.

Sigarni grinned and returned to the business of death.

Drada, with all hope of victory gone, tried to forge a path to the mouth of the pass. Beside him his carle captain Briga fought on, though a score of minor cuts poured blood from his arms and thighs. 'I think we are done, Drada,' shouted Briga. 'But by Vatan there's been some blood spilled today.'

Drada did not answer. Ahead of them a woman had climbed to a tall boulder and drawn back her bow. The arrow hissed through the air, thudding into Drada's throat, and with a look of surprise the Aenir leader fell sideways. Briga tried to catch him, but a sword slid between his ribs and he jerked upright.

He did not know it, nor would he have cared, but he was one of the last Aenir still alive in the Folly. His breath rasped in his throat and he dropped his sword as a great rushing noise filled his ears. Around him the pass was choked with bodies of the fallen, and Briga thought he could see the Valkyrie descending from the sky – the winged horses and the chariots of black. What tales he would tell in the Hall of the Dead . . .

He toppled from his feet, eyes still fixed on the black mass of crows and buzzards circling in the sky overhead.

Far to the south Asbidag, unaware of the clan victory, entered a thickly-wooded section of hills. He was breathing heavily and tired to the bone. Stopping by a stream, he tore the arrow from his shoulder and stripped his mail-shirt from him. He leaned over the water to drink. Looking down, he saw his reflection and just above it a face out of a nightmare.

Asbidag rolled to his back, scrabbling for his knife, but the were-hound's talons snaked down, ripping his throat to shreds. Blood bubbled from the ruined jugular and the creature's jaws opened. Asbidag's eyes widened as the fangs flashed down. The creature backed away from the body and squatted on its haunches, staring down at the ruined face. In its mind vague memories stirred, and a low whine came from its throat.

Pictures danced and flickered. Racing ahead of the pack and the horsemen, leaping at the stag as it turned to face them. Curling up in the day by the stables, warm and comfortable. But other, stranger, images confused it. A young woman with fair hair, smiling, her head resting on a cotton pillow. A child running, laughing, hands stretched towards . . . towards . . . it?

Lifting its head, the beast howled its despair at the night sky. Then moving back to the corpse the creature stretched out its taloned claw, pulling the dagger loose from the sheath. Turning the point to its breast, it plunged the blade home.

Pain, terrible pain . . .

Then peace.

Obrin found her hiding behind a boulder. He was tempted to slit her throat and be done with it . . . sorely tempted. He knew what she was, had always known.

636

The tall rider dragged her out by her hair. She was strangely quiescent, and her eyes were hooded and distant. 'I'd like to kill you,' he hissed.

Holding her hair, he led her past the bodies and out to the plain.

Sigarni was seated on a high-backed saddle placed before a small fire. She was drinking wine from a copper goblet and chatting to three of her lancers. She glanced up as Obrin hurled the woman to the ground at her feet.

'A surprise, my Lady,' said Obrin. 'She was with the Aenir, I'm told.'

Sigarni stood and pulled her gently to her feet. 'How are you, Morgase?' she asked.

The raven-haired woman shrugged. 'As you see me. Alone.'

'I know how that feels,' said Sigarni. 'Accept that the war is over, and you may return with us. I shall restore you to your father's lands.'

'In return for what? My promise of allegiance? My mother's soul would scream out against it. You saw my father slain, my mother raped. Kill me, Sigarni – or I will haunt you to your grave!'

Obrin's sword hissed from its scabbard. 'This once I'll agree with the bitch!' he said. 'Give the word, my Lady.'

Sigarni shook her head. 'Fetch her a horse. Let her ride where she will.'

Two soldiers took hold of Morgase and led her away. Twisting in their grip, she shouted out, 'I will find a way back, Sigarni. And then you will pay!'

'Your decision burdens my spirit,' said Obrin. 'She is evil, Sigarni. There is no good in her.'

'There is little good in any of us. We live and we die by the grace of God. A great wrong was done to her. It twisted her mind – as once such a deed twisted mine.'

By dusk the druids had come out from hiding in the woods around the Folly and had begun to administer to the wounded clansmen. Maggrig, ten stitches in his side and twelve more in his thigh, sat

637

on a boulder staring at the fluttering crows who were leaping and squawking over the stripped bodies of the slain.

The clan dead had been carried out of the Folly and laid together on the plain. A cairn would be built tomorrow. So many dead. Of the eight hundred Pallides only two hundred survived, many of these with grievous wounds. More than a thousand Farlain warriors had died, and another four hundred from the Loda and Dunilds. By a twist of fate both leaders had survived, fighting at the last back to back.

Maggrig sighed. The place looked like a charnel-house.

Leofas, his wounds stitched and bandaged, joined him at the boulder. 'Well, we won,' he said.

'Yes. And we old ones survive. So many young men gone to dust, and we old bulls sit here and breathe free air.'

Leofas shrugged. 'Aye, but we are a canny pair.'

Maggrig grinned. 'Have you seen Caswallon?'

'No. Come on, let's seek out the Queen. The least we can do is thank her.'

Leofas helped Maggrig to his feet and the two made their way through the bodies. The crows, bellies full and heavy with meat, hopped out of their way, too laden to fly.

At the mouth of the pass, beyond the tethered mounts, were the campfires of Sigarni's lancers, set in a circle at the centre of which sat the Queen and her captains.

Sigarni rose as the clansmen approached. 'Pour wine for them, Obrin,' she told her captain.

Maggrig thrust out his hand. 'Thank you, my Lady. You have saved my people.'

'I am glad we were here in time. I owe much to Redhawk, and it was a relief to part-settle the score.'

'Where is Caswallon?' asked Maggrig.

'I know not,' said the Queen. 'He asked us to meet him at the island of Vallon.'

Two riders brought high-backed saddles which they placed on the ground for the clansmen. 'Be seated,' said Sigarni. 'I wish to meet one of your clansmen; he saved my life today.'

'I think it will be hard to find one clansman,' said Leofas.

'Not this one. He has a blaze of white hair above his left eye and the eye itself is full of blood.'

'I know him,' said Leofas. 'If he lives I will send him to you.'

Obrin brought mulled wine and they drank in silence for a while.

The following morning, as work began on the cairn, most of the lancers had returned home through the Gate which had appeared in a blaze of light on the plain the night before. Sigarni remained behind with twenty men, including Obrin.

Leofas had found Gaelen sitting hand in hand with the Haesten girl in the woods skirting the mountains. 'Well met, young Gaelen,' he said.

Gaelen rose, introducing Lara to the older man.

Leofas bowed. 'I have seen you before, girl, but never prettier than now.'

'Thank you. I am glad you survived,' said Lara.

'We might not have done, had you not appeared with your archers.'

'A freak of chance,' Lara told him. 'We struck north to avoid the Aenir, and that meant we had to pass the Folly. How is it that the Queen arrived? Gaelen told me she was due at Axta Glen, and that's a day's ride from here.'

Leofas shrugged. 'I don't know, neither does the Queen. Caswallon's the man to answer the riddle. Now get a move on, boy, the Queen wishes to see you. But tell me, where is Layne?'

Gaelen looked into the old man's eyes, but could find no words. The smile faded from Leofas' face, and he looked suddenly so very old.

The white bearded warrior sighed. 'So many dead,' he whispered. 'Tell me how it happened.' Gaelen did so, and could find no way to disguise the horror of Layne's passing. Leofas listened in silence, then turned away and walked off alone towards the trees.

Gaelen watched him, and felt the comforting touch of Lara's hand. 'Come,' she said, 'the Queen wishes to see you.'

He nodded and together they approached the Queen's camp. Sigarni strode out to meet him, hand outstretched. 'Good to see you alive, my lad! There are a few questions I have for you.'

Gaelen bowed, introducing Lara. The Queen smiled warmly at the clanswoman. 'Now, what were you doing risking yourself to save me?' she asked, turning on Gaelen, her grey eyes glinting with humour, 'I expect that from my lancers, but not from strangers.'

'I owe you my life,' said Gaelen simply.

'For coming here with my lancers, you mean?'

'No, Lady. But I cannot speak of it. Forgive me.'

'More secrets of the enchanted realm? You sound like Redhawk. All right, Gaelen, I shall not press you. How can I reward you for your action?'

Gaelen stared at her, remembering the day she had saved them from the Beast. In that instant he knew where his road must lead. Dropping to one knee before the warrior Queen, he said, 'Let me serve you, my Lady. Now and for ever.'

If Sigarni was surprised she did not show it. 'You will have to leave this realm,' said the Queen, 'and fight beside me in a war that is not of your making. Do you desire this?'

'I do, my Queen. More than anything. I love this land, but I have seen my friends slaughtered, their homes burnt and their children massacred.'

'Then rise, for my friends do not kneel before me; they walk beside me. Will your lady come, too?' she asked, turning to Lara.

Gaelen rose and took her hand. 'Will you?'

'Where else would I go?' she answered.

'I love you,' he whispered, pulling her to him.

The Queen moved away from them then, joining Obrin at the fire.

With a high cairn now covering the clan dead, Leofas led the survivors back to Attafoss. Despite the victory the men were heavy of heart. Their loved ones were lost in the past, their friends dead in the present. Maggrig rode beside Sigarni, while Gaelen and Lara joined Lennox, Onic, Agwaine and Gwalchmai at the head of the column.

Gaelen was the only one of the surviving Beast Slayers to have emerged unscathed from the battle. Lennox carried a score of stitches, while Gwalchmai had taken a spear in the shoulder. Agwaine had been stabbed in the leg and he walked with a painful limp.

'Are you really going to go with the Queen?' asked Agwaine. 'And leave the mountains?'

'Yes,' answered Gaelen. 'I promised her years ago that I would follow her.'

'Will she take me too, do you think?' Gwalchmai asked.

'I believe so.'

'I shall not go,' said Agwaine. 'There is much to do here.'

'Without Layne there is little to hold me here,' said Lennox sadly. 'I'll come with you, Gaelen.'

An hour before dusk the column arrived at the invisible bridge to Vallon, and spread out along the banks.

A man appeared on the far shore, a tall man with greying hair, wearing a velvet robe the colour of dark wine. He lifted his hand. Glittering lights rose from the water to hover in the air around the invisible bridge, which darkened, gleaming like silver in the fading light. Stronger and stronger grew the bridge as the light coalesced, shimmering and sparkling, until at last it seemed built of silver and gems. The man lifted his hand once more and stepped out upon the silver walkway. From behind him came the men and women of the Farlain and the Pallides.

A great silence settled on the clansmen as hope flared again in their hearts.

The man approached, his grey-streaked hair billowing in the breeze. He was full-bearded and his eyes were the green of a distant sea. 'Caswallon!' shouted Gaelen, running forward to meet him.

Caswallon opened his arms, tears sparkling in his eyes. The two men hugged one another warmly, then Gaelen pulled back to look at his foster-father. Caswallon seemed to have aged ten years since last they met.

'What has happened to you?' whispered Gaelen.

'We will talk later. First let us enjoy the reunion.'

641

Wives and children ran to husbands and fathers, sons and brothers, and laughter swelled through the trees of Atta forest. 'A long time since that sound was heard,' said Caswallon.

Maeg was one of the last across the bridge. Silently she approached her husband, little Donal beside her riding on the back of the great hound, Render.

'Leave us for a while, Gaelen. I will see you later,' said Caswallon. He took Maeg's hand, kissing her palm. Her eyes were full of tears and she leaned into him.

'What have they done to you?' she asked, holding back the sorrow and stroking his greying hair.

'They? There is no "they", Maeg. Time has done this. But it was necessary, for otherwise I would never have found you. It took me eleven years to learn all that I needed to fetch you home. But every day of that time I thought of you and I loved you.'

Donal slipped from Render's back and tugged at the hem of Caswallon's velvet robe. He was crying. Caswallon lifted him to his chest and hugged him tightly.

'We won, Caswallon,' said Maeg. 'But the price was terrible.'

He nodded, it always is. But we are together now, and we shall rebuild.'

Maeg caught sight of a silver-armoured woman staring at them. 'Who is that?' she asked Caswallon. He turned and saw Sigarni swing away and walk alone towards the trees.

'That is the Queen, Maeg,' he said, taking her into his arms. 'She saved us all.'

'She looked so sad,' said Maeg, then turned back to her husband. 'Welcome home, my love,' she whispered, kissing him.

He couldn't reply. Tears ran from his eyes and she led him away into the trees.

11

Three days after the battle, Gaelen was summoned by an elderly
druid and led to Taliesen's chambers below the hall of the Gate
where Caswallon awaited him. In the harsh light of the chamber
Caswallon seemed even older; his hair was thinning and had turned
white near the temples.

'Welcome,' he said, gesturing the clansman to be seated. He
poured clear white wine into silver goblets, handed one to Gaelen
and then sat down in a wide leather chair.

'What happened to you, Caswallon?'

The older man chuckled. 'Do I look so bad?'

'No,' lied Gaelen, 'just older.'

'I *am* older. It is eleven years since I asked you to find Laric and
bring his warriors to Axta Glen. Eleven long years . . . lonely years.'

'The Queen told me you led her to the Chalice Gate and then
you stepped through. Within seconds you returned, only you were
older and dressed, as now, in robes of velvet.'

'It is not easy for me to explain it to you, Gaelen. When I reached
the Chalice Gate I was filled with fear. A dying monk told me the
Gate was not closed, yet I could see for myself that it was. The cave
was shallow and water dripped from the walls. I walked forward, sick
with dread, and reached out. My hand passed through the stone as
though through smoke. I walked on, and found myself on a plain
overlooking a city of golden turrets and tall towers of polished marble.

'A man was waiting for me. His name was Astole and he greeted
me like a brother, for I had saved his life in another place. He took
me to his home – a palace with many servants – and there he began
to instruct me in the Gates and the words of power to manipulate
them. I was filled with terrible impatience, but he promised he
could return me to within seconds of my departure. And I had to
trust him.

'The years passed slowly. Sometimes I would be filled with joy at my new-found knowledge and dream of exacting a terrible revenge on the Aenir. At other times I felt an awful dread, wondering if I had been tricked. But always I learned. Impossibility made reality. You have seen the stone that attracts iron?'

'Yes. Onic has one.'

'The force that pulls the metal cannot be seen, but its effects can be observed. It is the same with the power behind the Gates. Let me show you something.' Caswallon lifted a small box set with coloured stones. He pressed the ruby at the centre and the far wall darkened, then became a window overlooking the Farlain.

'As you can see, that is the mountain of Carduil on the borders of Haesten territory. That is *now*. We can see that image as the light is reflected to our eyes. Had we been here yesterday, we would have seen rain over Carduil. But we were not. Yet the image was still transmitted. Astole discovered that light images linger, leaving traces that can last ten thousand years. Hence, with the turn of a dial, we can see . . .' The screen shimmered and the mountain appeared once more, cloud-covered and dull, sheeting rain pounding the slopes. Caswallon pressed a stone and the image disappeared.

'Astole made machines that could trace the Lines of Time, allowing man to view his own past. But then the greatest excitement of all. Within the traces Astole discovered particles of matter that did not deteriorate. Unchanging, they existed from day to day, from century to century. They were unaffected by the passing of time. Indeed, they seemed to exist outside time's laws.

'During his experiments Astole trapped several particles within a field of force — similar to that which works the stone that attracts iron. The field and the particles disappeared without trace. Astole constructed another and suddenly the first field reappeared, but the second vanished. The following day he constructed a third field, and the same thing happened. Excited beyond his experience, Astole made plans for two large fields, preparing his assistants beforehand. He placed himself at the centre of the first field and activated it. He vanished instantly. His assistants, following his instructions, activated the second field and he reappeared. The particles had drawn him into a distant past. How, he did not know, but he had stumbled on the greatest discovery of them all, the Gates.'

'I don't understand any of this, Caswallon,' said Gaelen.

'I'm sorry, my boy. How can I tell you in minutes that which has taken a decade of my life? Anyway, I stayed with Astole, and I absorbed his knowledge. Together we journeyed to fabulous cities and kingdoms lost to the memory of man. We walked the Time Lines, seeing the births of civilisations and the deaths of empires. Finally he judged me ready and we journeyed to a desert, and there I met the man to answer all questions. As he spoke I felt my heart emptied and refilled. All dreams of vengeance died. Violence was washed from me.'

'Who was he?' asked the clansman.

Caswallon smiled and laid his hand on Gaelen's shoulder, if you thought the Gates were hard to comprehend, then do not ask about the man. He sent me home and I appeared in the Chalice Gate, even as you see me now. With my new words of power I activated the machines and scanned Axta Glen. You were not there. I searched the Farlain, coming at last to Icairn's Folly. Then I opened the Gate and the Queen led her lancers through.'

'But you did not ride with them,' said Gaelen.

'No. I am the Hawk Eternal, Gaelen, and I'll never wield a sword against any man again.'

'You have changed, Father.'

'All life is change. But I am the same man who carried you from Ateris, the same man who loves his people. Only now I love them more. It is strange. I could have destroyed the Aenir single-handed; but with the gift of that power, I lost the desire to use it thus.'

'How did Maeg take all this?' asked Gaelen.

'Hard. But love conquers all. And I love her – more than life.'

'Will you remain as Hunt Lord?'

'Do I look like a Farlain Hunt Lord?' he asked, smiling.

'No.'

645

'And I shall not be the Hunt Lord. I will remain here, at Vallon, and tend the Gates. There are many tasks before me, Gaelen, but first I must spend some time with Maeg and Donal. Then I will meet Astole again.'

'I am returning with the Queen,' said Gaelen. 'Lennox, Onic and Gwalchmai are coming with me.'

'I know. We will meet again.'

'Tell me, Caswallon, are you truly content?'

'More content than any mortal man has any right to be.'

'Then I am glad for you.'

'And I for you. You have a fine woman in Lara, and I know she will give you beautiful children. I wish for you a life enriched with love, for you deserve it.'

'I shall miss the Farlain. Will I be able to return some day?'

'Ask me when next you see me.'

'I must go. The Queen is waiting,' said Gaelen.

Caswallon rose and walked round the table. 'Walk always in the Light,' he told Gaelen.

Caswallon watched the clansman leave and his heart ached. He had seen pity in Gaelen's eyes and knew the bond between them would never be the same. For to Gaelen, Caswallon was no longer a clansman. He had put aside his sword.

What could he have told Gaelen to make him realise? Should he have explained about the man in the desert?

Caswallon grinned wryly and filled his goblet. Tell him about a man who allowed himself to be dragged through a city and murdered by the people he loved? Oh, yes, that would have impressed him. He finished his wine and turned to the black screen before him. Lifting the control box he tuned the image, watching Sigarni, Gaelen and his friends crossing the Gates of Time.

He felt a cold breeze on his back and turned to see Maeg standing in the doorway hugging a woollen shawl about her shoulders. She seemed so distant, so withdrawn. Caswallon swallowed hard, a sense of despair gripping him.

'You must be getting old, Caswallon,' she said, 'allowing yourself to be surprised by a woman.'

'Surprise, is it? When I heard the footsteps I felt it had to be a mountain troll come to life.'

She grinned at him then. 'My feet are not so large. But even if they were I think I'd sooner have that than vast areas of my head losing hair.'

'Did no one ever teach you to respect your elders, woman?'

'Is it respect you want?' she asked, moving closer.

He opened his arms and held her close. 'Do you still love me, Maeg?'

'I love you, clansman. Above all things. And you're a fool to believe otherwise. Now tell me what happened to you.'

For an hour or more they sat together until he had emptied himself of words. At last she led him from the chamber to walk under the stars above Vallon.

Epilogue

Agwaine ruled the Farlain for twenty-seven years, having first led his warriors in the sack of Aesgard. The city was razed to the ground and all its inhabitants put to the sword. Thereafter peace came to the mountains.

Deva lived in Agwaine's house for seven years, refusing all offers of marriage, her eyes constantly on the horizon – waiting for the man who would be King. One bright day in summer she was brushing her hair when she saw, in the mirror, the first grey hairs appearing at her temple. No suitor had approached her for two years now. Fear touched her and she went in search of Caswallon. She found him sitting in the sunlight in the garden behind his house, tending his roses.

Caswallon welcomed her, offering her a cup of honey mead, and she sat beside him on a long, carved bench. 'What is troubling you, Deva?' he asked.

'The prophecy hasn't come true, and if I wait much longer I shall be unable to bear children. Why hasn't he come, Caswallon?'

'Wait? Not so fast. What prophecy?'

'When I was born, a tinker-woman told me I would be the mother of kings. Taliesen told me it was true. But where is this prince who will ask to wed me?'

'Wait here,' he said, and walked slowly into the house. Deva sat in the sunshine for almost an hour, and was still there when the young Donal came walking in from the hills with the faithful hound Render beside him. Caswallon returned as the sun was setting, 'I am sorry to have kept you so long, my dear,' he said. 'Come, I have something to show you.'

Leading her into the house, he took a silvered mirror and placed it in her lap. 'Look closely at the glass and you will see the prophecy.' Holding it up to her face she looked into her own reflection, seeing the fine lines that were appearing round her eyes. The image faded, and she found herself looking down upon the scene in the front room of the old house. Cambil was holding a babe in his arms. An old woman was sitting on the rug before the young Hunt Lord.

The woman's voice came whispering into Deva's mind. 'She will see the great and the strong, Hunt Lord. And a future ruler will ask for her hand. If she weds him, she will be the mother of kings.'

The image faded. 'I don't understand,' said Deva. 'That was my prophecy. So where is this King I have waited for so long?'

Caswallon took the mirror from her hands, then he sat beside her. 'He asked for your hand, Deva, and you refused him.'

'No!' she stormed. 'There has been no prince!'

'The Queen who saved us named him as her heir and he will become King. He is a warrior and a great leader – and he loved you once.'

'Gaelen,' she whispered. 'He is to be King?'

'Yes. I am only sorry you did not come to me before this.'

Deva stood on trembling legs, then ran from the house. A year later she married a widower and raised three sons and a daughter.

Lennox returned twice to the highlands – once for the funeral of his father Leofas, who died twelve years after Icairn's Folly, and once to bring Gwalchmai home after an Outland spear cut him down at the siege of Culceister. Gwalchmai had asked to be buried above Attafoss.

Gaelen never returned. On the death of Obrin he took over as Captain of the Lancers and became known as the Queen's Champion. He and Lara lived contentedly, raising two sons and three daughters.

The clansmen served the Queen for thirty years. In the fortieth year of her reign Sigarni was called to battle by Morgase and the last great Outland army. The battle was fierce and close-run but, as always, Sigarni won the victory, leading a last charge against the shield-wall. Morgase took poison rather than be captured.

The Queen's wounds were grievous. Gaelen helped her from the field and in the last fading light of the dying sun carried her up the slopes beyond Citadel to the Chalice Cave – and beyond! There a young druid took charge of the Queen and Gaelen watched him half carry her towards a mountain cave.

Returning through the Great Gate, the ageing warrior removed his helm and scratched at his thinning grey hair. Idly he rubbed the ancient scar above his eye.

Beyond the Gate four boys were preparing for their first Hunt. The sun was a globe of gold and the future full of promise. At that moment there was no Beast, no danger, and the Aenir were a distant threat.

Gaelen turned back to stare down into the valley where the campfires blazed and the cairn was nearing completion. Below lay the bodies of the fallen, Highlander and Outlander together in death. Among them were Onic and Lennox. The giant had died swinging his massive club of iron and lead as the enemy swarmed forward. Onic had fallen beside him.

Now only Gaelen was left. 'Farewell, my Queen,' he whispered.

A shadow moved to his right. He turned and there was Caswallon, leaning on his staff of oak, his robes of velvet shimmering in the moonlight.

'And so it ends,' said Caswallon, his wispy white beard swirling in the breeze like wood-smoke.

'No, it begins,' said Gaelen, pointing at the cave.

Caswallon nodded. 'And now you will be King, Gaelen. How does that sit with you?'

Gaelen pushed his iron-grey hair back from his eyes, 'I'd give it all up to be young again.'

Caswallon turned and gestured to the Gate. 'But you are young, Gaelen. Through that Gateway is a youth, who with his friends is walking the mountains. Even now the wind is in his hair, and the future is before him, bright and golden. Just a few steps away. Would you like to see him?'

Gaelen smiled. 'Let us leave him to his life,' he said, taking Caswallon by the arm and leading him down the mountainside.

About the author

David Gemmell's first novel, *Legend*, was published in 1984. He has written many bestsellers, including the Drenai Saga, the Jon Shannow novels and the Stones of Power sequence. Widely acclaimed as Britain's king of heroic fantasy, David Gemmell died in 2006.

Find out more about David Gemmell and other Orbit authors by registering for the free monthly newsletter at www.orbitbooks.net.

VISIT THE ORBIT BLOG AT

www.orbitbooks.net

FEATURING

**BREAKING NEWS
FORTHCOMING RELEASES
LINKS TO AUTHOR SITES
EXCLUSIVE INTERVIEWS
EARLY EXTRACTS**

AND COMMENTARY FROM
OUR EDITORS

With regular updates from our team,
orbitbooks.net is your source
for all things orbital

●

While you're there, join our email list
to receive information on special offers,
giveaways, and more

●

Find us on Facebook at www.facebook.com/orbitbooksUK
Follow us on Twitter @orbitbooks

imagine. explore. engage.

orbit

www.orbitbooks.net